Forging H

Villains' Code: Book 1

By Drew Hayes

Acknowledgements

This book is dedicated to the toughest, most determined superhero I've ever known: my mom.

A big round of thanks to my beta readers as well. Without them answering the book-signal, this wouldn't be the same novel. Thanks TheSFReader, E Ramos E, Amanda Whatley, Bill Hammond, and Priscilla Yuen.

Chapter 1

Flames cascaded down from the vent, moving like poured mercury rather than fire. They crackled as they danced through the air, drifting slowly to the steel floor. At first the fire seemed to shrink back from the cold metal surface upon contact, but as the steel began to glow from heat, the flames spread out. They twisted and curled upward into an elongated column. As they rose, a shape began to form. It started as a rough humanoid outline and became more human with each passing second, until it was clearly that of a young woman with long flowing hair. She would have looked quite normal, and perhaps a bit comely, were she not composed entirely of sentient flame.

Then, with no warning at all, the fire disappeared, and only the young woman remained. She turned her head with great care, taking in every detail of the vault that encased her.

It was a massive structure, one that had taken no less than three months of planning and two accomplices to break into, even with her special abilities. Lasers, alarms, pressure switches, heat sensors, and a myriad of cameras were just some of the obstacles she'd overcome, and now she was in their deepest sanctum.

No mere trinkets were housed in this tomb of titanium, no coins or jewels. No, this was a central vault for Indigo Technologies, a leader in every industry that involved circuits or switches. Everything they released managed to be years ahead of their competitors. With the prototypes and plans available here, she would be able to advance her own research by decades as well as make a tidy profit. Finally, she could begin funding her own projects. All it would take was a bit of corporate espionage to get her off the ground.

She stepped forward with impossible care, eyes sweeping for some new trap ready to spring out at her. None of her considerable bribes, thieving, or threats had secured her information about the vault's interior defenses, so from this point on she was flying blind. There was no way Indigo would stop at merely protecting the outside, though, that much she was sure of. She crept toward one of the nearest walls, constantly on alert. When she reached it without incident, she tenderly opened the first drawer she could reach.

It was metallic, like all the box drawers she could see, and slid out from its nearly-seamless integration in the wall with a simple touch. The marking on its front—CX9-315—was gibberish to her, but she had to start the search somewhere. Perhaps she would get lucky and glean some sense of what the filing system meant from the box's contents, and if not, she would just keep searching blind.

Inside drawer CX9-315 was a single piece of paper. Clearly this project hadn't gotten very far off the ground, but if its mere concept was in a place this secure, then it had to be worth taking. She pulled the paper up to read it, unable to contain her curiosity. Curiosity was her fatal flaw, one that had resulted in her gaining her fire powers several years prior. But what met her eyes was not a project plan or a design schematic or even a rough sketch. Instead, it was two words in a bold, formal font, centered on the page:

"Well Done"

"The hell...?" she muttered, despite the fact that she was keenly aware of exactly what "the hell" was going on. Before she heard the vent system seal up or saw the glowing orbs crackling with energy rise from hidden compartments or felt the sudden dip in temperature—before all of that—she knew she was undone from the words alone. Someone had known she was coming, and Indigo Technologies was not the sort of company that failed to prepare for a guest appropriately.

"This is interesting," said a new voice, one coming from everywhere in the room yet at the same time from no single spot. It was a male voice, older but not quite at the cusp of aged. Rather than sounding upset or accusing, it seemed amused. That, more than anything else, set her teeth on edge. Angry people could be predicted; their actions would fall in the realm of reason. Someone amused, sounding like they'd found a new toy, could herald true horrors in store for her.

"Did you know that when we set this little trap for you, I was the only one who believed you had the skills to spring it? Everyone else thought you'd be snared by the lasers or the coolant cannons. Only I believed you had what it would take to make it all the way here."

"Trying to make me feel thankful?" She held the paper firmly in hand and it burst into flames. The fire spread up her hand to her elbow; within seconds there was nothing left but ash. Undone or not, she had no intention of going down gently.

"None of that, now. I was trying to tell you that you've just won me several thousand dollars and bragging rights. This means at the moment I am rather predisposed to like you, while my underlings are significantly miffed. You should probably just go along with things, because the other options in front of you are far less pleasant."

2

At his words, the temperature in the vault dropped noticeably. She suspected that if she'd had a normal tongue and pressed it to the metal walls, it would have stuck. Maintaining her flames grew significantly more difficult, but she persevered. She would not show weakness, not even if that was her final act of defiance.

"All things considered, if I have to die, then I think I'd like to wreck as many of your toys as I can on my way out," she spat.

"Die? Who on earth mentioned dying? Dear child, this is an opportunity."

"You just called it a trap." The flames spread farther along her arms even as the temperature continued to drop.

"It's that too. A trap, an opportunity, and an audition. We've had an eye on you for some time, Tori Rivas. We wanted to see just what you were capable of, given a bit of information and some competent cronies."

"Geraldine and Cooper... they work for you? You set this whole thing up?"

"We gave you resources; you're the one who decided how to use them. And to that effect, you used them very well. Breaking into this vault is no small feat; we designed it not to be."

"Why go to all this trouble? Why didn't you just approach me with a grant or a job offer?" Tori asked, looking up at the ceiling vaguely since there was no physical person to direct her questions toward. "Indigo Technologies is huge and well-funded, I'd have taken a job." Well, she'd have pretended to accept, and then used her access to find a much easier way into the vault, at any rate.

"Oh, Ms. Rivas, there is so very much to bring you up to speed on. Suffice it to say that we wanted to test far more than your ability to punch a clock and boil some coffee. Plus, we're well aware of your opinion toward conventional occupations. At any rate, I'd love to continue this discussion; however, you have yet to make a decision."

"A decision about what?" Her voice leapt and the fire flashed on her arms. Cold could dampen the physical capabilities of her power, but it held no dominion over the temper burning inside her.

"About your future. You are smart, talented, determined, and powerful. We have taken notice of you and of your potential. At this point, there are two ways we can regard you: as an asset or a threat. Assets are tempered, trained, and cultivated. Threats are eliminated."

"Do it then, call the capes! Let's see you explain your little mousetrap to them when they come get me. I'm sure some of the shit in here is illegal."

"I did not say threats were incarcerated. I said threats were *eliminated.*"

3

The floating orbs glowed more brightly. The temperature had fallen well below freezing. It would be impossible to fully transform in here now, and obviously her captor knew it.

"You can't do this. You're just a corporation; you don't get to kill whoever you want."

"A better grasp of America's history in third-world nations and its handling of union debacles would tell you just how wrong that statement is in general. But let's focus on the point that's most salient to our discussion: we are far from *just* a corporation. Talking time is done, Ms. Rivas. You have a choice to make."

Tori stared at the orbs, wondering if she could take them out. As cold as it was, she rather doubted it, but anything was possible. One never knew how a fight would end until it was over, that's what her father had always taught her. Still, even if she took out the orbs, they were bound to have other things, worse things, waiting in the wings. She didn't want to go down easily... but she also didn't want to die.

The flames on her arms burned away, leaving behind a woman who seemed far smaller and more frightened than she had only seconds before.

"Does anyone ever take the other option?" Tori asked, as she watched the orbs vanish back into the walls.

"More than you might think. Our kind is a stubborn, prideful lot, and many do not take well to being trapped and threatened."

"Our kind?"

The vault door opened, revealing a tall man in his mid- to late-forties, adorned in meta-armor Tori recognized at once. How could she not? It belonged to one of the most famous inventors of the last hundred years and one of the greatest criminals the world had ever seen. It had taken at least ten capes, working in tandem, to finally take him down. All that was missing was his trademark helmet, which was why Tori could make out the blue eyes and surprisingly warm smile on his face as he answered her question.

"Villains, Ms. Rivas. That is our kind. We are villains."

*   *   *

"Take that, vile monster! I smite thee with the shining light of justice!"

Clacking filled the air as thin, dexterous fingers danced along the keyboard and caused the shining knight on the screen to hack and slash with furious gusto. Each move was precise and calculated, decimating the wicked minotaur's health faster than the bull-headed being could recover. Victory seemed certain, until a gentle but very deliberate cough filled the air.

4

"Donald, what are you doing? We've talked about this before."

Donald spun around in his chair, one of the few orthopedic ones in the office, until his eyes rested on the tall man staring down at him. Ivan wore his usual pressed dark suit, crisp white shirt, and knotted red tie as he looked at his employee with a mix of weary exasperation and subtle displeasure.

"I'm just playing a game, Mr. Gerhardt. I didn't break the rules like before. It's my lunch break, and I brought my laptop from home, so I didn't think it would be an issue."

Ivan carefully considered the gangly young man in front of him. He could come down hard on Donald, scare the wits out of the poor boy so that he'd never step out of line again, but that would probably put him off working here. Despite his... *tendencies*, Donald was a talented programmer. Even with his knack for getting lost in side projects, he seldom missed a deadline, and the work he produced always ranged from good to excellent. Most managers would say that such things were irrelevant, that rules were rules and had to be followed. Ivan had been managing for some time, though, and he knew that cultivating resources was more important than being authoritarian. Besides, he had a bit of a soft spot for rule-breakers, as long as they stayed within the bounds that *he* set.

"Putting an unauthorized computer on the network violates several of Vendallia Industries' safety protocols," Ivan said at last. "That thing could have all manner of viruses, and without the safety software we put on the corporate machines, there would be no way to tell." This was bullshit, pure and simple. The corporate machines had cookie-cutter software that was easy enough for the management to use and cheap enough for the higher-ups to justify. Someone with Donald's skills undoubtedly had a more secure laptop than what the rest of the office was working on.

"Oh, right. I didn't think about that," Donald said. Ivan could see he was lying; even a man without his background could have read the anxious young man's face.

"Look, it's a silly rule, but if IT catches wind of you putting that thing on the network, we'll both get an earful. Do you really like playing games that much?"

"It just helps me relax, reset my head. I don't want to cause trouble, but this is sort of like my equivalent to a smoke break," Donald said.

Ivan nodded empathetically; it was a skill he'd spent years honing to get just right. "I can understand that. But at the same time, I can't let you break safety protocol. So here's what I'd like to propose: you're on the Elquey Project, right?"

"Yes sir, Mr. Gerhardt."

"That's a big project with a lot of money to be made, so the people up top are keeping a close eye on it. I need someone I can trust watching over the technical side. And Donald, I think you might be the man for that job."

"Me?" Donald's brown eyes widened, stretching so far that for a moment it seemed his eyebrows would make contact with the ends of his stringy red hair.

"That's right, Donald, you. That's what I came to talk about. I've had my eye on you for months, and I think this is your time to shine." Ivan carefully rested a hand on the wall of the cubicle, being sure to present body language that spoke to how open and caring he was. "The whole department needs this to go well, and I'm a firm believer in the right man for the right job. Part of that job, by the way, will entail needing a personal company laptop. You'd have to use it for all manner of work, and you'd be free to install anything on it, so long as it meets the company's general use guidelines." Ivan doubted Donald was stupid enough to watch porn on a company computer, but he also didn't want to have IT yelling at him about another hard drive caked in smut.

"So... I could play games on it?"

"When you're not on company time, yes, so long as they're not inappropriate, you'd be free to use the device as you saw fit. Now tell me, are you interested in the position, or do I move on to Williams?"

Donald's wide eyes suddenly narrowed. He and Rene Williams hadn't gotten along since they started. Rene was a ruthless kissass who never hesitated to steal credit or throw others under the bus. Ivan might have been inclined to reward such behavior if Rene also had the skills to succeed without others to feed upon. As it was, his main purpose was as a motivational tool Ivan could wield against his other employees. The moral and decent didn't want to see Rene Williams make any headway in the company, so much so that they would often take on extra tasks to prevent it.

"No sir, Mr. Gerhardt. I want the job. Please."

"Excellent, I'm glad to hear it. I'll put in the form this afternoon. By Thursday, you should be approved. Oh, and I'm sure it goes without saying, but no more breaking protocol. You understand that this is a big opportunity and a lot of eyes will be upon you, right?"

"Yes, sir."

"Good man, glad to hear it. Just send me an e-mail if you have any questions." Ivan turned and strode out of the cubicle, an expression of genuine happiness on his face.

Whatever manipulative methods he might have used to get his way, Ivan had meant what he said: Donald really was the best man for the job. He was talented, smart, and resourceful, not to mention so terrified of authority that

Ivan wouldn't have to put forth much effort to keep him in line. That would make Ivan's job, and therefore his life, easier.

He strode into his office—nothing too fancy, just four walls and a door that closed— and sat down at his desk. His computer had gone to sleep while he made his rounds, the dark screen showing his reflection instead of the spreadsheet program he'd left running. Ivan wasn't particularly handsome, though he did appeal to women who liked strong noses and pronounced chins. Both his eyes and hair were quite dark, a feature he'd inherited from his mother and passed on to one of his two children. Despite his age, Ivan looked like he couldn't be much older than his late twenties, a fact that everyone inevitably brought up when they met him.

There were a myriad of lies he used to explain the phenomenon: clean living, regular exercise, liberal use of sunscreen, and excellent genetics all making regular appearances. Soon, though, he'd have to think of something else—looking like this in his early forties was one thing, but once he was in his fifties, genuine suspicion would be aroused. Perhaps he'd lie and say he'd been doused with an experimental anti-aging serum. It would be strange, but not altogether unbelievable. It was certainly a far cry better than telling them the real reason his body refused to stop being youthful and fit.

Ivan glanced down at his desk and noticed the red voicemail indicator on his cell phone blinking. That was curious. Even down the hall, he should have heard his ringtone; that's why he'd felt comfortable leaving the phone in the first place. Picking up the device, he unplugged it from its charger (damn thing could never last more than half a day) and pressed the button to call his voicemail.

As soon as he heard the voice on the other end, everything made sense. Of course the actual calling process had been bypassed. The message probably wasn't even sent from another phone… more likely a convoluted system meant to bounce around signals and scramble listening devices. Ivan would have dismissed it as paranoia, if not for the fact that his friend had excellent reasons to be suspicious of prying ears. With a resolved grunt, Ivan leaned back in his own chair and listened to the message.

"Ivan, it's Wade. There's something I'm going to need your help with. Not the usual kind either. We've got a… well, I'll tell you in person tonight. This is me letting you know I'm coming over, so don't try and kill me as soon as I walk on your lawn or anything. See you soon."

Ivan set the phone back down and shook his head. One time, one time he'd almost killed Wade, and the man had never let him live it down. You break into someone's lair in the middle of the night, and you can't be surprised when they take a swing at you.

7

Especially not when that person had a reputation like Ivan's.

Chapter 2

Ivan lived in a two-story ranch-style house in a suburb of Ridge City. It looked exactly like six other houses in his neighborhood, save for the fact that Ivan had selected the beige trim while the others had gone with eggshell. It was a four bedroom, with one for Ivan, one that served as a home office, and the remaining two were for each of his children. Those were only in use every other weekend, but he liked to have a place for them to feel at home when they came over. In the front was a small patio adorned with a couple of wooden rocking chairs that looked homemade but had actually been purchased at a local chain store. Between them was a table in the same style, upon which there was a glass of iced tea waiting for Ivan as he stepped outside.

The heat of summer was dying out, giving way slightly to the brisk nip of fall. The battling elements made the evenings perfect for sitting out—enough heat to be warm paired with just the right amount of breeze to stay cool. As Ivan sipped his tea, he gave a polite nod to Mrs. Jefferson, the elderly neighbor who was making the trek down her driveway to check her mail. She was a sweet woman, likely a bit too frail to be living alone, but she refused to let a little thing like that stop her. Ivan and the other neighbors pitched in to help with her yard work and keep up her house. The others did so out of good-heartedness and likely a concern for property values if one home became derelict, and Ivan because he had a healthy respect for people who refused to do what they were expected to, even if it came at the cost of their own health.

A silver sedan pulled into Ivan's driveway, a familiar copper-haired man behind the wheel. Ivan was grateful that Wade had come in a normal car; heaven knew the billionaire had more than enough luxury automobiles to turn heads on this humble little street. Instead he was driving a nice, but not ostentatious, car that blended in perfectly with the neighborhood. Of course, knowing Wade, that vehicle was probably rocket-proof, could fly, and had a button that turned it into a robot. But so long as all that stayed hidden, it wasn't any of Ivan's concern.

The engine died and Wade emerged. Unlike Ivan, he was wearing his years appropriately. Though still tall and lean, a small pooch of belly had begun to accumulate around his midsection, no doubt the result of all-nighters filled with eating terrible junk food. His shiny copper hair was thinning, and within another decade, he'd likely be bald on top—unless he spared a day or so to find a cure. His eyes were still the same, blue and wild and full of life, barely able to contain all the thoughts of the brain behind them. He strolled up the driveway toward the walkway, avoiding Ivan's well-maintained lawn. Despite his wealth, or perhaps because of it, Wade always wore a similar outfit when he was going "mundane": jeans, custom shoes that supported his poor arches, and a plaid button-down.

"Evening," Ivan said, greeting his friend and one of the oldest acquaintances he had.

"Evening," Wade replied, settling down in the unoccupied rocking chair.

"Can I get you something to drink?"

"Maybe in a bit. How's life at the office treating you?" As Wade spoke, he pulled a small silver box from his pocket. It looked a lot like an oversized lighter, but as with everything else with Wade, looks were incredibly deceiving.

"Could be worse. At least the shitty economy means I've got a glut of qualified people desperate for work. Beats the hell out of the days when we were snagging any kid who could string three lines of code together." Ivan took a drink of cold iced tea, enjoying the excessive sweetness. He made his the old-fashioned way, with enough sugar to cause diabetes in a single glass. Life had taken away many of his vices, but this was one he refused to let go of. Besides, it wasn't as though a thing like sugar could hurt his body.

"Bad economy means it's an employer's market." Wade finished fiddling with his box; a small red light ignited near the base. He set it on the table, a safe distance away from Ivan's tea, and continued. "Okay, that should do it."

"I remember when you needed a room the size of my house and machines as big as your car to create your Cone of Silence."

"I don't care how much you liked *Get Smart* as a kid, we're not calling it that. It's a portable sound isolation and management system."

"Yes, your version just rolls off the tongue," Ivan said. He made sure to keep his usual half-smile on his face as he spoke. Wade's device would stop all forms of technological eavesdropping they'd discovered, not to mention distort the movements of their lips to prevent reading, and Ivan had wards all over his property that halted scrying, but none of that would stop people from noticing if they suddenly hunched over and acted secretive. The best way to do nefarious things was right out in the open, as if you had nothing to hide. "Now that we're cloaked and you're here, tell me what the big news is. I can't already be up in rotation."

"No, your work last month was superb; however, it left the others a bit uneasy about calling on your services again."

"That's what I was going for," Ivan replied.

"Clearly. The blood on the ceiling made that point abundantly obvious. I'm here about a different matter. Last week we picked up a new candidate:

10

smart, willful, and with a power that she's barely scratched the surface of. The rest of the board agrees with me that she has tremendous potential, but... well, I did say she was willful, didn't I?"

"Yes, you did."

"Very much so. She's not taking direction well, keeps bucking against us, toeing the line just enough not to fall out of our good graces completely. Some feel she'll never make the grade and we're better off cutting our losses. That there's no point in training a future code-breaker."

Ivan knew all too well what Wade was hinting at, and he was glad he'd made such a spectacle of his last job. He'd do his part, but he preferred that people be scared to call him in. It meant they wouldn't try to use him as some go-to exterminator.

"Personally," Wade continued, "I feel such actions are extreme and unnecessary at this point, but if things don't change, then sooner or later, that will be the unavoidable outcome. That's why I contacted you. Standard training isn't working for her, so I thought she might benefit from the old way we learned: master and apprentice."

"Hold the damn phone," Ivan said, setting down his tea so hard a bit sloshed over the side. "Look, I do what's necessary when I have to, but there is no way I'm going fully back in. Getting joint custody was hard enough; if I get busted, even if we beat it, I'll be lucky to see my kids before they graduate college."

"Calm down, no one is asking you to come back," Wade assured him. "This would be a modified program. No crime necessary on your part. You'd be a mentor: taking her under your wing and teaching her how things work. The rules, how to fight, picking targets, all the theory and legal training. Any real outings will be done by someone else with you in a supervisory capacity at the most."

Ivan settled back in his chair and plastered the fake smile back on his face, but the scowl in his eyes never quite lessened. "Fine, so I wouldn't have to go back in. Why should I do it, though? There are plenty of qualified people in your organization. Hell, you could do it yourself. I'm sure she'd love to study under the great Doctor Mechaniacal."

"Sure she would, and the minute I turned my back, she'd either try and steal everything off my hard drive or roast it when she failed. The woman is too smart and ambitious to trust around my lab. Luckily she's all science-minded, no talent or capacity for magic. Means you'd have nothing to worry about."

"Still not explaining why you need me instead of the others. Arcanicus has got to be bored as hell lately, and he's all magic too," Ivan pointed out.

"Look, I'll level with you: she's kind of a pain in the ass. Lots of us could try and train her, but no one wants to. Potential aside, they just don't see her being worth the investment of time and energy to properly mold. Add in the fact that a few folks are probably legitimately scared of her and it creates a pupil without a suitable teacher, save possibly for you."

"Why me?"

"Because you're a pain in the ass too," Wade replied. There was nothing accusatory in his statement; he told this to Ivan the same way he'd have given him the time. "You're stubborn, temperamental, willful, and you scare the shit out of a lot of members. Near as I can see, you're either the perfect teacher for her, or you'll kill her in two days. Either outcome solves my problem."

The prospect was certainly interesting, and Ivan could probably do with a new project. His last one, wood-working, had ended in a summer bonfire and a trip to purchase the rocking chairs he and Wade were sitting in. Still, an apprentice was a lot of work, and a fair amount of responsibility. It had the potential to complicate the life he'd worked so hard to keep nice and serene.

"I'll accept that I might be a good fit for her," Ivan said. "But that doesn't tell me why I should do it. I'm not the altruistic sort, you know."

"So you claim," Wade chuckled. He was one of the few people who knew all of Ivan's sides, the dark and the light. Admittedly, there was ample darkness, but he wasn't an empty monster. At least, not unless he had reason to be. "I already discussed it with the training board, and we decided that a stipend would be appropriate compensation for your troubles."

"My job pays fine, as you ought to know, so thanks, but no thanks."

"Fine, sure, but doesn't Rick start applying to college in a few years?"

"Janet and I have a college fund for both him and Beth."

Wade shook his head. "Ivan, you're missing the offer. Rick is a bright boy, and Beth is no slouch either, but with their current grades and extracurriculars, they're looking at a good state college, maybe a bit higher if they do very well on their SATs. I'm offering guaranteed, fully-paid, top-tier admission. Literally, pick a school, and they'll get accepted with a full ride. Rick wants to work for NASA, right? The Ivy League certainly wouldn't look bad on his resume."

"Malphorus came up with this, didn't he? I educate yours, you educate mine; it has the sort of symmetry he loves."

"It was his suggestion, but I thought the compensation would pique your interest. You've already earned a good, stable life for yourself. I assumed you'd be more inclined to help your children get closer to theirs."

From anyone else, Ivan would have taken this as manipulation, and his reaction would not have been kind. Wade was a friend, however, and in their former occupation, friends were a rare thing. He was truly looking out for Ivan, offering him something that would be unattainable through normal means. Wade was using his knowledge of what Ivan loved to create a better deal, not to try and con him into accepting against his better judgment. And, if Ivan were being honest with himself, it would take a lot of worry off his shoulders to know his children were getting a good first step into the adult world.

"I guess I can at least see what she's got," Ivan conceded at last. "No promises, though. If I don't think I can teach her, I'm walking away."

"That's what I'd want you to do anyway," Wade said. "I can take you to her now, if you're ready."

"In a minute." Ivan reached over and picked up his glass. "First, I want to finish my tea."

*   *   *

The skeleton let out a pathetic wail as the fireball struck its ribcage, exploding and shattering it into dozens of pieces. Nearby, another skeleton was caught by surprise as its target unleashed a torrent of flame that caused its bones to blacken and crack and shortly become too frail to hold together. More skeletons marched up to fill the ranks of their fallen brothers. They were many, but their opponent was strong. Strong... and dangerous.

"Almost makes me feel bad for the things," Ivan said, staring at the monitor as another trio of skeletons was taken out.

"She's able to destroy them nearly as fast as Arcanicus can conjure them," Wade said. On another monitor, they could see an older man, probably a decade ahead of Wade, wearing robes and weaving magical symbols in the air. Every couple of seconds, the symbols would form together and a new skeleton would appear in front of him. The man would point to a door, and the skeleton would totter through to its fiery destruction.

"Not much thought behind her moves," Ivan commented. "She's just throwing fireballs and blast streams. They're good range attacks, but what about up close?"

"I'd wager that's why she's in her fire-form," Wade replied.

Tori was indeed composed entirely of flames. She looked more like a tall inferno that happened to be human shaped than a woman who had changed her molecular chemistry.

"It's a potent ability, not overwhelming in strength, but with lots of versatility," Ivan said. "The guild seriously wants to be done with her so soon?"

Wade nodded, the gesture a bit stiff and weary. "Smart and strong as she is, Tori has also been steadily refusing to take her education seriously. We try and teach her about strategy, secrecy, and of course the code, but she keeps digging in her heels. From what I've gathered, she spent the last decade or so subsisting off of petty crime and a network of other crooks. Most of the ones pulled in to teach her feel she's too far gone, that all we're doing right now is strengthening a future code-breaker. And I don't have to tell you what the guild's policy on that is."

That subject was one that Ivan knew too well, perhaps even better than Wade. Useful power or not, if she seemed like a danger to the guild, then the threat would be neutralized. There was nothing else to say on the matter, so Ivan politely changed the subject.

"You're sure she's all science? I've never met a full-phase shifter without at least a little magic helping the process."

"Positive. It was an accident, so she's not certain how to recreate it, but the fact remains that Tori Rivas found a way to turn into sentient fire."

The two men were standing in a small office not far from the training facility where Tori was going through her daily combat training. They weren't in the guild's proper headquarters—aside from concerns about the length of her tenure, no one felt comfortable having people with powers test their limits in the same place where files and servers were stored. This was a training facility set up behind a secret door in what was, for the most part, a pork rendering plant. The smell alone was enough to keep all but the most determined of parties away.

"The power is impressive, sure, but with how she's using it, she'd never get above Delta Class. Just having Arcanicus switch to flaming skeletons would be enough to render her whole attack strategy useless."

"I told you that she had potential, not that she was ready to go," Wade reminded him. "If she were already adept and skilled, then your tutelage wouldn't be necessary."

"I guess. Does she just have the fire-shifting or did she get anything else?"

"She heals at a rapid rate, even more so when given time to shift between phases. Her body is tougher than a human's, though nothing approaching your level, and her basic speed and strength are augmented as well. What really shines through, however, is her intellect. The clothes she was wearing when the exercise started, the ones that phased with her? She made those herself. Invented a process all on her own with no funds or facility to speak of. The woman has a strong education, a bright mind, and a, forgive the phrase, burning ambition."

Ivan nodded and kept his eyes on the monitor. Creating fabric that could shift phases wasn't unheard of, but the rarity of needing it and complexity in making it meant that phasing outfits were very expensive. Like most meta-

14

tech, it was rare and hard to buy, unless you were the one making it. That she'd managed to create some without any resources did speak to a smart mind, but not so brilliant of one that Ivan understood his friend's interest in this woman.

"Be straight with me here, Wade. What's the deal? Is she the daughter of some guy in the guild who wants his kid in the business, or related to a cape that we're trying to stick it to by turning family, or something along those lines? She's got potential, I'll give you that, but I don't know that she has enough to warrant all the special treatment."

"What's the deal?" Wade repeated, his eyes never darting away from the monitors. He lifted a long finger and pointed to the image on the screen. "Arcanicus won't be able to keep pumping out skeletons for much longer. He's already beginning to sweat." Sure enough, the robed man was red-faced as he continued weaving magic and conjuring animated bones from nothingness. "I remember when he could curse a continent without so much as getting winded. Age is beginning to take him, as it will eventually take almost all of us." Wade shot his friend a targeted glance on the word "almost," and Ivan pretended not to notice.

"So, what, you want a successor? Then you should train her."

"It's not about an individual successor. It's about the impact we leave on the next generation. Some of the new members are hungry for violence and blood; they weren't around to see how bad things can get when we make war with the capes. Even Balaam, though appointed to the guild's council, constantly tries to move for amendments that would allow our members more freedom for carnage."

"There are always a few who want to go back to the old ways. We have a system for code-breakers," Ivan said. He didn't enjoy the system or his occasional role in it, but that didn't change the fact that it had to be there.

"But if enough like Balaam rise through the ranks, they can change the code. Rewrite it, strip it of meaning, and destroy the tenuous peace we've been able to create. I want more in our ranks like her: concerned with freedom over violence, someone who embraces this life because they refuse to bow down instead of wanting to cut others to their knees."

"Save it for the poetry slam. I get your point." Ivan looked at Tori once more, watching her tear through the last of the skeletons in the room. "You really think she can be someone we count on?"

"If she's taught properly, I know it," Wade said.

"Then I guess I should go meet her and see for myself. Tell Arcanicus to clear out. I'm administering her next test."

"I suspect he'll be overjoyed for the break," Wade replied. "Dare I ask what this test will be?"

15

"I'm going to see if she's got what it takes to learn under me," Ivan said. He gently stretched his arms behind his back, noting the rogue popping sounds from various joints. "Fair warning, though: either she passes her entrance exam or it will probably kill her. That going to be an issue?"

"No problem at all."

Chapter 3

The metal doors whispered open, but this time it wasn't more pathetic skeletons tottering through. Doctor Mechaniacal walked in instead, side by side with some guy who looked closer to Tori's age. She wondered if she'd have to fight this one too. She really hoped not: combat wasn't why she'd agreed to this training, and besides, aside from being fit, the new guy didn't seem exceptionally powerful. Not that looks meant much when dealing with meta-humans.

Ivan noticed the appraising look she gave him and kept his own expression neutral. From her body language, she'd drawn all the wrong conclusions about him. That didn't particularly bother Ivan; in fact, he took it as a compliment. He worked very hard to maintain his mundane facade. Her inability to see through it was just a testament to how effective it was. Of course, that wouldn't excuse the mistakes she was bound to make, but Ivan felt complimented all the same.

"Doctor," she said, keeping her tone flat but respectful. "I hope you're here to tell me I'm done fighting skeletons."

"Learning to deal with multiple opponents is an important aspect of training," Wade told her. "Though you could stand to work on your delicacy."

"If I'm fighting a room full of people, delicacy is going to be the last thing on my mind."

"That statement there sums up why you need to work on it," Ivan said. Tori was a bit surprised at the authority in his voice. He spoke with the sort of confidence and power she associated with older, more established people. "When you've got a room full of people coming for you, that's exactly when you should be delicate, not explosive."

"Explosive seemed to work just fine." Tori gestured to the fading bits of bone in the room. Most had already turned back into the mystic ether from which they were sculpted, but a few fragments were still dotting the floor.

"And if you're in a room with allies?" Ivan asked, stepping over a fading chunk of skull. Arcanicus's constructs tended to stain if one stepped on them while they dissolved, and these were new shoes.

"I'm sorry, aren't you all a bunch of villains? I didn't really think I'd need to learn about how to play on a team."

"Then you're even more foolish than I first suspected," Ivan said. "Of course we work together. The very existence of this guild should demonstrate that concept to you quite thoroughly." He turned to Wade, who was somehow managing to keep a cheerful grin fixed firmly in place. "You're really sure about this woman?"

"She has potential," Wade replied simply.

"She also has ears and doesn't like being talked about as if she isn't in the room." Tori glared at both of them for a moment then directed the bulk of her ire to Ivan. "Doctor Mechaniacal gets a pass out of respect for what he's accomplished, but I've got no inclination to take any shit off of you, Khakis."

"Actually, I'm the most important person in the world, so far as you're concerned," Ivan said, "because I'm the one who decides if you live to see another sunrise or not. The guild is thinking about terminating your association with them, but Doctor Mechaniacal has persuaded them to let you stay on as an apprentice. Of course, any apprentice needs a teacher, and that's what he's trying to rope me into doing."

"You're full of it," Tori snapped.

"No, everything he's said is perfectly true." Wade didn't even bother to look ashamed. To him, the situation was a purely practical one; there was no need to get caught up in sentiment over it. "You must have realized your attitude and refusal to cooperate would have consequences. Many of my colleagues feel you can't be made useful, and they advocate ending this experiment before you become too troublesome."

"Too... troublesome?" For the first time since Ivan had laid eyes on her, uncertainty flickered across Tori's face. Her eyes darted from him, to Wade, and back to him, repeating this cycle several times before she found her words. "Okay, maybe I haven't been a perfect little student, but it's not like I asked to join you guys in the first place."

"What you asked for is irrelevant. You're here, this is the situation. Standard training is clearly a lost cause. You'll either leave this room as an apprentice, or not at all," Wade said.

"Then be my teacher! You're the one I want to learn from, anyway. Please, help me out here."

"He's already convinced people who aren't easily swayed to give you another chance," Ivan interrupted. "Doctor Mechaniacal is the reason you ever got this opportunity at all, so be grateful for what he's done."

"But—"

"There are no buts." Ivan had crossed the room and was now close enough to feel the heat radiating off his prospective student. Either she was upset or just pissed; either way she was unconsciously cranking up the temperature. If he took her as a student, her first lessons would be on control. "I've been chosen to teach you. If I accept the job, then you get to prove Doctor Mechaniacal was right by not doing anything to make me have to kill you."

Tori stared at him for a few moments, emotions flickering through her eyes as she tried to make sense of a suddenly life-threatening situation. For the briefest of seconds, Ivan thought she would settle on panic, or worse, fear, but she pulled herself together and her eyes grew hard. She was letting anger carry her through this. It wasn't a bad call, provided she could keep it wrangled.

"Fine. So you're here to decide if I'm teachable, is that it? Then what do I have to do to prove that I'm worth the effort? I can roast skeletons all day, if that's your cup of tea."

Ivan shook his head. "No, I don't think that will be necessary. All I want you to do is survive a single punch from me. That's your test."

Tori tilted her head, ever so slightly. "Survive a punch? That's it? I guess I have to stay in human-form then."

"You can be fire if you want to," Ivan said. "You can also try to dodge or avoid it. I'm only throwing the one punch, so if you succeed, you pass. I'll even tell you where I'm hitting you: it's going to be dead center in your torso, right through your sternum."

"Is this for real?" Tori looked over at Wade, who gave her a small nod. "You know that when I'm in fire-form, physical attacks can't hurt me."

"I have things to do today. Let's move this along." Ivan took a few steps back and cocked his right fist back. "Take your time and get set. Let me know when you're ready, and that's when I'll punch."

Tori wasn't sure what to make of this strange man with dark hair and seemingly unwarranted confidence, but she was smart enough to take an associate of Doctor Mechaniacal's seriously. Her skin grew warm, then red, and then vanished completely as her entire form shifted to that of animated flame. She retained a humanoid shape for the moment; giving him a torso to aim at meant his moves would be easier to anticipate. Her fiery feet slid back along the floor as Tori braced herself, prepared to move in a heartbeat. After taking a few seconds to make sure there was nothing else she could do, Tori realized she was stalling. It was now or never.

"Ready." Her voice sounded like a fireplace crackling with fresh logs, but the words were still enunciated perfectly. Her attention was on the curious man in the khakis; she was ready to react the instant he moved.

It was this concentration that saved her life. In the sliver of an instant between when Ivan closed the gap between them and slammed his fist into her torso, Tori sensed the slightest movement. Acting on instinct more than strategy, she shifted a few millimeters back, turning his strike into a glancing blow instead of a direct one. She expected something strange to happen, for his hand to hurt when it went through her or for him to display a burst of cold powers.

19

What she hadn't counted on or imagined, not even for an instant, was that his fist would hit her as solidly as if she were still flesh and blood. She flew backward and crashed into the far wall; her form was undone as soon as she struck, leaving her little more than a flaming puddle smeared against the steel wall. She was in more pain than she'd ever experienced in this form, but Tori was still conscious. That meant she was alive.

"How... how..." Her voice crackled from the slowly reforming mass of fire; she was barely able to string words together.

Ivan, to his credit, kept his word and didn't throw another attack. Instead he just stared, watched her carefully through eyes that no longer belonged to Ivan the manager. These eyes were almost entirely black, aside from a series of runes burning from the center of each eye. Though the eyes didn't belong to Ivan the manager, they did belong to another identity of Ivan's, one he hadn't used for many years.

Tori finished pulling herself together and shifted back to her human-form. She was sweating and her chest hurt like hell, but she was alive. As she pulled her head up and looked at the man who had so easily bested her, she was treated to her first look at those impossible, unnerving eyes.

"Holy shit!" Tori yelped, terror momentarily forgotten in the rush of confusion and excitement. "You're... you're fucking Fornax! You're supposed to be dead."

"Fornax *is* dead." He closed his lids for several seconds, and when he opened them up, his eyes were completely back to normal. "My name is Ivan, but you can feel free to call me Mr. Gerhardt, Teacher, or just plain Sir. You have good instincts; you avoided the hit even when logic told you it wouldn't hurt. Let's see if we can develop those instincts into actual skills."

"Guess that means I passed." Tori slowly pulled herself to her feet. Neither man moved to help her, nor would she have accepted if they had. "Lucky me."

"That remains to be seen. There may come times when you curse yourself for moving, for not just dying when you had the chance." Ivan treated her to his best consoling manager smile. "I look forward to working with you, Tori."

He turned and left the room, Doctor Mechaniacal a few steps behind. Only when they were gone did Tori allow herself to fall against the nearest wall. She didn't know how he'd managed to hit her like that, but it was hardly surprising he was capable of it. Fornax was one of the original villains; he'd been as infamous as Doctor Mechaniacal in his own day. The man was as notorious as he was powerful, and he was renowned for being damn near unstoppable.

20

All of which raised the pertinent question: how on earth had he managed to fake his own death and hide for so many years?

*   *   *

"She's green, driven by emotions, and thinks she's a lot stronger than she really is." Ivan didn't bother stopping as they stepped out of the car and entered the guild's actual headquarters; he knew all too well how keen Wade's senses were. Or, rather, how keen the nanites in his blood made his senses.

"So you're saying she's you, back when we were starting out." Wade kept pace as they headed down the halls, already certain of the destination in Ivan's mind.

"Cute. Look, I said I'd do the job, and I will. I'll teach her to the best of my ability, but if she steps too far out of bounds…"

"The punishment for code-breakers is the same for every member of this guild," Wade said, "from its most senior members to its newest apprentices. If she can't work within our boundaries, then you'll do what is necessary."

"How is it you can say that with so much detachment, but you're the beloved billionaire and I'm still looked at as a monster?" Ivan finally arrived at the door he was looking for and nearly barreled through it.

On the other side was a medium-sized room with tables, plastic chairs, and vending machines serving up soda and microwavable fare. Ivan walked right over to the soda machine and pressed his thumb against a small touchscreen on the side. A barely visible panel in the wall slid away, revealing a set of ascending stairs, and both men began to climb.

"It's not like people know that Wade Wyatt is Doctor Mechaniacal. So far as the public is concerned, he's ancient history, and I'm the man who lets them listen to music on devices the size of their fingernail."

"Yeah, yeah, and Fornax has been dead since the Orion incident. I still feel like I get more hate than you do, and your persona isn't even 'confirmed' to be dead." Ivan emerged at the top of the stairs in a lush room with red carpet. There was an open bar, large tables with crisp white tablecloths, and an army of robot butlers ready to prepare any drink or delicacy one could imagine.

"You're just complaining to change the subject," Wade said. "I know you're worried about having an apprentice."

"Damn right, I'm worried," Ivan snapped. He flopped onto a cushy sofa and motioned for one of the nearest robots to come attend to him. "How are we even going to work this? I can't stay in guild quarters. My neighbors will notice if I suddenly stop coming home, to say nothing of my kids every other

21

weekend." The robot made its way over to Ivan, and he promptly ordered three BLTs and a glass of sweet tea.

"Yet you seem to have no qualms about using the senior staff facilities," Wade noted.

"Hey, asshole, you're the one who guilted me into taking a seat on the council. Executive break rooms are one of the fringe benefits, and I'm going to use it."

"As well you should. I constructed them with you in mind, after all. From the grand dreams of our ideal lair we used to have, back when we were squatting in abandoned warehouses."

"Don't you dare try to invoke 'the good old days' with me." Ivan rubbed his temples with his index finger and thumb, despite the fact that there was no physical pain in his head. It had been years since he'd gone up against anything strong enough to actually hurt him. "Let's just talk logistics: how am I going to train that woman? I guess I could come in on afternoons and some weekends, if I move things around."

"That would make you her coach, not her teacher," Wade told him. "You know perfectly well the way these things are done. She's going to move into your home, be under your tutelage and care for as many hours in the day as possible."

"Hells bells, Wade. My neighbors are going to have a field day if I suddenly have a twenty-something-year-old female staying at my place. The Jensens alone would start putting me in the prayer requests at church, and lord only knows how that gets the gossip fountain flowing. I have to live in that suburb, you know."

The two were interrupted as the robot returned with sandwiches and sweet tea in hand. Ivan accepted the plate, greedily digging into the first BLT as Wade addressed his concern.

"I've already been working on a cover story. She's your cousin's daughter, going through a bit of trouble at home and staying with you until things are sorted out." Wade reached into his back pocket and produced a small tablet. He set it in front of Ivan, who ignored it as he continued to eat, and gestured at the blank screen waiting to be unlocked. "In that is her cover, false history, and all pertinent information you might need. It's all airtight; every internet search they try will show Tori's history and bloodline to you. The movers currently setting up at your house are already chit-chatting with the neighbors and letting the pertinent details slip."

Ivan finished chewing a bite and slowly lowered his sandwich, glaring at Wade as he did. "Setting up at my house?"

"You told me you accepted her apprenticeship; I took you at your word and assumed you understood the duties."

"Where the hell is she supposed to sleep? I don't have any free bedrooms."

"The top of your garage is being retrofitted into an apartment. It won't be fancy, but she is in her apprenticeship, after all. Frills come with accomplishments. Of course, Indigo Technologies will cover the alterations and increased bills."

"You just think you're so damn smart, don't you?" Ivan drummed his fingers soundlessly on the squishy cushion of the couch. "There's a pretty big issue you skipped over, though. What about my kids? I'll do a lot for this council, for you, but there's no way I'm letting some half-cocked rookie anywhere near Rick and Beth. That's a deal breaker."

"Tori will have tutoring here on the weekends," Wade said. "Though her cover will be that she's undergoing counseling at a special facility. You'll be expected to train her when time allows, but I knew when I asked you to do this that there would have to be some exceptions."

"Gee, you think?" Ivan gulped down a few mouthfuls of the tea and grimaced. No matter how many times he had Wade tweak their programming, the robots just couldn't get sweet tea right. They made good sandwiches and coffee, though, so that was something. "I don't suppose I can use her as an excuse to skip council meetings, can I?"

"Sadly, no," Wade said. "Like all apprentices, she'll be expected to tag along and learn at your side. Speaking of, you remember we have one next Wednesday, right?"

"Unfortunately. Remember when being a villain was all about wild nights and brawls in the street?"

"Yes. I also remember being confined in a cell under so much security I could scarcely move," Wade reminded him.

"I didn't say it was all perfect, but now, I swear, we do more meetings and slideshows than we do at my office job." Ivan shook his head. "I wasn't built for this side of the business."

"Yet you continue doing an impeccable job. Chin up; if nothing else, I imagine your new apprentice will add some of the old excitement back into your life."

"That's what I was thinking, and why I didn't want one in the first place." Ivan leaned back in the chair, lazily holding his second BLT. "Honestly, a small part of me hopes I have to kill her. The other option is actually teaching her, which seems far more dangerous. I'm pretty fond of our world, but the last thing it needs is a disciple of Fornax."

"Fornax has been dead for over a decade," Wade said, crossing his slender hands in his lap. "Tori will be a disciple of Ivan. Nothing more, nothing less."

"Let's just hope that's not worse."

Chapter 4

Tori watched the streets crawl by, marveling at how impressively identical each of the homes were. Certainly, there were minor variations in design or decoration, but it was abundantly clear that each of the houses had been constructed from the same central design. She'd been to places like this before, usually on a quick burglary run to scrounge up money for components, and every time it overwhelmed her with an indescribable sense of horror. How could these people be so content to spin about aimlessly, like cogs in one of her earlier inventions? It boggled the mind, even one as impressive as hers.

The driver, a muscular man who had said nothing since she was led into his car that morning, turned left, bringing them into a different subdivision. It had taken a few days to get everything settled, but she was finally making the big move out to her new digs. She'd kept quiet about her dislike of the situation; the whole mess had apparently come about from how much she'd been dragging her heels in the first place. Plus, any place to stay was probably better than that pork processing plant she'd been kept in. It was nice not to be dead, and while she'd have much rather learned from Doctor Mechaniacal, Fornax wasn't a horrid consolation prize.

Except that he wasn't Fornax—Doctor Mechaniacal had been adamant about that point. It was a name she was never to speak aloud, to avoid thinking about if at all possible. Fornax had to be dead for Ivan, her teacher, to have any sort of life. Failing his training might result in death, but spilling his big secret would result in the sorts of punishments she'd rather die than endure. The way Doctor Mechaniacal had so coldly explained what was waiting for her if she slipped up still sent a shiver down her spine.

There a slight bump as the SUV turned off the street and pulled into the open driveway. It was adjacent to another house, one that was just like all the others. Completely indistinguishable in any way... except that one of the world's most notorious villains lived there. Tori felt her opinion of these neighborhoods rise slightly; there was something to be said for camouflage that let one blend with the herd.

Ivan stood on the porch, waving with a careful smile. It was smart, not appearing too happy about her arrival. After all, her cover story meant she was closer to a burden than a blessing. If he'd been overjoyed, that wouldn't have fit properly. Tori's opinion of Ivan was going up too; the man clearly had practice blending in. Or, she supposed, he was just unhappy to see her and didn't mind letting it show through.

With a grunt, Tori hauled her suitcase out of the back. Everything she needed was already up in the prepared apartment, but it wouldn't do to have her arrive without baggage. Tori had the feeling this wasn't the first time Doctor Mechaniacal had orchestrated something like this. She doubted it was even within his first hundred.

Despite the early hour, several of Ivan's neighbors were out. Some were mowing their lawns, others trimming hedges, a few even tending to well-kept flower beds, but all of them were clearly outside for the same reason: to get a look at Ivan's new tenant. For the most fleeting of moments, Tori was tempted to greet her "uncle" with a kiss on the lips, just to cause a stir. She resisted because she realized the momentary humor wouldn't be worth the complications it would create, and because she suspected Ivan would just dodge if she tried. Years of being "dead" aside, he was a legend for a reason.

"Tori," Ivan greeted as she drew near the porch. He reached down and took the suitcase from her, then pulled her in for a one-sided hug. It was as awkward as an actual embrace between distant family members, which sold the ruse well.

"Uncle Ivan," Tori replied. "Good to see you again."

"And you. Come on inside, let's get you settled in." Ivan opened his front door and held it for her as she stepped through the entrance.

Tori's first thought was to marvel at how mundane the foyer and living room were: a few pieces of bric-a-brac, some pictures on the wall, and a reasonably-sized television sitting across from a worn sofa. Comfortable and lived-in, the house had the kind of homey aura she'd never seen a fake dwelling accurately replicate… which meant, most likely, that it wasn't a fake at all. This was where Ivan laid his head—a head that would be at the top of the capes' hunting lists if they knew it was still on his shoulders.

Behind her, she heard the door shut as Ivan walked in and set her suitcase on the ground. Then came the sound of deadbolts being locked into place, followed by a few mumbled words that she couldn't quite make out. Magic, probably. No one, at least no one who talked to the public, entirely knew where Fornax drew his powers from, but they were obviously magical in origin. Tori turned around to see Ivan running his thumb along the seam between the door and the wall before he turned and faced her.

"Want something to drink?"

"I'd love a beer."

Ivan nodded. "Fine, just don't let the neighbors see you drinking anything. You're supposed to be here to get clean, remember?"

"I'll keep any drinking inside the walls with the blinds shut," Tori promised.

"Do that. And grab a seat." Ivan walked off into the kitchen, and Tori slid into an overstuffed green chair that had probably belonged to Ivan when he first got out on his own. She was surprised he'd managed to hold on to it this long—usually "bachelor décor" was the first thing to go when a man settled down. Ivan might not be married at the moment, but he seemed too put together to have lived so long as a bachelor.

Ivan came back from the kitchen with a cold beer in a bright orange koozie and a glass of iced tea. He handed her the bottle, allowing her to see that the koozie was from the "6th Annual Green Terrace Block Grill-Out." Tori twisted off the cap and kept her snickering to a minimum.

"I'm going to be honest with you, Tori. I've never had an apprentice before. The guild considers me to have a 'poor temperament' for teaching, which is probably why they let Wade pitch me as your instructor to begin with: they think I'll kill you and save them the trouble." Ivan took a draw from his glass of tea then took a seat on the arm of the couch, directly across from Tori. "I'm not telling you that to be mean, I'm just letting you know up front that I'll be making up a lot of this as I go along. I promised to teach you and I will, but you might have to bear with me as I chart the course. So, all of that said, let's start at the top priority for every guild member: tell me what you've learned about the code."

"The code is the slang term for the Villain's Code of Conduct, a document put together by the guild founders at its creation. It serves the purpose of keeping the capes from getting too aggravated by or interested in our activities, making sure that we never escalate to an all-out war with the superheroes of the world." Tori took a celebratory sip of her beer, feeling very confident in the answer she'd given.

"Textbook accurate, and also overall worthless," Ivan said. "The code is about survival: pure and simple. Some of it is to keep the capes off our asses, sure, but just as much is there to keep us from killing each other. For example, do you know why any villain planning to rob a building has to clear it with the guild first?"

"To be sure it's not a high priority for any of the superheroes or government agencies. If we accidently target one of their bases, it could bring down a lot of heat."

"Wrong. It's to make sure none of us, or the capes, have any friends or family in that location. If a villain acts without approval and accidently kills some other villain's sister, now we've got the start of a blood feud that's going to leave us with lots of dead bodies and more capes up our asses than we know what to do with," Ivan told her.

"You said you'd also want to make sure not to kill a cape's family. How would you even know if they had any in the building? Their identities are secret."

Ivan snorted then tried to play it off as a cough. He kept reminding himself that Tori was new; she'd been working off the public perception of how things functioned her entire life. "We know who pretty much every superhero is in their downtime. Between Wade's tech, some well-placed spells, and cell phone cameras, it's nearly impossible not to figure out who someone is under their mask."

"Then shouldn't you be targeting their friends and family? I mean, I'm not saying killing is great or anything, but isn't that the whole point of taking hostages?"

"And see, thinking like that is exactly why the code exists: to protect villains from themselves, and from taking actions they haven't thought all the way through." Ivan swigged a deep gulp of his tea. "Ever hear of a villain named Orbicorb?"

"Doesn't ring a bell," Tori admitted.

"Wouldn't expect it to. He was on the scene in the early days, same as Doc and me. Found out the secret identity of a small-time cape, and since there was no code or guild to stop him, Orbicorb took the guy's family hostage. Things went south, and he wound up killing the whole lot—wife and all three children. Know what happened next?"

"I'm going to take wild swing and say the cape killed your friend?"

"First off, he was a work acquaintance, not a friend. Secondly, you're right, but that was only the beginning. The guy went mad with grief, found Orbicorb, and tortured him for weeks before finally putting him out of his misery. Then he went after every known associate of Orbicorb's, down to the last toady and minion, and killed them too. In the end, we had to form a team specifically to bring him down, and he took a few more of us with him before he went. The lesson here, my young apprentice, is that if you take on a person with powers and leave them with nothing to lose, you have just stuck yourself in a whole wet mess of shit. That's why we have rules about clearing locations with the guild. That's why we have the code."

"Got it, code is super important. No breaky." Tori let herself show a half-smile as she finished her beer. Ivan could be a little scary when he got serious. Even if she hadn't known about all the power he was concealing, his demeanor alone would have had her defenses up.

"The code is the most important part of the villains' guild; it's the entire reason we're able to have a guild at all. Not all of us are traditional criminals; some of us just feel like we should be allowed more freedom with our powers than the law permits. At the end of the day, we're able to live together because we all follow the rules and keep our heads down. It's our constitution, our commandments, and our credo all rolled together." Ivan set his glass down and made sure he had Tori's eye for this next part, as it was likely the information most apt to keep her alive. "And, if you were wondering, the capes never get their hands on code-breakers. We keep our own house clean."

"For villains, you sure do have a lot of rules," Tori said. She'd taken his meaning just fine, but she refused to back down by saying something submissive.

"There are plenty of metas out there breaking the law and living however they choose; this frequently ends with them dead or in jail. We might have rules, but we also have longer lifespans and the ability to go outside. I'd say it's a good trade-off."

"I'll admit that you guys do seem to have your act pretty well together." Tori shook the empty bottle in her hand. "Another?"

"Nope, you'll need your wits about you," Ivan replied, rising from the arm of the couch. "Now that you understand the importance of the code, you're going to be learning it inside and out. I want you as familiar with that document as one of the founders who had to fight over what went into it."

"Oh come on, I thought weekends were going to be battle training," Tori said, moving out of her own seat as well.

"The rest of them will be, but I've always thought that if I had a student, the first thing I would do is drill the code into their head until they said it in their sleep. This weekend and future weekday afternoons are going to be spent reviewing it until I'm satisfied. Then we'll move on to more practical discussions."

"Afternoons? Does that mean I get the days to myself?"

"Absolutely not. You get your evenings and that's it," Ivan told her. "We'll talk about your weekdays tomorrow, once I finish up the details with Doctor Mechaniacal. Be assured, though, you're going to be under constant observation."

"I can really feel the love in this apprenticeship already," Tori said.

"You're not dead yet. That's about as loving as the guild can get. Now let's get you a copy of the code to look over." Ivan walked over to his bookshelf, hands skimming across thick, leather-bound books that Tori had initially assumed were just decoration. As he let his hand dance along the spines, he nearly hit a small picture at the edge of one of the shelves. It was too far away to make out well, but Tori was pretty certain she saw three people and a beach within the photo. He stared at it for a long moment, and then spoke.

29

"There is one more thing to discuss before we start. You'll figure this out soon enough anyway, so I might as well tell you now: I have two children that I get custody of every other weekend. You are never going to meet them, see them, or hear their voices. I understand that what we have here is not a completely voluntary arrangement, and I'm prepared to deal with the consequences of that. If you decide to try and kill me to escape from the guild, so be it."

Ivan turned away from the bookshelf and stared at her. His normal eyes were gone, and in their place were the dark orbs with the blood-red symbols in the center. Tori found herself overcome with the urge to look away but refused to let her neck turn or her eyes waver. Ivan was trying to scare her, and while it was working, she could still show him that she was able to stand her ground.

"I want to be very clear about this, Apprentice. What we have is between you and me, no one else. If you try to harm my children, if you injure them in any way—mentally or physically—I'm going to kill you." Ivan's voice was as empty as the darkness behind the symbols in his eyes. "I won't take any joy in it, I won't feel any glory from it, but I'll still do it. And much as I might dislike it, I am still very good at killing people. Do we understand each other?"

"Crystal clear."

"Good." Ivan turned back to the bookshelf and kept skimming the titles. "Go ahead and lug your suitcase up to the garage apartment and make sure everything is in order. We'll start when you get back."

Tori said nothing; she merely grabbed the suitcase and headed out the door, back into the world of sunshine and nosey neighbors. It was a sharp contrast to the half-lit living room filled with threats, intrigue, and one of the most powerful villains to have walked the earth.

*   *   *

The apartment was surprisingly nice, for having been constructed in only a few days. A bed took up most of the room, but there was also a small desk with a computer, a mini-fridge already stocked with sodas, a microwave, and a work table. The last component was the most important one to Tori, and she knew Doctor Mechaniacal had put it in for her specially. True, there were no high tech tools to play with, nor would she be allowed to make anything too dangerous while in this civilian area, but the work bench represented a space to create. It was a show of respect, scientist to scientist.

As she rested on her bed, a copy of the code lying next to her, Tori wondered when she would find time to begin a new project. Ivan had kept his word and drilled her relentlessly about the code all afternoon, quizzing her constantly with both technical details and hypothetical scenarios. It wasn't like the document was especially long or complicated. It was just important, in a way that was clearly very vital to Ivan.

Tori slid off the edge of her bed and padded over to her computer, jiggling the mouse to bring it out of sleep mode. With a few quick keystrokes, she'd brought up Fornax's Wikipedia page. There was a picture of him, blood-red mask concealing every inch of his face save for those dark eyes with the blood-red runes. He never had any sort of official costume; usually he just wore dark, sturdy clothing. Only the mask and the eyes were constants. Those and the power.

Scrolling down, she skimmed through his biography. Most of it was stuff that she already knew: his early career had started a few decades after the scientist who would become Professor Quantum accidentally introduced new elements to the world and changed the fundamental laws of the universe. Fornax came on the scene after capes were already entrenched and were thought to be unstoppable. In his first outing, he took down three of them; one was so mentally scarred by the experience that they quit the job altogether. When the press saw his eyes and the red glow that emanated from his limbs, some reporter compared his destruction to that of a black hole and named him after one of the few that wasn't just number and letters: Fornax. Only later on would smarter minds point out that this was the name of an actual galaxy, but by that point, the name had already stuck.

The early section covered his damage and criminal patterns thoroughly; Tori noticed that most of Fornax's big crimes were assault. He seemed to love fighting, especially capes. It was hard to reconcile someone like that with the controlled man who'd spent the day lecturing her. Ivan seemed... not weak, certainly, but measured. It was hard to imagine him going on a rampage like Fornax was known to do. Up until he was beaten, anyway.

Tori scanned the entry until she came to the section detailing Fornax's defeat. Lots of capes had gone up against him, but it had taken the girl with the golden glow to actually bring him down: Lodestar. Considered by most to be the most powerful meta-human in known history, she'd met Fornax one on one and brought him down. Granted, the fight had destroyed half a rock quarry and taken three hours, but she'd done it.

The only section after Fornax's defeat was about his death. Temporarily freed from prison, he'd been recruited to help deal with Orion when the mad meta-human tried to turn the earth into an actual black hole. A coalition of capes and villains had worked together and managed to bring Orion down, but only barely. The criminals who survived were supposedly given reduced sentences, though many were also supposedly lost in the fight. Fornax had been among those listed as killed, and Doctor Mechaniacal was "suspected dead" as well.

Tori tapped her finger on the desk as she read more about the incident and scoured the list of names. If Fornax wasn't really dead, there was no guarantee that any of the others were either. But why lie about it? She had a suspicion, a hunch that made her worry she was beginning to think like a paranoid kook. Then again, she reasoned, she was already a member of a secret organization composed entirely of criminals. Perhaps a little paranoia was in order after all. Either way, she intended to get to the bottom of this little mystery. Fortunately, she didn't have to speculate. She could get the information right from the source.

After all, Ivan was supposed to be teaching her.

Chapter 5

"It's called the 'Orion Protocol' for obvious reasons," Ivan told her as they ate breakfast the next morning. Tori had expected him to be cagey, or try and lie his way out of it, but Ivan hadn't even seemed surprised by her question. It made sense; he had to know the topic would be coming up sooner or later.

"Originally, there wasn't a name for it; there really wasn't even an 'it' to name," Ivan continued. "There was just a lot of panicking people desperate for any solution they could find. Since you're bringing this up, I trust you already know about Orion?"

Tori nodded as she spread butter on a pancake. "Former scientist who worked with dark matter, turned himself into some sort of living black hole. He's estimated to be one of the most powerful metas who has ever lived."

"Even that's an understatement," Ivan said. "Orion was terrifying in every sense of the world. Every scrap of humanity he had was burned away in his transformation. Fighting him was like going up against an act of nature. In all my years, I've only ever seen two other metas that *might* be on his level in terms of destructive potential. So, when he made it clear that he was seriously trying to destroy the world and then started to actually do it, a lot of influential people got very scared. Enough to where they were willing to throw anything they could at him."

"Including former criminals." Tori had finished the buttering and had moved on to adding more syrup than was either necessary or healthy.

"Precisely. Doc and I were crooks, and sort of jerks at the time, but we weren't sociopaths. Neither were most of the others locked up with us. We were just young, impulsive, and too weak to resist the temptation our strength offered. We were bad, but we didn't want to see the world destroyed. After all, we had to live here too. Orion put our crimes in perspective, and within a day of him destroying Detroit, we were getting pitched an offer we couldn't refuse."

Ivan paused, rising from the table to refresh his coffee, as well as get the jelly from the fridge. When he returned, he spooned a generous dollop of the purple glop onto his toast, and then continued. "Actually, that's not true. Many of us did refuse it. Not everyone had a life sentence, and even on the inside, we knew going up against Orion was probably suicide. Those of us willing to roll the dice, however, were offered a full pardon in exchange for bringing him down. Obviously, we succeeded, and the government kept their end of the deal. Most of us were too notorious to actually be released, so our deaths were faked and we were handed enough means to restart our lives as civilians, albeit with the caveat that one step over the line would land us back in a super-max."

"Hang on: if this was a one-time deal, then why have a name for the protocol?" Tori asked.

"Smart question," Ivan said. "Orion was a threat to the entire world, but he wasn't the last one. Usually, there's a real risk of Armageddon once a decade or so. When those come, the Orion Protocol gets activated. Not every criminal gets the offer: those who revel in slaughter or death are kept rightly where they should be. But the ones who were just greedy, or dumb, or got in over their heads, they get a second chance. Die fighting or live as a civilian. Luckily, the survivors aren't totally on their own anymore. Now when they get out, the guild is there to help them adjust to the new world and keep them on the right path."

"These people just got out of jail and you and your goons put them right back into a life of crime? That seems terrible from a moral and logistical standpoint. How do you even keep any members?" Tori had demolished half of her pancakes already and was reaching for more syrup. Ivan noted this, also taking her lean figure into the equation. He'd have to get her checked out to see if using her fire-form burned excessive calories. If so, they'd need adequate nutritional supplies on hand for training.

"Officially, the guild is a rehabilitative facility run by former criminals to help others readjust and prevent younger ones from going down the wrong path in the first place," Ivan told her. "We're actually registered as a non-profit. And honestly, a lot of that is true. We do help other villains get back on their feet, and if they want out of the life, then it's our job to help them stay clean. However, for those who can never content themselves with trudging about like a normal person while knowing that they could soar among the skies, we offer different services. Our people work smart, work safe, and keep from getting busted. You'd be surprised how much of what we do is technically legal, assuming you have good lawyers and a loose sense of morality."

"I have to call bullshit here," Tori interrupted. "The capes would never let that happen. They're all about no compromise and keeping the world safe. If you really formed an evil league of wickedness out in the open, they would totally come busting down your doors."

"It's been tried by a few whose reach exceeded their grasp, but most of the older superheroes tolerate us out of necessity. We minimize civilian injuries, we keep our activities out of the public eye, and, most importantly, we maintain order. The capes get to be adored and loved by the entire world, sign sponsorship deals and pull kittens from trees; meanwhile, we make sure the really terrible villains never see the light of day. We're on top, and we're not nice about how we stay there." Ivan sipped his coffee calmly, as though discussing casual murder was a regular breakfast activity.

34

"Some do still dislike us, there's no fighting that, but those in charge recognize the mutual benefits of our situation. They've seen what a world without the guild looked like, when it was constant war between us and them. No one wins in that situation: not us, not the capes, and certainly not the regular people just trying to get through life."

"The devil you know," Tori muttered, polishing off the last of her pancakes. She chewed slowly, savoring the sweet flavor while also contemplating what Ivan was telling her. The world was supposed to be cut and dry—the capes flew around keeping the peace, putting down all who stepped out of line. Now it turned out that they not only tolerated the presence of evil but also might depend on it. The situation, like most, was more complex from within than one could guess from the outside. Complex wasn't always bad, though. In fact, if one was quick, ambitious, and a bit morally flexible, complex could be quite lucrative.

"By the way, don't go depending on using the Orion Protocol to get a free pass on whatever crimes you commit," Ivan cautioned her. "We're quite adept at snuffing out the true world-enders before they rise too high, so such incidents are few and far between. Besides, you were fortunate enough to get recruited to the guild before being incarcerated. That means that if you do the sort of thing that would get you seriously locked up, the capes will never have a chance to find you."

Tori nodded. She was beginning to see why Ivan held the code so dear. It was a mutual shield, keeping them safe from the superheroes, as well as keeping most of the world safe from villains who reveled in senseless destruction. Order was profitable, chaos less so. Still, she was amazed that they'd managed to get so many criminals to go along with it. Tori would have imagined that many were too stubborn or prideful to accept the wisdom of restraint.

And Tori's instincts, as usual, were spot on, even if she didn't yet know it.

* * *

"There can be no doubt, a confluence is coming."

The woman speaking was hunched over a crystal ball on a polished wooden conference table, her face illuminated by the soft purple glow emanating from its smooth glassy surface. She made no gestures or incantation; her focus was solely on what lay in the swirling depths of the ball. The light cast itself on the nearby wall, clashing with the robin's egg blue paint that had been chosen for its soothing properties.

35

Across the room, a woman made entirely of metal and circuitry gave a slight nod. "That aligns with what our data models are suggesting. Scryanthos, can you discern any idea of when the confluence will occur?"

"Don't press her too hard," a young man cautioned. He sat next to Scryanthos, the woman reading the orb, and wore a white-toothed smile as he watched her plumb the ball's depths. Though he was currently out of costume, he favored the same color scheme in his daily attire. On this occasion, he was wearing a dark suit with a red shirt and a black tie. Aside from his irises, which were stained a dark maroon, he could have easily passed for a somewhat pretentious, but otherwise normal, human being.

"I just asked her to try," the metal woman responded. "There's no harm in that. I've got half of my people trying to pin down when they think it will strike."

"Ooooh, care to make a wager on whose department gets it right?"

"Balaam, enough. Xelas is merely trying to collect all the information she can. Since we're dealing with a confluence, I'd trust you to appreciate how important this is for the guild at least." This voice belonged to a woman older than any of the others looked, though she seemed at most to be in her late thirties. Her raven-black hair fell to her shoulders, where it landed atop a tasteful blouse that paired well with her slacks. Unlike Balaam and his irises, there was nothing that marked her as visibly inhuman, which was just the way she liked it.

"My apologies, Morgana." The young man, Balaam, turned to Scryanthos and gently rested his hand on her shoulder. "If you would, my dear, I think we would all greatly appreciate any details you can offer."

"It is... hard to discern," she said. Her eyes were glazed over as her head tilted slightly, straining to divine the unknowable. "But the clouds gather on the horizon. I can feel the pulse of the ley lines as they brim with power. Such a state cannot be maintained. It must come soon. By the new moon's rise, at the latest."

Xelas's digital eyes flickered for a nanosecond as she checked a file on her hard drive. "The next new moon is on Thursday the seventeenth. That means we're looking at a week and a half, assuming Scryanthos is right. I'll ask my people to reconcile the prediction with their own models to be certain."

"Double check all you like," Balaam told her. "Scryanthos is the top diviner among all of our mystics. If she says it will come by the new moon, then that's what will happen."

"I do not doubt her skill, but a deadline and a date are not the same thing," Xelas shot back. "Narrowing it down to a single day would greatly aid us in putting people in position."

"Double check," Morgana instructed. She loathed Wade for making her head up this committee; Xelas was enjoyable, if strange, but Balaam could be an unapologetic ass when he felt like it, which was often. Still, no one could question that the two of them certainly produced results. Morgana remembered a time when they got almost no warning at all of confluences, and then suddenly they were hip deep in meta-humans. This was better. Aggravating, but better.

"And Xelas," Morgana added, "send a message to the other council members. Tell them we're having a mandatory planning meeting on Tuesday. Even if we don't have an exact date, I want all hands on deck for this shitshow."

*   *   *

Once breakfast was done, Tori's education in the code resumed. It was still tedious and mind-numbing stuff, but she took to it with a touch more enthusiasm than she had on the previous day. Now that she understood the reason behind its existence, there was a desire to become familiar with it. It didn't make the morning any more fun; however, it did allow her to see the time as something other than a waste.

Not long after they broke for lunch, Ivan's cell phone began playing a swelling piece of classical music that Tori recognized but couldn't place. He scooped it up and exited the living room, leaving Tori to study on her own. What she'd assumed would be a five-minute call dragged on as Ivan's muffled voice drifted in snippets from the kitchen. The conversation took no less than an hour, and when Ivan returned, he looked weary. The older man carefully lowered himself onto the couch then glanced over at Tori.

"You're smart with technical stuff, right?"

"I built my own go-kart out of discarded parts before the age of five. Yeah, I've got a knack," Tori replied, bristling slightly.

"So you know how to work spreadsheets and databases?"

Tori looked up at her teacher, slowly lowering the document she'd been rereading for at least the fifteenth time. "I think I'd like to know why you're asking that before I answer the question."

"Because," Ivan said, letting out the word like a heavy sigh, "as of tomorrow morning at eight, you are officially my company's newest intern and my personal assistant. Answering phones, writing e-mails, minor scheduling, data processing, things of that nature."

"I beg your damn pardon." Tori's eyes narrowed, and the temperature around her rose by ten degrees. "Listen, I get that you all run on some archaic practices with the whole master and apprentice thing, and I'm on board with

37

that. But if you think you can drag me around as your pretty little secretary just because—"

"Tori, you have a high school diploma, a few college credits, and zero recent work history," Ivan said, cutting her off. "I don't even want to know what kind of strings Wade had to pull in order to get you this position, but I assure you it has nothing to do with your looks or gender." Ivan rubbed his temples carefully, idly wondering if he'd been that quick-tempered at her age. The answer was, of course, yes, but it didn't make dealing with her now any easier. "You need to learn how to blend in with normal society, and to be frank, I don't trust you enough to leave you on your own, so Wade arranged for you to be my assistant."

"And what is that you do, anyway?" Tori asked. She wanted to steer the topic away from her work history, and plus, she could only imagine what sort of position the man who had once held an entire state in terror commanded.

"Project management and coordination for a software company." Ivan gave a halfhearted shrug, as if to say that, yes, he knew how boring it sounded and he didn't have any way to jazz the position up. "I oversee a few departments to make sure products are on schedule and error free."

"Sounds... responsible." Tori couldn't think of anything else to say that wouldn't sound derisive and only barely managed to bite back a snicker.

"It's a safe, simple, uneventful job, which is precisely why I have it," Ivan told her. "For one thing, I have a family to support: the pay is both fair and steady. For another, working a job like mine makes me seem like a responsible member of society. It lends credence to the charade that I'm not actually a member of a guild of villains nor a famous former criminal."

Tori closed the book in her hand, leaning forward into the more interesting conversation. "But you said the capes already knew you were all full of it."

"They do, but my neighbors, friends, coworkers, and children all have no idea," Ivan said. "You're going to want some normality in your world, whether now or in twenty years. It's nice to talk with people about things other than how to loot a bank vault, and if you ever have a family, you won't ever want your children to look at you with the full knowledge of all the things you've done. I'm helping you lay the foundation so that you'll have a civilian identity when the time for it comes."

"A civilian identity? I don't even have a villain identity," Tori pointed out.

"Sure you do. It's all you have." Ivan stretched out his hand and gestured to Tori, moving his arm in a circle. "All of *this* is your villain identity. The woman who dropped out of college and joined a gang, who got along by

38

pulling smash-and-grabs to fund her scientific pursuits, who was nabbed by Doctor Mechaniacal and put into training. Tomorrow, your civilian life starts again. You become Tori, the lady who hit a rough patch but got a lucky break on an internship, and who might be able to work her way into a steady job. She's the identity you'll need to cultivate, to protect."

Tori rose from the chair, walking over to the bookshelf and setting Ivan's copy of the code amid the other tomes. She lingered for a moment, noting the various pictures of him throughout the years: Young Ivan and a pretty woman in a restaurant, Ivan fishing with several other men, Ivan and his children at a picnic. It was strange to see the man she'd read about last night, whose name was whispered like that of a legend or god, in such mundane circumstances. What was even odder was that Ivan looked so natural in them. This middle-management family man struck her as the true version of Ivan; it seemed impossible that he could actually be Fornax. Which, Tori realized, was exactly what Ivan wanted, and what he was trying to teach her how to do.

"If Tori is my civilian self, does that mean villain me needs a code name?"

"Eventually," Ivan said. "For now, Apprentice will do just fine."

Chapter 6

Tori wasn't sure how she felt about the pantsuit. Granted, the dark color paired well with her blue shirt, and the whole outfit wore quite well on her—Doctor Mechaniacal had clearly had it tailored—but the overall look wasn't the issue at stake. What bothered Tori was how the suit made her feel. It was like she was wearing a symbol of selling out, of giving up on her dreams of success and independence. She was going to work a shitty temp job, the very fate she'd bucked against by trying to make her own way in the world. This suit was mundaneness made physical, and it made her skin crawl when she thought about it for too long.

All that made the act of wearing it bearable was the knowledge that it was an act, a costume to protect her true identity. This was her mask; this was the facade that would keep her safe. If the strategy could work for someone like Fornax, then surely it could be effective for her. Besides, it wasn't like she had any choice in the matter.

With one last glance in her mirror, Tori stepped out of the bathroom and left her garage apartment on a course for the main house. Ivan had made it clear that tardiness was completely unacceptable. She wasn't sure that she'd keep heeling to his orders, but the relationship was a bit too fresh to push the boundaries already. Promptness wasn't an excessive demand, anyway, especially since she was supposed to be catching a ride with the boss.

Ivan was waiting when she entered the house, a crisp suit, white shirt, and crimson tie adorning his body. He handed her a bagel and a napkin before they'd even exchanged greetings. "Eat in the car. We need to get to HR in time to fill out your extra paperwork."

Tori cocked an eyebrow even as she accepted the breakfast and followed him out the front door. "I thought all of that was taken care of?"

"All the things that could be handled by others were," Ivan explained. He got into his car, checking his mirrors and buckling his seatbelt. Tori slid into the passenger seat and waited for the ride to start. Instead, she found Ivan staring at her, an impatient, pinched expression on his face.

"What?"

"I'm waiting for you to buckle your seatbelt."

"Seriously? You know I turn into fire reactively when something hits me, right? A car crash won't do jack."

Ivan drummed his fingers against the steering wheel but made no other motion to begin the drive. After a few moments of meeting his gaze, Tori reached up, grabbed the belt, and pushed it into its holder. "Happy?"

"Ecstatic." Ivan turned the keys and pulled out of his driveway. "As I was saying, the forms that could be done were. However, due to our special circumstances, we have to go in personally to fill out extra forms with HR."

"Is this a guild thing?" Tori asked her question through a mouth muffled by a big bite of bagel.

"This is a corporate thing. Since you and I are ostensibly family; your hiring would constitute nepotism if I were the one to orchestrate it. Even working together has the potential to be misconstrued. That's why we'll be signing documents allowing the company to intervene if there are complaints about the quality of your work and me not keeping you on task."

"Almost sounds like working under you puts a target on my back," Tori noted.

Ivan nodded. "In a way it does. You'll have to work harder to prove yourself than someone else in your position would, go above and beyond to show that you deserve to be there."

Tori finished off the last of her bagel, then brushed the crumbs off her pants. Ivan didn't wince as he saw them tumble to the floor of his well-maintained car, but only barely. "So, not only do I have to work a day job, I have to do it while people are muttering shit about me behind my back. Gee, thanks again for getting me this swell position, Teacher."

"I'm not thrilled about this either, but it was the only way to explain your residence at my home and our daily carpooling. If we'd tried to hide the connection that Doctor Mechaniacal established, it would have raised people's suspicions. That is the very opposite of what we are attempting to do." Ivan paused at a light and motioned for another car, merging illegally, to go ahead.

"Yeah, I've been wanting to talk to you about that," Tori said. "While I appreciate how much you all have done for me, I would like to make a return trip to my place at some point. There's some tech I'd like to recover, along with my clothes and my motorcycle."

"Your 'place' has already been emptied out and your possessions cataloged," Ivan replied, twisting the wheel to turn them down a narrow street.

"What? But how?"

"Standard protocol for new members. Everything that you've stolen and could be traced back to you, including your motorcycle, was either dumped or destroyed. The rest is put away safely into storage for when you earn a place of your own. Individual items can be removed by filling out request forms, though they don't often make exceptions for trainees. You aren't supposed to be *that* comfortable, after all."

Tori turned and looked out the window, watching the gray office buildings roll by as they entered the eastern part of downtown. They were so bland and boring, like a corporate version of Ivan's neighborhood. Soon, she would be one of the suit-wearing dots filtering through these places. A wave of nausea tried to rise up in her stomach again, but Tori forced it down. She had been through so much worse than this, and the opportunity in front of her wasn't one she felt inclined to let go of. Tori Rivas could smile and nod as needed, so long as she spent the rest of her time forging the new life being offered to her.

"There's a picture of me with both my parents. We're at a park, and it's in a faded gold frame. Any chance they'd let me have it?"

"Ordinarily, probably not," Ivan said. He drove slowly through the security gate, nodding at the guard on duty while a camera scanned the sticker in his windshield, and then pulled into his assigned parking space. "But I've got a little bit of clout around the guild. Do your best today, and I'll see what I can manage."

Tori nodded; she'd never expected a request to be fulfilled for free. That wasn't the sort of relationship she and Ivan had. In a way, though, it was comforting. She knew the stakes with him. There was no subterfuge or trickery. It was all there, out in the open, which made dealing with him far simpler than with most criminals.

With one last glance out the window, Tori unbuckled her seatbelt and left the car. The dull brown building loomed before her as a river of peons trickled into its glassy mouth of a door. Ivan began moving forward, and she followed suit. It was her turn to be devoured by this place, and she had to do all she could to make sure it didn't spit her back out.

*   *   *

The Alliance of Heroic Champions didn't have a council—or at least didn't call what they had a council, because councils (according to their PR department) tended to conjure up negative imagery associated with shadowy ruling criminals. Instead, they referred to their oversight committee as the Champions' Congress. Unlike in the villains' guild, those on the Congress were not selected by the various groups as representatives. Instead, the three who sat on it were either founding members or appointees who had been chosen by exiting members and ratified by the other two. At least, that's how the replacement system would work in theory. Since none of the original three had formally renounced their positions yet, it was still an untested method.

Fortunately for all involved, the Champions' Congress was only needed for major changes or decisions. The lesser tasks of running the AHC were appropriated to various subcommittees, which held elections every two years. On the same day that Tori was going in for her first day of work, the head of the New Acquisitions subcommittee was walking down a well-lit hallway with a thick folder under his muscular arm. Apollo wore no sleeves; he favored a sleeveless golden breastplate that paired with his armored kilt and sandals. They shone nearly as brightly as the blond curly locks atop his head, a wonderful accentuation to his blue eyes and perfect smile. There was a reason he had been chosen to head the New Acquisitions subcommittee for three elections in a row—the man knew how to turn on the charm when courting unsigned meta-humans.

He walked cheerfully up the hallway, enjoying the sunshine beaming through the clear windows. The AHC's base occupied a large block of drab city streets, but the sprawling compound was outfitted with artificial terrains to fit all walks of life, even those not originating from earth. For Apollo, all he needed was the sun. The shard of divinity he'd inadvertently taken from his namesake, the sun god of legend, reacted each time the light hit him. He felt suffused with power and strength, as though he were truly invincible. Apollo had been on the job long enough to know this wasn't the case, but he still enjoyed the feeling nonetheless.

As he arrived at his destination, Apollo gave three crisp knocks against the wooden door before him. It was unassuming, impossible to differentiate from any of the other offices throughout this floor, because the man inside simply refused to see his position as something that elevated him above the others. While the other two members of the Champions' Congress liked to work remotely or in private quarters when they actually came to base, Quorum viewed himself as one of the people. Well, perhaps not as *one* of them, but certainly not as being any better.

"Come in." The voice from behind the door was firm but friendly. Apollo opened the door to find Quorum typing on his computer. He wore a simple collared shirt and jeans, his usual attire when not functioning in an official capacity, and motioned for Apollo to have a seat.

"Good morning, sir," Apollo said as he carefully settled into one of the gray chairs with which Quorum and all the others had stocked their offices.

"Good morning to you, Apollo." Quorum looked at the younger superhero with a warm smile while his left hand continued typing away at the computer. Multi-tasking was just one of his many talents. "What brings you by this morning?"

"We've gotten wind of a confluence." Apollo set the folder on Quorum's desk; Quorum pulled the folder over and flipped it open with his free hand.

"All magical, astrological, and technological signs point to one striking within the next week or so," Quorum said, quickly interpreting the data before him. "If you don't mind, I'll hang on to this and see if I can't narrow down the window a bit."

"Of course, sir. We have plenty of copies already; that one is for you."

"Excellent. I'll alert Lodestar and Professor Quantum about this, but I trust you are already putting procedures in place," Quorum said. He continued to look at the folder's pages while his hand clacked away at the keyboard. This multi-pronged focus was disconcerting to watch at first, but over time, everyone more or less got used to it.

"We're doubling down on patrols for the next two weeks, as well as putting key people in every hospital, police station, and public area. When the new metas pop up, we'll be there to shake their hand, tell them it's going to be okay, and offer them an application."

"Wonderful work as always," Quorum said. "You're really going all out to prove how much you want that seat."

"It's just me doing my duty," Apollo said, working as hard as he could to keep his voice humble, though only marginally succeeding.

"Please keep it up. Trust me when I say your efforts are not going unnoticed." Quorum flipped through a few more of the pages on his desk. "Also, let's call a meeting for this afternoon. By then, I may have gotten a better idea of when the confluence will strike. The more precise a timeframe we have, the better a chance we're given to help the people dealing with such confusing new circumstances."

"Couldn't have said it better myself, sir," Apollo replied. That was true, whether he meant it to be or not; Apollo wouldn't have been able to keep himself from adding a snide comment to the tail of the statement, however. Quorum might be after these new metas out of pure altruism, but there were many others in the AHC who had different motives.

Most important among them: getting to the new metas before that damn villains' guild did.

*   *   *

"This is your cubicle," Ivan told Tori, gesturing to the small desk with gray felt walls running along the sides which separated it from the identical desks on either side. "There are many like it, but this one is yours."

44

"Does that usually get a laugh?" Tori asked. She set down the stack of papers that HR had given her, idly noting that all her cube came with was a computer and a filing cabinet.

"You'd be surprised. Some people around here think of me as the office cut-up." Ivan's face was stoic as always, his tone as flat as a forgotten soda. "I'll leave you here to get settled in and started on your paperwork, which HR needs to have from you by lunch. After that, we'll have a quick meeting about what your daily schedule should be for this first week as you get your feet wet."

Tori ogled the stack of papers before her, eyes going wide at how much reading and signature scrawling she'd have to do in order to have it complete by lunchtime. "And what are you going to be doing while I work on all this?"

"My job, obviously." Ivan extended his arm and checked his watch, making a small clucking sound with his tongue when he saw the time. "I'm already five minutes late for a morning meeting, in fact. I'll swing by here at eleven, sharp, to take you to drop off your paperwork and show you where the cafeteria is. Please be ready by then."

Without another word, Ivan was heading down the dull carpet under the florescent lights toward some meeting that Tori imagined would make her brain try to eat its way out from the inside if she had to sit through it. Then she looked at the stack of papers on her desk again, and suddenly an escaping, toothy brain didn't seem like such a terrible scenario.

"Hey there," said a new voice from beside her. Tori leaned back to find herself looking at a young man, roughly around her age, with oversized glasses and a shock of bright red hair. "You must be the new administrative assistant. I'm Donald, part of the programming department."

He offered his hand, which Tori accepted and shook. "Tori Rivas. It's nice to meet you, Donald."

"You too," he replied. "And don't worry too much about Mr. Gerhardt. He seems scary, but as long as you get your work done, he's actually really nice."

"I'll keep that in mind," Tori said, giving her cubicle-mate a professional smile. After a few moments of debate, she decided that since they'd gone to all the trouble of creating and telling HR her backstory, she should probably at least try to sell it a bit. "Actually, I already know Mr. Gerhardt pretty well. He's my father's second cousin; they've always been so close that he was like an uncle to me."

Donald's already wide eyes grew several sizes larger as he took in the news. "Oh, wow! No wonder you got such a large starter stack from HR."

45

"Yeah, I got here on my own, but then was put in his department, so, you know, rules are rules." Tori patted the stack of documents, which she could swear was growing every time she looked away, just for added emphasis.

"I wouldn't worry about it too much," Donald told her. "Mr. Gerhardt has a reputation for being fair. I can't imagine anyone will accuse him of giving you special treatment unless he actually does." Donald's pale skin grew suddenly flushed, especially the tips of his freckled ears. "Wait, sorry, I didn't mean to say that—"

"Don't worry, I got what you meant," Tori assured him. After weeks of dealing with the guild and years of being around crooks, she found it oddly endearing to see someone so worried about hurting her feelings. "And trust me, Uncle Ivan isn't going to take it easy on me. If anything, I'm on thinner ice than anyone here."

"In that case, maybe I should leave you alone so you can knock out all that HR paperwork." Donald glanced at the massive stack of papers on her desk; even with his years of corporate drudgery, he couldn't help but blanch at the sight.

"Sadly, I think you're right." Tori started to turn back to her desk but then paused. Much as it pained her to admit it, she'd barely understood half the lingo thrown about in the HR meeting. If all the papers demanded was a series of signatures, then she would be fine, but some of the pages seemed to have a lot of blanks, the sort she would be expected to put more than a name in. Much as she enjoyed being independently capable, Tori was not so prideful that she couldn't see the benefit in receiving help when stuck in an unfamiliar land. Besides, if Ivan had put her in a situation where she'd be facing unfriendly forces, it was best to accrue allies as quickly as possible.

"Hey, Donald, this is my first time working for such an... organized company. If I hit anything in this stack that I need clarification on, would you mind if I asked you for help?"

"Not at all," Donald said, a sheepish grin stretching across his face. "After all, we grunts have to look out for each other."

Tori wasn't sure how she felt about the "grunt" classification, but Donald's sentiment was exactly what she'd been hoping for. With a little luck, a bit of guidance, and all of her wit, Tori felt like she might just be able to fake it through a whole day of her charade.

*   *   *

Ivan had just made it into his office when he saw the shadow in the corner of the room. His eyes narrowed, and he readied himself for an attack. As

46

a member in good standing of the guild, and one of the seven councilors at that, there was no official reason he would have to fear being jumped. But when one dealt with villains, it was always best to assume a power grab or unexpected grudge could lead to assassination attempts at any given time. It had happened before, though the poor bastards that had come to Ivan's home that night had learned how little patience he had for his sleep being interrupted.

"Councilor," the shadow said, speaking in a whisper that Ivan instantly knew would be inaudible to anyone besides him. "I come to tell you that a meeting has been called for tomorrow night. It is high priority, and all seven must be in attendance, as per the code's agreements."

With still-watchful eyes, Ivan gave a small nod, and the shadow vanished. Arcanicus must have sent it; he was one of only three people in the guild who *officially* knew Ivan's identity. After a couple of coup attempts, Ivan had made certain that his civilian name stayed off all records, and had Wade scramble any digital footage of him when he entered the guild hall. He wore a mask at meetings and always used his official code name when dealing with most of the others, all to make it more difficult to find out who he was. None of this would stop the truly determined, of course, but it made it more difficult. Sometimes that was enough of a deterrent in itself, especially since he represented the segment of the guild least likely to care about an attempt to grab power.

Of the seven guild sections, Ivan Gerhardt was the chosen representative of those who were non-active members. The retired villains, as most called them, or the whipped dogs, as some of his more... asshole-ish colleagues liked to say.

Ivan went to his desk and grabbed some papers for the morning meeting. Mysterious messages and foreboding warning aside, he still had work to get done. Besides, if they were calling it a high priority, but not an emergency, then things probably weren't that bad.

He hoped.

47

Chapter 7

"Please tell me I'm not just going to be doing that all the time," Tori said as they walked through the front door of Ivan's house. "Because if so, you may as well go ahead and let the guild know that they can kill me. I'll take a quick death over god knows how many years of sitting in that place."

"When you become a full member, we can find a cover-job that suits your style better," Ivan said, following her in and locking the door. As always, he ran his hand down the seam between the door and the frame, muttering words that Tori could barely make out and had zero comprehension of. "Maybe something in the technological sector? I'm sure they can find space for you at Indigo Technologies."

"Um... Ivan," Tori said, her voice suddenly filled with uncertainty rather than annoyance. "I think you should see this."

Turning around slowly—it did no good to show fear to a potential adversary—Ivan's eyes followed Tori's gaze to the coffee table, where a large box with a bow rested in the center. It was done in a silver and black style that Ivan instantly recognized as Doctor Mechaniacal's. Still, he approached the package slowly, motioning for Tori to stay back. Looking like something his friend had left him and *being* something his friend had left him were two entirely different things. Ivan delicately lifted the top off the box, and then let out a sigh of relief.

"It's fine," he said. "They just dropped off your outfit for tomorrow night."

"Am I going to the ball?" Tori moved forward slowly, trying to get a better look at what lay inside the mysterious box.

"No, but I think this will suit you far more than some empty-headed gala ever would." Ivan reached in and pulled out a swatch of long, dark fabric trimmed with a fiery red color along the seams and edges. "This is your apprentice's outfit, and it's what you'll wear at all times when we're on guild business." He handed the box to Tori, who began pulling out the various components.

"Shirt, boots, pants, cloak, mask..." Tori laid each piece on the ground as she extracted it, assembling the whole outfit on Ivan's carpeted floor. "Sort of generic-looking."

"It's an apprentice's outfit," Ivan reiterated. "It's meant to be generic. Full guild members get to design their own uniforms, but until you graduate to that level, you'll be left to blend in with every other apprentice out there. We do this partly to remind you of your place, but it also helps from a training

48

perspective. By keeping the costumes neutral, it makes it hard to tie any crimes you might commit in your apprenticeship to the identity you ultimately assume. Sort of a clean slate, in case you make any goofs during your training."

"Wait, other apprentices?" Tori looked up at her teacher, who was examining the outfit she'd extracted. "I thought most of the newbies went through standard training. I only got given to you for being such a fuckup."

"Every guild member undergoing training is considered an apprentice," Ivan told her. "It's just that very few of them get teachers. See the red trim on your shirt and cloak?" He pointed to the areas, despite the fact that they were nearly impossible to miss in the otherwise endless sea of black fabric. "That marks you as a taken apprentice. The color matches what's on my outfit, so that anyone you deal with in the guild knows who is ultimately responsible for you."

"Just by the color?"

Ivan shrugged. "We used to do symbols, but as fewer people took apprentices, it got to the point where just color was enough to mark who was connected to whom."

Tori finished laying out her costume and eyed it critically. She'd have to try it on to be sure, but from a glance, it seemed to be perfectly crafted to her measurements. Since Doctor Mechaniacal had already gotten clothes for her, it was hardly surprising that the guild would have her new outfit tailored, but it was beginning to get her feeling a bit creeped out. It was something she supposed she'd have to get used to, though. Ivan had been worried by the mysterious box in his home, but he hadn't really seemed at all surprised by its appearance. Personal limits might be something she had to learn to reevaluate if she wanted to survive in this world.

"Where am I supposed to wear this to, anyway?"

"A meeting of the guild's council." Ivan left the living room and entered the kitchen, set on getting dinner started. It had been a long, late day at the office, and he felt that a solid meal would do them both good. "They've called an impromptu meeting, and as one of the seven councilors, I am obligated to attend. As my apprentice, you are expected to come along as well."

"Oh joy, you're dragging me to another meeting." Tori's mind went back to the day's activities, which had consisted almost entirely of paperwork, taking notes, and doing all she could to not fall asleep while people droned on about things she neither knew nor cared about.

Ivan turned to glare at her, an action which might have been more menacing if he wasn't holding two onions in his hands. Perhaps realizing the way his menace was undercut by the produce, he set the onions on the cutting board and grabbed a knife. "This is not merely 'another meeting' as you so flippantly described it. We are talking about all seven of the guild's councilors discussing high-level, important issues. Some guild members would give every item they own to attend such a gathering."

"Cool guild members?" Tori asked. "Like, guild members with a lot going on in their lives? Or guild members who are super boring and probably don't have much to do? I've got to be honest with you: I don't buy that a meeting is the happening place to be, no matter who's there."

Ivan glowered at her as he sliced the onions, clearly unworried by the fact that a slip of the knife would press it against his unguarded flesh. "It doesn't matter if it is 'cool' or not. The council is gathering, and we both have to go. Plus, it will be a good opportunity for you to meet some of the other guild members. Doctor Mechaniacal told me that you never graduated beyond the isolation phase."

"You just love throwing that back in my face, don't you?" Tori leaned against the wall and watched as Ivan expertly diced his onions. He hadn't even bothered to change out of his suit from work, yet he seemed neither worried about stains nor inconvenienced by wearing it. Sometimes Ivan reminded Tori of the uncanny valley: he was so close to being normal, but then he would give away his strangeness in subtle, unexpected ways. "Fine, so I didn't get to meet anyone besides Doctor Mechaniacal and the occasional trainer. Should I really be trying to make friends before we're even sure I'll survive my training?"

"I don't see why not. Every other apprentice lives with the same knowledge that they might die, and it doesn't stop most of them from making friends."

Tori choked a bit, despite her mouth being empty. "Wait, *every* apprentice has the 'fuck up and die' sword dangling over their head?"

"Certainly. We didn't make up the rules just for you," Ivan replied. He'd finished the onions and moved on to a tomato. "Any potential guild member who fails to meet expectations is terminated. The only difference between you and the others is that you already came close to meeting your end."

"Damn. That is some pretty extreme shit right there."

Ivan paused to look at his apprentice. He didn't glare at her, nor was he as disinterested as she was accustomed to. For what might have been the first time, Tori thought she sensed a bit of empathy in his eyes.

"We are not the good guys. No matter how structured or careful our code may be, never forget that we are an organization of criminals and potential killers. If the guild fails to neutralize threats early on, entire cities can be wiped out, and the tentative peace we've managed to cultivate becomes strained. Make no mistake: we cannot afford things like leniency or mercy. Not when dealing with the sort of people who join us."

Tori nodded, and Ivan went back to preparing dinner. Sometimes she let herself forget that not everyone would be like Doctor Mechaniacal and Ivan—decent men who simply didn't seem to care much for playing by the rules. Come the next evening, she would probably meet true monsters, the sort who were only constrained by stronger beings watching over them. Beings like Ivan.

Moving quietly out of the kitchen, Tori headed back into the living room and began picking up her outfit from the floor. If she had to step among the serpents, she'd best make sure her own snakeskin fit her properly.

* * *

After dinner was eaten and Tori had confirmed that her costume fit her as well as everything else she'd been provided with so far, Ivan took her into the living room for their evening training. Tori didn't ask questions; she just headed toward the bookshelf and prepared to pull out Ivan's copy of the code.

"Not tonight," he said, stopping her before her hand closed around the book. "You did well over the weekend. I think we can move to doing a weekly code review rather than spending all of our time on it. Let's begin your practical training instead."

Tori kept a solemn face as she nodded and walked back over to the couch, but the ripple of heat around her betrayed her excitement and nerves at this next step in her education. The temperature rise didn't escape Ivan's notice; in fact, it was the very subject he wanted to discuss.

"Next to the code, control is the most important thing for any meta-human to learn." Ivan motioned for her to sit, which Tori did. "Precision, power, effectiveness, subtlety: all of this comes from control. When you can use your abilities as you wish, and only use them intentionally, then the options spread out before you in any given situation are multiplied exponentially."

"Yeah, I know," Tori said, leaning back against the couch. "That's why I practiced so much when I first got my fire powers. I can light a cigarette from across a room without scorching the hand holding it."

"That may well be, but you can't seem to stop throwing off heat whenever you get worried, or excited, or experience any other sudden flux of emotion," Ivan countered. "Besides that, I've watched all your combat tapes from your time at the guild, and I was greatly underwhelmed by the amount of exploration you've done in developing your power's technique. All you did was throw fireballs or charge headlong into battle while in fire-form."

"I don't generally use my powers in the first place. I'm like Doctor Mechaniacal—all about the tech. I plan on building a meta-suit so advanced that it won't even matter if the wearer can turn into flames or is somehow made of glass."

"And there's nothing wrong with that aspiration," Ivan said. "However, until such time as you manage to complete that sort of suit, your abilities are all that distinguish you from a mundane human. You need to make the most of them, and you need to have them firmly in hand. Calling forth every bit of your power is how you survive as a villain; being able to turn it off completely is how you survive as a civilian. My goal is to help you reach that level of control."

It wasn't quite the "leaping skyscrapers" training Tori had been hoping for, but she was too pragmatic to deny the benefit of mastering her abilities. Truth be told, she'd tried on several occasions to find a cure for the cursed things—turning spontaneously into flames was more of a liability than asset when dealing with complex and delicate electronics. She'd eventually gotten them in hand, but Ivan was right in that she'd never really bothered exploring them. Her fire powers were just a thing she dealt with, not an asset she depended on.

"I guess I can get on board with that," Tori agreed. "Especially if I'm going to have to tag along with you to that office every day. Can't very well go warming up the entire building if one of the old guys slaps my ass."

"No, if that happens you come directly to me, and then we go to HR," Ivan told her. "Our company has a zero-tolerance policy on that sort of sexual harassment."

"I was kidding, sheesh. My point is that, yeah, if I'm throwing off heat unintentionally, then that's something I'd like to stop doing. The question is how? I already keep myself under pretty tight reins, but I don't know how to stop something that involuntary. It's like trying to learn to stop blushing when you get embarrassed."

"That is something else that you can, and will, learn how to do." Ivan left the living room and entered the kitchen, returning moments later with what looked like a small lighter. "For controlling your power, however, we're going to start by getting you accustomed to controlling your involuntary reactions. Today, you told me that your body automatically responds to damage by turning into fire, correct?"

"Always has in the past," Tori confirmed.

"Excellent. Does the method matter? Cutting, smashing, slicing, etcetera?"

"Well, burning doesn't work on me, for obvious reasons." Tori eyes were on Ivan's lighter, which he was fidgeting with absentmindedly as he stared at her. "Other than that, pretty much anytime I got seriously hurt, I went into fire-form."

52

"That is precisely what I wanted to hear." Ivan tossed her the lighter, which Tori snatched out of the air. "Would you mind lighting that for me?"

She turned the device around in her hands a few times, trying to figure out just what Ivan was up to. The lighter was made of silver metal and had a large plunger rather than the usual small wheel to flick. It was etched with a tasteful design, and seemed to be well-crafted from what little Tori knew about such devices. Having never been a smoker, her experience was limited to lighting candles and Bunsen burners. Tori rested her thumb against the plunger, and then, after one last glance at Ivan, pressed down on it.

"Son of a bitch!" The lighter fell to the ground as Tori's hand turned to insubstantial flames. The shift went all the way up to her elbow, where it thankfully stopped a few feet short of the t-shirt she'd changed into after work. "That damn thing shocked me!"

"Neat, right?" Ivan asked. "I had Doc whip it up based on a toy my son brought home a few years ago. It should hurt, but not do any lasting damage. Plus, it's fireproof and tough as hell, so you won't accidently break it. That lighter is now your training tool. I want it with you at all times, no matter where we are."

"The hell for?" Tori asked. She took a deep breath and willed her hand and forearm to resume their usual form. After a few seconds of concentration they complied, and the flickering light of her fiery appendage died out.

"You need to learn to control your involuntary responses. Since we can't shift your emotions about easily, the best path is through pain. You're to use that lighter until you can get shocked without shifting into fire-form."

"Oh, sure, that sounds just *super* easy." Tori bent down and picked the lighter back up, turning it over in her hands once again. Despite being unceremoniously dropped, it didn't bear as much as a single scratch. Ivan was right, the thing was sturdy.

"No, it will likely be one of the most difficult tasks I ask you to undertake," Ivan said. "But that's why I'm here to help. For example, just from observing what happened, I would say your first step is to focus on not overreacting."

Tori glared at her teacher with a pinched expression. "I am not sorry for cursing when you tricked me with a damn shock-lighter."

Ivan sighed—a long, weary rasp of air that puttered out from his lips—and shook his head. "Your transformation: that's where you overreacted. The only part of you being attacked was your thumb, but you shifted all the way up to your elbow. Try and focus on subduing that aspect first. Learn what it feels like when your body acts without permission, and then try to interrupt that action before it can occur. Starting with tempering the amount is easier than trying to stop it entirely."

"Why? I mean, I get the goal overall, but isn't going incorporeal when someone tries to hurt me a good thing? The reaction has saved my life more than once. I don't know that I want to try and get rid of it."

"That is... actually a very practical concern," Ivan admitted. He walked over and took the lighter from her, holding it in his own hands. "And honestly, you probably don't want to get rid of the reflex, not entirely. But there is a keen difference between something being eradicated and something being controlled." Ivan flipped the lighter open and pressed his finger against the plunger, locking eyes with Tori as he did so.

"Right now, my body wants to react by releasing a surge of power to destroy the thing attacking me. It's my instinct, and when I first got my abilities, it's exactly what I would have done. But instinct wouldn't explain away the shattered metal in my hand, so discipline is required to both keep me and my secret safe. Thus, I allowed a small ward to materialize on my thumb, stopping the mild electrical current from entering my skin."

"Really?" Tori looked down around his thumb to see if she could spot a telltale glow or the edge of a glyph.

"Indeed." Ivan raised his thumb, and she could see a small arcane pattern of light slowly fading away. "Although, to be honest, electricity of this level can't cause me pain... but you get the point of what I was trying to demonstrate. The first step is learning to limit your reaction to only the absolutely necessary. After that, you learn to will yourself not to react at all, in case you ever need to feign being truly human and vulnerable. Once you've gotten that down, you'll have the self-awareness to stop other, less immediate reactions, like letting off heat involuntarily."

"You can ease up on the sales pitch. I get the idea," Tori said. She held out her hand, and Ivan returned the lighter to her. Holding it carefully, she flicked the top open once more and stared at the plunger. He finger crept closer to the button she knew would send a shock through her arm, but before her thumb could land upon it, she looked back up at Ivan. "Just out of curiosity, do you mind if I ask what exactly your power is, anyway?"

He raised a single eyebrow, showing neither scorn nor acceptance. Tori was slowly learning that this was Ivan's "explain yourself" expression, the one he used when he wanted to hear all of someone's case before making a decision.

"It's... well, no one was ever totally sure what Fornax's power was. It was obvious he used magic—he could make those glyphs in midair that he used all the time—but he never seemed to cast spells and he fought like someone with enhanced physical abilities. You just said that electricity can't hurt you, which seems like it hints at limited invulnerability, but I've been here for days and I've yet to see you do any sort of spell or ritual that would provide that sort of protection. It's all really confusing and interesting, so I thought I'd swing for the fences and see if you'd tell me."

Ivan stared at her for several long moments before lowering his arched eyebrow. "First off, whatever Fornax's powers were have no significance; he is dead, after all. Second, I said electricity of that level couldn't hurt me, not that I was immune to it entirely. Enough power can bring me down, make no mistake of that. Lastly, I keep my abilities a secret for the same reason you should do the same: the less people know about what you can do, the more likely you are to be able to bluff them, or conceal vulnerability. That said, I will tell you where my power comes from... when I think you're ready."

That was actually a lot more than Tori had expected to get out of him. She knew she should be grateful for it, but she couldn't quite resist the urge to push her luck a bit more. "Conceal vulnerability? Does that mean that even you have a secret weak spot?"

The grin that spread across Ivan's face answered her question before he even spoke a single word. "No, I do not. That was just a general example." He tapped the lighter in her hand, careful to avoid turning it on himself accidently. "Now get to work. It will take a lot of effort to gain control of your reactions, and I'd like you as prepared as possible for tomorrow night."

Tori looked back at the device in her hand and pressed her thumb to the plunger once more. If this was the only way forward, she'd best get started down the path as quickly as possible, even if she knew it was going to suck for a long time before it got better.

Chapter 8

Tori's second day of work went better than the first, if only because it didn't require an uncomfortable meeting and a massive pile of paperwork. Instead, her morning (along with that of two other new hires) began with three hours of the "system training" that was mandatory for all new employees. The training centered on learning to navigate basic programs and utilize the company's proprietary software. She could appreciate the necessity for the instruction, and that it was given before any of them were asked to perform essential tasks. Unfortunately, Tori's intelligence and technical expertise allowed her to figure out each program within fifteen minutes, leaving her with over two hours of boredom to fill as she clacked away at the keyboard and tried not to groan when the others asked questions.

Despite what others in her life suspected, Tori's intelligence didn't come from any meta ability that she was aware of. It was simply a combination of having a knack for technology, an inquisitive mind, and the unwillingness to accept that any topic or material was beyond her range of comprehension. She knew how to figure out programs because she'd been researching software just as much as hardware since she was a child.

Tori was a prodigy, of that there was no doubt, but compared to the likes of Doctor Mechaniacal, she may as well have figured out a light switch. This limitation held back many of the would-be scientists in her generation, who were certain they would not contribute anything that the meta-geniuses of the world couldn't. Tori kept a more optimistic view of things; she understood that just because she couldn't make the breakthroughs others might didn't mean she couldn't add her own spin. After all, a genius may have invented the wheel, but someone with practicality thought of the axle.

After the system training was done, they took a break for lunch. It was catered, cold sandwiches from a nearby shop that were actually tastier than Tori expected. She made small talk with the other new hires, both of whom were older men named Stan, but the age gap made it difficult to find common ground in such a short time. When lunch ended, Tori and the Stans were brought back into their small training room to go over company policy for the rest of the day. It was still boring, but at least it was boring by nature, rather than due to Tori mastering the material. In a sense, she knew they were all suffering, and somehow that made the burden slightly more bearable.

At last, the day came to an end. Tori made sure to thank her instructor, a pleasant woman from HR named Barbara who insisted everyone call her Barb. It was important to make a good first impression on anyone who did the hiring and firing—even Tori knew that—plus, they were going to be stuck together for the rest of the week. Best to keep things cordial whenever possible.

After saying goodbye to the Stans, who had hit it off and were discussing the possibility of a fishing trip that weekend, Tori darted down the hallway, nearly knocking over a chair in her excitement to get to Ivan's office.

"Done!" Tori announced, flinging her hands in the air as if she'd just made a touchdown. Her foot kicked the door, knocking it closed behind her.

Ivan stared at her over the top of his computer monitor, then began shutting his system down for the day. Much as he wished she'd maintain a little more decorum, even Ivan hated dealing with the mandatory training sessions. Besides, her main job was to seem normal, and being glad to get done with a work day was about as normal as anyone could get.

"Let me power down my computer, and we can go," he told her.

Tori nodded then flopped into one of the two chairs Ivan's office boasted. While some took this as a mark of opulence, the chairs were in fact a mark of responsibility. They were there so that Ivan could call people into his office and have... *chats* with them whenever they weren't "living up to their potential," as Ivan liked to phrase it. Often, these were meant to motivate his employees so that they wouldn't fall below the threshold of tolerance and lose their jobs. Occasionally, however, Ivan had to fill the other chair with an HR representative, and let them know that wherever they ultimately lived up to their potential, it wouldn't be with this company.

"What's the game plan for tonight, anyway?" Tori asked. "Do we get picked up by a mysterious car that floats around the city? Or is there a hidden teleporter somewhere in your house that we use?"

"I'm driving us there," Ivan said, frowning at her attempts to discuss guild matters in public. Yes, his office was warded and soundproofed in ten different ways, but she didn't know that.

"Do we change here?" Tori looked around the room, scanning for some secret latch or hidden closet where they could don their costumes. Of course, since they'd still have to walk out to the parking lot, strutting around in those outfits would draw a lot of unnecessary attention.

"We change there," Ivan told her. "Masks go on once we enter the garage, and then there are changing stalls for us right inside the door. From that point on, the uniforms don't leave until we do. Exceptions can be made for fittings and potty breaks, but the masks stay on no matter what."

"Did you just say 'potty breaks'?"

Ivan's ears reddened, just a bit at the tips, and he turned back to his computer. "We are still in the workplace, and proper language should be utilized at all times."

"Uh huh." Tori wasn't entirely convinced, but she decided not to rib him too hard about it. They were, after all, about to walk into a building full of dangerous people. Pissing off the person she'd be looking to for guidance seemed like a risky move, even for Tori. "Why the mask emphasis, though? Do none of you know who the others are?"

"Some of us do; others have managed to hide their identities from the majority. Full members of the guild can forgo wearing a mask inside headquarters, if they should so choose. As an apprentice, however, you are expected to be in mask at all times when on official business. It's part of your training, learning to separate your identities."

"I'm with you; the mask marks the difference between Tori and Apprentice."

Ivan stood from his desk, reaching and grabbing the large briefcase resting beside one of the chairs. His apprentice was quick; many of the other initiates didn't catch the symbolism until they'd made the transition a few times. He also knew that she'd been up late into the night practicing with the lighter. Though he hadn't told her about them, the lighter had a few extra features built in. Along with the shocking apparatus, it also served as a GPS tracker, and it regularly broadcast data about its user to a server that only Ivan could access. That was how he knew that she'd shocked herself two hundred and thirty-two times after going to her apartment last night.

In spite of himself, Ivan was beginning to grow fond of his apprentice. She could be surly and snarky when the mood suited her, but she was also serious about learning once she understood the need for it. The more time he spent with her, the more he hoped he wouldn't ultimately have to kill her. The meeting would be a good testing point of that; if she could follow instructions and hold her own, there might just be hope for her yet. If, however, she made a serious error in front of the council, then Ivan would have no choice. It would fall on him to end her. That too was the responsibility of taking on an apprentice.

"You brought your costume, right?" Ivan asked.

"Stowed it in the trunk before we left this morning," Tori said.

"Good. Before we leave, you can dig out the mask. I'll let you know when to put it on." Ivan stepped forward and opened the door, ending their conversation of guild matters for the time being. He strode down the nearly empty hallway (Tori wasn't the only one happy about the end of a work day) and headed for the elevators. Behind him, Tori matched his pace, refusing to be left behind.

*   *   *

58

Morgana checked over the conference room for the fifth time, making sure everything was neat and in order. Though she was a councilor and there were robots and underlings to attend to such tasks, Morgana still liked to double check their meeting spaces before the council actually gathered. It was her own little ritual to keep her nerves at bay, like Wade's Sudoku or Ivan's eating. Looking at the pushed-in seats, the tastefully arranged plates of food, and the immaculately clean room soothed her, allowed her to feel as though things were under control.

That was a lie, obviously. Things were never truly under control in their world, and even less so when these seven people were in the same room together. Some were old friends, some loved each other like family, but a few had dislikes ranging from minor annoyances to outright grudges. That made seating important, as any buffer that could be put between certain parties minimized the chance of a meeting turning into outright war. With two exceptions, every person in the room was weak to another party's abilities, so fights could theoretically be neutralized before they got out of hand. As any experienced villain knew, however, what was doable in theory and what happened in practice were often very different things.

Morgana checked the seating position around the horseshoe-shaped conference table once more, certain all was in order. Gork was closest to the door, her chair the only one raised four feet off the ground and triple-reinforced to bear her considerable frame. Next to Gork was Xelas, since they were nearly inseparable friends. Gork's calm demeanor also had a soothing influence on Xelas, and often kept the mechanical woman from instigating a quarrel with Balaam. Ivan would be on the other side of Xelas, and next to him would be Stasis. Stasis often liked to sit with Balaam, but they goaded one another on too often, so it was best to stick her near Ivan. No one was entirely certain if Ivan's power could be the one thing to hurt Stasis, and thus far, she'd kept her nose clean enough not to find out. After Stasis would be Wade, who got along with everyone, and then Balaam, who trod on many of the older generation's nerves. Last would be Morgana herself, taking the final seat in the horseshoe since Balaam would be offended by it and she trusted herself not to rise to his endless antagonism.

It wasn't perfect, but then again, neither was the council, so this would have to suffice. At least this time they had an important subject to deal with, which would ideally keep everyone focused. The general meetings were always the worst, since no one wanted to be there and often made that fact known by acting up. Dealing with a confluence, dangerous as it could be, was at least exciting: things might go wrong, lives may end up on the line, and there was always the scramble to snatch up the newest recruits before the AHC did, once things settled down.

Morgana had a feeling that at least a few members would make some of those new rookies personal apprentices, once they were officially in the guild. Though nearly everyone would deny it, Ivan was still something of a trendsetter among the guild. Rumor had already spread that he'd taken a disciple, and many of the less-informed members were wondering why the other council members hadn't been allowed to do the same. It didn't matter that Ivan had done it as a favor to Wade, or that no one else had because the practice fell out of use for more pragmatic options. All that mattered was that some of the other seven felt that they were being compared to Ivan and coming up short, which was not something they could bear.

She felt a bit sad for Ivan's apprentice. He might be able to handle the weight of expectation and judgment on his shoulders, but Morgana feared it would break someone so new to the guild. There was nothing to be done for it, though.

Morgana took one last look around the room, helped herself to one of the catered sandwiches, and left to go put on her proper costume.

The meeting would be starting soon.

*   *   *

Tori hadn't gotten to see the guild headquarters when she was there the first time around. She'd just been escorted by Doctor Mechaniacal to various training activities and testing areas in the pork plant throughout the day, and then ultimately led to her apartment-sized quarters in the evening. Occasionally, she would be brought before another individual in a full mask and costume, sometimes to talk and other times to showcase her skill, but for the most part, her tenure in standard training had been a solitary existence. At the time, she'd taken it as a precaution against her learning too much information, in case things didn't work out. It was only after Ivan explained how close to the precipice she'd actually been that Tori realized the true reason she'd been kept alone: Doctor Mechaniacal didn't want anyone getting attached to her, in case she didn't ultimately make the cut.

It was a sobering thought she tried not to dwell on as she and Ivan walked down the long metal hallway leading out of the dressing rooms. She'd gotten to see her own outfit when she tried it on the previous night, but it was her first opportunity to see Ivan in costume. It was a far cry from his Fornax outfit, which had mostly been half-ripped clothes and a blood-red mask. These days, he wore a simple red-and-black costume with a mask that was all black, save for red trim around the eyes. It was so nondescript that she wondered how he managed to stand out among the other villains, then quickly realized he was trying to do exactly the opposite of that. He wanted to be unseen, unheard, and unknown as much as possible.

"Hey, wait." Tori stopped walking, and Ivan immediately halted as well.

"Are you nervous?"

"Huh? No, I got this shit," Tori replied quickly. The worry in his voice had caught her off guard. She was used to casually indifferent Ivan; seeing him show her concern was a curveball she didn't want to try and hit. "I actually just wanted to ask what I call you in here. You made a big deal about not using the F-X word, and I'm assuming you don't go by your actual name, so how do I address you while we're inside?"

"You will address me as Teacher," Ivan informed her, back to his usual authoritative tone. "However, should you need to know it, while in these walls, I am officially called Pseudonym."

Tori stared at him for a long moment, and then began slowly clapping her gloved hands together. "Woooooow. You must have really strained to come up with that one. I'd tip my mask to you, but, you know, that would break the rules about always having it on."

"Your sarcasm is not appreciated," Ivan said.

"I bet it's not." Tori stopped clapping and shook her head. "Geez, did you put any effort into your name at all?"

"No, in fact, I did not," Ivan replied. "My goal was specifically to show how little I cared about what they called me here. I am a retired member. I do not wish to strike fear into hearts or be known across the continents. All I want to do is the bare minimum required of someone of my station and be left alone."

"Then why... why are we here?" Tori shied off at the last moment from her real question— asking Ivan why he'd taken her as an apprentice if that was how he felt. It wasn't that she feared he'd dodge the question or lie. In fact, she knew Ivan would be completely straight with her, which was part of why she stopped herself from asking. She wasn't sure she really wanted the answer.

"I mean, you keep saying you don't like this stuff, but they still call you in for emergency meetings and you show up," Tori continued. "Is this what retirement means? You don't do the crime, but you still have to come to all the meetings?"

"My case is special," Ivan told her. He began walking again; Tori followed, easily keeping pace with her teacher. "I was elected by the other retirees to serve on the council as their representative. That's why I'm still on a leash, even though I've officially quit the game."

"Hang on, there are elections? I knew there was a council, but I just assumed it was occupied by whoever had the most power."

Ivan gave a slight nod. "That is a big part of it; no one wants a weakling representing their interests. We still choose our leaders, though, once every six years. Every meta-human gets to vote based on their classification, in order to be sure that each group has an equal voice at the table."

"Let me take a guess at this: one of the classifications is obviously people who have retired, hence you, and I'll bet another is people who build stuff, like Doctor Mechaniacal."

"You're correct," Ivan replied. "There are also groups for those who use magic, those with innate abilities, artificially-created beings, nonhuman naturally-occurring beings, and those who achieved their meta-status by having their bodies or genetics fundamentally altered."

"Which makes seven." Tori paused for a moment, mulling the information around in her head. "What about me? I'm genetically altered, and I plan to use gadgets like Doctor Mechaniacal, so which group would I get to vote in?"

"You'll make that decision if and when you ascend to full guild membership status," Ivan told her. "Around that time, you pick your group. We're not so concerned with people having a foot in more than one pool; the main issue was making sure that everyone, no matter how unique, has someone looking out for their interests."

Ahead of them loomed large metal doors. Instinctively, Tori knew that beyond them was the guild, the real one, not the small selection of cells she'd seen before. This time, she felt the heat rise around her as her stomach tightened. Ivan clearly noticed but said nothing, which she was thankful for. They both knew she was working on it—pointing out her slip-ups would do no good for either of them at this point.

"I've said it before, and I'll say it again: for an organization of villains, you sure do have some strange policies in place," Tori quipped, trying to keep her mind off the prospect of what lay beyond the doors.

"And as I've said before, there is a reason for that. Many meta-humans become criminals because they see no other path forward. They have power, but are still suppressed by society. Eventually, they see their abilities as their only avenue toward being heard, which leads to acting out. We created a system that emphasized giving everyone a voice because it makes them less likely to try and start an uprising." Ivan walked over to a small console and pressed his eye up to a small, glowing green spot.

"Welcome, Pseudonym." As a voice from the console spoke, the doors before them parted. Slowly they moved until the room beyond could be seen. Inside of it were several people milling about.

Tori took a deep breath, gathered her willpower, and took her first steps forward into the guild of villains.

Chapter 9

The large, red-carpeted lobby wasn't quite as full as Tori had expected. She counted a half-dozen people lounging about in costumes, most either working on laptops or making small talk. Tori was about to ask Ivan for an explanation when she put the pieces together on her own: this was an emergency meeting for the council. There was no reason for a lot of the other guild members to be present. The small group made her feel a bit more at ease as Ivan continued walking forward. His aim seemed to be the large staircase at the edge of the room, though he soon veered off course as they drew closer. It appeared he was going to at least do perfunctory greetings if nothing else.

"Evening," Ivan said, walking up to a man who was at least ten feet tall and apparently entirely made of muscle and his conversational partner, a small fellow with dark hair dressed in a pinstripe suit.

"Evening to you, Pseudonym," the man in the suit replied. His beady eyes wandered over to Tori, who met his gaze without wavering. "So the rumors are true; you took one under your wing. Looks like Thuggernaut owes me ten bucks."

The giant of man—Thuggernaut, it seemed—pulled a crumpled bill from a hidden pocket on his black and purple pants, and then set it down in front of the pinstriped man. "I pay this under protest. I'm pretty sure you had some sort of inside information."

"Pay it however you want, long as I get the cash." The man in the suit swept up the bill and gingerly deposited it in his own pocket. That done, he rose and stepped toward Tori, pausing to give a deep bow. "Pleasure to meet you, Apprentice. My muscular companion is Thuggernaut, giant of strength and speed, while my villainous moniker is—"

"Why don't we just have her call you Johnny," Ivan interrupted.

"I don't know," Johnny replied. "I mean, what if she gets me mixed up with another villain, or worse, one of the heroic lot? Seems best to give her my proper handle."

"There is no one else whose code name starts with Johnny," Ivan countered.

"Ah, but there could be. Especially with the confluence nigh; who knows what new names folks will choose after they've made it to the appropriate rank."

Ivan shook his head, but he did it with a sense of resigned annoyance that Tori recognized as him giving up on a pointless fight. "Fine; it's your guild name, I can't stop you from using it."

"Much appreciated." Johnny turned back to Tori and gave another, though smaller bow. "As I was saying, you can feel free to call me Johnny, though my proper code name is slightly longer. It's Johnny Three Dicks."

Tori let out a noise somewhere between a snort and a cough then quickly tried to pass it off as a chuckle. She wasn't so prudish that the name particularly offended her, but it did open up a whole slew of questions that Tori both dearly wanted to ask and very much hoped Johnny wouldn't answer. Thankfully, Ivan retook control of the situation.

"I still think you chose that name just to see people's faces when you said it. At any rate, I need to go greet the others. If you'll excuse us..."

"Nice to meet you," Thuggernaut said, giving Tori a wide smile and small wave, which she returned without thinking. Johnny gave her a grin too, though his was sopping with twisted humor.

After parting from Johnny and Thuggernaut, Ivan introduced Tori to a group of three people—Kilo, Meg, and Gig—who were punching away on computers. Kilo was a short man with glasses and an awkward stutter, while Meg and Gig were a pair of brunette women who looked so similar that Tori suspected they might be sisters, or at the minimum cousins. Ivan told her that they were collectively known as "the Bytes" and handled most of the hacking and sinister software services for the guild. While each person was pleasant, they were also clearly busy, so Ivan kept the chitchat short.

The last person Ivan led her to was a young man who appeared to be in his mid-twenties, sitting in front of a television playing an 8-bit video game that Tori recognized from her childhood. Unlike most of the others, he wore no mask or costume—the only thing slightly obscuring his face were the strands of dirty blond hair that hung down to nearly his shoulders. When Ivan spoke to him, Tori noticed an unusual note of tension in his voice. On impulse, she looked around the room and noticed that everyone else seemed to be looking at them, waiting to see what would happen.

"Good evening, Kristoph," Ivan said. "How are you doing?"

"Pretty good," Kristoph replied. He paused his game and stood up from the small chair he'd been resting in. He was tall and broad, though not as large as Ivan. Even so, as Kristoph's gaze fell upon Tori, she felt a shiver run down her spine. Somewhere in the depths of her mind, she remembered her grandmother saying that those feelings came when a person walked over your grave. Then, as quickly as the feeling had come, it passed, and Kristoph was holding out a hand to her.

"Nice to meet you, new apprentice. I'm Kristoph. You don't seem like a bad person, so you can come talk to me whenever you like."

Tori accepted the handshake, noting as she did that the balloon of tension that had filled the room was rapidly deflating. Without another word, Kristoph settled back into his chair and resumed his video game. Ivan took Tori by the arm and headed toward the stairs. She managed to wait until they were out of a regular person's earshot before her curiosity got the best of her.

"Okay, what the hell was that about?"

To his credit, Ivan made no attempt to pretend that something very strange hadn't just occurred. Instead, he merely lowered his voice to barely above a whisper while they ascended the carpeted stairs.

"Everyone in the guild has to meet Kristoph during their apprenticeship. It's a time-saving device, since we don't want to spend all the effort of training someone only for Kristoph to kill them the first time they meet each other."

"Wait... you thought that guy might have tried to kill me?" Tori stopped dead on the stairs. Being deemed an irresponsible asset was one thing, she could at least see the argument in that, but putting her in front of some guy who went on random murder binges was a whole other case entirely.

"Not tried, succeeded," Ivan replied, his tone neutral and unapologetic. "Kristoph is probably amongst the most powerful meta-humans alive, villain or cape. I've dealt with a lot of heavy hitters, and he could give a run to even the most legendary of the lot. If he decided to kill you, then no one could have stopped him, and none of us would have tried."

"Wha—"

"Kristoph doesn't kill indiscriminately, Apprentice. He searches your soul for a very special type of sin, and if he finds it, then his power manifests. That's the other reason we bring apprentices in front of Kristoph: this is a guild for villains, not monsters. We don't want the kind of people Kristoph kills walking around this planet, and we certainly don't want them in a place that is home to some of our own families. Many of us are parents, after all."

"What does... shit. You're talking about people who hurt kids, aren't you?"

"Merely scraping a knee or delivering a spanking won't leave the sort of stain Kristoph searches for," Ivan replied. "But those who kill or do lasting damage to the innocent are marked in a way that no spell or ward can camouflage."

Tori's eyes widened and she glanced back at the young man playing video games. "Ohhhhh. Okay, I'm with you now. But why is he here, then? That sort of work seems like it puts him on the side of the capes."

"No doubt he'd be welcome there, except that Kristoph doesn't bother with things like due process or proof. Soul-gazing isn't exactly the sort of thing that's admissible in court, and even if it were, Kristoph wouldn't bother submitting it. Even that might be overlooked... if not for the fact that the deaths Kristoph gives are not the quick, merciful sort."

"Do I want to know?"

Ivan contemplated for a moment before responding. "The tamest way I've seen him kill someone was to animate their skeleton so that it clawed its way out from the inside while the person was kept alive to feel every excruciating second. Would you like to hear more than that?"

"Not really," Tori admitted. "Although, knowing what the skeleton guy must have done, I do sort of want to buy Kristoph a beer."

"A sentiment we all echoed, which is why he lives here and has his needs provided for. But Kristoph is not our concern tonight, Apprentice. The time for the meeting is almost at hand."

"Well then, let's get to hopping," Tori replied. She and Ivan ascended the stairs, back on course for the clandestine meeting with the other members of the villainous council. Even in the midst of actually doing it, Tori was keenly aware of how ridiculous that all sounded.

*   *   *

Apollo arrived late for the Alliance of Heroic Champions' Congress meeting, and he was fuming as he did so. In an effort to get more notoriety and become well-known, he'd made a point of recently helping some of the others with their own PR issues and debacles. That act of generosity had backfired, unfortunately, as it ultimately made him the de facto person to deal with Karl and his impossibly bad Heroic Champion persona. No matter how hard they tried to convince him to change identities, the man was steadfast in sticking to his current one, and his civil case had barred them from booting him just because no one liked his identity. Karl actually had to screw up to get thrown out, which made his boy-scout clean record a point of aggravation instead of something they could laud to the public.

The large doors slid open, revealing a massive conference room that surely must have been built to hold more people than sat on the current Champions' Congress. Sitting at the vast wooden table was Quorum, who had a pad and pen with him despite the fact that he never really needed to take notes. Technically, there was no one else in the room, though there were two small devices resting a few feet away from Quorum. Each was generating a holographic projection of a different symbol: one featured the two entangled atoms that represented Professor Quantum, and one had the blazing astral design that was the symbol for Lodestar. The room was silent as Apollo entered, a peace broken immediately as Quorum took notice of his entry.

"You're late." He didn't sound particularly perturbed by the tardiness, merely announcing it factually, as though he were saying Apollo's golden hair was curly.

"My sincerest apologies. Whitest Knight put out some fires downtown earlier today, but then he stopped to pass out more of his 'informational pamphlets,' and I'm sure you can guess how the media reacted."

"You must be kidding me." The voice was female, strong yet youthful, and emanated from the device projecting Lodestar's symbol. "That jackass is still registered with us?"

"The court ruled his persona to be constitutionally-protected free speech," replied an older man's voice, this one coming from the device with Professor Quantum's symbol. "So long as he adheres to our rules and does his job well, we cannot expel him from our ranks."

"Please, friends. Karl is not our concern tonight," Quorum said. As the only member of the Congress physically present, it fell to him to keep the discussion on topic. Admittedly, this was true even back in the days when his fellow members didn't telecommute, though that had certainly exacerbated the problem. "Apollo, please take a seat and listen closely. As someone who seeks to sit on this Congress one day, tonight's meeting will be of the utmost relevance to you. We have many duties as upholders of law and order, but few quite as important as aiding those who suddenly find themselves thrust into a situation beyond their control or understanding."

"Of course, sir." Apollo slid into one of the many, many free chairs and took out a small notebook of his own. He'd been with the AHC long enough to have dealt with these situations before, but it was his first time to see the process from the top level of management.

Quorum nodded to the devices, which Apollo assumed were being fed video as well as audio. "Professor Quantum, if you would start us off."

"Certainly. I won't bore you all with the science I used to determine my estimates, but the long and short of it is what we're all already keenly aware of: a confluence is coming, and it will be here quite soon."

*   *   *

Tori was somewhat underwhelmed by the conference room itself. Once upon a time, in her childhood, she'd been brought along with her parents to work and seen more impressive ones. Certainly the table was nice, and she rather enjoyed the decor, but overall it seemed like a room that had been built to accommodate those using it rather than impress others who might see it, which went counter to the purpose of every other conference room Tori had previously observed.

The people, on the other hand, were a whole other matter. As soon as she walked in she recognized Doctor Mechaniacal, clad in his meta-armor for the first time since she'd first met him. He still didn't wear the helmet, though, which made sense for a meeting, when she thought about it. The copper-haired inventor gave her a small smile as she entered, which she returned as formally as she could manage.

Tori also instantly recognized the metallic woman talking with an eight-foot-tall gray creature as Xelas, who had won a landmark case for the rights of artificially intelligent beings. Every inventor knew the story of how Tech Lord, a member of AHC, had created Xelas as a sex doll, only to accidently construct her so well that she developed free will. When she sued for her freedom, it was the first time a machine was legally seen as anything more than property, and it was why every inventor now had to be sure not to make their machines so smart they could emancipate themselves. Xelas had clearly been given a lot of equipment changes and upgrades, but she still wore the same metal face that Tori had seen in the history books. None of that explained why she was now with a villains' guild, though Tori could make a few guesses. She'd heard Tech Lord hadn't taken losing his toy and having his fetishes dragged out in public view very kindly.

The large person with gray skin was a stranger to Tori, as was the blonde gal wearing street clothes and chatting it up with a younger man in red-and-black robes. He at least looked somewhat familiar, though she couldn't place where she'd seen him. Probably from a crime scene, which he'd then bargained his way out of the consequences of by killing an even worse person. As though sensing her thoughts were on him, he gave her a long glance paired with a toothy smile. Tori noted that his irises were stained a deep maroon. She had no doubt the look was meant to be intimidating, which made it less effective. Even before being paired with Ivan, Tori hadn't been one to rattle easily. Sharing a house with a living incarnation of destruction had only increased her idea of what constituted as scary.

The last person in the room, aside from Ivan and Tori, was a middle-aged woman with raven-black hair and a costume done in deep reds. She made a beeline around the table, coming right up to Ivan and giving him a big hug, followed by a peck on the right cheek.

"Must I schedule one of these every time I want to visit with you?" the woman asked. "It wouldn't kill you to come around here more often."

Ivan nodded slightly; he seemed to be just the tiniest bit uncomfortable by this strange woman's open display of affection. Tori's suspicion was quickly confirmed when he dodged the question entirely, gesturing to her and saying, "Morgana, this is my new apprentice. Perhaps you should introduce yourself."

"Apologies," she said, not seeming particularly sorry in the slightest. Still, she turned to Tori and gave a slight bow. "My name is Morgana, and I am the councilor who represents meta-humans that were innately born with their abilities. It is a pleasure to meet you, Apprentice."

"Pleasure to meet you, too." Tori wasn't entirely sure what to make of this woman, which was par for the course with nearly every other villain she'd met so far. At least Morgana seemed pleasant, and she certainly held herself with an air of earned confidence. Then again, if everyone here was on Ivan and Doctor Mechaniacal's level, there was no reason they shouldn't feel confident.

"Sadly, I don't think there's time to do proper introductions around the room, but I can fill you in quickly," Morgana offered. She turned, pointing to Xelas and the gray-skinned creature still deep in conversation. "Over there are Xelas, the robotic one, and Gork, the tall one. Xelas represents artificially-created beings, be they mechanical or biological, while Gork is the representative of all naturally-occurring nonhuman and alien creatures."

Tori was hoping Morgana would also elaborate on just what the hell Gork was, but she kept right on going, pointing to the lady in street clothes and the man with red eyes. "Over there are Stasis and Balaam, Stasis being the woman. She represents all our meta-humans who were turned via accident, experiment, prototype serum... you get the idea. From what I've heard about your powers, she would be your councilor."

"I'm actually planning on using my technical knowledge to build meta-suits," Tori said quickly. Morgana shot her a look that spoke to surprise, curiosity, and perhaps just a hint of attentive interest.

"Well then, that will put you under Doctor Mechaniacal, who you are already acquainted with, since he represents all our science and gadget users. Anyway, Balaam oversees our magic wielders, regardless of the source of their power. And since you likely know that Pseudonym is the representative of our retired members, that should catch you up to speed." Morgana flashed Tori a dazzling smile, nothing like the dry attempt at intimidation Balaam had thrown her. Tori decided that she liked the woman; it took more strength to be welcoming and kind than scary.

"Everyone," Doctor Mechaniacal called, clapping his hands together. "If you could all please take your seats, I think it's time we got this meeting under way."

The rest of the attendees made their way around the horseshoe shaped table, some snagging one of the provided sandwiches as they took a seat. Morgana leaned in and gave Tori a quick hug, pausing only to whisper in her ear.

"Try not to let them scare you too much, but don't forget that they are scary people."

Then she was gone, hustling across the room to sit on the end of the table. Tori found herself wishing the older woman was seated nearer to Ivan, who plopped down between Xelas and Stasis. She was the first person to show Tori more than perfunctory kindness, and if the warning held any value at all, Tori was going to need every friend she could get.

Chapter 10

"As you all know, the reason we've called an emergency meeting is that we've got a confluence on the horizon, and a much wider window than we prefer working with," Doctor Mechaniacal said.

Ivan had always found it impressive that Wade could deliver his speeches in a way that was affable yet still held an air of authority. Leading this group was never an easy effort; hold the reins too loosely and they'd run wild, too tightly and they would rebel. Only Wade, with his gentle expressions and powerful mind, had managed to do it consistently and well over the years. Once or twice, he'd tried to get Ivan to take on leadership roles, and each attempt had been an unmitigated disaster.

"We've had our mystics consulting oracles and looking for portents while the tech department analyzed data on geospatial anomalies and quantum oscillations," Doctor Mechaniacal continued. "All signs point to the window for the confluence opening up on Thursday night and closing by Monday morning. That means we've got a little over seventy-two hours where the confluence could strike, and by current indications, it's going to be a doozy."

"That's putting it mildly," Balaam interrupted. He paused for a moment to look around the room, clearly curious to see if someone would call him out on his small act of rebellion. Those dark red eyes lingered on Ivan longer than anyone else, but when Balaam was met with silence, he continued with a slight smirk on his face.

"Two crystal balls cracked when their seers tried to look into the heart of the energies gathering, and from the fire that broke out this morning, I'd wager the AI oracle department had issues as well."

Some of the councilors turned to Xelas, who gave a slight nod, then narrowed her metallic eyes and glared at Balaam. Though she did in fact have ocular lasers, Xelas merely chose to metaphorically drill a hole in him for the slight of pointing out an issue in her department.

"Balaam is correct," Doctor Mechaniacal agreed, retaking control of his meeting. "By every measure we've utilized, this confluence will be the biggest we've seen in at least a decade. That means a lot of new metas, many of whom will have extremely potent abilities."

"Psssst."

Ivan closed his eyes and tried to will away the soft voice whispering in his ear. For a sliver of a moment, he thought he had succeeded, until the voice spoke again, this time louder.

"*Psssst*. What's a confluence?" Tori asked.

"Does Apprentice have something she wishes to add to the meeting?" Balaam's voice was much louder than when he'd made his own interruption, and from the gleam in his eyes, it was clear he'd been waiting for Tori to make just such an error in etiquette.

Ivan readied himself to respond but realized Tori was talking before he could get a single word out.

"I was asking what a confluence was. I've been in the tech world for a long time, and I've never even heard of one of these things." Tori's voice was earnest but unapologetic. It left little to object to, aside from the interruption itself, which Ivan considered a shockingly diplomatic move from her.

"Oh yes, certainly," Balaam said. "Let's just pause this highly important meeting so we can explain to an apprentice something that does not, and likely never will, concern her."

"Balaam motions that we pause the meeting to explain to Apprentice what confluences are, and I second it." Morgana, who had been looking a bit bored off in the corner by Balaam, seemed to positively glow as she stole his dickish remark and twisted it to her use.

"Wait, what?" Balaam's clearly rehearsed evil smile fell away as the meaning of Morgana's statement sank in.

"Motion has been announced and seconded," Doctor Mechaniacal said. "All in favor?"

Ivan, Xelas, Morgana, and Doctor Mechaniacal raised their hands, while Balaam looked around frantically as his joke quickly turned against him.

"Doctor, come on, I was obviously being sarcastic."

"The council of villains does not recognize sarcasm, Balaam; you were told that on your first day here. It's the only way we manage to get anything done," Doctor Mechaniacal replied. "The motion carries. We will now pause the current discussion so that Apprentice can be brought up to speed. I would like to recognize Balaam's motion for its commitment to the continuing education of our next generation of members."

Ivan barely suppressed a grin as Balaam crossed his arms and fumed silently. No doubt he was going to hold this against Tori, but since she was Ivan's apprentice, there was already inevitable enmity there.

"A confluence, in the simplest of definitions, is what its name would suggest," Doctor Mechaniacal said, turning his attention to Tori. Ivan could practically hear her straighten up to listen more closely. "It is the gathering of many forces simultaneously, causing unexpected reactions that can neither be predicted nor reproduced. We still don't understand what causes confluences; however, we have learned to measure the indicators of their gathering. Now, while many of the effects of a confluence are benign, there is one that happens with great frequency that concerns us greatly: during a confluence, the number of meta-humans created increases exponentially."

"Not only that, but those that occur during a confluence tend to be more powerful than average," Stasis added. As the councilor representing meta-humans created by external elements, she was the largest expert in the effects of confluences. "Most people at this table were either born during a confluence, created during one, or arrived during one, in the case of Gork. It's true of the big name capes as well: Quorum and Lodestar were both made during a potent confluence, and it's believed that Professor Quantum was part of, if not the cause of, the very first confluence we know of."

Behind Ivan, Tori nodded her head. There was scarcely a person alive, let alone a meta-human, who didn't know about Professor Quantum's famous experiment and how that had created the first known meta-humans and apparently opened the doors to the creation of others. No one was quite certain what he'd unleashed that day; all they knew was that all of a sudden, the hard rules of science and reality had gotten much more malleable.

"As such, the time during a confluence is very important for both our organization and the Alliance of Heroic Champions," Doctor Mechaniacal said, resuming his portion of the impromptu lesson. "The more meta-humans that can be identified as they are created, the less wanton chaos we have as people try to adapt to their abilities. Not to mention that it certainly helps to get first choice of the new crop."

"So, it's basically the cape and villain version of NFL draft day, only with just two sides and you have to be really on top of scouting," Tori said. "Plus, if you fuck up, someone might level a building."

"That part is their problem," Balaam snickered, still slightly sulking in his corner.

"That part is everyone's problem," Ivan said, speaking for the first time since the meeting had begun. "When new metas do that level of damage, the capes end up making examples out of some of us to calm the public's nerves. It's in our interests to minimize those instances as much as possible."

"Make examples out of 'us,' you say? You must be confused, little puppy; only real villains live in any danger, and we're all strong enough to handle it." This time, when Balaam's eyes flashed, there was nothing faked in his vitriol. He wasn't trying to be scary at all; he genuinely hated Ivan and had no qualms about letting it show. This, funnily enough, made him far more terrifying than when he put on his cheesy attitude to seem scary.

"Balaam, none of that." Doctor Mechaniacal's voice grew a few shades harder, a difference too slight to notice in most men, but from him, it was as blatant as if he'd aimed a gun at Balaam's face. As kind a man as he could be,

Doctor Mechaniacal had not been forced to fake his own death without reason. Anyone who forgot what he was capable of was a fool, and often a short-lived one.

Before Balaam could reply, Doctor Mechaniacal turned to Tori, gave her a reassuring nod, and continued with the explanation.

"Apprentice, your analogy was an apt one. Confluences are when we have the chance to gather top-tier talent before they are hauled away by the AHC or give in to their base urges and commit the sort of crimes that will get them courted by gangs or locked up. Thus, it is important that we have a strong system for locating new meta-humans, as well as dealing with them when their powers manifest. The goal for this meeting is to coordinate shifts throughout the window, trying to make sure we have the ability to mobilize as many of our people as possible once it begins."

"I understand. Thank you for taking the time to explain." Tori dipped her head respectfully and Doctor Mechaniacal let a genuine smile light up his face. Most people couldn't tell the difference, but to Ivan, there was no mistaking a falsehood for the genuine article.

"It is our duty to pass on knowledge to those younger than ourselves. But now that you've been brought up to speed, please hold all questions until after the meeting, so that we can finish at a proper time."

Doctor Mechaniacal turned to face the rest of the conference room, and all eyes moved to him.

Including the pair that didn't belong to any of the invited guests.

"Pardon me, is today Tuesday the eleventh, and are you a clone of Wade Wyatt, or the original?" This voice was weathered, strained, and all too familiar to every member of the council. Only Tori found it foreign. She spun around to see who had spoken, only to let out a half-strangled gasp as her eyes fell upon the intruder.

"N-*Nexus*." She instinctively gripped the arms of her chair and made to rise; Ivan put his hand on her shoulder for reassurance. He would have been more surprised if she didn't have this reaction to Nexus. Even aside from his unique appearance, he was easily the most famous criminal of all time. Nexus rarely acted, but when he did, entire cities were wiped off the face of the earth. Despite the best efforts of every cape the AHC could throw at him, and even a few villains on occasion, no one had ever managed to kill or incarcerate Nexus. He could be stopped, occasionally, but never taken out for good.

Tori's head whipped around so quickly that her mask came loose at the corners, nearly covering her left eye. The discomfort didn't even seem to register as she stared at Ivan with an expression of naked distrust. "Is he part of this organization?"

"Not in the slightest," Ivan assured her. "But no one knows how to stop him from turning up wherever he pleases. Since sometimes he drops useful information, we've all learned to deal with it."

"Ahem; still waiting. I've gotten a little turned around and the clone thing would help a lot." Nexus stood patiently as Tori recovered and the others sat awkwardly in their chairs. His appearance was the same as it had been since he first surfaced: dull brown hair and a two-day stubble across his narrow face. He wore simple clothes and a dusty brown overcoat that nearly swallowed up his lean body. Nexus could have passed for human if not for his kaleidoscope eyes like a sea of shattered glass, always twinkling and swirling, shifting each time they met another's gaze, never the same twice. For all their remarkable appearance, he barely seemed to use them, head bobbing about as he stared at what appeared to be empty space to the rest of them.

"No, I'm not a clone," Doctor Mechaniacal said at last.

"Really? Is this one where you secretly are but are hiding it? No, you almost always try to kill me when I ask you about it in those. Hmmm. I could have sworn I—oh! Never mind. Another me found the one I was looking for."

Nexus gave a slow shrug, as if to say he was sorry for the interruption. As he gazed idly through the room, his broken eyes fell on Ivan and Tori. His eyebrows raised ever so slightly.

"She's finally here? I thought she was never born... must have just come along later than in the other ones. Already the apprentice, huh? Well, that's no surprise; you always end up learning from Ivan. At least, in the ones where Ivan is still alive. And you're still alive. At any rate, welcome aboard. I look forward to seeing which you choose when the time comes."

"What in the hell are you talking about?" Tori asked. Now that the initial shock had faded, she puffed herself up, determined to regain the ground she lost earlier.

"The metal or the flame, of course," Nexus replied, tilting his head slightly to the side. "That choice is usually inevitable, no matter how other things play out. Such a simple thing, yet it carries such consequences."

"Look, are you going to tell us anything about this upcoming confluence, or are you just here to dick around?" Stasis was on edge—no surprise to any of her fellow councilors. They were all aware that she was the only one with cause to actually hate Nexus, and yet she was also the only one who was proven to be beyond his reach.

"Oh, you're here, Stasis. You should have said something earlier, would have saved me the trouble of getting my bearings. As for your question, how could I tell you about the confluence? I can't see the future. At any rate, I was looking for a different Wade. Since that's done, I suppose I'll go try wiping out one of the surviving Tampas and see how that alters things."

In the span of a blink, he was gone. There was no effect or visual cue; Nexus merely stopped being in front of them and presumably started being someplace else. Tori turned to Ivan, who met her uncertain eyes with a simple nod. It was unnerving the first time anyone met Nexus, and often never stopped being so on subsequent encounters. He would explain things to her, but not here.

"I'd like to motion that we take a ten-minute break before resuming the meeting," Stasis said. From the way she was gripping the sandwich in front of her, Ivan suspected that there would be at least two more broken pieces of equipment by the time she'd worked off her anger in the gym.

"Seconded," Morgana chimed in, receiving a grateful look from Stasis for the support.

"All those in favor," Doctor Mechaniacal said, calling for votes.

Despite Ivan's hopes to make it home at a decent hour, he still raised his hand in support of the short break. They all had people who pushed their buttons; he couldn't fault Stasis just because it was hers that happened to show up. It just as easily could have been Lodestar who crashed through a wall, and then he'd have been the one needing a break.

Though ten minutes would not have been nearly enough.

*   *   *

"... and if we have Baron Peppermint cover everything south of 95th Street, that should close out the schedule nicely." Quorum finished filling in the last lines of the grid he'd drawn on his paper, sketching "BP" into the final unoccupied box.

"With all due respect to the Baron, are we certain he's capable of keeping watch over such a wide swath of land?" Apollo asked. "He isn't exactly what I'd consider one of our heavier hitters."

"I'll grant you that our new Baron Peppermint hasn't quite reached the level of his mentor, but those gumdrop minions of his mean he can have eyes and ears, relatively speaking, over a massive area," Quorum pointed out. "Besides, we don't need heavy force on the ground. Most of the new metas will be scared, confused, and completely mystified by what they're suddenly able to do. Our role is to calm them down, help them come to grips with their new lives, and get them on a healthy path toward understanding."

"Our presence helps us recruit any of the truly powerful ones," Professor Quantum added from his teleconferencing device. "Once they feel a sense of debt toward us, it becomes all the more difficult to turn down our requests that they join our alliance."

"All these years and PQ is still just as heartless as always." Lodestar might have meant this to be good-natured ribbing, but the weariness in her voice made Apollo feel as though it were likely more honest than she meant it to be.

"Not heartless, merely objective," Professor Quantum rebutted. "The more we get on our side now, the fewer are likely to become serious threats later down the line."

"You seem to have forgotten many of the occasions when I had to go haul criminals out of their meta-max cells to help us bring down one of our own," Lodestar snapped back. "Their arch-nemeses wound up being all that kept certain cities on the map."

"This is not about good or evil." Quorum's voice was a combination of the other two, both detached and passionate in a way that made Apollo's head hurt if he thought about it too long. It was easy to understand how Quorum could be of many minds about something, but many voices was a bit harder to deal with.

"What choices a person makes are their own. Our goal is to keep them from giving in to the panic when confronted with an unexpected twist in the world they knew. Once they have control of their faculties, whether they use their new powers to help or harm is a decision only they are capable of making. But until that time, it is on us to help them through the terror that is first becoming meta. I don't have to remind any of you what it was like when you first turned."

Apollo actually would have loved to hear those reminders, both because he was hungry for more information on the members of the Congress and because his own turning story hadn't been traumatic in the least. He'd just knocked over a jar at the museum, had a surreal, dream-like encounter with the real sun god, and woken up with his powers fully juiced up. For a scrawny kid with no special traits to get incredible powers and appeal suddenly... well, it was pretty much the opposite of traumatic.

"You're right," Lodestar said over her device, bringing Apollo back to the moment at hand. "No one should have to go through that alone. I'm sorry I can't be there in person to help out with the patrol."

"It will be fine," Quorum said. "Our own Apollo has volunteered to take many of the shifts himself, easily covering any gaps we might have had in the schedule."

"Keep it up, young man, and you may just get your wish granted yet," Professor Quantum said.

Apollo merely nodded his head humbly, as if the duty were nothing more than an afterthought. In truth, it was nearly all he could think about, day in and day out. It was no secret that Lodestar was on her way out; she hadn't been seen in public for over seven years, and it had been a solid four since she came to the AHC base. Sooner or later, she'd retire officially, and when that day came, Apollo had to make certain that he was the only viable candidate to replace her.

All of his beautiful, glorious plans depended on it.

Chapter 11

It was well after midnight by the time Ivan and Tori finally pulled into the driveway. She'd been largely silent throughout the rest of the meeting, either cowed by the sudden appearance of Nexus or bored by the minutiae of coordinating a readied response among all of the council's departments. Ivan had been braced for a myriad of questions once they were out the door; however, her embargo on words had continued as they changed from their costumes and drove across the city.

Tori exited the car before he could say anything, not that Ivan had anything he planned to say, and made a beeline right for the house. At least she didn't slam the door as she entered; that would have certainly gotten a few of the neighbors interested.

Ivan stepped through the front door to find Tori standing only a few feet away, waiting for him. Taking the cue, Ivan quickly locked the door and conjured a few wards, adding some to keep sound in on top of those for security. So far, she'd been exceptionally controlled, especially for her, but there was no sense in taking unnecessary risks. Once they were sealed in, Ivan gave her a slight nod. It was all the permission Tori needed.

"What the *fuck* was that? I'm not crazy, right? That was Nexus, one of the world's most wanted terrorists. We're not talking about you or Doctor Mechaniacal, people who just robbed companies or started fights with capes. Nexus is... bad. I mean, really terrible. He's killed thousands of people and no one even knows why, and you all barely batted an eye when he came sauntering in through the front door."

Tori slumped onto the couch, the ever-present fight in her eyes slowly beginning to dim as she stared up at him. Ivan could see it hitting her at long last. She'd been a criminal when Wade recruited her, but it was only a means to an end. When she signed up for the guild, she'd no doubt expected to rub elbows with people like herself and Doctor Mechaniacal. She was finally beginning to understand that living in this realm, a place outside of law and society, meant that she shared it with more than just the opportunistic and the brash. She was also in the same world as some truly evil motherfuckers.

"Nexus isn't a friend, neither of mine nor anyone at the guild," Ivan said. He made a point to keep his voice as even as always. It wouldn't do either of them any favors to seem like he was coddling her in this moment. "But he's impossible to kill or capture so far as we know, which means we have no way of stopping him when he pops in. For whatever reason, he likes us more than the capes, so he comes around every so often to drop cryptic clues and ask insane questions. Do not, for a single moment, think that any of us would call that man a friend, let alone an ally."

"Honestly?" If Ivan had been lying, it would have been the most effortless one he ever told. Tori was in so deep, she desperately wanted to believe that the organization had some lines it refused to cross. That would at least give her something, a sense of morality to hang on to.

"It's the absolute truth," he told her, because it was. "But make no mistake: we do have members whose death tolls, while smaller than Nexus's, are still considerable. Nexus could be a member of our guild, were he willing to follow the code and pay the appropriate dues. It is not morality that bars him, only his own impulsive actions."

Tori's face, which had begun to fill with life as Ivan told her that Nexus was not a friend, deflated. It was as if he had drained the very hope from her smile, which he was keenly aware that he had, in a way.

"I've told you this before, Apprentice: we are not good people. Our guild is not the place where those of strong morality and goodness come to lay their heads. We are villains, rogues, and scoundrels. The people we bring into our fold are of that ilk as well. That is the organization that found you, that is what you seek to join. Never, under any circumstances, should you delude yourself about what we, and you, are."

"Jesus, Ivan. I... I didn't want something like this. I know I don't have the cleanest record— maybe I'm too quick with a punch or casual about theft— but... I'm not that *bad*. I don't know if I can do this. Even if death is waiting for me on the chance that I fail, I don't know if I can live the rest of my life surrounded by that sort of people." Tori turned her head to the ground and slowly rubbed her left hand with her right one. In the short time they'd been together, Ivan realized it was the first time he'd seen her completely let her guard down. It was good to know that she could, when the occasion demanded it. Some people got too stuck behind their walls and were unable to break free, even when they desperately wanted to.

"If you thought you could handle it, I'd be worried." Ivan walked across the living room, heading for the bookshelf. "Tori, what did I tell you was the most important thing that I could teach you as my apprentice?"

"The code," she replied automatically. He'd drilled it into her endlessly since her arrival, in no small part as preparation for precisely this moment.

"That's right: the code, the law that all members of the guild follow. People who have no care for the laws of religion, man, or society are still bound by the ones we have set down. For the vast majority of our members, it is the only set of rules they respect, let alone obey." Ivan took his worn, leather-bound copy of the code off the shelf and walked back over to Tori. "All members of the guild, regardless of who they were before recruitment, are bound to the code. Or else."

He held it out to her, the book steady in the care of Ivan's powerful grip. Slowly, with the soft light of comprehension beginning to glow in her eyes, Tori reached out and took it from him.

"The first of us who were set free weren't the worst of the lot, though we were some of the most powerful. More than anything, I think we valued freedom and adventure over society's regulations. Perhaps, in another time, we'd have been cowboys, or pirates, or settlers. Sadly, when you pair the kind of power we had with that spirit and youth, you often end up with criminals. But after being chained down, we saw that our kind needed *some* rules, even if they were only bare-bones, so that we could have that freedom we craved so dearly. In the course of it, we also realized that some metas would never be cowed by the threats of those chained by law. They would only respond to the thing they respected: power. In that way, the guild was founded to guide those of us who sought freedom and to contain those of us who sought destruction."

Tori held the book in her hand and stared at Ivan with an expression he'd yet to encounter on her face. He'd seen mere glimpses of it when she glanced at Wade, but never had such sentiment been turned in his direction. It wouldn't be until later that night when sleep evaded him—as it often did after a Nexus visit—that Ivan would begin to suspect the truth behind her expression.

It was admiration.

"The code is the most important thing I can teach. It's the most important thing you can learn. It's the most important thing the guild has ever produced, and upholding it is the most important job you will ever have, should you become a member."

"Sort of seems like you're doing the capes' work for them," Tori noted. She held the book tightly, and as she did, the weight that had dragged her down seemed to lift, if only a pound at a time.

"Keeping wanton destruction in check is everyone's work," Ivan replied. "I don't want some sociopath wiping out my home, or my friends, or my family, any more than a human would. Besides, the capes aren't allowed to dish out the sort of penalties we can. Our jobs are entirely different."

"I'm beginning to see that," Tori said. She pulled herself off the couch in a single fluid move, tucking the book under her arm as she did so. "I'm going to hit the hay. We've got work in the morning, after all."

"Spoken like a true mundane assistant. I'm verging on proud." Ivan smiled at her, not because he felt particularly cheerful, but because he knew she needed it. Tough as Tori was, facing some truths required a bit of support.

"But tomorrow evening, I want to learn more about the guild," she continued. "And about Nexus, since he said a lot of weird stuff you didn't seem fazed by at all. I'm guessing you've got more information on him than the masses."

"Why would you want to know more about that man?"

"Because he's not one of us, which means he could easily be an enemy one day. I'm a thinker, remember? I like to go into these situations with as much information as possible."

Ivan said nothing but gave her a polite nod. It was a good answer, and that made it a good reason. She wasn't wrong, either. No one knew when, but it was always possible that Nexus could make himself an enemy. When that day came, they were all better served with a few countermeasures, or at least plans, in place.

"Oh, one question before I head out, though. I'll probably forget if I wait," Tori said, turning around from her trek to the garage apartment. "That Balaam guy clearly hates your guts, and I'm sure there's a story there, but why did he keep referring to you as a dog? He called you 'little puppy' like three times, and when your water went down the wrong pipe, he suggested you had kennel cough. The hell is that about?"

Ivan suppressed a sigh; he'd expected her to be astute enough to pick up on that. Of course, that didn't always mean he was happy to be right. "Balaam, along with some other members of the guild, like to refer to the retired members as 'beaten dogs.' They feel that the only way for a villain to retire is in the permanent, graveyard fashion. Anything less is seen as weakness, as though we had the fight kicked out of us and have gone home to lick our wounds."

"Great, so on top of unstoppable monsters and heartless killers, you also have run-of-the-mill douchebags." Tori shook her head, sending her dark hair tumbling about. "Tell me that, if it came down to it, you could at least beat that guy."

"Councilors are forbidden from actually doing battle with one another in all but the most extreme of circumstances," Ivan told her.

"I sort of figured that when no one threw a punch tonight, but I'm not talking about next week. Just, you know, some magical hypothetical time and place occurs and you two could scrap it out. Would you win?"

"In that very unlikely situation, assuming I could safely engage him without betraying the code I helped write or the guild I helped create..."

Ivan paused. Tori twirled her finger in the air, the universal sign to get on with it. Generally, as a rule, he avoided bragging, but as Ivan contemplated his answer, he realized that he had no qualms with merely telling his apprentice a truthful answer to her question.

"In that case... I would whip the shit out of him."

Tori raised her eyebrows and let out a low whistle. "Now that's what a girl wants to hear from her teacher."

*   *   *

Unlike Ivan and Tori, Balaam hadn't gone right home after the meeting was over. Instead, he'd headed down to his department and begun doling out assignments for the upcoming confluence. Magic users were, by and large, a nocturnal bunch, so his task was far easier to accomplish while the sun was down. Of course, if he were asked about it by any of the other councilors, Balaam would have claimed he did it because he didn't need rest when top-priority events like these were at hand.

Once all the mystical messages, teleported whispers, and e-mails had been sent out, Balaam retired to his quarters inside the guild's offices. They were spacious, and he'd spent a fair bit of effort customizing them once he earned the penthouse-level accommodations that came with a seat on the council. Blood-red walls decorated with tasteful pieces of art that were either stolen or expert reproductions ran throughout the space. In truth, Balaam would have preferred something a little more color-neutral, but certain sacrifices were necessary when one had an image to keep up. His furniture, at least, had a more modern flair that suited his sensibilities. Décor was one thing, but he refused to compromise on comfort. Since decadence was sort of evil-ish, he felt like this suited his persona well enough to get away with it. And if it didn't, then so be it. One of the perks of the position he'd worked so hard to attain was that he was allowed to break rank on occasion. He was the one people had to impress, not vice versa.

A quick shower purged away the day, and Balaam was debating between reading his weathered, ancient tome of a spellbook or watching reality television when a sharp needle of pain flashed behind his right eye. Most men would have been alarmed by the sudden discomfort, but Balaam merely grumbled to himself as he went to his work desk and pulled a silver mirror from a carefully-padded black box in the bottom drawer.

Unlike the majority of the bobbles and trinkets he'd either inherited, acquired, or stolen, this mirror was a true artifact. Most magical items had merely been given some modicum of enchantment by a competent mage, but the mirror resting before him had an actual magic core inside that powered it, as did its twin. The set comprised one of the most valuable pieces ever to have entered Balaam's collection, and he'd gotten excellent use out of the twin mirrors since almost the moment he acquired them.

The pain throbbed again, and Balaam bit back a curse. He could have set any manner of notification spell for when the mirror's twin called out, but he'd chosen pain for many reasons—the most important of which was that it was something only he could perceive. Sounds were overheard, glowing runes noticed, but pain belonged only to its owner. The moment he rested his hands on the mirror's cool, slick surface, the ache faded into nothing more than a memory.

"Took you long enough." The voice filled his head and caused his fingers to tingle, but otherwise was nothing more than a phantom.

"No need to be snippy, I've had quite the busy day." Though Balaam could hear these words as he spoke them, no sound actually left his mouth. Instead, it carried through his body, into the mirror, and filled the mind of the recipient just as their voice came to him.

"As have I. The confluence draws near, and it seems that this will be the biggest we've borne witness to."

"There's no question about that. We're going to see a lot of new metas, though only time will tell whether or not they are actually top-tier."

"Quality or quantity, so long as we get enough, I think we'll finally have what we need to make our move."

"I like the enthusiasm, but I'm going to see what we actually reel in before I start planning the fish-fry." As soon as the words were out of his mouth, Balaam wished he could reclaim them. That was an idiom of the river-dwelling child he'd been, not the mystical master of the occult he was.

"Accurate, if a bit oddly stated. We'll see what sort of crop the confluence reaps, then make our plans from there. But I must tell you, I'm growing impatient at all this waiting."

"You and I both," Balaam agreed, thankful that his partner had let the phrase pass largely unremarked on and a bit jealous of the much-cooler reaping analogy. "Living in the shadows, hiding our glory at every turn... this guild is scarcely any better than Pseudonym and his ilk. Our tails have been tucked between our legs for far too long. It is time we reclaimed the pride that is rightfully ours."

"Couldn't agree with you more. Soon we can move, but first, we'll see what gifts the confluence delivers."

"Then let's cross our fingers," Balaam replied. "And hope that the next few days prove to be very, very interesting."

Chapter 12

Much as Tori loathed to admit it, she was getting the hang of being an office drone. The work wasn't challenging: not for most employees and not for someone who'd been able to build functioning robotic cars before she'd tested out of the third grade. The hard part was bearing through the pointlessness of it all. So much of Ivan's work, and therefore her work, fell into the category of metrics. Forms, files, and hours of people's days were dedicated to tracking what they, and those in their departments, were doing.

Wednesday morning, during a period where she had nothing to do but tried to look busy, Tori did some rough number-crunching and estimated that no fewer than two hundred billable hours were being pissed away every week on such tasks. When she brought it up to Ivan, he simply nodded, then told her she'd lowballed some of the values she used for her calculations.

Realizing that much of her day job was pointless had been a bitter pill, though Tori was able to take great comfort in the knowledge that for her, thankfully, it was nothing more than the bland coating disguising her exciting true life. She wasn't sure how the others in the office managed to cope with such a harsh reality, though the bloodshot eyes and obvious hangovers sported by many gave her a solid guess.

Donald seemed to find relief in video games, which had taken Tori all of half a day to figure out. Aside from the figurines he kept on his desk, Donald also liked to wax on at length about *Legacy World*, the MMO he spent great swaths of his free time playing. Adding in that he kept a handheld device to play during his lunch hour, which was actually a carefully-timed thirty-five minutes, and Donald couldn't have been more obvious in his geekery unless he showed up to work dressed like his game avatar.

Strangely, Tori found she enjoyed working next to Donald in spite of his passion for games, or perhaps even because of it. Dealing with Ivan and the others in the guild could be tiring, and for the last several years, she'd been around no one but ruthless criminals and petty inventors, sometimes even people who fell into both categories. It was nice dealing with someone as straightforward as Donald. There was no hidden agenda or unseemly secrets; the man simply loved his games and was happy to share that with anyone who would talk to him.

Plus, it was nice chatting with someone who wasn't entirely technologically incompetent. Donald certainly wouldn't be able to keep up with her or Doctor Mechaniacal, but as he described his new computer setup over their Thursday morning coffee, Tori found herself somewhat impressed by the amount of technical acumen he'd put into creating it.

"Anyway, the last piece comes in tonight, and that's the power supply. By the time I log in for my guild's raid, I'm going to be sporting a system that no one short of a tech company can rival," Donald boasted.

He took a sip from his coffee mug, and then quickly pulled it away from his mouth. Tori was keeping count, and in the time she'd been at the company, Donald had burned his tongue on his morning coffee no fewer than eight times. She drank from her own, unbothered by the degree of heat a mere recently-boiled liquid could impart. Even if it had been scalding, Tori would have barely noticed. She didn't consider her powers to come with many perks, but being essentially fireproof was useful, especially for someone who tinkered about in a lab so much.

"Why do you need that much processing power? Any mid-range desktop can run *Legacy World*, no problem. Hell, they ported it to the new Indigo Gamesystem. If a console can handle it, your computer sure could." Tori hadn't actually played the game herself, but she'd done some light research in the interest of keeping conversations flowing with her cubemate. Tori had also looked up local gastro pubs, dog shows, and rare kinds of tea in order to fit in well with those she met in the office. Ivan had heartily approved.

Donald stared at her as though she'd just suggested he scrap all of his gear and start over as a level one character. "It's not about just being able to run it; it's about being the best. Every advantage you can get, every drop you manage to snag that bumps your stats, every bit of lag they have and you don't, all of it is essential to becoming the strongest player on the server. There are people out there with higher levels and better gear than me, so while I level up the software part slowly, I'm also doing my best to keep ahead on hardware."

In a strange way, Tori got what he meant. Being an inventor out on one's own meant struggling against people with entire corporations working for them. The odds were stacked infinitely in their favor, so she'd had to grab on to every advantage she could. Donald had his over-clocked computer; she had a guild of semi-murderous villains.

"Wait, how are you not at max level yet? That game has been out for two years," Tori said.

Donald blew on his coffee and took a tentative sip. This time, it didn't cause him to wince in pain, so the burn count stayed at eight. "There was an expansion released this week. People who don't have jobs got to play for days on end, but I'm stuck coming here, so I can only play for like twelve hours a day."

Tori did some quick math and realized that after eight hours at the office, plus some time for driving, that meant Donald was only sleeping two to three hours a night. She marveled that he hadn't slammed a coffee drip straight into his veins.

"But it's not all bad," Donald continued. "The raised levels and new dungeons came with a whole slew of new gear. My guild was so far behind the others in terms of top-tier equipment that we'd have never caught up. All the old stuff is pretty much useless now; it's an even playing field as we all try and get the new top-of-the-line stuff."

"You sound weirdly happy for someone who just had all of their previous hard work invalidated by a single expansion," Tori pointed out.

"I guess I could see it that way, but I prefer to think of it as a new challenge. Besides, if I want a game I could just win and be done with, I'd play through one of the *Blaster Brahs* sequels again. MMOs are fun mostly *because* they always keep going." Donald glanced down at the small digital watch on his wrist. Tori had thought it was a joke or ironic statement when she first caught sight of the black plastic band, but it seemed Donald actually saw use in wearing a timepiece despite his cell phone being perfectly able to tell him the current time.

"Darn, we need to head back to our desk," Donald said. "Break ends in three minutes."

Tori sighed, but picked up her mug and rose from the small plastic table they'd been sitting at in the break room. If she and Donald weren't checked back in at their computers by the time those three minutes were up, the scheduling software would peg them as being out of compliance with their timetables. Her fingers itched as she thought about how easy it would be to modify the programming so that she was no longer chained to a schedule, but she resisted. In a workplace full of computer people, someone had surely beaten her to the punch and no doubt the company had safeguards in place. Much as Tori believed she could get through them, that wouldn't really be in the spirit of blending in. Instead, she took her coffee back to her desk and logged in like the good little intern she was.

"So, obviously, I'm spending my weekend testing the system and maxing out my level," Donald said, plopping down in his chair next to her. "What are you going to do with yours?"

"Might go check out the town," Tori said. In truth, she was either going to be by Ivan's side dealing with the confluence or at a guild location beginning her next round of combat training. It all depended on how things went down. On the upside, at least either option seemed more exciting than another day of office drudgery.

"This is really short notice."

The woman on the other end of the line was terse, which was to be expected, but it still made Ivan want to dig his hands into the side of his desk. He resisted, partially because such displays of power would raise far too many unnecessary eyebrows and partially because he was quite fond of his desk. He'd worked hard to rise high enough in the company to warrant a nice one.

"I recognize that, and I've already apologized. Believe me, the last thing I want to do is go without seeing them, but I'm afraid there's no way for me to get out of this work event. I'm just asking to switch weekends. Please."

Janet huffed on the other end of the phone, a sound he knew all too well was accompanied by a roll of the eyes and a soft toss of her dark hair. He felt for his ex-wife, truly he did. They had never been meant to be tied together in any lasting capacity. She'd been going through a bad boy phase; he was about as bad as they came. Once Rick was born and Ivan was freed from prison, they tried to make an honest go of it, which was how Beth came along. Even so, it became clear within a few years that they were only making each other miserable. Now she was connected to a man she had nothing in common with save for children they both loved and was burdened with keeping his secret from those same offspring. It wasn't a fun position for anyone, let alone when the ex-husband in question was an internationally-known criminal.

"Fine," she said at last. "Juan has been wanting to check out the museum's new post-meta art exhibit, and it closes this weekend anyway. He'll be glad we can bring the kids along. Just don't make a habit out of this, okay?"

Ivan winced inwardly. That had, sadly, been the easy part of the conversation. Next came the real hurdle. "Actually... why don't you and the kids—and Juan, of course—take a mini-vacation? There's an amusement park that just opened outside New Denver. I went ahead and grabbed VIP passes for everyone. Go and have a fun time; think of it as my apology for the inconvenience."

"Ivan, what are... oh hell." Static and shuffling filled the phone as Janet relocated to somewhere he assumed was more private. When she spoke again, her voice was a hushed whisper. "Ivan, are you ditching your children for a... *thing*?"

"I am not *ditching* them, we're trading weekends," Ivan snapped. He knew better than to take her bait, but the insinuation that he was trying to be rid of his kids irked him. After a few deep breaths to calm down, he tried again. "Listen, Janet, I'm not sure what you think a 'thing' is, and I don't feel like over the phone is a great place to talk about it. This is just an act of goodwill from me. Even if you don't accept, I think it's good for the kids to get away once in a while. See new towns, get some real life experience. Really, taking them anywhere outside Ridge City would probably be good for them this weekend."

Janet's silence stretched for several moments, and Ivan feared she was trying to build enough steam to protest his suggestion. Thankfully, when she finally spoke again, it was with a tone of acceptance, albeit a still hushed and whispered acceptance.

"Maybe that's a good idea. Perhaps we should even take a long weekend, if needed."

Ivan had little love in his heart for his ex-wife, but he was constantly thankful that she was smart and pragmatic. She might not know much about what he did with the guild these days, but Janet still trusted that when he said to get the kids out of town, it was for a good reason.

"I'd leave this afternoon, if you can. No one learns on a Friday, after all. As for coming back, they'll probably have all the experience they need by Sunday evening. Just pay attention, I'm certain you'll know if they need longer."

"We'll be sure to do that," Janet said, her tone back at a normal conversational level.

Ivan hung up and let out a soft sigh of relief. He would have done whatever it took to get them out of town during a confluence. Meta-humans would be all over, many with powers they had no idea how to control. Even with the capes about trying to keep the peace, there would be some casualties. There always were. Between the needs of the guild and dealing with Tori, Ivan couldn't secretly watch over his family like he had so many times before. Better to get them clear than see them hurt, or worse... turned into metas. The last thing Ivan wanted was for his children to get powers, an eventuality that would make them viable targets for the many enemies he'd racked up over the years. As humans they were safe, and Ivan aimed to keep them that way.

That tended to, he checked his schedule, a paper one that he had the perk of managing himself rather than having his time tracked by a computer. It was a light day in terms of meetings, which was actually unfortunate. Now that his family was safe, Ivan didn't want to dwell on the other issue that lay heavily on his mind: namely, the risks of having an untested apprentice during a confluence.

The tall man rose from his desk and picked up an empty coffee mug. If the schedule refused to keep him busy, he'd just have to go check in on his employees. They were bound to have enough problems and excuses to at least help him stay mildly entertained.

"Wade, do you have a moment?"

Morgana stood outside Wade Wyatt's metal and glass office, waiting patiently until he glanced up from the laptop he'd been diligently clacking away on. Officially, she worked for Indigo Technologies as a freelance associate consultant. This meant no one knew what exactly she did, but they also didn't think anything of her stopping in to chat with the boss at odd hours. It was a job Wade offered to any of the guild's councilors that he trusted, though only Morgana and Xelas had taken him up on it.

"Of course, Lynn. You know I always have time for you." Wade felt a touch strange using her mundane name in any setting. This wasn't the case with all guild members, but he felt that Morgana's moniker fit the woman he'd spent years working alongside far better than something as simple as Lynn.

She walked in, firmly shutting the door behind her. Between the built-in anti-surveillance technology and the weekly-refreshed wards, there was scarcely a safer place in the world to speak without being overheard, so she wasted no time in broaching the subject at hand.

"I wanted to talk about Pseudonym's apprentice. Specifically, whether or not she needs to stay at his side after what we're expecting this weekend."

"The council already voted in favor of letting him try to train her before we dismissed Tori as a lost cause," Wade said. "In fact, it was a measure you voted in favor of. Why the sudden urge to dispose of her?"

Morgana shook her head quickly, eyes widening as she realized how Wade had taken her words. "Nooooo. No no no. I don't want you to kill her. Shit, Wade, why is that always where your mind goes?"

"I oversee a group of criminals and villains. Murder is the first proposed solution more often than not." Wade gave a slight shrug by way of apology, then folded his hands on top of the massive desk (far bigger than Ivan's middle-management one), closed his laptop, and assumed his "I'm listening" face.

"Look, I don't want to kill her—in fact, I rather liked the girl. She's smart, she's got some guts, and she's able to exercise at least a little self-control. My point was that after the confluence, we're expecting to have at least a few new recruits to the guild once the dust settles. I know Tori didn't take well to being trained on her own, but I think, in a classroom environment, she might thrive. Having others going through the same things as she is could be a boon, plus it might get a little competition brewing."

"The last thing Tori Rivas needs is more incentive to excel," Wade replied. "On top of an already impressive power, she's strangely driven in regards to creating new technology. I suspect there's a reason for it; however, so far my investigations into her past haven't turned up anything compelling. At least, nothing connected to meta-suits."

"Did you need a personal tragedy or driving force to build your first meta-suit?" Morgana asked.

"Certainly not. I was driven by scientific curiosity coupled with the desire to test the limits of what my brain could do. But I didn't have the power to shift into fire. If I had, that would have doubtlessly become the subject of most of my study."

"Guess Tori is different than you," Morgana said. "But I wasn't talking about *her* needing the competition. A bunch of new metas, all at the apprentice level... it might be good to have someone in the group with a head start. Should do a great job of pissing off the rookies and inspiring them to catch up to Tori."

Wade tilted his head slightly as he mulled over the idea. He unfolded his hands and reopened his laptop, typing away while still keeping his gaze on Morgana. After several seconds of nothing but the clacking of keys filling the air, he finally finished thinking and began to speak.

"You raise valid points, Lynn. Tori could be very useful in getting the new recruits on their feet. Her somewhat abrasive personality would go far in making sure they wanted to surpass her, if nothing else. However, I don't think we would need to go so far as to separate her from her apprenticeship to Ivan in the process."

"Are you saying we should have one apprentice under a guild councilor and the rest lumped together in a class? I don't think that's going to work quite as well. They won't see Tori as a true peer, so it won't light as much of a fire under them when she pulls ahead." Morgana resisted the urge to put her hands on her hips or show defensive body language. Wade was a reasonable man, the most reasonable she'd ever known, and he was willing to discuss something endlessly so long as he believed the other party hadn't dug in and shut down.

"It may be less effective; however, I think it's the best solution all around for several reasons," Wade said. "Firstly, you forget how many of the guild members still look to Ivan as a legend and leader. Circumstances are irrelevant; the mere fact that he took an apprentice has reignited an interest in many of our members to do the same. I predict most, if not all, of whatever recruits we can scrounge from the confluence will be under a guild teacher before the weekend is over. Thus, they will be in the same situation as Tori, if with somewhat less infamous teachers."

Morgana nodded her head slowly; Wade was right about how Ivan was viewed. Outside of Balaam and the others who believed no one should be allowed to retire, Ivan was still treated with as much respect and deference as Wade himself. She'd also considered the possibility that he might reignite the trend of taking on apprentices, but she hadn't expected Wade to be so on board with the idea.

"Secondly, I'm hesitant to put any sort of plan in motion until I see what the components before us are. We may indeed get a large amount of recruits from the confluence; however, we could also come up empty-handed or with very few. It's certainly happened before. There's no sense in planning for a situation we don't know is even going to occur. The third reason I don't want to separate them is the most important, though."

Wade paused for a moment, typing a few more things on his computer, and then slightly lowered the screen.

"Right now, Tori's association with Ivan is both her greatest threat and protection. When we voted before, she was a nameless recruit that no one had interest in. So long as she is in her apprenticeship, only he has the right to kill her. Now that I've aligned her with Ivan, Balaam and his faction would vote to have her removed the minute she was up for discussion. The vote last time was too close—only apathy kept her alive, a protection she no longer possesses."

"I get it," Morgana said. "Tori Rivas either finishes her apprenticeship under Ivan, or she won't live to have any other chance."

Chapter 13

Thunder rattled the house although no sounds of rain joined it. The only accompaniment, besides the continuous blasts of lightning, was the barking of the neighborhood dogs, yelping enthusiastically with every boom of sound. Ivan left the kitchen with a glass of sweet tea and a can of beer, the latter of which he set down before Tori.

"Is it okay for us to just be eating dinner like this?" Tori accepted the drink and eyed her plate of pasta hungrily, but at the same time, she couldn't shake the feeling that something was off. "I mean, with shit about to go down at any given minute and all?"

"A confluence is a gathering of forces," Ivan reminded her. "This strange storm front may well be one of them, but on its own, it poses no more danger than any other sky full of clouds. Even once the confluence starts, it's not as though a buzzer will sound and chaos will descend upon the city. Only those aware of what's happening and the few caught up in the side effects will ever realize what has transpired."

Tori popped open her beer and took a sip. It was still cold, despite the tension in her gut about all the impending unknowns. Ivan's lessons on control were definitely taking; Tori couldn't remember the last time she drank something while nervous and didn't accidently heat it up.

"That seems kind of far-fetched. You all made it sound like powers would just be raining from the sky." Tori got the words out before another clap of thunder drowned her out, but only barely.

"Let me put it this way: before you joined the guild, you had never heard of a confluence. You'd never even suspected such things existed, because the only aftermath is an influx of new metas, which both we and the capes manage carefully. So, if someone as smart as you never put together that metas were often created en masse, why would you suspect mundane minds to be capable of piecing it together?"

"Using my own ego against me, that's a low blow." Tori speared a large bite of pasta and promptly wolfed it down before continuing. "I did notice the grouping, though; most people do. We just associate it with the big events that create lots of metas. Stuff like the discovery of that magical city beneath Indianapolis, the alien ship that blew apart and scattered debris across Nevada, and, of course, the original explosions at Wilshire Applied Technologies back in the forties. All were big events that saw the rise of people with new powers, and I'm guessing all occurred during confluences."

"Some, but possibly not all," Ivan said. "New metas spring up outside of confluences all the time. This is just when we see a wide range created at once."

"That's good." Tori stabbed at her food with a bit more gusto this time then quickly reeled in the pasta violence. It was almost a subtle enough change for Ivan to miss it. "I'd hate to think people were on watch every time a chemical lab blew up or an experiment went awry but chose to do nothing because they wanted more metas in the world."

"You sat in on the council meeting where we made plans to deal with the impending confluence. As of right now, you see exactly how much information we have to work with," Ivan told her. "Do you feel as though we can do much to alter however this will play out?"

"Nope. Feels like we're going to end up being caught flat-footed, dicks in our hands, and have to scramble to do what little damage control we might manage."

"That's a crude and somewhat inaccurate analog—"

Ivan was interrupted by another clap of thunder, this one so powerful that his dishes rattled across the table. From outside, he and Tori both saw a bolt of what appeared to be purple lightning strike the street, lingering longer than any bolt of true electricity would. Before the thunder's echoes had fully faded, they were both out the door, spilling out into the street along with the rest of the neighborhood.

The asphalt was warped and melted where it had been struck, and Ivan held his breath as he waited for some manner of animated road monster to pull itself into being. After a few heartbeats, it seemed that the lightning hadn't been enhanced, or at least wasn't that powerful. Ivan let the air slowly slip from his lungs. Tori tapped him on the shoulder, softly at first, but with increasing fervor until he finally followed her gaze skyward.

Overhead, the dark clouds of the impending storm were colliding with strangely-colored smoke from one of the corporate laboratories outside the bounds of Ridge City. Multi-colored veins crept through the clouds, arching in irregular patterns as they wove through dark swells of rain and lightning.

Ivan could feel threads of magic up there, weaving about amid the warping storm. He wasn't entirely sure why, but it didn't matter. Understanding the cause was a job for after the dust had settled. From the growing chatter among his neighbors, it seemed this wouldn't be one of the low-key confluences. People knew something was up, and that would put them on edge.

"We should get inside," Ivan announced, as much to the people around him as to Tori, who he took lightly by the shoulder. "Whatever that stuff is doing, the strike was too close for us to be out here in a lightning storm."

The chatter seemed to swell with consensus, and to his relief, Ivan saw many of his neighbors follow his lead and head back into their homes. Right now, the guild members on standby would be getting prepped; he and Tori weren't due for a shift until the following night. That didn't mean he might not be needed before then, though. Until Ivan was called in, the best he could do was encourage his neighbors to stay safe and make sure he had privacy to work.

Ivan slammed and locked the door behind him as another clap of thunder tore through the sky, followed by the soft patter of raindrops finally slapping against his roof.

Just like that, the storm was upon them.

*   *   *

She flung open the attic door and was nearly pushed back by the wind screeching through what had been a window only moments before. The rain soaked her clothes as she struggled to find something to block the hole with. The lightning had struck through a window, of all things, and as another bolt flashed outside, a glimmer of light among the boxes it had struck and charred caught her eye.

Kicking aside the smoky remains and debris, she uncovered a strange pendant. It was silver, with runes etched across it and some sort of creature in the center. One of her great-grandmother's "treasures," no doubt. The woman could have been on that hoarding show if it had been around when she was alive. There was always someone in the family who said they were going to tackle the boxes in the attic and see if she had left behind anything valuable, another bit of real worth aside from what was already lost, yet somehow it never got done.

The wind and rain seemed less important the longer she stared at the pendant. Everything around it was burned or destroyed, but this was completely unharmed. Her delicate fingers brushed against the surface, and she almost drew away in surprise at how warm the silver object was. In fact, she tried to pull back, but her body wouldn't listen. Her hand wrapped around the pendant, lifting it reverently from the ground as water continued to pelt her. It had gone from warm to hot in the span of seconds, and as she stared at the curious bobble, she saw a flicker of movement.

That creature in the center had flinched, moving its long scaly head so that silver eyes were staring into her own. Wings stretched from its back and a spiny tail whipped about from behind. The burning of the metal had gone from hot to unbearable, yet she could have no more let go than she could have torn off her own hand.

A clap of thunder drowned out her first scream, but not any of those that followed.

*   *   *

He staggered through the street, trying to let out a yell of pain and instead releasing only a high-pitched roar. The windows of nearby cars cracked at the sound, but he paid them no attention. The pain in his body, the shifting of his bones and the growing of mass, it was all too much to bear. Despite lobbying against gun ownership for most of his adult life, he'd happily have put one in his mouth at that moment if it would have made the pain stop.

A crunching sound reached his ears and he realized he'd hip-checked a car, the feeling so minor that it hadn't even registered. The car, on the other hand, had a serious dent and looked like it had been shoved away from the curb. A low moan escaped his lips, and he pushed onward.

Overhead, he could see streaks in the air, along with a strange cloud that was sending out oddly-colored lightning bolts. Probably metas—or, rather, *other* metas. That thought was bitter as it scorched across his brain, but there was no denying what was right in front of him. Whatever was in that drug he'd taken, it was clearly not FDA approved. All this because of his damn blown-out knee. Now he not only wasn't going to play football again, he'd be lucky if they let him back in his college.

"You look like hell," said a man hovering a few feet in the air. He was golden in hair, clothing, and the glow that emanated from him. Landing gently on the drenched sidewalk, the man approached, showing no concern for the monstrosity facing him.

"Ap-ol-lo." Words didn't want to form with this strange new tongue, but he forced them out anyway. This was Apollo, one of the greatest champions in the world. If anyone knew what was happening, could help him, it was Apollo.

"That's right, I'm the great Apollo. And you seem like you could use a hand."

*   *   *

People were crawling away from the debris slowly but steadily. She'd been farther back than most of them, never much of a fan of poetry readings. Her job was just to pour the coffee while customers piled up on the couches and listened to people read. No one had expected that weird guy's book to start glowing, for him to read in a strange, twisted language that seemed to carve its

97

way through her ears. She still wasn't sure if it was the lightning or him that had created the explosion, but from the remains of his cheap boots still smoking on the stage, she was betting on the latter.

The weird flash, though, and that wave that had burst forth from him... those were beyond insane. She shook her head, refusing to let herself get distracted, not while crawling through a half-destroyed coffee shop with a torrential rainstorm spewing down around them. Pushing forward, she stumbled to her feet and glanced in what remained of the rear wall's mirror.

Soot covered her face and stained her short white-blonde hair, but she didn't see any serious injuries. She looked a fright, but that was nothing compared to what some were dealing with. Besides, with a good shower and a little time at the hospital, she might just be able to walk out of this.

"I'll be fine," she muttered to herself, turning away to look at the rest of the people still trapped. "Fit, fine, and right as rain."

The words had barely left her mouth when the storm moved inside, relentless drops pelting her and the others as though they were lying on the ground outside. It washed over her, sending her stumbling back to trip over one of the cushioned chairs. She huddled behind it, shutting her eyes tightly and praying that this night would end soon.

"Chin up," she reminded herself. "You can do this; it's always darkest before the dawn."

Screeches filled the air as the last of the emergency lights cut out, leaving everyone stranded in inky black darkness.

*   *   *

Nexus stood on top of the Quincy Hotel, seemingly unaware of the raindrops soaking his coat and the thin body beneath it. At this altitude, he was technically at risk for being struck by lightning, but that didn't worry him. On the rare occasions it happened, he'd always made arrangements to be elsewhere just before impact. Besides, this was one of his favorite events. He tried to get a good seat each time it happened.

Not that it always did, of course. The multiverse was sprawling, technically infinite, though after a certain point, the worlds were so far removed from his that they were essentially alien and therefore uninteresting. Still, in the core worlds he visited, this storm almost always happened. The causes changed, and with them the effects, but in some form or fashion, this storm would soak Ridge City.

Though there was ample entertainment throughout the night, the real fun would begin once the sidewalks dried and the sun hung overhead. So many new people with gifts previously unseen. So many new possibilities for how they would be used and eventually use others. Nexus had seen it play out in countless worlds already, and there were countless more to witness, but this was a show he was especially excited about.

After all, this world had not one but two wholly unique people in it, unseen anywhere else in the multiverse. Nexus was quite anxious to see how they would play these new cards being dealt to them. Perhaps good would triumph; more likely it would be evil, but no matter how things went, he would be entertained.

And when someone was in a situation like his, that was the component they cared the most about.

*   *   *

"Aaaaaand done!" Donald's voice rang through his apartment, partially drowned out by the sound of pounding rain, but he made the announcement nonetheless. Despite the rain, he could hear the soft hum of power as his new system came fully online for the first time. It hadn't been an easy endeavor; half the parts he used were either custom or personally modified to make them function as needed. But now, at long last, Donald was finally going to see the fruits of his efforts.

All three screens flickered to life as he sank into his worn but sturdy chair. Behind him, a blue light glowed from his system's massive new power source, casting azure light on the rows of electronics lined up on either side of him. Additional monitors rested directly to his left and right. Although these hadn't strictly been necessary, he still felt it created a more immersive environment. His hands wove around the custom controllers set up on the armrests of his chair, and before his eyes came the most beautiful sight he'd beheld to that point: the *Legacy World* loading screen, rendered so crisp and clear Donald felt like he could practically reach through the screen and take hold of his character.

"I am sooooo calling in sick tomorrow." He hoped Tori wouldn't rat him out when he said he had a stomach bug, but either way, there was zero chance Donald could tear himself away from this new toy so soon. Besides, Tori seemed solid; he doubted she'd tattle.

The hum of his electronics grew stronger as the claps of thunder seemed to come faster and faster. Ordinarily, he would have shut everything down and pulled the cord from the walls, but Donald hadn't spent all that cash on a power management system to fear something as weak as surges. According to the specs on what he'd bought, it could, and had, been used to regulate entire sections of an old Russian nuclear test site. He couldn't imagine why they'd been willing to let it go so cheaply, and Donald wasn't going to pry. He had the equipment, the tech, and now, finally, the power. It was time to reach a whole new level.

When Donald woke up the next morning, he would find out that one of those strangely-colored bolts of lightning had hit his building's transformer, blowing out the electrical system for the entire complex. Donald didn't have a chance to register what was happening in the moment, however, as energy burst through his oh-so-foolproof power source, flowing through his gaming array before arcing outward into the nearest conductive source: Donald himself.

The upside was that it all happened so fast that there was no time to register any pain as the bright blue volts struck him from nearly every conceivable direction, filling his body with electricity along with a myriad of other things. When it finally stopped, he slumped over in his chair briefly before tottering forward and slamming his head to the floor.

Eight hours later, when he finally rejoined the land of the living, that bruise on his forehead would be the only injury Donald found.

Chapter 14

"As responders continue to comb through the wreckage of a laboratory registered to Granco Pharmaceuticals, the hopes of finding any more survivors are dwindling. Many of those that were rescued have cooperated with investigators, shedding much-needed light on the accident that sent unexpected blasts of multi-colored lightning tearing across Ridge City last night. While much of the information remains classified, confidential sources have said that it all stemmed from yet another attempt to recreate the infamous Wilshire Applied Technologies experiment that gave the world, among many other things, Professor Quantum."

Tori muted the television as Ivan walked into the living room with two plates of scrambled eggs and bacon. She'd been stuck to the screen all morning, but it had been more or less a loop of the same information. Occasionally, there would be an interview with a clearly-panicked and lying Granco executive to spice things up, and those Tori was relishing. There was no compassion in her heart for sloppy, irresponsible scientists—a suitable classification for anyone who would try that experiment so near a city. Even Professor Quantum, the world's leading expert on meta-elements (and a testament to them, since his powers were due to high levels of setlium exposure), had moved his work to a remote island in order to minimize possible casualties.

"You ever wonder if the rest of the Science Sentries get pissed when they're lumped together as 'other things' every time someone talks about the professor?"

"It's been a long time since I had any dealings with them, but even back then, they weren't particularly fond of living in his shadow," Ivan replied. "I was in prison when they officially split up as a team, so I can't say for certain as to what drove them apart. I believe the official story was that the others were getting too old, since they didn't get his seemingly endless youth; however, my guess would be that his ego finally succeeded in driving them away."

"Bit of a prick despite the family-friendly image?" Tori asked.

"Professor Quantum might be the only living person I've ever met who is as smart as Doctor Mechaniacal, and the accident gave him physical powers that put him on par with me. I can't imagine any situation where a man like that doesn't turn into some form of asshole." Ivan took a large bite of eggs, thankful he'd spent the time to dice and add fresh garlic before scrambling them.

"I always imagined most of the big names were assholes when the cameras went off," Tori said, turning her attention to the bacon before the eggs.

101

"Professor Quantum always seemed like the coldest of them, but I bet Quorum and Lodestar are no better."

Ivan's fork scraped the plate ever so slightly. He disguised the twitch of his fingers by digging out an extra-large scoop of eggs. "Quorum is probably the fairest person any of us will ever meet. All those voices give him a lot of perspective. He can be a bit stuffy at times, but truthfully, the man is almost entirely without ego. Not surprising given what his sense of self must be like. As for Lodestar..." Ivan hesitated, unsure of exactly how to put this for his apprentice. The capes were, ostensibly, the enemies, but there wasn't exactly a bounty of negative things to say about the woman with glowing hair and lavender eyes. "She's... well, she's the real deal. Almost every cape I ever met and fought was in it for their own reasons. Even if those reasons led them to do good, the core was driven by some sort of selfishness; they were still people, after all. Lodestar's a true hero, which makes her the hardest person in the world to fight against. She won't turn or run or back down, no matter the opponent."

"Guess some people do live up to the hype. Hope I never have to fight her," Tori said. She could see something flickering in Ivan's eyes, though she had no clue whether it was vitriol for the cape who beat him, admiration for such a powerful fighter, or some emotion that was entirely unexpected.

Ivan snorted through a bite of his bacon and shook his head. "There is no situation in which you should try to go up against Lodestar. It's entirely futile. Words can't convey what it's like watching her drop from the sky in an explosion of golden light, the crushing sense of defeat you feel tearing through you. As soon as we saw that meteor-like drop, we knew it was over."

"That's quite a statement, given your track record and acclaim."

"I'm sure you researched all the footage and articles, so you already know that I could never beat her. Pretty much everyone else, sure, but never her. And that was in my prime. Now, I doubt I'd last more than a minute against her, tops."

"You still look young and spry to me," Tori pointed out. She finished off the last remains of her breakfast and idly glanced around to see if Ivan had brought toast.

"My body might not age much, but I haven't been in a real fight in years. There's no room for being rusty when going up against one of the greats."

"Not like she's been all over the news lately, either. Actually, I can't remember the last time I saw Lodestar make an actual appearance."

"No doubt she's locked herself away to train up the next generation of capes," Ivan said, perhaps a hair too quickly. "At any rate, since our docket is clear today, I thought we might swing by the guild headquarters and see how the cleanup is going. They say it's all under control, but there might be some tasks we can assist with. Who knows, perhaps you can even sneak a peek at some of the new recruits."

"Ooooh, spying, I likey." Tori set her plate down on the coffee table and checked the screen, which was currently showing the blacked out section of downtown Ridge City. "Any chance we'll get a four-day weekend out of this?"

"Power should be back on at the office by early afternoon. We're lucky they let us telecommute the whole day as it is," Ivan replied.

"Yet we're not telecommuting at all. You want us to play hooky and go mess around with guild business."

Ivan rose from the couch and paused to pick up Tori's dish off the coffee table. "Come on, now, you've been at the company for over a week already. Don't tell me you really think anyone actually telecommutes, especially not on a Friday. This is the corporate equivalent of a snow day."

"And just like during real snow days, I have to spend it inside studying," Tori said. For the briefest of moments, her eyes seemed to grow slightly wistful and a touch sad. Then she blinked and it was gone. She turned quickly to see if Ivan had noticed; he made a point of facing the TV. It certainly didn't fool her, but it allowed them to skate over the moment without comment. To both of them, that was the best way to treat momentary displays of emotion.

"It's not just studying," Ivan corrected. "Since my kids are out of town and the confluence came early, you and I have some free time this weekend. I was thinking that perhaps it's time to start some light combat training."

"Seriously? That's awesome!" Tori leapt up so quickly that she nearly smacked her shin on the coffee table. As fast as the excitement had come, it transformed into concern as she studied her teacher's stoic expression. "Wait, you're not going to try to kill me again, right?"

Ivan smiled and turned toward the kitchen, dishes clinking lightly as he walked.

"'Try' is a bit of a strong word. Let's just say that whatever happens, happens."

*   *   *

Quorum stood atop the overlook, staring through the one-way glass at the motley collection of people assembled in the sizable room below. Many looked benign, though a few had the telltale signs of recently-transformed metas. One older woman was hovering a few inches off the ground; a child had blue sparks flashing periodically from his eyes. Then there was the seven-foot-tall man who seemed closer to an anthropomorphic beast than a human: head of a tiger, body of a gorilla, talons of an eagle, and that was just what Quorum

103

could make out from up in his vaulted position. Most of them would be able to readjust to their changed lives, having the option either to return to the mundane world they'd known or embrace their potential to be champions of good. The tiger-headed man, however, would likely get no such option. Whatever path lay ahead for him, the life he'd held before was forever out of reach. Quorum felt for metas like that. After all, he was one.

"Quite a crop this year," said Apollo, walking over with a stack of files in hand. "Most we picked up scared and confused. The only one who did any real damage was Ren Tanaka, and honestly, I can't blame the kid. If I'd been turned into some sort of weird chimera monster, I would have accidently broken some windows too."

"How are they in terms of power?" Quorum asked calmly. There were certainly more metas out there, ones that hadn't been so distraught or easy to find, to say nothing of those who would stumble upon remnants of the confluence and be created later. Most would be lower-level, not suited for lives donning the cape nor intriguing enough to be courted by Wade Wyatt and his team. The strongest ones usually popped out the first night, though not always. Quorum estimated there would be a few surprises showing up in the weeks to come, perhaps even a determined solo hero in a homemade costume. He was rather fond of the upstarts; they reminded Quorum of how things had been back when they were first beginning. No uneasy alliances, no global organization, just a bunch of people who'd been handed power trying to do the best they could with it.

"We haven't gotten to do any real testing yet," Apollo said. "I've got Stalwart Iron rigging up some dummies in the practice chambers for a baseline physical exam. Surprisingly broad range of origins, though. Several accidentally mutated, as we'd expected from the storm, but there are also a fair amount of activated inner powers and even a few who are testing positive for magic. Data Mine thinks that the people at Granco were employing mystical substances in their experiment."

"That would account for the energy spikes we saw throughout the night," Quorum agreed. "Combining magic with such a high level of experimental technology is bound to produce unexpected results. Do any of them have hope of reversal?"

"A few are showing tangible cores of power. There's more testing to do before we know if it's safe, but separating them from those cores could return them to human." Apollo flipped through his folders as he spoke, skimming to make sure the information he provided was accurate.

"I don't suppose Ren is one of those few." Quorum already knew the answer; he'd been around for too long not to know how cruelly the world worked.

"Afraid not," Apollo confirmed. "He was on an experimental drug trying to treat a blown-out knee. We think that's what the lightning he was hit by reacted with. No one is even sure what it did to him yet; all we know is that his DNA has been seared like a flank steak. Whatever he was before, there's no way to turn him back from here."

"Thank you for the update," Quorum said. "Those people have been kept waiting long enough, I believe. It's time to start my address. Hopefully I can sway them toward lending us the strength of their talents."

Apollo closed his files hurriedly as Quorum started down the hall. "You'll do great. We always have a big crop of recruits after you rally them. Heck, that's what got me to sign up initially."

"One never knows just how things will go," Quorum said. A small smile pulled at the edges of his mouth as he remembered seeing Apollo for the first time over a decade ago. He'd looked much the same as he did now, only with a touch of fear in his eyes where confidence currently dwelled. "I appreciate the encouragement, though. Pay close attention as I talk with them, Apollo. There may come a day when you are the one who must greet the new metas."

"I could only hope to be a pale shadow of you, sir." There was nothing small or soft about the smile blazing on Apollo's face as he trailed down the hall after Quorum.

*   *   *

"Only three?" Tori didn't bother masking her disappointment as Xelas told them the results of the previous night's storm. "I thought there would be, like, a whole new litter of meta-humans out there."

"Oh, no doubt there's a shitload," Xelas replied. Despite her metallic form, her voice was warm and lively, probably the most carefree Tori had heard in her time with the guild. "But the capes are the ones who scoop up most of them. We usually only run into ones that are on, or building toward, a rampage near something we're protecting. Capes play offense, we play defense. It means we get fewer, sure, but ours are more destructive."

"Are there any of particular note?" Ivan asked.

"They're all fairly neat. One guy keeps accidently creating powerful spells and wards by drawing simple symbols, another summons swarms of insects, and then there's a woman with a transforming power. In the two hours

105

we've had her, she's done two distinct but similar shifts. Arcanicus thinks that's barely scratching the surface. She even put some hurt on Thuggernaut before he was able to take her down."

Ivan gave a slight nod while Tori let out a long whistle. "Thuggernaut? That massive guy who looked like he could crush me between his fingers when I met him? That's who this new gal beat up?"

"Thuggernaut is a good man with a firm head on his shoulders, but technically speaking, he's not the most powerful of metas," Ivan informed her.

"Still, for a rookie to leave a mark like she did, the lady is working with serious mojo," Xelas added. "Doc is out testing the lot of them right now, using a different suit than his usual." She turned to Tori, since this comment was clearly for her benefit rather than Ivan's.

"Since these folks didn't get caught busting into a vault, they still get a choice before joining," Xelas continued. "The ones who have control and want normal lives are cut free; typically we tell them we're a group of metas who like to help newbies figure things out. The ones who have control and who Doc thinks will go criminal are joining whether they like it or not; that's part of what the guild is here for. The ones who don't have control, but he believes will be able to attain it, are given a little more information to work with. They can either sign on and get training, be cut loose to try and live normally, or go work for the capes. However, they are also given a firm warning that if they lose control and we have to deal with them, it's going to be in a permanent fashion. Getting turned into a meta isn't their fault, but choosing to be a loose cannon around others is."

"Geez, you all really don't fuck around," Tori said. "Also, someone besides Pseudonym calls Doctor Mechaniacal 'Doc'? Is this an old-friend thing, or can any guild member use the cutesy nickname?"

"Perks of having known him for long enough and being on the council," Xelas shot back. Her robotic features had no trouble relaying heaps of smarmy sarcasm in the grin she flashed Tori. "Put in enough years of service, and maybe you can get away with it too."

Ivan cleared his throat to bring Xelas's attention back around to him, though the devious sparkle remained in her mechanical eyes. "Since Doctor Mechaniacal and the new recruits are out, I assume Tunnel Vision is on the property?"

"Sure, they're in the break room down the hall." Xelas motioned out the door of her small, cramped office into a winding hallway of dark carpets and strange people. Tori had barely been able to keep from swiveling her head about as she and Ivan marched in from the parking garage. There weren't a whole lot

106

more people than she'd seen on her first night, but each one was fascinating and unique enough to warrant a good stare.

"Thank you," Ivan replied. "If Doctor Mechaniacal returns, let him know that Tunnel Vision has taken us out to one of the training grounds."

"Roughhousing? Ooo ooo! Can I come watch?"

Tori waited for her teacher to say no, to tell this metal woman that such sessions were meant to be a sacred act of learning between master and disciple. Instead, Ivan gave a half-shrug and waved for Xelas to follow as they walked out her office door.

"I am so glad I had my optic cameras upgraded last week," Xelas crooned, so excited that she was weaving as they meandered through the halls. "There's just something magical about the first time you watch a rookie get demolished."

Chapter 15

Ivan ducked nimbly to the side. The blast of flame careened harmlessly over his head as Tori scrambled to get a new line of sight on him. From a nearby cluster of rocks, Xelas hooted loudly, the sound of her applause like trash cans being slammed together in a compactor. Tori bitterly wondered how long she was going to keep cheering. They'd been at it for half an hour and she'd yet to so much as even singe the lining on Ivan's costume, let alone land a clean hit. When she went in for melee, he easily tossed her aside, and when she tried to snipe him at a range, he dodged the fireballs like he had all the time in the world.

"Can we pause for a minute?" Tori asked, phasing into her human-form. Overhead, the sun beat down on them, making the dry sand around them so hot that it likely would have been intolerable if one weren't partially made of fire, entirely mechanical, or a goddamned legendary powerhouse. She didn't know where they were, but Tunnel Vision (a pair of fraternal twins who shared one code name) had evidently taken them somewhere set aside for guild training. It made sense that they'd be out here—not even Ivan could do more than turn the big rocks into smaller rocks.

"Your enemies won't give you any quarter just because you're tired," Ivan replied, standing stoically as he carefully watched his student.

"I'm not tired, ass. I'm just not sure what I'm supposed to be getting from this." Tori could barely feel the weight of her own costume resting on her body. It breathed in a way she'd never found a fabric capable of. "Yeah, you're a lot faster and stronger than me. Does me firing pointlessly at you for hours really have a point? Shouldn't you be attacking me a little too?"

"Unfortunately, I'm not yet confident that you could survive one of my attacks," Ivan said. "As for the futility of training, did you imagine you'd close the gap between us in such a short time? The best way to improve at fighting is like any other task: do it relentlessly. You have to *find* a way to hit me, whether through creative tactics or increasing your core abilities. Either way, there's no better training than doing the task. Even in failure, you'll still grow stronger for the effort spent."

Tori idly conjured then released a fireball in her hand as she mulled over Ivan's words. Essentially, fighting him was like trying to play a video game with the difficulty cranked up to maximum. She probably wouldn't beat it anytime soon, but after enough time, the easier modes would seem ludicrously simple. The idea wasn't necessarily flawed, though one glaring problem did stick out to her.

"If that's the case, then shouldn't we be doing this once I have my actual costume?" Tori gestured to the dark, layered material she had worn upon entering the guild's halls. "We both know I want to build a meta-suit. That's the kind of villain I'm going to be. Why not train me how to fight with one of those, instead of with my fire abilities, since I never plan to use them?"

"The girl has full elemental phasing *and* she wants a meta-suit? I can't tell if that's spoiled or ambitious." Xelas tilted her head and tapped her cheek several times. "I'll go with ambitious, since she said she intends to build her own."

"Intentions are well and good, but I can't train you on something that might or might not one day exist," Ivan replied. "Aside from which, the world is an unpredictable, dangerous place. Even if you have no intention of using these abilities for whatever reasons you've dreamed up, there may come a day when they are the only thing that will keep you alive. Better to have the skills and not need them than need them and not have them."

"Thanks for the cliché, Pop Pop. I'd still rather be training with the actual gear I'm going to be spending my life building and using."

"Well then, I'll make you a deal," Ivan said. "Once you have successfully constructed a meta-suit, feel free to bring it to our training sessions. In fact, any equipment you make is fair game..."

Ivan's words tapered off as Tori bolted through the desert sands until she reached the small pile where they'd set their duffels. He had brought along water, bandages, and some minor painkillers in case of emergencies. Tori quickly unzipped her bag and produced what looked like a gauntlet made of wires, sheet metal, and duct tape. In moments, she'd fastened it to her right arm and was scrambling to get back into position.

"Made this in my downtime," she said, answering a question no one had asked. "Doctor Mechaniacal was kind enough to provide me with a workspace and some materials in my apartment. It's just a prototype, you understand. I'll need much higher-end tech to create a model that will hold up long-term."

"She's confident," Xelas said. "Pseudonym, you got yourself a fun apprentice. I'm a little jealous."

"Would that I could hand her over to you," Ivan muttered. "Very well, Apprentice, I am a man of my word. You may now use that new piece of equipment in our exercises for however long it holds up. Can we finally resume your training now?"

"Hell yeah!" Tori slapped a few buttons and switches with her left hand and the gauntlet softly but audibly buzzed. Flexing her fingers, the glove piece moved, albeit stiffly. As Ivan watched, the dark material of the glove began to glow, turning from a rust color to hot red-white, like a sword pulled fresh from the forge. It was certainly an interesting spectacle, he would give her that.

Ivan slid carefully into a defensive position, eyeing his apprentice closely as he waited for her attack. Though it didn't seem so compared to his skills, Tori was actually a reasonable combatant already. It was true that she couldn't hurt him, but dodging her attacks without tapping into too much of his power actually demanded some attention on Ivan's part. Taking the fireballs head-on wouldn't teach her anything, so right now he was focused on improving her ability to land shots.

Tori licked her lips as she raised her right hand and took aim. No subtlety in her approach, but he supposed that was to be expected when using a piece of untested equipment. From the size of the thing, Ivan was guessing it would send a bigger blast of fire at him, augmenting her existing power. It was the smartest way to utilize what she had to get what she wanted.

The white beam that shot out from Tori's hand was roughly as thick as a soda can and moved so quickly that Xelas would have to replay it at a sixteenth of its actual speed for others to see what had happened. To those who didn't have trained or enhanced senses, there was merely a flash, then a brief motion as Ivan stepped back, and a line of glass that suddenly materialized between Pseudonym and his apprentice.

Ivan felt power surge through his veins before he even registered the threat. Time slowed as his eyes took on their trademark almost-entirely-black appearance, his magical energy reacting to the impending danger. He could see the beam scorching through the air, set on a course for his chest. She hadn't pulled any punches, and for some reason, Ivan felt a flicker of pride at that fact. He could have avoided it entirely, but Ivan's curiosity was piqued. If it had triggered his power, the beam must have been something notable. As her teacher, it was practically his duty to test what she could do.

The beam struck him square in the shoulder, slamming into him like a burning hammer. It was so forceful that Ivan felt himself take a single step backward under the assault. Then it was over, and Tori was stripping off the gauntlet hurriedly as it smoked and popped, a meltdown already beginning.

For his part, Ivan carefully examined the patch of sand that had been turned into glass from the cast-off heat, and then checked his shoulder. The fabric had been cleanly burned through, but his skin was largely unblemished. At the center of the circle, however, there was a small red spot. He touched it delicately and nearly winced in surprise. No doubt about it; that was a burn. As the spot faded, Ivan looked over at Tori, who had successfully freed herself from the glove before it began throwing off sparks like a busted transformer.

110

She had managed to wound him with that garage-made device. Granted, he hadn't been using any shields or wards, but it was still impressive. Untested and untrained though she was, Tori had done something entire legions of capes had failed to accomplish: put a wound on Ivan's flesh.

"Hot holy damn!" Xelas yelled from her perch on the rocks. "That one is going in the Christmas highlight reel."

*   *   *

Chloe sat in the back of the small room, quietly filling small Styrofoam cups with dark coffee as she pretended not to listen. The people gathered around in metal folding chairs paid her no mind; they were used to half-concealed eavesdropping and lingering stares. After all, if being a meta-human was easy, they wouldn't need support groups.

"I made it to a third date with the girl I told you all about," said a man wearing a battered toupee. His announcement was greeted by soft applause, and a light blush filled his round cheeks.

"She knows I'm a meta, though I haven't told her exactly how it works yet. I'm planning to tell her on our next night out. If you see me coming to extra meetings next week, you'll know the reason why." He chuckled anxiously and touched his toupee unconsciously. Chloe wondered what secrets the patch of fake hair was hiding as the others chattered with assurances that things would go well.

She wasn't quite sure why she'd volunteered to provide the coffee for this meeting. Yes, Ridge City Grinders did have a reputation for giving back to the local community, but that wasn't why she felt uncertain. Truthfully, Chloe was chiding herself for being too much of a coward to just own up to what had happened and take a seat at one of those metal folding chairs. She'd created a convenient lie to come here while the coffee shop was being fixed, or at least made workable, because she didn't want to admit to anyone, even herself, what the previous night's storm had done to her.

Her hands wavered slightly, and she focused on not talking. Not a mumble, or a whisper, or a word. Chloe had yet to figure out what caused the strange occurrences around her, but more often than not, they came after she spoke. Until she had control, or at least understanding, she was doing her best to stay mute.

Chloe Henson refused to be beaten by mere blackouts, explosions, and strangely-oriented rain. She'd get the hang of what was going on, sooner or later. Chloe wasn't ready to resign herself to one of those chairs.

Not until she knew for sure just what had happened to her.

"That is... impressive." Wade watched the video once more, carefully examining each detail, from the speed of the beam to the transformation of each grain of sand. On the desk next to the television sat the remains of Tori's gauntlet. Ivan stood behind him, eyeing the video as Wade rewound and advanced to various parts. "There are flaws, of course. The beam's power isn't nearly constricted enough if it let out sufficient heat to turn the sand to glass. Speed could use work, as well. With that much blasting power, she could get it at least fifty percent quicker. And, of course, the fact that it burned out after a single shot speaks to some serious longevity issues. Overall, though, it's quite an impressive accomplishment."

"Impressive would be if she'd had a month and real tools," Ivan said. "Not a week of spare nights and a miniature junk shop above my garage."

"Now, now, I did provide some quality components for her to use," Wade replied, rewinding the tape once again. "True, I wasn't certain what she'd be able to do with them, but I wanted to give her a chance."

Ivan walked around to the front of Wade's desk. Unlike his office at Indigo Technologies, the desk Wade sat at here didn't sit in front of a glass wall that provided an excellent view. Instead, there were bits of tech scattered about the room, as well as a pile of half-finished inventions on Wade's desk. Ivan often remarked that Wade was as messy as he was brilliant, which was a remarkably high bar on both accounts.

"Wade, you need to shoot straight with me here. Did you give her anything that accounts for being able to build something that powerful? She managed to burn me, *me* of all people. I might not have been at full power, but I was definitely braced for the blow. If she could churn out something like that..." Ivan's voice trailed off as the implication flooded his mind. He could count on one hand the number of people who could build a device like that so quickly, and one of them was standing on the opposite side of the desk from him.

"When I first brought Ms. Rivas to your attention, I mentioned her powerful intellect," Wade said. "From the moment I began testing her, it became clear that her greatest limitations have always been finances and resources. Given appropriate funding, your apprentice would have likely already constructed a meta-suit that would put my first generation ones to shame."

Ivan ran a hand through his dark hair and leaned against the edge of the metal desk, turning his eyes to the television once more. "You said she was smart, but that's like Thuggernaut saying someone is tall. You're both towering so far above most everyone else that it seems like you're guessing at what everyone else's standards are."

"Then let me clarify: Tori Rivas is smart by my definition of the word. Her technological prowess rivals any that I've ever seen. She still has much to learn and a long road before her, but I have no doubt she could be an inventor of legendary stature one day. Perhaps her creations will even eclipse my own." Wade clicked off the television and picked up the smoking husk of her gauntlet.

"So why in the nine hells aren't you her teacher? Think of what that woman could do with a real scientist leading her."

"She doesn't need scientific guidance." Wade jiggled the gauntlet, causing a slight tinkling sound to fill the room. "That was proven by her little side-project here. If I train Tori, she will become a second generation version of me. She possesses the potential to be much more than a poor copy; she can be a powerful entity all her own. To get there, however, she needs to learn about more than science. Did you know that Tori was up for three grants during her time in high school?"

"It didn't come up over dinner," Ivan said.

"Each time, she was the frontrunner but refused to comply with the requirement that would split a percentage of credit and income for her discoveries with the grant's investors. She has chosen to walk the path of poverty and crime rather than allow anyone else to have claim over her creations."

"Sounds a lot like someone I know, someone who got pissed at a company for stealing his designs and decided to wipe out their assets by force." Ivan could still remember the first time he'd seen Doctor Mechaniacal in action—lasers blasting, energy missiles singing through the air, the high-pitched squeal of his sonic stun gun tearing at people's ears. It had been all he could do to resist fighting him right then and there.

"Precisely. Tori and I are too similar. Under your guidance, she will become a more adult, independent version of herself. Under mine, she would likely end up following in my footsteps, which is pointless. The world already has a Wade Wyatt. I think it would be better off experiencing a Tori Rivas at her true capacity."

"That's all nice and well-intentioned, but look at what she made." Ivan tapped the side of the gauntlet lightly, causing a piece to fall to the ground. "We can't ignore that. Think about what she could do with real resources. It's criminal to make her piss away time with me when she should be pursuing her true calling, and not the kind of 'criminal' that we actually enjoy."

"No, you're quite right there," Wade agreed, setting down the gauntlet before Ivan could do any more damage. "I gave her a few coins and she returned with a golden harp. Ms. Rivas has proven her innovation and intelligence to a degree that even I wasn't expecting. It's high time we allowed her to start constructing that meta-suit she's always going on about. The materials will be pricey, but I don't mind putting them on loan until she begins to earn for the guild."

"Perfect." Ivan walked over and sat forcefully in one of the chairs next to Wade's desk. "We can keep the apprenticeship going, but I'll have her move into guild quarters where she can have a proper lab. As soon as Xelas is done showing her around, we can give her the good news."

Wade took a seat behind the desk. This was not done out of a need to show Ivan which of the two of them was in charge, but because it put a large, heavy object between Wade and his friend. "Actually, there's no need for that. As I mentioned, Ms. Rivas did better than I expected, but I realized she might need a true workspace from the first time we met."

"What did you do?" Ivan's eyes narrowed and he gripped the edge of the desk.

"Nothing too extreme; we merely had a lab built for Ms. Rivas at your residence. It locks from your side and has every safeguard you can think of. She could set off anything short of a nuke and it wouldn't singe your wallpaper."

"Uh huh. And why haven't I noticed this lab anywhere around my house?" Ivan's irises hadn't vanished yet, but darkness was beginning to creep slowly through his sclera.

"Well, obviously, because we put it in the basement," Wade replied.

"I don't have a... Wade, what did you *do*?"

Wade coughed lightly, a signal that activated many of the defensive measures he'd set up throughout the office. "Since we had the opportunity when we were renovating your garage and moving Tori in, I may have left behind some bots to construct a basement that would make a suitable laboratory. It can be stocked with everything your apprentice needs by day's end."

"Just so we're clear—" Ivan stood up, the entirety of his eyes now cloaked in darkness with only the glowing red runes remaining "—you violated my house without permission, left your little builder-bots around to do whatever they pleased, and built a subterranean level without so much as consulting me?"

"I also took the liberty of stocking a few initial components while we were having this chat," Wade added. If it was going down, he might as well get everything settled at once.

"Get your suit and call Tunnel Vision," Ivan instructed. "We need to have a... *chat*... about the importance of personal boundaries."

Chapter 16

Tori walked into Monday's weekly meeting tired, sore, and exhausted, yet it was still the most cheerful any of the staff had seen her since her arrival. Training with Ivan had been a wearying experience, but it had all been worth it when he showed her the secret basement tucked under the house. She wasn't entirely sure why he had seemed so grumpy as he'd given her the tour, but the moment she'd set eyes on her new workstation, Tori hadn't cared enough to try and guess.

It was gorgeous—barrels and buckets of parts, along with a computer that could actually handle her calculations and software. There had even been a piece of decoration, the gold-frame painting of Tori and her parents she'd requested to have returned. While Ivan had plodded about like he'd never seen the basement before, Tori dove headfirst into exploring, cataloguing, and—most importantly—planning. She'd barely gotten any sleep. Ivan had to drag her away for Sunday's combat training, and he had actually cut her off from lab access at ten that night so she would get a few hours' rest before they had to go back to work. Her brain had been buzzing, though, and while Ivan could stop her from physically tinkering, he couldn't do a thing about her making sketches in her head.

Tori was still riding the high of mentally solving how to couple together her forearm and bicep joints when Donald plopped into the cubicle next her. Like Tori, he looked as though the weekend had taken a bat to him. Unlike Tori, he wasn't surfing a wave of possibility and endorphins as he sluggishly logged in to his work computer.

"Good morning," Tori greeted cheerfully. "How was the weekend of raiding? Get back up to the max level?"

"Ugggggggghhhh." Donald's head tilted forward slowly until it fell against the top of his small desk with a slight thud. "Stupid, damned, evil, wicked, horrid, villainous, total dickhole of a storm torched my building's electrical system and every item that was plugged in at the time, including my new setup."

Tori sucked in a gasp of air through her teeth, then let it out slowly as she said, "Shiiiiiiiiiit. Were you able to salvage anything?"

"Not so much as a RAM stick," Donald said, his face still smushed on the desk. "I went from having the best gaming set-up in the state to playing all weekend on my three-year-old backup laptop. Yes, my backup one, because I had my main wired in for additional processing power. I just *had* to get that extra burst of speed. Hubris, thy name is Donald Moss."

"Maybe it's a chance to start over, you know? Build something even grander than before?" Tori didn't have a lot of hope that this would cheer him up; she knew a shitshow situation when she saw one.

"And until then, I will clack away on my tiny keyboard like a total noob." Donald let out a grunt and pulled himself up, quickly logging on to the corporate system. Sad as he might be, getting dinged for being late wouldn't make it any better. "Still, it wasn't a total loss," he muttered at a volume he thought was inaudible.

"How so?"

Donald froze at Tori's question, quickly stumbling through an array of falsehoods, each more intricate than the last, before realizing he could hide his mistake in the truth. "Well, I still got to play at least, and my guild was able to log some serious levels. We even got enough intel to make a real attempt on one of the raid dungeons next weekend."

It was clear Donald was hiding something; anyone with half a brain could expend two seconds of effort and crack through the sweaty, uncertain veneer he had built up. Tori decided not to push it, though. Whatever Donald was actually thankful for, it seemed like it was something he dearly didn't want to talk about. Probably a "personal" folder that was salvaged or backed-up before the system crashed.

"Just goes to show, you don't need top-of-the-line stuff to have fun with your friends," Tori said, her leftover pep adding an unexpected tone of encouragement to her trite line.

"Completely true," Donald agreed.

Though the sentiment was quite accurate, neither one was currently ascribed to the philosophy of minimalism. Tori was focused on perfecting her suit, and Donald... well, Donald desperately needed to get a better setup and probably some peripherals.

The part of his weekend he wasn't sharing with Tori had turned owning such equipment from a desire into a requirement.

*   *   *

One man hurried down the street, three cups of coffee from the wrecked shop nearby clutched in his hands as he got into the passenger side of an idling sedan. He handed two of the cups to the other men who had been waiting, then glanced around nervously to see if anyone in the bustling downtown area had taken notice of him. No one had, as they were all busy going about their day, most of them inconvenienced by the fact that their de facto

116

coffee destination was under repairs and only had a small stand at the front to serve the swarms of caffeine-starved workers.

"What are we supposed to be watching for, anyway?" said the man in the back seat, sipping tentatively at the still-steaming coffee.

"Just watching," said the driver. "Getting a sense of the comings and goings in the building. We have to figure out when things are the slowest, but there are still enough people. That's when we'll want to strike."

"Seems like a lot of work to rob an office." The man who had brought the coffee continued to watch people as he spoke. With the amount of money on the line for this gig, he was damn sure going to do a good job.

"It's a weird scheme," agreed the driver. "But this is the place he wants hit. Something about corporate espionage, I think. For what he's paying, I didn't ask too many questions."

The backseat rider took another long sip and stared up at the building. "Are you sure we should be trusting this guy?"

"If you want to walk away, feel free. More money all around," said the passenger.

"I'm not quitting, just saying... I don't know, whole thing seems weird."

"In this town, weird comes with the highest paycheck," said the driver. "Now, watch people's movements. We've only got a couple of weeks before he wants to do the job."

With a long draw of his coffee, the man in the back seat turned his attention to the sizable office building that hosted multiple companies, hundreds of employees, and, unbeknownst to them, one retired super-villain of global infamy.

*   *   *

Ivan was unsurprised to find Wade's seemingly simple silver sedan in his driveway as he pulled in. After their conversation had somewhat lapsed during the "sparring match," it was clear they still had things to discuss. Plus, Wade had been kind enough to leave a voicemail warning Ivan of his arrival. He sat patiently on Ivan's porch, rocking back and forth in one of the purchased wooden chairs as though he were nothing more than a friend who had stopped by before the homeowner returned. It was both gracious and prudent, for while the locks on Ivan's house would do nothing to stop Wade, some of the wards might very well have proven troublesome.

"I'm guessing this means one of us is in trouble," Tori said.

117

"Not at all; Doctor Mechaniacal and I simply have some guild business to discuss." Ivan popped open his door and Tori followed suit. In moments, Ivan had the house unlocked and had shooed everyone inside, lest they give the neighbors more cause for speculation.

"Tori, why don't you go work on your suit for a while?" Ivan said. He nodded his head toward the wall where an entrance to the basement had been constructed and hidden, all without his consent. It stirred a bit of anger in him, but he forced himself to let the sentiment go. Ivan and Wade had beaten each other up for the better part of two hours; it was time to put the cause of conflict in the past. Not being able to let go in their world made having any sort of friendship essentially impossible.

"Twenty-three years old and I'm still being sent to my room like a kid," Tori muttered. She still slid the wall aside, though, hurrying down the stairs to her project below without so much as changing out of her work clothes first.

Wade waited until the door was sealed before settling into one of Ivan's chairs. "I came with news about the recruits."

"For the love of... I do not want to kill some stupid rookie just because they had the bad luck to get a power they can't handle. You have a whole guild of villains, I'm sure one of them can handle it."

"Actually, there's no need to dispatch any of them," Wade replied. "All three have decided to join our organization."

"Seriously? We never bat a thousand on recruitment runs." Ivan crossed his arms and leaned against the nearest wall, studying Wade's face carefully for any signs of falsehood.

"The one who summons swarms is excited about his power and very ambitious about developing it. He doesn't care where he receives the training. Our symbol-wielding mage is a standard anti-social type, hungry for power, status, and probably more than a little vengeance. Truthfully, we may end up with a code-breaker in him, but he at least gets a shot to show he can handle the responsibility first. Lastly, the woman with the transformation ability is terrified of her powers and wants control above all else. Evidently, she nearly killed a few members of her family by accident before Thuggernaut brought her down. I suggested she head to the nearest AHC headquarters before I offered her a spot, but it seems she has no love for that organization in the slightest. Thus, The Guild of Villainous Reformation has three new apprentices."

Ivan resisted the urge to groan inwardly at the guild's full name; he always felt it sounded like a cult more than a gathering of like-minded people. Wade had won out in choosing the name. Ostensibly it was meant to sound like a group of villains trying to find their way to the straight and narrow; the cheeky use of "reformation", used literally in this case to mean "to make different"

118

rather than with its more common connotation, pleased Wade too much to let it go to waste. He got off on wordplay and hiding in plain sight. Had it been up to him, Ivan would have chosen a simple, unobtrusive name like "Joe's Meeting Group."

"Poor kids. I'd hoped one of them would have better decision-making skills," Ivan said. "Why'd you feel the need to come out and tell me that, though? I'm not taking on any more damn apprentices, if that's what you're after."

"Perish the thought," Wade said. "No guild member can have more than one apprentice at a time in the first place, and in the second, all of them are already spoken for."

"Spoken for? What the hell, no one does the mentorship thing anymore. I only did it as a favor to you."

"But you still did it, and others in the guild took notice," Wade replied. "Having an apprentice has become an overnight status symbol. Balaam had officially taken the one who can draw magic symbols almost before I accepted him into the guild. Arachno Bro found much in common with our insect summoner, so he has requested to be his teacher and I approved. As for the dragon woman—"

"Hang on, what's this about dragons now?" Ivan interrupted.

"Ah, right. Things devolved before I brought you fully up to speed. The young woman who can transform does so into multiple types of dragons. Thus far, she has become a red dragon with extremely hot fire-breath and a green dragon with greatly enhanced physical properties."

"Versatile," Ivan noted.

"Quite. At any rate, two people are interested in becoming her teacher: Wildwood and Thuggernaut. As she technically falls under the magic category, Wildwood has a stronger claim, but I wanted to get your input before making an actual call."

Ivan weighed the options in his head. As a magic user, Wildwood might have a more technical right to the young woman's education, but that didn't mean he'd be the better teacher. From what Wade had described, she was functionally a brawler so far, which meant Thuggernaut could probably impart more wisdom about how to use her powers rather than just understanding their source. It was also true that Wildwood was a trusted confidant of Balaam's, and Ivan wasn't so self-aware that he could be certain he was seeing the issue objectively.

"You're the one in charge of the rookies, you make the call," Ivan said. "Right now, her power is still fresh; it's unlikely anyone can be sure how it will work or max out. Today, Thuggernaut seems like a better fit, but her next dragon-form might be purple with the power of spell-casting, which puts Wildwood back in as a solid teacher. If you had to use something as the criteria for choice, maybe ask them why they want her as an apprentice."

Wade leaned back in the chair and smiled. "Funny, I had a very similar thought. Wildwood sowed some malarkey about wanting to pass the knowledge of magic on to the next generation of capable adepts, but it was clear he was following either orders or a trend. Thuggernaut told me that, after fighting our recruit firsthand, he thought she could be much stronger if properly trained."

"Then you already know Thuggernaut is the better choice," Ivan said.

"I do indeed. But I was curious how you would handle the situation, given your respective associations. Our guild's newest recruits are going to be spending time together during their training. It seemed only prudent to see if your prejudices extended to those even associated with Balaam, as his do to you."

"Relax; just because the kid got snagged by that bastard doesn't mean I hate him. Bad luck can happen to anyone," Ivan uncrossed his arms at last and walked over to his sofa, where he nestled into a comfortable position. "But what's this about them spending time together? It's classes or apprenticeship, not both."

"We haven't had the chance to do both," Wade pointed out. "Some camaraderie could be good for them, build alliances and friendships that will keep them alive later on. Plus, we can use one of the greatest teaching tools ever afforded to mankind."

Ivan grinned as he took Wade's meaning. It was the force that had driven him to fighting endless numbers of capes during his youth, that had caused Wade to work tirelessly in developing cutting edge technology, that defined those born of greatness and those burdened by mediocrity. With four rookies all starting around the same time, it provided a perfect opportunity to use that tool and carve stronger, better people out of them. Ivan's voice came out barely above a whisper, yet the excitement and potential in his tone caused it to carry throughout the entirety of the living room.

"Competition."

*   *   *

No amount of air fresheners could mask the scent of burned plastic that wafted through Donald's apartment. He was tempted to try candles, but the landlord had a pretty strict policy about open flames, and after already losing his computer system, Donald couldn't emotionally handle being evicted. The charred husk of his beautiful system still sat in the corner of his apartment, likely the reason he was unable to cleanse the smell of melted plastic from his space.

Donald paid the shrine of lost potential no mind as he set up the video camera on his uneven kitchen counter. It was cheap, one he'd bought from the discount bin of a local electronics store, but it would record images and that was all Donald really required for now. He had to create proof, to know for sure he wasn't losing his mind. True, if he were crazy, then his brain could make him see madness on video as easily as in real life, but it was a step forward. That was what he was focusing on: just moving one single step at a time toward acceptance and understanding.

Propping up his lone remaining laptop (aside from the work one that he dared not risk in this experiment), on a wooden TV tray took some time, but Donald refused to rush. This was in part because if something went wrong and he lost this computer, he was going to have to get truly desperate, but also because part of him feared what would happen if he tried this and failed. Or, perhaps worse, succeeded.

He clicked the red button on the camera then hurried back into what he hoped was the proper frame. Upon review, Donald would discover that he'd actually cropped the top part of his head out of the shot by standing too close. He also wouldn't care because that was the least interesting aspect of the video Donald was about to record.

"Ahem. Hi. Um, my name is Donald Moss. And this, I guess, is trial number one of... well, one so far. If you're watching this and something has happened to me, then things probably didn't go that well. Mom, Dad, Sheila... I love you all."

Nervously shuffling about, Donald debated on where to go from there. He hadn't planned the "just in case" goodbye; this was supposed to be for his eyes only. Still, since he'd already gone down that path, he might as well see it through. The other option was stopping to re-record the introduction, and Donald wasn't sure his willpower would hold up for long enough to allow that.

"Last Friday, I was at my computer when the building was hit by one of the lightning bolts from that lab's weird storm. It fried my system and zapped me unconscious. I thought that was all it did, but the next night, when I was on my game... maybe at this point it's better to show than tell."

Donald leaned over and typed quickly on his laptop's keyboard, pulling up the predetermined program he'd carefully selected for the experiment. With a deep breath and an unsaid prayer, he got everything loaded and prepared to proceed.

"Here goes nothing."

Chapter 17

"Here are the—and I want you to look up from your desk so you can see my hands—" Tori paused, raising her index and middle finger like bunny ears and then lowering them halfway twice "—*vital* spreadsheets you need for today's meeting."

She dropped the stack of paper on Ivan's desk, far enough away that he had to lean forward to reach it. "You know, some employees actually show me respect, seeing as I'm the one in charge of hiring and firing them."

"True, but those employees aren't supposedly family members with attitude problems. If I didn't give you shit, wouldn't that seem more suspicious?"

Ivan quickly checked to make sure his office door was closed and then leaned back in his chair. Tori had a point, but as it was the kind of point that let her continue getting away with doing what she wanted, he didn't trust it. At least she was aware enough to make such cracks out of earshot from the mundane office workers. Much as Tori liked to test boundaries, she clearly knew where the unmovable ones lay.

"Just don't take it too far. Remember, you're an intern, and an under-qualified one at that. Even I can only justify so much in the name of nepotism." Ivan flipped through the sheets carefully, admiring the work. Tori might moan and complain about her boring day job, but even when she was half-assing it, she was still the most competent assistant Ivan had ever worked with. "Also, tomorrow after work you will not be coming home with me. I've arranged to have a car with one of Doc's drivers pick you up from here. If anyone asks, tell them you have to go in for one of your 'meetings' and show discomfort. That will likely make them let the topic be."

"Oh, right; the kiddos are coming to the house again, aren't they?" Tori had heard very little about Ivan's children, and she'd made a point not to pry. His warning from her first day was seared in her mind, and as much as she was growing fond of her surly teacher, she didn't doubt for a minute that he wouldn't make good on his threat. "Another weekend at the pork plant for me, then. I'll pack a bag tonight."

"No need. You'll be heading to the guild this time. Everything you need will be provided for the weekend. From what I understand, there is quite an array of training planned for you all."

Tori tilted her head and arched an eyebrow. "Sending me to the park to play with the other kids? About time, it's already been two weeks since the confluence. I was wondering when—"

The sound of an explosion filled the air. Through the small window in Ivan's office, Tori saw a bright green blast of light burn through the sky. She looked at her boss and teacher, waiting for him to give her an order, to tell her they needed to get to safety. Clearly some heavy shit was going down, right?

Instead of doing any of those things, Ivan let out a heavy sigh and pulled a small radio from his desk. He clicked it on and an excited, static-filled voice burst forth from the black plastic box.

"*—moving to a shelter on Magnolia and Ave E. To all those just tuning in, there is currently a fight occurring in uptown Ridge City by the Alfred Settler Memorial Plaza. Two men with strange powers just robbed Ridge City Savings & Loan and are currently engaged with Stalwart Iron as they try to make their escape. Again, if you are in the area, please seek a safe place to hide. All those out in the open can go to the just-opened shelter at Magnolia and—oh my goodness! It's Battle Cry, Blunderbuss, and Apollo arriving to assist Stalwart Iron. Such an array of talent and power I personally have never seen—*"

Ivan dialed down the volume knob until the radio was barely audible. "This is going to happen a fair bit for the next few weeks. Lots of new metas out there, testing their powers, figuring out what they can do, you get the idea. Eventually, some will build up big enough heads of steam to try and pull a poorly-planned plot like robbing a bank in the middle of the day. Capes are on high alert, so this is the time when any villain with a brain in their skulls goes deep underground until the capes get complacent."

A knock sounded on the door and Barb, the woman from Human Resources Tori had met during her orientation, poked her head in. Atop it was a small plastic fireman's hat with the words "Safety Officer" emblazoned in yellow letters.

"Hey all," Barb greeted. "I'm sure you heard about the fight going on outside. Nothing to worry about, it was miles away and we got word that it's already wrapped up."

"I had complete faith we'd be evacuated if the situation was otherwise," Ivan replied. "Thanks for keeping us in the loop, though."

Tori could barely manage a nod as Barb ducked out and presumably headed off to the next office in the hallway. She stared at the shut door for several moments before finally forcing her tongue to work again. "You all take this stuff really well. I mean... creepily well."

"We work downtown in the city where the AHC has its global headquarters," Ivan replied. "Between idiot upstarts testing their power, the propensity to use capes in place of cops, and being near the tempting target of the financial district, meta fights are just part of our work week. Especially after a confluence."

"Score one for crashing in the slums, I guess. Nothing to steal means the capes rarely get called out." Tori gazed past Ivan to the world she'd spent too many wasted years in. For an instant, she could practically see the beaten-down warehouse where she'd set up her makeshift lab, but she blinked and it was gone. Strange as her circumstances with Ivan and the guild were, it was all still a big step up from where she'd been not so long ago.

"Anyway, you said I was going to be doing group training? Should I pack up a bag of my tech to bring along?"

"No, for this exercise, you will only have access to yourselves and what you can find," Ivan replied, turning his attention back to the spreadsheets in front of him. "You'd do best to assume it will be something quite rigorous and mentally prepare yourself. I trust I don't need to tell you to bring your A-game, right? After all, you're representing me as much as yourself, and I have quite the reputation to uphold."

Tori was pretty certain she caught a whisper of a smirk on Ivan's face, but it vanished so quickly she suspected it might have been a trick of the light. There or not, she didn't need visible sarcasm to know that Ivan didn't give two wet shits about his reputation. He probably did, however, know that being Fornax's apprentice would put a target on her back right out of the gate and wanted to make sure she was aware of it going in.

"Nothing to worry about," Tori said. "I'm going to show those other rookies what a real apprentice is made of… which is fire. Real apprentices are made of fire. Wrapped in electronics. With a kicking smile and awesome wit and a sharp—"

"Pleeeeease stop stalling and go back to work." Ivan looked up from his spreadsheets to glare at her, but only for a second. There was a meeting to prep for, after all.

"You are just no fun at the office. No fun at all." Tori stuck her tongue out at him while his head was down, then opened the door and headed back to her cubicle.

*   *   *

Apollo floated gently down to the floor, grinning as applause from the trainees reached his ears. Stalwart Iron was already on the ground, having deactivated the thrusters on his legs. Though some of the others felt Stalwart Iron was a bit stiff, Apollo actually found himself fond of the robotic champion. What he lacked in emotion, he made up for in being willing to do grunt work, and that was a trait Apollo always enjoyed in his lackeys.

124

"That was great, sir." It was one of the trainees. Apollo hadn't bothered to learn most of their names yet, so rather than reply he just gave a smile and a thumbs-up. From behind the rookie, Blunderbuss appeared, massive gun strapped to his back and a pair of would-be criminals unconscious in each arm. Bridge stepped out of the wormhole she'd opened, followed by Battle Cry. A quick motion from Bridge and the warp in space vanished as though it had never been there. Bridge was one of the least well-known capes in the AHC, but she commanded salary and accommodations nearly on par with Apollo's. Utility was almost as important as prestige. Almost.

"Class, please circle around me," Stalwart Iron commanded. "Apollo has graciously agreed to lead a discussion over the event you all just saw, so we are going to review the footage from multiple angles in order to make sure you're adequately prepared."

This bought Apollo time to grab a shower and a sandwich, the former of which was most important. It wouldn't do to have them noticing the flecks of blood splattered across his bronze skin. It wasn't even his fault that the bigger goon had been so roughed up. The guy had certainly looked like he could take a punch, after all.

"You sure about leaving the kids with gearhead?" Battle Cry asked as they left the giant hangar designated for landings and entered a much smaller, more intimate hallway. Behind them, Bridge and Blunderbuss dragged the two cuffed and unconscious crooks off to processing, where the police would pick them up for trial after their abilities were adequately sealed off.

"Did you want to lead a half-hour long fight recap?" Apollo asked.

Battle Cry shook her head, sending the straight dark hair of her wig spinning slightly through the air. Underneath her red leather costume and wig, Battle Cry was a normal-looking woman who could and did pass as a regular civilian when at her day job as a local news station's production assistant. "I just always feel weird about trusting robots. Yeah, he's nice now, but you never know when one will get uppity and use Xelas's Law."

"Stally isn't going anywhere," Apollo said. "He's technically free and loves working for us. Not all of them turn out like Xelas. Besides, do you know literally anyone else in this organization who doesn't complain when the cleaning staff is off and the toilets need scrubbing?"

"Okay, you make a strong point. Any thoughts on what you'll tell the trainees?"

"Probably just stick to the usual: assess the situation, use only the necessary amount of force, always go for the capture instead of the kill unless given special authorization. All the shit we're supposed to teach them. The ones who actually make it through will figure out how things really work pretty quickly."

"It's not a bad crop. Some of them could be really strong with enough training. I saw Blunderbuss working with that Ren kid, and man, for a rookie, he could take a beating," Battle Cry said.

"Regenerative properties are off the charts. Whatever weird cocktail he had in his system didn't go dormant once the changes were done. It's still in him, bubbling around and fixing anything we try to break. He's my frontrunner in the class, for now."

Battle Cry leaned back, staring at Apollo uncertainly. "What, you think one of those others will pull ahead? I haven't paid much attention, but it seems unlikely."

"No, most of them are destined to be second-string," Apollo replied. "I'm more looking forward to when we see the ones who were smart enough not to get found that first night. Unlike the dipshit brothers we brought in today, there are bound to be a few metas testing and training themselves, exploring their powers on their own. Out of that lot, there are always a couple of standouts. Could be some serious talent, assuming they're smart enough to join our team instead of bothering with the chump change of robbing a bank."

"Or before those damned guildies get their hooks in them," Battle Cry added. "I cannot for the life of me figure out why we don't just kick their doors down and take them all out once and for all."

Apollo grinned, an expression that made his face literally light up as his ever-present golden glow intensified. "Can't very well go attacking them for ostensibly trying to support each other in keeping their noses clean, now can we? They're too smart to get busted doing any amateur-level shit, so we don't have cause. And besides, I think it's useful to have all of them gathered together in a guild like they are."

"Why on earth is that useful?"

The glow around Apollo grew just a bit brighter, shining off the metal floors of the hall as they walked. "Because when the day for dealing with them finally does arrive, it's more convenient if they're all grouped up in the same spot. It'll make for a much cleaner assault."

*   *   *

"Gather round, gather round, the betting is about to open." Johnny spun the blackboard at his back around, revealing a simple table with the names of all four rookies' teachers along with a selection of numbers on each person's name. "Since our wonderful guild members did the service of choosing apprentices this

126

year, you can bet on which one you expect to do the best in this weekend's special training."

Johnny Three Dicks stood on a box that was full of protein bars so he could see over the small sea of villains that had gathered to participate in one of their favorite forms of entertainment: betting on each other. The sizable break room, stocked with games and snack machines, was almost filled by the crush of people that had turned out to piss away some of their hard-stolen money. Johnny gleefully spotted a few councilors and felt his greedy heart swell with cheer. If they had turned up, this truly was going to be quite the event.

"For the record, I do not approve of this," Thuggernaut grunted. He was sitting at a nearby card table, playing a round of hearts with The Bytes. Around them, the other guild members scrambled to see the board better.

"You gave Pseudonym's girl the best odds?" Wildwood asked, staring at the chalk writing. "No one has even seen what she can do yet."

"Some of us may have filched a file or two," Johnny replied, "all in the name of research, of course. But regardless, she's had several weeks' head start on the others, so she's not paying out as much if she wins."

"I'll drop a hundred on her," Xelas said. "She's got spunk. Let me get fifty on Arachno Bro's boy as well. You humans do not take well to bugs."

From the rear of the small crowd, a man in a popped collar with spider mandibles sprouting from his mouth gave a nod, then motioned to Johnny that he wanted to put two hundred on his own apprentice.

"Give me two hundred on Balaam's guy," Wildwood said quickly. Several other members of the magical division also placed bets on Balaam's apprentice. Whether they believed he would actually win or not was irrelevant. What mattered was making sure Balaam knew they supported him and his endeavors.

Gork called out for three hundred on Pseudonym's apprentice, and others quickly piled in, despite the crappier payout. Stasis broke the mold by betting on Arachno Bro's apprentice. After her, Trilogy was next, and true to his motif, he bet on three of the apprentices, despite the fact that he was functionally guaranteed to lose money no matter who won.

Thuggernaut sat patiently as the bets poured in, villains from all departments of the guild throwing down a few hundred here or there. As he listened, he noticed more and more that his own apprentice was being bet on significantly less than any of the other three. The favor shown for Pseudonym's apprentice was one thing—she did have a head start and a legendary teacher—but the other two weren't anything special. In fact, Thuggernaut considered his own apprentice, Beverly, the strongest of those living at the guild, perhaps even more powerful than Tori. The longer he listened, the more bothered he became by the trend, until finally he laid down his cards and stood forcefully from the table.

The crowd parted before him and he approached the small box that Johnny was standing on. He surveyed the blackboard, taking careful note of each student's odds, then looked his best friend in the eyes.

"I would like to make a bet."

"Seems I recall someone saying this game was 'gauche, barbaric, and uncivilized.' If only I could recall who said those things..." Johnny tapped his fingers together, looking as though he were genuinely plumbing the depths of his mind for the memory.

"That was because it seemed inappropriate to liberate money so easily from a friend. Since you decided to press on, though, I suppose I have no choice." Thuggernaut paused briefly, doing some quick tabulation in his head. "I'd like to bet ten thousand dollars on my own apprentice."

Johnny's whistle carried over the heads of the nearby people who were chattering amongst themselves. Dropping that kind of money was no small feat, and he was her trainer. Maybe he knew something the rest of them didn't.

"Now that is one hell of a bet," Johnny said. "But per guild rules, I can't accept anything over five hundred. Pot gets too big and people start getting antsy."

"Then put me down for five hundred," Thuggernaut replied. He returned to his card game, only to lose a few moments later. It didn't particularly bother him, however. In fact, he was showing a slight grin as Gig reshuffled the deck.

From the way people were betting now, it was clear no one was ignoring his apprentice anymore.

Chapter 18

It was strange to be approaching the guild's headquarters in a car other than Ivan's. Tori hadn't realized how at home she felt with the silent, brooding man until he was replaced by a robot built to look like a human driver—particularly given that, on the surface, this should have been a fairly good substitute for her teacher.

The experience also left her wondering why on earth Doctor Mechaniacal hadn't started selling these self-driving robots to the world at large, since it did a marvelous job of taking her through traffic. It was honestly better than most humans she'd ridden with, which meant it would be worthwhile for both the guild's pocketbook and society as a whole. It was possible he didn't release them *because* it would help society, but Doctor Mechaniacal had never struck Tori as that type of villain.

After disembarking from the car, which she watched drive off and park itself, Tori let herself in to the changing stations that separated the garage from the guild proper. As Ivan promised, one of her Apprentice costumes was waiting there. She slipped out of her work suit and into the comfortable, now-familiar feel of a guild outfit.

She stepped out and was surprised to find someone waiting for her, though she likely shouldn't have been. Xelas wrapped Tori in a powerful hug, squeezing so tightly that it almost triggered Tori's fire-form before letting the softer woman go.

"Are you excited?" Xelas asked, her voice literally buzzing as she spoke. "Getting to meet your fellow rookies, sharing stories and experiences, fighting to the death to see which of you we actually keep?"

"I'm kind of—what the *fuck*?" Tori yelped, her brain catching up to her tongue midway through the reply.

"Calm down, I'm just screwing with you," Xelas said. "Come on, do you really think we'd force you all into a death match for some artificial reason?"

"Let me meet your question with a question: do you really want me to answer that honestly? Remember, I've already got a death threat dangling over my head."

"Pshhh, we all have those at some point," Xelas replied. "Honestly, if I don't have at least three people actively trying to kill me, I feel like I've pissed away a week."

129

Tori stared at the metal woman for several very long seconds. "Okay, cards on the table: I can't tell if you're serious, being glib, or just outright fucking with me."

"Why pick one when all three seem like great options?" Xelas crooked a finger and motioned down the hall. "Now, come on, your classmates are anxious to meet you."

Moving slowly but steadily, Tori followed Xelas down the hall. "Are they really? Like, do they know there's a fourth apprentice?"

"Of course. They've got their own teachers, so each one was brought up to speed on the current situation of the guild. They're also probably all gunning for you, since you're considered the top seed as Pseudonym's apprentice."

"Faaaantastic. Don't suppose you'd care to even the playing field and tell me a little about them?"

"Technically, since I'm a councilor I'm supposed to be completely neutral, which includes not letting any trainees have advanced information." As Xelas clipped through the words, it was the first time Tori had ever heard her actually sound robotic, a tone that quickly vanished when she continued. "But screw that, where's the fun in being a villain if I can't ignore some rules?"

Xelas and Tori turned down a hallway Tori had never been through before. It was largely bare, save for the usual red trim and a single dark wooden door at the end. Something static seemed to race down Tori's arm as they drew closer—extra security, maintained by magic, technology, or probably both. At least she knew they were heading in the right direction.

"Thuggernaut's apprentice is a fellow lady, one who can turn into dragons from what I hear. Balaam has a guy who can do magic by scratching symbols on things, which is weird even for a magic user. And lastly, Arachno Bro is training a kid who can summon swarms of insects. Have lots of fun with that one; just seeing those things makes me glad my skin isn't soft and vulnerable like you humans."

"Bleh. I might spend more time in fire-form than I expected," Tori said. Insects didn't send her scurrying up the walls, but she still wasn't a fan. "Any hints as to what we're going to be doing for training?"

"Sorry, even I know there are lines not to cross. Besides, Doc is way too excited about seeing the surprise on your faces for me to take that away from him." Xelas reached out and pulled open the door, revealing a staircase that went steeply downward, obscuring whatever lay at the bottom from view. "Here endeth your guided tour. Good luck down there, and remember: don't start anything, but don't take people's crap either. Grudges run deep, as do memories of weakness."

"Cheery," Tori muttered. "Thanks, though. When this weekend is done, maybe I can buy you a martini, or whatever your equivalent of booze is. You know, to show my gratitude."

"Taste sensors are fully equipped, so a martini works fine by me." Xelas pointed down the staircase with a long metal finger. "Now quit stalling and get down there."

With a deep breath and a long stare, Tori began her descent. No sooner had she passed the first stair than the door closed firmly behind her. She didn't need to check to know that it wouldn't budge if she tried to open it. The message was clear: Tori and the others were being put here. Escape was not an option. At least, probably not yet.

Moving briskly lest anyone at the bottom mistake a slow pace for fear, Tori emerged from the staircase into a spacious room. Multiple large chairs and couches were scattered through it, and at the center was a massive table laden with food and drinks. Tasteful art hung on the walls, and an empty fireplace was set against the far corner. The whole place reminded Tori of a high-end lounge, or at least how she'd pictured them from movies and television.

Three other people were already in the room, each wearing a costume quite similar to her own. One was a broad-shouldered man who was helping himself to a plate of thick sandwiches that rested amid the array of food. Another was a thin, almost sickly guy who was sitting in a chair, eyes darting about the room. The final apprentice was a woman, taller than Tori and leaning against the far wall next to the fireplace.

All eyes turned to her as she stepped off the staircase and into the room. To her surprise, the gazes weren't as unfriendly as she expected. The thin man gave her a courteous nod and the woman kept a neutral expression. Only the one stuffing his face had a non-subdued reaction. He set down his half-eaten meal and strode across the room.

"You must be our fourth apprentice! Damn, nice to meet you, we've all heard nothing but great things." Before Tori could react, he'd swept her hand up in his and was shaking it firmly. "Seeing as we're all technically named 'Apprentice' for now, how about you just go ahead and call me Lance. I don't see any harm in giving you a first name."

"I... um... Tori. My name is Tori." She wasn't sure why she was giving out her name so easily; it was just that Lance's friendliness had taken her off guard. That was not how she had expected to be greeted by her fellow apprentices.

"Tori. Well, that's a lovely name, if I do say so. The fellow over there who needs a sandwich is going by Warren right now, and our silent, strong lady at the far end is Beverly. Seeing as I'm sure someone with your connections

131

already knows who we're apprenticing under, that probably gets you all the way caught up." Lance released her hand and headed back toward the table, where he waved his hand over the food. "We're supposed to eat our fill while we wait for training to start. They seem to think the food is poisoned or something, but I'm five entrees deep and have to say that it must be some damn tasty poison."

"Feel free to ignore him," the lanky lad named Warren told Tori. "We've already begun to."

Tori contemplated ignoring the food like the others, but she didn't really see the point. If they were trying to drug them, there were easier, less obvious ways to go about it. Besides, she'd had a light lunch thanks to Ivan suddenly dumping a bunch of work on her, and the food did look pretty yummy.

"Screw it; there are worse ways to go." She walked over and joined Lance, helping herself to some chips and chicken fingers, along with a cold soda. There was also beer in the bucket; however, that seemed to be tempting fate a touch more than she should. No matter what was coming, Tori suspected she was going to need her wits for it.

If Ivan's training was any indication, whatever was waiting for them would be neither gentle nor easy.

*   *   *

"Hey, Dad." Rick gave his father a brief hug before letting go and scurrying in the house. Ivan tried to remind himself that his son was simply at that age where being around any parental figure was, to quote, a drag.

"I missed you, Dad!" Beth jumped up and gave him a big hug, and Ivan took the opportunity to squeeze her tightly. Though she too had entered her teens, Rick's younger sister hadn't yet developed the inevitable impending allergy to parental affection. It would be a sad day when they both reached that point, and Ivan intended to get every drop of affection while he still could.

"I missed you, too," Ivan said, finally setting his daughter down and ushering her inside. From the Jeep in the driveway, Janet gave a solemn nod to her ex-husband, which Ivan returned. Avoiding each other made keeping up a peaceful appearance much easier, especially given how much they couldn't talk about in front of the kids.

Shutting the door firmly behind him, Ivan turned to find Rick sprawled out on the couch with the television already turned on, while Beth sat in a nearby chair. "I'm so sorry I had to reschedule our last visit. Did you all have fun at the theme park at least?"

"Heck yeah, we went on a ton of rides," Beth said.

"But we missed the freaking event of the year in town," Rick grumbled from his slouched position on the couch. "All everyone at school is talking about is that weird storm. They say a bunch of people even got superpowers from the lightning. Maybe if we'd stayed, we could have been able to fly or something."

"Or maybe you'd have been turned into a fly-like monster with a proboscis for a face and tattered wings for arms," Ivan countered. "These accidents are very dangerous things. Not every meta is happy about what they are, you know."

"Progress comes with a price." Rick clicked through the channels until he came upon a documentary about NASA's newest probe being sent off in the direction of the last alien debris that had rained down on Earth.

"I'm set with a regular face and arms," Beth replied. "Roller coasters beat weird chemical storms any day of the week."

"And that's why she's the smart one," Ivan said. Despite his teasing tone, he actually meant it. Rick might have a knack with mathematics, but Beth was the only one of the two who seemed to realize that metas and aliens and subterranean species weren't always good things. More than one person with a relentless interest in metas had found their way to join the inhuman ranks, often with terrible results. Had Ivan possessed the power, he would have shielded his children against anything that might steal their humanity. Sadly, that was beyond even his exceptional abilities.

"Off the couch and go get ready for dinner," Ivan commanded. "I've made a big enough meal that even the two of you should get full, but only washed hands get to eat."

Beth took off quickly with Rick moving at a weary trudge. Ivan watched them go then turned his attention to the remaining work in the kitchen. He glanced at the table and noticed he'd forgotten to set a place. He quickly realized that no, he'd been right the first time. For a moment he'd forgotten that Tori wasn't in the house with them and therefore wouldn't be joining the family for dinner. It was a relief not to have to worry about her tinkering away in the basement, perhaps courting an explosion to blow up his house's foundation. But, if he were completely honest, it was also a bit strange not to have her raiding his fridge and peppering him with questions he didn't want to answer.

Ivan shook off the sentiment and continued into the kitchen. There was no point in worrying about his apprentice. She was in capable hands that would give better training than he could ever hope to. Assuming said training, or the other apprentices, didn't find a way to kill her, of course.

*   *   *

Tori was on her third bag of chips when they heard the thumping of steps coming down the staircase. As soon as the figure stepped into view, it was instantly recognizable to her and she suspected to the others as well. Doctor Mechaniacal stood before them in all his metal-suited glory, spiked glowing helmet fixed firmly over his face. This was not the councilor or instructor she had met previously: this was the leader of their guild and the overseer of their future.

"You all have been chosen for the chance to join our organization. This is a burden we will place on you, a trust you must guard carefully, and a privilege few will ever see. Our lives are not easy, nor do we have the luxury of being soft people. Therefore, over the next few days, I will test the strength of your bodies, powers, and minds. If you can endure this hardship, you will be one step closer to true membership, and all that comes with it."

From behind Doctor Mechaniacal, Tunnel Vision stepped into view, separating to flank their leader. The sister, who Tori suspected was Vision but had yet to confirm, stiffened as her eyes began to glow. Her twin brother, the most likely candidate for Tunnel, raised his hands and pressed them to a nearby wall. Before their eyes, the red-painted plaster disintegrated, revealing a long stretch of plains similar to the one Ivan had taken Tori to the weekend prior. Gasps came from Lance and Beverly, though Warren seemed oddly unfazed. Tori wondered if he'd already seen this trick before. Hell, for all she knew, he could do it himself; it wasn't as though anyone had been forthcoming about their powers so far.

"All of you, step through." Doctor Mechaniacal pointed to the open gateway to clarify, as though there were another place they could go. Tori bit down a sarcastic comment and followed orders, moving from the cool, air-conditioned room to a hot, arid landscape. By her guess, they were probably in the same general area where she and Ivan had trained, though this spot had mesas looming over them, partially blocking out the cloudless sky.

Lance, Warren, and Beverly followed suit, all three squinting as their eyes adjusted to the bright sun now glaring down on them. Doctor Mechaniacal followed, stepping out of the side of the cliff where the portal had manifested. Tori still wondered how they knew where to set the connecting spots up when they made these tunnels through space, though she had a theory that involved telepathy and far-sight.

"Your test for the following days is a simple one," Doctor Mechaniacal informed them. "Scattered throughout this area are an array of robots designed to attack you on sight. Additionally, there are hidden caches containing food, supplies, and other useful items. Your primary goal is to survive. Anyone who is so injured that they require intervention is deemed a failure. On top of that,

134

however, there is a secondary goal. Every robot has a metallic core inside of them, ones made of copper, silver, gold, and platinum. The more valuable the metal, the more difficult the robot holding it will be to kill. Those who survive and bring back those cores will be paid for what they collected. Copper wins you ten dollars, silver a hundred, gold a thousand, and one of the rare, precious platinum cores is worth ten thousand dollars. Additionally, whoever gets the most money is deemed the winner and receives one hundred and fifty percent of their orbs' value."

Tori's eyes went wide. She could practically feel the excitement humming in her fellow trainees. That was a *shitload* of money up for grabs, all for the simple task of beating up robots. Then again, these were robots designed by Doctor Mechaniacal, so she'd be a fool to assume they'd go down easily. But damn... ten thousand dollars would buy a lot of high-end tech, and no doubt the others had their own uses for such large sums of money. For training villains, cash in hand was the perfect motivation.

"At sunset on Sunday, you will be here, waiting for us to bring you back. Failure to do so is just that: failure. Your test begins now," Doctor Mechaniacal informed them, stepping back through the portal into the cool, safe room they had all walked away from. Seconds later, the window across space was gone, leaving them all staring at the plain, craggy side of a brown cliff.

A smile crested Tori's face as she surveyed the landscape, wondering where those wonderful robots bent on her destruction might be hiding. The real training had officially begun.

Chapter 19

Warren hunched over and began to scrawl symbols on the dusty ground. Before Tori's eyes, each one glowed as his finger traced the strange, arcane shapes into existence. When they were completed, each flashed with an emerald light before causing different effects. The first rune sent a wave of energy rippling out, washing over the four apprentices and continuing off in all directions. Warren's second rune solidified the dirt around it, transforming it into a green stone that he plucked from the ground and stuck in his pocket. The third and final rune conjured a green fire before burning out, leaving an arrow pointing toward one of the nearby cliffs.

"That should buy us a little time," Warren informed them. "My blast will scramble just about any manner of detection software the robots are using. You have perhaps an hour, at best, so I suggest everyone find a safe place where they can hole up and wait this out."

"With orbs worth ten grand out there? No way I'm ducking down." Lance reached out and a small swarm of flies materialized in front of his palm. The swarm grew exponentially, doubling in size every few seconds, until the sound of tiny flapping wings filled the air and set Tori's teeth on edge. At last, Lance made a small gesture and his myriad of miniature minions took to the air, scattering in every direction as they buzzed through the dry desert air.

"And what exactly did that accomplish?" Warren asked.

"I'll tell you if you explain the rock and the arrow," Lance replied.

"Neat as both tricks were, don't any of you think that maybe we should talk strategy?" Tori suggested. "Seems like there's a lot of money at stake; might make sense to come up with some sort of coherent plan."

The other three turned to stare at her with expressions that made Tori wonder if she'd somehow insulted their mothers, lovers, and honor all at once with her proposal. It was Beverly who finally spoke, voicing the sentiment that the others were clearly feeling.

"What strategy do we need to talk about? Everyone goes out, kills all the robots they can, and reaps what they earned. Or do you think you deserve a cut of everyone's winnings just because your teacher is on the council?"

"The fuck?" Tori jerked a thumb at Warren, who did his best to look inconspicuous. "His teacher, Balaam, is on the council too, not that it matters in the first place. I wasn't trying to take control or demand a cut, just pointing out that it might make more sense to work together, or at least coordinate. Think about it: four tiers of robot, four of us. Doesn't it seem like maybe we're only going to be able to take down the tougher ones working as a team?"

136

"Perhaps your teacher has placed you under some serious misconceptions," Warren said. "We are all training under a guild of *villains*, people who personify the self-reliant ideology. While some collaboration is necessary for the guild's survival, it is certainly not meant to be the focus of our training. Look at the challenge itself: those who take the risks reap the rewards. All of it was built around the idea of us getting our own winnings."

Warren, it seemed, either already had Balaam's unwillingness for teamwork or had been taught it in their short time together. It wasn't exactly a surprise to Tori; she'd hoped for better, but had expected the worst. What she hadn't expected was Beverly and Lance to nod along with the sickly-thin young man, clearly on the same page. They were wrong, though; Tori had seen firsthand how much focus the guild placed on working together. The council meeting, the groups of friends, the code—all of it indicated that guild members were never entirely on their own, for better or worse.

"Look, I think you aren't really seeing everything about this challenge. If we coordinate with one another—"

"So sorry that we foolish newcomers don't have your depth of perspective," Warren interrupted. "But I think it's you who is missing something: no one cares what you think. We all know this is a competition, and we won't let you trick us into wasting our time so you can pull ahead. Keep chattering if you like; I for one am done listening."

With that, Warren jogged away from the rest of the group and toward the direction his arrow had pointed him in. Lance looked at Tori and gave a half-apologetic shrug before heading off at a brisk pace in another direction. For a moment, only Tori and Beverly remained.

"I get what you were trying to do," Beverly said carefully. "Thuggernaut told me you probably wouldn't be as bad as the rumors made you out to be, and it seems like you really were thinking of what was best for everyone. That said, I can't work with anyone else. It's too dangerous for all of you."

Tori watched as Beverly headed north. Her stomach sank as she realized how blinded the three of them were by their fears, ambitions, and inherited prejudices. In a way, the schism among them was her fault; these three weren't just new to the guild, they were new to being meta-humans. To them, this was as much about testing their new abilities as it was racking up the cash, and she'd just stepped all over their egos by suggesting they'd need help before she even saw what they could do. Tori still didn't think she was wrong in how they should have approached the trial, but it was clear there were more diplomatic methods she could have utilized.

With little other choice, she headed off in the direction no one else had, which she estimated to be south based on the sun's position overhead. Night would be coming within the next few hours, so she'd need a place to hole up and maybe some supplies to tide her over. Tori's form flickered as her flesh turned to flames, and soon she was racing across the landscape. Fire-form was faster and weighed less, not to mention kept her less vulnerable, so for the moment, it was her best option to explore with. Once night fell and she'd stick out like a burning beacon, Tori would have to switch to other tactics.

She just hoped she'd come up with some by the time the sun dipped below the horizon.

*   *   *

"Not the strongest of starts," Johnny noted. He, Thuggernaut, Xelas, and Gork were holed up in Xelas's quarters, watching the apprentices scatter to the four points of the compass toward dangerous robotic adversaries. Xelas had a screen that comprised an entire wall of her living room, one that could show a single picture or multiple feeds, making it the perfect place to monitor the various cameras showing the rookies as they trudged through the desert.

"I thought Thuggernaut's girl was going to get wise and join up for a minute there," Xelas said. "Would have given those two a big damn advantage right off the bat."

"Sadly, Beverly is not yet confident in either her control or in another's ability to withstand her power," Thuggernaut said. "Against Tori, I doubt she could do much, but until she gains confidence, she'll keep separating herself and trying to work alone."

"She will get there in time, as we all did." Gork patted Thuggernaut with a wide, stony hand, and smiled at him in a way that made people run in terror. He knew the showing of all her teeth was meant as a sign of empathy, however, and returned her kindness with a grin of his own.

"She has a strong heart and a good mind. Nearly trampling her family on the night she changed left a deep scar, but I believe she can work past it as her experience grows. Truthfully, I'm hopeful that losing to some of Doctor Mechaniacal's creations will show Beverly that her power does have limits."

"Personally, I'm hoping at least two of them get knocked out," Johnny said. "Almost no one bet on complete drops, which means I'll make a tidy sum if they go down."

"You are all heart," Xelas said.

"So says the Tin Woman. Can you really blame me for looking on the bright side, though? As it stands, those kids might make it through some

138

coppers, perhaps even a silver or two, but the minute the golds come into play, they're all toast. At least in my perspective, someone is making a little money off of it."

"Don't count your coins yet, Johnny," Gork cautioned. "This is an interesting crop. I would be careful about assuming any outcomes until they actually happen."

Johnny reached over to the table and grabbed a handful of popcorn from a bowl. "Look, no one is hoping for a turnaround more than me. The better a show they put on, the more bets I'll get for the next event. I hope they all make it to the end, or at least go down fighting a platinum core."

Xelas let out a trilling, unpleasant sound. "A platinum? We want them to learn, not die."

With a shrug, Johnny downed his fistful of popcorn in a single bite. "Guess they'd better learn quick, then."

*   *   *

A high-pitched whine filled the air as Tori's flames melted the hovering robot's rear rotors and singed its already-exposed circuitry. It managed to squeeze off a few more bolts of concentrated electricity, spraying the rocks to Tori's north with small, crackling white blasts before it finally gave out and crashed to the ground.

For good measure, Tori blasted the thing with a torrent of flame until it was little more than a melted hunk of scrap. Only then did she walk over and dig into the exposed shell, working her fingers around until she produced a small orb roughly twice the size of a marble.

"More copper." She hadn't expected anything different—after all, this was the third of the drones Tori had taken down, and the other two had also carried copper cores in them. As far as opponents went, they were quick and annoying, but not much of a threat to someone who could render themselves functionally intangible. There was some amount of danger—the electricity made her feel weird when it shot through her, and she assumed enough of it would cause serious problems—but overall, she could easily survive the weekend if all she had to do was pick off copper enemies.

Moving carefully, Tori headed back into the small alcove she'd found along a cliff's edge. It wasn't great cover, but it did come with the oh-so-homey touch of having a cache of supplies hidden inside. It had contained meal replacement bars and bottles of water, which Tori recognized for the treasures they were immediately. There was also a scroll sealed with some strange symbol she couldn't recognize. After carefully trying to break the wax and open it, Tori decided to let the scroll be when it resisted. Ivan hadn't taught her much about magic, but one of his key lessons was not to mess with it unless she knew what she was doing. Given the context clues around the scroll, it was an aid clearly not meant for her, so she left it in the bottom of the metal box that held her discovered supplies.

With the patrolling robot gone, she turned her attention to the project it had stolen her away from: digging through the weak spots in the sand to deepen her alcove. One thing living as a criminal had imparted to Tori was the importance of having a home base. She would need somewhere to stash her supplies, to hide out if things got bad, and to recover if she became injured. It would take a lot of effort, but she estimated it would be possible to build up enough dirt to cover her entrance and get some much needed rest. There were two more days of this to go, and Tori assumed the first afternoon had only been a warm-up.

Idly, she wondered how the others were doing. Warren was probably set; the versatility of his power almost certainly lent itself to creating a shelter. She wasn't sure he'd fare as well on offense; though, without seeing all he could do, there was no way to tell. Lance was a toss-up, as she wasn't exactly sure how his power worked. With enough insects, Tori supposed he might surround himself in a giant swarm that could serve as a shield. Beverly was the one that Tori most worried about. That dragon-form of hers might be tough enough to fight Thuggernaut and therefore resilient enough to shrug off tiny blasts from the copper drone bots, but there was no way it would lend itself to a restful night of sleep.

"Idiots should have listened to me," Tori grumbled as her hands tore deeper into the sandy dirt pressed against the cliff. "Warren could have given us shelter, Lance's bugs could have been an early warning system, and then Beverly and I could have handled anything that broke through." It was an optimistic dream, both in terms of what people could do and in assessing their willingness to work together. Still, it was a nice image to cling to as her hands shoveled the dirt.

Deep down, Tori knew that her worries were also based in fear. What if she was the only one having any trouble with this stuff? What if each of the others had torn apart heaps of robots and built a shelter from their scraps? She pictured them sitting on thrones of hidden caches. The realist in her knew this was unlikely, but without a firm grasp of what each of them could do, it was impossible to rule anything out. Tori might not have cared about being the only apprentice in the guild or even the expectations set on her because Ivan was her teacher. What she did care about was the idea of losing, of slipping into last place, of failing.

The dirt around her wavered. For an instant she was back in that hospital room, the endless beeping of the monitors like a drill boring through her skull. Both of them were lying there, staring at her with what little willpower over their bodies they still possessed. Then the vision was gone, and Tori realized she'd accidently heated up her alcove by twenty degrees.

She stepped out into the air. The evening was a cool contrast from the now scorching hideout, even if it did put her at higher risk of being seen by a patrolling bot. She could use a break from being alone with her thoughts, and violence didn't seem like such a bad way to clear her head. Besides, sooner or later she would have to go on the offensive. The world was a hard place; Tori Rivas knew she had to rise through it by her own force of will. She'd learned that lesson long before she was assigned to learn under Ivan.

Her eyes wandered to the starry sky, a gorgeous tapestry of twinkling lights perfectly visible through the clear air. No city lights to obscure the view. Tori enjoyed the stars; not as much as when she was a child, but they still filled her with a sense of wonder to look up at them and sense her small place in the cosmos.

Small for the moment, anyway. Tori was nothing if not ambitious. She turned away from the comfort of the night sky and plunged back into the alcove, determined to fortify her defense as quickly as possible. Once her home base was secure, she could turn her attention to the next step in her plan.

Come sunrise, Tori was going hunting.

Chapter 20

Ivan tapped his finger against the center of the mouse, not hard enough to click anything, just loud enough to cause an annoying rattle of plastic. He was on his laptop in the kitchen while his children still slumbered upstairs. If Wade ever found a way to convert teenage sleeping abilities into an energy source, he'd be able to power North America for centuries with just this generation. Glancing at the clock, Ivan decided to give them another half hour before forcibly dragging them into consciousness.

The news items on his feed scrolled by, headlines that Ivan looked at without seeing. His own sleep the prior night had been restless, and as the morning sun streamed through his blinds, there was no denying the cause: Tori. He was worried about his apprentice. Guild training wasn't often intentionally deadly, but accidents had been known to happen. Wade liked to test people thoroughly, to see how they reacted in the most pressure-filled situations. True, it was a good way to see how well people kept their heads when the world was burning down around them, but it carried the sincere risk of them being caught up in the flames.

Shutting his laptop firmly, Ivan got up from the table and went to his fridge to pull out some eggs and bacon. Cooking would take his mind off Tori and would hopefully help wake up his children. It wasn't as though he needed to worry about her, really. Tori was smart, strong, and had a solid ability, even if it was one she seemed dead set on letting stagnate. Pride aside, so long as she used her head, she could avoid whatever big threats Wade had put into play. Assuming she didn't get stubborn and try to pull out a win for no reason, of course.

The pan sizzled as Ivan dropped the first few eggs into its burning embrace. He was trying to make himself not worry about Tori by working from the assumption that she wouldn't act prideful or stubborn... this was, to put it mildly, completely ridiculous.

Turning the day's schedule over in his head, Ivan remembered that Beth was going to the pool with her friend. Rick would certainly end up walking aimlessly around the mall. There might be time to slip over to the base and check on his apprentice. Just the thought made Ivan's tension ease. He would pop over, reassure himself that his apprentice was fine, and then enjoy the rest of his weekend unconcerned.

Mind made up, Ivan pulled the bacon from its package and laid it carefully in a pan before sending it to roast in the oven.

Tori was thankful she had heat-based powers as the morning sun bore down on her. The others were probably sweltering by this point, unless they had an ability to block out the endless rays. An image of Lance with a cloud of flies acting as a living umbrella popped into Tori's head and she choked back a snort. The copper cores in her pocket were already making enough noise as it was; she didn't need to draw any more robots before she was ready.

Her morning's hunt had gone well, netting four more cores to add to her collection. She'd been keeping them on her person, which was a pain given how they would fall away during her phase shifts, but she wasn't quite ready to drop off her winnings at the alcove she'd renovated into a near-proper cave. After dispatching so many copper-cored robots, Tori's confidence was beginning to grow. She wasn't certain she was ready to take on a silver yet, but she'd like to at least find one. Research was as much a part of hunting as actual engagement.

A loud explosion from one of the nearby mesas sent Tori spinning into a crouch, a fireball conjured in each hand as she readied for attack. When none immediately came, her posture relaxed. She stared in the direction of the explosion, near the top of the mesa. Someone else must be fighting, and she'd never heard one of the copper-cored drones make a noise like that. Tori surveyed her surroundings quickly, wondering if there was a way she might be able to scale the cliff face quickly enough to catch the show. It was only about thirty feet high, but she wasn't exactly a practiced climber.

Before she could figure out if it was worth the risk, a big, scaly green figure came into view near the mesa's edge. It didn't look like any dragon Tori had ever seen, but by process of elimination, that was all it could be. The thing certainly seemed built for damage: sharp claws, powerful limbs, and a hide armored with hundreds of scales. Tori found herself thankful she didn't actually have to fight Beverly to win the contest.

As quickly as the thought entered her brain, Tori saw the dragon jerked backward—flung through the air, in fact—toward the center of the mesa, out of Tori's line of sight. Even without the somehow panicked expression on Beverly's now snout-wearing face, Tori could have put the clues together.

Her fellow apprentice was getting her green ass kicked. Badly, from the sounds of the scuffle that reached Tori's ears. It was very, very tempting to turn around and pretend she hadn't seen anything out of sorts, but Tori immediately dismissed the idea. Aside from the facts—that Beverly had almost definitely seen her and that almost every guild member she'd met had warned her to avoid grudges— Tori just honestly didn't want to leave the woman in harm's way.

This place was dangerous, and it just as easily could be her in over her head if she went
 the wrong way. She'd tried telling them there was merit in working together; now it was time to try showing.

All of which was a good thought, but as Tori pulled out her copper cores and stashed them under a nearby rock, she realized her initial hurdle had yet to be dealt with: how the hell was she going to get up the cliff in time? She could practically hear Ivan's voice, telling her over and over again that exploring her power would pay endless dividends when she found herself in tough situations.

"Come on, there's a way up there," she muttered, staring at the sheer rock face as her physical eyes vanished in a burning wave that cascaded across her body. In fire-form, she had less mass, so it was possible she could take the cliff in a series of jumps. The trouble was that she also lost almost all the strength she'd need to launch herself. Aside from burning and rolling across, Tori had limited capacity to interact with physical objects. Ivan would have told her to find a new way to go at the problem, just as he'd told her to try new tactics when attacking him. He wasn't even here and he was nagging her, which made it all the worse. Tori would have blasted his face with a fire beam if he'd actually shown up at that moment.

In fire-form, Tori could not blink, but she gave it her best shot as a rogue idea entered her head. It would be risky, no question about that, and her control would be imprecise at best. Still, there was no reason it couldn't work, as long as she kept her focus. Besides, at this point a maybe was better than nothing.

Leaning forward, Tori pointed both of her arms toward the ground and began to blast the sand with twin streams of steady fire. As the dirt heated up below her, Tori focused on tightening the streams, increasing the heat while decreasing the surface area of each beam. They grew smaller and fiercer until at last Tori felt her flame feet lift up slowly from the ground. Tilting her arms slightly, she angled her rise so that it put her on course with the looming cliff where the sounds of battle still filled the air.

It wasn't the fastest way to fly, but Tori still felt exhilarated as she rose higher into the air. Before, her concern had been with keeping a low profile, not letting people know what she could do. Never in her life would she have imagined soaring through Ridge City, let alone actually tried it. Yet now she was lifting off the ground, moving through the sky on no power but her own. It was thrilling, scary, and firmly confirmed what Tori had hitherto been wavering on: her meta-suit would definitely have flight capabilities.

As she crested the top of the mesa, Tori finally saw the conflict she'd been listening to for the last several minutes. Beverly was lumbering about, moving as fast as her sizable body would allow while a giant silver orb on four thick legs tracked her every step. Metal tendrils snaked out from its right side, whipping at her thick hide and trying to wind themselves around her limbs. Beverly leapt back, clawing and snapping as they came near, then tried to turn the tables by charging her attacker. The orb's left side opened up, a whole section swiveling freely, connected by a single large arm. Though Tori couldn't see exactly what happened, she did notice the air between Beverly and the robot ripple for the span of several seconds. Beverly crashed to the ground, aborting her charge and letting out a roar of pain. She backpedaled quickly as the metal tendrils tried to capitalize on her injury.

"Fuck me," she muttered. "Sonic attacks on one side, big metal whips on the other." It was a good system, perfect in both a melee or ranged context while also dealing with problematic people like Tori. She wasn't sure how a concentrated blast of sound would affect her fire-form, but she had a hunch it wouldn't be pleasant. On the other hand, judging by the gashes Beverly left in the robot's tendrils when they came near enough to strike, she'd probably tear it apart if she could get close enough.

All of it added up to one inescapable and very depressing conclusion: Tori would have to be the distraction if they were actually going to drop this damn thing. It sucked like hell, but she still tilted her arms slightly left, circling around to land behind the metal bastard. If she was going to do this, she was going to make damn sure it would be effective. As long as she could make it turn its back on Beverly, the dragon apprentice could hopefully do the rest.

It occurred to Tori as she landed carefully on the mesa's flat surface that she was leaving an awful lot of her rescue mission to maybes and ifs. By that point, though, she was already committed, so she pushed the thought from her mind as a massive fireball built in her hand.

"Beverly! When this thing comes at me, don't you dare fucking hesitate. If I get killed from this, I am going to haunt the living shit out of you!"

A slight roar over the whir of robotic limbs was the only response, which Tori decided to take as a signal of understanding. It wasn't like she had a lot of choices left, anyway. Taking careful aim at the rear of the metal orb on legs, Tori let loose a torrent of flame, blasting its body with a column of fire as thick as a baseball bat.

To her surprise, the orb didn't rotate around to face her. Instead, panels near the areas she was pelting with heat opened up, glassy camera lenses fixed on Tori as she poured as much energy as she could into the attack. They watched her as she dug in, but from the sounds of scuffle coming from the robot's other side, it seemed she wasn't making enough of an impression to split its focus.

"All right, you big testicle. Come get some." Tori concentrated the beam in front of her, tightening it just as the she had the ones that lifted her off the ground. In principle, it was the same technique she used for small-scale soldering and welding, though she'd never tried it on something this big before. As the beam shrank down, Tori could see sparks beginning to fly from the spot where her beam connected to the robot's body. It wasn't much, but it gave her the encouragement to keep going, narrowing her blast further until a cascade of sparks shot out of the robot's weakening body.

Tori knew she'd succeeded when she saw the sonic cannon flip around and point at her. She dimly made out the sound of charging footsteps before her entire body seemed to explode in a wave of pain. Her focus was shot and the beam dissipated as Tori struggled to hold her body together. The endless, pulsing waves ripped through her, trying to scatter the sentient flames that made up her consciousness. Tori couldn't see or hear or think; all she could do was hold herself together by sheer force of will.

Then it was over, agony replaced by a loud crunching sound barely audible through the ringing in her ears. Tori slowly realized that she did indeed have ears again, and that her hands were pressed over them. Pulling her palms away from her head, Tori could see streaks of blood smeared from her thumbs to her wrists. That sonic cannon had seriously not been screwing around.

Moving carefully, Tori pulled herself up from the ground where it turned out she'd been kneeling, her head hammering in pain with every inch she progressed. As Tori reached a fully standing position, the world around her spun violently and she lost her footing. She fell backward, waiting to feel the sting of impact against the mesa's hard surface, only to instead be greeted by wind whistling through her ears.

Right... she'd stood on the edge of the mesa. It had seemed like a good idea at the time, allowing her to slip over the lip if she needed to dodge. Plummeting through the air, however, Tori recognized that it might have been a strategic mistake. She closed her eyes and tried to shift back to her fire-form, but for the first time she could ever recall, her body rebelled.

Tori glanced upward, back to where she had fallen from, and was shocked to see another form closing in fast on her. She let out a small yelp as it snagged her in a pair of powerful claws. Then, at long last, the part she'd been expecting arrived.

Her fall, as all falls do, came to a sudden and abrupt stop.

Chapter 21

Tori rejoined the world of the living slowly, with pain being the first and most persistent thing to greet her. The sun stung her eyes, the ringing in her ears had yet to fade, and her arms felt like they'd nearly been pulled out of their sockets. She wasn't dead, though, and considering how things had been going when she blacked out, that was an unexpected improvement. Moving slowly lest another bout of unconsciousness take hold, Tori raised herself to a sitting position and took stock of the world around her.

She was lying on top of the mesa where they'd done battle, a fact made obvious by the sparking and smoking husk of a robot resting twenty feet away. From the position of the sun in the sky, she guessed she'd only been out for a couple of minutes, though it certainly felt like a lot longer. To her surprise, Beverly was still there, though no longer wearing the form of the hulking green dragon nor of the creature that had snatched her out of the sky. Tori's fellow apprentice had shed her mask and seemed to be taking in the sunshine. Without the obstruction, it was clear that Beverly was quite beautiful. Well-crafted cheekbones, skin like light cocoa powder, and piercing green eyes all made her quite captivating, and that was without even taking the dragon-powers into account.

"I didn't know you had a form that could fly," Tori said, snapping Beverly out of her restful daze. She scrambled up quickly, watching Tori carefully to see if a fireball was impending.

"Why did you help me?" Beverly took two steps back, and her eyes seemed to glow slightly. Their natural green tint darkened and the tips of her nails seemed to elongate by several inches.

"Whoa, shit, chill." Tori raised both of her hands upward in a sign of surrender. "I didn't really have some sort of grand plan going in. It just looked like you needed help, and I hadn't gotten the chance to see what one of the big bots could do... which, by the way, please tell me that bastard was at least a gold-cored."

Beverly shook her head slowly, reaching into her pocket to produce a gleaming metal ball. "Silver, if you can believe it. These things are on a pretty steep difficulty curve."

"Shitballs. I'm not sure I even want to see a gold if that thing was a silver." Tori had been expecting the higher value models to be tougher, but that thing had nearly taken down the both of them. Then again, it wasn't as though they'd used a coordinated attack or strategy. With a little planning, she and

Beverly could probably bring one down without too much risk. Going at it solo, however, would be pretty much impossible without her tech.

Fluctuations in the ringing sound filling her ears alerted Tori to the fact that Beverly was talking, though the words were impossible to make out since she'd lowered her voice.

"Huh? Sorry, damn bot did a number on my ears. You have to speak up."

"I said THANK YOU!" Beverly yelled, a touch of red tingeing her cheeks as she shouted to repeat herself. "For helping me take that thing down. I wasn't sure how I was going to deal with it."

"Seeing as you saved me from doing a swan dive into the ground, I think we can call it even." Tori lowered her arms slowly, making sure Beverly wouldn't think she was about to attack. "Look, I'm in a fair amount of pain here, so I'd like to switch to my fire-form to heal. I don't want you thinking I'm about to do something stupid, though, thus I am formally giving you warning that I'm about to turn into living flame."

Beverly hesitated for a moment and then nodded. Tori focused on shifting to her other form; waves of relief filled her as her body complied. Part of her was reassured to know the sonic cannon hadn't done any serious damage or blocked her power, but the vast majority of her brain was overwhelmed by happiness as the pain shrank to a dull ache. It would take an hour or so for her body to completely regenerate away her injuries; in the meantime, she'd feel a lot less pain without actual nerve receptors to send the signals.

"Hot damn, that is a neat trick," Beverly said. "And yes, pun very much intended."

"Coming from a gal I watched go from ripping up a robot to soaring through the skies, that's quite a compliment." Tori scanned the area around them as they talked; it wouldn't do to have their conversation broken up by more attackers.

"Yeah, actually didn't know I could do that." Beverly slowed lowered herself to the ground, picking up her mask and slipping it over her face. "My powers didn't come with much in the way of instructions. Just found an old amulet in our attic and then poof, suddenly I'm gigantic and tearing apart the house."

"Coolest thing I ever found in my family's attic as a kid was an old mannequin head," Tori said. "My parents told me it belonged to my grandpa, but now that I think about it, he worked at a meat processing plant, why the hell would he own... actually, I don't think I want to see where that train of thought ultimately leads."

"I'd say that's a smart call," Beverly said. "My great-grandmother used to collect weird artifacts and charms. Most of it was supposed to be junk, but I guess she found a few pieces of the genuine article."

"Or it used to be junk and turned into a genuine article," Tori pointed out. "No one really knows where all these magic talismans keep popping up from. We're pretty sure magic used to not be real, though."

"Well, it damn sure is now. I'm the living, sometimes fire-breathing proof of that. Just wish I at least knew what all I could do. Flying would have made getting up here the first time a hell of a lot easier."

Tori could relate, now that she'd tasted a bit of air mobility herself. "So you flew just because you were trying to save me?"

"Thuggernaut thinks my intuition is to access the power reactively. First time, I was scared and in pain, so I turned into a big green dragon that's made to give and take punishment. Second time, they were making me fight a bunch of targets that kept pinning me and then fading back, which pissed me off. I got so mad I ended up turning into my red dragon-form and blasting them with fire breath. This time, I didn't want your death on my conscience, and lo and behold, I sprout some wings for arms. Pretty sure that form had white scales, though I don't always get the cleanest view."

"Definitely white," Tori confirmed. "I can remember it perfectly. Honestly, I doubt I'll ever get the image of you barreling down toward me out of my head. Which, um, thanks, by the way."

Beverly waved her hand through the air. "Like you said, we're even. And if I happen upon you getting owned by one of those things, count on me to jump in. Competition or not, I can do at least that much."

"What if neither of us had to get owned by another robot?" Tori had been biding her time, hoping to build slowly to the topic, but from the way Beverly had started to rise, it was clear she had to take her shot or lose the opportunity. "What if we worked together, this time from the start? With a little planning, the two of us could tear those things apart."

"Look, I was in the fight too. I know it would be easier if we teamed up. But I'm still learning to control these powers of mine. What if next time I'm the one who accidently injures you?"

"Claws, fire, and wings aren't going to hurt me, at least not easily," Tori said. "Unless you're keeping a hidden form in your arsenal—which is not me prying, if you are—then you don't have to worry about doing anything worse than the robots can do. I'm a lot tougher than I look." To prove her point, Tori flowed upward from the ground, expanding to add a bit of presence to her fiery visage.

"And you look pretty tough as is." Beverly sighed and shook her head. "Even aside from putting you in danger, doesn't working together defeat the entire point of this exercise? We're clearly pitted against each other. Teaming up probably breaks the rules."

"Doctor Mechaniacal never said anything about us not being allowed to help each other or splitting our winnings. Sure, this contest implies that we're supposed to be on our own, but short of anything being stated outright, it's a gray area at best. Besides all of that, though, you're overlooking the most important reason why it doesn't matter."

Beverly pursed her lips as she stared at this strange fire-woman and the increasingly convincing madness she was spitting out. "And what exactly is that?"

"We're training to be villains. Half the fun of that is ignoring the rules when it suits us. And right now, I'd say it suits both our interests quite well."

*   *   *

Ivan was unsurprised by the festive atmosphere in Xelas's room when he arrived; that everyone seemed relatively sober and no argument had broken out was by far the bigger miracle. He'd have much preferred to check things out with Wade; however, Doctor Mechaniacal's full attention was rightfully on the trial he was coordinating. Since Ivan had refused anything more than a bare-bones quarters where he could rest if needed, that made sitting in with Xelas and company his next best option to assuage his worries about his apprentice. Not that he would admit that's what he was doing, of course. Ivan was merely looking in to evaluate her performance, as any good teacher would.

"And here he is, coming in halfway through the second day," Johnny cried as soon as Ivan stepped into view. "Who had Saturday afternoon?"

Gork raised one of her massive, thick-fingered hands. "Had a hunch."

"All right, everyone, that's a hundred apiece, since Gork won the pool." Johnny pulled a crisp bill from his pocket. Thuggernaut took his from a small pouch at his side and Xelas seemed to have one dispense from her wrist. All three slapped the money down in front of Gork, who quietly collected her winnings and squirreled them away.

"If everyone is quite finished having their fun, perhaps one of you could catch me up on how things are going." Ivan glanced down at the modest watch adorning his wrist, a timepiece that cost less than Gork had won only moments before. "I do have a daughter to pick up in an hour."

"Calm down, spoilsport," Xelas chided. She motioned for Ivan to come over and have a seat. As he did, she pointed to the many screens displayed before them. "Tori and Thuggernaut's girl, Beverly, just decided to work together after tag-teaming a silver. Right now, they're on their way to Beverly's hideout to grab the cache she found. After that they'll probably head back to the cave Tori dug."

Ivan sat down in one of the many plush leather chairs Xelas stocked her room with—the mechanical woman was famously fond of entertaining guests—and took note of the two apprentices trekking through the hot desert sands. On the other monitors, he could see a thin young man trapping a silver-cored robot with a series of complicated symbols etched in the ground. The fourth of the group was nowhere to be found, though there was a massive consolidation of insects on top of one of the mesas, a churning miasma of fluttering wings.

"Lance—that's Arachno Bro's guy—has been pumping out bugs like nobody's business, tracking and overwhelming coppers since yesterday. Warren is the one using magic—he's Balaam's, as I'm sure you know—and so far, he's managed to bring down two silvers solo. Looks like he's working on his third from what I can see." Xelas effortlessly charted all the feeds, simultaneously watching the drama unfold from every angle as only one with a robotic brain could.

"It's a sound, if slow, strategy," Ivan said. "Though I highly doubt he'd be able to take down a gold-cored robot with such tactics. Nonetheless, from what you've described, it seems as though Balaam's apprentice has a commanding lead."

"For the moment." Thuggernaut leaned forward from his own chair and scooped a pear cider from the open cooler resting in the middle of the floor. "There's still a day and a half left though, and it looks like our students are the only ones who've figured out the importance of teamwork."

"True; with no tech and only her powers to work with, Tori might be able to bring down a silver-cored on her own. Paired with someone who has power like Beverly, I can't imagine they'll have any trouble handling a challenge of that level," Ivan agreed. "Even splitting the winnings, if they make a conscious effort to go on the offensive, they'll easily pass the others in no time."

"Let's hope they manage to get a little practice in before sunset." Johnny nodded to the small clock at the top of the massive screen set before them. On it, a clock with golden numbers was slowly counting down toward zero. There were several hours remaining, yet second by second the time was falling away, as all time was wont to do.

Every person in the room already knew what would happen when time ran out, just as they had when the clock was silver in color and counting down on the prior day. The clock signaled the time remaining until the difficulty was going to be kicked up, when the next level of enemy would be released into the field. Gold-cored robots were hours from entry, and when the time for their entrance came, it would mark a real turning point in the training exercise.

Gold-cored robots were powerful enough that they could, and had, killed full members of the guild before. If an apprentice went against one unprepared, the class might just get a little bit smaller.

*   *   *

"This is it." Beverly gestured to the cave, its entrance half-hidden in a mesa's shadow.

Tori stepped inside, pausing to marvel at the impressive method used to open up the area. Unlike her, Beverly had torn through rock rather than moving sand as the scattered remains of rubble and deep claw marks through the cave attested. It culminated in a far more intimidating, but also vastly smaller, space. Taking up a fair chunk of the limited room inside was a metal case identical to the one Tori had found in her own cavern, tucked carefully away lest anyone wandering by should notice its existence.

"Looks like we had the same idea," Tori remarked as she surveyed the surroundings. "I dug out a big hole in a place like this not too far away. Mine was a bit larger, though, so if you wanted to sleep in shifts tonight, we could stay there."

"I'll think about it." Beverly had clearly warmed to the idea of taking on robots with Tori's help, but it seemed outright trust was still a point yet to be crossed.

Tori could hardly blame Beverly for the wariness—part of her wondered if reaching out like this would culminate in getting stabbed in the back. If so, then there wasn't much to be done about it. Succeeding in this environment was going to require risk; that was obvious. She'd either have to take heavy chances with strategy fighting the robots or by trusting one of her fellow apprentices. This way, at least, seemed moderately less likely to get her killed. Since Beverly still appeared on the fence, Tori decided that it was time for a show of good faith, or as close to one as she could manage under the circumstances.

"Well, if you decide to take me up on it, at least I've got plenty of rations there. We wouldn't have to haul anything over from your cache." Meal bars and bottles of water weren't the world's best olive branch, but Beverly nodded in appreciation at the offer, so Tori counted it as a small victory. At least her fellow apprentice wouldn't think she was trying to mooch. "Oh, and I had a scroll of some sort in mine too. My powers have nothing to do with magic, so I

152

didn't bother opening it, but if you can get some use out of it, then it's all yours."

"Are... are you sure about that?" Beverly's large eyes widened even further, visibly taken aback by the unexpected display of generosity.

"Look, I'm not pretending to be a saint here. If I thought that thing would give me any kind of edge, I'd keep it for myself, but it's useless in my hands. Maybe even dangerous. Better I hand it off to the person I'm working with instead. At this point, giving you a leg up helps me too." Tori leaned slightly outside the small cave, scanning the area for any sign of movement that might indicate a robot attack. They'd run into a few copper-cored ones on just the walk over—pesky things seemed to be increasing by the hour.

"It might not be useful for me, either. The amulet has been confusing enough to try and figure out." Beverly gestured to her neck, though whatever lay there was buried under the dark fabric of her apprentice costume. "But I'll take a look at it. Highly doubt it could make things much worse."

Beverly walked over to her own metal box and undid the latch, flipping it open to reveal the remaining contents. She'd gone through more food and water than Tori had—which made sense since she couldn't spend half her time in the form of living energy—but Beverly didn't reach for any of the foodstuffs. Instead, she dug down to the bottom of the cache, eventually coming up with a small leather case. With a quick motion, she popped it open, and then held it out so Tori could get a good look inside.

"Mine didn't have a scroll, but it did have this stuff. Couldn't make heads or tails of what it was or how it was supposed to be used, though obviously it's some sort of high-tech toolbox. Since we're pooling resources, you can have it, as long as you can use it."

Tori suppressed her desire to drool as she stared at the array of instruments before her. Most of the assortment laid out in the leather box was familiar to her, things she had lower-quality versions of in her own lab, but a few were new even to her. The only part that struck Tori as odd was that this was clearly a case meant for someone to tool around with advanced technology, yet the desert they were in was barren of materials.

The whirring sound of a passing copper-cored drone echoed across the landscape outside. Beverly checked over Tori's shoulder to make sure it wasn't getting close, her eyes already glowing their telltale green. For Tori however, the sound was not the harbinger of battle about to commence; it was a wake-up call correcting the misassumption she'd made only seconds prior. There were, in fact, tons of raw materials out in the desert, provided one had the combat acumen to procure them. That drone and all its siblings were stuffed with all manner of electronics Tori could twist to her own designs.

"I think I can get some solid use out of those," Tori said at last, accepting the case and snapping it shut. "Let's swing by my cave to drop this off and let you look at the scroll. After that, I want to get back into the field while we've still got daylight. If we work hard enough this afternoon, we may be able to kick the shit out of this place tomorrow."

"Sounds like you've got a plan," Beverly remarked. A coy, half-fanged smile danced on her lips as she remained partially shifted to her green dragon-form.

"Calling it a plan seems a bit grandiose; it's more of an outline. But it all rests on laying the groundwork today." Tori slipped the case down to her side and peeked carefully out of the cave. So long as she was carrying those precious tools, shifting to fire-form was out of the question.

"Given how little there is to do here, I'm going to take the wild guess that this groundwork centers on fighting robots," Beverly said.

Tori shook her head then stepped back out into the sun's burning light. "Not fighting. Hunting. There is a very key difference. You see, from here on out, we're going to use every part of the robot buffalo."

Chapter 22

By the time evening fell, Tori and Beverly had managed to down six of the silver-cored robots and a dozen or so more coppers. It was rough going at first as they gained a better sense of how to combat the spherical enemies as well as how to work together. During the first two battles, there were times when their attacks overlapped, each nearly striking the other. Those were tenuous, dangerous seconds during which their fragile alliance easily could have shattered. The need to win, however, drowned out any petty squabbling that might have occurred, and by the time their opponent was down, all thoughts of dissolution were driven from their minds.

As the day wore on, coming closer and closer to dusk, their teamwork grew stronger. Each woman began to understand the other's natural attack style, and they soon fell into a rhythm. Tori darted in and out, zipping around to draw attention while Beverly charged in and smashed the most pivotal pieces of the robot's anatomy. By the time they killed their sixth silver-cored robot, they were functioning like a well-calibrated machine themselves, tearing through the last opponent in only a few minutes.

Much of a roll as they were on, neither wanted to press their luck as the sun began to set. Surprise was the element that had given them the most edge in their fights. With Tori standing out like a beacon against the dark sky, that aspect of battle would be turned against them. Better to hole up, rest, and conserve strength for the next day's fights.

They made it back to Tori's cave just as the last specks of sunlight were fading from the horizon, covering the desert in a blanket of stars and darkness. It would have been an easier and faster trip, if not for the fact that Beverly was forced to spend it hauling most of the mechanical remains from one of their silver-cored opponents across the desert. When they finally reached the cave, she set it carefully down outside, and then shifted from her green dragon-form back to the lovely, weary young woman Tori had first met.

"All right, that's four of the damn things. If you can't work with that, drag the next one yourself." Beverly made a show of stretching her back and arms, despite the fact that they weren't really all that tired. She was still learning about her dragon powers, but her green form seemed almost impervious to fatigue.

"Should be plenty," Tori assured her. "With this much raw material, I think I can whip together a useful tool or two by sunrise. How about you? Going to take another crack at the scroll?"

"Maybe after dinner." Beverly had already opened the scroll stuffed in Tori's cache, though there hadn't been any effect that they could discern. After a few minutes of study, Beverly came to the conclusion that whatever magic lay amid the arcane runes burned into the parchment would require some sort of activation. Since daylight had been dwindling, she put it away as a project to look at during her time on guard duty.

With night upon them, both women turned their attention to fighting hunger and dehydration by downing most of the remaining supplies stashed in Tori's metal box. If they wanted to last another day in the desert, it would mean either relocating to Beverly's hideout or hauling over her supplies. Each could easily go without the food and water for a day if needed, but constant combat would take its toll unless they were properly sated.

"What's your deal anyway?" Beverly asked as she dug into her third meal bar. It seemed the slender woman either burned a lot of calories while in her dragon-form or possessed the not-so-super ability of having a tapeworm. "You've got a really cool ability where you turn into fire, but you want to spend the night tinkering around with busted robot parts?"

For a brief moment, Tori contemplated hiding her plans for the salvaged components, concealing her true abilities from this woman who might end up being her competition. That idea was quickly tossed aside, primarily because Beverly would quickly see Tori's talents when her devices were used but also because lying seemed a poor choice. Ivan appeared to have a lot of friends in the guild; if Beverly made it to full member status along with her, Tori could use a few comrades of her own. That sort of relationship was built on trust, though, especially among villains.

"I'm actually more of a tech-head than a fire-user. Right now I'm working on a meta-suit, and I've been inventing more or less since childhood. Truth be told, I really don't like using my powers this much, but Pseudonym wouldn't let me bring any of my gear."

"Living off the land seems to be the theme of this weekend. Well, sort of." Beverly took a long draw from a bottle of water, emptying it out and setting it aside. "I guess I can see why you're supposed to be a big deal, though. Having those powers and the smarts to build your own tech... that's a hell of a combo."

"My teacher is the big deal, not me," Tori quickly corrected. "And the only reason I got him was that no one else wanted me. My attitude is seen as 'problematic' and 'uncooperative' and other shit like that. I mean, I still think I'm awesome, but I doubt anyone else in the guild really believes that. Not yet, anyway."

"Thuggernaut thinks pretty highly of Pseudonym, that's for sure. As strong as my teacher is, I get the feeling he's a little wowed by yours," Beverly said.

"He is something of a legend." Tori finished choking down her lone meal bar, the texture roughly akin to what she imagined eating Styrofoam would be like. "But tell me about Thuggernaut; I've only gotten to meet him in passing. Is he really as strong as he looks?"

"More," Beverly replied. "That first night when I ran into Thuggernaut, I thought I was going to kill him. After a couple weeks of training, I realized that the only thing holding him back was him trying not to seriously injure me. I'm really lucky he took me on as an apprentice, otherwise I doubt I'd have even this much control over all this... stuff."

"I don't mean to pry, and if this is overstepping, I understand, but I have to ask. Since you seem to view these powers as more burden than blessing, why not just take off the necklace?"

Wordlessly reaching up to the top of her costume, Beverly carefully undid a clasp and pulled the neckline open, exposing the top of her sternum. Her dark skin was smooth and flawless at first, but then a pattern began to glow with silver light. In moments the symbol, which ran up around her throat like a necklace, had lit the cave with a soft, candle-like glow.

"Nothing to take off. The moment I put the necklace on, it fused with me. Thuggernaut's brought me to every person he trusts in the magic division, and none of them have any idea how to separate me from it. Like it or not, for now, I'm stuck with these powers. If I want any shot at my old life back, it means getting them under control."

Tori nodded her head at the three torn-apart robots resting just outside the cave door. "Seems to me you've got things pretty well in hand."

"Being the dragons is the easy part; it's keeping them at bay that's tough. Every time I get scared or mad or surprised, I can feel them pushing to get out." Beverly bowed her head. The intricate silver tattoo faded away, plunging them once more into darkness. "I'm making progress, though. There was a time I couldn't even get it to disappear, which would have really cut down on my wardrobe options."

"Not to mention swimsuits would pretty much be out, unless you could dig out one of those giant frilly dress ones from the thirties," Tori added.

"Yeah, that shit was not happening. I don't do frills or ruffles, no exceptions." Beverly glanced out the opening of the cave, taking in the soft night sky. "For what it's worth, I'm glad I ran into you today. This has been a lot easier with someone to watch my back."

"Imagine how we could have torn through this if everyone worked together," Tori replied.

"Wish in one hand, spit in the other." Beverly's eyes began to glow, this time scarlet instead of their usual emerald green. "If you want to bed down, I can take first watch. My red dragon has solid night vision."

"Thanks, but I'd rather get to work." Tori stood from her sandy seat and walked over to the cave's rear where the case holding those precious tools was stashed. "I've got too many ideas whizzing around in my head. Even if I wanted to sleep, I doubt—"

The explosion was far enough off that neither woman thought they were under attack, though they did both react immediately to the threatening sound. Tori dropped the case, her body turning to flames before the metal even hit the soft, sandy floor of the cave. Beverly's body lengthened and grew, covered with bright red scales as she took on the only one of her forms Tori had yet to witness. Both peered out the narrow doorway for a few seconds, waiting for more explosions or the sound of approaching enemies.

After a few minutes of peace, Beverly leaned out, sniffing the air carefully as she scanned the thick night. Eventually, she pulled herself back in and shed her inhuman-form, an expression of worry draped across her face.

"There's a faint scent of smoke coming from the southwest, but it seems pretty far off. Nothing approaching, as far as I can tell. Best guess is that one of the boys decided to try and do a little night-hunting to grab more cores."

"Let's hope so." Tori shifted from living fire to perfectly normal-looking young woman, although her brain was still shooting adrenaline through her system. "Well, I wasn't anywhere near sleep before, and now it's definitely not happening."

"No kidding." Beverly's eyes still glowed with a faint red light as she made her way across the cave, lying down with her head against the rock wall at the rear, gazing directly out the entrance. "I may stay up for a while and watch you work. Just until my nerves settle."

"Feel free," Tori told her. "But fair warning, when I get in the zone, I'm not very chatty."

Beverly reached out to the nearby metal box and plucked the scroll from its depths, carefully unrolling it between her narrow fingers. "Somehow, I think I'll manage."

*   *   *

Lance limped through the desert, only his myriad of insect helpers supporting him. His leg was probably broken; enough high school football had taught him the basics of what such injuries felt like. He couldn't manage to put even the smallest amount of weight on the limb, so that was also a dead giveaway. The swarm of dragonflies and bees pushing upward on his left shoulder acted as a makeshift crutch, giving him what he only prayed would be enough mobility to complete his escape.

All those sentries and scouts he'd positioned around the desert and none had given Lance adequate warning. That robot had come after him like there was a target on his chest, turning so many of his conjured minions to ash under its laser blast. Those that survived served as a smokescreen to cover his escape, which was more falling off the top of a mesa than any daring plan to make himself scarce. Whatever that robot was, Lance knew from the moment it arrived that he wasn't going to be able to win the fight.

The silver-cored ones had been challenge enough; he'd had to practically choke their interior electronics with swarm after swarm of insect sacrifices to shut them down. This one didn't seem keen on letting anything get close, not even a seemingly harmless bug. Lance couldn't imagine how any of the four apprentices were going to be able to take it down. If the other three were that far out of his league that they could dispatch something that powerful solo, what was the point of making him train alongside them?

Lance would have slowed down as the realization struck him if he could have afforded to. Tori had been right from the beginning; they were supposed to work together. It was the only way any of them had even half a hope of stopping something that strong. Lance cursed himself for not listening then turned his attention away from the mistake and on to what could still be done.

Raising his right hand, Lance conjured a handful of assorted flying bugs and tossed them into the air. There was a day left yet. If he could find Tori or one of the others, maybe he could convince them to team up with him. True, he was injured, but his power had never been physically-based in the first place. Even if they demanded some of his orbs in exchange for working together, it would be worth it.

By Lance's reckoning, that robot he'd fought was either a gold or platinum core. If it was platinum, that was bad enough, but if it was gold, then they were in a world of shit. A gold-cored robot doing that much damage meant he hadn't even seen the final opponents, and with the way they seemed to exponentially grow in difficulty, Lance wasn't sure he'd survive a platinum encounter.

With his bugs on the wind searching for those who might be allies, Lance focused on limping along as fast as he could, desperately searching for somewhere he could lie low until sunrise.

*   *   *

Ivan sat in his living room, a glass of sweet tea in his hand as he watched the evening news. Beth was asleep upstairs, worn out from her long day, and Rick had snuck out his window only a half hour prior. It was always tempting to bust his son when he clumsily tripped through wards and traps that would have incinerated him had they not been keyed to leave him alone, but Ivan resisted. He had, after all, once been that age, and the trouble he'd gotten into was far worse than anything Rick was likely to manage. Ivan followed him on occasion, staying to the shadows and keeping watch to make sure intervention wasn't needed. Usually, all Rick did was sneak over to a friend's house or to the parking lot of a local gas station where he would hang out with the same friends. All teenagers went through some form of rebellion; at least Rick's was largely harmless.

Still, Ivan planned to catch him when he came home tonight. Rebellion had risks, and getting caught came with consequences. He couldn't stay on top of his son all the time, not if he wanted Rick to learn how to live on his own, but Ivan knew too well the problems that came for those without limits. Occasionally catching and grounding him would remind his son that there were rules in his life, curfew included, and breaking them still had consequences.

A video of the daring rescue from a few days prior cycled across the television screen. The various news outlets had been playing the fight footage ad nauseam, no doubt at the AHC's urging. While none of the old guard went in much for that sort of promotion, it was common knowledge that the founding three were getting more and more hands-off as time wore on. The media relations team was likely almost completely comprised of younger, more ambitious capes, eager to make their organization seem like the gold standard in superpowered heroics.

Technically, none of the original three needed to step away from their leading roles. Quorum's age was slowed down to a point where it was nearly irrelevant, Professor Quantum seemed to have found a way to permanently lock his appearance to that of a late forty-something, and Lodestar... well, Ivan understood why she'd let her position in the organization diminish. Life was often cruel in its little tricks, offering gifts with price tags not understood until long after they'd been accepted. Not that she'd ever really been given a choice. Lodestar's power was thrust upon her. She wasn't like the hungry ones who'd sought it out. She wasn't like Ivan.

Ivan's mind turned, as it had ceaselessly since the weekend's inception, back to his apprentice and the trial she was undergoing. Tori had been doing

160

well when he left Xelas's room, having paired up with Beverly to fight the silver-cored robots. She was a smart woman and had made finding a place to hide top priority. There was little chance she'd be caught unaware once the gold-cored machines were released, and even if she was, at least she had backup. Beverly seemed to be an exceptional meta herself, and Ivan had implicit trust in Thuggernaut's guiding hand. The two of them together could likely overcome a gold just as they were, albeit not without some injuries. If they managed to make use of the supplemental supplies in their caches, they'd be able to pull it off without issue.

Though, Ivan still planned to look in on them again tomorrow after Janet picked up the kids. It was simply good form for her teacher to be waiting when the trial was done, after all.

Chapter 23

"You know, in spite of the green scales and leathery skin, I'm not actually a purse, right?" Beverly slung the makeshift sling and its bulky contents around her shoulder and fastened it in place as best she could. It still bounced and rustled when she moved, but at least it seemed to stay on her.

"I'd love to help out, but since neither the scroll nor the robot parts were made of morphing materials, they won't turn to fire with me. That means if I'm carrying I either stay totally human—and therefore useless—or go into fire-form and drop or burn everything I've got." To illustrate the point, Tori switched to the incarnation of living flame and ran her hand along the cave wall, leaving a scorch mark behind.

"Guess they gave you a uniform made of the morph stuff," Beverly said, taking note for the first time that Tori's clothes changed with her. "Makes sense. Mine's made to shrink and expand as needed. Too bad it didn't come with a backpack." She adjusted the sling once more, and the two women stepped from the safety of their cave into the early morning sunlight.

"We going after more silvers today?" Beverly asked, her eyes already beginning to shift into the white iris of her flying dragon-form.

"Or whatever is out there. Given the explosions we heard last night, I wouldn't be surprised if someone fought their first gold. Maybe even platinum. Can't afford to fall behind."

"Especially not since we have to split our winnings." Beverly's skin lightened as scales appeared from its formerly smooth depths. "I'll do the usual circle around, see what's visible, and then come back so we can start moving toward our target."

"Perfect. Meet you on top of that mesa." Tori pointed upward to one of the many patches of raised land surrounding them and then began to push off the ground using controlled blasts of flame. After discovering the new technique on the prior day, she'd become determined to get as much practice as possible while safely away from civilization. While flight didn't come as easily for her as it clearly did for Beverly, there was still a primal thrill in ignoring the limits of gravity and soaring, or carefully bobbing, through the air. One day, she'd make a meta-suit that would slice across the sky, but this would do until then.

Beverly nodded, finishing the transformation. Her white dragon-form was as large as the others, though in place of her arms, a pair of massive, leathery wings extended from her torso. With one kick from her mighty hind legs, she leapt into the sky, quickly pulling herself higher with a few powerful flaps. In seconds, she'd risen high enough that Tori had trouble distinguishing her fellow apprentice from the white clouds.

Turning her attention to her own ascent, Tori slowly rose upward toward the predetermined mesa, so intent on keeping stabilized that she didn't even notice the wasp, clearly not indigenous to the area, that buzzed by and abruptly stopped as soon as it saw her.

*   *   *

He'd found her. Not just a fellow apprentice, which would have been good enough, but the only one to advocate working together. She was some ways out—it would take him an hour or so to reach her—but at least he had a location. The wasp would stay on her, and he could adjust his course as she moved. While there was no denying this was a long shot, it was still a shot. And he'd take what he could get.

Poking his head out from under the shelf of rock where he'd taken cover, Lance slowly pulled himself up from the dirt. His leg hurt even more than it had last night, and the rest of his body had begun to add its own lyrics to the symphony of pain. Taking that kind of tumble, even with his swarm to slow his fall, had left Lance with more injuries than he'd realized. It was an important issue, one that warranted dealing with… something he fully intended to do as soon as the trial was over. Until then, he would soldier on. If anything, it would just make his eventual triumph all the more impressive.

The thought of coming out on top in spite of his bruised and battered body was all that gave Lance the strength to push himself forward. The crutch of bugs was back in place, its individual denizens more numerous than before thanks to a few hours of summoning under the cover of night. Lance hobbled forward, cutting a brisker pace than the day before, eyes set on the sunrise. Soon he'd reach Tori and hopefully be able to make a case for teaming up. If he was lucky, she'd have seen the robot he fought already; that thing made the case all on its own. Either way, he'd feel better once he wasn't out in the open, alone.

Lance just had to hope the robot didn't find him before then.

*   *   *

Tori barely made it onto the mesa before she heard a roar rip through the sky. Glancing upward, she caught sight of Beverly tucked into a dive, careening toward the mesa at breakneck speed. There was a moment of total, unmediated confusion as she watched her partner on what seemed like a death

163

dive for no reason. Then, from behind the cover of a cloud, the robot came into view.

It was smaller than the silver-cored ones, but slightly larger than Beverly in her current form. Unlike the others, however, this one was human-shaped. As Tori watched, it raised its right hand at the fleeing dragon, releasing a bolt of red energy directly at her. Beverly, operating on what had to be sheer instinct by this point, tucked her wings and rolled, avoiding the blast by mere inches. The red bolt tore through a nearby mesa, causing a massive explosion and showering the whole area in fragments of broken rock.

That was a hell of a weapon. This was no nonlethal armament like the silver's sonic cannon. It was meant to kill, albeit messily. And if that's the tool it was opening with, Tori had to assume there was more powerful gear stashed away in its metal body.

Beverly skidded to a stop on top of the mesa, her powerful claws leaving deep grooves in the rock as she killed the momentum from her dive. Before she'd even fully stopped her scales began changing from pearly white to an emerald green, wings vanishing in exchange for thick, muscular arms. Reaching up with one newly-altered appendage, Beverly sliced through the knot on the makeshift sling, sending it tumbling to the ground with a rattling thud. Swiveling her reptilian head toward Tori, Beverly spoke—the first time she'd done so in a dragon-form since they met.

"It's strong." Beverly's voice was harsh and rough, like a rattlesnake who'd managed to evolve vocal cords.

"I can see that." Tori watched the robot descend, both of its arms raised and ready to fire, no doubt waiting for the opportune shot. "Can you buy me enough time to use my gun?"

"Use it fast." She whipped her head back around, keeping a watchful eye on the robot as it landed across the mesa, its arms still raised. Without another word, the green dragon-woman barreled forward, racing toward the mechanical opponent that had chased her out of the sky.

Before she'd even made it three steps, the robot fired off a bolt of focused blue energy from its left hand that crackled as it cut through the air. Beverly wasn't entirely able to get out of this one's way, and she roared in pain as it burned through part of her bicep. As much as it hurt, she kept right on barreling forward, refusing to be stopped so easily. Green blood dripped from her arm as she rushed to close the gap.

While Beverly charged, Tori shifted back to human-form and hurriedly dug through the sling on the ground. During her evening of turning salvaged parts into workable electronics, Tori had imagined the adversaries she might use her inventions on when the sun rose. In her mind, though, the situation hadn't

164

been quite so desperate nor had it come so soon. But what her imagination had failed to anticipate in terms of setting, it had certainly accounted for regarding necessary power. Jerking her invention free of the sling, Tori turned just in time to see Beverly getting into range for a melee attack.

As the powerful green monster tore across the mesa's rock surface, the metallic humanoid watched her come. It squeezed off one more blue energy shot, which Beverly managed to dodge. It quickly became clear that this was not a fight that would take place over a long range; Beverly fully intended to use those powerful claws and muscles against the robot's comparatively slender form. Just as she was one step away from paying back the damage she'd taken, her metallic opponent leapt upward, taking flight and putting itself completely out of her range.

"Right idea," Tori muttered, carefully drawing a bead on her now-floating target. "Wrong opponents." She pulled the barely-fastened trigger and the entire apparatus she had braced against her shoulder began to vibrate. With enough time and parts, she could have built in stabilizers to get rid of the device's shaking, but those were luxuries not afforded to her. Instead, Tori grit her teeth and kept her aim, refusing to lose this chance. There was no guarantee they'd get another.

The reason Tori had wanted to go after the silver-cored robots wasn't just because of their size. She'd wanted a sonic cannon of her own from the instant one knocked her all the way back to being human. Of course, the ones inside the bots were too big for her to carry, let alone wield. That was why she'd spent the night piecing together a version that was smaller, light enough that even she could utilize it. Of course, with a bit of ingenuity and four robots' worth of parts to work with, Tori had done more than just shrink the cannons. She'd also cranked up their output.

As the sonic blast tore through the air, a massive wall of vibration that slammed into the floating robot as it took aim at the dragon below, Tori was glad she'd given it all the stopping power she could. Even as their opponent seemed to lose control and fell toward the mesa once more, she didn't trust it... she wouldn't until the thing was torn into pieces and scattered through the sand.

"Beverly!"

Tori's shout was all her partner needed; the dragon-woman was already reared back and ready to jump. The moment Tori screamed, Beverly leapt, meeting the humanoid in midair with an audible crunch. Her claws were tearing through its torso and her powerful jaws were crushing through its left shoulder before they even hit the ground. Whether this was payback or pragmatism was up for debate, but there could be no doubt it was effective. The two slammed into the rocky top of the mesa, sending a spray of dust and rock everywhere.

165

While the adversaries fought, Tori dug through the sling once again. She pulled the smoking circuit board out of her makeshift sonic cannon and threw it to the ground. Overclocking the device came with a serious drawback: the internal system got fried after every shot. Since she'd had four robots to salvage from, she only had four chances to fire her cannon. Well, three, now.

Slamming the second circuit board into position, Tori quickly aimed at the dissipating cloud of dust. Firing into the fray was only going to be a last ditch effort. Large as the blasts were, she'd definitely hit Beverly if another shot was needed, but that would be a far better fate for her than taking one of the robot's explosive shots at point blank range.

A wave of relief washed over Tori as the dust finally fell away to reveal Beverly, still in her green dragon-form, standing over what looked more like an upended bin of spare parts than the remains of an actual robot. In her claw, shining bright in the mid-morning sun, was a golden orb the same size as the lesser ones they'd already collected. Tori lowered her gun back to the ground and made her way across the mesa, intent on checking out the remains for herself.

"You didn't leave me much to work with, did you?" A few rogue sparks still crackled from the debris that had only moments ago been a deadly opponent, but there was little chance of it suddenly springing back to life and attacking them. Not unless it was built to self-repair or was actually made of far, *far* tinier robots all working together.

"All that sonic blast did was stun it. Bastard was already getting its shit together when I attacked. Decided not to take any chances." Beverly's voice had lost its husky quality. Tori glanced over and found herself staring at the human version of her fellow apprentice, no worse for the wear despite her injuries.

"Do you need me to look at your arm?" Tori offered.

"It's fine." Beverly pulled back her sleeve to show a bare, unmarked bicep. "I told you, my green dragon is tough and can heal like nobody's business. I'm just glad he didn't get off another one of those red explosion shots while I was coming at him."

"I'll have to look it over to be sure, but I'd wager it didn't because it couldn't. Attacks that strong take a lot of juice; it probably needed to recharge after the first shot." Tori hunkered down in a squat and began sifting through the claw- and tooth-marked remains. "There's other stuff in here, too. Shield system that it didn't get to use thanks to the cannon, smaller weapons, even a few for melee. Keep watch while I pick through this."

"Think you'll find something you can use?" Beverly asked.

Tori shook her head. Even if there'd been time, Beverly had done too good a job turning her opponent into scrap. "Nothing physical, but if I'm lucky,

I might see what little tricks this one was hiding. That way the next one won't take us by surprise."

"Take your time, then." Beverly's eyes began to glow white as scales manifested over her body. "There's bound to be a lot of those out there. I'd like to see how many we can take down."

*   *   *

"And first kill on the golds goes to Thuggernaut's apprentice, with Pseudonym's getting a respectable assist," Johnny announced. While he was still wearing a pinstriped suit, it was at least a different one than the day before.

"An assist? What fight were you watching?" Xelas made a motion to the wall; one of the screens began to rewind until it was showing Tori's blast once more. "Without that shot, dragon-girl had no chance of making the hit. If anything, Tori got the kill and Beverly got the assist."

"Tori's contribution was invaluable, that's why she gets an assist." Johnny pulled out the laptop he'd brought along and made a few quick keystrokes, updating the betting pool along with how much he stood to make himself. This was a big one; almost no one had picked Beverly for the first kill of a gold-cored. "The one who spills the blood, or in this case circuits, gets the credit. You know it as well as I do."

"Johnny is right," Gork said. Her voice was nearly as rough as her words were heavy. Gork's people had a heavy emphasis on honor and protocol, which made her quite a stickler for the rules… or at least the ones she agreed to follow. When it came to matters of fairness, regarding both the letter and spirit of their rules, Gork was universally considered as impartial a judge as could be found in a guild full of criminals and outlaws. Had the AHC greeted Gork as a friend instead of assuming her people were a threat, they might have gained powerful allies beneath the Earth's crust. Unfortunately, force had won over diplomacy, and Gork's culture had *very* firm ideas about dealing with unwarranted aggression.

"See, from the part-rock woman's mouth herself." Finishing his entry, Johnny slid the laptop back into the bag by his feet and turned his attention to the screens once more. "That said: it was one hell of an assist. Can't believe the gal put together something like that out of spare parts in a single night."

"I'm starting to see why she's so insistent on being in Wade's department," Xelas agreed. "I've got a few upgrades in mind I've been tinkering with, might have to see if she has any thoughts worth sharing."

"No loading the rookies with too much work until they actually become full members," Gork reminded her.

Xelas crossed her arms and frowned, an exaggerated gesture that set off red lights around her cheeks. "Stop trying to rain on all my fun. First you break up a me-and-Johnny fight, now you tell me I can't use an apprentice for grunt work."

"I just said you had to wait to do that," Gork pointed out. "If you can't be more creative in your hazing, then you really don't deserve to mess with them anyway. This is *you* we're talking about."

"Ouch, foiled by my own reputation. Fine. I'll find more ways to amuse myself at their expense," Xelas conceded. "I plan to take it easy on Pseudonym and Thuggernaut's kids, though. They seem the type to want payback and are a little more competent than I prefer my victims."

"Beverly definitely is," Thuggernaut confirmed. "And while I don't know Tori that well, she *has* survived as Pseudonym's apprentice for nearly a month."

Xelas looked back at the screen where Tori was pulling apart one of the larger pieces of the robot's chest, trying to crack open an undamaged section of its electronics. "Let's hope he wasn't going easy on her. There's still daylight left before this thing is done."

Chapter 24

Warren slid his back along the rocky wall separating him from the hovering, human-shaped robot currently scanning for his location. The symbol he'd drawn on his torso cloaked him from most of its sensors—at least, he hoped so—but the spell wasn't strong enough to keep him safe if the thing caught sight of him. He'd been overconfident; taking down a half-dozen silvers on his own had bolstered Warren's opinion of his abilities, and he'd gone up against the new opponent without enough research. To say that had backfired would be like saying Fornax had been mildly disliked by the local police during his heyday. As it was, Warren desperately needed to escape, regroup, and strategize. Despite the wounds on his legs and the blood dripping from his chest, Warren still believed he could win against what he assumed was a gold-cored robot.

But it would require planning, preparation, and time to heal, none of which he was likely to have if that thing caught hold of him. Balaam had made it clear—this was not a gentle trial. No one was waiting in the wings to leap in and save him. It was just as it was in the real world: to fail was to die. And Warren didn't intend to die. Not in this robot-infested desert, not for failing to impress the guild, not under Balaam's heel for not living up to his expectations.

Warren would survive. It was what he did. What he had always done. The only difference now was that the stakes were higher. That, and the fact that Warren finally had some power of his own to swing around.

Dipping his finger into one of the many wounds torn open by rock debris from the explosion, he began to scrawl a new symbol on the wall behind him. It took a few more dips in the leg wound to get enough blood, but eventually, he finished his work. He pressed his hand to the symbol and it immediately began to glow, just as the matching one he'd scrawled days before did. That symbol resided on a small outcropping between two mesas over a mile away, sheltered from elements and sight.

When the glow faded, Warren was no longer anywhere near the robot that had attacked him. The symbol, its work completed, crumbled into dust that caught on the late morning breeze. Seconds after he vanished, the only proof Warren had ever been standing there at all was the small pool of blood drying in the sand.

*   *   *

Hunting the golds was much different than going after the silvers. Silver-cored robots, formidable as they were, excelled in a castle-style defense. They were big and well-armored but suffered from poor mobility. Golds took an opposite approach: they zipped through the sky as they searched for targets, preferably ones they could catch unaware. In a way, their technique was similar to the copper-cored drones from the first day, though those were obviously far easier to handle.

This meant that Beverly couldn't fly around scanning from a safe distance for targets like they'd done for the silvers, going airborne now came with serious risks. Since it would make her vulnerable in one of her weaker forms, the women quickly brushed aside the idea of having Beverly do any more solo air scouting. Instead, they decided to use the fact that they were being hunted to their advantage.

Beverly waited patiently atop a mesa in her red dragon-form, scanning the sky for any flying enemies. When one was spotted, she would let loose a blast of flame in its direction. These attacks were, of course, much too far away to be effective, but they succeeded in their true purpose of drawing the robot's attention to her. As it would get close, the gold-cored would take a few shots at Beverly, who would immediately shift to her green form. At such a long range, she was easily able to dodge any attacks, even the red blasts. This helped them to gain some critical information: Tori had correctly assumed that the red blasts needed to be recharged after firing. Finding its tactics ineffective, the robot would then drop height, seeking to shorten the range of the shots and remove Beverly's ability to dodge.

That was when Tori took her shot, blasting it from her hidden nearby position with the sonic cannon. With its shields down since it thought it was safe, the robot was stunned long enough for Beverly to attack, shredding it to pieces just as she had the first.

Their first attempt at using the strategy was rough: Tori nearly missed due to the robot's last-minute shift, and Beverly wasn't quite quick enough off the line. The robot had nearly regained its senses by the time she arrived, which made for a tense moment as she attacked, uncertain whether her opponent would be able to activate its defenses in time. Luck was on their side, though, and the metallic enemy dropped to the ground as mere scrap metal under Beverly's assault.

The second attempt went much more smoothly; the poor robot never even had a chance.

"Three cores down." Beverly pulled the golden orb from the scattered electrical remains, her claws and glowing eyes the only remains of the dragon-form she'd shed moments prior. "That's fifteen hundred apiece. Not too shabby for a long weekend of work."

"You're counting wrong." Tori yanked the circuit board free as she walked over, dropping it to the ground like the trash it now was and pulling out their last functioning unit. "Since killing this many means we'll win, one of us should turn in all the cores, getting the bonus. That turns three thousand into forty-five hundred, netting us two thousand, two hundred and fifty dollars apiece, plus some extra from the silvers."

Beverly stared carefully at the half-distracted woman as she tucked the orb away in her pocket with the others. Their partnership had worked out well so far, but they'd yet to reach the point that would truly test it. When money and credit were on the line, there was always the chance that one of them would decide alliances were worth less than what could be won.

"And which of us would do the claiming?"

"Since you obviously think I'm doing this as some sort of trick, why don't you turn them in?" Tori suggested as she loaded the final board into place. One shot left on the sonic cannon, and since they hadn't seen many silvers out since the prior night, it was best not to expect any chances at reloading.

"You'd trust me to just give you your cut? Not to mention giving up all the credit for these kills?"

"Trust me, the guild knows exactly who killed what. They've probably watched everything we've done since arrival. The only people who would think more of me for turning in a bunch of orbs are you three, and I think there are already enough expectations being thrown my way as it is." Tori set her cannon down before turning to face Beverly properly. "And yes, I will trust you with collecting the money. Best case scenario, you and I build a little more trust between us, something that is very useful to have in this place. Worst case scenario, you betray me and I learn you're not to be trusted. Two thousand dollars isn't a cheap lesson, but better I learn it now before it costs me far more down the road."

Stepping away from the robotic wreckage, Beverly shook her head and let out a muted chuckle. "Jesus Christ, it's kind of creepy how logical you are. Sure you aren't part Vulcan?"

"Nah, Spock wasn't that big on revenge. I'd definitely make you pay for screwing me over. But I don't really think it's going to come to that," Tori said.

"This place is already weird and scary enough. Last thing I need is someone with a grudge against me... especially when that person could be an ally instead." Beverly stuck out her hand and Tori grasped it, giving a firm shake.

171

"I like to think we could even make it all the way to becoming friends," Tori added. "From what I've seen, having those is half of what it takes to survive in this guild."

"In that case, I suspect you're about to find my proposal very interesting."

This voice came from neither Beverly nor Tori. Both spun toward its source, Tori's whole body immediately morphing into living flame while green scales engulfed Beverley's form. What met their eyes was not a threat, or at least not something that seemed particularly threatening.

Lance sat on the edge of the mesa, hands high in the air in a motion of clear surrender, a swarm of bugs helping keep him balanced as he rested. "I come in peace. Is that Star Trek? Damn it, I knew I should have watched those shows. Point is, I don't want trouble. I came to talk about working together."

Tori slowly lowered her hands and the fireballs burning at the ready in her palms, though she didn't turn back to her human-form just yet. Taking in the man before her, she noted that his leg looked to be in rough shape, and he had the weary, hunkered appearance of someone fighting sleep deprivation and dehydration.

"You barely look like you can sit up straight; meanwhile, we're taking out golds with ease. Feels less like you want to talk about teaming up and more like us dragging you along."

"True, I'm far from in peak condition, but my power has never been one that required me to do much dirty work. Besides, from the number of circuit boards left and what I saw through my bugs, I'd guess that fancy shooter of yours is on its last bullet, so you'll have to change strategies soon. I can lend a hand with that on the combat side, or at least my bugs can. And on top of that, I bring something to the table that neither of you has: surveillance and tracking. Imagine if you knew where those gold-cored robots were at any given time. Might make getting around and hunting them a lot easier."

"He talks a good game," Beverly said, words a half-snarl through her scaly snout. "But how do we know he can back it up?"

A single wasp flitted through the air, rising from Beverly's back and floating until it landed on Lance's outstretched finger. He smiled as the realization dawned on the others and considered letting the moment speak for itself, but ultimately decided to really drive the point home. "I found you, didn't I?"

Tori slowly shifted back to her human-form, then walked over and picked up the sonic cannon. While she didn't actually point it at him, the implied threat was more than enough. Tori didn't need words to drive her points home, not when they were better used for making her demands.

"All right, Lance, tell us what you're thinking."

*   *   *

"Beth, don't forget your phone charger." Ivan's voice echoed up the hall into what he only hoped would be his daughter's room and mind. Well-intentioned though she was, Beth couldn't seem to keep track of her chargers no matter what lengths he and Janet went to. Were she a more malicious child, he'd have suspected the losses were intentional simply because he couldn't fathom one person genuinely going through so many.

The upstairs bustled as the sounds of packing filled the air. It often seemed like his children had barely arrived before they were stuffing their lives back into suitcases and heading out the door. During those moments, Ivan had to force himself to remember how lucky he was to have even the weekends he did. After all, it wasn't as though Janet didn't have good cause to dispute the joint custody. He liked to think it was respect for his parenting abilities that kept her from trying to keep his children away, but in his heart of hearts, Ivan always suspected that fear was her primary motivator. While he would never hurt his children by taking away their mother, Janet likely still believed that crossing him so severely would be bad for her health.

Sometimes, it was hard to remember the harsh, worried woman as the wild girl who'd had a thing for bad boys. Time had changed her, as it had him, and as it did all, eventually. There were many moments in Ivan's life he'd have altered given the chance, but his time with Janet was certainly not among them. Not for fond memories of her, which a bad marriage and worse divorce had soured. No, Ivan wouldn't dare risk changing the past because it might steal from him two of the only things in the world he truly cared about.

Rick came bustling down the stairs, bag slung over his shoulder, phone conspicuously absent from his hand. His and Ivan's discussion the prior night had been a long one, heavy on responsibility and trust, and while it ended with a grounding, such was done more in service to formal rule observation than out of anger. Ivan wanted his son to understand the importance of consequences; it was a lesson his life would have been better served if he'd learned it earlier. As the young man, the near spitting image of Ivan at that age (sans a few scars and pounds of muscle) reached the end of the stairs, he looked up at his father with a touch of embarrassment.

"Dad, I just wanted to say I'm sorry again about last night."

"We went over everything, and it's fine. You know what you did wrong, and you're paying for it. So long as the lesson is learned, there's no need to keep raking yourself over the coals." Ivan grabbed his son and wrapped the

173

boy in a powerful hug. "Just don't go thinking you can slip past your old man so easily."

"Trust me, I've got that figured out." Rick hugged back, even though they both knew it was only a matter of time before he tried something again. This was the age where he tested his limits. Few people in the world understood that better than Ivan.

"Daaaad, have you seen my charger?" The voice carried down from upstairs, causing Ivan to wince while in mid-hug. He glanced down at Rick, who quickly shook his head to the negative. Wordlessly, he reached into a drawer on the desk resting at the foyer's edge and removed one of a half-dozen identical white cords with specialized ends.

"It's down here!" Ivan called upstairs. He pressed a finger to his lips and stared pointedly at Rick, who took the message. "You left it on the kitchen counter."

The goal was not to teach his son not to lie, but that lies were tools best used for purposes that suited them. Keeping a young girl from worrying over the loss of yet another cord, for example, was an excellent use of a well-timed lie. As was what he'd told them both he planned to spend the evening doing: reading and getting a jump on the next day's work. No good would come of his children knowing he was off to check in on his apprentice in a guild of villains. It would only pointlessly change the way they looked at him, seeing a vision of who had been rather than who he was.

After all, it was no lie that Fornax was dead. He'd passed away the moment he was pulled from his cell and shown the picture of the newborn baby bearing his DNA. From that moment on, only Ivan had remained.

Chapter 25

The afternoon sun sank further toward the horizon as Beverly finished clawing her way through their fourth gold-cored robot. At this point it was almost—*almost*—easy. Despite his injuries, Lance hadn't been bluffing about his ability to keep summoning and controlling bugs; not only had this been helpful in scouting, hunting had also become much easier with his ability to send clouds of bugs as bait to draw their adversaries in. After a quick run to the cave for some supplies to at least bring him halfway back to life, the young man had sent scouts across the sky in search of more robots. Shortly thereafter, a gold-cored arrived to take them down. Tori ambushed the robot in fire-form alongside a green-dragon Beverly; their mechanical opponent barely had the chance to throw up an energy shield that hissed and crackled as Beverly's claws cut through it. Her hands were bloody as it fell to the ground, but by the time the robot was in pieces, her wounds had healed. It seemed the green dragon really could take quite a bit of punishment.

"And this makes four." Tori pointed to the gold core, which Beverly quickly scooped up, using her claws like pincers and slipping it into the pouch on her expanded uniform. "Though, Lance, you're only getting a third of the ones you help bring down."

"Tell you what, why don't you just go ahead and keep my share too?" Lance said. He pulled himself slowly up from behind the rocks where he'd been hiding, his swarm replaced by an actual crutch Tori had fastened out of leftover parts from their salvaged silver-cored parts.

"You helped us destroy it," Tori reminded him.

"Sure, but you helped bandage my leg and gave me food and water. Never a good idea to overextend one's position in a deal. I'm lending aid as thanks for you two helping me survive this long, and hopefully until the end of the trial." Lance looked up at the dipping sun, taking in the splendor as its light danced across the mesas. "And seeing how much assistance I'll need getting back, let's just say I feel more comfortable trading my help for yours rather than getting greedy."

"He's smarter than he looks," Beverly noted, the last of her dragon-self slipping away.

"To be fair, given my size and appearance, that's a pretty low bar." Lance shrugged his muscular shoulders and smiled with the sort of willful innocence that really had no place on an apprentice of the villains' guild. "But I am smart enough to know we're starting to get near the end of our time. We can try and hunt one more if you want, though I'd be surprised if getting back is really going to be as easy as just walking over."

"Four golds are enough for me," Tori said, turning her fiery head to Beverly, who nodded as well.

"Plenty enough to win, especially the way we're doing it. I'm all for playing it smart and getting back to the meeting point." To illustrate the point, she shifted back to her green dragon-form and walked over to Lance, lifting him from the ground as if he weighed no more than a few pounds and cradling him in her massive arms.

"Win or lose, I cannot imagine Arachno Bro isn't going to give me shit for this," Lance sighed from the crook of Beverly's arm. "Still beats not coming back at all, though."

"You can say that again." Tori turned back to full human-form, something she'd tried to avoid any more than necessary around Lance, and pushed aside a small set of rocks near the wall where she'd stashed her cannon. Turning it over carefully in her hands, she slowly made her way back across the mesa and held it out to Lance. "Here, I want you to hold this."

"Isn't that what the sling is for?" Lance pointed to the twisted fabric around Beverly's back, now largely empty except for the lone scroll resting inside.

"She can't carry us both, and I can't hold this when I'm in flame mode. If something gets the jump on us, you can still shoot, so you get tasked with holding it. Just remember: you only have one shot, and if you use it on either of us, the other will make you regret it." Tori shook the cannon once, moving it a few inches closer to the injured man in the dragon's arms.

"Trust me, there is no gain in me taking a shot at either of you. But if something attacks, I'll be ready." Lance reached out and wrapped a meaty hand around the cannon, clutching it carefully against his pecs.

"Good. And don't miss. Like I said, one shot left," Tori reminded him.

"Think there will be trouble?" Beverly growled.

"Look at who we're dealing with. The question isn't *if* there will be trouble, it's *how much* we're about to step into." Tori's form grew blurry as she once more morphed to flame then pushed herself gently into the air with her controlled blasts. "Lance, keep your bugs on alert. I'll try and scout as best I can. Beverly, if we get caught off guard, scatter first, then regroup."

"Let's finish strong." Beverly's gravelly voice echoed off the mesas as the three apprentices started on the final leg of their trial: the journey back to the start.

*   *   *

176

The platinum timer ticked away steadily, shedding seconds as the time for the final confrontation drew closer. In Xelas's room, the cheerful atmosphere had subsided significantly as each spectator watched the screens with more rapt attention than they had before. As veteran members of the guild, they knew that everything in the previous few days had merely been sport and spectacle, a way to test the mettle of each apprentice as well as entertain the watching guild. What was coming was the true test, their actual trial.

Of everyone present, no one was more nervous than Thuggernaut. While the others had met and enjoyed some of the rookies one on one, he was the only person present with a vested interest in seeing one make it back alive. Beverly was strong and had a good head on her shoulders, but she was still green. He could only hope that the last few days were enough to teach her that she wasn't invincible. If she didn't think through what was about to happen, it could cost her more than spare change and bragging rights.

As he watched worriedly, Johnny laid a hand on the massive man's shoulder.

"Relax. She's a good one, and Ivan's kid has solid instincts. Add in that they've got the insect guy's powers, and those three have a real shot at making it."

"We've seen others with shots make bad choices," Thuggernaut replied, eyes unwavering from the screen.

"Maybe so, but none of them had you as a teacher. You know Beverly better than anyone here, and I've got no doubt you prepped her for this as much as you could. Now it's time to have some faith." Johnny leaned forward, nodding to the ticking clock with highlighted platinum numbers. "They can do it. And hey, you'll win a few bucks in the process."

"There's that classic Johnny way of navigating a moment," Xelas said. "But he's right. Those two are kicking ass, and adding in Lance only makes the group stronger. If anyone should be crapping themselves right now, it's Balaam. His apprentice hasn't exactly been going strong since the golds came out."

"Warren got one," Gork reminded them. He'd managed it after a morning of recovery, and while the effort was impressive, especially since he'd done it solo, it was still far too little to close the gap between him and the others.

"And if that were the real test, he'd be looking great. As it is, he has to know he's behind, and with only a few minutes left until the big game enters the field, the kid might be desperate enough to try something stupid." Xelas glanced at the clock, even though she was perfectly able to keep track of the time on her own. There was something a touch more dramatic, more human, about watching the tool with the others.

"Good or bad, looks like we're about to see how things are going." Johnny gestured at the screen where Tori, Beverly, and Lance were nearing the drop-off site. Tori blasted a few copper-cored drones out of the air, seemingly clearing out the area. Of course, she didn't know what was still waiting. After all, there were still twenty minutes until sunset.

But more importantly, there were ten minutes left on the digital clock with platinum numbers.

*   *   *

"That was actually pretty easy," Tori said as the last of the copper-cored drones fell to the ground in fiery scraps. From behind her, a loud, pronounced groan filled the air.

"You just had to say that, didn't you? Haven't you ever heard of a jinx?" Lance was propped against a pile of rocks, sonic cannon still in his hand, while Beverly rested nearby. She seemed intent on staying in dragon-form until they were safely out of the desert, a precaution that no one questioned the validity of.

"There's no such thing as a jinx."

"Says the lady who is made of living fire, to the boy that can summon swarms of insects, who is sitting next to the woman that turns into a massive dragon creature through what I'm assuming has to be magic," Lance countered.

"Fine, jinxes are real, but you don't activate them just by commenting on the fact that we weren't attacked much on way over," Tori replied.

"That probably depends on the jinx." Beverly's stout neck swiveled as she craned her head around to sight any incoming threats. Above them, the sun was dipping deeper toward the horizon. By their best guesses, sunset was likely only a half-hour away at the most. "You know, if it was a trap."

"Who would, or could, lay a trap for us that was triggered by us talking about the fact that we didn't get ambushed by robots on our way to a meeting place?" Tori demanded.

"Well, we do know that Warren uses magic," Lance pointed out, grinning despite the subject matter.

With a fiery huff, Tori lifted off into the sky to help Beverly scout. Buzzing overhead was Lance's cloud of gathered insects, a swarm that steered clear of the burning woman as she pushed herself free of gravity's tireless clutches. She rose partly to get away from the conversation and partly to sweep the area from a new vantage point, but mostly because she didn't know when her next chance to fly would be. Ivan was a good teacher, and despite his

178

demeanor, she suspected he cared about her, but he wasn't big on getting her much practical training. Now that she'd finally pushed herself enough to learn she could leave the ground, it was an experience she wanted to repeat as often as possible.

Tori's annoyance was the only reason she was in a high enough position to see the movement. While Lance's bugs and Beverly's eyes scanned the sky, Tori happened to glance down at her fellow apprentices just in time to catch the shifting sand that was moving toward them. Something was burrowing beneath the surface, on a course directly for Lance and Beverly, who were just standing around unaware. With no time to think, Tori hurled a fireball just to the right of them, scorching the dry desert sand and immediately grabbing the pair's attention.

"Ruuuuuun!" Tori screeched the word, desperate to be heard through the great distance. Her flaming hands gestured wildly to the moving lump of sand, trying for all she was worth to get them to look over.

Mercifully, it was Beverly who trusted her enough to look away from the apparent attack. Her scaly eyes widened as she caught sight of the thing heading for them. Grabbing Lance by the shoulder, Beverly flung him through the air. He crashed in a groaning heap nearly forty feet away and immediately tried to right himself and figure out what had happened. As for the dragon, Beverly leapt backward, putting some distance between herself and the approaching enemy. Fast as her reactions had been, she still only missed the attack by a matter of inches.

A metallic pincer as long as green-dragon-Beverly was tall burst out of the sand. It sliced through the air, chopping the space where Beverly had been only seconds before. Red energy flickered between the two razor-sharp blades as they came together, filling the air with a sickening sizzle. As quickly as it appeared, the pincer sank back through the sand and rock, as easy as a shark through water, vanishing completely save for the slight bump that gave away its movement.

It headed for Beverly, but she'd already taken a cue from Tori. Emerald green turned to pearly white as her scales shifted, arms turning to wings almost midair. Beverly took to the sky, rising upward with two powerful flaps before reorienting herself toward Lance.

The large, injured young man was no slouch at discerning a situation. While the sand robot had gone after Beverly, Lance had called every nearby insect he had to converge on his location. Together, hundreds of tiny wings were slowly bearing him away from the perilous position on the ground. It was clearly a struggle, though; he was less than four inches above the sand when the bump turned and headed toward his direction.

179

Strong, foot-like claws grabbed Lance by the shoulders and yanked him higher as Beverly beat her wings for all she was worth. While neither she nor the bugs could raise him quickly enough on their own, together they managed to get fifty feet off the ground by the time the sand bump would have been in striking range.

"What the hell is that?" Lance yelled, mostly for Tori's benefit since she was still flying over to join them.

"Platinum core, I guess," Tori replied. She eased off the fire blasts as she drew close, not wanting to careen into the swarm and kill any of the helpful bugs.

"Too easy," Beverly snorted. In this form, her words came out half-garbled. Evidently, the white dragons were less suited to speech than the green ones. "We can just fly away."

"We can, sure, but how many apprentices have flight powers?" Tori reminded her. "Though I'll give you that it does seem like a pretty serious design flaw, especially if it's meant to be as dangerous as the gold-cored ones."

"Um, you know how you didn't believe in jinxes?" Lance said, pointing to the sand below them.

From the depths beneath the desert, the robot began to rise. It was a massive beast, long as a line of buses and three times as big around. Out of its front extended a pair of sharp pincers, along with mandibles and dozens of glowing red eyes. Stretching up from the back was a long, metallic tail that whipped freely through the air with what appeared to be a glowing blade and some sort of cannon affixed to the end. Three thick legs extended from each side, half buried in the ground as it kept itself low. Along its back were dozens of turrets and guns, all of which were quickly rotating, aiming in the three apprentices' direction.

"Fuck me," Tori said, taking in the instrument of death as it gazed at them with countless glowing, *targeting* eyes.

"Holy shit, it's going to blast us. Scatter!"

Chapter 26

Tori blasted upward, racing away as fast as her flames would take her. Beverly let Lance go and went into a dive, zipping through the air with half-tucked wings. For a moment, Tori thought Beverly had taken the heartless route, but as the first shot ripped through the air, it became clear that dropping Lance had saved them both. He'd fallen faster than she could have moved while bearing him. Meanwhile, his insect swarm had slowed his fall and was steering him toward the relative cover on top of a nearby mesa.

The robot, some strange bastardization of a weapons depot and a scorpion, didn't take long to recover, reorienting its aim even as its targets tore through the sky in different directions. Beverly's grunts of pain reached Tori just as she felt a bolt of energy race through her own insubstantial leg. It didn't hurt, not exactly, but it definitely wasn't a pleasant experience. She knew from her experience with the sonic cannon that too much damage could push her back to human-form, and there was no reason to doubt these blasts' effect would be any different. Too much from them and she'd be a sitting duck. Strike that: a falling, flightless duck that would be finished off by the robot monster if the landing didn't kill her outright.

Forcing herself to turn up the intensity of her blasts, Tori cranked up the speed just in time to dodge the next volley of shots. This plan was no good; the damn thing could track and attack them all individually. As it was, they were simply treading water before they got shot down; counterattacking wasn't even on the table. They needed a moment to think, to plan, to recover. She glanced down at Lance, whose bugs had set him down on the mesa's top out of the massive thing's eyesight. Of course, given that it could somehow swim through rock and dirt, that wouldn't keep him, or any of them, safe for more than a few minutes.

Unless, of course, it had something else to attack.

Banking hard to the right, Tori sacrificed some of her precious altitude to drop within shouting distance of Lance. She couldn't chance slowing down or changing direction, so she screamed, "Lance! The bugs! Send them out as one giant swarm right now. Make them stick close and draw its attention!" With that, she was past the mesa, only able to hope he'd heard her and that he trusted her enough to follow the seemingly crazy order.

Turning up her speed again, Tori raced through the sky, taking a few more bolts for her trouble. Pushing past the fear and first rumbling of pain, she raced onward, getting close to the white dragon that was ducking and dodging under the hail of fire.

"Get to the mesa!" Tori screamed the words as she and Beverly zipped past each other, the predicament of their situation not allowing for any more conversation than that. At first, she feared her ally hadn't heard, but seconds later, Beverly took a sharp turn and flapped her way in the direction of the mesa.

A giant cloud of insects was slowly rising off of said mesa like buzzing steam from a boiling pot. Tori hurtled toward it, noting with some relief that the robot's volley had begun attacking the bugs as well. She turned wide, passing behind the cloud of bugs before rocketing down, not so much landing on the mesa as crashing into it, her fire-body spreading like a dropped egg before reforming itself.

Getting up from the ground, Tori turned human and checked the sky. Beverly was coming in for a landing a few feet away, and the cloud of insects still seemed to be taking the endless onslaught, both of which meant they still had a fighting chance of living through this.

"Lance, you can see through the bugs, right? Is that robot moving or just attacking?"

"Hang on." Lance closed his eyes for several seconds, long enough that Beverly landed with a mighty *whump* nearby before they snapped open again. "Just attacking. Do you think it doesn't know we're here?"

Tori quickly shook her head. "It's a robot, running on programming. This one seems to seek out targets and engage them. I think as long as it has some target to fight, that protocol wins out over chasing other ones. At least, that's what I was hoping when I noticed it didn't try to come after you after you left its line of sight."

"Great, so we use the bugs to keep it distracted then run by once the doorway opens?" Beverly had shifted to her green form. The half-dozen wounds on her arms and legs began to heal before Tori and Lance's eyes as the dragon-woman limped over.

"No. It has no problem targeting multiple enemies at once, as we just saw," Tori told her. "The bugs will buy us a few minutes, maybe, but the minute we step off of here, we're right back in the fight. Assuming we can wait it out until the doorway opens, we just have to think of a way to get past it."

"You don't want to try and take the thing out?" Lance asked.

"Too strong. Maybe with a full day to hunt it and learn its weaknesses, we could have given it a shot, but as things stand, I think we need to focus on surviving." Tori looked between the others, carefully checking each of their expressions. "Unless one of you knows of a way we can beat it."

"I'm trying to figure out how we'll survive even getting past it," Beverly replied.

182

"I'm on board with running, I just expected one of us to be more gung-ho about taking it down," Lance said.

"Nope, pretty sure we all want to not die. If that's even on the table." Tori moved slightly nearer to the edge of the mesa's cliff where she could look down on the landscape below. The cliff face where the portal would open was a few feet behind the wildly flailing tail that whipped through the air. No way around it; they'd have to pass the robot to make it out.

"Beverly, I hate to say this, but I think you need to get the scroll out."

"Whoa now, I told you I don't know what it does," Beverly said, turning to face Tori so quickly that her claws left marks in the rock beneath them. "The most I could figure out was how to activate the thing."

"Which is why we agreed it should probably be saved for an emergency," Tori said. "Maybe we're getting different reads on the situation, but this feels a lot like an emergency to me. As it stands, I've got no idea how we're going to get past that robot. We need to change something, because this is not a good situation for us."

"And what if it impairs me?" Beverly suggested. "If it's a trap, then we're even more screwed."

"At this point, the degree in which we're screwed is largely academic. We can only die once. And besides, everything we found in the caches—*everything*—was helpful. If there was ever a time to trust a mysterious magical scroll, this is probably it." Tori glanced back at the area where the doorway would appear. She thought she caught the slightest waver on the earthen surface but dismissed it as a heat shimmer.

Grumbling under her breath, Beverly reverted to her human-form and pulled the sling free from over her shoulder. With a few motions, she unwound it and produced the scroll, which looked a bit beaten around the edges but otherwise no worse for the wear. Carefully, she unrolled the item, laying the parchment flat against the mesa's rough surface, until a single circular symbol at the bottom was exposed. With a slight exertion, Beverly turned her left hand's fingernails into sharp claws and pricked herself on her right thumb. As the red bead swelled atop her pierced flesh, she looked up at Tori once more.

"You sure about this?"

"Not even a little bit, but if you have a better plan, I'm open to hearing it."

Beverly gave her answer by pressing her thumb into the small circle at the bottom of the scroll. "Commence," she said, her words barely above a whisper.

Immediately, the symbol began to glow, the parchment turning into golden light and weaving itself around Beverly's arm, working its way upward until it reached the magical tattoo etched around her neck. As soon as the two sources met, they exploded outward, completely engulfing Beverly and forcing the others to cover their eyes.

When the light finally cleared and Tori blinked away the last of the static-like spots from her eyes, a wide grin split her face as she took in what stood before her. Lance chuckled as well, and for the first time since they'd arrived on it, the mood atop the mesa turned hopeful.

"Yeah," Tori said, taking in Beverly's altered form. "I think we can work with this."

*   *   *

Ivan stood positioned in a line with Thuggernaut, Arachno Bro, and Balaam, all four men staring at the wall where Tunnel Vision was about to open a doorway through space. Doctor Mechaniacal was in front of them, counting down the seconds until it was time to give the apprentices a way back. Only their mentors were allowed to be present for their return, a precaution meant to make the apprentices feel safe as well as ensure no staff were harmed in the retrieval process. These four were more than capable of handling anything a simple robot threw their way.

"Gentleman, in a few moments I am going to open the doorway. I want to remind you that once I do, it is prohibited by guild law for you to interfere with what lays beyond. Whether it be to help your own apprentice or hinder another, your influence can be nothing more than the training you imparted to them previously. I trust there are no objections?" Doctor Mechaniacal made a point of turning his helmet since his eyes were obscured, making sure each guild member knew he was looking at them. When no one replied, the helmet turned to Tunnel Vision with a curt nod.

"Do it."

As the wall before them began to shimmer, Thuggernaut leaned in and whispered to Ivan, "Nervous?"

"More than I expected. You?"

"Same." Thuggernaut paused, checking to make sure the portal wasn't open yet. "When Doctor Mechaniacal came to get me, they'd just released the platinum robot. I didn't get to see any of the fight."

"You know that isn't really—"

"I know. Still, have to keep up appearances," Thuggernaut said.

"Just checking. At least they made it this far, and from what you said, they took down a few golds in the process. I wasn't expecting them to do quite this well," Ivan admitted.

184

"It's an interesting group, full of surprises. I never thought ours would pair up, or that AB's would join them later. Kids today. You can never tell what they're going to do."

Thuggernaut's voice faded away as the wall in front of them turned transparent and then opened to a hot desert landscape. Initially, all they could see was the massive tail whipping about from the robot's rear, but almost immediately a new sight caught their attention. Even the veteran council members found themselves slightly taken aback.

"Full of surprises, indeed," Ivan chuckled.

*   *   *

It was not a subtle plan. Given what the scroll had done to Beverly and the goal set before them, it would have taken someone with a mind far greater than any of the three gathered to work any sense of covertness into the tactics available. Recognizing that limitation from the outset, they didn't bother to try. Instead, they opted for a strategy that put Beverly's temporarily-altered state to good use. All things considered, the plan wasn't a bad one. But it was literally as subtle as a giant green dragon barreling through the desert with an insect summoner and a fire-conjuring woman clinging to its back.

The scroll, as it turned out, increased the size of its user tremendously. Tori marveled at the massive limbs tearing through the sand as Beverly charged the scorpion-like robot head-on. In the back of her mind, Tori knew that Beverly's limbs should be insufficient to support her new weight, that the enlarged woman should have been immobile. Yet science seemed to have taken the day off as the twice-transformed woman raced across the sand. Magic played by its own rules, and Tori was beginning to understand why so few people could straddle the scientific and the arcane.

"Are you okay?" Lance asked, yelling from his position on Beverly's back. He and Tori could both hear the shots striking her scaly hide, but they didn't seem to even register with Beverly, let alone slow her down.

"Can barely feel them." Her voice shook loose debris from the nearby mesas as they raced past them. Tori could actually feel the sonic waves shake her too-human body as it worked to hang on. Fire-form would be safer, but she needed a good grip if she wanted to catch a ride.

Tori chanced a glance over the shoulder she was tucked behind. Not only were they close to their goal, but that the doorway had actually opened. Tori could make out a few figures just beyond the cliff's entrance—no doubt Doctor Mechaniacal and some helpers to welcome them back or collect their remains. It was only a little farther, given Beverly's pace, but to get there, they'd have to pass directly by the robot. It clacked its pincers in anticipation, and the tail that had been whipping wildly about halted, twisting itself around so it was pointed directly at the approaching dragon. Acting more on instinct than logic, Tori lifted herself up, right next to Beverly's ear, and screamed as loud as she could.

"Get down!"

The giant dragon had barely thrown herself to the ground before the massive red beam of energy shot overhead, sizzling through the air where Beverly had been only seconds before. Scrambling to get up lest she make an easy target, Beverly still took a minute to twist her head around and stare at Tori with a gigantic eyeball. Though she didn't speak, the implied question was evident.

"The last two models had cannons. Seemed like a good chance this one would too."

Beverly let out a huff and hurried forward, eager to get moving again. If the tail needed to recharge, there was a good chance she might be able to get past before it succeeded. If it didn't... well, they were probably screwed no matter what she did.

Mercifully, a second blast didn't follow the first, and Beverly raced forward until she was nearly within striking distance of the scorpion-bot.

"Laaaaance," Tori called, noting that they were getting closer than she wanted to be.

"Give me a damn second to line this up. You're the one who made me hold the gun with only one bullet." Lance was propping himself over Beverly's shoulder, one hand holding the gun as it rested on her scales and one clinging on to her miraculously-expanded uniform for dear life. He took a deep breath, drawing as tight a bead as he could, and gently pressed his finger against the trigger. "Firing in three!"

"Heard!" Tori raised herself slightly, fireballs forming at the ends of each of her hands. There was no telling how much of a window Lance would be able to open up, if any. She had to do as much as possible with whatever chance they were given.

True to his word, three seconds later, a familiar boom rang through the air as Lance fired the final round of the sonic cannon. When the plan had been hurriedly conceived atop the mesa, there was ample debate about what he should aim for. A leg might knock the creature off balance, but taking down a pincer would remove half the melee threat. Ultimately it was Beverly, the only one among them who knew what it was like to be a powerful, armored creature, who told Lance where his shot would count the most.

The blast of sonic energy tore forward, smashing directly into the scorpion robot's dozen or so glowing red eyes. It let out a high-pitched screech. That was all Tori needed to commence her own attack. Fiery bolts burst forth from her hands, scorching across its already wounded eyes as the scorpion robot scrambled to recover. While Tori doused its eyes in fire, Beverly swung wide, veering around the pincers as she made a run for the doorway. Within seconds, Tori's angle of attack was gone, the eyes shielded from view as Beverly passed the metal monster's legs. She returned her focus to the act of hanging on with all her might. The time for doing damage was over; now they could only hope it had been enough.

Hurtling forward, Beverly quickly closed the gap between herself and the doorway. The robot, much to their relief, didn't try to turn around and catch her as she ran past. That relief was cut short when Tori realized the tail was raised carefully overhead, tracking their movements as a familiar red energy began to glow from deep within the cannon's depths.

"Round two is coming!" Lance hollered, having noticed the same ominous glow as Tori. Beverly let out a snort of awareness but said nothing. Words would be wasted at this point. The cannon would be firing from point blank range if it got its shot off. They either made it through the door or died in the charge. No one had any tricks left up their sleeves.

Pumping her legs with all her considerable might, Beverly took three more steps forward then vaulted into a horizontal leap toward the doorway. Hands extended forward like she was sliding for home, it was clear that in only a few seconds she was going to crash into the side of the cliff, since she was far too large to fit through the doorway.

"Release!"

A sharp pop, like a balloon bursting, filled the air as giant-dragon-Beverly vanished, leaving behind only the normally large one. Despite the change in size, her momentum was still going strong, sending her, Tori, and Lance forward like they'd been thrown from a catapult.

There was a moment of uncertainty among the figures awaiting them, followed by a hurried scramble to get out of the way as they realized the three apprentices had almost no control over where they'd be landing. Beverly smashed through a table that was filled with soft drinks and sandwiches; Lance felt a rib break as he crashed into, and then through, a chair; and Tori was whipped about through the air until she slammed back-first into the room's far wall.

Whether it was due to exhaustion or her focused effort on staying human, Tori's body didn't shift, in spite of the impact. Her breath fled her lungs

187

and her eyes opened wide, terrified words trying to escape but with no air available to form them.

Since she was facing the doorway, Tori could see the glow of the robot's tail as it took aim directly at the room they were now all gathered in. Her hand shook as she pointed toward it, trying to make the others notice, but before anyone else's head so much as swiveled, the tail cannon fired directly at them.

Tori's eyes clamped shut as she waited for the wash of pain followed by what she presumed would be an infinity of nothingness. When neither came, she slowly allowed her lids to part and see how she'd survived. What greeted her wasn't particularly surprising, at least not given all she'd learned in her apprenticeship, but it was still damned impressive nonetheless.

Standing at the edge of the doorway, looking more bored than strained, stood Ivan. He'd raised a single hand, around which rotated a circle of runes. The massive blast of energy, so much more powerful at this close a range, burned harmlessly against his shield before flickering out and dying entirely.

Ivan, task handled, lowered his hand, pausing only to pop his knuckles. He turned to face his apprentice. He cleared his throat and took one quick glance over his shoulder where the angry giant robot stormed across the desert before addressing Tori.

"That was... satisfactory."

Chapter 27

"Kiss my ass, 'satisfactory,' that was fuckin' awesome!" Arachno Bro raised a hairy arm and slapped into a high-five with Lance, lifting the muscular young man off the floor as though he weighed nothing more than a forgotten dream. Thuggernaut walked over to Beverly, who was already scrambling up by the time he reached her. Tori and Ivan's gaze never left each other as she pulled herself back to her feet, the spasming in her lungs finally under control.

"I think you mean dangerous, unnecessary, and very poorly thought out," Balaam said, somehow managing to look bored despite the spectacle he'd just witnessed.

"Someone's just grumpy that his apprentice didn't make it back with the others," Arachno Bro snickered.

"Actually, I used a rune and slipped in while they had the robot distracted." Warren emerged from behind one of the larger pieces of shattered table where he'd been hiding, hurrying over to Balaam's side.

"What a fine use of planning and tactics, as well as capitalizing on the flaws of the lesser." Balaam patted Warren's head as though he were a child, awkwardly ruffling the younger man's hair.

"I wouldn't go throwing around words like 'lesser' until we know who actually came in first." Thuggernaut didn't seem aggressive, but his tone was stern as he steered Beverly over toward the metal-suited man who was Doctor Mechaniacal. "Apprentice, present your winnings."

Beverly's hands were nearly back to human as they plunged into her pockets, coming out with four golden orbs, a half-dozen silver ones, and a handful or so of the coppers. Doctor Mechaniacal took the lot from her, and after holding them for several seconds, announced his count.

"Four thousand, eight hundred and twenty dollars' worth of orbs. Quite impressive, Apprentice. Who would like to go next?" The orbs he was holding seemed to vanish, though keen eyes could spot them rolling into a compartment located just above his wrist.

Warren was there before anyone could so much as speak, plunking down his orbs unceremoniously in Doctor Mechaniacal's now empty hands. This assessment was shorter, as it was clear even from a distance that Warren didn't have nearly as many orbs as Beverly.

"One thousand, four hundred and ninety dollars. Very good indeed, but as of now, you are in second place." Again the orbs vanished. As Warren trudged over to Balaam this time, the older man didn't look particularly happy with his apprentice's placing.

189

"I might as well get this over with," Lance announced, half-hobbling across the room and plunking a pocketful of orbs into the doctor's hands. There was plenty of copper and more than one silver, but not a gold in the lot was anywhere to be found.

"Six hundred and forty dollars," Doctor Mechaniacal announced. He refrained from commenting on the paltry sum as he and the rest of the room turned to Tori.

"Oh, yeah, I got nothing." Tori held up her hands to show they were empty. "I'll take the last spot. Bev is the big winner."

A snort, followed by boisterous laughter, filled the air, all coming from Balaam. "Well now, that is an interesting surprise. Looks like Pseudonym's puppy has as much killer spirit as her teacher. I can't say I ever recall anyone surviving the first trial and yet still coming back empty-handed. Truly, you *are* his pupil, aren't you?"

Despite all the work she'd been doing on keeping her power under control, Tori knew the air around her was heating up as she stared down the red-eyed jackass and his ear-to-ear grin. She didn't know which was more aggravating—him insulting Ivan or her. It sort of all got swirled together in the miasma of pissed off churning through her.

Tori's mouth was halfway open, her tongue already intent on telling Balaam to go fuck himself, when she felt Ivan's hand rest firmly on her shoulder.

"It seems you're right, Balaam. Though since my apprentice did pass the trials of survival, cunning, and temptation, I'd say she showed great potential in this weekend's activities. Not to mention she was the only one who took the reins and tried to lead. Prioritizing safety and survival over pocket change... no, I can see why you wouldn't appreciate the value in an apprentice like that. Luckily enough, I do."

Tori's tongue fell silent as Ivan's words drifted through the room. Balaam stared at Ivan with such unmasked hatred that, for a moment, she really thought the two of them were going to get into it right then and there. Given that Ivan had just displayed how powerful he still was in a *very* visible way, she didn't imagine things going well for Balaam if they did come to a head.

Clearly he reached the same conclusion. Balaam turned on his heel, swirling his red-and-black robes as he did, and began to march upstairs with Warren in tow. "Come, my Apprentice. Let us celebrate the good work you did, as well as discuss the ways you might improve."

Something in his inflection made Tori wince. She felt a kernel of pity for Warren as he was dragged up the stairs by his teacher. Could that have been her, if Ivan had passed on the task of being her mentor? No; from what he'd said, they likely would have simply killed her outright. At the time, she'd thought he was being dramatic just to keep in line, but over time, Tori had started to realize that there might be fates worse the one hanging over her head.

"Now that that unpleasantness has passed, I suggest you all celebrate," Doctor Mechaniacal informed them. "We'll have some fresh food and drinks brought down; no need to worry about trashing the tables. It happens so often during these things that we've learned to keep extras on hand. Enjoy yourselves. You must be famished from your time out there. Your money will be put into your respective bank accounts on Monday, with the added bonus going to Thuggernaut's apprentice for her exemplary performance."

Doctor Mechaniacal paused, walking over toward to the staircase that Balaam had ascended. Their teachers followed him, albeit a few steps behind. When the doctor reached the edge, he turned his helmet toward them once more. "Your teachers will each discuss your performance with you one on one, making sure you understand the lessons presented. But today, you have passed a hurdle toward guild membership, and as such, your involvement in our world will increase. Next weekend you'll understand what I mean. So take this time to rest and enjoy yourselves, deepen the friendship that has begun to bloom, and remember that not all obstacles can be overcome on one's own. That is a lesson the capes taught us firsthand, and it's a mistake this guild is dedicated to teaching you to avoid."

With that, he headed up the stairs, Thuggernaut, Arachno Bro, and Pseudonym all close behind. As they stepped out the door, Arachno Bro closed it firmly behind them, and Doctor Mechaniacal let out a long, low sigh of relief.

"Whew; the kids are taken care of. Now everyone to my quarters for the real party! I'm already there, waiting."

*   *   *

While Lance and Beverly were no doubt predominantly grateful to be back in a room with air-conditioning, with Lance being especially thankful for the handful of pain killers he'd been given for his injuries, it was the table of real food that filled Tori with gratitude for being back in the civilized world. Grabbing a paper plate, she darted for one of the tables they hadn't smashed and began piling it high with chips and sandwiches, even helping herself to a cold beer. After the ordeal they'd been through, she felt entitled to at least a little relaxation. Lance was only a few steps behind her, and Beverly quickly followed. None of them were on the verge of starving, but protein bars were a poor replacement for actual culinary creations.

Lance and Tori made it through two sandwiches and Beverly four before the eating slowed down enough for conversation to bubble up. At first, they talked about the insanity of their last robot opponent, all blown away by how strong it had been. This turned to a discussion of how they would have fought it if given enough time and preparation. Eventually, the discussion gave way to the same topic every new meta-human focused on sooner or later: their powers.

"I've been collecting bugs since I was a kid," Lance said, somehow managing not to slur a single word despite the ceaseless stream of chips entering his mouth. "We lived out in the deep country, and there was only so much to do after chores were finished. My granddad taught me about them, helped me learn the ins and outs of catching and respecting bugs. I kept it up even after moving to the city, as best I could. On the night of that big storm, I was in the museum's entomology exhibit when an old statue of a scarab started glowing. All I remember after that is a lot of buzzing, some loud noises, and then when I woke up, things were different." Tipping back a beer of his own, Lance cleaned it out in a single gulp, and then reached for a new one.

"Probably magic then, like me," Beverly surmised. "Did you get any weird scarab designs on your skin?"

"Not that I'm aware of, and no one mentioned it to me after I got checked out the next morning." Lance popped the cap on his beer using only his thumb, a motion so fluid that Tori could only imagine how many times he'd done it. "But weirdly they don't think it's magic. Doesn't give off the same vibes or whatever. The current leading theory is that it was some codex from an ancient civilization, but that's far from proven."

"Then I guess you're stuck in a mystery as well, at least as far as where your powers come from. How about you, Tori? You told me yours came from an accident, care to elaborate a bit more?" Beverly's tone was almost inhumanly polite as she pried into something that clearly wasn't her business. It was a strange contrast to the gruff way she acted when channeling her dragon powers.

"There isn't much to tell," Tori replied. "It was a few years ago, when I first started to work on the plans for my meta-suit. The hardest part of those things is creating a power source, you know. Any idiot can slap a rocket pack on a localized shield generator, but producing enough juice to run it is a big problem."

Beverly and Lance exchanged glances, as both were reasonably certain her idea of "any idiot" seemed to require someone with far more technical expertise than them.

"So I was trying to crack that part first; you know, why build a car frame if you can't make an engine? Most inventors use a meta-element like

192

blagrinite or setlium, but I wanted something more stable. Anyway, I had this idea about converting the organic life found all around us, germs and bacteria and the like, into energy via a chemical reaction. When I fired up my prototype, it turned out I'd made a few miscalculations. Overload, explosion, and poof: here I am."

"A self-created meta. I respect that. There aren't a whole lot of those out there," Lance noted. "I tried to ask Warren how he got his powers, but that guy apparently talks no more than he absolutely has to."

"Somehow that doesn't surprise me," Tori said. She wasn't sure how to feel about Warren. Sure, he seemed like a dick, but with Balaam as his teacher, it might be more reactionary and protective than malicious.

"I have to ask, did you ever figure out a way to power your meta-suit after that first failure?" Beverly had finished her plate of food and was absorbed in the conversation, leaning forward to carefully study the expressions of her fellow apprentices. Tori got the feeling it had been a while since Beverly was able to relax. Probably since the night she first turned into a massive dragon, if Tori were to place a bet.

"Well, yeah. I mean, my prototype didn't exactly go as planned, but it did give me my power source." Placing her own plate on the ground, Tori allowed her head and hand to engulf in fire, staring at Lance and Beverly as she did. "Fire's not the most efficient energy out there, but since I never run dry, it should still work fine for my purposes."

"Damn... you're going to use yourself as a battery." Lance took another long draw from his beer and nodded with approval. "That's smart. Kind of weird, and definitely outside the box, but smart. Starting to see why the guild thinks you're the one for us to beat."

"Maybe I was before, but as of now, Beverly is the one who cleaned house at the trials. I came in fourth," Tori pointed out.

"If I didn't know better, and I'm not sure I do, I'd think you planned it that way to get some of the pressure off you," Beverly said. Her tone was gentle, but a glint of suspicion twinkled in her eye.

Tori chuckled, turned off her flames, and picked her food back up. "I wish I could claim to have thought that far ahead. I might be—okay, I *am*—brilliant when it comes to electronics and mechanical stuff, but I'm awful at planning or scheming. I was basically flying by the seat of my pants out there, just like you two."

"My cynical side wants to doubt you, but it's pretty hard seeing as I was flying right there alongside you," Beverly admitted. "Though part of me wishes you were a schemer. It would be nice to believe one of us has this all in hand. That might have been all the flying my pants can take."

193

"Let's just hope all our pants last for the rest of training," Lance said. He lifted his beer up slowly, and after a minute, Tori figured out what he was doing. She tapped the glass of her bottle against his with a soft "clink." Moments later, Beverly joined their toast with the side of her soda can.

"To the apprentices." Lance's voice was subdued for a change, the sudden touch of gravity in his words making him seem far less jovial. "May we all become the people we want to be."

Everyone took a long drink, contemplating Lance's words and thinking about how much still lay ahead of them.

*   *   *

Like all parties held by the villains' guild, the one following the apprentices' first trial was filled with fine food, excellent liquor, and an endless sea of reminiscing. Soon it would turn to boasting, both about feats accomplished and of ones that would have been so, had things been different. Ivan never minded the boasting, even if he never saw fit to take part. He was fine with others reliving what they considered to be their glory days, riding the high of their previous adventures. If it kept them satisfied and obeying the code, he didn't care if they spent all day, every day bragging about what they'd done.

Not minding it wasn't the same as enjoying it, however. Shortly after they arrived at Doctor Mechaniacal's quarters, Wade's shock of copper hair visible even as the Doctor Mechaniacal suit walked itself into a power station to recharge, Ivan piled up a plate with decadent food and did his best to project an unapproachable air. This had nothing to do with magic or his powers; it was a skill that involved lots of vacant stares, frowning, and pretending not to see people when they waved at him. He'd developed it over the years and was quite proud of how effective it was. Sadly, some of his guildmates were simply immune to his talents, even when his frown was set the deepest.

"No cash, but your girl put on a hell of a show." Xelas plopped into a chair next to him, or at least pretended to. Had she actually dropped the full weight of her metal body on the chair, it would have been in splinters; Xelas was well-practiced at appearing to bound about as easily as any normal human.

Morgana arrived a few steps behind Xelas, settling down into her seat with a natural grace. "She did seem skilled at making them work as a team." Morgana had ignored the food, instead choosing to help herself to the bottles of wine Wade had set out. Each was worth thousands of dollars, and they were for most of the guests to avail themselves of. Wade had but one rule when it came to expensive wine: only those who would appreciate it were allowed to drink it. Curiously, no one knew what would happen if that rule was broken, as it had yet to come up. Few in the guild had the power to disobey Doctor Mechaniacal, and of those that did, none had the inclination.

Ivan slowly set down the small fork he'd been using to spear escargot. "Your congratulations are appreciated but would be better directed toward my apprentice. She earned her own glory this weekend."

"Ah, but we didn't come by to congratulate; we came by to give fair warning." Xelas's ever-present, playful smile deepened, a sight which pushed her toward the uncanny valley and often made those she spoke with uncomfortable. "Morgana and I have been talking it over, and I think the council ladies are going to take the new gals out on a test drive."

"Nothing unseemly," Morgana assured him. "Just a little meet-and-greet, since Thuggernaut's apprentice didn't get to sit in on a council session like yours did. Plus, we thought it might be fun to get to know them. A girls' night out, if you will."

Looking back and forth between the two women, Ivan picked his fork back up and speared a fresh snail. "Is anything I say going to change this?"

"You could fight us if you reaaaaaaaally wanted to, but is it worth the effort?" Xelas asked, leaning back slightly in her chair. "Besides, you know talking with council members is good for newbies. We can give perspective, help them make connections, and generally get them more comfortable."

"Your idea of comfortable is what I'm worried about." Ivan pointed at Morgana with his fork and the butter-coated morsel at the end of it. "Are you going to be in charge of this?"

"Would Doc let us do it otherwise?" Morgana shot back.

"Fair point. Then I suppose I have no objections, so long as I can have enough warning to account for it in her training schedule. Also—and I feel this should go without saying—don't get too attached. One trial does not a full member make."

"Come on. We're not the ones who're rookies. We know the deal." Xelas allowed her chair to hit the ground and rose fluidly to her feet. "I'll get you a date as soon as we talk to Thuggernaut. In fact, I see the big man over there by Johnny. Morgana, let's hustle."

"Thanks for being a good sport," Morgana said, smiling briefly at Ivan before Xelas half hauled her across the room.

Ivan popped the escargot into his mouth as he watched them go. Xelas was as brilliant as she was crazy—and the mechanical maiden was easily mad as a hatter—but she knew which lines were suggestions and which not to cross. Furthermore, Morgana was probably the most responsible person on the council, next to Wade, and if Gork was going too, then that would only make things easier. All in all, it likely would be an excellent opportunity for Tori to make connections and learn from experience.

In fact, it was so good he was a bit surprised there wasn't an effort underway to have a similar night with the male trainees. A moment's consideration and Ivan realized that would mean putting the apprentices around himself and Balaam with only Wade as a buffer. No wonder that idea hadn't been suggested. One night of that would be enough to make even the most dedicated apprentice throw their next trial just to find the sweet release of death.

Maybe Johnny could put something together, though. Ivan decided to speak with him about it; after his meal was done, of course.

Chapter 28

"Drop me off here." Tori pointed toward the coffee shop on the corner halfheartedly, her eyes drooping as she struggled to keep them open. In all the excitement and celebration of their victory the night before, it had completely slipped her mind that she had work in the morning. Ivan, however, had suffered from no such memory lapse. The heartless bastard had nearly dragged her out of her apartment, hustling her into the car with no concern for either her sleep-deprivation or mild hangover.

"There's coffee in the office." Ivan, despite having been out as late as Tori, looked just as ready for the day as he always did. She wasn't sure if it was an aspect of his powers or a learned skill; all Tori knew in that moment was that she hated him for it.

"There's cheap pisswater and non-dairy creamer in the office. My body will not accept any imitators today; only the real deal is going to get me moving." Tori tapped her finger carefully on the car's clock. "We're still twenty minutes early, and the office is literally across the street. I'm on my time, and I'd like to spend it funneling caffeine down my throat so I don't fall asleep at my desk."

The traffic light changed, and Ivan pulled the car forward. Making a split-second decision, he eased over into a free parking spot and motioned to the door. "Don't be late, and drink as much as you need to be functional. We're coming up on quarterly reviews, so there's a lot to get done."

"Yeah, yeah, when isn't there?" Tori popped the door open, unbuckled her seat belt, and slid out of the car before Ivan could change his mind. No sooner had the door shut than Ivan pulled back into the street, going all of thirty feet before taking the left turn into the company parking lot. While the sudden movement made her headache a bit worse, the fresh air filling her lungs helped her feel awake for the first time all morning.

Downtown Ridge City was a lovely place; the city went to great pains to make it that way. Carefully chosen trees were spaced out along the sidewalk, shading the dozens of corporate drones walking to their offices in the early morning sunlight. All of them wore slacks, polos, or suits like Tori's, and despite the fact that it was Monday morning, some had even donned smiles as well. The good mood was so contagious that Tori allowed herself a slight smirk of her own as she pushed open the front door of Ridge City Grinders.

The place had cleaned up nicely since the night of the confluence, or what almost everyone in town thought of as 'the big-ass storm'. While Ridge City Grinders had been flooded and lost most of its windows, there had only been a short delay before it reopened. In a town with this many capes, collateral damage was bound to happen, and as a result, people were used to putting things back together. It certainly didn't hurt that the AHC often funded cleanup efforts after a big bout of destruction.

Tori slipped into line and quickly scanned the board to see what seemed good. With chains, she always knew what she wanted, but in local shops, she tried to explore the specialties. Nothing really caught her eye as the line moved briskly forward, and before she knew it, Tori had arrived at the counter with no idea what she wanted to order.

"Morning!" The perky barista had short bleached-white hair and the name "Chloe" emblazoned on her apron. She was easily the cheeriest person Tori could ever imagine meeting on a Monday, let alone encountering in real life. "What can I get for you?"

"I... uh... shit. I sort of blanked out. What do you recommend?" From over her shoulder, Tori could hear the passive-aggressive shuffling and sighs from the people in line. If she'd been in their position, she'd have done the same, but this was how things were, so they were going to have to deal with it. She needed her damn coffee.

"Well, if you're looking to really wake up, we do some of the best espresso in the entire town. Smooth and tasty but with enough kick to get your day off right." Chloe, at least, was unfazed by the grumpiness in the line behind Tori. Tori could only imagine putting up with pissy, under-caffeinated corporate drones all day. She'd probably light someone on fire before the end of her first shift.

"Sounds great. Give me four. To go, please."

Chloe's blue eyes widened so much that Tori could make out the lines of her contacts and the telltale stripes of her brown irises underneath. "Are you sure you want that much?"

"I've got a good tolerance. Four, to go, please. The name on the order is Tori." Tori whipped out the debit card tied to her meager bank account and scanned it through the register, pausing to key in a decent tip for the cheerful barista who hadn't gotten mad at her for holding up the line.

Less than five minutes later, another worker called her name and handed her a tall cup filled with hot brown liquid. Taking a tentative sip, Tori noted that it was scalding hot—not that such things bothered her—but also surprisingly delicious. Usually the espresso she got had an acrid, harsh taste, but this one was mellowed out. From the way her heart rate increased the moment the first drop hit her tongue, it still had the expected kick too.

Tori lifted her cup to Chloe as she headed out the door, and the blonde barista replied with a big smile and a wave. All in all, it was a pleasant start to a

Monday. Tori headed toward the office feeling hopeful that just maybe this wouldn't be such a bad day after all.

*   *   *

Unnoticed by Tori as she walked from Ridge City Grinders to her office building, a blue sedan sat in front of a recently-expired meter. Its occupants noted her approach to the building just as they'd taken down all the comings and goings for the last several weeks. Ten years earlier, such behaviors might have seemed suspicious, but these days, three men in suits typing away on laptops just looked like a group that was trying to finish up a presentation before it was due. No one walking through downtown spared them more than a passing glance, forgetting about the men inside almost as soon as the sedan faded from view.

"Has the girl ever stopped for coffee before?" The man in the driver seat watched Tori make her way briskly across the street, gleefully chugging a beverage that he had no idea would scorch the roof of anyone else's mouth.

"Not since we've been watching." This came from the thinner man on the passenger side. He held a laptop on his... well, lap, with a spreadsheet program open. On it he noted the time Tori entered the building, next to a small note that she'd stopped for coffee, breaking her established pattern.

"Unexpected, but there's always going to be a few variables that are impossible to account for," Driver remarked. "On the whole, it looks like morning is still going to be our best window."

"Oh, come *on*, guys. Who does this kind of shit in the morning? Nighttime, that's when it'll look the coolest." These remarks came from the wide-shouldered man in the back seat who leaned forward and rested his elbows on either side of the center console. "We want to be taken seriously, don't we? We need to make sure this comes off as fucking sweet as possible."

Passenger punched in a few more keystrokes while Driver scanned the street, both of them doing their best to ignore Back Seat. Neither of them had been particularly happy about adding him to their plans, but there was no help for it. Annoying as he was, Back Seat was necessary if they wanted to succeed. After all, only an idiot went into an operation like this without a contingency plan for meta-humans. The damn things could hide in plain sight; anyone from the girl at the coffee shop to that nerdy red-headed programmer slipping in the building's side door could be one. It was impossible to tell, so the only sensible thing to do was to make sure they had one on hand.

"The slacking copper-top makes up the last of the early morning group," Passenger noted. "About fifteen people will be on the Vendallia

Industries' floor for the next twenty minutes. After that, the rest of the staff arrives to barely make it in on time."

"So this is our window. Get in and get things secured while the number is small enough to deal with." Driver carefully rested his hands against the wheel, thinking all the possibilities through. "Any variations in the last week?"

"Aside from the coffee, only minor ones," Passenger confirmed. "This timeframe is going to be our best shot."

A loud groan came from behind them and both men resisted the urge to turn their heads. "Seriously? This early? Fine, whatever, but this isn't going to impress anyone." Back Seat removed his elbows and leaned back, his sizable frame barely contained by the sedan's rear. "Should we just go do this thing, then?"

At last, Driver turned around to face the car's third member, a scowl visible even behind the designer sunglasses on his face. "We are most certainly not going to 'just do this thing,' either today or when the time comes. This is a carefully planned, formulated strike, and under no circumstances will we burst in there without proper preparation. Now that we know the best time to work in, we'll need to gather supplies, which will take—"

"About three days," Passenger interjected.

"About three days." Driver glanced away from Back Seat, staring at Passenger, who was still clacking away on his laptop. "Wait, really? Only three days?"

"I did most of the groundwork in advance. All that's left is to make and fill the orders… about three days. Which is good; we want to work as soon as possible, while our data is still fresh. If we wait, things might change."

"Huh." Driver swung around to Back Seat, who was grinning from ear to ear. "Okay then, looks like we'll be doing this in three days. Try to constrain yourself until then."

"You're the boss," Back Seat replied, using a tone that made it clear that while his words might be technically true, neither he nor anyone else believed them.

Driver ignored it, turning back to the steering wheel and twisting the ignition key. With a quick change of gears, he sped off into the street, narrowly avoiding the parking attendant who'd been coming over to write them up for the expired meter.

*   *   *

"Uuuuuugggghhhhhhh." The half-grunted moan came from Tori's lips as her head rested heavily on her desk. Her good mood and sense of optimism had both evaporated along with the caffeine high from her espresso. Several cups of the office coffee had allowed her to keep trudging along, but by the time she'd finally gotten enough time to eat lunch, she was seriously beginning to wonder if maybe it wouldn't be better to torch the office and just deal with the guild's retribution. The sole bright spot in her day had been getting the bank alert that Beverly had transferred over half of the weekend's winnings.

What Ivan had failed to tell her about "quarterly review week" was that the workload quintupled as they prepared charts, reports, and endless graphs explaining what they'd spent the last three months doing, all while performing the actual work for which the department was responsible. Adding on to that were the interviews every employee had to go through where they ensured they'd hit all their targets and sett new goals for the coming quarter. For most of the staff, those meetings were just one annoying hour. For management and management's overworked assistant, they ate up more time than a watch-devouring goblin.

"And miles to go before you sleep." Donald peered over from the slim wall that divided their desks and threw her a look of pity. He'd taken his own lunch hours before, as had most of the people not completely bogged down in the miasma that was quarterly reviews. "On the upside, they only make you do this once every three months, and it usually only lasts a week."

"Oh no. Fuck that. Fuck a whole wet sloppy mess of that. Next quarter, I am at least not going to be dealing with the management side of this." Tori lifted her head off the desk, bloodshot eyes brimming with determination. "If nothing else, I will be a regular employee and only have to deal with the simple side of things."

"Well, that'll be pretty easy to manage." Donald reached over to her keyboard and struck a few keys, quickly pulling up the company's home site. "Vendallia keeps an internal job board just for the employees to use. We're supposed to choose career paths and work toward them, so this lets us see what's available and what it takes to make it there; that way we can tailor our resume to fit it."

"That's surprisingly helpful," Tori said, skimming through the listings at the top of the page. Most of them demanded more formal education than she had, though a few allowed for time at the company and the passing of skill tests in place of a degree.

"Training costs money and lowers efficiency," Donald replied. "If they can keep everyone in-house instead of letting them learn skills and get recruited away, it works out better for the bottom line in the long-term. Nothing like dangling a carrot to keep us plodding along, you know?"

"Mmhmm." Her eyes kept flitting through the jobs one by one. Management was out of the question—she did not want to deal with these reviews again, and besides, they all demanded at least five years with Vendallia before one could even apply. The tech jobs, on the other hand, were well within her skill-level. Heck, she'd likely have to pretend to be worse than she was just to avoid arousing suspicion.

Donald leaned back, putting himself more in his cubicle than hers. "I'm glad to see you're thinking about staying. Be nice to still have a friendly face around, even after your internship is over."

"Oh. Right." Tori's hand stopped, finger frozen just above the mouse. Right... this was supposed to be temporary. She was only working here because of Ivan. Her apprenticeship, and therefore her internship, would end when she made it into the guild. After that, she wasn't required to work a regular job anymore. Granted, no one had told her what the other choices were, but she assumed they existed.

For the first time since Tori had been told she was in a "pass or die" situation, her mind turned to what would come after graduation. Could she work on her inventions in peace? Would she be required to participate in heists? Was there a crime quota? She'd been so focused on making it across the finish line, she'd never bothered to ask if the road on the other side was even paved.

Suddenly, the rest of the day's meetings were no longer the most bothersome thing on her mind.

Chapter 29

"A quota? Like, we make you mug so many people in a week? No, the guild doesn't impose a mugging quota."

Ivan set down Tori's plate across from her, the pork loin still steaming as butter from the peas melted against its side. He lowered his own dish too, piled high with food that Tori had quickly learned only represented a fraction of what had been cooked. The man could eat, there was no question about that, and as he took his seat across from her at the dinner table, his fork was already in his hand to do precisely that.

"Obviously not a mugging quota. I just meant..." Tori waved her hand through the air in wide, vaguely circular motions. "I don't know, some allotment of crime we had to fulfill. It is a guild of villains and criminals, after all."

"No, it is a guild of people who do not always enjoy the confines of the law and who prefer to stay out of jail and the ground." Ivan sighed then chewed a few bites of food before continuing. "Crimes are committed by members of the guild and organized on guild premises, but in case it has slipped your notice, the vast majority of your education has emphasized survival and not getting caught."

"I'd say you talked more about the code than anything else," Tori pointed out.

"What did you think I meant by 'survival'?" Ivan countered.

Tori swallowed; though, to be fair, she had also taken a bite of peas, so it could have been necessity rather than reaction. Either way, Ivan trusted his point was made and decided to put her mind at ease.

"You're going to learn the specifics this weekend, but essentially the guild functions as an organizer and approver of criminal plans. Someone comes up with an idea, puts together a proposal, runs it by those of us who have the experience to see any potential flaws, ideally receives approval, gathers a team, and then executes their job. At no point in that process is anyone forced to pull capers against their will. We even have an entire department and seat at the council to represent all of those who choose to have no involvement with criminal activity whatsoever."

"I sort of figured that was something you had to work your way into. Like, put in ten good years, you earn the right to retire," Tori admitted.

"Not at all. In fact, many of those who make it into the guild immediately put themselves in my department. Remember, Tori, the goal of this organization is not to increase crime: it is to make sure crimes are committed in a way that keeps us protected. Choosing to do nothing doesn't counter that philosophy, so it's a perfectly valid choice."

"I get it. I can opt to do jobs as long as I run them through the guild, or I can work a nine to five like you. The only thing I can't do is break the code, right?"

Ivan smiled slightly, a rare accompaniment to dinner, and nodded. "That is the sum of it. Upon graduation, the path you choose is up to you, so long as you stay within the guidelines we've provided."

"But I bet I'm going to have to pick up at least a little side work if I'm going to get the parts for my tech or pay off the loaners Doctor Mechaniacal put in the basement." Tori mulled it over as she chewed her pork. Now that she knew she wouldn't *have* to be a criminal, the idea wasn't nearly as scary. In fact, snatching some extra cash from time to time might be a useful option to have. "Tell me more about how jobs work."

"I think it can wait until this weekend. In some cases, it's better to show than tell." Ivan stood from the table, his plate miraculously clean, and headed for the kitchen. "Can I get you seconds on anything while I'm up?"

"Yeah, peas, please," Tori called. The mysterious job-talk had her curious, but after weeks with Ivan, she'd learned that when he said no to something, it was fairly permanent. Besides, after the spectacle that had been put on over the last weekend, she probably would rather just see whatever they had planned. Thinking of jobs did raise another concern, however. As Ivan returned with his freshly filled plate along with a bowl of peas for her, she decided that since they were already talking about the future, she may as well push her luck.

"Am I allowed to keep working at Vendallia after my apprenticeship is over? Or is it just a temporary thing, like my living here, and as soon as we're done I'm going to have to find some new job?"

Ivan stared across at her, his plate rattling slightly as he set it on the table. For a second, Tori couldn't read his expression, and then she realized why. She'd caught Ivan by surprise, which meant he was making a face she rarely got to see.

"To be honest, it never occurred to me that you'd want to," Ivan said at last. "Your work is fine, but you've never shown any interest in the company as a whole."

"I work in a cubicle farm for a faceless corporation. How much interest were you expecting to see?"

"Right around the exact amount you've shown, hence why I assumed you'd want to move on when your time was done," Ivan told her.

"Okay, I guess that's a fair point." Tori dragged her fork through the bowl of peas Ivan had brought out, trying to find the right way to phrase her curiosity. "I don't love it there or anything, but maybe it's not as bad as I'd thought. Well, except this week. This week is fucking awful. Overall, though, it's not such a terrible place to be. And if I wanted to keep at it, maybe even apply for a real job where I made good money and got to use my brain, I just wanted to know if that was on the table."

A slight clink filled the air as Ivan set his fork down, nicking the side of his plate in the process. "Tori Rivas is an employee of Vendallia Industries. Your identity is on file there. Your social security number. Your face on the badge. Tori Rivas, not my apprentice. Assuming your performance reviews are satisfactory and you don't do anything to get fired, there's nothing to stop you from staying with the company, regardless of role." Ivan picked his silverware back up but held it gently in his hand, not yet turning it on the food that still remained.

"That is the benefit of having an identity outside your guild one. That is why I forced you to be an intern in the first place. You have a place in the real, normal world now, and it's one that no one in the guild has the right to take away from you. They only have power over Apprentice, not Tori."

"Unless I fuck up and they kill me," Tori added, eating a forkful of peas to punctuate the statement.

"In that case, I would say Apprentice had to die and Tori was unfortunate collateral damage. But you've made it this far despite what others might have thought. Perhaps you should continue thinking about your future, lest it blindside you when the time comes. Oh, and pick a code name early on. Ever since Johnny slipped his through, we made the approval process more rigorous."

Tori snorted in spite of herself and barely managed not to spit peas across the table.

*　　　*　　　*

"Ren, my man, just the animal-human hybrid I was hoping to find."

Apollo slipped a friendly arm part of the way around Ren Tanaka's giant shoulders, somehow managing to hold on to his aura of authority even as he was dwarfed by the creature Ren had become. Scales had sprouted beneath his initial fur, and a long tail with a razor-sharp blade at the end swung freely from his rear. He'd also grown slightly, albeit more outward than upward as his already muscular, inhuman body easily packed on mass.

Around the break room, the other rookies shot them both dirty looks as Apollo led Ren into the hallway. In the past few weeks, it had become all too clear who the most powerful of the new recruits were, and the older capes hadn't bothered to hide the favoritism the frontrunners were receiving. These were the top choices, the first draft, and they wanted to keep them all happy enough to stick around.

For his part, Ren ignored the mutterings and glares, even though he could hear their movements so well he could even hear their displeasure in the creaking of their bones and blood. Adapting to his new senses had been one of the hardest parts of the transition, but after Data Mine created a special chamber to cut him off from the world when he slept, the worst was over.

"Ren, it's time we swing by the office of some people you're going to love because they make sure everyone else loves you." Apollo was as confident as ever as he guided the hulking giant through the spacious halls, made extra-large specifically for people like Ren. He beamed at everyone they passed, pearly white smile and golden glow both as intoxicating as ever. It was bullshit, obviously—no one was that cheery all of the time—but it was the sort of bullshit that was hard to call someone out on. There was no way to say a person was too cheerful without coming off as an asshole. Ren should know; he'd racked his brain trying to come up with a way.

"Where are we going?" Despite still having full use of his cognitive faculties (Ren was in fact starting to suspect that he'd gotten smarter), talking was still something of an ordeal. His tongue was wide and flat, not quite suited for making words as much as it was for cleaning his fur. But over the weeks he'd learned to manage basic communication, though every word took such focus and effort to pull out that these days he spoke briefly when he spoke at all.

"Why, right here!" Apollo let go of Ren's shoulders and pulled open the door to a large conference room. Standing inside were a man and a woman wearing matching dark colors in their professional clothing who stood as soon as they saw Ren. It wasn't a fearful leap. It was a respectful rising to acknowledge that he'd entered the room, and Ren found himself oddly appreciating it.

"Meet Jessica and Barney, the Alliance of Heroic Champions' top image consultants," Apollo explained quickly, shutting the door and slipping into a cushy leather chair. There was one next to him that was identical save for the fact that it was three times as large and no doubt heavily reinforced. Ren sat down in it as quietly as he could manage, sliding his bladed tail through a small slit in the back.

"And we are just thrilled to meet you," Jessica said, a slight southern twang under her sophisticated voice. Ren wasn't sure if anyone else could hear it or not; he was still working out just how different his senses had become.

"Sure are. Why, everyone we've met just tells us the best things about you." Barney was the first person Ren had ever met whose wide smile and ample enthusiasm matched Apollo's. He didn't quite have the act down as well, though, and Ren could see the small ways it was already wearing on him. Hopefully that would at least mean this was a short meeting.

"See, Ren, since we all know you've got what it takes to make it here at the AHC, I thought we should get a jump on everything so that once it becomes official, you can be ready to go," Apollo said. "And the first thing we have to nail down for any worthwhile superhero is their name."

Jessica and Barney both nodded along as Barney pulled a stack of files from his briefcase. "Given your imposing looks, we felt it was important to find a name that captures the essence of who you are while also making you accessible to a family-friendly audience," he told those around the table. "After several focus groups and some market testing, we got it down to a few."

"First off was Chimera," Jessica said, picking up smoothly where Barney left off. She snagged a paper and laid it down. The name and a graph of marketing data filled the page. "Now, technically there was already a Chimera back in the pre-AHC days. But since he died before any solid trademarks were filed and since chimeras are creatures of legend, we felt it would be an easy win, legally speaking. The problem is that Chimera doesn't test very friendly, and it's a bit on-the-nose given your powers."

"After that, we were leaning toward Grendel, an obvious allusion to Beowulf and well within the public domain; however, after seeing the test scores, we decided that we could do better. We could get you something that the people loved."

Ren could hear Barney's heart speed up as he finished his sentence, followed by Jessica's as she prepared to talk. This was the name they were really trying to sell him on; their bodies were giving away the nerves that their smiling faces masked. He wished they'd just hurry it up. Teeing up two toss-outs just to make him more receptive might be good for sales, but it was a pain in the ass to sit through.

"After going back to the drawing board, talking with some experts, and really poring through the people's reactions, we finally found what we were looking for." Jessica tossed down the paper, which, to her credit, did boast a graph showing far better numbers than either of the other two.

"Med-ley?" Ren asked, sounding out the word as he read it from the top of the page.

"That's right, Medley. A mixture of many things, but in a way that's harmonious," Barney said. "I have to tell you, people really reacted well to that name. It made them feel good, safe, and as though the person sporting it was someone to be trusted."

Both of them were staring at Ren now, fake smiles and eager eyes waiting to hear if they were going to have to spend more time on this kid who wasn't even fully in the AHC yet. Next to them was Apollo, who Ren found impossible to read, grinning in his own more practiced way.

The name was fucking stupid; there was no way they didn't know that. Ren looked like he'd escaped from a deranged zookeeper's nightmare, so they were trying to pin the most milquetoast name possible on him to balance out his image. He could still say no if he wanted to. He could tell them to take a flying fuck at the moon, pack his shit, and be out the door. But then what? His old life, his old body, all of it was gone. Ren Tanaka was dead in every way that mattered. This was his new world, his new life. What did it matter that the name was stupid? If it made some kid he pulled out of harm's way a little less scared, then that was worth it.

"Medley," Ren said again, this time getting the word out in one go. "I like it."

The wave of relief from Jessica and Barney was so tangible it nearly pushed Ren's chair back from the table.

Chapter 30

It was probably a good thing Ivan had forced Tori to get her sporadic heat bursts under control, because by the time Wednesday afternoon rolled around, she was so worn out and annoyed that half the office would have been suffering from heat stroke. As she marched down the dingily-carpeted hallway, a stack of files that it really would have made more sense to move digitally filling her hands, Tori kept focusing on not letting her frustration roll off her in palpable ways. Her morning espresso from Ridge City Grinders had already stayed hot in her hand much longer than it should have, so she was being extra careful.

"Delivery of more cr—stuff," Tori announced, barely stopping herself as she remembered they were in the Vendallia offices, not at home or the guild. Ivan either didn't notice the near slip or, most likely, chose to let it slide as he continued working on the small mountain of paperwork at his desk. He did pause his pen, but only long enough to motion to a free area on a filing cabinet where Tori could put the pages.

"And with this done, I am officially taking a coffee break." Tori set the pages down carefully, all too aware of how much time had gone into getting them properly organized and unwilling to do such a tedious job over again.

"Try to keep it in the building, there's still more to do."

"Hey, how I take my fifteen minutes is up to me. If you insist on having me do all this junk, the least I can do for my tired body is fill it with caffeine that doesn't taste like forgotten dumpster water," Tori replied.

Ivan looked up from the pages and glared at her, then slowly shut his eyes in resignation. "Vendallia policy is that you can go off-site if you so desire, so long as you're back at your station when the fifteen minutes are up, which I will check to ensure is the case."

"Deal!" Tori spun on her heel and was halfway out of the office before Ivan's voice called her back in.

"If I may ask, is the coffee over there really so much better than what we keep on hand?"

"As long as it's not counting against my fifteen minutes, you can ask me anything you like, boss." Tori stayed partway out the door, making it clear what her answer would be if she was talking through her break time. Ivan gave her a nod and motioned her back inside. She happily complied: any non-break time not spent working on quarterly reviews was fine by her.

"Yes, Mr. Gerhardt, the coffee over there is a lot better than what we stock. More varieties, more flavor, and just an all-around better product. The discount store barrel stuff they buy us here is probably great for the bottom line, but you can't really expect it to compete with the real deal."

Lowering his pen again, Ivan began scrawling something once more. For a second, Tori thought the meeting was over, but then Ivan ripped the sheet of paper off the notepad he'd been writing on and held it up.

"Take my company card and get me this order, please, along with whatever else you were going to get. Also, see if they do catering work, and if possible, grab a sheet with their prices and hours. I realize this will take longer than fifteen minutes, and as such, I won't be counting the coffee run as your break time." Ivan pulled his credit card out from his pocket and offered it to Tori along with the paper in his hand.

"What's with the sudden interest in java?" Tori quickly grabbed both items as she spoke, not about to give him the chance to change his mind. Free coffee and an actual break when she returned? This was, sadly, going to be the highlight of her day.

"Everyone has been working hard for the quarterly reviews, and I'd like to thank my department with a treat on Friday to celebrate reaching the end of things. I was planning on just getting donuts, but there's probably enough room in my discretionary budget to squeeze in some coffee too. Assuming it's as good as you say it is, I think it will do wonders to help lift people's spirits."

"Don't worry about that. I'll have Chloe make sure to hook you up with the good stuff."

Before Ivan could point out that he actually wanted to taste what their average product was like, Tori was out the door, this time determined to get clear before he could stop her. Ivan stared at the empty door for several seconds then turned his attention to the massive pile of work still looming before him. He really hoped the coffee turned out to be worthwhile. Tori wasn't the only one who could use a pick-me-up today.

*　　　*　　　*

Tori took her time heading across the street to Ridge City Grinders, a stark contrast to the brisk pace she would have used if she were on her actual break time. Her mind was filled with thoughts of wonderful caffeine and curiosity over what the weekend would hold when she was back at the guild. No matter how torturous it might be, there was no way it could compete with quarterly reviews. That much was obvious.

She was so distracted by her musings that Tori didn't notice the three men sitting in a sedan with open Chinese food containers on the dash, as they appeared to be nothing more than workers enjoying a quick lunch. Had she paid more attention, it might have struck her that this car had been parked around the area an awful lot.

"That Mexican gal sure does drink a lot of coffee," Back Seat noted as they watched Tori head in and greet Chloe with a wave.

"Pretty sure the term is Hispanic," Driver corrected, barely looking up from his container of noodles and pork.

"Actually, I believe in recent years the more acceptable phrase has shifted to Latino or Latina, depending on the person's gender," Passenger pointed out. "Though Dirk would actually be in the right with Mexican, assuming he had knowledge that she was from Mexico."

"Hey, I've got a question: why do either of you give a shit?" Dirk, the man previously known as Back Seat, laid his sizable arms on the seats of his companions, making his weight felt so he couldn't be ignored.

"Saying it wrong just sounds ignorant. We might be robbers, but we're not assholes. Do you want to be like that cape who flies around in the mechanical Klan suit?" Driver said.

"Shit, man, I was just asking. Don't put me in the same league as the Whitest Knight." Dirk pulled away and rested his back against the rear of the seat, causing the car's suspension to shift visibly from the outside. "I'm just bored back here. We already know the schedule, why aren't we busting in and getting things done?"

"Because it's not Friday, when we'll have all the gear we need," Passenger informed him. "So our time is best spent acquiring as much information as we can. The better we know the people who'll be in the building, the easier it will be to handle them. Besides, if any of them happen to be metas, there's always the off-chance that they'll slip up and show us their powers."

"Though I think Abner is being pretty hopeful with that one," Driver added. "Then again, we did have that freak storm a few weeks back. Never know who might be still figuring their shit out."

Dirk chuckled and tried to pop his knuckles, though he only succeeded in producing weak sounds from the middle and index finger of his right hand. "Don't you worry about that, Nelson. I've had years to learn how to handle myself. No newly-turned meta is going to be a challenge for me."

Abner sighed from his spot in the passenger seat and made a few clicks on the keyboard. "A new meta would be fine. We have to worry about someone with actual practice hiding among them. Though, given that we're expecting a staff of maybe fifteen during our operational window, the odds of that are staggeringly low. The chances of anyone in that building having meta powers are practically zero, especially ones strong enough to interfere with our plans. No one with any real juice would spend their time working in a dreary office."

Abner didn't know it, but in a way, he was dead right. On the day of their heist, there would not be *one* meta in the offices of Vendallia Technologies with them.

There would be four.

*   *   *

When Beverly had gotten the offer to stay on guild premises during her apprenticeship, she'd immediately steeled herself for a worst case scenario. Her parents, both Marines, had told Beverly enough stories about their time in boot camp to give their daughter a healthy fear and respect of the lifestyle. Since that was the military and these were freaking villains, Beverly had gone in expecting to get a cot, a toothbrush, and a communal shower if she was lucky. What Beverly had failed to take into account was that criminals often turn to such activities to feed their hunger for a life of luxury, and in a guild full of them, that nature tended to impact how rooms were designed.

Her shower complete, Beverly changed into a t-shirt and yoga pants and tossed the damp towel into the laundry hamper, where it would vanish in the morning only to be replaced with a fluffy new one by lunch. The steam from her bathroom, small but private, was still wafting into her room as she slipped into the hallway. Shutting the door on her bed, computer, television, and moderately-sized bookshelf, Beverly charted a course for the nearest communal area. When she first arrived, they were places she had avoided, but once she realized no one was going to jump out and attack her, Beverly had grown bolder. Besides, after the weekend she'd had, it was becoming clear just how important making friends could be.

The break room on their floor was ostensibly only for rookies who hadn't yet made the cut. As such, it was more sparsely furnished than the ones she'd seen on other floors: just a pool table, foosball table, game rack, big flat screen, Indigo Gamesystem 4, couch, recliners, stove, oven, fridge, and pair of vending machines with sodas and snacks. Because this room was often without occupants, many of the other villains still ducked in out of habit. Plus, the sodas in the machine were only a quarter, which Beverly was pretty certain made it the last of its kind in the known world.

This evening, she could hear the sounds of explosions echoing down the hall long before she set foot inside. Sure enough, perched on the couch with a controller in one hand and a bag of chips in the other was Lance, whose on-screen avatar was shot in the head just as Beverly got a good look at the screen. A respawn counter popped up and Lance set down the controller, turning toward the soda machine and finally noticing Beverly.

212

"Hey! What's up?" He hopped off the couch and practically threw a quarter into the soda machine. He grabbed the resulting root beer and raced back before the counter ran down.

"Not much. You playing with Arachno Bro again?" Unlike rookies, Arachno Bro had an IG4 in his room and played via online hook-up. At first, Beverly had taken it as an antisocial way to game until Lance explained that Arachno Bro had to use a specially-designed controller due to his arachnoid hands and was a bit self-conscious about it.

"We've got Xelas on too, though to be honest, I'm not sure if she even uses a controller. I swear I saw her walk by when her character was taking out an enemy sniper." Lance popped the top on his drink, grabbed his controller, and waded back into the action as his muscular, gun-toting avatar reappeared on screen. "But man, this is a tough match. Most of the others are good, but they've got one guy who—motherfucker!"

On-screen, a creature that looked like a teddy bear mixed with a lizard darted by, not even pausing as it shot Lance's tough guy straight through the skull. A new respawn counter appeared, and Beverly fought to resist the urge to chuckle as Lance seethed at the screen.

"I don't know who Don Doomald is, but I wish I could send a swarm of bees to that dude's house. He is freaking tough. They just opened up the shooter arenas in *Legacy World*, and the damn guy plays like he's been doing it for years."

"Maybe he does a lot of shooter games," Beverly pointed out. She pulled a half-eaten sandwich out of the fridge and plopped down next to Lance. Oddly, no one had ever touched her food, even when she left it in the communal area. She wasn't sure if it was courtesy or just pragmatism (not everyone ate things that were technically "food"), but she appreciated it all the same.

"Please. I've played my way through every game in the *Blaster Brah* series twice; that wouldn't account for this kind of skill. Besides, judging by his level and gear, this guy is dedicated to the MMO. The expansion only came out a couple weeks ago, and he's already at max level and wielding a top-tier staff of explosions. This is someone who has logged more hours on this game than Thuggernaut has at the gym."

"That's not a hard bar to hit; Thuggernaut doesn't go to the gym much. His muscles are just a power side effect," Beverly informed him.

"Well, just pretend I said something more fitting then, because I'm going back in." Lance held his controller at the ready as the timer ticked away once more. He licked his lips and narrowed his eyes, ready for the instant his character reappeared. The time came at last. His avatar lifted what looked like a steampunk rocket launcher high on his shoulder and raced across the forest map

213

they were playing on, big legs pumping and camera spinning as he searched for a target. It was thanks to the spinning camera that Lance caught sight of the teddy bear/lizard just before his character's head was separated from his shoulders.

"Dude, are you fucking trying to sink us?" Xelas appeared outside the break room, glaring at Lance while her bird-like character swept down from the trees and rained fire on the screen.

"No! That little shit keeps getting the drop on me."

"Then start looking around a little instead of running blindly through the jungle. Whoever wins this match has a chance to get the Vorpal Wings, and I will be downright *incensed* if you keep me from flying around and cutting people's heads off. Pull it together. We like you, but it's not too late to dump you in a river." Xelas pointed at her glowing eyes, then at Lance, then back at her eyes. Beverly was reasonably sure that this was the metallic woman's way of saying she was watching him.

Lance, for his part, took a deep breath, along with a drink from his root beer, as he tried to calm down and focus. Beverly found it strangely amusing that in this hive of scum and villainy, the biggest issue of the night was getting beaten in a video game. The longer she hung around this lot, the more she was starting to see the people underneath the reputation. Slowly she was coming to realize that the guild might be more than just a way to get her powers under control.

That was a thought for the future, however. For now, Beverly focused on eating her sandwich and watched Lance desperately try to stay alive.

Chapter 31

Chloe moved quickly but carefully as she set up the cups, real sugars, fake sugars (pink, blue, *and* yellow), straws, creamer, and, of course, cardboard sleeves to keep people from burning themselves. Her large cart, formerly burdened with all of those necessities, still held the equipment for making the actual coffee, but that would come in a moment. People liked their java hot, and Ridge City Grinders made a point of delivering that.

Mr. Gerhardt, Tori's oddly serious boss, had explained that people tended to filter in depending on their personal responsibilities in the morning, so the bulk of the office would arrive a bit later than he and Tori. In Mr. Gerhardt's estimation, she'd only need one carafe of coffee to start, but once the others started rolling in she'd need to get brewing as fast as she could. Chloe had, of course, happily agreed. Rebuilding the coffee shop hadn't been cheap, and her boss had made it clear that scoring more catering gigs like this one would help bring in a lot more cash. He'd probably have done the job himself just to make sure it went well if not for the fact that Chloe had struck up something of a friendship with Tori, who'd brought them the work in the first place.

"Yo, how's it coming?" Tori poked her head around the edge of the break room, a wide grin on her face. As they'd let Chloe into the building and helped her up the elevator, Tori had explained that this was the final day of a very shitty week, so the overall mood in the office was likely to be ridiculously cheery. It seemed that even extended to her, as her often-somber veneer had been replaced by one verging on bubbly.

"Should have the first batch up and ready to go in five minutes," Chloe explained. "Is anyone going to mind if I move your usual equipment?" Chloe nodded to the drip-coffee maker on the counter where a half-full pot of unpalatable room temperature liquid sat undrunk from the previous day.

"I personally wouldn't care if you threw the fuuuuu—er, *freaking* thing out the window. But better go check with the big man first, just to make sure. This place has some ridiculous rules about safety, I don't want to get you in trouble." Tori checked over her shoulder to make sure no one had caught her nearly cursing and then headed down the hallway toward Ivan's office.

She passed by Donald as he unpacked his laptop when three people in motorcycle helmets burst out of the elevator, quickly targeting the employees with the weapons in their hands.

"Everyone stay calm and put your hands on your heads! If no one does anything stupid, you're all going to get out of here just fine. If you get any ideas about being heroic..." The speaker, his sex betrayed by his voice, lifted his gun overhead and fired a single shot into the ceiling. While he spoke, his shorter companion ran through the cubes, forcing those few people at their desks to stand. The biggest of the lot lumbered his way down to the offices.

Tori forced herself to stay calm. She was so close to Donald that there was no way he wouldn't notice a spike in heat. Instead of being angry, she focused on thinking the situation through. The group was wearing masks and thus hiding their identities, so there was at least a chance they meant what they said about letting everyone go. The rest of their bodies were covered in leather with oddly-shaped bumps inside: most likely some kind of body armor. At the moment, they were herding everyone together, and the main guy's warning shot had been into the ceiling, not a human being. While she could probably tear all three of them apart without so much as a scratch, the same couldn't be said for her coworkers. Everything pointed toward playing along, at least until she had a better understanding of the situation or found an opportunity to strike.

Moments later, she got confirmation that her thoughts were at least somewhat on point. Ivan calmly walked down the hall in front of the big one, hands on his head, his expression so calm that it was like this was just another day of performance reviews.

"This is the only one in the offices," said the big one in a clearly-male voice. Tori would lay odds that the third was male as well, but it was impossible to tell under all the padding.

"Guess that makes you the man in charge," said the middle-sized one, who Tori suspected to be the leader.

"Normally, no; I'm merely middle management." If Ivan was at all nervous, he hid it well. She noticed his eyes quickly scan the room, making sure everyone was unharmed—at least so far. "However, given that you are the one with the gun, I would say that for today, you're the man in charge."

"That is exactly right. You seem like a pretty smart guy. Just keep acting smart and we can all get out of here safe and sound. Do what we say, keep it simple, and don't try to be a hero."

Tori felt fairly certain she was the only one in the room who noticed the slight tug at the corner of Ivan's mouth before he responded. "I can assure you that is the last thing I ever intend to be."

"See, what'd I say? Smart guy. Now, tell all your people to gather up in the break room. They'll be watched over by one of my guys while you come along and give us a hand. Your cell phones are jammed, landline is cut, and the exits are sealed, so it's just us here today." The man motioned to his smaller accomplice, who slowly and firmly herded people back toward the break room.

"May I ask what it is you're after?" Ivan was still calm, but his attention was split as he watched his employees being corralled. Barb, the

216

pleasant woman from HR whom Tori had learned was obsessed with her pugs, was taking a little long, resulting in the small criminal jabbing her in the ribs with their gun. Barb let out a small yelp of pain and hurried along.

The blow was largely for show, even if Barb would no doubt have a bruise later on, but Tori felt her inner fire try to rise up all the same. That was expected, though; that was who she was. What took her by surprise was, for a fleeting moment, the twitch of an expression on Ivan's face that she'd almost never seen before. As Barb yelped and everyone half-glanced at her, Ivan's mask slipped ever so slightly. What lay beneath it was nothing but naked fury. He was beyond livid at what these people were doing.

In that moment, Tori knew with unequivocal certainty that no matter what these three thought, this day would end in blood. And some of it, if not all, would be theirs.

"Now why would I go and bother telling you a thing like that?" The group's leader had obviously missed what Tori had caught, otherwise he'd have either emptied his clip in Ivan's skull or started running as fast as he could. Neither would have saved him.

"This floor of our company deals in software, so if you're here to steal something related to that, I'd need to talk to one of our programmers," Ivan explained, his veneer of calm fixed firmly in place once more. "Depending on the extent of what you're trying to take, I might need to bring one along. As I said, I am only middle management, so I have my technical limits. I'd hate for this to come up later on and you take me as being uncooperative."

"Don't you worry about that. We know exactly what we're here for. You just do as you're told and everything will be fine." The leader swung his head around slightly and nodded at the big thug behind Ivan. "Go help round everyone up, then keep an eye on the lot while we handle everything else. If they're good, then be nice. If not... well, we warned them."

A light tug on Tori's wrist pulled her attention from the conversation. Donald, laptop bag still slung over his shoulder, was trying to head toward the break room and he'd grabbed the cuff of her jacket to pull her along. Much as she loathed to leave the scene before her, Tori let herself be led away. Ivan would be fine with two wannabe criminal masterminds. Hell, Ivan could probably take on half the AHC and be okay. The others, however, weren't legendary villains hiding in plain sight. They might need looking after. And with the man formerly known as Fornax otherwise occupied, it fell to his apprentice to handle that job.

The big guy followed them into the break room and positioned himself in front of the entrance. There was no door to lock—something to do with fire safety—but with his wide shoulders, he easily filled the role. If not for

Thuggernaut and some of the others in the guild, Tori would have thought him huge. As it was, she still wondered if he was a meta. It might change how she acted when things went bad, but at the moment, it had no impact. She was just going to be good and sit between a pale Donald and a clearly nervous Chloe.

Tori would wait. Like a jungle cat crouched in the grass, she would wait.

*   *   *

Ivan was sorely tempted to kill both his captors the minute his colleagues were out of sight. None of these idiots were with the guild; Vendallia was a well-hidden subsidy of Indigo Technologies, and as such would never be approved for a job. It would be akin to robbing one's own piggy bank. The only thing that stopped him from tearing the taller one's arm out of its socket and beating the other to death with it was the simple fact that he was here as Ivan Gerhardt. Not Pseudonym, and certainly not Fornax. If he ripped these two into shreds there would be a lot of questions and attention on him. His best bet was to wait it out and see if he could find a way to handle them in a way an office drone in his forties could easily do. Ideally, he'd be able to pin the glory on someone else, but the odds for that were shrinking by the moment.

"Everyone else is in the break room," said the smaller one, a high, somewhat nasal voice emanating from under the helmet. Ivan imagined it was a struggle for him to move under all that padding and leather. Slow reaction times, then… something to keep in mind.

"And now we get to see just how smart you really are. You're going to take us to your office and log on to the protected system, the one where Vendallia can access every fancy design or piece of code that's ever been put together." The leader motioned with his gun back down the office hallway and Ivan complied, even as everything fell into place.

Vendallia did work across a dozen industries, but with the effort these three were going through, they either had to be after data for banks or national security. A bank was far more likely, as they seemed at least smart enough to avoid pissing off the entire government. So they were likely bank robbers after the security protocols to bypass a bank's electronic deterrents. If Ivan were a betting man, he'd have guessed that they were killing two birds with one stone and using this as a trial run of their robbery.

The walk to his office was a short one. Without prompting, Ivan sat at his desk and reached for the computer. A *click* hit the air just before his fingers made contact. Ivan glanced up to see the taller one had pulled the hammer back

218

on his gun. Given that he was holding an automatic, it was a pointless gesture done purely for the drama, but Ivan lifted his hands skyward all the same.

"I'm sorry, I thought you wanted me to log in?"

"We do, but that's all we want you to do. No trying to send out a call for help."

The smaller man reached over and quickly typed on Ivan's computer. He had to give them credit; they'd certainly done their homework. It took no time until the secure server's log-in screen flickered up, at which point the short criminal pulled back and offered Ivan the keyboard.

"Now it's your turn," said the leader, waving his gun at the keyboard.

Ivan tried to pretend he wasn't insulted by the implied need for direction; instead, he simply went to work. The server they were after was tied to one of Indigo's, which meant it had been built by Wade. As a criminal himself, no one was more safety-conscious than Wade Wyatt. As such, every member of the guild who worked a mundane job was given two access codes for secure systems: one to actually access them and one to log in to a dummy screen designed to stall anyone who went hunting for data while simultaneously alerting the guild.

If he really wanted to get out of this unscathed, accessing the true system was the right call. These men clearly hadn't come with the intent of killing, and whatever they took could be documented and dealt with. It was the safer choice.

Without hesitation, Ivan entered the second password. These three idiots had stepped into his office and pointed guns at his employees. They'd unknowingly walked into the territory of monsters far beyond their comprehension. A debt had been incurred, and Ivan would see it paid in blood before the day was done. He might be nothing more than a lowly dog of the guild, but he was at least a guard dog.

"You're in," Ivan lied, pulling his hands away from the keyboard.

"Nicely done," the leader told him. "We'll leave my friend here to work while you go join your colleagues. Just a little while until we get what we want, then you're all free to start an early weekend."

Moving slowly, hands still visible, Ivan stepped out of his chair and yielded it to the smaller robber, who hopped in and began typing without so much as a pause. The guy was obviously good. In other circumstances, Ivan might have offered him a job. Sadly, with a few notable meta exceptions, dead men didn't code very well.

The leader walked Ivan into the hallway, away from the offices and toward the cube farms. His gun was still there, always close enough to Ivan not to miss but far enough away that it couldn't be taken. Certainly not an amateur,

Ivan had to give him that. Yet to make such a stupid mistake as to come in here... it seemed fate had decided this man's time was up. And really, no time like the present. They were apart from his friends and Ivan's colleagues with no witnesses to what would occur. Taking down two armed men? Impossible. Getting a lucky shot off? Unlikely, but a lot more believable, especially now that Wade was aware of the situation and would doctor all records as needed.

"May I ask you a question?" Ivan's tone was as peaceful as ever, and he kept moving with the same slow, plodding pace.

"You just did," replied the hostage-taker.

"Then another one. Did you know, when you came in here? I'm honestly curious. Did you have any idea just whose property you were stepping onto? I dearly want to believe you're just unlucky, but part of me wonders if you really are just that stupid."

"You think I'm scared of some big corporation? Money won't stop bullets."

"There are worse things than bullets." Ivan stopped walking and turned slowly around. He couldn't see the man's face through the helmet but he could hear his heartbeat quicken. Fear was spilling off him as he came to realize the situation was not as in control as he'd thought. Deep within Ivan, in a part he'd worked so very hard to seal away, something rattled against its cage, and the echoes resounded all the way to Ivan's brain.

"What do—" Those were the only words the robber got out before Ivan's hand wrapped itself around his neck like a vice. The power was bubbling up, and he knew that the last thing this man would see were his eyes, pitch black save for the glowing red runes.

"Sshhh." His voice was like a whisper from the shadows of an abandoned cemetery. "Time to suff—"

The *crack* of the gunshot cut him off. Ivan turned his altered eyes downward in disbelief. Somehow, through all the terror and asphyxiation, the son of a bitch had kept his head and squeezed off a shot. Of course, the bullet had bounced harmlessly off Ivan's skin, but he could already hear the people in the break room stirring. There were only seconds to work with... otherwise his entire life outside the guild would be nothing more than ash.

"Fucking hell." In one motion, Ivan snapped the man's neck and dropped him to the floor. An instant later, he fell down as well, casting a minor illusion as he went. By the time he landed, it appeared to anyone looking that he'd been shot through the side of his stomach and was slowly bleeding onto the carpet. His hand snagged the dented bullet; in seconds it was burned away to vapor.

Thinking quickly, he also scorched a few words into the carpet. If luck was on his side, it would fluster the robbers enough that they wouldn't see the real threat. Plus, it would be interesting to see how his apprentice handled herself. Training opportunities like this were few and far between.

Chapter 32

Everyone in the room started at the sound of the gunshot, even the large man blocking their way. He started to lunge from the doorway, clearly intent on racing out, but stopped long enough to turn back in their direction.

"Nobody move, nobody try anything." He punctuated this point by slapping his palm on one of the break room tables, shattering it to splinters. Admittedly, they weren't exactly made from the finest of materials or the highest construction standards; however, it still got the message across. He was strong, and he could do the same to their bodies just as easily.

For Tori, she actually found some comfort in seeing him use his power. Like any good scientist, the more information she had, the more she could do with it. Knowing the big guy was a brute meant he'd be tough to bring down through physical means, but what he could manage was limited. She'd already hit on an idea to incapacitate him, assuming she could get the opportunity. By her estimations, Ivan had gotten a similar chance and taken it.

"What are you doing?" Chloe's voice drew everyone's attention. The bodies in the room noticeably stiffened as they realized Donald had slipped his laptop out of its bag and was rapidly typing away on the keyboard. Barb whimpered under her breath, huddling closer to one of the Stans—the one with the bushy mustache.

"The wireless is down, but I saved a few local copies, just in case." Donald glanced up from his screen and nodded at the door. "Can... can someone tell me when he's coming back? I think I have enough time, but I need to be sure."

"Enough time for what?" Tori's question was barely out before Stan started coughing into his hand. Without pause, Donald slapped the laptop shut and slid it back into his case. By the time the hulking figure appeared in the door again, it was like the device had never been removed.

"All of you, come with me," demanded their captor. His voice was different than before, more tense. Something had gone off-plan, and Tori needed exactly one guess to know what. Or rather, who.

Everyone in the room stood and filed out. The Stans went first, the clean-shaven one slightly ahead of his mustached counterpart who was trying to comfort Barb; then, of course, went Barb herself. Rene and Carol, two of the programmers in Ivan's department, went next. Tori tried to angle herself so she could bring up the rear, making her the muscle-man's first target if things went bad, but Donald slipped behind her as Chloe moved forward, leaving himself in last place. That idiot. What was he thinking? This was not the time to pretend to be a hero.

Thankfully, no one was assaulted as they were marched into the cublicle area. That was a lucky break, as they'd all have been caught off guard, so absorbed were they with the sight that met their eyes.

Ivan was lying on the ground, a small pool of blood leaking from a gunshot wound in his side. His chest was still moving, so they weren't supposed to take him for dead, but he did look paler than Tori recalled. When this was over, she'd have to ask him how he faked an injury with so little time.

Next to Ivan, limbs splayed akimbo, was the very evident corpse of the man who'd been leading the criminals. His helmet had been removed by the shorter goon, and they could see his face. It wasn't one that would stick in any of their heads, partially because it was nondescript, but mostly because the jagged angle of his neck made it hard to stare at.

Shocking as both bodies were, it was the scene next to them that really drew one's attention. Burned into the cheap office carpet were three words, small tendrils of smoke still curling up from the edges:

You Missed One

"Do any of you know about this?" The big man was behind them, waiting for someone to show a single sign of recognition. He was angry, that was easy to tell, but he was also scared. This was a strange scene to walk in on, one that hinted strongly at exactly one possible solution: there was an uncaptured meta loose in the building.

"All I know is Mr. Gerhardt's bleeding out pretty quickly. If we don't stabilize the wound, he might die." Tori slid her foot slightly forward without taking the actual step. Showing intention was probably acceptable, but they might try to shoot her if she acted without permission. In a crowd this tight, even if it went through her fire-form, it would still end up hitting someone.

"Why do I give a shit about that?" The rumble of his voice was directly behind her, and Tori had a feeling that if he didn't like the answer, a gun wouldn't come into the equation. She could take this chucklefuck, but not without giving away what she really was. And letting that secret slip might *actually* get her killed.

"Because whatever did this, Mr. Gerhardt might have seen it," Tori shot back. "If we can get him stabilized and wake him up, then he can tell you what happened. Or do you prefer going up against something that can do... that—" Tori gestured to the corpse on the ground "—with no knowledge about it whatsoever?"

"Or maybe he's the one who did it," the smaller one piped up, turning its gun toward Ivan. "Maybe he's a meta, and we should just gun him down right now."

"Whoever heard of a meta that can snap bones but gets put down by a handgun?" Donald asked, piping up just when Tori didn't want him to. "We've all worked with Mr. Gerhardt for years, he's never done anything remotely unnatural. Plus he's literally bleeding out on the ground! Do you think he managed to carve an ominous message in the carpet while he was shot?"

The crowd muttered in agreement, and Tori could feel both of their captors grow tense. Taking hostages was one thing, killing them was another. Once death was on the table, being good little boys and girls didn't seem like quite as smart of a play. With the possibility of a pissed-off meta in the building, the last thing they needed was an unruly crowd to deal with. Killing them all was an option, but one that removed any leverage they might have if the threat did turn out to be real. The wheels in their heads were almost audible as they spun, until at last the small robber moved his gun away from Ivan.

"Where's the first aid kit?"

"Break room," Tori replied quickly.

"Take him back in there then, get him patched. I want to know the minute he's conscious. Everyone else is going with my big friend there. He's going to put you in an office so we can make sure all of us stay safe. While they're in there, I want someone combing through the HR records of every person who works here; see if any of them are self-outed as meta."

"But that's confidential," Barb protested, earning her a sight down the barrel of the small one's gun. To his credit, Stan pulled her closer, doing as best he could to put himself between her and the bullet.

"Looks like we know who'll do the searching. Take them to the office next to the one I'm using. I'll make sure the girl and the boss man are properly restrained." He waved at the hallway, and the large man started herding the group back toward the offices.

"I'm going to need some help," Tori protested. "I can't just drag him across the floor. He needs to be lifted and carried carefully if you want him to live long enough to talk. I can manage with two others, unless you feel like helping out."

"Fine," snapped the shorter one. "You, coffee girl, you come help. And ginger-boy, you too."

Chloe and Donald broke off from the pack and went with Tori to stand over Ivan. He was still breathing, though the motions of his chest seemed to be getting more shallow. Somehow she doubted Ivan intended to fake his own death, so it probably wouldn't get much bleaker looking than this. Not unless the situation demanded it.

"Donald, you're on legs. Chloe, take his left arm; I'll get the right," Tori ordered. Together, they lifted Ivan off the ground and delicately hauled him to the break room under the watchful gun of the littlest hostage-taker.

As soon as they'd set him on the clean linoleum floor, the robber went to work. He pulled zip ties from his pockets, cuffing Donald's hands to the fridge and Chloe's to the front latch of the soda machine. Tori he left free as she went to the clearly marked area on the wall and pulled out the first aid kit. Only after she'd set it down next to Ivan did he take one of her hands as well, tethering her to the nearby cabinets.

"You'll need one free to work with," he explained, rooting though her supplies to make sure there was nothing sharp. "But try anything stupid and a bullet is going in each of your heads. I don't know what's going on. I just know that if something wants me dead, then I'd rather take people out with me. Clear?"

"Completely," Tori said. Chloe and Donald both nodded from their spots in the corner.

With order firmly established, the small man left, presumably to check on his accomplice. This left Tori with the task of trying to figure out how to give first aid to a man who was faking injury.

The only silver lining she could see was that, even as badly as the day had gone so far, it was still marginally better than doing more quarterly reviews.

*   *   *

"Doctor Mechaniacal, sir?" Isotrix stuck his head tentatively through the office door where Wade was working. One of the upsides to being an eccentric genius inventor and head of a company was that no one at Indigo Technologies ever questioned his need for a private, off-site work area. Granted, they didn't know its location was actually smack dab in the middle of a guild full of former or potential villains that he'd helped found, but the only person he technically had to divulge that to was the IRS, and even then only if he wanted to take a deduction.

"What can I do for you?" Wade didn't bother to look up from the device on his work table; there was nothing that could be said which would require enough attention to draw his focus. Besides, he wanted to get this doodad knocked out early. After it was done, he'd have to find enough ways to dumb it down so that Indigo could replicate and manufacture it, which took far longer than the actual inventing, and then have it properly tested and marketed by the time Christmas rolled around.

"We got a ping on the security network, one of the high priority ones. Assistance teams are already mobilized, but this was on the list of networks you wanted to be personally notified about." Isotrix shuffled from foot to foot; even after spending four years as Wade's assistant, he still felt awkward interrupting the man's work.

"Wait, don't tell me. It's the one tied to Pseudonym." Wade let out a sound that was a strange combination of chuckle and exasperated sigh as he shook his head.

"That's correct, sir. Did someone already tell you?"

"No, just a hunch. When you've been at this for as long as I have, you learn to play the odds. And the odds always say that if there's trouble, he'll be a part of it." Wade set down his tools and turned to Isotrix, an act that only made the younger man grow somehow more tense. "Tell the teams that he's more likely to need cover-ups and explanations than extractions. First priority is containment of his and his apprentice's identities. Have them tweak personnel as necessary to make that happen."

"Right away, sir." Isotrix nodded so quickly that he inadvertently gave himself a headache. "Should they begin breaching immediately?"

"Oh, I'd give it a few minutes. Something tells me that by the time they make it, there won't be much of a threat left." Wade picked his tools back up and returned to his invention, a sly smirk on his face.

"After all, you can't take the Fornax out of the Ivan."

*   *   *

It was almost impossibly frustrating to work on Ivan, keep pressure on the wound, wrap it in gauze, and pretend to be concerned all while knowing he was perfectly fine. This was what it meant to protect one's identity, though, and now that she'd managed to get a small slice of life for herself, she could see why Ivan didn't want to give his up. Nonetheless, it was annoying, and when the other two were looking away, she made a point of being as ungentle as possible.

"Damn it." Donald's curse was whispered and fierce as he tried in vain to pull apart the zip tie that bound his hands to the fridge. "If I could just get to my laptop—"

"Then what, you'd send out a call for help?" Tori snapped. "They barred the doors on a Friday morning and shot off a gun. People know shit is up, and by now, someone has already called the cops. My guess is that they already accounted for that."

226

"No, I wasn't trying to call anyone. I was... look, this is really easier if I just show you than tell you," Donald replied.

"Yeah, well, unless you're going to get a whole lot stronger in the next five minutes, good luck with that." Tori could all but taste Donald's frustration, but that was for the best. Whatever half-cooked idea he had was only going to get him and probably others hurt. She needed to think of a plan, and the first step was finding an explanation for why her zip tie had suddenly melted into plastic goo.

"Do you really have a way to help us?" Chloe's voice sounded almost alien. She'd gone silent since the criminals had burst through the front door. Something in her had changed, evidently, because now she was staring at Donald with an intensity Tori had only ever seen the woman use when working an espresso machine.

"I do. At least, I think I do. I've never tried this in real life before. Just lots of training."

"You *think* you do." Chloe took a long breath then glanced at Tori and Ivan's supposedly severely injured form. "I guess that's better than nothing. I don't want to die here. Not this young, not so randomly, and for damn sure not in my barista apron." She turned to Donald, resolve set in her face. "What was your name?"

"Donald. Donald Moss."

"Well, Donald, things are going to be really weird for the next minute or so. You just need to roll with it and not make any noise if at all possible." Chloe didn't bother waiting for a reply; she closed her eyes and took a long, deep breath. When she spoke again, her voice was the same, yet worlds different. There was a vibration to them, something that rippled through the air. Later, when she had the chance to think about it, Tori would realize the feeling reminded her of when Beverly had used the scroll.

"*What doesn't kill you makes you stronger.*" Chloe's eyes snapped open as she spoke, and for a moment, her strange words hung heavy in the air like they were taking up a space of their own. It was an oddly tense moment that seemed to stretch on endlessly.

Then Chloe reached her leg out and kicked Donald squarely in the ass, which sort of broke the spell. It was only thanks to her warning that Donald stifled a yelp, and Tori heard a nervous giggle that she realized had made it past her own lips.

"What the hell?" Donald hissed, staring at her from his confined spot at the fridge.

"Are you dead?" Chloe shot back.

"No!"

"Then suck it up." She kicked him again, and again, smacking the rear of his khakis with the toe of her shoe over and over. Finally, after around ten kicks, she pulled her leg back and nodded. "Okay, try it now."

"Try what now?"

"The zip tie, dipshit." Chloe rolled her eyes, and Tori found herself wondering if they could hire the blonde barista on as permanent staff.

Donald, suspicion evident on his face, tried to pull apart his zip ties again. This time, they started to give as soon as he began. With one burst of effort, they tore off with a slight pop. He stared at the broken binding device on the floor, then looked at Chloe, then back to the zip tie.

"What the hell..." he muttered softly.

"I don't totally understand it myself, but when I use really old, cliché advice or sayings, they sort of... come true. My kicking you in the ass didn't kill you, so you got stronger. Speaking of, '*A penny saved is a penny earned*.' There, now you should be normal again. Didn't want you to break your laptop by accident."

"So, you can only do one at a time?" Tori asked as Donald quickly and quietly dug into his laptop bag.

"Yup. Soon as I use a new one, the old one cancels out. Took me a while to figure that out, or that I had powers at all. That weird lightning storm a couple of weeks ago was the cause, I guess. Now you both know my dirtiest secret: I'm a meta."

"There's nothing wrong with that," Donald said, his face half-lit by the glowing screen of his computer. "Though I do appreciate you revealing your secret just to help us out. Turning into a meta is a scary experience, but sooner or later, they all have to share the truth with someone."

Donald pounded on the keys for a few seconds more, then turned to look at Chloe and Tori, his eyes half-watered up with excitement and fear.

"I guess it's my turn."

Chapter 33

No one aside from Donald was quite sure what he was doing as he reached toward the computer screen, especially when sparks and flashes of light started to erupt near his hand. The confusion only got worse when the light show stopped, because that was when Donald lifted up something that definitely hadn't been there before. To Tori it looked like an idiot had tried to build a gun—the thing was large, clunky, and had various flashing lights that would do nothing but give away one's position.

Chloe, on the hand, had a different reaction.

"Is that... is that the gun from *King Commander Cold*?"

"Good eye, and yes, it is," Donald confirmed. "I was affected by the storm too, only I got the power to pull digital stuff into the real world."

"Holy fuck," Tori said, her eyes going involuntarily wide. "You can bring out dragons and monsters and shit?"

"Well, no. It's only items. I can't bring out anything with an AI," Donald admitted. "But the things I bring out function just like they do in the games, which means I now have a way to harmlessly freeze these guys in place."

"Unless they shoot you in the head," Chloe pointed out.

"I do have more than one game on here." Donald tapped a few more keys. This time, he pulled out a buckler made of metal and glowing green light. "The Endless Shield from *Knights of the Cyber Hell*. It can handle any projectile they send my way."

"Awesome. Got anything in there to get us free?" Tori asked. While she had to admit that Donald's power did seem pretty impressive, it didn't change the fact that at least one of their captors was smart, or that the other seemed to be a meta himself. If Donald went out there alone with a freeze ray and fancy shield, he was probably going to end up smeared against the wall.

"Ummmm, all the swords would be too big. Oh, I know."

Donald calmly stood and walked over to Chloe, made a few adjustments on his weird gun, and fired at her hands. She let out a small squeak, but when the blue ray vanished, not one bit of her flesh had been frozen. The same could not be said for the zip tie or the hunk of soda machine it was tied to. With a single twist, Chloe snapped the frozen zip tie into pieces, angling her legs so they hit her pants rather than the floor.

"The ability to freeze only objects so you wouldn't hurt allies was a groundbreaking design feature in *King Commander Cold*," Donald explained. He walked over to Tori and took aim, sending a wave of panic through her.

Sure, it might not have hurt Chloe, but Chloe wasn't partially composed of fucking fire, now was she? Still, it was either let him shoot her hand or have them try to fix things on their own. Powers or not, neither of them had any experience in this or any sort of combat, probably. If worse came to worse, there had to be someone at the guild who could patch her up. Hopefully.

A small flash of light, a deep cold feeling, and it was done. She'd gotten lucky; Donald's toy hadn't accidently iced her hand clean off. Snapping her zip tie easily, Tori rose from her half-crouched position over Ivan and popped her back.

"Okay, look," she said, thinking fast. "We need a plan. Donald's items are really cool, no pun intended, but they've still got a lot of our friends hostage. Stopping these guys isn't worth it if it means innocent people get killed."

Chloe and Donald nodded in agreement, because of course they *did* agree; they were actually good people, not apprentice villains trying to fake their way through this. But it struck Tori that her words weren't entirely for show. She really didn't want any of her coworkers dead—not even Rene from programming, annoying kissass that he was. Tori sort of liked these people, at least enough to not want them listed as casualties. And Ivan wasn't the only one who had a problem with people stepping onto his territory.

"Sooner or later, one of the guys is going to come check on Mr. Gerhardt—probably the little one so that the big fellow can keep an eye on people who aren't supposed to be bound to office furniture. If we can freeze him before he screams for help, then we might be able to get the drop on the other one. Donald, does that thing do more than just act like liquid nitrogen?"

"It was made for a kid's game, so it's supposed to freeze people solid, but they melt—unharmed—after an hour or so. I've tried it out on roaches and a mouse in the alley near my house, and all of them seemed to be fine when they unfroze," Donald explained.

"I was actually asking if it kept people from yelling, but total body freezing works pretty well too," Tori said. "So the key to this will be you getting off the shot before he realizes anything is up. Think you can handle that?"

"I've been practicing," Donald admitted. From the way his eyes dropped, though, Tori had a feeling he knew he wasn't the best shot in the west yet. That was okay. With a little planning, they could still find a way to get him the window of opportunity he needed.

Unfortunately, it was just then that Tori heard the sound of soft footsteps coming toward the break room. They were officially out of time to plan or scheme in any capacity. That left Tori with only one option left: winging it. She felt oddly comfortable with that realization—at least flying by the seat of her pants was something she'd had practice with.

"Everyone, get back in your spots and pretend to be held. Donald, I'll find a way to get him distracted. Whatever you do, don't miss the damn shot."

*   *   *

Unnoticed by anyone in the office, a ragged man with kaleidoscope eyes wearing a beaten coat appeared near the edge of the cube farm, tucked away in the office's entrance alcove. Nexus had no intention of interfering, of course; only on the rarest of occasions did he see a need to influence things directly, at least in this world. In certain others, he tended to be a bit more... hands on. But today, he had merely come to watch the show. It would be interesting to see how things played out here in one of the most unique universes he'd ever discovered.

Gathered in the break room were four people with the potential to change the world before them astronomically. Here, in this encounter, many possibilities would be destroyed while a myriad of others would be created. How this fight went often determined the paths of all four of them, though one's path would be far shorter than the others.

This universe was certainly unique, so it might surprise him, but in the overwhelming number of times Nexus had watched the next five minutes, one of the four almost always died. The only question today was who.

Leaning back so as not to be seen, Nexus carefully watched as the short man in the body armor made his way to the break room, unknowingly setting the wheels of fate in motion.

*   *   *

Despite her bold promise, Tori actually had no idea what she was going to do to distract their captor. Her brain whirred with activity as the steps grew closer by the second, her eyes darting about the room as she worked to think her way through the situation.

The zip tie was in chunks, and while their captor might not notice Chloe and Donald's farce at first, she'd be busted the minute he stepped through the door. Subterfuge was out, which meant her best bet was to catch him off guard with an attack the minute he walked in. Of course, since he was pretty much protected from head to toe, the only strike that might work would require showing her powers to everyone in the room. Even that might not be effective enough, as the leather would protect him from the heat for at least the first few seconds—long enough for him to shoot at the others. She needed a way to hurt

231

him so badly that he couldn't think straight, let alone take aim. It was the only way Donald would get a safe, clean shot.

Tori's wandering eyes stopped on the drip-pot with the plastic orange handle, full of cold coffee still sitting from the night before. An idea, seemingly from nowhere, popped into her head. Granted, it would still require using her powers, but in the ensuing chaos, she doubted anyone would notice. It wouldn't be quiet either, which was a big strike against it. Unfortunately, she couldn't come up with anything that would deliver on that element, so it was better to pick the alternative that at least kept them all alive. Besides, the footsteps were almost at the door. She didn't have the luxury of thinking up something smarter.

In one motion, Tori snatched the coffee pot off the cold warming plate, doing her best to shield it from Donald and Chloe. One of the side effects from Ivan making her learn not to emit heat waves was that Tori had grown intimately aware of just how that aspect of her power functioned. For a change, she focused not on stopping her heat output but on directing it. She poured all of her anger, frustration, and general annoyance into that half-congealed coffee sludge. In mere seconds, it had reached a rolling boil. Tori kept at it. She turned up the heat as high as she could for as long as she could, using every last instant before the short man in leather walked through the break room door.

The moment he entered, Tori threw the coffee at him. She didn't aim for his head, where it would have bounced uselessly off the helmet, or his chest, where the leather would have taken the worst of it. No, Tori aimed right for his neck, spraying the super-heated liquid in the length between his collarbones. True, this part too was protected by leather, but the helmet was far from airtight. Burning steam poured upward into the helmet and their attacker's face.

Tori barely had time to shout "Now!" before the criminal's own yell drowned her out, unexpected and horrible screams tearing from his throat. They were mercifully cut short as Donald fired. Their would-be captor suddenly froze in mid-panicked flail, his torso stretched backward and his hands clutched futilely at the helmet that had sealed in the painful steam. Even without being able to see his face, they could practically feel the pain just from his stance. Everyone made a concentrated effort not to look at him as they gathered together in the middle of the room.

"We got him," Donald said, holding his freeze-gun at the ready. "But it wasn't exactly the silent take-down we were hoping for."

"Sorry about that, I sort of panicked and went with the first thing I could think of. I've gotten blasted by the steam from enough cups of coffee to know it would at least hurt. Guess it was hotter than I expected." Tori tilted her head to the drip-pot maker, still sitting useless on the counter. As far as covers went, it wasn't a great one, but she highly doubted anyone would fact-check it.

"Maybe we got lucky and the big guy didn't hear it," Chloe said.

"Abner?" The voice called out through the office, nearly rumbling the tiles as it did. No such luck: the big guy had heard the screams. Their best case scenario was that he'd try to come kill them. Worst case would be if he was smart enough to use the hostages; though, given that he seemed to be using the frozen crook's real name, that seemed somewhat unlikely.

"What do we do?" Donald looked at both of them, gun shaking slightly as his eyes went wide.

"You're asking *us*? I'm an administrative assistant and she makes old sayings come true. You're the one with the ability to turn video game shit real," Tori pointed out.

"Right," Donald said. His shaking gun slowly steadied, and a determined gleam seemed to twinkle in his eye. "You're right. This is mine. I can handle it. He might be strong, but he probably still freezes just like anyone else."

Tori chanced a look at Ivan, who was still doing an excellent impression of someone who'd been shot and poorly bandaged. She dearly wished he would stop the act and talk to her, if only for a few moments. The truth of the matter was that without knowing what sort of meta the big guy was or where his powers came from, there was no way of telling how Donald's beam would work on him. Even Tori's flames might be useless, depending on exactly what abilities and immunities he had. Her time in the guild had shown her just how broad the meta spectrum really was, and she knew well enough to take nothing for granted. But... it wasn't like they had any better options, was it?

"You shoot him; Chloe and I will try and distract him," Tori said.

"How do you plan on us doing that?" Chloe didn't look scared, not exactly, but she was eyeing Tori in a new way. It looked more suspicious than anything else, which caused Tori a twinge of worry, but she'd just have to deal with that later.

"Easy. We shoot him too." Reaching over to the frozen man wracked in pain, Tori pulled a pair of handguns from the myriad of weapons strapped across his body. They were mildly cold, more like they'd been left outside in autumn than stuck in a freezer, so she hoped they would still fire. Tori checked the clip on one then handed it over to Chloe.

"Only shoot at the big guy, and don't even try that if he has a hostage." As Tori spoke, the rumblings of heavy footsteps slammed through the office. "He's strong, so he's probably tough on top of having body armor, which means the most we'll do with these is annoy him. Donald, we're counting on you."

"Don't worry. I can handle this." No one was sure if Donald was trying to convince them or himself, but there wasn't time to argue. Those heavy thuds were growing louder, and no one wanted to try and deal with the big man in an enclosed space.

"As soon as we're out the door, spread out," Tori ordered. "He's big, so although we might be faster, there's a good chance he'll barrel right through the furniture and cubicles. Don't count on them for cover. Stay spry, keep moving, never let him pin you in a corner. And for heaven's sake, let's all try not to get anyone killed out there, especially ourselves."

Chapter 34

The bulky kidnapper was thudding through the cubicle area when all three of the former hostages burst out of the break room. Despite having been brought on for muscle more than brains, he could still tell when a situation had gone sideways. Three office workers storming into view with guns in hand tripped his awareness pretty handily. And so it was that the man threw himself down and rolled to the side, easily avoiding the freezing beam of Donald's first shot.

"That's a weird-looking gun you got there." He stayed low, peeking up as little as possible to see where the three had fanned out. "Is that the gun that made Abner scream so loud?"

"Nah, your little buddy just can't handle his caffeine." Tori fired a bullet near the hulking man's position, clipping the top of a felt-covered cube wall. It was nowhere close to a clean shot, but she hadn't really expected to hit him. All she'd wanted to do with the first shot was make sure the gun worked and draw his attention. On the first goal, at least, she succeeded; however, his helmet-shielded gaze stayed aimed right at Donald. Damn. He was smart enough to keep his eyes on the prize—in this case, the prize being the one of them holding unnatural equipment. Tori read him loud and clear: handguns were useless on him, but the mystery gun might not be, and thus needed to be carefully observed.

She really hated when her opponents weren't idiots.

"You can still walk away from this, you know," Tori called out. "Both of your cohorts might be down for the count, but you can probably smash right through this wall and make your escape. The job is a bust. You must see that. Your best bet is to get clear and live to rob another day."

Of course, that day would never come; she'd seen the look in Ivan's eyes. One way or another, this was the date that would be on the big man's headstone.

"Yeah, that's probably the smart call." His hands moved somewhere out of sight, and Tori had just enough time to register a slight crunching sound before a dark object whipped through the air. "'Course, I'm not all that famous for my smarts."

The object, a tower wrested from one of the many desktops scattered about the cubes, rushed forward on a beeline with Donald's skull. It was too fast for him to dodge; she doubted he even had the chance to register it. Luckily, Donald hadn't walked into the fight without some protection of his own. The buckler on his arm flashed, and for a moment, Donald was surrounded by a perfect sphere of light. Loud smashing and clattering filled the room as the tower slammed against the light, turning to debris and tumbling harmlessly to the floor.

"I'll be damned. You have some pretty neat toys. Surprised to find you working in a place like this." Their opponent didn't seem bothered by his failed attack. He stayed low and crept through the cube farm. More muffled crunching sounds were the only warning Tori had that he'd restocked his supply, not that it would do any good. Donald's defenses were top notch.

It hit her just before she saw the desktop tower screaming toward her chest: Donald wasn't the only viable target in the room. Years of petty crime, fighting off muggers, and perhaps a little of the guild's training all kicked in at once. Without a thought, Tori leapt to the side, narrowly avoiding the hunk of electronics that shattered on the wall near her. Chloe, however, didn't have all of her experience and training.

"Fuck!" On the upside, Chloe had managed to get partly out of the way, but her yelp coupled with the audible crunch as the tower struck her hips made it clear she'd taken an injury. Worse than that, even from across the room Tori could see it was an obvious effort for her to keep standing. She'd be unable to pull off even another half-dodge.

Tori watched the blonde barista mutter something under her breath. It was impossible to tell what the words were, but the most Tori could hope for was that there was an old saying that made people immune to flying computers.

"Looks like the girls don't have fancy shields or guns." He was moving through the cubes again, no doubt reloading. Periodically, Tori would get good shots at his limbs or shoulders—there was too much bulk to completely conceal—but she didn't bother taking them. Wasting ammunition wouldn't do them any good, at least not for the moment. She needed to think of a way to draw him into the open, to give Donald an actual shot. And she needed to do it soon.

"How about we make a deal? You throw down the gadgets, I promise not to hurt any more of these nice people. Maybe you've got connections or powers, but we both know you aren't a cape. Keep pretending and you're going to get someone hurt."

Donald's eyes swept the area, searching for his chance, but Tori could already see his determination wavering. The huge jerk wasn't wrong, after all. Donald was as far from a cape as one could get and still be considered a meta. Shit, Tori was closer to a cape than he was—at least she'd had some training and combat experience. Cape or not, though, Donald was the closest thing to a champion they had, so he would have to do. By any means necessary.

"Hey, Donald, same deal as last time," Tori called. She brought her gun to the ready and lowered her stance. All that talking and moving about had given her a clear idea of where the last hostage-taker was in the array of cubicles. He was too low to shoot at, true, but that didn't mean she couldn't find him. "Whatever you do, don't miss. Even if you have to take two instead of one."

Before Donald could manage more than a half-formed attempt at a question, Tori was off, racing through the cubicles. It took all of ten seconds and two quick turns to find the near-giant crouched down on the ground, a small pile of desktop towers at his feet. Though she couldn't see his face through the helmet, she still noticed his visible shock as she came whipping around the bend in a head-on charge. Shock was the right emotion, too. After all, he was a powerful meta and she looked like nothing more than an average woman ready to face the final workday of the week—what could she hope to accomplish with such a pointless attack?

Without slowing down, Tori leapt on the large man's back, jammed the gun under his helmet as best she could, and pulled the trigger. Even those who could shrug off a lot of damage had some places on their body were tougher than others. If he was going to have a spot weak enough to let a bullet through, the top of his neck and area under his jaw were her best bets.

Tori squeezed the trigger three times before a large hand wrapped around her own. He easily yanked her off his back, squeezing her hand so tightly it was a miracle her fingers didn't completely shatter.

"This one has guts," he said, his body still hunched over even as he dangled Tori a foot off the ground. "I admire that, I really do. Tell you what, out of respect for her guts, I'm going to give you until the count of three to—"

His next demand or threat would forever remain a mystery. The entire room filled with a thunderous roaring that shook the very desks. It sounded like a wolf the size of a bus had broken in to demand a tribute of flesh. The criminal, Tori still clutched firmly in his hands, leapt up from his hiding spot on pure instinct. Meta or not, humans were hardwired to react in certain ways when a predator was nearby, and the first course of action was to locate the threat.

Unfortunately for the large man, Donald had somehow kept his cool in the face of the noise. No sooner had the crook crested the top of the cubicles than a bright blue beam struck him in the chest. His grip on Tori loosened and she wriggled free, dropping to the ground and rolling away from her opponent. Springing back to her feet, she quickly surveyed the room for the source of the noise, only to find Chloe opening and closing her mouth in sync with the terrible barks. Strangely, the blonde woman had bruises forming around her jaw and a trickle of blood seeping out of her mouth, but her eyes were full of fire.

When she finally halted the wall-shaking distraction, Tori asked the obvious question. "What in the nine hells was that?"

"My bark is worse than my bite." Chloe winced with every word she spoke, her eyes watering from what Tori assumed was pain. The halfhearted explanation left Tori with many questions, but she wouldn't get to ask them quite yet.

"I haven't felt that kind of cold since I was kid and my dad locked me out of the house in January." Moving slowly, but still very much moving, the large man reached up and slapped his chest three times. He turned his helmet to face Donald. "Guess I've gotten tougher since then."

"Fuck us all, he's resilient," Tori whispered softly. It was just what she'd been afraid of: the bastard was a meta that could withstand the effects of certain attacks, freeze-guns evidently included. A strong enough strike could still overcome his defenses, but Donald had shown them the best his blaster could do and all Tori's tech was half-built and stashed under Ivan's house. Unless Chloe had a super powerful phrase up her sleeve, they were out of options for stopping this guy. Even if she blasted him with heat, he could probably endure it. The only one of them who could easily stop this son of a bitch was down in the break room, pretending to be shot.

Stealth, it seemed, was no longer deemed necessary by the wide-shouldered criminal. Without turning his head from Donald, he barreled forward, taking two more shots from the freeze-gun as he tore through the desks like they weren't even there. While each blast did seem to slow him, he kept right on coming, reaching back and throwing a punch that would easily tear Donald's head from his slender body.

Just before impact, the glowing sphere reappeared from Donald's buckler, valiantly putting itself between his too-frail skull and the meta's fist. This didn't deter Donald's attacker in the slightest; he kept right on slamming his fists down on the shield over and over. That alone would have been worrisome enough, but after the first few attacks, Tori noticed that the sphere seemed to be flickering on impact. Not even video game shields had infinite energy, after all.

Donald had a minute before he would be no more than powdered bone and organs, if that. Tori had to work fast. She could only think of one way that might stop this jerk, or at least draw his focus, and she'd need to work quickly to make it happen.

Rushing over to Chloe, Tori grabbed her fellow hostage by the shoulder and shook, pulling her attention away from Donald's predicament.

"Chloe! That thing you did with Donald, the 'what doesn't kill you' thing: does that work the way it looks? The more you get hurt, the stronger you get?"

Chloe blinked a few times then slurred out a response. "It's proportional, from what I've seen. I don't think you could get hurt enough to stop him, though." Her eyes flicked back to the man pummeling Donald's shield, a shield that was beginning to flash violently on every punch.

"Do it to me. Now. Please."

With a curious, sidelong glance, Chloe muttered, "*What doesn't kill you makes you stronger.*"

"Thanks." Tori lifted the gun in her right hand, pressed it to her own left arm, and fired. Those lessons from Ivan were paying big dividends: she forced her body to resist its instinct to turn to fire and accepted the wound as it tore apart her flesh.

Chloe yelped in shock, but neither Donald nor the man trying to kill him seemed to notice the gunshot. Nor did they notice the next one Tori used to shoot lower down her arm, nor the next, nor the next. After the pain from gunshot number four nearly caused her to pass out, it was time to roll the dice. She wouldn't do much good if she gave in to shock, now would she?

Racing forward, trying dearly to ignore the throbbing pain in her ruined left arm, Tori ran up behind the man trying to murder her friend and punched the back of his motorcycle helmet with everything she had. The helmet exploded into fragments. He hurtled forward, tumbling through the air until he slammed violently into a wall. Face exposed for the first time since arriving, the man turned and stared at Tori with a combination of confusion and annoyance.

Donald, on the other hand, was panting on the ground, seconds away from a panic attack as far as she could tell. The buckler on his arm was flashing with a red light, which, by video game logic, probably meant it was about to run out of juice. She'd been just in time.

"How did you—"

"Same way you broke the zip ties, I just didn't have time for Chloe to kick me in the ass," Tori snapped. "Now, up and at it. Big Papa isn't out of this fight yet."

"No, he isn't," rumbled the large man as he hauled himself up. He carefully rubbed the back of his head, wincing visibly at the touch of his own fingertips. "But you three are turning out to be quite the annoyance. I don't even give a shit about the job anymore; I just want to pay you back for causing this much of a headache."

"Hey, Donald, this is just me talking here, but I'm betting that your gun is like every other gun out there: it works a lot better when you shoot people in the head. Especially now that it's exposed." Tori didn't bother whispering; they were all too close together for the target not to hear. Besides, he wasn't that stupid. With the helmet gone, he knew where the next shot would be aimed. He'd probably dodge it, too, which was why Tori didn't plan on giving him the chance.

She barreled forward, charging the big man before he could do the same to them. With Tori starting from as far away as she had and telegraphing the move so clearly, he had ample time to dodge out of the way. Just as she'd hoped, he went for a counter instead, grabbing her around the chest and locking her in place. For a guy with his strength, it was probably pure reaction to render someone nearly helpless and then pound them into submission. What he hadn't had time to adjust to yet, however, was the fact that Tori had some extra strength of her own. Rearing up her right hand, she punched him in the calf as hard as she could, savoring the slight popping sound she heard from the bone.

It was less satisfying a moment later when he buried his fist in her stomach. Despite the fact that she jumped with the punch to disperse the momentum, Tori nearly lost control right then and there. Her instincts screamed at her to go into fire-form. She'd probably need to spend the rest of the day in flames to regenerate—her ribs felt like shrapnel more than bones and her arm was gushing blood in a streaming torrent. But that would come later. For the moment, he'd done a great job of hurting her worse than a gunshot, and with the added benefit of not killing her.

Tori grabbed the arm holding her and squeezed, finding his flesh more pliable with the extra addition of strength. A slight yelp of pain and surprise escaped his lips and he released his hold; no doubt he was trying to regroup and understand what just happened. Tori was having none of that shit, though. She would end this, right here and now.

His arm firmly in her grasp, she yanked it around to his back, half-wrenching his giant shoulder out of its socket. This time she didn't need to give Donald his cue. Flashes of blue light lit up the large man's pain-stricken face one after the other until the arm clutched tightly in her hand went limp. She held on through a few more shots before releasing her iron grip and letting him slump to the floor.

"If one of you would be so kind as to dial emergency services, I think my assistant and I are in need of medical attention." Standing in the door-less doorway of the break room was Ivan, still pale and seemingly covered in blood, but smiling in a way Tori had only caught glimpses of. The old bastard was beaming with pride, and as her consciousness finally gave way to the pain and shock flooding her system, Tori realized that he wasn't the only one.

She was pretty damn proud of herself, too.

240

Nexus vanished from his hiding spot and reappeared across the street, watching as guild members pretending to be police and EMTs rushed into the building. Normally they'd be bagging a body before anything else, but today it seemed that only some spot-healing and basic cover-up work would be needed.

In truth, he wasn't that surprised to see everyone make it through alive. This universe was always unpredictable; it had been from the moment it created Quorum instead of a hole in the ground like literally every other iteration had. It surprised him, intrigued him, always kept him guessing. In a way this was Nexus's favorite piece of the multiverse, though it was also the one he hated the most, for the same reasons.

At least things would remain entertaining now. A world where one dodged the computer, one's shield held out, and one jumped just enough to not be killed by the punch to the stomach... that was a world where many fascinating things would certainly occur.

All for Nexus to watch, and—perhaps on occasion—influence. Interactive entertainment was his absolute favorite.

Chapter 35

Tori awoke to find herself in a room full of white light, the pain in her arm and stomach greatly reduced, but not entirely gone. She started to sit up only to feel the white room spin underneath her.

"Go slowly. You're going to be dizzy for a while." Ivan was seated on a small stool in the corner of the room, the tablet in his hand occupying most of his attention. "The genetic regeneration and reconstitution rooms are handy for getting people back on their feet, but all that healing in such a short time tends to leave people with a bad case of the spins."

For once, Tori didn't argue and eased herself slowly into a sitting position. Bit by bit, the room stabilized until she was able to admire the tech surrounding her. Fixed to the ceiling at various points were large, strangely-wired lamps that were dousing her in that curious white light. Obviously, it wasn't just light; they must have been pumping out some sort of beams or radiation designed to promote inhumanly-accelerated healing.

"You know, if every hospital in the world had one of these rooms, a lot fewer people would die," Tori pointed out.

"Unfortunately, the R&R rooms only work on meta-humans, and not even all of them, at that. If you think they should come standard in hospitals, talk to Professor Quantum; he's the one who invented the technology." Ivan rose from his seat and walked slowly over to Tori, tablet still firmly clutched in his hand.

"How nice of him to share his breakthroughs with a bunch of criminals," Tori replied.

"Did you think you were the first scientist to realize that sometimes stealing tech is easier than recreating it? We *are* a guild of villains, after all."

"Hopefully that means you didn't kill off everyone in the office to cover our tracks." Tori was mostly joking, but in her time with Ivan she'd learned not to underestimate the people she'd been thrown in with. Fun as they might be, it was her folly if she forgot the lengths they would go to, should the need arise. It was just like Ivan said: they were a guild of villains, after all.

"Now, why would we need to go and do a thing like that?" Ivan held the tablet out in front of her and pressed the play button on an archived video feed from a press conference. Standing in front of the office building where they'd been taken prisoner, surrounded by a sea of reporters, was Donald, looking far more scared than he had while taking on the men with guns. Next to him was the familiar face of Apollo, arm wrapped around Donald and white smile catching the flashes of all the cameras.

"As the story is being reported, Donald Moss, a recently altered meta, used his powers to defeat a gang of thieves out to steal restricted data from a programming company. He did so without losing so much as a single life, though some members of the staff were injured in the chaos. Those sustaining injuries were rushed to a top-tier medical facility staffed with metas with healing abilities at the expense of their employer. Donald was the lone meta on the scene, though he made sure to mention that without the help of his coworkers, this victory would not have been possible. The Alliance of Heroic Champions has already offered him membership; they're not the kind to let a golden PR opportunity like this slip away."

"But Donald wasn't the only one, not even just besides us," Tori protested. "Chloe—"

"Chloe is a very brave young woman who doubtlessly helped save lives today, but she is also happier living outside the limelight, at least for now. It was at her request that Donald took all the credit. She convinced him that he would be protecting her secret. This life, his or ours, isn't for everyone."

"You're not going to try and recruit her either?" Tori found herself skeptical, though she had to admit Ivan wasn't one to make false claims. Usually he just told her how things would be, whether she liked it or not.

"We don't 'recruit' like that. We take in those who are likely to run afoul of us by breaking the code, if we can get them early enough, or those whose powers are too dangerous to run rampant without training. As you might recall, you were only dragged in here because you broke into a secure facility."

"Does that mean the big dude we stopped is going to be joining the other rookies?"

Ivan's face darkened, only for a moment, but Tori knew what she saw. "No. He doesn't quite possess the self-control we look for in our recruits. Had he taken the chance to run when you offered it, perhaps an exception might have been made. But he chose violence over prudence, and that is not our way. Besides, your crime was managed and performed in private, while his was broadcasted across the news. We have to set a standard of expectations for what happens to those who try and break into our companies."

"I get the feeling I don't want to know any more about this, so I won't ask," Tori said.

"Smart call."

"But that doesn't mean I don't have other questions. Like: how are you going to explain away your little message in the carpet? So far as everyone else in the office knows, there was another meta on the scene who killed the first guy."

"Ah, you must mean when I struggled with the man who had a gun on me, knocking him against the edge of the desk and accidently breaking his neck after he shot me. True, he did have some acid that spilled and corroded the carpet, but calling it a message is a bit of a stretch." Ivan reached up and tapped one of the suspended lamps blaring light on Tori. "We've got more than just physical aftermath covered; several of our guild members have either the magic or the abilities to cloud the mind. Obscuring whole memories would be tricky and temporary; however, nudging the details a bit is so subtle only the most self-aware of people notice it."

"Well, that's peachy for you. If I'd known we had memory changers I might have come up with a solution besides shooting myself in the arm four times." Tori tested her left arm, finding it stiff and painful but once again functional. Good as the lights no doubt were, she'd feel a lot better once she went into fire-form and fixed herself up.

"As I said, *small* changes are easy. There's a reason I had to play dead, after all. But I think, even with the restrictions placed upon you, you did very well, my apprentice. You protected your friends, you took down the intruders, and you managed it all without using your powers in an overt manner. The caution and prudence you showed today will go a long way toward your membership in this guild."

"Oh man, please tell me you didn't set this whole thing up just as a way to test me," Tori said.

Ivan laughed softly under his breath, yet somehow it still managed to fill the room. "Sadly, even my level of conniving has limits, and this is one of them. Fate is often a far better teacher than we could ever hope to be."

"Thank goodness." Tori leaned back in her bed, shutting her eyes to diminish the waves of dizziness that accompanied all movement. "When we get home, the first thing I'm going to do is start working on some portable tech to keep in the office. Next I'm putting a prototype of my suit together. If today has taught me anything, it's that I do not like being caught unarmed."

"With strong powers and a good mind, we are never truly unarmed," Ivan replied. "But I'm afraid you won't be going home tonight. Since there is apprentice training tomorrow, it was decided that you would stay the night here to fully recover. After all, we neither have the lights nor a fireproof room at the house."

"Wait, is this bed fireproof?" Tori looked down at the sheets and firm mattress under her; so far as she could tell, they seemed completely normal.

"Fire-resistant is a better way to put it; nothing is really fire-proof. So long as you don't actively try to burn it, you should be fine. A few sets of sheets were commissioned the first week you were recruited, well before you became my apprentice. The softest of these are in your room here, by the way."

"Oh geez, that fucking cot back at the training facility? Thanks, but no thanks." Tori had slept on worse during the darker times in her life, but not by much.

"No, that was a cheap measure while the fireproof ones were being made. I'm talking about your room here, at the guild," Ivan replied. "Every member has one, even apprentices, and you are no exception. They aren't extravagant, but sometimes we just need a place to hole up; this allows us to do so. When your apprenticeship under me comes to an end, presuming it's a good one, you'll be allowed to move in here, if you so choose."

"That's awfully generous of the guild," Tori said. She'd seen the way members were treated and it was always kind, but free rooms would take a lot of space and get highly expensive.

"We find that people make fewer stupid mistakes when they know they always have a place they can call home," Ivan said. "Sometimes just having a place to go back to gives them the mental strength to keep on the code's path."

That actually rang true. The most desperate, harshest times Tori could remember were when she was scrounging for a home base, a place to be safe amid the chaos. Even in last week's trials, the first thing she'd done was find a safe spot to hunker down. It was human nature. Providing such a luxury had probably saved the guild from having to deal with several of its members going off the rails throughout the years.

"I guess I'll check it out once the dizziness fades, if that's okay," Tori said.

"It won't fade while you're under the lights, but I'll get you a wheelchair and bring you over to it myself." Ivan turned toward the door, but Tori's hand grabbed his sleeve and held him in place.

"Be honest with me: how much more of this do I have to go through? I like learning from you, and I'm grateful for what you've done, but the longer this sword dangles over my head, the heavier its shadow gets. Give me a quarterly review so we can plan my next steps if you have to; just paint me a finish line."

Ivan slowly turned back to her and gently rested his hand on top of hers. "This weekend, you're going to learn how jobs with the guild work. For the next two weeks after that, you'll be getting field training every night. At the end of that time, you will participate in a job, one you can orchestrate either by yourself or with others. How you do on that job, coupled with the judgment you've shown during your other trials, will determine if we believe you can adhere to the code. I can't tell you how that job will go, Apprentice, only that when it's done, you will either be a member of the guild or dealt with accordingly."

Tori tried to release her grip, but Ivan held firm for a few seconds longer. "I should also add that as your teacher, my opinion is considered the highest prized regarding whether you can join the guild or not. And as things stand now, you have impressed me at almost every turn. Keep going the way you have, and I will fight tooth and nail to win you the admission you'll have earned."

A slight smile appeared on Ivan's face as he released her hand and eased the heaviness of the discussion. "And you'll be glad to know that since we were both injured on company property, they're going to complete the rest of the quarterly evaluations without us."

"You know, I think that's actually worth the broken ribs and bullet wounds."

*   *   *

Abner sat in the jail cell, no longer clad in leather or armor, listening to the small sound of leaking water as it dripped from somewhere in the building's concrete depths. Dirk was being held someplace where his strength couldn't be used to free him, and Nelson was dead. He'd been so careful in planning everything, in doing the research, in learning everything he could about the people who worked there. How could it all have gone so wrong? The entire plan shot to shit, his face still burned from that fucking steam, two of them in jail, and all because some lone meta had managed to get the drop on them. The buyer for the information was long in the wind by now; he'd kept himself far enough removed that Abner couldn't point a finger, even if he'd wanted to.

The sole bright spot Abner could see was that Dirk and Nelson had been the only ones to get their hands dirty. He'd never fired so much as a single shot at anyone, even after that bitch threw coffee on his face. The mere thought of it caused the burns on his skin to flare up with pain, which Abner dutifully ignored. There was a chance he could skate by on this; after all, he'd let them tend to a wounded man. If he claimed that Nelson had spearheaded it and Dirk had forced him along, there was a chance he could beat the charges. Dirk was confirmed to be violent and Nelson was dead; there was no one left to give credible testimony against him. It was a rule he lived by: never leave unnecessary witnesses. It had cost him a few bullets and shallow graves, but this time, fate had been on his side. Without so much as a drop of blood on his hands, he could coast to freedom.

"Hello."

246

Abner jumped in shock at the voice then turned to stare at the man with long, dirty-blond hair who had appeared in his cell. He wore an almost serene expression as he moved toward Abner, kneeling down to look the seated man in the eyes.

"Who are you?" It wasn't the most apt question to ask at the moment, but Abner's brain was hardly firing on all cylinders.

"I'm Kristoph. They let me go in first to check people, just in case." That serene expression darkened. Abner felt his stomach churning in fear even before his brain could process why.

"You... are a bad man. You killed them in Guatemala, just because they saw you loading your bags. You killed them and threw their bodies into the river."

Abner's eyes went wide in shock. He'd never told anyone, not even Nelson, about the two children he'd murdered to keep his face unknown. Yet Kristoph knew. As he rose to his feet, a new energy swirled through the air. On the concrete walls of the prison cell, Abner noticed the moving shadows and saw what was sprouting from Kristoph's back.

"You are a bad man." All peace was gone from his voice; it was as though Abner was hearing the very judgment of a wrathful god. "And you will suffer for your sins."

By the time the guards made it to the cell, the screaming had finally stopped, though what remained there would haunt their nightmares for years to come.

Chapter 36

"My oh my, the ability to turn digital items into real things. That is incredible." Apollo was sitting across from Donald between two constantly-smiling people he'd introduced as Jessica and Barney. "And to have such a public debut, why, you've done the bulk of the work for us, which we always appreciate. Now, since you'll be pulling out and using material that is trademarked or copyrighted by a slew of various companies, we'll need to either get some waivers signed or have the lawyer get a defense ready to go when the lawsuits come rolling in."

"Storybook already set the precedent with her literary minions," Jessica replied, barely looking up from her laptop as she took down Apollo's requests. "Courts ruled that a meta conjuring protected material doesn't violate the copyright, so no damages can be sought."

"Really? That's a surprisingly favorable decision for the meta," Apollo noted.

"It was right after Storybook helped save an entire city, and the company suing her was found to have some unethical dealings with child labor overseas. The PR was a tidal wave they couldn't surf," Barney explained.

"Well then, new tactic. Let the owners of the video game companies know this is happening and if they want to design some gear especially for our new recruit, they can do so for a hefty fee. Branding isn't free, after all."

"I'm not sure that will work," Donald said. It was the first time he'd found his voice since the introductions. Everything that had happened throughout the day was so overwhelming; he was halfway running on autopilot. "I've tried to just code items before, but it doesn't work. For whatever reason, they have to be a piece of a game world, though I've got no idea why it would matter."

"Best not to overthink these things," Apollo said, waving his hand as if he dismissed such issues every day. "Our powers themselves are often a mystery at the outset; the deeper you dig, the more confusing things get. So, only real game items will work then. I feel like we can still make something happen there, but let's table it for the moment. Instead, let's focus on getting you equipped, Donald. Barney, what's the turnaround on getting a portable unit for our new man, one preprogrammed with every video game and item screen on the market?"

"We could get a halfway decent version in a few days, but if you want something top-of-the-line, we'll have to wait for Professor Quantum to make it," Barney replied. "And you know his turnaround times."

"Order the weaker one as a stop-gap measure; it'll have to do until we can get Professor Quantum to work on something besides his pet projects," Apollo instructed. He glanced at Donald and offered up a comforting smile. "The man is a legendary genius, and like most people with that sort of intellect, he's prone to getting caught up in his research. I'll talk to Quorum and see if he can't speed things along. In the meantime, someone schedule Donald a meeting with our costume people. He'll need some protection while he's learning the ropes."

"Already got him booked for tomorrow morning," Jessica said, hands still whizzing across the keyboard. "The press is hounding us for a name, though. You know how these things go; if we don't give them something soon, they'll start using a nickname and it'll be hell to unstick it from him."

"How can we forget the way Cuddle Monster got his name?" Apollo let out a sigh as he shook his head, and even Jessica and Barney's smiles dimmed significantly. "I suppose that means picking a name is the next item on the agenda. Donald, you have my sincere apologies. Normally, we allow our new members to have their names researched and market tested before making them settle on one, but this is a downside to having a debut like yours: things just move faster. Now, you've obviously been training on using your abilities for some time now. Have you given any thought to what you might call yourself?"

Donald had, in fact, given a tremendous amount of thought to that ever since he realized the storm had given him powers. However, he'd thought about it in the same way he thought about what he would tell his online friends if he managed to score a supermodel girlfriend: it was always more fantasy than actual problem. Yet here he was, sitting across from Apollo, *the* Apollo, being asked what the name he'd use when he donned his costume would be. It was so far beyond what he'd ever considered possible that it was surreal. Donald kept expecting to wake up suddenly or find out he'd died in the fight. It was taking all he had to keep his sanity together, so the words that popped out of his mouth did so without bothering to get his brain's approval. They knew the brain had bigger issues to deal with.

"I sort of thought... maybe... something like Cyber Geek? You know, turn an insult into a positive, and since my powers relate to digital stuff, I thought it would be cool..." Donald trailed off as he registered the vacant stares from Jessica and Barney. Apollo, however, clapped his hands together so loudly it startled everyone in the room.

"Cyber Geek, huh? I like it! Not too stuffy or proud, a very down-to-earth name. Shows you know where you come from. The Internet is going to love you. Jessica, any issues?"

"Oh, um, one second." She clacked away on the keyboard, pulling up several databases and punching his proposed name into each one. "No prior claims on it, no trademark issues, and nothing in private domain. If he wants Cyber Geek, it would be his free and clear."

"Handling his own debut and picking a name we don't have to pay for; Donald, I am liking you more by the second." Apollo stood from the table and motioned for Donald to do the same, though neither Jessica nor Barney were given such orders. "You two get it registered. I want that name released to the media in the next hour before they try and give him one. As for you, Donald, with the paperwork out of the way, how about I show you around the facilities? The Alliance of Heroic Champions has top-notch gyms, spas, recreation areas, and housing, should you decide to avail yourself of any of that. All of it's here at your disposal to help you be the best superhero you can be."

Donald allowed himself to be led from the room, still uncertain of what, if anything, to say. Apollo seemed to have things well in hand, so Donald let the glowing man keep helping him through the paces. He did wish they'd let him visit Tori and Mr. Gerhardt, though. Assurances were nice, but he'd like to be certain they were okay. Oddly, no one he mentioned it to seemed very worried about them. In fact, if he didn't know better, he'd have said that Apollo was almost annoyed by the mention of Mr. Gerhardt.

He knew he was imagining it, though. Why would a world famous superhero be annoyed by a middle manager?

*   *   *

"You know, I was coasting on a pretty good wave of respect and self-esteem after last weekend, but then Little Miss Attention had to go and get half the guild talking about her again."

Tori looked up from the sandwich she'd been eating—her third one since leaving her room—to find Beverly standing in the door of the lounge. Ivan had told her that it was usually only rookies on this floor so her chances of seeing anyone were greatly reduced, but somehow, she'd had a feeling it wouldn't be that simple.

"Maybe step your game up," Tori replied, kicking out an empty plastic chair on the other side of the small table. "Or get a day job where you're likely to be a target of organized thieves."

"I have a day job, thank you very much. I do freelance articles for an online fashion company. Haven't even missed a deadline during all the chaos of turning meta." Beverly stopped by the refrigerator and pulled out a half-empty soda bottle, then took the offered seat across from Tori. "It's weird being in here without Lance playing his games. Too quiet."

"He must have gone to bed early. Apparently we've got a big day ahead of us tomorrow," Tori said, digging into her sandwich. Spending three hours in fire-form had healed up most of her injuries, but as soon as she turned human Tori realized that she'd gone the whole day without eating. With the nausea fading and her stomach back in place, she'd begun throwing food down as quickly as she could get it from the vending machine.

"Lance? Nah, guy's a night owl. Wait, those eat bugs. Maybe a night wasp or something. Point is, I'm usually up pretty late, and I always turn in before him. More likely he's hanging out with Arachno Bro, getting mentally pumped for whatever they're going to throw at us."

"Not the worst idea." Tori looked around the lounge, admiring the big screen, vast couch, cushy recliners, game tables, and well-stocked vending machines. It seemed like it was made to accommodate far more than just the four apprentices that were currently being trained. She wondered if they'd once had larger groups of recruits, and if so, why that number had dropped off.

"What about Warren? He usually hang out here?" Tori asked.

"Once in a blue moon. Balaam likes to keep him around for training pretty much all the time. People who actually cast magic have it rough; they have to study their asses off to know what they're doing, otherwise they can accidently start some serious shit," Beverly explained. "Not unlike you science types, actually. I'm glad my power is straightforward: turn into dragon, kick ass, turn back."

"I could have used you on my team today," Tori admitted. "You never realize how much you need someone who can throw a good punch until you don't have one."

"If nothing else, we're always in demand." Beverly smirked as she twisted the top off her bottle of soda and drained a quarter of the remaining contents.

"Maybe you should pick up a book on dragon myths," Tori said. "The flying wyvern, the fire breathing beast, the armored monster; all of your forms seem to be based on popular legends. It might not hurt to see if you can find out what else is in your amulet's arsenal."

"Way ahead of you. I've read more about dragons in the last month than I ever wanted to know. I even got halfway through a role-playing game manual before I realized there were no actual dragons in it. It's given me some ideas about what I might be able to do, but try as I might, nothing has come from it. Seems the only way to unlock them is to need them, which is only handy until I get in a situation where the dragon I need doesn't exist."

251

"That's what you have friends for." Tori finished off her sandwich and walked right over to the machine to get another. Her stomach was quieter now but far from satisfied.

"I don't think every hurdle we face is going to be like last week's trial," Beverly said.

Tori stuck a wrinkled dollar in the machine and made her selection, peeling back the cellophane as soon as she'd gotten the well-made morsel into her hungry hands.

"Maybe not, but this place runs on teamwork more than you'd think," Tori replied, returning to the table. "And trust me: if there's one thing today demonstrated, it's the importance of having good people watching your back. If it had just been me and Pseudonym, our covers would have been blown and our coworkers might have been killed."

"Or you could have both played along and just let the robbery happen," Beverly countered.

A grin that had nothing to do with her sandwich crossed Tori's face. "Now, I think you know there's no chance that could have happened. Pseudonym didn't become known as a villain because of his willingness to take people's bullshit."

Beverly leaned back in her plastic chair, looking at Tori appraisingly as she devoured her fourth, and not final, piece of dinner. "And what about you?"

"What do you think? I *am* his apprentice, after all."

*   *   *

"Uncle Ivan!" The small girl barreled into Ivan's legs with such ferocity it might have knocked him off-balance had she been several tons heavier. Her arms curled around his legs, hugging him in the unashamed way that only children ever seem to manage. It was a tragedy that humanity lost that skill as it grew older—perhaps the world might have been a better place if everyone were so free with their affection.

"Good to see you, too." He reached down and mussed her mousy brown hair with his free hand, the other laden with bags from a nearby restaurant. At his touch, she hugged his legs tighter. Ivan made no move to pull her away.

"That's enough, Penelope. You have to let Ivan go if he's going to make it in the door." From down the hall, Helen stepped into view. A lovely woman in her mid-twenties, she looked only a few years younger than Ivan, though both of them were keenly aware of just how deceiving appearances could be. "Oh, for the love of—I told you that you didn't have to bring dinner."

252

"It was the least I could do after not stopping by for so long." Ivan took a step forward as Penelope released her grip on him. He shut the house's bright red door behind him. It looked a touch out of place with the rest of the white exterior, but Helen had never been a woman who shied away from standing out.

"Then it's an apology meal, is it? In that case, I hope you picked up the little cakes I like." Helen met him halfway down the hall, gripping Ivan in a hug of her own. It was not as honest and open as Penelope's, but in her firm embrace was a familiarity and tenderness that spoke to how much had passed between them. "Seriously though, do you have to get attacked at your office before you can free up the time for a visit? Because I still know some people..."

"It's more that I've had a houseguest who has made it impossible to slip away," Ivan replied. Their hug ended and he made his way into the kitchen, setting the bags down on the island and beginning to unpack them.

"You can bring them along; I don't mind meeting new people." Helen hopped onto one of the stools around the island and swept a long strand of her brown hair away as she watched Ivan work. "Though I'm shocked you actually know someone you're willing to let stay with you."

Ivan's voice fell a few octaves, quiet enough that Penelope, who was still ambling about near his legs, wouldn't hear. "I didn't. My houseguest is a new intern at my job... at both of my jobs. Which is why I've made sure to keep her as far from here as possible."

Helen's eyebrows shot up and she leaned back in her stool. "Whoaaaa. *You* took an apprentice?"

"Mommy, what's an apprentice?" Penelope asked from down near her mother's feet.

Helen reached down and scooped her daughter up, setting the girl on her lap to be part of the conversation. "An apprentice is like a student, but the teacher is only teaching them instead of a whole class. Mommy is surprised because Uncle Ivan always swore up and down that he'd never take one."

"Why not?" Penelope leaned forward, staring at Ivan with unabashed curiosity. "He helps teach me stuff when he comes over. He's good at it."

"Uncle Ivan just never thought he had anything worth teaching someone enough to have a full-time student," Ivan replied. "And he didn't exactly take this one easily. There were... circumstances."

"Must have been some pretty interesting circumstances," Helen replied. "This apprentice of yours, they someone I should keep an eye out for?"

"Highly unlikely. She's smart, shouldn't do anything to stir up trouble." Even as he said the words, Ivan found himself doubting them. Tori was bright, that much was undeniable, but she also had a genuine talent for putting herself right in the thick of all manner of chaos.

"If you're teaching her, she's got to be something of a sparkplug."
Helen lowered Penelope back to the ground as she got restless, allowing the six-year-old to dart about once more. "Got a lot longer left on her apprenticeship?"

"Only a couple of weeks," Ivan said, pulling out a Styrofoam bowl of gumbo and popping off the lid. "In fact, I slipped out tonight because she's going to spend the weekend learning about how to job hunt."

"Wow, she really is near the end then." Not bothering to be even marginally polite, Helen reached into a white paper bag, pulled out a loaf of bread, tore a piece off and dipped it in the gumbo. "My old place has a class of recruits just about ready for their debuts too. These things always seem to move in cycles."

"That they do. Anyway, in a few weeks, my home will be my own again and I'll stop being so elusive."

"I guess it's forgivable," Helen relented. "You're just trying to keep us secret, so I won't hold it against you. Assuming..."

Ivan sighed, then reached into the bag and pulled out a large box. Opening it up, he revealed half a dozen mini-cakes topped with chocolate icing.

Helen let out a slight squeal of happiness and clapped her hands together, a joyful outburst that that immediately drew Penelope back to her side.

"I'll give you this, Ivan. It took a while, but you finally learned how to make a proper apology."

Chapter 37

"Insecticide?"

Lance frowned at Beverly, an unnatural appearance on his usually cheerful face. "That's what you call something that kills insects. Completely the opposite of what I do."

"Well, you didn't like Bug Lord," Tori pointed out.

"It's not that I didn't *like* Bug Lord, it's just that it seemed a bit ostentatious for me," Lance protested. "I'm a simple man. I'd like to have a simple code name."

Tori, Beverly, and Lance were all sitting on the couch in their floor's lounge while Warren stood near the entrance. They'd been given directions to gather there that morning, though with no indication of what would follow. It was a setup they were all getting quickly accustomed to, so rather than spend their time fretting over what was to come, they'd begun discussing what code names they would submit to the guild.

"Simple is overrated. I'm going with a classic: Bahamut, king of the dragons," Beverly declared.

"Not to be 'that guy' or anything, but you're, um, more queen than king," Lance stammered out slowly.

"Somehow I highly doubt anyone is going to be checking my dragon-form to see if it's got a scaly cock and balls dangling down there," Beverly shot back. "Besides, I want people to make the wrong assumptions about who might be behind the dragon's form. If I ever do slip up and get the capes looking for me, it'll be all the better if they're searching for the wrong sex."

"Damn, that's pretty smart." Tori set her hand against her chin, adding the idea to the possibilities already swirling around in her head. "I'll have to keep that in mind."

"If this leads to someone suggesting I go by Queen Bee, let me save you the trouble: no, and it's already in use," Lance said.

The sound of heavy, clanking footsteps silenced their conversation. All three scrambled up from the couch. Several long moments stretched out, and then at last the familiar helmeted head of Doctor Mechaniacal came into view from the doorway. He scanned the room, ensuring all four apprentices were present, and then motioned for them to come forward.

"Today, you will all be allowed into a secure area of the guild. Understand this: most of where you've been are recreational areas, open freely to all members, regardless of status. That will not be the case where we are headed. Only full members in good standing can proceed to this area. It is a place with secure, dangerous information, and I expect you all to behave appropriately. Be silent unless you have a question, and listen hard. This is where you'll truly learn how our guild functions."

Without another word, Doctor Mechaniacal spun on his heel and headed out of the lounge. Everyone fell silently into line behind him, keeping a respectful distance yet never dropping behind as he made his way through the winding hallways. Soon, he took a set of stairs down three levels, and then walked over to a large wall with a single hole in it. Producing a device from the machinery around his right finger, Doctor Mechaniacal inserted it into the opening, and moments later, the wall slid away to reveal a wide, spacious elevator.

They piled in, with Doctor Mechaniacal removing his odd key and stepping in last. There were no buttons to press; the door merely slid closed once more and the elevator began to move downward. There were no windows—only metal walls enclosed them as they moved lower, farther than the bottom floor of the building could possibly be.

"This elevator is the only way in or out of where we're heading," Doctor Mechaniacal informed then. "It's made to contain and neutralize all but the most powerful of meta-humans. Should an unauthorized person gain entry, it will immediately immobilize and defuse the threat. If the threat cannot be contained—remember that I did say it could only stop *most* metas—then the area below us will be completely destroyed, including, unfortunately, any personnel who happen to be down there. Remember, above all else, the safety of the guild is paramount. If evidence of what we do were ever uncovered, it would ruin the organization as a whole. Compared to that, a few lives are a smaller cost to pay."

No one objected to his analysis of the situation, even as they grew nervous about the fact that they would soon be in such a place. The guild had its own ways, after all.

Slowly, the elevator came to a smooth halt, and the door opened once more. Stretched out before them was a long metallic hallway, filled with cameras, lasers, and all manner of odd devices that not even Tori could puzzle out the use for. Doctor Mechaniacal wasted no time, stepping forward into the room without so much as crooking a finger in their direction. They all took the message anyway and hurried to keep pace behind the metal-suited man.

"Here, every person entering is scanned on multiple levels, ensuring that they are indeed a member of this guild with permission to be here. Everything from their fingerprints to the very strands of their DNA are evaluated. We have no shortage of wards and special cameras to detect trickery. For today, your respective genetic signatures have been given authorization.

This will not be the case again unless you prove yourselves worthy of full membership. As you can imagine, those who try to gain unauthorized entry are dealt with in all manner of unpleasant ways, most of them quite permanent. And, as before, should those measures fail, everything beyond here will be purged."

His heavy steps echoed off the metal floor as he walked, yet Doctor Mechaniacal's voice overwhelmed them as it rang clearly through the air. Everyone followed, some with tensed nerves as they waited for an unseen trap to spring out and attack them. Eventually, they reached the end of the hallway where a large but simple metal door awaited them. Doctor Mechaniacal reached forward, pressed a small button at the side, and stood back as it began to open.

"We tried to think of a good term for this place, something unassuming that still conveyed the importance of it. Sadly, the more theatrical among our ranks won sway over the vote. Nonetheless, it is with no small amount of pride that I introduce you, Apprentices, to the guild's inner nerve center. Welcome to Sanctum."

*   *   *

There was a small knock on the door of the room. Well, not *the* room. *His* room. Apollo had showed Donald to it the night before, explaining that his very public debut meant it wasn't safe for Donald to go home just yet. At best, as a public persona he would be hounded by the press for the next few weeks, and at worst the people he helped stop might have friends that wanted payback. His room in the AHC headquarters was nice, a bit like a hotel room in one of the places that tried to replicate apartments. They'd stocked the fridge and brought over some of his clothes, which made getting dressed that morning less stressful. Given that he was in a strange place with his whole life turned upside down, nothing was without at least a little stress, though.

Donald opened his door before the third knock, nearly leaping backward in shock at the creature before him. It looked like someone had hurled a half-dozen killer animals into a genetic blender in the hopes of putting all their muscles, scales, and claws into one body.

The thing in front of him seemed unsurprised by his reaction, waiting patiently until Donald seemed a bit more composed. "Morning." Its voice was thick and rough, the sort of sound one might hear in a nightmare just before waking and staring wide-eyed around a darkened room. "My name is Ren Tanaka. Apollo asked me to come down and get you for your fitting."

"R-right," Donald stammered out. "I mean, sorry, nice to meet you. I'm Donald, Donald Moss." Donald began to stick his hand out for the customary handshake, an impulse so ingrained in him by years of corporate schmoozing that his arm was halfway in position before he realized that Ren might accidently shred his hand as easily as shake it. Still, by that point, it was too late to pull away without seeming rude. Donald steeled his nerves and finished the gesture, trusting Ren to have the necessary control of his abilities.

"Nice to meet you." Ren easily shook Donald's hand without leaving him with so much as a scratch. "And don't worry about jumping, most people do far worse the first time they see me. At least you didn't scream."

"If I'm being honest, it was touch and go for a second there." No sooner had the words left his mouth than Donald wished he could yank them back in. Curse his stupid, nervous tongue! He readied himself to apologize again, but before he had the chance, he noticed a deep rumbling coming from Ren's chest, like a cat's purr mixed with a soft bark. It took him a moment to put the pieces together, but eventually logic prevailed and Donald realized that Ren was laughing.

"Nice to meet someone who doesn't tiptoe around all of... this." Ren gestured to all the misshapen strange bits of who he now was. "Most of the other rookies are too put off to even be around me, let alone actually discuss the fact that I look like something out of a bad *Island of Dr. Moreau* knockoff."

"I'd say it's far too well-designed to be a mere knockoff. You're a penny dreadful of your own, if you're anything." Donald had no idea what he was saying, but the large, sharp-toothed grin on Ren's face grew wider, so he assumed things were going well. Or he was about to get eaten. With that expression, things could really go either way.

"Dreadful is going to be the right word if you're late to costuming. Come on, let's get you down there."

Donald didn't pause to lock his door as he followed Ren down the hall. For one thing, there was nothing inside but a few t-shirts, boxers, and a spare pair of khakis. For another, Apollo had explained how every door was keyed to the person supposed to open it. Made things much easier all around.

"I'm curious... since you're on a different track than me, did they get you a name yet?" Ren asked.

"Excuse me, but different track?"

Ren nodded, an action which sent his fur to waving. "Yeah. You're someone who debuted on his own. Along with training, most of us are still being primed for our debuts; everything will be planned, researched, and carefully controlled. The AHC likes to start all of its new superheroes on a good public footing."

"That sounds... so much smarter than what I did." Donald had imagined showing up on the AHC's doorstep and being turned away because his ability was so useless. It had never dawned on him that they might have programs up and running specifically to get him up to snuff.

"I don't know. The longer I'm cooped up in here, the more I wish I'd gotten to do things your way. Jump right into the action, use these powers for something good. Though, without the PR department here managing my debut, people probably would have assumed I was the villain in any situation," Ren admitted.

"Probably beats some giant smashing on your shield, trying to turn to you into a pulped programmer." Donald shivered slightly at the thought, quickly steering the conversation back to more pleasant topics. "I do have a name, to answer your question. Picked it out yesterday. I'm going by Cyber Geek."

"Not too bad." Ren thrust a clawed thumb into his own chest. Only his scales kept him from piercing his sternum. "They're calling me Medley."

"Medley, you say?" Donald turned the name around in his head, trying to find something positive to same about it. "That's certainly..."

"Idiotic? Asinine? Flat-out dumb? Don't worry, I'm well aware." Ren shrugged his massive shoulders as they turned down a new hallway. "But if I want to help people, they can't be scared of me. A name like that helps soften my image, at least according to the market research."

"They market-researched your name? Wow, you weren't kidding about them going all-out on prepping stuff for your debut," Donald noted.

"You don't know the half of it," Ren said. "And if you're lucky, you never will. Let's just say I've had my fill of paperwork and image management. I'm ready to get out there and start actually making a difference."

Donald looked his fellow aspiring superhero up and down, taking in his size and natural defenses. If Ren had been there, the fight with that big meta in the office would have probably gone a lot differently. Then again, if Ren had been there, the robbers probably would have taken one look at him and gone screaming for the hills.

"Is your debut soon?" Donald asked. He had a feeling there would be a lot of criminals watching their shit once Ren took the streets.

"End of this week or the start of the next one," Ren replied. "Almost everything is in place. Once the last few bits are done, it's just a matter of waiting for the right crime. They have a fellow member come out with me, just so no one mistakes me for a bad guy, and then let me help save people or stop bad guys. Afterward, there's a press conference—more or less what you went through."

"What do you do if there's no crime?" Donald had lived in Ridge City all his life, and while things could get crazy on occasion, the big incidents were often weeks, if not months, apart. There were only so many metas dumb enough to tangle with the Alliance of Heroic Champions where they lived, after all.

"There's always crime," Ren told him. "In a city this size it's inevitable, and the AHC keeps watch over way more than just Ridge City. Now, not all of it is meta-human crime; in fact, that's a minority by far, but there's still enough of it that not even us and the police can stop every petty thief and mugger. We try to prioritize our responses to do the best we can. First priority is meta-humans, obviously. Then come situations where we're in less danger than normal cops would be. After that is the mundane stuff, just pitching in where we can."

"Gotcha. Guess I'm going to have to learn about all this," Donald said.

Ren stopped walking, reached over, and patted Donald carefully on the shoulder. "Don't sweat it too much. They've been training new superheroes in here for decades; they know how to prep us for the real world. Just do your best, and hopefully you won't make any big screw-ups that get people killed."

"Well, that's encouraging," Donald muttered.

"That's the gig," Ren said, giving another giant shrug. "Anyway, this is your stop. Just go through the door behind me and you'll be whisked into a world of fittings and fabrics. Try and endure it as stoically as possible. Think of it as a rite of passage, if that helps."

"Did it help you?" Donald asked, grabbing the doorknob and beginning to turn.

"Hell no. But you'll get through it. And afterwards, we can get some lunch and I'll introduce you around."

Donald smiled and nodded. His first full day in the AHC and it seemed like he'd actually managed to make a friend. "I'll look forward to it."

Chapter 38

For three of the four apprentices, what was revealed behind the door was initially anti-climactic. For Tori, whose mind and study had long been devoted to cutting edge technology, Doctor Mechaniacal might as well have opened the pearly gates and ushered her directly into heaven itself.

In the spacious room were a bevy of devices visibly branching off into several distinct hallways, scattered about as if they weren't technological marvels worthy of being put on display. With a single glance, Tori recognized a spatial anchoring apparatus (meant to stop spatial manipulators like Tunnel Vision from breaking and entering), a quantum entanglement relay (to talk with people over any distance), and what she took to be a cellular recombination machine, or techno-teleporter, which had heretofore had only been discussed on a theoretical level. This was on top of the dozen or so smaller wonders as well as a massive hub of computers.

The remainder of the apprentices entered behind Tori, who was fighting not to sprint ahead of Doctor Mechaniacal with all her self-control. They turned their attention to the room's natural focal point: a large digital display showing several columns of information.

"This is what we colloquially refer to as 'the job board.'" Doctor Mechaniacal pointed to the display, more to direct Tori's attention to where the lesson was meant to take place than anything else. "Nothing in this area can be connected to by outside sources, regardless of what powers or tech they're using. Any internet access is run through various hubs that are all set to disconnect the minute anything non-requested tries to come through the system. The reason for all the security is that in here, in this place of safety, we plan and discuss the crimes committed by guild members. The job board is where it all begins and ends."

He moved forward once more, walking down the metal stairs onto the crisp white-tile floor below, followed by the apprentices. Soon they were standing directly beneath the digital display. Now closer, they could make out that within each of the columns were various listings, each with a title and short description. They could also see that the columns were color-coded: red, yellow, and green.

"When a member of this guild has the idea for a job, they submit it to their council representative for review," Doctor Mechaniacal continued. "After it's been vetted and we're sure there are no conflicts with the code, it is posted down here on the job board. You can access this feature from any terminal in Sanctum, learning all the details about what's planned, seeing who has signed on in various capacities, what the expected score is, what roles are still needed... you know what? This probably a lot easier if I just show you a sample."

Doctor Mechanical waved his metallic hand at the screen, and to their surprise, one of the listings in the red column expanded, filling the entire gigantic display. After reading over it for a minute, he turned back around so that the front of his helmet was facing them.

"That will do nicely. What you see here is a planned robbery of an art house in Madrid. As you can tell at a glance, Pointillism is listed in the 'Leader' role, as she's the one who put this job together. She created the plan, she calls the shots while in the field, and she is entitled to a larger cut of the proceeds. In fact, if you glance below her name, you'll see she's offering a fifty-fifty split, where she takes fifty percent of the profits and the other fifty is split equally among the others who do the job. I should note that usually leaders will take a bit less than this, but because Pointillism has a reputation for pulling off flawless jobs, she's able to demand a bit more of the take."

A quick crook of the finger from Doctor Mechaniacal and the screen zoomed in on the section below Pointillism's name. This area was filled with basic role descriptions, though most of the sections next to them were empty. There were, however, two names gracing the lower list.

"As you can see here, Pointillism needs two people with enhanced strength—roles that Smash and Grab have filled. These three often work together; in fact, Smash and Grab may have been included on the plan submission itself. The other openings on this job are for a teleporter and someone who can hack the computer security. Since this opening just went up today, I wouldn't at all be surprised if applications have already been submitted. I imagine those roles will be filled before this evening. Like I said before, Pointillism has a reputation for clean plans and solid executions. She only works with good people, and the scores she goes for are usually large. In this case, she's aiming for around twenty million dollars' worth of sculptures."

Everyone could clearly see the giant total on the screen, a mind-boggling amount to most of them. Even with Pointillism taking half, that would work out to two and a half million dollars per person for what seemed like a few days' work, max. Tori suddenly understood why just being in this guild could lead so many into the arms of crime. With only a few jobs like that, she'd have enough seed money to start all the companies she wanted.

"I should also point out that the guild charges a three percent tax on the gains from all jobs here—far less than the government would, but enough to help keep the lights on," Doctor Mechaniacal added. "As far as being the leader of a job goes, right now you're all no doubt thinking it's a cushy gig. Submit a good plan, approve some competent cohorts, and take home the lion's share of the profits. You should know, however, that being in the leadership role comes with more than just a higher payday: it also means you are the one held accountable if things go awry. I'm not saying the mistakes of others will be laid at your feet, but should a job you pull turn into a problem for us, and especially if the code is broken, then you will be held accountable for that failure. At this point in your training, I trust I don't have to explain what that means."

Doctor Mechanical made a motion and the screen shrank, the three color-coded columns and their accompanying listings having shrunk back to their original size. "Now then. What we just looked at was a red job, meaning it was illegal and came with serious risk for all those involved. That's not the only way to apply our talents, though, which is why there are other colors." He flicked his finger at the screen, and suddenly the middle column grew to dominate the digital space.

"Yellow jobs, as seen in the middle column, are jobs that, while often criminal adjacent, pose a low risk of arrest. We often get requests to arrange transportation for people that wish to move about unseen by law enforcement, to provide a bodyguard for an unstable and illegal situation, or to obscure unscrupulous bank transactions. Those requests are received by our people tasked with such work, and those we accept go in the yellow column."

Another motion and the final column became the largest on the screen.

"Green jobs are ones that occur within the guild itself. Maybe someone needs help getting rid of some scrapped robots or a councilor wants a new assistant. These are done for a fair wage, which is specified in the listing. Since this is a guild of villainy, there is always the chance that taking a green job will result in light criminal activity, but it should never be anything too extreme."

Spiel complete, Doctor Mechaniacal allowed the display to go back to its default setting. He carefully examined the faces of the apprentices before him to make sure they had absorbed the information. It wasn't that complicated; in fact, the council had worked hard to keep things exceedingly simple. But the system was deeper than it seemed on first glance. Having to assess jobs, both the risks they carried and the rewards they offered, took a lot of practice, and that was without even factoring in the skills of the people one would be working alongside. This would be the bread and butter of their activities in the guild, unless they all made a beeline for Ivan's department, which was doubtful. It was hard to walk away once those dollar signs danced in front of one's eyes.

"This will, of course, all come to you assuming you prove yourselves worthy to be members of this guild. To achieve that, we will spend the rest of the weekend on more training, but we won't be stopping there. For the next two weeks, you will be shadowing guild members on jobs, sometimes in mock situations, sometimes in real ones. At the end of that time, you four will be expected to put together a job of your own. Think of it as a demonstration of skill."

Though she'd known it was coming, Tori still pretended to reel a bit like the others. Ivan had been right; they truly were coming to the end of their time as apprentices. Soon it would be all or nothing, and she could scarcely wait. When the time came, she had no intention of coming up short.

Especially if she had her meta-suit ready.

*   *   *

"All right, sorry about that. The fire is more or less under control, so we can get back to the meeting."

Professor Quantum's voice held no signs of distress over the sudden explosion and fire that had come from his side of the call. Others might have been more surprised by his calm demeanor, but after years of working alongside one another, Quorum and Lodestar knew to take such things in stride. As a being with nigh-incomparable intellect and almost unstoppable physical powers, Professor Quantum simply did not rattle easily.

"Glad to hear it. I hope none of your assistants were injured," Quorum said. He sat alone in the conference room with only the remote relays used by the Congress's two other members to keep him company. It had been this way for years now. First Lodestar had taken her leave, then Professor Quantum had begun spending more and more time in that island lab of his. It didn't bother Quorum from a social perspective—alone was one of the few things he could never feel—but it certainly didn't do much to help the other members feel looked after. That was, in fact, the point of the day's meeting, and why Apollo hadn't been asked to sit in on it.

"Where were we?" Professor Quantum asked.

"Quorum was making the case that one of us should officially resign our post and let the new kid take up the slack," Lodestar informed him.

"Apollo has been with the AHC for nearly a decade now. He's one of the most popular, respected members of our organization and has worked hard to learn every aspect of how things are run," Quorum replied. "He is anything but 'the new kid' by any measurement. I believe it will do the others good to see him move up to the Champions' Congress. Absentee overseers are not helpful for morale."

"Personally, I never much cared for the boy," said Professor Quantum. "Too overt with his ambitions. He's blatantly had his sights set on a Congress seat since almost the first day he was brought in. I believe those on the Congress should be able to conduct themselves with a bit more discretion."

"If this kid's worst sin is wanting to take on a hard, thankless job and working his way toward it, then maybe he does deserve a shot." Lodestar and Professor Quantum disagreed almost by tradition at this point, though she had always tended to be the one to give people the benefit of the doubt.

"Apollo is not perfect," Quorum said. "That can also be said about any of us. Yes, he is ambitious and poor at hiding it. He also puts on a show of constant cheer and encouragement to keep up a positive image, despite having as wide a range of emotion as any of us. He is young and brash and sometimes a bit too quick to jump to battle when talking could work. However, he has great potential and the desire to serve this Congress well. Better to bring him in now, flaws and all, so that he can have two experienced members to learn under. If we ever intend to pass the reins of the AHC to the next generation, this is a necessary first step we'll one day have to take." Many of the voices in his head were already correcting Quorum's words, but he ignored them. This was the decision that he'd made, and he would see it through.

Silence stretched across the untold distances while his fellow superheroes, founders of the very organization tasked with helping to keep the world safe from rogue meta-humans, pondered what would be best for the AHC's future. All of them had the ability, or curse, to live long lives, but if they never relinquished leadership, then eventually the AHC would atrophy. Fresh blood, new perspective, those things were essential to keeping an organization moving forward. They all knew this, had discussed this, yet still it was hard for any of them to let go of what they'd worked so hard to build, even a little bit.

"He can have my spot," Lodestar said at last. "At least on a trial basis. I'll still listen in and check up on things, but if he can show me that he's really got what it takes, then we can do the full hand-off and make things official. Quorum's right: our people need to see their leaders putting in the work just like them. Since I can't do that anymore, the best thing for me to do is find someone who can."

"We will be sad to see you go," Professor Quantum told her. "Perhaps I'll even arrange a trip to Ridge City so I can attend a few of these meetings in person with Apollo. In a few months, when my schedule relents, of course."

"Of course," Quorum said. "We all know how busy you are."

"Busy and productive," Professor Quantum replied. "Come this time next year, I daresay I'll have quite the interesting package to send your way."

"I'll look forward to that. In the meantime, I'll bring Apollo in and let him know that he's officially to begin training for replacing Lodestar on the Champions' Congress. We'll keep it private for now until everything is official; although, I'll need to upgrade his security clearances if we're going to teach him to do the work," Quorum said.

"I know you'll take him down to the vault, but try and keep him from touching the pleasure orb we took from that alien with the nineteen heads and fire breath," Lodestar cautioned. "Unless he has willpower like iron, he'll be down for a week at least, and then you'll have to get his mind purged of the memory or he'll be addicted."

"Please also instruct him that the ancient device we uncovered south of Egypt is to be looked at, not touched," Professor Quantum added. "I do not have time to undo another rip in dimensional space that allows dinosaurs to come stomping about."

"I assure you both, we will observe full safety protocol when touring every bit of the restricted areas, including the vault," Quorum promised. "Now, if there are no more objections, I will go fetch Apollo and we can give him the good news."

"Go for it," Lodestar replied, her voice present even as her body and mind sat elsewhere, pondering the idea of truly stepping out of the AHC. "We might as well get this over with."

Chapter 39

Sunday evening found Ivan waiting patiently for Tori, as well as cleaning the kitchen while he had the opportunity. Since Wade had arranged for the robotic cars to drop her off at the end of the weekend, it meant a bit more alone time for Ivan. With the kids at their mother's and his apprentice undergoing training, the weekend had been the first real bit of peace he'd gotten in weeks. This was how it used to be before Wade showed up talking about a stubborn woman who needed guidance. It was a calm, measured, safe existence. It was what Ivan had fought so hard to obtain all those years ago, and after two days of it, he was ready to climb the damn walls with boredom.

There was no doubt where the blame for this shift in attitude lay; it was unquestionably Tori's fault. She'd been dragging him back into the guild's world a bit at a time, whetting his appetite for intrigue and adventure. Ivan felt like a long-sober alcoholic who'd accidently taken a sip of vodka. The cravings he'd thought were gone came surging back through his brain as if it were the first day all over again. Once upon a time, his hunger for excitement, chaos, and battle had led him to take on every cape he came across. Now older and wiser, Ivan didn't quite feel the urge to charge up the AHC's front door and pick a fight, but he also wasn't quite as content with cleaning the kitchen as he once might have been.

A slam from the front door echoed through the house, signaling that his apprentice had arrived at last. Ivan stepped out from the kitchen, dishtowel still in hand, just in time to catch Tori making a beeline for the secret entrance to the basement. She looked weary—a weekend of guild training would do that to nearly anyone—but there was excitement burning in her eyes as she rushed toward the bookshelf.

"Not even a hello?" Ivan said, watching his apprentice carefully.

"Hi, how's it going? Life good? Family healthy? Nice catching up, then, talk to you later." Tori spat the words out as quickly as she could, racing all the faster for the hidden doorway now that she knew Ivan was trying to stop her.

"Freeze," Ivan commanded. To her credit, Tori immediately complied, though her eyes never really looked away from her destination for more than a few seconds. "What's the rush to get down to the basement?"

"What do you think the rush is?" Tori replied. "I've got two weeks until we're supposed to pull a job to prove we can get into the guild, a job which will literally have my life on the line. I need to get my meta-suit in working order by then; otherwise, I'm going into yet another situation with a hand tied behind my back."

"Most people would consider your powers advantage enough," Ivan pointed out.

"Maybe so, but most people can't build what I can build, so they don't have a good perspective." Tori nodded to the wall, her whole body leaning slightly forward in excitement. "Now, I've spent all my downtime this weekend planning how to get it up and running with the little windows I'll have to work in between the office and the night training, so can I please go get in some work before my whole plan goes to shit?"

"You can if you really want to. My apologies for holding you up," Ivan said. He watched as she bolted over to the wall, but before she could trigger the door, he spoke again. "I just thought I'd tell you that we're both going to have next week off from the office."

"Waaaait, who the what now?" Tori's hand paused halfway to the door's opening device, unable to continue forward. "Why are we off? People knew we were getting transported to a place with fancy metas as doctors."

Ivan set the kitchen towel on the living room table and took a seat. Though he made no gestures and said nothing, seconds later Tori walked over to join him. Now that she knew there would be more time to work, her curiosity was winning out over her drive to jump into the basement.

"Yes, we will make much faster recoveries than anyone would expect without meta involvement," Ivan assured her. "However, particularly in situations like the ones you and I found ourselves in, a weekend is too short a time to return to work. Assuming our physical injuries could be healed that quickly, which is suspect for people as unimportant as we are supposed to be, there's also the mental health issue. We were both attacked. I was shot, and you had your ribs broken. As the nice, normal office workers we're supposed to be, don't you think we might need a little bit of time to emotionally process all of that?"

"Right... I sort of forget we're not supposed to be badasses," Tori admitted.

"It's the kind of small detail that on its own might slip by unnoticed, but if enough of its kind accumulate, someone could put things together." Ivan gently tapped the table, making sure he had his apprentice's attention. "When you're on your own, if you choose to keep this civilian identity, that sort of attention to detail will help you last a lot longer."

"I'll keep that in mind." There was no sarcasm in her tone; after fighting so hard to retain her secret only days before, she'd begun to realize how important her mundane life was. It was a place to get away from the madness of the guild, something that gave her perspective on the world and how things were supposed to work. Among people with tremendous power and flexible morality, it was easy to lose sight of what things were like in the real world. "So, what's the story, anyway? Are we spending the week in the loony bin?"

"We're undergoing counseling, which will continue after we return to work," Ivan told her. "The guild will falsify all the necessary paperwork and doctor's notes, which no one will question because right now, the management views us as both heroes and potential lawsuits."

Tori leaned back in her chair, not quite so far that she risked tipping but enough to stretch her tired back. "That's so nice of them, considering I got shot in the arm four times."

"To be fair, you did that to yourself," Ivan reminded her.

"Yeah, well, Chloe's power isn't the easiest to work with. Speaking of, can I go check on her at some point? I know you said she's okay, but given how much she helped, I feel like I owe her a face-to-face."

"Chloe is doing well, though she's actually going to be taking the week off and getting some counseling, too, just to make certain she's all right," Ivan said. "And don't worry; we're footing the bill for her treatment as well. You can check in on her next week, when you're both supposed to be back at work."

"Guess that will help sell the story all the more." Tori rose from the table, waiting for Ivan to stop her. When nothing came, she turned toward the wall, mind already intent on the basement. "You're really good at keeping up the act, I have to say. One day, I'm going to get you tell me why you really decided to hang up the costume and go mundane."

"Was the offer of freedom coupled with the fact that the world was ending not a believable reason?" Ivan asked.

"Back then, sure, but we've been at this for a while now. I've gotten to know you pretty well, and you're a stubborn guy. For you to have completely turned over a new leaf, to commit as hard to this as you did, I know there's something else at play."

For the second time that night, Tori was nearly to the basement entrance when Ivan's words stopped her dead in her tracks.

"I'll trade you."

"Trade me what?"

"The truth. The whole story of why I took the offer, why I adhered to the Orion Protocol. In exchange, I want you to tell me why you're so dead-set on living the way you have. With a brain like yours, you could have gotten a job at any tech company in the world. With powers like yours, there was never any need for a meta-suit. Yet you keep on pushing, taking the hardest path possible. So I'm up for a trade, if you're amenable to the terms."

Ivan sat still at the table, patiently waiting for a reply. He wasn't pressuring her or forcing her hand, merely making an offer: tit-for-tat, information for information.

"Seems to me like you're asking for more than you're offering." Tori turned around slowly, locking eyes with her teacher. "I think I can fill in a lot of the gaps for myself on your story; all I'm seeking is details. You, on the other hand, are asking for some pretty personal shit."

"Is this you saying no?"

"This is me saying sweeten the pot," Tori replied. "A trade is only fair if it's equal."

Ivan turned this over in his head a few times, debating on what he was willing to offer to know his apprentice's secrets. He'd found out much on his own through research, but there was a large difference between reading a file and hearing a person tell a story. So much more could be learned from the latter that the two were hardly even worth comparing. Of course, that was just as true for him as it was for her, which meant he had to be careful how much of his own past he gave away.

"I will tell you the root of my power," Ivan said. "Not the story of how I acquired it or any useful details regarding how it works, however. Truthfully, this will leave you with more questions than answers, but it's still something precious few people know. If that isn't good enough, then I suppose we don't have a deal."

"No, I think that'll do. But you're going first." Tori walked past Ivan into the freshly cleaned kitchen and pulled a cold beer from the fridge. Much as she liked to be clear-headed when she worked, this sort of talk called for at least a little liquid fortification.

"Only for the first part. My power, we save for last, otherwise you'll want to ask me more questions instead of offering up your story," Ivan countered, calling through the doorway.

Halfway back, Tori stopped, reopened the fridge, and poured a tall glass of sweet tea for Ivan. He might want a little fortification of his own, after all. Gripping both drinks, Tori walked back into the living room, set the tea down in front of Ivan, and retook her seat.

"I guess that's fair," Tori said at last.

Ivan reached out and took hold of the glass, treating himself to a long sip of the cold beverage before he began to speak. "I'm sure you know Lodestar was the one who finally brought me in, got me locked away in Rookstone with the other criminal meta-humans. We fought several times, but I always managed to get away when she had the upper hand. I was convinced I could beat her if I only had the right strategy, could build up enough power. When the day of our

270

last fight came, I gave it everything I could manage. All my power, all my strength, every tactic and trick I could conceive of, and it just flat-out wasn't enough. She beat me, defeated me in a way I'd never experienced before. Now, much as that sounds like the start of a story of lifelong vengeance, it's hard not to have some amount of respect for an opponent like that. I guess she felt the same way—there weren't many metas who could challenge her—because even after hauling me off to jail, she would still visit from time to time."

"Wait, you and Lodestar hung out together?" Tori didn't exactly doubt the story, but she was definitely having trouble wrapping her head around it.

"Think of it more as community outreach. Lodestar believed that there was potential in me, that I could be more than a battle-thirsty punk. Of course, she saw the good in everyone, so it wasn't that surprising, but even now, I think she took a special interest in me. Maybe she really did see something, or maybe she just knew the day might come when she needed an ally like me. Anyway, once Orion turned into a cataclysmic threat, she was the one they sent to talk to me, to make me the offer."

"Damn. I was not expecting it to be friendship with Lodestar that turned you around." Tori sipped at her beer, entranced by the story but keenly aware that her turn was fast approaching.

"It wasn't," Ivan told her. "When Lodestar showed up that day, she didn't come empty-handed. She brought along a picture of a baby, only a few months old at the time, and put it down on the table in front of me. I'd slept with a woman who had a thing for bad boys before Lodestar brought me in, and, well... I wasn't making the best decisions back then, ideas about protection included. When Lodestar made the pitch, she didn't lean on the part where I'd have a shot at freedom. Instead, she just showed me the picture and explained how things were. Orion was trying to destroy the world and every living creature on it. One of those creatures, as it turned out, was my son."

Ivan paused, looking down at the glass in his hand, drops of condensation running down the side, one at a time. "I don't expect you to understand. Up until that moment, I don't think I possibly could have either, but there's something primal about being a parent. Something powerful. Suddenly, Orion wasn't just some threat trying to wipe out existence. He was threatening my family, my blood. As soon as Lodestar showed me that photo, I knew I would charge the very gates of hell if it meant keeping that baby safe. That's why I took the deal. That's why I tried so hard to honor it, too. Even gave it an honest go with his mother, which is how his sister came about. We live in a strange, powerful, dangerous world. I decided I would be there to watch over my children, even if it meant setting aside the life I'd known until then. Fornax died

271

the moment I knew I was a father, though I did borrow his name one last time to end Orion."

"Shit. I suspected it had something to do with your kids, but I didn't imagine it went down quite like that," Tori admitted. "Pretty shrewd of Lodestar to save her trump card until she needed it."

Ivan chuckled and shook his head. "Lodestar doesn't think that way. She never told me about my son because she thought it would be cruel; I was in a place where I could never see him, never talk to him, never hug him. It wasn't until there was a chance for my freedom that she decided to tell me."

"Guess that morality is why you just trusted she wasn't making it all up," Tori said.

"That, and a few talents of my own." Ivan took a draw from his tea and stared at Tori. He didn't bother telling her that it was her turn; that much was obvious. Instead, he let her get her thoughts together and speak when she was ready.

"My story isn't as long or fancy as yours," she said at last. "It's just a hard life lesson I learned early on. My parents were both scientists—Dad a biologist and Mom a physicist. They worked hard, gave me a solid education from the day I was born, nurtured my mental talent as soon as they recognized it. Both of them had such high hopes for me. Then, one day there was an accident at the lab where they worked. Might have been a confluence, actually, since more than a few people left that day as metas. My parents weren't among them."

The air around Tori shimmered softly as she spoke, and her grip on the beer bottle tightened. Ivan knew how hard she'd been working to gain control of her emotions affecting her powers, which made it all the more worrying to see the heat slipping out.

"They just got sick. Bad sick. Like a meta-version of cancer. It ripped through them so fast. In only a couple of weeks, they were so filled with tumors... well, you get the idea. There were treatment options, of course. With all the metas in the world, there's always someone who can fix what ails you, be it by spell or machine or just talent, but those options are impossibly expensive. And the company they worked for, the one who owned the lab that made them sick, refused to pay what it would have cost to save them. Said they'd signed non-liability agreements, that the lab wasn't culpable. They just let my parents sit in that goddamned hospital room and rot away from the inside out."

Tori was crying now—not a full-on sob, but small, short-lived tears that evaporated before they were halfway down her face. Ivan had seen many tears throughout his life, and he knew enough to tell that these were not shed from grief, but from anger.

272

"I sat there, watching them die by the hour. And in that time, I realized something important: my parents spent their lives working hard to help other people, and when the time for repayment came, those other people skipped out. I wasn't going to go down that path. I would work for myself, make my own way in the world. I'd never be left on a bed, slowly dying because my fate ended up in some corporate asshole's hands. That's why I went out on my own. That's why I decided it was better to scrounge and steal than indenture myself to anyone else."

"You have my condolences," Ivan said simply. There was nothing else to tell her, nothing she didn't already know. It was a tragedy. Had he been there at the time, he'd have done all he could to change it. But it was long over, and not even metas had the power to bring back the dead. "Is that also why you work so hard on the meta-suit? So you'll be able to live under your own power?"

"That was part of why I started," Tori admitted. "I had to create inventions and that seemed like a good place to kick things off. But, to be honest, I think I really picked up the project as a memorial. My mother loved meta-suits. She believed they could bridge the gap between metas and humans. Everyone who has made one so far has kept the tech all to themselves, which means that if I manage to develop one that anyone can use, I'll be able to launch a huge company and make my mother's dream come true all at once. Double-whammy, you know?"

"Two birds with one stone, indeed." Ivan finished off his tea then rose to go get another glass. By the time he'd returned with a fresh beer that hadn't been nearly boiled, Tori had regained her composure. She accepted the drink with a nod of thanks, taking a long draw before addressing her teacher.

"So, did that satisfy you?"

"It answered many of my questions, yes. And my story?"

"Explained a lot about you," Tori replied. "Though there is one part left unfulfilled. If both of the other parts are done, you owe me an origin story."

"No, I owe you only what the root of my power is," Ivan corrected. "No story, no explanations, only the simple source of my meta-abilities."

"Yeah, I get it, more questions than answers; just get on with it already. I'd still like to squeeze in a little work tonight, if you don't mind."

"Fair enough. My powers come from a magical source—which is no surprise—that I encountered in my youth. While the exact relationship I have with that source has altered tremendously since the beginning, I'd say things have been constant for the last several decades. Explaining that relationship though... how shall I phrase this?" Ivan drummed his fingers, took a drink from his tea, and finally found the right combination of words that suited his needs.

"To put it as simply as possible: I ate a god."

Chapter 40

"We're not doing it tonight," Morgana said, barely resisting the urge to slam her hand on the table. "That's their first day, and it's an imprudent way to start things off. They *do* need to get some actual field training in."

"Plus, it's Monday," Stasis added. Unlike Morgana, she wasn't taking things too seriously, which was par for the course with how things went when they were both involved. Leaning back in her chair, feet on the table, Stasis might as well have been doing her nails, had she actually been able to do anything to them. Instead, she was skimming through a beat-up romance novel starring a swarthy Latin hero named Rodrigo. "There's nothing worth doing on a Monday."

"Well, we can't do it on the last day. Doc will say they need to have a level head for their upcoming planning session," Xelas shot back. Next to her, Gork laid a reassuring hand on her metal friend's shoulder, a simple act that helped keep Xelas's sharp tongue in check.

"Training runs for two weeks," Gork said in her slow, lumbering voice. "Let's do it on the first Friday, the one coming up. It will be a nice break in the middle."

"Friday works for me," Stasis said. "That's when there's shit actually worth doing."

"I can swing that, though I'm still not sure I should," Morgana admitted.

All four of the female councilors were gathered together in a meeting room that was technically only supposed to be used for official crime-planning purposes. Given their high position in the guild, though, they'd commandeered it for their own use without feeling guilty about it in the slightest. There were certain perks to being villains, after all.

"Come on. It'll be good for the apprentices, and for us," Xelas said. "When was the last time the four of us all went out to tear up the town?"

"Literally? That incident in Canada a few years back. Figuratively? I feel like it's only been a little while." Stasis leaned so far back that her center of gravity should have tipped the chair over, yet she remained supported. "Let's see, I'd just won my second term on the council, which was... holy shit, it has been a while, hasn't it?"

"That's what I'm saying!" Xelas thrust an arm in the air, a gesture either meant to rally the others around her or signal victory; no one was entirely sure which. "We go out in ones and twos on occasion, but we really need to do something together regularly. We're on the council, we need to bond."

"If its bonding you're after, why not invite the guys too?" Stasis asked.

"Because then Balaam would come," Morgana said, intercepting the question. "And no one considers him and Pseudonym bickering at one another a good time. Plus the dog shtick got tired a long time ago."

"Bal's not so bad on his own," Stasis defended. "But yeah, he does have a stick up his ass when it comes to Pseudonym. Fine: we keep it as a girls' night, just us four and the two female apprentices."

"That's what I like to hear." Xelas glanced at the plasma television mounted on the conference room's wall. Seconds later, it turned on and displayed an itinerary on its high-definition screen. "Now that we've got the date down, it's time to decide what we'll do with them."

"Let's try not to get either of them killed, either that night or by expulsion from the guild," Morgana suggested. "Pseudonym and Thuggernaut are both quite fond of their apprentices, whether they'll admit it or not."

"Nothing to worry about," Xelas assured her. "Truth be told, I sort of like them as well. They've got spunk. We'll keep things nice and low-key, nothing that will get them in trouble."

The room was quiet as the three other women stared at Xelas. None of them spoke; they simply waited patiently for what would inevitably come next. After having worked together for so long, none were surprised when a mischievous twinkle sparked through her mechanical eyes and a slight smirk turned up on the side of her lips.

"Well, not *that* much trouble, I mean."

*　　　*　　　*

When Donald showed up to work that morning, he hadn't been quite sure what to expect. The stares were strange, but that much had been anticipated, along with the whispering. What took him by surprise was the way people gave him a wide berth, doing little more than wave from across the cubicle lanes. He hadn't shown up in costume or with the new wrist computer they'd given him or anything; he'd shown up as regular old Donald Moss, programmer for Vendallia Industries for over five years.

He should have expected something from Apollo's reaction when Donald told him he had to go to work that day. There were too many projects still left undone, and he didn't want to leave his coworkers in the lurch by up and quitting all at once. Plus, he still wasn't entirely sure how superheroes got paid, which made the idea of giving up his income stream a frightening prospect on top of everything else. Apollo had listened, nodded, and then said he would arrange some transportation and protection, just in case someone tried to sneak attack him. That seemed normal enough. What struck Donald as odd, though, was that Apollo had made sure he knew the car would be on call all day: whenever Donald was ready to come back, it was only a phone call away.

He was only halfway to his lunch break, and Donald had already figured out why Apollo drove the point home. This place wasn't the same anymore; people looked at him completely differently. He'd helped keep them all safe, and they did seem appreciative of that, but it didn't change the fact that they were also afraid of him. Donald wasn't just Donald anymore. Now, when they looked at him, what they saw was a meta.

"Mr. Moss? We weren't expecting to see you in today."

Donald spun around in his chair, slightly startling the suited brunette standing just inside his cube. Mrs. Espinoza was Mr. Gerhardt's boss; she worked on a different floor than they did and usually only showed up for special meetings or when someone was in trouble. Before he could answer his own question with a little thought, Donald blurted out the first thing that came to mind.

"Where's Mr. Gerhardt?"

"The hospital, of course," Mrs. Espinoza replied. "Even with exceptional care, gunshot wounds take some time to recover from, at least for most people. I'm filling in for him while he's gone."

"Right." Right. Mr. Gerhardt would need some time to recover from getting shot in the gut, to say nothing of Tori and all the wounds she'd accumulated helping him. At the thought of Tori, Donald felt a pang of guilt about covering up her help that day. Even if it was to protect Chloe, taking all the credit still felt wrong. "Do you know what hospital they're at? I'd like to bring flowers and visit, if I can."

"I'm sorry, since they were taken for... special treatment, we weren't given the name or location of their hospital. Protected secret, I'm sure you understand." Mrs. Espinoza looked him up and down once more as if she were waiting for him to grow horns and attack her. Which maybe she was; Apollo had made a point of not telling the press exactly what Donald's power was until they'd created his identity, so no one in the office had any idea exactly *how* he'd stopped two armed men and one meta.

"Anyway, Mr. Moss, may I ask what brings you back here today?" Mrs. Espinoza continued, still keeping a careful distance from him.

"It's Monday, I wasn't injured in the fight, and I didn't get any e-mail about the office being closed," Donald told her. He tilted his head slightly, trying to see what she was getting at.

"No, I understand that work is proceeding as normal today. I was just wondering why you felt the need to show up."

"Because..." At last, comprehension dawned on Donald. "Wait, did I get *fired*?"

"Certainly not, Mr. Moss, certainly not," Mrs. Espinoza protested, her voice rising a few octaves, as if she wanted others to be aware of the conversation that was taking place. "Vendallia Industries would never violate federal law by firing someone upon discovering they were a meta-human, especially a meta-human who helped safeguard our office only days before. We just all assumed that, when the AHC scooped you up, you'd prefer working with them to your simple job here."

Donald glanced around, noticing that nearly everyone else in earshot had stopped what they were doing to watch the scene that was unfolding in his cubicle. He wasn't sure if they were hoping he would deck the boss or slink out the door, but it seemed pretty clear they'd been waiting all morning for exactly this discussion to take place. Much as he wanted to be annoyed or even angry, Donald reminded himself that only a month or so ago he'd have been staring with as much, if not more, curiosity. Metas were nothing if not fascinating.

"Nice as the AHC has been, I didn't feel right leaving my work unfinished," Donald said at last. "Besides, I like working here; the people are nice and pay is fair. Maybe once I get a little more settled in my new... side job... that will change, but for the moment, I'm happy to be here doing my part."

"And we're happy to have you." In spite of the forced smile on her face as Mrs. Espinoza fled his cubicle, he had a feeling that management was anything but happy to have him around. A meta was one thing, but a meta who'd openly come out as a cape and might be targeted for retribution, that was a whole other kettle of fish.

Staring at the code on his computer screen, Donald wondered if he was selfish for trying to come back here. This wasn't his world, not anymore. All he was really doing was disrupting the lives of people who had normal jobs to get done. Maybe it would be better if he just stayed at the AHC headquarters and spent this time training. There was obviously some sort of stipend available; pretty much zero famous capes held day jobs.

Donald started to push away from his desk, turning on reflex to tell Tori he was heading out, when he realized he'd be talking to an empty workstation. He paused, then pulled his chair back to its proper position. He couldn't leave, not just yet. The least Donald owed Tori was a proper goodbye, and an apology for leaving her out of the story. One week of working amid the stares and whispers wasn't that high of a price to pay if it meant setting things right.

Plus, if Donald were completely honest with himself, he wasn't sure he'd ever see her again if he left without saying something. And he definitely didn't want to have seen the last of Tori Rivas.

*   *   *

Balaam sat in the small media room, one occasionally used for classic film screenings or bad movie nights. It had a dozen leather chairs set up in a tiered seating system, a popcorn machine in the corner with a soda fountain adjacent, and a massive screen at the far end of the windowless room. Although he'd availed himself of the popcorn—that smell made it nearly impossible to resist—it wasn't a movie that Balaam sat watching in the darkness. At least, not a fictional one.

On the screen before him, Fornax leapt off the ground, so much magical energy pouring off him that the camera warped and stuttered, barely able to sustain its task. There were precious few records of this fight, or any of Fornax's battles for that matter. Of course, Balaam had pored through the accounts and testimonies from witnesses at the various scenes, but that was a poor substitute for watching the action himself. And was there ever action.

He watched as Fornax collided in midair with the glowing figure that was Lodestar. While his name was a silly reference to a black hole, hers was actually a well-chosen moniker. People often described the aura Lodestar put off as golden, but it only appeared that way in the after-streaks it left behind. When one gazed into the genuine article, they could see it was a silver-white color, like the twinkling of a star on a dark night. Except that she didn't twinkle: she burned like the heart of a demon.

In a single swing, Lodestar whipped Fornax around, smashing him into the concrete and sending the amateur cinematographer scrambling for cover. When they reemerged, she stood on top of Fornax, raining down blows that would have shattered mountains. Yet he took each one with that madman's grin he'd been so famous for. Seizing an opportunity, he kicked her in the stomach, barely moving her back an inch but giving himself time to move. In a blink, he was behind her, and the fight began anew.

Balaam had watched this and every other known video of Fornax's fights more times than he could actually count, just as he'd watched the ones of Doctor Mechaniacal, Xelas, and Morgana. Of the entire guild, they were the only four who might be strong enough to stop him, should a fight ever occur. Gork and Stasis, while powerful in their own right, were easily circumvented, at least.

As a spellcaster and a man who had embraced that title in every sense of the word, Balaam had long been a believer in preparation above all else. Even if the possibility of a fight with his fellow councilors didn't loom on the horizon, he preferred to be ready anyway. One never knew what others were scheming, after all. That was why he took time out of his schedule to watch these tapes. Hell, that was why he'd had Warren watch the video from the desert trial over and over again until his apprentice knew the capabilities of the others backwards and forwards. The more one knew, the more one could be ready for, and the higher the chances of victory in any given situation.

This all sounded good on paper, though if one were to check the logs of Balaam's viewing habits, they might notice that he watched the Fornax videos far more than any of the others. If pressed, he would have defended the choice by saying that, as one of the most dangerous metas on record, Fornax warranted the most research. Or, if the query came from someone who knew him well, he would simply say that he enjoyed watching Fornax get pummeled, which Lodestar certainly achieved. But while both of those answers had some merit, neither of them would be entirely true. Because the simple fact of the matter was that, much as he might loathe Ivan Gerhardt for tucking his tail between his legs and giving up on what had made him great, Balaam felt the same as he had when he first saw these fights as a child.

They were thrilling, filled with tension and excitement, the power of the two individuals involved palpable even through the camera. This moment in time, this battle between demi-gods, was what encapsulated metas more than anything else in their history. This was what they could be when truly pushed to be their best.

This was what they would be again, when Balaam was finished.

Chapter 41

After Friday's attack on the office, a full weekend of combat training at the guild, and spending all of Monday locked in the basement working on her meta-suit, coffee and willpower were the only things propping Tori up as she got dressed for their first night of field training. Ivan had sent her over to the guild headquarters early, and she'd found a simple black outfit waiting for her in her room. Unlike the apprentice costumes, this one wasn't meant to mark one as anything special. It was dark, certainly, but also purposefully mundane. Anyone who looked at Tori in it would think she was just another person on the street, maybe walking to a restaurant or bar. Had she just arrived at the guild, Tori would have found the choice strange. After learning from Ivan for so long, however, she understood the value of blending in.

The only part of the outfit that wasn't spectacularly normal was a silver pendant with a stone that had a rainbow of shifting colors set in the center. Obviously it was magic, which meant Tori instantly found herself somewhat distrustful of the curious accessory. There was no sense in fighting the inevitable, though—another lesson she'd picked up from Ivan—so she slipped it carefully over her head. A light tingle ran through her body as soon it fell against her chest, but after a few seconds of waiting, she didn't notice anything else. With a shrug of acceptance, Tori finished getting ready and headed out the door.

She was the last to arrive in the lounge area; Lance, Beverly, and Warren were dressed in similar, but not identical, clothing to hers, and each boasted a pendant of their own, all with the same odd moving colors swirling about in the stones. No sooner had she taken a few steps into the room than a familiar voice greeted her, although it was one she hadn't heard in quite a while.

"Good evening, everyone. For those of you who don't know me yet, my name is Arcanicus." He looked the same as he had the last time Tori laid eyes on him, same lightly-wrinkled visage and crisp purple robes. His eyes, however, were more alive than they had been back then; clearly, he was more excited for this task than he'd been while conjuring skeletons for some upstart rookie to firebomb.

"Tonight, we begin your training outside this guild. Different nights will call for different tactics. Sometimes you will be shadowing guild members as they go on actual jobs. On other occasions, you'll be completing small tasks for me. These won't be anything ostentatious: merely exercises to get you past the first-time jitters and accustomed to working in the field."

Seeing as Tori had logged plenty of time out in the real world and had, in fact, gotten recruited by breaking into one of the guild's holding facilities, she wasn't feeling any of those jitters Arcanicus warned them about. All the same, it wasn't a bad strategy for rookies. Getting their feet wet in a relatively safe environment would give them the chance to get past any fears that might surface. Better then than in the middle of a real job when they could let people who needed them down.

"Since tonight is your first outing, we're going to take things slowly," Arcanicus continued. "We'll do a little walking around downtown, getting used to moving as a squad, and then swing by the diamond exchange where Pod Person is scheduled to do a quick break-in. If you have any questions during that event, please hold them until after we're back at the guild and they can be asked safely. Before we get to any of that, however, I should probably brief you on the equipment you've been issued."

No one needed prompting to look at the pendants hanging from their necks; they knew immediately what Arcanicus was referencing.

"Those are stones of obfuscation, handcrafted by yours truly. So long as you're wearing them, you'll be unmemorable to anyone who sees you. No one will be able to give an accurate description of what you looked like, people you know won't recognize you, even cameras will turn warped and blurry when you're in frame. The exceptions to this effect is others who are wearing the pendants—that's why you recognize each other—and the creator himself, of course. They are very expensive, so take care not to lose them or you will be billed and it will not be cheap. They'll be returned to me each night at the end of training and reissued the next day. For reference, I also rent these out to guild members to use on actual jobs, so if you ever need one, just come see me to negotiate the price."

Tori looked at the stone with new respect; the ability to hide them all from being noticed or remembered was pretty incredible. What's more, it was something she didn't think she could easily accomplish with science or technology. Much as her natural inclination went against it, she might have to learn a little more about the arcane arts. They were proving too useful to disregard.

"All right, everyone, follow me. I've got Tunnel Vision on standby, waiting to transport us across the city. Other nights we'll take a car, but I thought it would be pleasant to begin on an easier foot." Arcanicus headed out of the lounge and the apprentices followed, eager and nervous as they headed toward their first night loose in the real world amid villains of the guild.

*   *   *

In spite of all the buildup, or perhaps because of it, their night started off rather boring. Arcanicus walked them around downtown, letting them get used to the way people's eyes seemed to slide off them under the spell of the obfuscation stones. It was disconcerting initially, but once the strangeness wore off, they each began experimenting more with the limits of what the magical pendants could do. Lance tried to strike up a conversation with some women walking to a club and managed to hold their attention for all of half a minute before the sound of a honking horn distracted them and he fell out of their attention. Tori dropped an empty soda can on the ground in front of a cop, who frowned when he saw it then put it in the garbage. Warren slipped into a bar, ordered a drink, and then emerged without bothering to pay, the bouncer not even giving him a second glance.

Only Beverly kept her interactions normal, stopping someone to ask for the time, trying to bum a cigarette off a few guys gathered outside a club, and getting directions from the same cop who had thrown Tori's can into the garbage. The difference was that Beverly did all three of these things on a loop, waiting first five minutes, then three, then one between each round. On the final occasion, one of the smoking men squinted at her like she seemed familiar but still handed over a cigarette. Beverly rejoined the others, tossing the tobacco stick into the trash on top of Tori's discarded can.

"Looks like too much interaction either wears them down, or coming back too soon makes you recognizable," Beverly reported.

"Very good," Arcanicus said, nodding and shaking the purple robe. No one they met had commented on Arcanicus's strange attire, which didn't surprise any of the apprentices. A man who could make items like what they were wearing no doubt had a few tricks of his own in use. "The stones, like all magic, have limitations," he explained. "No power is infinite, and those with truly strong wills can sometimes pierce the illusions cast by such items. Beverly was smart to assess the limits of her new tool in a practical method that carried little risk. Whenever you're counting on new equipment, you need to know just how far it will take you."

Warren seemed annoyed while Lance and Tori gave Beverly small looks of respect. It was easy to forget how good a head she had on her shoulders when contrasted with the hulking forms she could assume. Arcanicus headed away from the bar area where they'd been hanging out for the last half-hour, and they followed his lead.

"Many years ago, before we implemented the current job approval system, we used to mark every building that was off-limits to guild members,"

Arcanicus told them. "This included buildings owned by guild holdings, places where family of members worked, and anywhere that a cape was suspected to have loved ones of their own. It worked well, for a time, but there are obvious flaws in any system like that."

Moving his hand up to the exterior brick wall of a mortgage company, Arcanicus muttered under his breath and tapped his finger to the cold surface. A softly glowing rune appeared on the bricks, hovering in place for several seconds before vanishing.

"There are plenty of magic-users among the AHC, and they eventually discovered the marks we'd left. Additionally, some of the other criminal metas found them too, which made for a far more dangerous situation. The system inadvertently told them all the places where useful holdings and hostages could be acquired. Eventually, we got around the mistake by just marking every building in town, as well as putting down any of the groups who tried to attack them. These were a bloody few years, and when they ended, our guild had inadvertently become the underworld's overseer. We established ourselves as the collective king of the criminals, and ever since then, we've made sure to keep that spot by whatever means are necessary."

Arcanicus turned and looked at the apprentices, measuring the determination in their eyes. "But that will come later. As I said, tonight we start out slow. Pod Person's work will begin soon; let's head that way."

All five of them walked through the downtown Ridge City streets, seen but unremembered. It was an almost surreal experience for Tori, trekking from block to block, neighborhood to neighborhood, all under the light of stars and streetlamps. They passed upscale apartments and condos then made their way through a patch of the city known for being more dangerous. Capes and cops did have limits, and spots like this were where those breaks in the seams showed. No one bothered them as they walked calmly across the streets, though. That was probably for the best, as no low-level pusher with a gun would possibly be prepared to try and mug this group. It occurred to Tori that perhaps the pendants were as much for the protection of others as themselves. Guild members weren't exactly the sort that would hold back in a fight, so this kept the body count low, which made things easier on everyone involved.

They walked past a few more clusters of apartments before heading into another business district. While the first had held mostly bars and shops, this was clearly a place where money changed hands. Banks were all over the place, as were the logos of several Fortune 500 companies. Most telling of all, though, was how many buildings bore no labels beyond an address. They were the sorts of places that people only went to if they knew they had business there. Walk-ins need not bother.

Sitting on a bench in front of one of the banks, eating a salted pretzel nearly dripping with mustard, was a man Tori recognized from the guild's halls but couldn't have put a name to if her life was on the line. Given that he wore an identical pendant to theirs, however, it seemed like a logical bet that this was Pod Person, the guild member with the job going down that evening.

"Hey there, Apprentices." He rose from his seat, gobbling down the last of the pretzel in a few hurried bites, then wiping his hands on the napkin and tossing it in the trash. "Arcanicus, you're cutting it a little close on the time."

"Foot travel is not exactly an easily predictable tactic," the older man grumbled. They shook hands quickly, and Arcanicus sat down on the sidewalk, chalk suddenly appearing in his hand. He mumbled something under his breath as he began to draw lines on the concrete.

"While Arcanicus sets up the barrier for you all to watch behind, let me introduce myself. I go by Pod Person, and in exchange for free use of one of his fancy necklaces, I agreed to let you all observe my heist tonight. We only have a few minutes left before the others and I arrive, so let's go through the ground rules for you four as spectators."

Everyone shared a confused look at the words "the others and I arrive," but all remembered Arcanicus's warning about questions and so kept their silence. Besides, this seemed like a question that would answer itself if they were willing to be patient. It was a good thing they didn't try to ask, because Pod Person didn't slow down his speech, continuing right along without pause.

"The barrier Arcanicus is setting up will shield you from view so long as you stay behind it. There's also a little bit of protective magic going in to the barrier, but if you're in this guild, then I doubt you'll need it. Here's the most important thing you need to remember tonight: no matter what happens, you do not get to intervene. This is my job. I submitted it to the council, I got it approved, and I am the one who is allowed to work it. If things go bad, if I look like I'm in trouble, if you hear me screaming desperately for you to help, you still stay put. The *only* possible exception is if I've severely miscalculated and you end up in danger, at which point Arcanicus will give you permission to do something, probably run. Don't expect it to come to that, though. There's a reason this job was picked for you to watch, and part of it is because there's very little chance of catastrophe."

Behind Pod Person, Arcanicus rose from the ground, chalk still in hand. He made a wide, sweeping gesture over the runes he'd drawn. A ripple appeared to run through the air in front of them. It stayed there, shimmering softly in the streetlights, giving the effect of looking down the road on a hot summer day.

"That'll do it," Arcanicus announced.

"About time, I'm going to be here any minute." Pod Person reached into his jacket and yanked out a nondescript black ski mask. Pulling it over his head, his features disappeared under what appeared to be exceptionally scratchy wool. "Time to call for reinforcements."

Every one of the apprentices jumped back slightly when Pod Person first spat on the ground, giving him a wide berth as he hocked up loogie after loogie. With each expectoration came a small green object, like an unripe bean, that landed on the sidewalk without so much as a bounce. The beans grew at an incredible rate before their eyes until, mere seconds later, they were the size of an adult human. That turned out to be appropriate, as one by one they split open, revealing perfect copies of Pod Person, lacking only the enchanted pendant.

"Boys," Pod Person announced to his recently-hatched clones. "You know what to do. As for the rest of you, stay put and get ready for a show."

Chapter 42

Pod Person's... pod people had scarcely tucked themselves out of sight in a nearby alley when a car came speeding down the road. It pulled up in front of one of the many unlabeled buildings, and from its depths emerged four men wearing masks. The disguises were nothing fancy like what the guild would have issued; they looked like cheap balaclavas not much different from the ones Pod Person and his copies were already wearing.

"This is what we call a Trojan Horse job," the original Pod Person, identifiable by means of his pendant, explained. Unlike his duplicates, he'd stayed behind the barrier with Arcanicus and the others, evidently to provide color-commentary. It seemed imprudent to be speaking so freely with strangers only just across the street, but precautions must have been in place because not a single head turned in their direction. Instead, all four men were gathering up near the door of one of the buildings, the smallest of them typing away on some handheld computer.

"Basically, this crew has been pulling heists around town, and while they aren't technically doing anything to bring down the guild's full wrath, they did step on a few toes," Pod Person continued. "One of the men over there is me; he's been working for weeks to get in good with them as a safe-cracker. Tonight, once they've successfully robbed the diamond exchange, I'll use my knowledge of their plans to ambush them with all the other versions of me."

"We rarely do jobs in Ridge City," Arcanicus told them, not paying attention to the four men as they successfully opened the door and poured inside. "While the AHC has a presence all over the world, working in their backyard is unnecessarily risky. Generally, the only work we do around here is enforcement, which will be covered on another night. Pod Person is an infiltration specialist, however. Since he has the ability to bail out of a situation when the need arises, he gets cleared to do certain local jobs."

"I'm not big on travel." Pod Person gave a hearty shrug, slightly rattling the pendant around his neck. "I've got another me for that. He's in London at the moment, which I will say is a far more beautiful city than pictures really do justice capturing."

Arcanicus and Pod Person spoke a bit more, going over the details of how Pod Person had wormed his way into the crew over the last few months. Things seemed to be going smoothly when suddenly a noise like a muted firecracker echoed through the air. Pod Person let out a long, annoyed sigh and turned in the direction of the building being robbed.

"Those two-timing rat bastards. They just shot me in the head. Can you believe that? Sure, I was going to rob them too, but I wasn't planning to kill any of them. And what, for my part of the score? What if they need another safe-cracker? That's just unprofessional, that's what it is."

Pod Person remained still, but from the nearby alley his clones poured forth, arranging themselves closer to the entrance while remaining largely hidden from view. One enterprising double skulked forward, sliding under the car and pulling out a large knife that gleamed in the streetlight.

"I guess it's a good thing it happened, sort of. Lets me show the rookies how to adapt to changes," Pod Person said. "See, I was going to use the me inside to know exactly when they were emerging so I could catch them perfectly by surprise and cut off their chance to run back inside. With that option gone, I'll have to be fast instead of precise and ambush them the moment they pop out. Just to be on the safe side, I'm also cutting off their escape route. On a job, you can never count on things going to plan. That's why it's so important to always be... ready... to..."

His voice trailed off as he stared at the small, blinking red light coming from the watch on his left wrist. A quick glance at Arcanicus, who pulled back his robe to show a crystal pendant that was also blinking red, seemed the solidify Pod Person's certainty regarding the situation.

"Well... tits. This just got a lot more complicated. Arcanicus, full evacuation, do you think?"

"I'm actually leaning away from that," Arcanicus replied. "None of us are doing anything illegal; we're all just out on a nightly stroll. It might be a good opportunity for them to see the capes in action. Not to mention to observe how you handle such an unexpected development."

"You're a real bastard when you get the inclination, you know that?" Pod Person glanced over his shoulder, then up into the sky, before turning to face the apprentices once more. "Okay, rookies, what Arcanicus and I just got warning of is that superheroes from the Alliance of Heroic Champions have been dispatched to this scene. Guess the crew's alarm specialist wasn't as good as he thought he was. Anyway, in a situation like this, the very first recourse for a guild member is a simple one: bail. If at all possible, bail, run, and get clear of the situation. Which reminds me..."

Lifting his hand into the air, Pod Person snapped his fingers. The seemingly innocuous gesture was anything but given that each nearby copy of him exploded into a cloud of green goop. The muck splattered all over the ground, steam rising from its viridian depths. Before their eyes, the puddles grew smaller. They soon realized that the steam was more than just effect: the goop was rapidly evaporating.

"There we go: did the one inside too just for good measure, which is no doubt freaking out those double-dealing douchebags." Pod Person reached up and pulled his mask off, handing it over to Arcanicus, who turned it to ash with a single bright flash of fire. "Ideally, Arcanicus's spells will keep us off any of the capes' radar, but with other metas, you can never take things for granted. However, as of now, none of us were involved in the burglary. We're all just out walking the town, helping our wizard friend test his new enchanted items. That is still, admittedly, suspicious as hell, but without solid evidence, they won't try to push it. The guild of villains has far better lawyers than they do. Like watches over like, as the saying goes."

"I know we're supposed to wait until we get back to ask questions, but seeing as things have gone off the rails, do you mind if I slip one in?" Lance said, stepping slightly forward.

"Is it about the watch?" Pod Person asked.

"It is definitely about the watch," Lance confirmed.

"There's nothing too special about it. The AHC tries to coordinate with police whenever possible—no need to double-book the same crime or put human police in the middle of a meta-brawl. Doctor Mechaniacal wrote a program that monitors all the emergency channels and lets off a warning if the GPS chip in the watch senses we're near where the capes have been dispatched."

"There's also a magical relay system." Arcanicus pulled back his robe sleeve again so they could see the glowing crystal. "Since many of us who use the arcane arts have a tendency to short out electronics, it just sends the information from the computer version through a different method."

"It's a good tool to have, but you should never count on it," Pod Person added. "The AHC *likes* to coordinate with other agencies; that doesn't mean they always do so. Especially if they think we're involved and it might tip us off. Then they use discre—"

Pod Person was cut off by a thunderous blast filling the air. The car went up like there had been dynamite hidden inside, along with the remains of Pod Person's double still steaming beneath it. The combustion let out a blast of heat so intense they could feel it across the street. No one had to bother speculating on what had caused the explosion, as seconds later the familiar form of Blunderbuss came crashing to the ground, the end of his mighty weapon still smoking slightly. Squat, thick, and with the all-but-trademarked beard, Blunderbuss was impossible to mistake for anyone else, even without his giant gun. Above him swirled the familiar winds of Roto, who descended gracefully with another person gripped carefully in her flying vortex.

Although to say *person* might have been a bit of a stretch. The creature that landed on the concrete was a hybrid of dozens of animals, none of them

288

exactly what one would call cuddly. Despite such a fierce appearance, the creature immediately swept the area upon landing with a quick, cunning intelligence. Its eyes, feline and golden, squinted slightly when they rested on Arcanicus's barrier, but eventually that gaze continued past them.

"That should put the fear of all nine hells into them," Blunderbuss declared, whipping his gun around and resting it on his shoulder. "Now, go charging in and take their weapons away. After that, you bundle them up nice and tight for the police. Been tracking this crew for a while and none of them are meta, so it should be an easy fight. Just remember not to be too hard on them. Scratches and bruises can make for the wrong kind of sympathy."

"Good luck, Medley," Roto said, her voice so soft it was nearly impossible to hear from across the street. "We're here if you need us, but you can handle this. It's your debut, so take your time and do the best you can."

The creature—Medley, presumably—nodded its shaggy head and moved toward the door. For a split second, its eyes veered off track and he looked at Arcanicus's barrier again, but soon the sound of a gun cocking echoed, drawing its attention to the task at hand. With more grace than its form would have betrayed, Medley leapt inside, greeted immediately by the screams of the would-be diamond thieves.

"Lovely, lovely. Sounds like he's handling them no problem," Blunderbuss said. Gun shots filled the air, their tinny pops nothing like what he'd let loose yet still unmistakable. The sound halted suddenly a few seconds later. "Roto, is the press on their way?"

"The call was supposed to go out three minutes after we left, so based on current response times, it seems likely," Roto replied. "Apollo *definitely said* we shouldn't have Medley debut in the daytime, right? Having him work under cover of night... I feel like it's going to do more harm than good."

"Testing data shows people were far more weirded out by seeing Medley in sunshine than shadow. His presence at night, at least, meshes with what they expect of someone who looks like him." Blunderbuss glanced at the flickering fire of the freshly exploded car. "Maybe we should move this a little out of the way, though. Might make him look menacing."

"I told you not to shoot it," Roto said as she created a new swirling vortex beneath what remained of the vehicle. The wreckage rose slowly but progressively until she shifted it several feet out of the way and placed it back on the ground.

"I didn't want the damn crooks to scatter," Blunderbuss defended. "Hunting them down would have thrown off the timetable. This got them all to hole up in one spot."

"Maybe so, but you also flung debris and what looks like brake fluid all over the ground." Roto leaned in closer, examining one of the small still-steaming puddles of goop. "I mean, it can't be oil, that much is obvious, but I've never seen brake fluid this color, either. Car must have really been in need of a tune-up."

"Wait a damn minute..." Blunderbuss hunkered down to his knees, carefully inspecting the remaining goop on the ground.

"And that, my dear rookies, is our cue to leave," Pod Person announced. "Between the fact that cops and reporters are en route and ole Blundy preparing to put two and two together, we're best getting while the getting is good."

"I'll keep a barrier woven over us until we're out of sight," Arcanicus said. "Doing one on the fly means I won't be good for much else, but I should be able to manage for at least a block." With that, he lowered his head, pressed his hands together, and began to mutter softly under his breath.

Pod Person took charge, guiding Arcanicus by the shoulders and motioning for the apprentices to follow along. Together they walked as quietly as they could away from the scene, not pausing or stopping until they were several blocks away from the action, at which point Arcanicus let his spell end. They proceeded to head back to downtown, protected now only by the pendants around their necks. It seemed things had gone their way, in the end. A good demonstration of dealing with capes, a little knowledge of how to work in the field, and no one had gotten seen or noticed. They'd made it through their first night without any apparent negative effects whatsoever.

*   *   *

Apollo watched as the group walked through the streets, his golden glowing eyes easily piercing the pathetic spells of a tired mage like Arcanicus. He stood perched atop a nearby building, careful to stay unseen by both the villains and his fellow capes. Medley was a powerful meta with ample potential and while he wanted to make sure the debut went just as they'd planned, Apollo couldn't have the others know he was checking up on them. That would be bad for morale and worse for trust.

"Going to stop them?" Lady Shade stood near him, her cloak of endless shadows concealing his constant glow. It wasn't often that Apollo needed to do things covertly, but when the occasion arose, she was the one he trusted to make it happen. It certainly didn't hurt that her powers made getting around much easier and that she trusted him enough to not question his orders.

"Certainly not," Apollo said, grabbing his chest as if wounded. "For one thing, we've got no proof they had anything to do with tonight's robbery; that is to say, we've got nothing a capable lawyer couldn't turn into reasonable doubt, anyway. Besides, the last thing I want to do is split the media's focus. Tonight is about Medley and his spectacular debut, not about us bringing in bystanders with magical equipment for questioning. He caught his criminals red-handed; the whole thing tied up so nicely I may as well have put a bow on it for him. More arrests complicate things, and the debut needs to be simple."

"If you say so, but you sure were watching them closely for someone you don't want to bust." Lady Shade glanced over the edge of the building. Unlike Apollo, she could only make out six distinct shapes amid the crew of escaping villains. Details were lost to her; even their relative size and shape were hard to pin down. Despite both having powers that were magical in origin, it was clear she and Apollo resided in entirely different leagues.

"Perhaps you can't tell, but of the six down there, four are people I've never seen before." That wasn't entirely true, actually. One of them, the woman with the long brown hair, did seem familiar, but Apollo couldn't figure out where he might know her from. He knew she'd never been hauled in for villainy, though; that would have stuck in his mind. "I'm committing their faces to memory, making sure I'll be properly prepared for when they don their masks and come mucking about in our nice, orderly world."

"Newbies, huh? Guess that confluence gave their guild a few fresh recruits as well." Lady Shade squinted, the pale skin around her mousy eyes bunching up as she tried to make out more details in the vague shapes below. "But doesn't it make more sense to try and pop them now before they're skilled enough to actually be a problem? You could at least zip down and put a healthy dose of fear into them."

Apollo reached out and put an arm around Lady Shade, the sort of friendly gesture she'd long ago learned was meant to be reassuring, not romantic. So far as she knew, Apollo didn't have time for romance in his life. All he saw was the AHC and his place in it.

"That, my friend, would be doing a disservice to our own new recruits. Do you know what superheroes need, above all else? What gives us purpose, reminds the people that we matter, ensures that we will always have a place in this world?"

"Villains," Lady Shade replied. "We have to have criminals and metas to fight, otherwise why would we be needed?"

"Precisely," Apollo said. "They are evil, certainly, but a necessary evil. And when our new group of heroic champions is ready to go into the world, they will need villains to fight. The older, more experienced members of that guild are too wily and too dangerous to be their prey, but the new ones... now, they're the sort that might just make some mistakes. I don't want to stop them tonight; there's no point in picking a fruit before it's ripe. Better to wait until there's a need to take them."

He watched the group move through his street, golden eyes gleaming in spite of Lady Shade's efforts to dim them.

"Even villains can have their uses, from time to time."

Chapter 43

By the time Friday morning rolled around, Tori was equal parts grateful to Ivan for getting her the week off and mutinous at the thought of having to deal with work and training when the next week started.

Thus far, the week had gone well, or at least less chaotically than their first night out. Tuesday, Arcanicus had sent them off into town with a list of various items they had to retrieve, the only condition being that they turned over their wallets first. Some had turned to shoplifting to complete the list; others used charm to get their way. For her part, Tori simply found a shipping warehouse that had everything she needed, snuck in as living fire, then made her way out under the cover of darkness.

Wednesday was another tagalong event, this time in Greenland, where they watched a bank get expertly robbed. Double Down and Slipshod were masterful to watch. They even slipped in counterfeit money in place of what they took, long delaying anyone's realization that a theft had even occurred. It was strange to see the scale the guild worked on, from low-level capers like the one Pod Person had planned to elaborate international heists that brought in millions of dollars. It really was a place where everyone worked at their own comfort level so long as they stuck to the code.

Thursday had left her the most drained since it entailed a whole evening walking into various locations to try and spot undercover cops, or worse, capes. The endless rotations of clubs, bars, and street corners coupled with the fact that she'd tied with Warren for fewest undercover officers noticed meant Tori had to drag herself through most of Friday's work on her meta-suit.

Much as she might have wanted to take a break, she knew there wouldn't be any chance to work on it through the weekend since Ivan's kids would be coming over again. That meant more combat training at the guild, which barely gave her enough free time to eat, let alone solder delicate circuitry in place. Things were going well, though; she had her fingers crossed that by this time next week, she might just have a functioning prototype. There would be improvements to make, there always were, but for the moment, she just wanted something that worked. Whatever job they decided to pull off, Tori would feel a lot better going into it with a full suit of tech strapped to her body.

It was past one in the afternoon when she finally emerged from the basement, bleary-eyed and with a crick in her back from so many hours spent bent over the table. To her surprise, there was a plate of sandwiches sitting out, carefully covered with saran wrap. Ivan generally held to the belief that she could eat during mealtimes or prepare food herself, which made the gesture nice but suspicious.

"You look like hell." His voice caught her by surprise, and she spun to find him sitting in a recliner, a thick book open in his hands. He cocked an eyebrow at her reaction, and Tori fought down the urge to blush.

"Yeah, you look like... I don't know... an old guy who isn't old enough for as old as he... fuck, I've got nothing." She went to the fridge and reached for a beer, then thought better of it and grabbed a soda. There was still a lot of daylight to get through, not to mention night training once the sun set. She was better served by a caffeine boost than by alcohol, even if it was in small amounts.

"I think you should take a nap after lunch," Ivan said once she returned to the kitchen table. Tori fumbled with the saran wrap, needing three tries to get to her sandwiches.

She took a large bite of the nearest sandwich she could grab. "It'd be nice," she agreed. "But I've got too much work to do. I'll fuel up on coffee and energy drinks before we train tonight, don't worry."

"Perhaps you misunderstand. I was not saying that as Ivan your caretaker. I was saying it as Pseudonym, your teacher."

Tori swallowed her bite of sandwich hard, feeling it move through her throat like a small brick. Ivan didn't play the apprentice card too often; he liked to let her make her own mistakes as she learned. If he was throwing it down now, it meant things were either about to get very serious or he was sincerely worried about her safety.

"Do I need the sleep that bad?"

"You'll be far better served if you have your wits about you this evening," Ivan replied, turning his attention back to his book. "And caffeine is a poor substitute for genuine awareness. Spend your afternoon as you wish, this is just my opinion on the matter."

Both of them knew his opinion was usually more than just that, at least when he cared enough to share it. Tori wolfed down the rest of her lunch, the hunger she'd been ignoring all morning finally making itself known, and guzzled down her soda. Once that was done, she considered heading back to the lab for a few more minutes, just to finish up what she'd been working on. But before the idea could take root, Tori recognized it for the slippery slope it was. As soon as she went in there, time would lose all meaning, and before she knew it, the hour to head off to the guild would have arrived. Granted, that had been her plan until a few minutes ago, but she decided to heed Ivan's advice instead.

Heading up to her garage apartment, Tori squeezed in a quick shower, dressed in some comfortable pajamas, and laid down in her bed. She had a book in hand, anticipating needing a little winding down time before her brain would allow her the sweet release of slumber. This proved to be unnecessary. No more than a minute after her head hit the pillow, Tori Rivas was fast asleep and softly snoring.

Hours later, when a knock on the door from Ivan startled her awake, she would swear she had just closed her eyes seconds prior, which only went to show how right he'd been about her need for sleep. Especially with the long night she had ahead of her.

*   *   *

"I seriously hate you for dragging me into this," Johnny said, hefting a case of mid-range beer higher in his arms. It was clearly weighing him down, which was all the more embarrassing when contrasted with the fact that Thuggernaut was carrying an entire poker table over his head. Even Arachno Bro was easily carting around a dozen shopping bags on his long, furry arms.

"Hate all you want, just don't jostle the beer," Thuggernaut ordered. He kept walking at the same pace, refusing to let Johnny's whining slow them down. "And don't sneak any either, they're for tonight."

"Which I maintain is something the male members of the council should be doing, since all the women are the ones putting together the girls' night." Johnny adjusted his grip on the beer once more, trying to keep the cardboard from cutting into his palms. While the villain known as Johnny Three Dicks had plenty of talents, enhanced strength wasn't one of them, nor were invulnerable palms.

"Great idea," Arachno Bro said, his words coming out slightly slurred due to the mandibles protruding from his mouth. "We'll just get Pseudonym, who only comes for required guild matters, Balaam, who's even an asshole to his own apprentice, and Doctor Mechaniacal, the man burdened with running a Fortune 500 Company and a guild of criminals, to spend their Friday night hanging out with a pair of apprentices."

"I never said it would be easy," Johnny mumbled halfheartedly.

"Doctor Mechaniacal was nice enough to give us access to one of the fancier lounges and let us expense all the refreshments," Thuggernaut reminded them. "If we want to welcome the guys in, it's up to us to put in the actual work."

"I think Pod Person and Arcanicus might stop by too." Arachno Bro stepped carefully to the side as Thuggernaut navigated through a doorway with his table, then let Johnny putter past. "Said they wanted to see the rookies off the clock."

"Or they heard we'd have free booze," Johnny pointed out, "which is how you baited me into this, so I suppose I can't give them too much grief. Though I should point out that they aren't here helping us haul the supplies."

"No, they actually helped out with the training," Thuggernaut said. They arrived outside of a wide metal door none of them had been through before. Reaching over, Thuggernaut pressed his thumb to a digital pad adjacent to the handle. A small beep could be heard and the door swung open. Carefully maneuvering his table, Thuggernaut walked up the red-carpeted stairs into a sweeping room.

"Damn." Johnny let out a soft whistle as he surveyed their surroundings. "This almost makes me want to earn enough to make it to the Executive level. I didn't even know we had spots like this." The room was covered in the same lush red carpet that swathed the stairs. Several recliners and a large couch were scattered around, far nicer than the ones in the general lounges. A bar staffed by a pair of robotic butlers occupied the far corner of the room. Televisions were dotted about, as were tablets for those who wanted to surf the web while hanging out.

"This is nothing," Arachno Bro told him. "Once I robbed a gold reserve and actually made it to the guild's top ten percent of earners. You should see the Executive break rooms. More robots, free everything. It's nuts. I spent so much time enjoying the facilities that I forgot to pull any jobs, and after a month it was back to the common quarters."

Thuggernaut set the table down in a clear spot near the center of the room. He was only guessing, but he suspected that Doctor Mechaniacal had specifically altered the room's layout just for their use; otherwise, the arrangement of furniture didn't make much sense. "I think it's smart of Doctor Mechaniacal to let us use this space. Good chance to show the kids what they can get, if they put in the work."

"Ugh, that word." Johnny shivered, shaking his shoulders so hard that the lapels of his suit began to flap. "If I wanted to *work* I'd have stuck to a normal life, thank you very much. I prefer to do things that are fun, especially if they result in me taking home a significant amount of someone else's money."

"Right, so Johnny doesn't get to talk tonight," Arachno Bro suggested.

"I've known him for over a decade; if you can find a way to shut him up, I'll pay you half my earnings for the next six months," Thuggernaut offered.

Johnny's ears perked up visibly. "If that deal goes to anyone in the room, I think we might be able to make an arrangement."

"Not happening, you'd just find some loophole to weasel through." Thuggernaut adjusted the table once then grabbed a few of the recliners and began setting them up around it. As he worked, Arachno Bro and Johnny took their supplies to the bar, where the robots immediately began putting things away. By the time they finished watching the MMA fight at the Ridge City Arena and Civics Center, everything would be properly chilled or heated as serving demanded. They'd come back to play cards with a big meal waiting for them.

If pushed, Thuggernaut might have admitted the festivities were a little trite for his sensibilities—he much preferred the opera to physical combat, seeing as he got enough of that in his line of work. Dealing with two young men, however, meant playing the odds and picking things that were most likely to be at least a little fun to all involved. Violence and drinking were solid bets for their age group, especially when one factored in that they were the type of people to join a guild of villains. Regardless, the point of the evening wasn't the activities themselves; it was the bonding that would occur during them. Now that the rookies were this far along, it would be beneficial to give them some roots and connections beyond just their teachers. The more people they knew, the better off they'd be if they made it to full membership.

Thuggernaut tried not to think about that "if" as he continued to set things up. The best he could do was prepare his own apprentice and hope that when the time came, she proved herself worthy. Plus, if he started worrying now, he'd inevitably let his mind begin to ponder exactly what Xelas had in store for the women. And if he started down that path, he'd be a useless bundle of nerves all night long.

*   *   *

"There's my guy!" Apollo walked into the gym, breezing past the half-dozen other rookies who were giving Ren a wide berth as he used the bench press. Donald was standing over him, technically a spotter though they both knew anything Ren couldn't lift was well beyond his league. While Donald wasn't really the gym type, Ren was constantly exercising, and since he was the only friend Donald had made in the AHC, he'd decided to try and share the interest. It helped that a week of working in an office full of people that were wary of him had left Donald with the uncharacteristic desire to burn off some frustration.

"Medley, my boy, your test scores have been coming back and they are just great," Apollo announced. With one hand, he grabbed the bar laden with weights, lifted them easily from Ren's clawed hands, and set it down back on the rack. Several noticed this feat of strength but few were surprised by it. Apollo wasn't one of the world's most famous superheroes for nothing.

297

"They are?" Ren sat up carefully, a bit dubious of such claims. He'd been warned over and over again that his looks might hinder the public's response to him, which was why his image needed to be so carefully managed.

"They are! You're testing about where we expected with adults—most find you scary, but since you're on the side of the good guys, they're okay with it. But guess what? Kids, the most marketable and impressionable demographic out there, they freaking love you. Think you look like a creature from some animated movie or such nonsense. Point is, you are scoring way above what we predicted with them." Apollo lifted his hand high overhead, and after a moment's pause, Ren took the cue and gave him a high-five. At least with Apollo, he didn't have to worry about accidently breaking his bones or stabbing him with his claws.

"That's great," Donald said, patting his friend on the furry/scaly shoulder.

"It sure is, and in celebration, I come bearing a gift," Apollo said. From behind his back, he produced a silver bracelet no less than five inches wide with runes and inscriptions etched all over the metal surface. "Truth is, we'd ordered this for you a while back, but it happened to be ready today, so I'm going to call it a congratulatory present."

"Um, thank you." Ren accepted the odd piece of silver—more gauntlet than bracelet, if he were being honest. It was certainly interesting looking, though Ren wasn't sure it went well with the primal image he had.

Apollo, clearly noting Ren's confusion, only smiled wider. "Try it on, Medley. I promise, you won't be disappointed."

Ren carefully fitted the bracelet over his thick forearm, surprised by how much give it had. No sooner had it slipped across his flesh than the bottom part clicked, the two sections interlocking to form a complete circle around his wrist. The gasp from Donald was the first clue that something had changed, and as Ren examined the flesh around his wrist, he realized what it was. There was *flesh* around his wrist: pink, human, normal-looking flesh. Tentatively, he reached out, running a finger along the skin. It felt real... sort of. If he pushed too hard, he could sense the fur and scales that were really there, but that was only if he really tried.

"It's just an illusion," Apollo cautioned, watching as Ren rose from the bench to examine himself in one of the gym's many mirrors. "As you know, we can't give you back a true human-form. But with this, you can go back out into the world. Hit a bar, eat at a restaurant, do anything you want."

Ren stared at the face looking back at him. It wasn't his own—the size of his new body would have made that impossible. Instead, he looked like a competitive bodybuilder, all wide shoulders and a thick, nearly nonexistent

298

neck. No, this face wasn't his, but it *was* human. A tear slid down the pink skin of his normal face as Ren turned around to face Apollo.

"Thank you. Thank you so much." Even his voice sounded different, less animalistic. For the first time since the night of the storm, Ren felt a flicker of hope in his stomach. A normal life was gone, that much was true, but now... now he wasn't quite as trapped as he had been. Now there were possibilities other than being a monster.

"Hey, you earned it," Apollo said. "And if you're going to do this job, you need to be able to go out and let off a little steam here and there. In fact, I order you to do exactly that tonight. You too, Cyber Geek. Go out and take the bracelet for a test drive. Try a bar or a club or something fun. We already had some clothes brought to your rooms, so you can pick a stylish outfit to go with the new look."

Donald wasn't really one for going out to loud, social places, but one glance at Ren told him that refusal wasn't on the table. Somehow the illusion was conveying his expression on the false face, and Ren was so overwhelmed with excitement by the idea that Donald was shocked he hadn't sprinted out of the gym already. Whether it was his kind of scene or not was irrelevant; Ren was his friend, and this night would do him a world of good. Plus, it would mean ending the workout early, which Donald most certainly *was* in favor of.

"Let's hit the showers," Donald said. "After that, you can come to my room and we'll make a game plan."

Chapter 44

"Tonight, we are your instructors," Xelas intoned.

No sooner had Tori arrived at the guild than she'd been hustled upstairs, into a large room she'd never seen before, filled with every female member of the council as well as Beverly. Lance and Warren were nowhere to be seen. Whatever was on the docket, she found herself grateful Ivan had urged her to take the nap. This was clearly more than just another night of training.

"We have planned an itinerary, secured transportation, and provided you with the necessary equipment. You are to go into the changing rooms we've set up and get ready for the night's activities, which will only be revealed to you once we are en route." Xelas pointed to a pair of curtained-off areas, no doubt only set up hours before, given their level of construction. "Beverly, you are in stall number one. Tori, you're in stall number two. The rest of us will wait out here until you're ready."

Behind Xelas stood the other three councilwomen, expressions unreadable. Morgana and Stasis weren't adorned in their usual costumes, Tori noted. Instead, they had sweeping cloaks that covered them from head to toe, even their faces obscured by the hoods drawn high overhead. Gork looked as she usually did, which was to say giant and gray, though there was a gleaming headband just above her eyebrows that Tori didn't recall seeing before. No one was talking, so it seemed the only way to learn what was going on was to follow orders until they let her in on the secret.

Tori and Beverly made their way to the makeshift changing rooms. Pulling back the curtain, Tori found herself staring at a wide space with a small rack of clothing, a mirror, and a wide chair. All of that aligned with what she'd been expecting, but as she checked the outfit waiting for her, Tori got her first surprise of the night. It was not a new costume or some sort of camouflage. Instead, it was a black and red ensemble that would look more at home on a model than a villain.

"Um, Xelas," Beverly said, sounding uncharacteristically uncertain. "Why are we dressing like this?"

"Sorry, Apprentice, but we're not taking questions right now," Xelas yelled back. "All you need to know is that tonight, you'll learn how to blend in without the use of magical pendants."

That explained more than Tori had hoped for; Arcanicus had told them he rented out his obfuscation pendants, so using them all the time was bound to be expensive. Learning to blend in, despite being out of their element, was a skill that was bound to come up more and more as they took on new jobs. With a grunt of determination, Tori shed her apprentice costume and slipped into the outfit they'd assigned her.

It fit well—perfectly, in fact—which was a bit worrying until Tori remembered they'd taken her measurements for her costume. She wore black pants, a red blouse, a cropped black jacket that slipped over her shoulders, and a pair of red heels she nearly tumbled out of after the first few steps. Tori had worn heels before, it just hadn't been for quite a while. By the time she'd slipped on the last of her accessories, she'd reacquired the knack and emerged from the changing room with steady steps.

Beverly had finished first and was clad in a green dress that matched her eyes and wrapped around her in a way that left most, but not quite all, up to the viewer's imagination. What was most striking about Beverly had nothing to do with the outfit, however. That honor went to the fact that she was staring, mouth slightly agape, over at the council members. Tori followed her friend's gaze only to sport her own dumbfounded look seconds later.

The apprentices, it seemed, were not the only ones who had been changing. Morgana and Stasis had both shed their cloaks, revealing the stylish outfits beneath them. They'd styled their hair and done more elaborate makeup as well, making them almost unrecognizable as the two council members Tori had met before. More shocking even than them, however, were Xelas and Gork. Gork still towered over the rest of the group, though by far less of a margin, but now she did so looking like a model. Long, pale-blonde hair and a creamy skin tone made her appear as though she hailed from Norway or Sweden or one of those countries Tori knew housed women who were lovely, tall, and blonde. As for Xelas, there wasn't a trace of metal to be seen; she now looked like a tan woman with dark, short-cropped hair. It was really only the mischievous grin that gave away her identity, and even with that, Tori wasn't sure she'd have recognized Xelas if not for process of elimination.

"As I said, tonight is about blending in, something we all need to do from time to time," Xelas told them. Her voice, at least, was still the same. "Some of us do it with heels and makeup, while others use advanced holographic technology complete with bio-feedback. Point is, you never know when you have to be able to go down and mingle with the masses. And, after you both do your makeup, you'll both be ready to join us."

Morgana plucked a pair of small pouches from the ground and walked over, handing one to each of the apprentices. "Don't worry," she whispered while standing between them. "Xelas just likes putting on a show. Tonight will be a fun one."

"Ahem, if my cohort would stop undermining my attempts at fear-mongering, I'd greatly appreciate it," Xelas said. "Now then, if you'll both go to the bathroom and get your war paint on, we can head into the urban jungle that is Ridge City."

With little else to do in the way of options, Tori and Beverly complied and headed toward the restroom. As she walked, pouch of makeup in hand, Tori wondered what on earth Lance and Warren were going through. If they were stuck with the male council members, she didn't envy them in the slightest. Much as she respected Ivan, he wasn't exactly a barrel of fun. And whatever else one could say about the female councilors, the prospect of a night out with them was far from boring.

Dangerous and chaotic, almost certainly; just not boring.

*   *   *

Though Tori didn't know it, at that moment the male apprentices had finished changing into suits and were heading to the garage with Thuggernaut, Johnny, and Arachno Bro. Like Xelas and Gork, Arachno Bro was employing camouflage to conceal his true appearance, while Johnny and Thuggernaut just used nice outfits. Thuggernaut was still obviously a meta-human, as not many normal people were ten feet tall and essentially carved from muscle. Since he didn't have to worry about being recognized, Thuggernaut didn't bother hiding what he was, though he did make sure to buy the seats behind him at any given sporting event he went to so as not to obstruct anyone's view. While this might have been viewed as an act of kindness, it was also one of self-protection. People who got blocked sometimes decided to be confrontational, and Thuggernaut preferred to keep a low profile, something that was hard to do when forced to beat people senseless.

Unlike Tori and Beverly, the men hadn't been given even the slightest of hints at where they were going. All they were told was to change, not ask questions, and be ready for anything. Lance was convinced they were about to go rob a casino, while Warren worried they were being marched to attend a guild member's funeral. Luckily, they wouldn't be in the dark for much longer, as it was a short trip to their first destination where all would be made clear. While Warren would be greatly relieved by the truth, Lance would find himself just the slightest bit disappointed. He'd been pretty set on the casino robbery idea.

That would come later, though. At the moment, they merely marched down the stairs, flanked by their senior guild members who were working as hard as they could not to smirk and giggle. It was supposed to be a serious time, at least until they got to the fight, but the silliness and fun of what they were doing kept worming through their minds. They fought to suppress the smiles that wanted to bloom on their faces, but in their attempts to look stoic all three men appeared to be suffering from stomach issues, which only confused Lance and Warren all the more.

So it was that five men, three looking like they were fighting the urge to sprint for a toilet and two looking extremely confused, entered the garage only about ten minutes before their female counterparts. They made it into the SUV five minutes before Tori and Beverly's transportation arrived, which turned out to be a piece of very fortunate timing. Luxurious and practical though the SUV was, the guys would have been stricken by envy at the sight of what waited to bring the others out on the town.

*   *   *

When Tori laid eyes on the limo, her first thought was that it would probably cost more than her yearly pay at Vendallia just to fill up its gas tank. Her second was to wonder why on earth they needed not only a limo, but one that looked like it had been cross-bred with a Humvee. That question, at least, was quickly answered as Gork ducked her head as she squeezed through the back door. Tori had allowed herself to forget that, holograms aside, this vehicle was still carting around a woman who was made entirely out of metal as well as one who Tori suspected to be at least thirty percent rock. That sort of weight was bound to wear down the shocks on a regular vehicle. Plus, this afforded them all enough room to travel in comfort. While appearing ostentatious, it was in fact a purely pragmatic way to get about town.

Had she floated this theory by Xelas, the robot woman would have blinked a few times, then completely agreed with her that of course that was why this limo had been chosen. She would have done so in spite of the truth that Xelas merely liked it. Tori did not offer up her theory, however, so she didn't get the chance to have it disproven through a lazy, halfhearted lie.

Once everyone was boarded, Morgana pulled out one of the many champagne bottles from the large cooler in the bar area of the limo, popping the cork with an expert flair and not letting so much as a single bubble spill onto the carpeted floor.

"Tonight, we are heading out on the town," Morgana said, filling the first champagne flute and passing it off to Stasis, who kept handing it along. "And as such, we will be pretending to be civilians. That means from this point on, we are no longer to refer to each other by our guild names. As of this moment, you can call me Lynn. Stasis will be Stacey, Gork is Gretchen, and Xelas is Alexis. You two already know each other's names, obviously."

She continued to pour, filling flute after flute until the only empty hand in the limo, robotic driver notwithstanding, was her own. Morgana—Lynn, for the evening—carefully filled her glass, set the bottle back in the cooler, and lifted her own flute.

"Now that we're officially out on the town, it's my pleasure to tell you that this evening's training is in networking. Specifically, getting to know your superiors in the guild and having a little fun while you're at it. We do have quite a night planned, though none of it involves crime. At least, not until Xelas— pardon me, Alexis—gets a wild hair up her ass to cause mischief. But we're going start things off with a toast to you two, the apprentices who've made it this far. While neither of you might have chosen this path if given the choice, we're glad you did. Both of you have the potential to be fine members of this guild, and when the time for your last trial arrives, know that we'll be rooting for you from the sidelines. Cheers."

Lynn tossed back her glass of champagne, and moments later, so did everyone else. Gretchen was the only one not to finish hers, merely taking a respectful sip before setting down the glass. It rested in the mobile cup holder for no more than a few seconds before Alexis snatched it up and guzzled down the bubbly liquid.

"So, I have a question," Beverly said, choosing her words carefully. "But I'm not sure if it's offensive to ask or not. The last thing I want to do is start this night off by making a social error."

"Oooh, she'd do well if she ran for the council," Stacey commented.

"Your sentiment is noted," Lynn replied, ignoring Stacey. "Go ahead and ask. We'll tell you if it's out of line."

"Okay. I was just wondering, Xel—I mean, Alexis, how do you eat and drink stuff? Wouldn't it mess up your circuitry?" Beverly asked.

Alexis killed the last of Gretchen's champagne and set down the glass with a smile. "That's probably a borderline question in general, but since it's me, you're fine. Without getting too bogged down in the science of it, I have a system that turns the food and liquid I drink into energy, just like with humans. It's part of what helps power me, though it's easily the least efficient method in use… one of the holdovers from my days as a *fuck-toy*. It's actually the same reason I came pre-equipped with a holographic generator. Tech Lord liked to be able to take me out without people realizing he'd built his own girlfriend."

Her usual half-mad cheer seemed to dissipate at bit toward the end of the explanation, a venomous thread of hatred worming its way through Alexis's words.

Beverly's eyes got so round Tori could see the lines where her eyeshadow ended. While Tori had recognized Xelas from the moment they met,

304

Beverly wasn't a technology-obsessed science geek who would know about the first artificial intelligence to sue for its freedom. Before Beverley could blurt out something that might be taken the wrong way, Tori set a hand on her fellow apprentice's arm.

"Did you know all artificially-created intelligence of a certain level has the right to emancipate itself from its creator? It's called Xelas's Law, named after the courageous mechanical woman who sued to be free from the cape who crafted her," Tori explained.

"Had a feeling you'd know about that," Alexis said. The dark tone seemed to vanish from her voice, replaced by more of the happy noise that Tori was only now beginning to suspect covered much deeper scars. "Most of the original me has been changed out over the years, but I like food, so I kept the stomach. Added some taste buds though so now I can actually appreciate what I'm eating. Speaking of which, how far out are we from the restaurant?"

"Only another five minutes or so," Stacey told her.

"Five minutes? Sweet Jesus, someone hand me that bottle of champagne. I'm not going to survive if I have to wait an entire five minutes." Without waiting for anyone to actually comply with her request, Alexis reached over, grabbed the neck of the open bottle, and gleefully sipped down the remainder of the sparkling wine.

"Nice to know this won't be different than any of our other girls' night outs," Stacey chuckled under her breath. Tori and Beverly exchanged worried glances, which only went to show that the weeks spent training with the guild had succeeded in heightening their ability to sense impending trouble.

Chapter 45

Not for the first time that evening, Donald adjusted his tie. While he'd been perfectly content to go with Ren wearing a t-shirt and jeans, Barney and Jessica had been waiting for him the minute he approached his room. As a new member of the AHC, he had a certain image to project, which meant not going out to high-end clubs looking slovenly. And the clubs they were going to *would* be high-end, as would the restaurant where they grabbed dinner. While the AHC wouldn't go so far as to alert the press that one of the town's newest superheroes would be out and about, they certainly weren't going to risk people snapping pictures of him in jeans at a burger joint.

So they'd dressed him, made reservations at a restaurant Donald couldn't imagine being able to afford, and booked a roped-off VIP area in a newly opened club (all on the AHC's dime, thankfully) before car service picked him and Ren up. Unlike Donald's own expression, his friend's false face was brimming with excitement, his squat neck swiveling as he looked out the windows at the lights of downtown Ridge City. It occurred to Donald for the first time that, aside from busting the would-be diamond thieves, Ren probably hadn't left headquarters since the day he was transformed. Moments later, another thought struck him, and Donald's eyes went wide as a curse escaped his mouth.

"Oh, shit."

"What?" In an instant, the joy was gone from Ren's face. In its place was a primal, fierce gaze. He was ready for whatever threat might have interrupted their night and intended to make anyone responsible for ruining his first evening of freedom pay dearly.

"I just realized, I'm known outside my mask, but your face is brand new. If we go out like this, you'll be linked to hanging out with a cape and your anonymity goes out the window."

"Is that all?" Ren eased back into his seat, the tension melting away as an easy smile took its place. "Don't worry. Apollo already briefed me on that and taught me how to deal with it. Turns out the doodad they gave me is more than a one-trick pony."

Ren held up his wrist, where a projection of a fashionable watch concealed the magical bracelet. Touching it gently with his left hand (it looked to Donald as if he were simply adjusting the dial), Ren's face and skin tone began to shift. In seconds, he no longer resembled the man Donald had gotten into the car with. With another quick spin, the image shifted once more, going back to the original setting.

306

"Multi-functional, in case I ever need to have different cover identities," Ren explained. "They went all out on it. So don't worry; even if people see this version of me tonight, I can always look like someone else if I want to go unnoticed later. But I don't mind having an identity that's associated with the AHC. If I'm doing the work, it might be nice to get a little recognition from time to time."

"Doesn't seem like there's much chance of that not happening." Donald peered out the window, noting all the people on the streets making their way to various places of entertainment. His usual social anxiety had his stomach churning, a sensation made all the worse by the fear that people might recognize him. The weight on his own wrist, a compact device tucked away beneath his sleeves and pre-programmed with a myriad of digital items to draw at his fingertips, seemed much heavier than it should.

Given the choice, Donald would have left without it, but on that point, there had been zero wiggle room. Every member of the AHC was expected to have whatever tools were needed for their power on them at all times. One never knew when trouble would break out or they'd be called into the field. For better or worse, he was a superhero now, and that meant there was no true time off. If the need arose, he was expected to act.

Donald tried not to think about that as they rolled down the streets. It was a Friday evening in a town that most of the nation's superheroes called home. Things would be fine. He and Ren would have a fun night out, that was all.

He hoped.

*　　　*　　　*

Dinner at the Gerhardt home that evening was a simple, though tumultuous, event. Ivan made pizzas in the oven—a Friday tradition dating back to when he'd had no free time and simply ordered them from a nearby delivery place—and had planned on settling in with his kids to watch a movie. Unfortunately, Rick's chief goal was to slip away from the family event and go off to a party with his friends. A reminder from Ivan that he was still grounded for sneaking out had gone over about as well as could be expected with a teenager.

Eventually, Rick gave up and settled in to watch the movie, an easily-forgettable comedy that left Ivan wishing he were still inclined to break the law, as he would have happily beaten his rental fee out of the actors on screen. With nothing in the movie to distract his thoughts, they inevitably wandered to the guild and what was occurring that evening.

Tori would be fine; Ivan had no worry about that. In spite of how she could come off, Xelas was dependable when the occasion truly demanded it. Not to mention she was one of the most powerful members of the guild—working hand-in-hand with Wade had elevated her technology to a place no one else on Earth would easily match. Paired with Morgana, Gork, and Stasis, no army in existence could harm the apprentices, to say nothing of the sort of things they might encounter in Ridge City. Certain capes of near demi-god level notwithstanding, of course.

Strangely enough, what Ivan found himself more concerned with was the fact that Thuggernaut and Johnny were hosting a guys' night for the other two apprentices without a single council member in attendance. Not that there weren't good reasons—Wade was far too busy, and Balaam wasn't exactly at the top of anyone's guest list—but he felt a curious pang of guilt at the fact that he could have made time for it. Ivan couldn't imagine why he cared about such an event; he'd worked as hard as he could to stay only tenuously linked to the guild. He'd probably missed countless such nights without even a single thought spared. Yet here he was, wondering if he shouldn't at least try to make an appearance.

Part of it was Tori's influence, obviously. She'd dragged him further back into the guild than anyone in years had managed; Ivan suspected that was part of why Wade tasked him with teaching her in the first place. But it was more than just that. Now that he was partially back in, he was seeing more, knowing more, and consequently caring more.

Absentmindedly, Ivan reached out and ruffled his daughter's hair. Rick was too grown to enjoy such displays of fatherly affection, but thankfully Beth still embraced them. Ivan cared for very little in the world, but he loved his children dearly and was impossibly grateful they'd been spared from seeing his world. It was only luck and lots of planning that had kept them away from any confluences or accidents that might turn them into metas. There had been numerous occasions where, if things had gone differently, they could have been the ones found wandering the street, causing wanton destruction with their new powers. How involved would he have been if they were the ones the guild brought through that door, scared and desperate to understand what has happening, hoping against hope that they might find a way to control the unnatural abilities thrust upon them?

It was impossible to say for certain since a hypothetical was just that, but he suspected he would do more. And perhaps he still could. Only after the movie was done and his children were asleep, obviously. Helping at the guild was all well and good; however, Ivan always put his only family first. No matter what else might occur, he would protect these two above all others. That was a truth Ivan clung to, one he used to help keep his more irresponsible urges in check. It was a reason that fueled him when the rare true monster threatened to destroy the entire planet. Nothing else mattered more: not old grudges or alliances, not even working with people he hated. His children made him take up fights he would have never bothered with, and oftentimes the presence of Ivan Gerhardt had made an important difference.

Though they didn't know it, Rick and Beth had, albeit inadvertently, saved the world on several occasions.

*   *   *

After the lively affair that was dinner, in which "Gretchen" put down five entrees in front of an astonished staff and "Alexis" ran up a three hundred dollar tab on wine, everyone piled back into the limo and headed off to the next destination. Tori knew they were going to hit a club or bar—she couldn't imagine the councilors had gotten everyone this dressed up just to eat—but her dearth of knowledge regarding the Ridge City party scene meant she didn't recognize the glow of neon and flash of spotlights as the limo pulled up to a four-story building with a line stretching around the block.

"No freaking way," Beverly said, staring out the window like there was gold littering the streets. "You got us into Specter Lounge? I know a dozen people who've tried to get in since it opened and none of them had any luck."

"Your associates don't have our connections," Alexis replied cheerfully. "Let's just say that, between money and influence, guild members don't often bother with lines or waiting lists."

The limo pulled to a stop next to the curb, where those stuck waiting with the faintest hope of entry watched as the six women piled out of their ride with as much grace as each could manage. This turned out to be a pretty fair amount, with the exception of Tori, who lost her balance thanks to the damn heels and nearly took a tumble to the ground. Before she'd fallen more than a few inches, a firm grip had wrapped around her shoulder and halted the descent. Alexis, her reaction-time expectedly inhuman, smiled casually as she righted Tori—a grin that said all too clearly the apprentice would be getting ridiculed for her slip once they were indoors.

Outside the limo and with both feet finally on the ground, Tori took the opportunity to get a sense of the building and was suitably impressed. It was a vast expanse of real estate, probably formerly an office building now converted for its new purpose. A silver sign rested just above the entrance, the words "Specter Lounge" lit by white neon around the letters. Spotlights from the top of the building flashed and wove intermittently, drawing the attention of everyone on the street, not just those trying to gain entry. From inside, a slight bass throb could be heard pumping through the walls.

A sharp whistle from Beverly broke Tori's spell. She looked around to find that Lynn was leading the group up to the three bouncers who stood overseeing the line. The largest of them saw their approach and stepped forward. He met them with careful, assessing eyes, trying to figure out if they were asking an innocent question or about to make trouble. Tori couldn't make out what Lynn said to the muscular man, who she'd have considered more impressive if not for time spent around people like Thuggernaut, but in the span of ten seconds, his tough-guy persona melted away. In its place was a man who could not have been more accommodating as he pulled aside the decorative rope and pushed open the front door. Like a caged tiger, the music came bursting through the entrance, nearly bowling Tori over with its ferocity.

"Don't worry," Stacey assured her. "Where we're going, it's not nearly as bad."

Though not at all certain what to make of such a cryptic statement, Tori followed the others as they walked forward, noting the angry whispers that rose up from the people in line. She couldn't say she blamed them; if this were a place she actually wanted to be, it would have been infuriating to watch others stroll in so casually. Then Tori was through the door and all thoughts of the world outside or the people still in line completely vanished from her mind.

Specter Lounge was decorated entirely in a scheme of silver, white, and purple. Those hues ran through the entire establishment, from the numerous bars stationed throughout the area, to the massive dance floor that occupied almost the entirety of the ground floor, to the DJ booth overlooking all the writhing bodies, to the three upper floors that provided a panoramic view of the giant orgy of motion that occurred below.

Even more striking than the place itself were the people inside. Tori had felt a bit overdressed at dinner, but now she felt like she'd wandered into a fashion show wearing sweats and a stained t-shirt. Every person she saw was dressed like they were about to step onto a runway. Most were so stunning and sculpted that her brain soon overloaded and lost the ability to distinguish between them. People were wearing designer everything, outfits that cost more than her old motorcycle—and that wasn't even counting the high-dollar accessories.

Stacey's gentle hand on her shoulder guided Tori away from the entrance, bringing her back to reality while simultaneously steering her to their next destination. A few feet away from the front door, guarded by a pair of men that were slimmer than the bouncers yet immediately recognizable as more dangerous, was a silver elevator. Again, Lynn said something Tori couldn't hear over the music pounding through her ears, and again the guards parted cordially. All six women easily fit inside the spacious elevator, and when the doors shut, Tori found herself overcome with the sudden crush of silence.

"Thank goodness," she muttered, her own voice sounding strange to her battered ears. "I felt like I was taking another one of those silver-cored robots' sonic attacks by the end."

"Yeah, they keep it pretty unwelcoming on the first floor," Alexis agreed. "No idea why, but somehow that makes it all the more exclusive. I tell you, the things these places pull, yet somehow we're the criminals."

"Fortunately, the VIP areas offer much more enjoyable accommodations." Lynn pressed the number four on the elevator's panel, which it lit up after a moment. The elevator began to move. "Of course, such areas are highly restricted. Generally, only the extravagantly wealthy and famous are allowed up to the fourth floor."

Stacey chuckled darkly to herself. "There's no movie star on earth better known than some of us. I'd say we definitely fit the famous part."

"Don't be silly, those are the old versions of us," Lynn corrected. "Tonight, we are merely well-connected, which I find to be far more enjoyable than infamy ever was."

The ding of the elevator's arrival interrupted their conversation, doors sliding open to reveal more guards. This pair quickly stepped aside, revealing a sprawling area that visibly wrapped around the open section in the middle of the building. True to Lynn's word, the music was greatly reduced this high, turning more to background noise than an overpowering presence. Tori suspected the club had implemented carefully-designed acoustics to achieve such an effect; the odd shape of the walls was all the confirmation she required.

This area had the same color scheme as the ground floor, though that was one of the few similarities they shared. Here, clusters of seats were carefully grouped together, tables full of various mixers and liquors set on each one. Tori didn't deal much with the club scene, but she knew enough to understand what bottle service was, along with the fact that it was idiotically expensive. Then again, they were probably on Doctor Mechaniacal's tab tonight, and billionaires had the luxury of making such indulgences. She hoped everyone else up there had a similar fiscal situation, otherwise it was shamefully wasteful.

While by no means deserted, the top floor of the club was hardly at full capacity either. Scanning the tables already in use, Tori was surprised to recognize a few of the faces present. One had been on a sci-fi show she grew up loving, another was a famous anchorman who did war correspondence, and one was someone she was pretty certain she'd seen plastered on billboards selling hand cream. It was curious to see the familiar in such a strange place, and as she turned her head to keep scanning the room, Tori saw a face she knew well. Much too well, in fact.

She felt her stomach twist at the realization that her two separate worlds were about to collide. Sadly, her stomach didn't share this information with her mouth, which spat out words of surprise before she could even consider trying to slip by unseen.

"Holy shit. Donald?"

Chapter 46

Every ounce of residual annoyance Donald felt toward Barney and Jessica for making him dress nicely evaporated the moment he heard Tori's voice say his name. Turning in his chair, he nearly fell over at the sight of her. She'd always been pretty—he'd noticed that on the first day she walked into the office—but there was also a bit of tension that seemed to constantly linger in her, as if she were too aware of her actions and speech. Whether it was the clothes, the makeup, or the company, something had lightened her mood, and with an aura of cheer around her, Tori was so beautiful it nearly took his breath away. It certainly stole his mind, as he gazed at her for several dumbfounded seconds until a very light kick on the shin from Ren reminded him that words were appropriate in this situation.

"Tori? Wow, I didn't expect to see you until Monday." Donald rose from his chair, oblivious to the people taking notice of his movements as they would note any recently debuted superhero. Before his brain could fully kick back into gear and nix the idea, he gave her a brief, friendly hug. After they parted, he finally got a good look at the five other women with her and began to wonder just how a meeting like this was possible.

"I thought you were in the hospital," Donald said, noting the analytical stares Tori's friends were giving him.

"Oh... yeah. I was. Got out today, decided to go celebrate. You know, seeing death makes you want to live life, that sort of thing. These are..." Tori's brain raced, trying to think of a plausible reason she'd have to be hanging out with five distinctly gorgeous women in the VIP room of an exclusive club. She jumped on the first thought that popped into her head, which was part of the backstory Ivan had spun for her all those weeks ago.

"These are my friends from the program. The mandatory one. That I go to on weekends."

Donald knitted his eyebrows together in confusion; then, all at once, comprehension set in. "Oh! Right. The, um, the... thing."

"It's okay, Donald, you can say drugs." Without a moment of hesitation, Lynn stepped forward, taking his hand and giving it a firm shake. "I'm Dr. Faye, but please call me Lynn. I'm the group's supervisor. You must be one of Tori's coworkers."

"Yes, ma'am. We're cubicle neighbors," Donald confirmed.

"How lovely. Well, these are my other patients: Alexis, Beverly, Gretchen, and Stacey. Tonight, everyone is out for a night of proving to themselves that they don't need drugs to have fun."

The other women nodded, seemingly unbothered by having their business put on display. Tori, however, looked like she wanted to dig a hole and climb inside. While Donald searched for something to say, one of the other women—Alexis, he was fairly certain—clapped Lynn on the shoulder.

"No drugs, no doubt about that, but booze is still on the table, right, doc? I didn't use my father's connections to get us in here for nothing."

Lynn frowned slightly but gave a nod of her head. "While I don't recommend it, controlled, carefully monitored drinking is all right, since none of you have any history of alcoholism." She turned back to Donald and gave a small shrug. "This is a readjustment group, and part of that process is allowing them to define their own limitations."

"Donald, who's your friend?" Tori asked, less out of curiosity and more out of a desire to get her supposed drug-abuse history out of the limelight.

Spinning around, Donald realized that Ren had gotten up from their couch to join the group and was now waiting patiently to be noticed. "Crap, I'm so sorry. Everyone, this is my friend Ren. We know each other from... the gym."

As soon as Donald finished speaking, he knew he'd made a mistake. Six sets of mascaraed eyes told the clear story that they weren't buying his shit. While Ren looked like he probably lived in a gym, Donald would have been out of place even changing the towel bins. Even Ren seemed surprised by the explanation, which didn't help sell the story in the slightest. Donald fumbled, trying to think of a more believable reason that would also account for the lie, but, fortunately for both of them, Ren was a little more composed under pressure.

"Donald, it's okay, you don't need to be embarrassed," Ren said before facing the women. "We're actually in the same raiding party in *Legacy World*. I just moved to town for work, and Donald was nice enough to offer to show me around. He's a little skittish about admitting that we're friends from an online game, though."

Unlike the gym lie, this went over almost without question, as it was easy to believe Donald was the sort who'd spend hours playing around in the digital world. The only one who found it suspicious was Tori; she'd worked with Donald long enough to know he was anything but shy about his love of the MMO. It was an issue she might have pressed if she weren't so concerned with keeping her own lie undiscovered.

"So, Donald and Ren," Alexis said, sliding forward while carefully avoiding touching either of them. "I know how we got up here. What's your deal? One of you invent a search engine or something?"

Tori's stomach, finally recovered from the shock of seeing Donald in such a strange environment, fell through the floor. In all the oddness of seeing a

314

coworker while out with her guild-mates, she'd nearly forgotten why she hadn't seen Donald all week in the first place. While she was supposed to be in the hospital, he'd no doubt been getting settled in at his new job... with the Alliance of Heroic Champions.

The slender hope she held out that Donald would be too modest to mention it evaporated as Ren threw an arm around his friend's shoulder and proudly proclaimed, "Guess you folks haven't been watching the news. My buddy here single-handedly stopped an attack on his office last week. He got scooped up by the AHC within hours."

"Wait," Beverly said, her eyes darting back and forth between Donald and Tori. "You mean he's..."

"That's right," Ren confirmed. "Standing before you is one of Ridge City's newest professional superheroes."

*   *   *

On the far side of the fourth floor, across the open space that looked down on the dance area, sat a man with kaleidoscope eyes, all but bathing in the awkwardness of the scene unfolding across the way. He shouldn't have been there, of course, as he was not a VIP, or at least not the sort that was ushered into high-end lounges. He also shouldn't have been able to see or hear what was occurring with any clarity, but Nexus had long ago learned how to extend the range of his senses with a few pinhole-sized rips in dimensional space. It was fascinating to see the budding metas squirm as they met each other on unfamiliar ground, both spinning lies as quickly as they could conceive of them, but it wasn't why Nexus had come out this evening.

Stasis so rarely indulged in leaving the guild headquarters; he liked to be on hand to watch what might occur when she did. This was not a habit predicated on anything about her, in particular; across infinite multiverses, she was among the few creatures that only occupied one. There were many versions of her as she'd been before, of course, yet she was the only one to transcend. The lone Stacey to become Stasis. Nexus was fascinated with all the singulars he encountered. Singulars were beyond rare, and this world hosted two of them. Nexus often wondered if Quorum's existence was part of why Stasis had survived her accident, though he'd never been able to find a tangible string of events to tie the two together. It might be chance—that was always in play—but the longer Nexus ricocheted through the multiverse, the more he found almost everything was connected in some manner or another. Occasionally, Nexus would wonder if he was, in fact, the inadvertent cause of Stasis surviving when every other version of her perished or survived unchanged. While he couldn't

315

fathom how he might have impacted things, the potential was impossible to deny. After all, the accident that created her had been based on *his* theory and experiment.

He sipped a cosmopolitan taken from the corpse of the man who'd actually rented out this area. Around Nexus were smoldering bodies, flash-fried in a burst of heat from a dimension that was almost entirely composed of lava. Nexus had never been big on sharing his personal space. Unlike the general VIP lounge, this spot had a closed door and low lighting, making it the perfect place to sit peacefully and observe the evening's events.

As the women went over to Cyber Geek and Medley's table and had the staff bring another couch and chair over, Nexus frowned. Things weren't spinning out of control as he'd hoped. After going through so much trouble to pick a good seat, it would be a shame if there was no show to enjoy. Fortunately, Nexus was not a mere spectator. With a bit of effort, he could provide entertainment for everyone to enjoy.

It was just a matter of choosing the right props.

*　　　*　　　*

What Tori was most taken aback by was how unfazed everyone else seemed to be by the revelation. Gretchen was quiet and stoic—no big surprise given Gork's usual personality. Alexis had clapped her hands and began fawning over Donald, asking to hear the story of how he'd saved the office. This was weird, sure, but no weirder than any of the other behaviors Xelas exhibited. Stacey seemed unbothered by the revelation—a bit bored if anything—and Lynn had merely smiled politely and complimented Donald on his prestigious position.

The only one to actually seem surprised and uncertain by the revelation was Beverly, who shot Tori a curious glance. Tori replied to with a shrug that said, "Yeah, I know it's weird. I'll explain later; this isn't the time or place to talk about it." She hoped it said that, anyway. Regardless, Beverly let the silent exchange end, following the others to the section where the guys had been camped out as Alexis had the staff bring in more chairs.

Within moments, everyone was comfortably seated, a few with drinks in their hands, as Donald regaled the table with the harrowing tale of how he'd stopped the three armed gunmen that had taken their floor of Vendallia Industries hostage. Tori noticed that Donald squirmed a bit when he got to the parts where he had to glaze over Chloe, and, by extension, her own contributions to the story, so every time he looked over, she gave him a reassuring smile. She liked that he felt guilty. Tori had never been fond of those who liked to steal

316

glory, but ultimately this version of the story was for the best. Powers had unquestionably altered the course of her life and the lives of everyone seated around her, with the possible exception of Ren. If Chloe wanted to live as a normal person, Tori could understand why. As fun, exciting, and tumultuous as the meta life was, it also came with a lot of danger and uncertainty. For some people, that wasn't a worthwhile trade.

"... and I managed to get off a shot to his face with my freeze-gun, which finally did the trick and knocked him out," Donald said, concluding the harrowing yarn of his triumph. "After that, things were kind of a blur. Cops came pouring in, EMTs rushed Tori and Mr. Gerhardt to the hospital, and then the last thing I could have ever expected happened. *Apollo*, of all people, showed up to help me make sense of things. He told me the AHC was impressed with what I'd pulled off and wanted to offer me a spot in their ranks. After that, it was pretty much just a press conference and paperwork."

"Wow! *The* Apollo came to court you? That's got to be something special. Your power must be really incredible." Alexis would have come off as sarcastic if not for her wide eyes and properly captivated tone. Tori was impressed with her senior's acting chops, as well as a bit surprised at how much she seemed to be enjoying her role. She also felt the slightest twinge of annoyance; even if Donald didn't know he was being mocked, Tori still did, and it felt unwarranted. Regardless of what jackasses other capes might be, Donald was just some guy who'd gotten powers tossed in his lap and was trying to do his best with them.

"It's not all that amazing," Donald replied, fidgeting nervously as Alexis inched closer to him. "Like I said, I just manifest digital objects. There are lots of way cooler powers than mine out there. I mean... did you catch that new guy, Medley, on the news? He's got some real strength, if you ask me."

"Well, strong or not, Medley wasn't the one there when our whole office needed help," Tori replied. She lifted her drink—soda with the barest splash of gin—higher than needed off the table and held it in the air. "Here's to you, Donald Moss. You saved a lot of lives that day, mine among them. I hope you get to spend the rest of your career saving many more."

The others joined in, clinking their glasses and drinking to Donald's honor. As she sipped her own, Tori wondered if there would ever come a day that she could tell Donald four members from the council ruling over a guild of villains had toasted to his good fortune as a superhero. Probably not; in fact, she might even take a little heat for it once they were back in the limo. That was fine, though. Donald was her friend, and he deserved to feel good about what he'd done. Besides, heat was one thing Tori never had any issues handling.

317

"That's... strange." Ren tilted his head to the side like a dog trying to puzzle out the mysteries of a doorknob, a crease of worry appearing on his forehead. "Why are people... ?" Without another word, he rose from his seat and darted over to the edge of the railing which encircled the entire floor. The others joined him, more curious than concerned.

As she walked over, Tori realized what had caught Ren's attention. While it was hard to hear over the pumping music and carefully-designed acoustics, a new sound was emerging from the dance floor. It wasn't bass or treble or even people hollering their drink orders at overworked waitresses. No, this was something she'd heard before, and never on good occasions.

People on the dance floor were screaming. Screaming in fear, panic, and pain.

Tori peered over the railing with a gasp that escaped her lips without waiting for permission. There amid the chaos on the ground level was a bizarre creature that looked like a mix between a rhinoceros, a gorilla, and a truck. Dark, scaly armor coated nearly every part of its body as four muscular, misshaped arms reached out and snared the innocent dancers that tried to run away. Its thick, trunk-like legs cracked the ground as it moved, far too nimble for a creature of its size. It dropped screaming people into a toothy maw mere inches below the six-foot horn on its face.

"What... what the hell is that thing?" Donald was even paler than normal, no small feat for a man with his complexion, and his hands were shaking as he stared down at the monster currently murdering people by the handful.

Though the question hadn't been addressed to her and she doubtlessly didn't intend for Donald to hear the answer, Stacey still muttered a single word beneath her breath. Since she was next to Tori, it was just barely loud enough to make out each syllable, and when Tori put them together her blood ran cold.

"Nexus."

Chapter 47

There was no telling how long Donald would have stood there clutching the railing and watching innocent people die if a firm, slightly painful squeeze to the shoulder hadn't brought him back to reality. Ren was staring at him as he gripped Donald's flesh, clearly waiting for something to click. But what was there? They should be safe up here, hopefully. Probably not forever, but at least until the capes arrived.

That was when it finally hit him—*they* were the capes. This mess, this monster, they were the ones who had to deal with it. No cavalry was coming because it was already there. Donald nodded—a weak, shaky gesture that made him feel slightly dizzy as he did it—and Ren let go of his shoulder. Moving more on instinct than intent, Donald unbuttoned his sleeve and yanked it up on his arm, revealing the small, black digital pad. He brushed a finger across the surface and the device hummed to life. A half-dozen categories were there to greet him. He clicked on the very first one: weapons. He needed something to stop that monster, and something told him a freeze-gun wouldn't cut it this time.

"Donald?" Tori was looking at him, clearly worried. He wasn't sure if it was for her own safety or for his, as even he knew he must look like a wreck. "What are you doing?"

Donald took a deep breath, trying to force himself to calm down. If he panicked, if the cape lost his composure, then everyone else would too. Beyond his responsibility to keep them safe, he also had to make them feel safe, even if he was lying out of his ass. That was part of what it meant to be a superhero.

"I'm grabbing something to deal with the rhino-monster down there," Donald said, much louder than he needed to for Tori to hear. It wasn't just for her; it was for all of the others up on their floor, the scared men and women who'd just been forcibly reminded of how very mortal they all were. He skimmed through the digital display, looking for an item with high damage that would still give him a controlled shot. Power was useless if it caught innocent people in the crossfire. It took three screens, but Donald found what he needed. A spark of blue electricity came from his hand as he pulled the item out of the screen, out of the game program running in the interface's background and into the real world.

"The Buster Burster Blaster should handle this." Donald nearly fell backward under the weight of the massive gun, almost as long as he was tall, but he managed to keep his balance long enough to rest the edge of it on the railing. Peering through the eyepiece in the back, Donald suddenly felt a wave of familiar comfort wash over him. The display was just like in *Blaster Brahs*, only this time, he was the first person whose perspective was being used. With a flick of the wrist, he cycled through the settings, choosing the plasma ray and locking on to the massive target below. Of all the elements the gun fired, this would be the most precise. Plus, it had a massive damage output, even if the cool down cycle was annoying. It would be okay, as long as Donald could end this in one shot.

"Here goes everything," he muttered under his breath. Exhaling slowly, he squeezed the trigger, a soft whir of gadgetry filling the air just before the plasma beam cut through it.

Though Donald was the one firing, it was everyone else in the room who got the best view of what happened. A blinding white light tore from the oversized gun, heading directly for the creature's torso. At the last instant, displaying more speed than anyone would have believed if they hadn't seen it, the monster turned to the side. With this new angle, the beam struck the creature just to the right of its shoulder. The beam hit the dark, chitinous armor and for a moment, the plasma ray was actually stopped. Less than a second later, a loud crack filled the air, followed by an inhuman roar from the beast. As the beam thinned and vanished, one of the creature's arms fell to the ground with a mighty thud, dark orange blood trickling out from the stump.

"Well, it stopped eating people," Alexis said from behind him. She was right, too. The alien rhino-monster wasn't attacking random dancers anymore. Now its attention was solely focused on the gun that had taken its arm and, of course, the red-headed man shakily holding it. With two steps forward, it reached up a giant hand, gripped the edge of the second floor, and began to climb.

"Shit... shit, you all need to get out of here." Donald pulled away from the gun, only pausing to check the remaining cool down time. It would be over a minute before he could get off another shot, and at the rate the thing moved, he wasn't sure he'd live that long. "Ren, get everyone to safety."

"Yeah, your buddy slipped out of here while you were fiddling with your tablet," Alexis told him.

"Why would he—"

The familiar roar from below answered Donald's question before he'd fully formed it. A glance over the railing confirmed that Ren, now back in his furry glory as Medley, was charging across the bloody dance floor. He leapt onto the creature's back. His claws, always so sharp, were scratching ineffectually on its hard armor, causing annoyance rather than pain. Still, it was enough to make the monster swat at him, which slowed its ascent. At this point, Donald would take whatever good fortune he could come by.

"Tori," Donald spun his head around before realizing that she was directly next to him, giving himself a small fright in the process. "Tori, can you get everyone out of here? I don't think they want to be around when that thing arrives, but with it up here, you should all be safe to evacuate out through the front doors."

"And what about you?" Tori shot back. "I highly doubt that thing is coming up here to shake your hand and compliment you on the good shot."

No, it was coming up here to kill him. He knew that—hell, everyone in the room knew that—and honestly, Donald suspected that it would likely succeed. But he couldn't admit that fact. Not to the scared civilians, not to Tori, and most importantly, not to himself. If he did, his resolve would break, and he'd end up putting everyone else in danger. So Donald dug deep within himself, reaching all the way back to when he was a child watching the capes beat impossible odds time after time. Donald looked at the situation through the eyes of that naïve kid who truly believed good would always triumph and asked himself a single question.

What would Lodestar say?

"You're right, it's coming to try and kill me." Donald hefted the gun up from the railing, walking with more confidence than he felt and resetting his perch with the barrel of the mighty machine propped against the top of a couch. "But it's going to find me waiting for it with another hot blast of plasma, and this time, I'll take more than a shoulder."

Tori stepped slightly forward, but Beverly caught her arm. Eyes darting between her friends, the strangers cowering in fear, and Donald, Tori finally locked eyes with him once more. "Are you sure about this?"

"I've got this under control. Just get everyone to safety. Trust me: I'm a superhero."

"Looks like you really are. Credit where it's due, kid, I've known worse superheroes than you." This came from Alexis, whose bubbly, vacant expression had completely vanished. In its place was the gaze of a woman who had lived too long and seen too much, a bizarre juxtaposition with her youthful appearance. Then it was gone, and she whirled around, letting out a high-pitched whistle. "Monster is coming, morons. Everyone out the fucking door unless you want my heel up your ass."

For a split second, no one moved, so Alexis grabbed the person nearest to her—a minor TV celebrity—and shoved him forward. "Are you deaf as well as talentless? I said MOVE IT!"

The shove and the scream did the trick. Everyone began rushing for the stairs that sat on the opposite side of the room from the elevator. Gretchen and Lynn stood near the door, forcing people to go through one at a time so a jam

321

wouldn't impede their escape. In seconds, the floor had emptied, with Tori and Beverly being the last to go. Donald breathed a sigh of relief as he watched Tori vanish into the stairwell, noticing that she did pause to throw one last look at him. If he was going to have to die tonight, he'd prefer to do it alone.

Of course, dying wasn't exactly Plan A.

As a massive hand wrapped around the edge of the railing, Donald stuck his eye back on the viewer. Only a couple of seconds left and he'd have another shot. It was close, but Medley had bought enough time.

They weren't out of this fight yet.

*　　　*　　　*

"Are we going to do something?" Tori demanded. Beverly was beside her, and the four council members had stopped on the landing just above the next floor's exit. The panicked scuffle of bodies hurrying to freedom masked their conversation, which was good because Tori wasn't in the mood for covert whispers.

"We are doing something," Stacey replied. "We're getting out of here like your buddy wanted. Just waiting for things to thin out a bit." Though she'd affected her usual disinterested tone, it was clear Stacey was bothered by what was going on. Or, more likely, by the man they believed to have caused it.

"I meant about Donald. That thing is going to tear him to bloody chunks if we don't help." Tori glanced back up the stairs, even though they were too far down to see any of what was happening on the fourth floor.

"What do you suggest we do?" Stacey asked. "Go bust out our powers, our very well-known and distinctive powers, to save the very people who would try to haul us off to Rookstone if given half a chance?"

"Donald wouldn't do that," Tori protested.

"Tonight? Probably not, but sooner or later, he would," Stacey countered. "It's inevitable. They all turn out that way, caring more about the prestige than the good they do. Maybe it's better that he dies tonight; at least he'll get to go out while he's still the genuine article."

Tori threw the punch before she even realized she'd made a fist. It connected perfectly with Stacey's jaw, and then stopped completely. It wasn't like Tori had hit a wall or someone super strong. It was like she'd just thrown the energy of the punch away; it vanished as soon as it met Stacey, who smiled at Tori's suspended attack.

"Well, well, our little rookie has some guts to her. You're lucky I like guts. A different member of this guild would tear your spine out for that." Stacey calmly reached up, grabbed Tori by the forearm, and lowered her fist.

322

Tori tried to resist, but it was pointless. Stacey wasn't strong: she was inevitable, as though every movement of her body was the orbit of a planet, too tremendous to even entertain the idea of halting it. "But I think you've forgotten something pretty important here: we're not the good guys. We don't jump in whenever people are in danger. We take care of ourselves and our own. End of story. If you wanted to run around playing hero, you should have signed up with the AHC."

Stacey released her grip on Tori's arm just as the sound of another blast filled the air. This time the screech of the monster was so loud it rattled their teeth. It sounded pissed and definitely hurt, but not dead. Not dead was bad. Bad for the club, bad for anyone who didn't get out, and most immediately, bad for Donald.

"I thought we were also supposed to defend our turf." Tori was grasping at straws and she knew it, but the idea of leaving a friend behind was too much. If she was ever going to get a good night's sleep again, she had to at least try her best to save him. "Someone either just unleashed or turned into a monster in a club with four of the guild's councilors. That sure seems like an act of aggression to me, the sort of thing our terrifying and powerful guild should mount a response to."

"Oooh, going for the pride *and* the politics, now that's a nice move," Alexis said, leaning against the concrete wall and gazing down the stairs as people flooded out. "Pseudonym wouldn't have had the patience for that play."

"Whose side are you on?" Stacey snapped.

"Whoever's is more interesting," Alexis replied. "And, on a personal level, while I loathe almost all the capes out there, the ones like that kid aren't so bad. He knew he was probably going to die, and he still tried to get us all to safety without making us worry. That type, I don't mind so much."

"Oh, great, then you and the rookie can both go up there to save everyone." Stacey turned, her stoic mask slipping to show the fear and frustration ripping through her. "And then when that insane fuck lets loose three more monsters, you can kill those too. Then fight back the lava, or the tundra, or whatever else comes because you can't *beat* Nexus, you idiots. All you can do is wait until he gets bored."

For a moment, there was silence, punctuated by the thump of something hitting the wall upstairs. When Lynn finally spoke, it was with the same measured, calm voice she'd affected while pretending to be the group's doctor, a facade Tori was quickly realizing might be more truth than fiction.

"Enough. Tori, I understand he's your friend, but the AHC has their own way of handling things. Stacey, we all know you and Nexus have a complicated history, but please don't antagonize our rookie, who is only worried about a friend's safety. Alexis... well, I'd ask you to stop stirring the pot, but those would be wasted words. Now, we're all going to get out of here, right now, and anyone who wants to argue more can do so once we're back in the limo."

"But I—"

"Tori," Lynn said, cutting her off before a new argument could begin. "Your friend has chosen a very difficult path. It will be fraught with peril just like this. Unless you plan to follow Donald around and fight his battles for him, you have to accept that he's going to end up in danger more often than not." Lynn walked over and set a reassuring hand on the apprentice's head, gently stroking her hair. "Much as we might have our quarrels with the AHC, they are not in the habit of giving such attention to weak metas. Try believing in Donald instead of worrying about saving him. If given the chance, he might just surprise you."

"If it'll make you feel better, I've hacked into the security cameras," Alexis said. "He's not dead yet, but things are getting interesting. I can put it on the screens in the limo, once we get there."

"Yeah. Please. I should watch, if nothing else." Tori wasn't certain if she'd just agreed to be a witness to her friend's death or his unlikely triumph. All she knew was that if these were Donald's final moments of life, someone should see them.

Chapter 48

In spite of logic, odds, and all belief in a practical universe, Donald Moss wasn't yet dead. He darted to the other side of the room, barely dodging one of the monster's grabbing hands as it tried to snap his bones and turn him into food. The monster, now less one horn thanks to a plasma blast that was just a bit too early, thundered about, trying to snare the vulnerable human flesh in its murderous claws.

Donald, still dragging the massive gun, was barely able to avoid the attack. The reverberation as the beast hit the wall shook the very floor beneath his feet. Though shooting off the horn had been an accident, Donald had started to suspect it was actually a stroke of luck. The grace that this rhino-like beast had displayed down below was suddenly absent, leading him to theorize that the horn somehow served to help it balance the unwieldy bulk of its body. This made dodging difficult but still doable.

On the other side of the room, Medley slowly rose to his feet, and Donald breathed a small sigh of relief. When the monster had hurled his friend against the wall, leaving a massive dent in the stone material, Donald had feared the worst. Luckily, Medley was far hardier than most and was slowly shaking off the worst effects of the blow. Unluckily, the time he was taking to regain his wits meant Donald was on his own, running away from a clumsy, angry, deadly monster intent on turning him to pulp.

"You okay?" Medley called, his powerful voice barely audible over the cacophony of stomping monster.

"*Do I look fucking okay?*" Donald screeched as he hurled himself to the side, nearly losing a grip on the gun, his greatest asset and liability all rolled into one slowly recharging package. Though there was no time to glance in the eyepiece, he estimated that it had to be nearly recharged by now. Not that it mattered—it was taking everything he could to get away from this damn creature. Lining up a shot was out of the question. If only he could actually lift the thing, maybe he'd have a better chance of connecting. Of course, the pressure of knowing that without a power-up, the gun had a three-shot limit certainly didn't help matters. If he did get another shot, it would be the last one.

With a shake of his head, tossing his mane like it was caught in the wind, Medley reared back and charged at their opponent. This time he didn't bother grabbing on to its back; the armor there was too thick, and its unnaturally jointed arms could still easily reach him. Instead, he took advantage of its missing horn and launched himself right at its face. Using his own claws to grip the scarce amount of exposed flesh, Medley snapped and tore at the area that

325

appeared to be its eyes, a small open patch barely visible under the armored ridge of its brow.

As a gamer, Donald knew a delay tactic when he saw one. Mounting the end of the gun against the edge of a sofa once more, he peered into the viewer and readied himself to take aim. Unfortunately, what greeted him was not the aiming mechanism that would help him lock on to his target, but a timer that was just going down past the thirty-second mark. Shit, had it really only been a minute since the last shot? Time flew when one was dodging for their life, apparently.

Medley let out a sound between a whimper and a roar as the monster's claws raked across his back. While Medley had some scaly armor of his own, it wasn't nearly enough to stop those powerful arms from driving into his flesh. Donald tried to think, tried to focus on what he could still do. Medley wouldn't be able to hold out for a whole half a minute more, and when he went down this time, there was no telling how long it would be until he managed to get back up, if he managed to get back up at all. Without a distraction, Donald had zero hope of pulling off anything but a wild shot. Damn this gun! It was so stupidly heavy and cumbersome. Who had designed it like this? They'd had to add a whole special armor to *Blaster Brahs* just to explain how they wielded ...

"Medley! I need ten more seconds!" Donald wanted to smack himself on the head and feel like an idiot, but there wasn't time for self-loathing. He'd have to sneak that in later, assuming they both survived. Slapping the display on his wristband so quickly that the screen wobbled, Donald backtracked out of weapons and into the armor section. Of all the things he'd experimented with during his time by himself, it had never occurred to him to try to manifest and equip something other than handheld items. He wasn't even sure his power worked that way, but worrying was a luxury he didn't have at the moment. Either it worked, or they probably died.

So it had damn well better work.

Finally, Donald found what he was looking for and thrust his fingers, crackling with blue sparks as usual, into the display. As he pulled the item from the digital world to his, he focused on it not only coming through, but coming through already wrapped around his weak, tender body. Closing his eyes and tossing a prayer up to any god that might listen, Donald gave the final jerk.

Lines of code suddenly turned into metal and electronics. Lifting his eyelids as slowly as he dared, Donald was overcome by a wave of excitement as he realized he was peering through the visor that topped the helmet of the Master Brah's Armor. It was all there—meters for shields, speed-boosts, even thrusters. As he pulled himself up, Donald realized he could easily lift the gun now, swinging it about one-handed, as if it weighed no more than a wooden toy.

That was why the weapon was so heavy: in the lore of *Blaster Brahs*, they needed specially enhanced armor to use it. In the upper right-hand corner of his visor display, Donald noted a replication of the countdown timer. Only about fifteen seconds left to go.

From Medley's bloody gouges and lilting stance, it didn't seem like he'd last that much longer. The fact that he'd managed to hang on for so long under such a powerful assault spoke volumes about the determination that lived in Ren Tanaka. Donald was impressed—wowed, to be honest—and made a mental note to buy Ren a beer once things were settled.

"Get clear! I'm on this."

For a moment, it seemed like Medley was going to hang on anyway, determined to go down swinging. But Medley understood enough about guns to know that being in the way when a giant plasma beam fired was a futile gesture. After a moment of scouting for the best path of exit, he leapt between the monster's swinging arms, which were intent on slicing him to pieces, and landed deftly on the carpet fifteen feet away.

As soon as Donald saw his friend go, he charged forward. He still had ten seconds left, but he'd be damned if he was going to let Medley buy them in blood. It was time to stop hiding—behind Ren, behind Chloe, behind Tori. He'd told the world he was a superhero, that he could be counted on to save the day. Ten seconds and one more shot; that was his window to prove it.

Between the adrenaline, fear, and relentless pressure of having something unworldly trying to kill him, Donald moved almost entirely on instinct. It was like he was in the hardest part of the game, difficulty settings cranked up as high as they would go. Thought failed to exist; it would only slow him down. Donald didn't even know how he'd activated the armor's speed-boost, shooting backward at the last second as he avoided a powerful blow. Fragments of couch flew toward him, striking the armor's shields and slightly lowering their value. The speed-boost gauge had also been drained, over a third gone from that one move alone.

For the first time, it occurred to Donald that merely loading the games and items onto a wrist-sized computer display hadn't done dick in the way of leveling them. He was basically playing with starter gear. Contrary to how that news should have hit him, Donald smiled as he speed-boosted back from another blow, bright blue flames shooting out of his back as they carried him away. Sure, he'd have liked a little more oomph in his weaponry, but he hadn't spent most of his adult life playing games because he shied away from a challenge. Real life had always been terrifying. Deep down, he knew he should be a quivering mass of fear at what was happening around him. But he wasn't. Maybe it was the digital display that made things seem just a bit unreal. Maybe it was the cocktail of adrenaline and worry soaking his brain. Maybe he had just gone too far into terror and become momentarily numb to it.

All he knew was that as he used the last of his speed-boost gauge to avoid a set of claws that would have cut him to ribbons, Donald realized he was actually having fun. It certainly didn't hurt that as his speed gauge went empty, the numbers in the upper right-hand of his visor ticked down to zero. Suddenly, the targeting system came online. Donald raised his gun and saw the now-hornless monster light up like it was the only thing in the room.

Unfortunately, it wasn't just raw muscle and violence; it had learned what Donald raising that gun meant. The beast charged forward, determined to crush him before he was able to get off another shot. Donald's heart was slamming in his chest so loudly that he could hear the blood rushing through his ears. He tried to think of a way out. No speed-boosts left, and if chair debris drained his shields, then they had no shot of surviving a direct hit from the rhino-monster. Normal dodging was out, and so was standing his ground, which left Donald with only one option. Granted, it was an option that had very little chance of succeeding, but after cheating death so many times in such a short span, Donald felt like he was on a roll. Might as well make the big bet while riding a hot streak.

With a mighty leap that would have made Medley proud, Donald jumped straight over the railing that ran around the fourth floor and into the open air above the dance area. As soon as he was airborne, he kicked on the armor's thrusters. It couldn't fly, technically, but the Master Brah's armor did have the ability to hover for short windows of time. In the case of unleveled armor, that window was especially tiny—the thruster gauge on Donald's visor began dropping like it had sprung a leak. With no time to spare, he spun in the air, locking his weapon directly on to the alien creature as it slammed into the wall where he'd been standing.

For a moment, just one precious moment amid the chaos of the evening, the creature was stunned by a combination of surprise and impact. It was exactly the chance Donald had been waiting for. He fired the last plasma beam without hesitation, striking right in the monster's center mass. The armor held as before for just an instant and then the beam was through, boring a hole directly in its torso. Not wanting to take any chances, Donald swung the gun, the laser carving a path of burned flesh from the middle of its torso up to its alien head. The beam puttered out just before his thrusters, and suddenly Donald was freefalling through the air.

He slammed into the ground, the shields saving him from some, but not all, of the impact. To his surprise, the armor dissolved into flashing numbers and sparks of electricity as soon as the shield gauge hit empty. Seconds later, the gun, flashing a red light on its side that indicated it was out of shots, did the same. Donald had never seen that happen before, but he'd also never completely used up or broken any of the digital items he brought over. Surprising as it was, the disappearing gear was the lowest possible item on his list of priorities.

Donald sprawled on the dance floor, listening to the music still somehow blasting through the air, and waited. His back ached and his ears were already starting to hurt from being so close to the speakers, but he didn't dare move a muscle. Not until he knew for sure that the fight was over. If that thing was alive, if he'd failed to hit any vital organs, Donald wasn't sure what moves he had left. Wait peacefully for death seemed the most likely, but after fighting this hard to live, he somehow doubted he had it in him to just lie down and die, no matter that he was already lying down.

Finally, the furry head of Medley popped over the railing's edge. He yelled something down but Donald was in a crush of bass—no mere words could cut through. When Donald failed to reply, Medley quickly put two and two together. Rather than continuing to scream, he merely held out a clawed hand with a raised thumb—the universal sign for "things are okay."

His friend's furry thumbs-up was one of the most beautiful things Donald could ever remember seeing. He returned the gesture with one of his own, letting Medley know that he was bruised, not broken. Then, to no one's surprise more than his own, Donald let out a whoop of unfettered joy. On its heels came laughter, nervous and wonderful and paired with tears, which Donald wouldn't notice until several minutes later.

They'd done it. They hadn't just survived, they'd stopped the monster. Maybe he'd exaggerated his way into the AHC; maybe he didn't really have what it would take to be a big-name cape; maybe tonight was just a fluke. But tonight, none of that mattered. He'd still managed to do the job.

Tonight, Donald Moss was a superhero.

329

Chapter 49

"Come on now, even we have to admit that was pretty cool," Alexis said, refilling her glass of champagne.

Thanks to her and Gretchen shoving people aside, they'd made it back to the limo just in time to watch Donald summon his armor. Tori sat, mouth wide open in amazement at what she'd just witnessed. Donald, *Donald* of all people, had just pulled that off? It hadn't felt like she was watching her coworker at all. Had she not known better, Tori would have guessed she was witnessing the fight of a real, true-blue cape.

Which, now that she thought about it, she sort of had been.

"Good for you," Tori said, eyes still on the screen as Donald laughed himself to tears amid the blaring music.

"He fought bravely," Gretchen agreed.

Lynn cleared her throat and shot a look to Alexis, who took the cue and turned off the video feed. With the limo once more silent, she moved to a position near the front where everyone could see her.

"Though tonight was planned to be more fun than educational, it seems fate intervened and gave us a teaching moment after all," Lynn said. "Capes are not, in and of themselves, our enemies. We do not antagonize them; in fact, much of the code is based around staying out of their way. We can even respect them, on a personal level, if we deem them to be strong or worthwhile in a way we acknowledge. Friendship is... well, not unheard of, but certainly a bit tough. Nonetheless, Tori, I'm glad you didn't have to bury a friend tonight. With all of that said, can either of you apprentices guess why Alexis was monitoring the feed before anyone asked her to?"

"She wanted information," Beverly replied, no hesitation in her voice. "Those guys are new to the AHC, right? Medley popped up this week, and Tori's friend only came on last Friday. In case they survived, she—no, the guild would want to know what they could do."

"Precisely." Lynn turned to Tori, who'd suspected that to be the reason even if she didn't want to say it out loud. "So, using that information, Tori, if Donald were to come up on you while in costume and on a job and catch you red-handed, what methods would you use to avoid capture?"

Tori opened her mouth to reply then closed it a second later. Her first instinct was to assume Lynn was asking how she'd kill Donald, but that hadn't been the question. In fact, the guild emphasized evasion over engagement at pretty much every turn. Mentally flipping back through the fight, she realized that they now all knew of a very easy way to slow him down long enough to slip away.

"I'd blast his armor until it dissolved, then run away before he was able to reform it," Tori replied at last. "Since the gun died too, there's probably a limit to how much he can use his items. If I could dodge them long enough and slip away before he had the chance to reload, I could take off my costume and just be regular Tori again."

"Which addresses why costumes are mandatory," Lynn said, giving Tori a slight nod. "Yes, that would be a viable option. In contrast, you also now know that the one called Medley has exceptional recovery abilities. Nothing short of extreme damage is likely to take him down, and even then, only for a short while. This means he can be dealt with more firmly without risk of killing him."

Lynn took a glass of champagne from the bar and carefully sipped its contents. "Remember, unless you are specifically authorized by the council, killing a cape is to be avoided at all costs. They get angry when their own die, just as we do, and that anger can lead to problems for the entire guild. Much of why we gather information is so that, should engagement become unavoidable, we can slip away without doing lasting harm. Control and precision are far more crucial to our survival than mere power."

"Of course, when the need does arise, and the council gives that permission, it also helps to know what their weaknesses are," Alexis added. "Though you won't have to worry about that for a long while. Killing capes, especially covertly, isn't easy, and it definitely isn't something we saddle rookies with."

"When do you kill them?" Tori asked. "I've had to learn the code backwards and forwards, and I've yet to see a clause outlining when we knock off superheroes."

"It's covered under the 'threats to guild security' section," Stacey told her. "If the council feels a cape is stirring things up too much, focusing on coming after us instead of the people who aren't so careful with their crimes, then we try to dissuade them. First politely, then less so."

"It doesn't happen often," Lynn said. "Nowadays, the AHC largely plays along with the peace. In the early days, things were less stable. But none of the capes in charge are gung-ho about coming after us. They know the gain isn't worth the loss, so they usually squish any attempts by others to get on our bad side."

"If it ever did come down to a fight between us and them, who do you think would win?" Beverly asked. She seemed oddly interested in the idea, a fact that Tori filed away for consideration at a later date.

"No one knows," Gretchen said.

"Yeah, we'll talk a lot of shit in front of the masses, but at the end of the day, it's a toss-up," Alexis added. "They've got more people than we do, but we have more major league hitters than they do. People who get the insane, world-changing powers are more likely to seek self-betterment than saving the world. It would be a good fight, but there's no way to predict the winner."

"Which is why we work so hard to avoid it," Lynn said. "Win or lose, an all-out war between us and the capes would shatter the enjoyable lives we've built for ourselves. No one, at least no one in the guild, wants to go back to being wanted fugitives with our faces plastered everywhere. Not when we can have champagne, VIP lounges, and limos along with anonymity."

"War: the only way to win is not to play." Tori wasn't sure that everyone would get the *War Game* quote, but the casual nodding and smiles told her that at least the sentiment had made it through.

"Exactly," Lynn agreed. She reached up and knocked gently on the divider between them and the robo-driver. Seconds later, the car smoothly pulled into motion. "Which is why we stay out of their business, they stay out of ours as long as we don't flaunt it, and everyone wins. The people get peace, the capes get acclaim, and we are about to go get some cheesecake."

Weird monster fights and cheesecake weren't exactly how Tori had expected the night to end, but, given the company she was with, things certainly could have turned out worse.

$$*\qquad*\qquad*$$

The soft sound of palms striking one another snapped Donald to attention. The hair on the back of his neck stood on end as he readied himself for another fight. The sound repeated itself, and again, and again, and he finally realized what it was. Apollo was standing in the door of the infirmary, giving him a slow clap that was gradually picking up speed. From anyone else, he might have taken it to be sarcastic, but the beaming grin on Apollo's face made it all too clear how sincere the applause was.

"You, Donald Moss, are full of surprises," Apollo said, walking through the door and sitting down next to the tank of goo Donald was currently submerged in. Supposedly, it rapidly accelerated the healing process and minimized long-term damage—an invention Professor Quantum had come up with some time before. All Donald knew was that from the moment he'd been put inside, his back had stopped hurting, which was no small feat since it was bruised from his neck to his ass.

332

"I have to tell you, when I heard that there had been a dimensional rip with an unfriendly breaking through, I assumed the worst. Then they told me it was at the club where we sent you and Medley, and all I could think was that I hoped you got the call out for backup in time. But you and Ren, you didn't even need backup, did you? The two of you handled an Epsilon Class inhuman presence on your own, and that is impressive. Damned impressive, if you want to know the truth."

"We caught some lucky breaks," Donald admitted. Much as he enjoyed the praise, it felt a little excessive to accept wholeheartedly. The last thing he wanted was for Apollo to think he could handle that sort of fight regularly.

"Oh, there's no question about that. I'd say seven out of ten times, that thing would have torn you both apart," Apollo agreed. Despite the seemingly negative words, his cheer didn't dim. If anything, it seemed to increase. "But three out of ten is much better odds than I'd give the majority of the rookies we've got right now. With time and training, each of you will be able to smoke something like that single-handedly."

Donald couldn't imagine ever being that powerful; however, before tonight he couldn't have imagined himself going toe-to-toe with a giant alien monster in real life either. He was starting to think his imagination was going to have to expand its limits, though he wasn't too keen on testing Apollo's assertion anytime soon.

"Let's hope I get a long while before I have to try soloing anything of that level," Donald replied. "What was that creature, anyway? Another meta-human?"

"Maybe, in the dimension where it hails from." Apollo sat over one of the uncomfortable plastic chairs, hovering in place a few inches above the surface. "Or it might be something akin to a deer for all we know. Sometimes, for one reason or another, the walls between the dimensions bleed or outright break, and on those occasions, it's possible for things to slip through. What you fought was one such example. Some of the smarter superheroes have tried cataloguing them, but there are more dimensions out there than there are stars in the sky, so no one has had much luck figuring out any sort of pattern in the bits we discover."

"Do they at least know what caused the rip tonight?" Donald had an uncomfortable fear sitting in his stomach as he pictured the way he pulled his items into existence. What if he was yanking them from another dimension and in doing so was weakening the borders between them?

"Oh yes; security cameras caught a glimpse of the criminal named Nexus watching the show from a corner of the club. We had a few of our metas with dimensional abilities do a sweep and they confirmed it: he caused the rip."

Much as he'd expected to feel relieved, Donald instead felt a new fear crystalize inside him. "Nexus is the guy who wiped out the original Denver, isn't he? Why on earth would he bother unleashing a monster in a club?"

"No one knows why Nexus does what he does." Apollo shrugged his tan, muscular shoulders in a way that seemed strange for one so blessed with authority. "He's untraceable, unpredictable, and seems to be totally insane. Sometimes he changes things in ways that help people; on other occasions he unleashes wanton destruction for no apparent reason. Maybe there was someone in the club he wanted to kill tonight. Maybe he was just interested in seeing what you two could do. Maybe they messed up his drink order, I honestly have no clue. You're better off not worrying about it too much. Think of Nexus like a force of nature: don't look for reason in the destruction he causes."

"If he's that dangerous, why hasn't the AHC stopped him?" It was something Donald had wondered even back when he was looking in from the outside, but now that he was here, inches away from Apollo himself, the question seemed even more important. They had so many metas, so many resources. Why was a maniac like that allowed to run free?

"Look, you find out a way to do that, you can pretty much write your own ticket around here," Apollo replied. "Everyone has tried to stop him, even Lodestar and Quorum. We've captured him a few times, though it never lasts, and even killed him once or twice, not that it matters. He just turns right back up. We don't know how his powers work, only that they let him open holes between dimensions. Trust me, the minute someone actually finds a way to neutralize that asshole, it will be all hands on deck."

Apollo leaned forward until he was only a few feet away from Donald's face, his eyes suddenly serious. "One thing about me, I have no tolerance for the villains of this world. It's our job to stop them, and I take that job very seriously. No matter what opinions our other members might have."

Before Donald could ask a single clarification question, the moment was past. Apollo was back to floating above his seat, ever-present grin right back in place. It happened so quickly, Donald almost wondered if he'd imagined the whole exchange.

"But we'll talk about that later. Tonight, you just need to focus on recovery," Apollo told him, floating forward and putting his feet on the ground. "Tomorrow we're going to have a press conference and some celebration for you and Medley. You both managed to score your first big collar before we'd even put you on patrol. Rest up and make sure you're in tip-top shape."

Apollo walked to the edge of the room and looked back at Donald, the shadows from the hallway hitting his face in a way that distorted his constant smile into something almost like an insane grin.

"You need to take care of yourselves. I've got big plans for the both of you."

*   *   *

Thuggernaut, Johnny, Arachno Bro, Pod Person, Arcanicus, and Ivan, who had slipped out once his kids were good and asleep, along with Lance and Warren, were seated around the poker table when the other apprentices and their guides walked in. Xelas—Alexis no more as she'd shed her disguise along with the others—glanced around in confusion before slapping herself on the head, causing a clank that echoed across the room.

"Shit, I forgot you had this place tonight. We'll go find another room to unwind in." Xelas turned, motioning for the others to head back down the stairs, but Johnny called to her before she got free.

"How'd your night go? Have a nice, fun outing at the club? We've been getting pretty rowdy ourselves."

Every female member of the council, along with Tori and Beverly, stared at Johnny with individual combinations of disbelief and contempt. Wordlessly, they filed back down the stairs in search of another lounge where they could drink wine, relax, and unwind from a night that had gone spectacularly off the rails. The slam of the door from downstairs was the only cue that they'd officially left. No one even bothered to call out a goodbye.

"Guess they're jealous we had a livelier time," Johnny said with a shrug. He threw a few more chips into the pot, hoping to bluff his way out of yet another bad hand.

Chapter 50

Tori was a bit surprised by the hangover that woke her up on Saturday morning. While she liked the occasional beer, she rarely drank enough to actually catch the 'brown-bottle flu', as her father had called it. Yet in the midst of all the craziness the night before, she'd probably put down more booze in one evening than in the rest of the month combined. It was, mercifully, an easy fix as she pulled herself out of bed and trudged toward the bathroom.

Before stepping in (making certain she was on the tile, just to be safe), she pulled off the t-shirt and shorts that served as her pajamas and turned into living fire. Regeneration was a handy aspect of her abilities, one for which she'd been constantly grateful over the years. Using it to cure a hangover might not qualify as the most noble of pursuits, but with a day of guild training ahead of her, the last thing Tori wanted was to start off sluggish.

She stood there for about five minutes before shifting back, her once more human anatomy now completely cured of any lingering hangover effects. That problem solved, she hopped in the shower, scrubbing off a night of excitement, panic, and worry. Once clean, she dried off and dressed in her apprentice costume, the default outfit for all guild endeavors. Glancing at the clock, Tori realized she was up a full hour earlier than necessary. With nothing else to do before training started, she decided to head over to the rookie lounge and grab some breakfast. It wouldn't be as good as the stuff Ivan made, but it would be filling enough to keep her going until lunch.

When Tori walked into the large room, she immediately noticed that she wasn't the only one with a hankering for caloric intake. Beverly, adorned in her own generic apprentice costume, sat in front of the television watching the news as she wolfed down a breakfast burrito from the vending machine. Based on the wrappers at her side, it was her third or fourth so far.

Neither said anything as Tori plunked her money in the machine, getting two burritos of her own along with a soda. Things had been a bit strange between them ever since Beverly found out Tori was friends with a cape. She'd expected that reaction from the older members, who'd turned out to be unbothered by it, but not from Beverly. Silence wasn't fixing anything though, so as Tori took a seat on the couch, she decided it was time to try the other thing: actual talking about the issue at hand.

"Are we cool?" She hated the words even as she said them, but Tori Rivas had not been blessed with the gift of subtlety. Beverly looked over at her, so she decided to just power through and get things done. "You've seemed kind of bothered since last night when you met Donald."

"Guess we had to do this eventually," Beverly muttered. She picked up the remote, turned the television on mute, and then gave her attention back to Tori. "Look, I get it. He was your buddy at work, you became friends, and then he got turned into a cape. Completely impossible to predict and nobody's fault. Well, sort of his for choosing to be one, I suppose, but I'll admit it sounds like things sort of snowballed on him. I don't have any problem with Donald as a person or you for being his friend. I just *really* dislike the AHC."

"Why? I mean, sure, we're villains and technically enemies, but you heard Morgana last night. We mostly stay out of each other's way."

Beverly shook her head. "I've disliked that place since long before I got these powers. It's part of why I stayed with the guild; I needed to learn control, and I sure as shit wasn't going to the capes to get it. Remember how I told you that the amulet I found was among my great-grandmother's knick-knacks? Well, I wasn't the first in my family to come across an artifact from her collection. My grandpa found one, a special one she'd kept tucked away in a safe almost no one knew about. It was a crown, silver and studded with three gems in the center. When he put it on, grandpa was suddenly adorned in medieval armor. He was strong, fast, could fly, and had a few other powers as well. He figured that after a lifetime of hunting and hoarding, great-grandma had actually found one item of genuine power."

"I'm guessing your grandfather joined the AHC," Tori said.

"Tried to, anyway. This was way back in the day, before Quorum and Lodestar, before the AHC was even called that. Professor Quantum was the biggest powerhouse around, and he was in charge of what was then the League of Metas. My grandpa went by there after learning how to use his powers, wanted to join up and make the world a better place. Their response was that they didn't have a spot for him on the main roster, but they were working on a 'Colored Division' to do some lesser jobs and they thought he'd be a great fit."

"Hoooooly shit." Tori set down her breakfast burrito, appetite momentarily lost.

"Yeah. The fifties, you know? That wasn't even the worst of it, though." Beverly put her hands together, using each to stop the other from trembling in anger. "When he rightfully told them to go fuck themselves, guess what they said? If he didn't want to join up, that was perfectly fine. He could leave anytime he wanted. The crown, however, stayed with them."

"No fucking way. They couldn't..."

"Different times," Beverly replied. "Media was carefully controlled, and there were no internet or cell phone cameras to record that sort of thing. Grandpa hadn't gone out and done anything heroic yet—he wanted to get training so he could be as effective as possible—so no one out there even knew he existed. Just like that, those fuckers took away the source of his power, saying it needed to be in the hands of someone who would make proper use of it. They took the heart right out of grandpa along with it. To the day he died, there always a sadness around him, like a piece of him was missing. I guess because there was."

"God. Damn. No wonder you hate the AHC," Tori said. "I'd be trying to light their building on fire if I were you."

"Not going to lie, the day I discovered the red dragon power, I was a little tempted," Beverly admitted.

"Probably for the best you didn't, at least for now." Tori shook her head in disbelief and picked her breakfast back up. Terrible as Beverly's tale was, it didn't change the fact that she couldn't train on an empty stomach. "Do you know what happened to the crown? Like, which cape is out there using it?"

"Strangest thing, actually," Beverly replied. "We've never seen hide nor hair of anyone out there wearing it. It's possible that the appearance is different depending on who uses it. Or maybe it only works for certain people, limited by genetics or inherent goodness or something. Trust me, if I did know who had it, I'd be beating it off the top of their head right now."

"If that day ever comes, just let me know and I'll hold them while you hit them," Tori offered. "But, and please don't hate me for saying this, that was a different organization than the AHC. I've got no love for capes in my heart, either, but it's not like it was when they did that to your grandfather."

"You know you're talking about the same organization that has a member who flies around in a robotic Klansman's outfit, right?"

"We all know they tried to kick out Whitest Knight," Tori reminded her. "The lawsuit was a media circus for the full year it took. I'm not proposing we drop out of the guild and run to see if they'll let us join, just advocating for a clear perspective when dealing with them. That kind of grudge can lead to mistakes, the sort that might end in breaking the code. And, in case you didn't notice last night, I'm not big on the idea of seeing my friends killed."

"I might have picked up on that. Sort of surprised me, actually. I mean, who'd have guessed that the terrifying Pseudonym's apprentice was actually a big ole softy?" Beverly chuckled. "I'll take the point to heart, though. I don't plan on taking many, maybe any jobs once the apprenticeship is over, but I also didn't plan on getting dragon powers. Best to be ready for anything."

Beverly reached over, picked up her pile of wrappers and began smushing them together into one greasy, wadded-up ball. "And to answer your question, yeah, we're good. It isn't your fault you had a friend go cape, and it isn't his fault that they did what they did to my family. I might not like the organization, but I'm trying to judge the people on a case-by-case basis."

338

Leaning back, Beverly tossed her paper ball through the air, where it arced gracefully before plopping down a solid two feet away from the open trashcan where she'd been aiming. "Guess it's a good thing no one expects me to handle ranged fighting."

"Not when they've got me on hand." Tori balled up her own wrapper, took careful aim, and proceeded to miss the exact same shot, her wadded up ball landing a few inches away from Beverly's. "Well, shit. Maybe Lance has a good aim."

"We can only hope," Beverly agreed.

It was a silly, simple conversation, but by the time breakfast was done, both women felt a lot better. There were few people they could trust and lean on in a situation like theirs; losing that trust with each other would have made things much harder.

Especially as they drew closer to their goal, when they'd need to rely on the other apprentices more than ever before.

*   *   *

"Come in!" Donald didn't bother getting up from his bed, controller still in hand as he fired several rounds into the alien hides of his attackers. From the door, an audible click could be heard as it unlocked, responding to his voice command and allowing the person outside to step through. Donald wasn't sure how he felt about every aspect of the AHC, but the accommodations they had in place were nothing to sneeze at.

"What the hell, man?" Ren pushed open the door, once again cloaked in his human illusion. Instead of a suit, he was wearing a tank top and basketball shorts, having no doubt come right from the gym. "When I asked what you were doing at breakfast, you said you were going to spend the whole day training. I've been in the gym since this morning and you haven't set foot in there."

"I'm doing a different kind of training," Donald replied. He punched the pause button, freezing the screen as his character looked over a small hill where an ambush was no doubt waiting to try and surprise him. "Last night, I noticed something that had never come up before. I explained that the items I pull have to come from real games, right? They can't just be pieces of code."

"Yeah, that's why your fancy wrist pad has like twenty whatchabytes of memory on it. It's running a dozen or so games at once in the background."

"Exactly. Well, when they built it, they installed fresh copies of all the games. Which means all I can access are the default, unleveled versions of the items. If I'd had a fully fleshed out blaster and armor last night, I could have lit that monster up before it even managed to climb the wall."

"Your items have levels?" Ren stared at the screen, then at Donald, then at the wrist computer that sat on the floor, wires connecting it to the television screen. "I do not get you video game guys."

"Some have levels, some are just shitty until you find upgrades, and sometimes you have to play through to the end of the game to get the really cool gear," Donald explained. He held up the controller in his hand and pointed at the screen. "That's what I meant by training. I'm playing through *Blaster Brahs* so next time I can actually take a few hits and not need ninety seconds between every shot."

"Weird," Ren said. "I mean, I get it, or I think I do anyway, but it's still strange to me that you sitting in here, playing games, is going to make you stronger. Are you even sure it will work? What if you still pull the default item?"

"It took me an hour and a half to figure out how to hook up a controller and television to that thing, so I definitely made sure it was worth the time first," Donald assured him. He hopped off the bed and walked over to a small desk where his laptop, the one he'd gotten for his project at Vendallia, sat humming softly. "This morning I logged into my *Legacy World* account and created a new character. When I took a sword from him, it was just a sword, and kind of a shitty one at that. When I switched over to my usual character, I was able to pull the same sword that had gone through some serious upgrading and gem-crafting."

Donald wiggled the mouse, bringing up a screen that showed his small character sitting in a pub, head down on the table, asleep. With a few clicks, he opened the item screen, reached over, and plucked the sword from inside the game. Ren took a step back on pure instinct. The blade in front of him was glowing with a dark purple light. Power seemed to radiate off it, occasionally appearing in short bolts that crackled between the blade and the guard.

"The upgrades definitely carry over." Donald let go of the blade, which quickly dissolved into sparks and numbers. "Hence why I've been in here playing *Blaster Brahs* all morning."

"Why not just use items from the game with the sword?" Ren asked.

"MMO's require constant internet connections, the sort that are hard to manage wirelessly." Donald cast a long, lingering glance at the computer screen still acting as digital portal into *Legacy World*. "Much as I'd love to pull out some of my *LW* character's items, the wrist-unit can't reliably connect, which means it's too dangerous to count on them. Instead I've got to work with stuff I can keep offline copies of."

Ren held up his hands in surrender. "You win. I give up. This somehow counts as training. But you still need to hit the gym sometimes. Basic strength and cardio are useful no matter what your power is."

"Plus, who else there has the courage to spot you?" Donald closed the laptop and went back to his bed. Nice as it was to hang out here, he was looking forward to the AHC finally making his apartment safe enough to go back to. This was like living in a giant dorm, which was not something Donald had enjoyed even during his college days. Though it wasn't quite so bad now that he had a friend.

"Heaven save us if you're actually needed to help lift," Ren replied. "I guess I should get back to it. I've been feeling pretty confident in my own strength lately, but last night made me realize just how lacking I am. You burned a giant hole through that thing; I could barely leave scratches on it."

"Whoa there. The *only* reason I lived long enough to get that shot off was because you were there to draw its attention," Donald said. "Given how it was smashing through freaking everything it touched, I'd say it's outright amazing that you were able to last like that."

"Maybe so, but there's still a long way for me to go."

Donald didn't have a good reply to that, because Ren was right. Both of them were only just starting out; it would probably take months, if not years, before they were even semi-competent superheroes. They might have different ways of doing it, but they each understood how important training was.

"When you finish at the gym, feel free to swing by," Donald offered. "This can be a two-player game, you know."

"Appreciate it, but..." Ren held up his hands, turning them carefully so his palms were facing Donald. "They only look human, remember? Not sure the claws are built to handle fragile electronics."

"We had someone build a computer that fits on my forearm and runs more than twenty video games all at once," Donald replied. "I bet they can create a controller that you'll be able to use. I'll tell them you're my training partner. It's a lot easier to level in these things when you have a friend."

Ren hesitated then lowered his hands. "If you can get me the gear, I'll play some games with you. But you have to agree to keep hitting the gym with me. Deal?"

"Deal."

*   *   *

In his chambers, Balaam was perusing a tome of ancient power, searching for a spell he could use to properly reheat an old stew without boiling it over, when he felt the familiar twinge of pain behind his right eye. With a heavy sigh, he shut the book, went to where his carefully concealed and padded box was stored, and removed the silver mirror. His hands rested against the smooth surface, dulling the pain that told him it was time to converse. A familiar voice entered his head.

"*Balaam, how go your preparations?*"

"As good as they can with no actual deadline to work with," Balaam snapped. How were *his* preparations going? He wasn't the one holding things up, though even Balaam would admit that his task was the easier of the two.

"*That, I'm happy to say, is no longer good enough.*"

A trickle of excitement, tentative but undeniable, wormed through Balaam's heart. Could it be? After all these years, were things finally progressing? He kept his voice stoic—even if no one but the mirror's other holder could hear him, there was still a certain way evil wizards were supposed to act during these things.

"Are you saying that the time has come?"

"*I am saying it draws near. Very near. Within a week, perhaps two, I will finally have the last pieces we need. I have prepared my loyal ones as much as I can. A few days to bring them the rest of the way into the light and purge those who dissent and we will be ready to move.*"

Balaam resisted the urge, barely, to lift his hands off the mirror and clap with enthusiasm. With that timetable, it would be only two or three weeks until they could begin. Amid his excitement, he also felt fear slither its way in. For so long they'd been plotting. For so long it had been but a scheme that was more mad dream than tangible plan. Now that it was finally turning into reality, it was a bit scary. What they were about to do could never be undone.

"Very well. I'll bring the ones I trust in and get them up to speed. There will only be a few of them, of course, but it should suffice for what's needed on my end."

"*A few will be plenty. Once the fuse is lit, others will be drawn in whether they like it or not. We only need enough to get things started. Move forward. I will tell you when things are ready on my end.*"

With that, the voice faded. Balaam slipped the mirror back into its box. He put it away and didn't even glance at the tome of spells he'd been perusing earlier. Balaam now had far bigger concerns than reheated stew. There was much work to do, many contingencies to plan for, and so many pieces to put in motion. He'd done the vast majority of the groundwork already, but what remained was no small task.

All that aside, there was still one part of his job Balaam had no idea how he was going to pull off. Pseudonym as he was now posed very little threat to the plan. However, should the man be sufficiently motivated, there was always the chance that Fornax might once again raise his ferocious head and emerge from the weak shell of his current self. Should that occur, the entire plan could be thrown off course.

Balaam needed to find a way to deal with Ivan Gerhardt, and he needed to find it soon.

Chapter 51

The jingling of the bell overhead as Tori shoved the door open was both familiar and depressing. On one hand, it was nice to be back at Ridge City Grinders, and she was looking forward to checking in on Chloe. On the other hand, she was only here because Ivan had dropped her off while he parked the car, meaning she still had a full day of office work in front of her, followed by more guild training that night, and a few hours working on her meta-suit before she grabbed a quick nap to do the whole thing over again. The vacation was over, and now she had to go back to living her double life. At least field training would only last another week. And there was coffee, which was something to be grateful for.

Thankfully, the line was light for once, and Tori quickly made her way to the counter. To her surprise, Chloe's cheerful face wasn't there to greet her; Tori had been certain she'd seen the other woman's shock of white-blonde hair when she stepped through the door. Seconds later, a soft tap fell on her shoulder, and she turned to find her favorite barista standing behind her with a pair of extra-large cups in hand.

"Morning!" Chloe said cheerfully. "If you've got the time, I took my break and thought we might catch up a little."

"Of course." Tori wasn't actually all that sure she did have the time, but there was bound to be a little residual sympathy in the office she could milk if the talk made her late. Besides, she'd accidentally drawn Chloe into a dangerous situation with robbers and a crazy meta. The very least she owed the woman was a morning chat.

Chloe led her through the store, past the clustered tables and toward a pair of soft purple chairs set up by a window. Tori couldn't be certain, but she felt pretty sure they hadn't been positioned so out of the way last time she'd been in the store. It had been a week, though; some other customers had probably screwed with the layout. As they arrived, Chloe passed Tori the cups and grabbed a small table barely wide enough to hold a laptop. She placed it between the chairs; Tori set both coffees down on top of it.

"Let's start with the most important part," Chloe said as she and Tori settled into their seats. "Are you okay? Doctors gave you a clean bill of health and everything?"

"Fit as a fiddle." Tori raised her left arm and stretched it, flexing her fingers and making a fist. "No long-term damage; they even patched me up so well that I won't have scars from the bullet wounds. What about you?"

"I didn't need much treatment," Chloe replied. "Though I'm glad that someone sprang for a meta with healing powers, otherwise the jaw stuff might have taken a while."

"Yeah, in all the confusion, I didn't get to ask what happened there. How did your face get so hurt in the fight?" Tori could vividly recall the bruised, disjointed angle of Chloe's jawbone, almost impossible to picture now against her perfectly uninjured face.

"Oh, that. I sort of... I did that to myself." Chloe broke eye contact as she quickly glanced around, making sure no one else was near enough to overhear them. "You guys needed a distraction, so I... well, I punched myself in the face a few times with a stapler until I felt my jaw break, then said my bark was worse than my bite. With a broken jaw, you have a really crappy bite, which was why my bark was so loud and scary."

"Huh. Sort of seems like if you took that statement literally, it should have given you a shitty bark," Tori pointed out.

"That occurred to me later on, but I guess my power works more on what's meant than what's said. After all, the sayings aren't always literal. Or maybe my own intent matters. I'm still sort of figuring it all out." Chloe paused to take a sip of her coffee, wincing slightly from the heat of the liquid. "That's part of why I wanted to talk with you this morning."

Tori felt a prickle of worry dance down her vertebrae. "Did you want me to give you Donald's number or something? I'm sure you want to talk to another meta now that you know one."

Chloe stared at her friend for a long moment, then sighed and set her cup back down on the table. "I was hoping it wouldn't come to this, but I had a feeling it might. *Liar, liar, pants on fire.*"

Her words echoed through their small space, and Tori immediately glanced down to see if her khakis were combusting. Mercifully, they were still fully intact. Then again, all her clothes were built to be able to shift forms with her, so there was no guarantee fire would harm her outfit. It would make a hell of a scene, though, and Ivan had a tendency to frown on those.

"When we were trapped in the break room, you threw coffee on one of the robbers to give Donald a distraction. The thing is, the pot you used was full of cold coffee left over from the night before. We both know it shouldn't have hurt him, but he screamed like he was burning. Steam even came off it. Donald's power wouldn't have let him do that, and neither would mine. That only leaves you, Tori. You were the meta who heated up the coffee."

Tori considered her words carefully. Chloe's power was hard to predict and seemed to obey a set of laws unlike anything she'd encountered. Still, the effects always held true to the saying that Chloe used, so assuming she didn't tell a direct lie, there was a good chance her pants wouldn't suddenly ignite.

"That's a pretty big assumption to make just from me throwing a pot of coffee at someone."

"It is," Chloe agreed. "But after I made it, everything else that happened began to make a lot more sense. The way you charged into the fight despite being a paper-pusher, how quickly you figured out ways to use my and Donald's powers, even the determination you showed when you shot yourself in the arm. At the time, I took it as you being you, and while that's probably still true, I think there's more to it. Part of the reason you were able to do all those things is that you have a power of your own, and you're accustomed to using it."

"Well, it's an interesting theory," Tori said. "Let me ask you, though, if I say something is hypothetical, and it's not true, does that count as a lie?"

"Not sure, but I doubt it," Chloe told her. "Like I said before, intent seems to count. If you're trying to tell a lie, that's what will set it off."

That made things even murkier, which was precisely what Tori had been trying to avoid. There was no way out of this without some sort of risk, though. Even if she got up and left, she'd more or less confirm Chloe's suspicions. Plus, there was no telling how long her weird curse would last. Better to see things through for now and find out where that led.

"Let's say, hypothetically, that your theory was right. That I was a meta with a power of my own. Why call me out like this? What are you hoping to get from me? If it's money, you're out of luck. The office job pays decent, but not enough to be worth blackmailing."

"Huh?" Chloe tilted her head in surprise then gave it a hearty shake. "Whoa, no, no, no. I don't want to blackmail you or anything. I want *help*. I want to stop guessing at how this power works and actually figure the damn thing out. I keep setting it off by accident if I don't watch what I say. If you're a meta, you're obviously not a new one like me and Donald. I just need someone to help get me through this until I've got a handle on this stupid ability."

"Oh." It occurred to Tori that perhaps she'd been spending a bit too much time around supervillains. While the morally corrupt might want to profit from Tori's secret, it made sense that Chloe would desire help above all else. She hadn't been taken in by the guild or the capes; she was just stuck with a power that didn't come with instructions, trying to muddle through her life while keeping that strange ability a secret. Tori had been lucky; she'd understood what happened to her and had the skills to control it. Heck, even Donald had it better; at least his power could only be activated under certain conditions. Chloe's could turn on at any time just by accidently picking a poor turn of phrase.

"Okay, Chloe, let's assume I am a meta for a moment. What if my power is nothing like yours? I mean, yours is clearly rooted in magic. Maybe my hypothetical power came from a science mishap. Even if I wanted to help you—which I do—I'm probably one of the worst metas out there to do it."

"I'll take the worst over no one." Chloe fidgeted with the coffee cup clutched in her hands, staring down into its half-drunk contents. "I need to get this under control. It's fun, and it could be a really neat power in its own right, but I have to figure out how to use it properly. Otherwise, it's just going to keep causing me trouble."

"Have..." Tori hesitated, unable to believe the words that were about to leave her mouth. "Have you considered going to the AHC? I'm pretty sure they have classes and training specifically for new metas. They're bound to have someone there who can help you." Much as it galled Tori to put another friend on the path to being a cape, Chloe needed help, and better she get it from the good guys than entangle herself with the guild.

"I thought about it, but I don't want to be a superhero. Honestly, I don't think I even can; my power just isn't that offensive," Chloe admitted. Tori was inclined to disagree, seeing as it had let her punch out a strength-based meta, but she said nothing as Chloe continued.

"Going to the AHC, it feels... dangerous. Like I'm putting myself in a world that I might not want to be in. Once I do that, there's no going back. They'll know who I am and what I can do, and if for some reason they ever decide I might be necessary as a tool, I might not have a choice. Meta drafts have happened before. That's why I don't want to get involved with some mysterious organization. I'm just asking someone I consider a friend if they'll lend me whatever help they can."

"Forcing me to tell the truth or burn was a bit heavy-handed," Tori pointed out.

"True, but my break is only so long, so this saved us both fifteen minutes of you trying to lie your way out of admitting what you are—what we *both* are. But you're right, I'm asking a lot. It's time I showed you some trust. *A penny saved is a penny earned.*"

"How does that one work, exactly?" Tori didn't feel any different physically, though her mind was far more relaxed knowing that she wouldn't be in danger of having her trousers set aflame for one little fib.

"Every time I resist the urge to spend money, whatever I would have spent doubles," Chloe explained. "It only works with cash, though, and I have to be both genuinely tempted and able to buy it. No pretending I want a house, resisting, and watching my bank account swell. It just earns me a little extra grocery money here and there."

"Pretty useful," Tori said. "So, look. I meant what I said about being the worst person to help you, but that doesn't mean I won't still try. That said, I do know a few other people who might be better suited to figure out how this ability of yours works. Are you okay with me sharing your secret? It would only be with people that I trust, I promise."

Slowly, tentatively, Chloe nodded her head. "If you trust them and really think they can help, then I trust you. Let's just not broadcast it all over town though, okay?"

"Don't worry; I've only got one or two in mind. The first would be the best, but unfortunately, that one is also a super long shot. The second is like us: still inexperienced, but I have a feeling she'd definitely help out. One more thing, though. We won't be able to start until next week. I'm sort of swamped every day and night until then."

"That's fine," Chloe said, a relieved smile cresting her face. "Honestly, I wasn't even expecting that much. It'll give me time to try and figure out where we should start."

Tori glanced at the clock and confirmed that she would indeed be stepping into the office late. So far, it was in the forgivable bounds, but she needed to hurry if she didn't want to catch hell from Ivan, especially since she was about to try and con a huge favor out of him.

"I've got to head in," Tori said, picking up her cup and rising from the chair. "But you've already got my number from when we set up the catering, so text me next week and we can work out the details. Just keep things vague, you know?"

"Nothing to worry about there," Chloe replied. "I'm a big fan of keeping things private."

"Figured as much." Tori began to turn toward the door then stopped, facing Chloe once more. "Just out of curiosity, why go through all this to come to me? I mean, you know Donald too, and wouldn't have had to strong-arm him into admitting he was a meta. I get not wanting to go to the AHC, but why not ask him for help?"

"I thought about it; I even picked up the phone to call you and get his number a few times. It's just that... well, he's a superhero now. He's out there stopping crime. Just last Friday, he fought this giant monster in the middle of a club. I feel like he's got better things to do than help out some untrained meta that doesn't want to sign up with the heroes."

It made a certain amount of sense; Tori could see where Chloe was coming from. But at the same time, this was Donald they were talking about. He'd have definitely made time for someone he thought needed help. At least, the Donald she'd made friends with would have, but that Donald wouldn't have tried to take on a giant monster. His new job was clearly changing him.

She just hoped it wasn't into someone she had to count as an enemy.

Chapter 52

"Are you asking me for help or permission?" Ivan seemed unfazed by Tori's rundown of her unexpected coffee discussion, taking it all in with a passive, almost bored expression. She'd expected him to at least be annoyed. Instead he kept clicking away on his computer as she spoke, no doubt clearing out the backed up emails from his week away.

"Um, both, I guess?" Tori was still taken aback by his disinterest in the issue at hand, but she steeled herself to press on, apathy be damned. "Let's start with the help part. Is that something you're willing to do?"

"Depends," Ivan replied, eyes still trained on his monitor screen. "By 'help,' do you mean train a meta that owes no allegiance to our guild, or do you mean dispose of someone who knows about your secret? If it's the former, then no. If it's the latter, then still no, but I have some other people I can recommend for reasonable rates."

"Oh, pretty please let that just be a terrible joke," Tori said, unapologetically glaring at her teacher.

Ivan finally turned from his computer and set his hands heavily on the desk. "The guild does offer certain services like that, but no, I wasn't serious about killing the barista just because she figured out you were a meta. I was, however, serious about not wanting to train her. As you might recall, I'm not big on students, especially ones I wouldn't be educating in the guild's code first."

"Chloe isn't asking to be turned into the next Lodestar; she just wants to get better control over her power."

"You would be surprised how quickly 'better control' turns into 'all the power,'" Ivan said. "If Chloe wants help from me, or someone with better qualifications, then she is welcome to enlist in the guild. Of course, as you well know, that is neither an easy nor safe path. However, as I have a vested interest in a meta not accidently causing havoc or chaos in our city, I have no objections to you helping her gain better control and understanding of her power."

"Really?" Tori backed away slightly from the desk, accidently betraying her shock. "I expected you to fight me a lot more on that."

"Tori, you have one more week of field training and a single test remaining before you can become a full member of the guild. One of the things that will change at that point is the amount of hand-holding and supervision you receive from me. Your time is just that: yours. So long as you don't violate the code, you're free to spend it however you see fit. If you want to train this woman then I won't stop you. But if she becomes a problem, then she becomes your problem… yours to fix or to be dragged down by. Understand?"

"Understood," Tori replied. "But let's go back to the thing about less hand-holding. Does that mean you're not going to be my mentor anymore?"

"I will still be around in some capacities," Ivan told her. "A mentor and student are always bonded, which is why so many guild members avoid taking them. But you will have gotten past the largest of the hurdles and proven yourself to be worthy of membership. From that point on, you alone will determine how you further your education."

"Guess that means no more nightly quizzes of the code or you drilling me with hypothetical scenarios and seeing how I would deal with them." She'd meant the words to sound playful, but to her surprise, they came out tinged with sadness. Her time with Ivan hadn't necessarily been easy, and heaven knew she was tired of his endless emphasis on the code, but at the same time, it had gotten to be a comfortable, familiar routine.

Ivan coughed slightly into his hand, the first time he'd betrayed a sense of discomfort since she'd barged into his office. "To be frank, Tori, after you've become a full member of the guild, you won't be residing with me anymore. This was an arrangement done only for the time in which you needed my guidance and supervision. You'll be free to move into the guild headquarters or find a spot of your own."

"I just can't stay." She wasn't surprised, not really. In the back of her mind, Tori had always known that her garage apartment in the heart of suburbia was a temporary arrangement. And at least she had a place to go—even if it was a place stocked full of criminals and weirdoes.

"Would you even want to?" Ivan asked. "I imagined this would be more akin to opening a cage than handing you an eviction. You'll be free to go where you like and live in whatever way pleases you, which I imagine will involve a cluttered, messy lab with little more than two plates, a microwave, and a miniature television."

"That's a weirdly accurate description of my last few places," Tori admitted.

"Don't feel bad; I based the guess on Doctor Mechaniacal's first apartment. Anyway, the point is, I'm not kicking you out the door as soon as your last trial is over. You'll be free to apartment hunt and figure things out as you need to. While neither of us might have precisely wanted this arrangement, it's not so bothersome that I can't hang on for a little while longer." Ivan smiled at her, betraying the fact that he'd actually just said something bordering on nice.

"Yeah, you're not as bad as I expected. At least you can cook." Tori decided it was best not to push her luck; after all, she'd gotten permission to help her friend and a kind word out of Ivan. Best to quit while she was still

351

ahead. "All right, boss, time for me to head back to work. After a week away, there are a ridiculous number of meetings for me to schedule."

"Oh, that reminds me, don't make any plans for lunch," Ivan told her. "The office is throwing us a surprise 'welcome back' party. My understanding is that they got Thai from that place three blocks over."

"That's really nice of them." Tori found herself unexpectedly touched by the gesture, in spite of the fact that she'd seen how close the office was when they were taken hostage.

"The people here are good, decent folk," Ivan said. "And they tend to look out for their colleagues. Which brings up another thing: have you seen Donald today?"

Tori shook her head; Donald had been stuck in meetings all morning. The rumors around the break room were that he was having his project load assessed and reassigned in order to free him up in case the AHC had to call him in for an emergency. A lot of people thought it was the first step in getting him to stop coming in to the office. They speculated that after this he'd be given the "opportunity" to telecommute as much as he liked, and eventually, he'd likely get paid for doing nothing. Capes weren't exactly attacked in the street, but the non-guild criminals out there sometimes tried to hit them when they thought their guard was down. The bigger Donald's profile got, the more risk there was that someone would try to come after him while he was on Vendallia's clock.

"You may want to reach out to him and see how things are going. From what I understand, things have been a bit tough for him around here since he became a cape. A little friendship might go a long way."

"Nice as that sounds, you'll understand if I'm a little suspicious about why you want me to reach out to a superhero," Tori said. "Putting up with a friendship is one thing, but that borders on you encouraging it."

"Of course I encourage it." Ivan turned back to his computer, the rhythmic clacking of the keys resuming. "The continued existence of our guild is predicated on us being more trouble to fight than to tolerate. A few friendships across the moral lines only make us less tempting as targets."

"I guess that's true, even if it feels a bit manipulative." Tori regarded her teacher carefully as he punched away at the keyboard. "Does that mean you've got a few friends over at the AHC as well?"

"Don't be ridiculous. Who on earth in that organization would have wanted to befriend Fornax?"

"Well, Lodestar—"

"Lodestar reaches out to everyone she thinks she can help," Ivan said, cutting Tori off. "And it paid off in the form of us stopping Orion. She was the only one who saw recruiting me as a good idea, though. Trust me: Fornax has no friends at the Alliance of Heroic Champions, which is why it's all the more important that his apprentice keep the one she managed to make. You never know when you might need someone over there to speak on your behalf."

"Let's hope it never comes to that." Tori left the office, though her mind stayed with Ivan. Stoic as her teacher was, she'd been around him long enough to get a bit of a read on him. Something told her he wasn't revealing the whole truth about having friends among the capes. It was something she'd dwell on later, when there was time.

For now, she still had a whole Monday to get through.

* * *

It wasn't until lunch—which was both delicious and heartwarming; the rest of the floor had gathered to wish her and Ivan a happy return—that Tori finally found herself free at the same time as Donald.

He emerged from a conference room with the telltale combination of weariness and relief that spoke of a long meeting that had finally come to an end. She hadn't noticed in the chaos and surprise of the club, but he seemed different than Tori remembered him. Not physically—he was still a wiry young man with red hair and freckles—but the way he held himself had shifted. No longer did Donald Moss merely trudge through the hallways, visibly counting the minutes until he was free of their fluorescent-lit cage. Now he had an air of confidence about him. He moved like a man who knew his surroundings were temporary, and that something far greater awaited him on the outside.

Donald noticed Tori in her cube and smiled, giving her a nervous wave; suddenly the illusion vanished. But Tori knew what she'd seen. Donald was changing, bit by bit. And really, how could he not? He was a cape now. No one could take on a job like that and remain the same as they were before.

"Glad to see you're all right," she told him, standing up from her seat and giving him a brief, office-appropriate hug.

"That's supposed to be my line," Donald replied. "I was really worried you wouldn't make it out of there, but I didn't have your cell, so I couldn't check in to make sure you and your friends were okay."

"We all escaped fine, thanks to you and that other guy… Medley, I think the news said his name was?" Tori knew perfectly well what the other cape's name had been. She also had a sneaking suspicion that in another form he resembled Ren, Donald's friend, but she had an image to keep up, even if it meant playing dumb.

"Yeah, he's another new guy at the AHC," Donald confirmed.

353

"He seems like a tough SOB. The news was showing surveillance footage and stuff people shot with their cameras, and it was an incredible fight. Weren't you scared, though? That thing seemed like a real monster." Tori didn't consider this part to be a lie—that rhino-creature had been flat out terrifying. She wasn't even sure how she would have fought it, at least without her meta-suit. But Donald had managed in spite of everything.

"Oh yeah, I was freaking out during the whole fight." Donald didn't seem at all embarrassed about his fear as he sat his laptop down on the cubicle desk and settled into his uncomfortable chair. "There were at least three times where I was a thousand percent sure I was going to die. Only Medley and way too much luck got me through it."

"You seemed so composed when you told us to leave." That part was total bullshit and they probably both knew it, but the guy had tried to put himself between innocent people and a monster. He deserved a little bit of flattery for that sort of bravery. "Didn't you even consider trying to run?"

"Honestly... it was the first thing that went through my mind." Donald's pale cheeks flushed slightly, and he busied himself with opening his laptop to avoid Tori's gaze. "Like I said, I was scared. All I could think of when that thing started coming after me was how to not die."

Tori settled back into her own chair but stayed far enough away from her desk that she could continue watching Donald as she spoke. "So, why didn't you? There's bound to be some gadget in your computer that would have let you get out of there." This was a question Tori had been burning to ask ever since Donald decided to stay behind in spite of being able to run. She didn't understand it, simply couldn't fathom why he'd lay down his life like that. Fighting for friends and family was one thing, but they could have evacuated with the rest of the club, and everyone would have probably been safe. Instead, Donald and Medley put their lives on the line to protect the retreat of strangers. The survivalist mentality Tori had spent half a lifetime honing simply couldn't square up with such actions.

"I mean... I wanted to, really badly. But if I had, then who would have stopped that creature?" The flush in Donald's cheeks began to fade, and he managed to glance back over at Tori as he spoke. "Medley can take a beating, but he wasn't able to hurt the monster very much. And sure, the AHC could have dispatched someone else, but there's no way of knowing how many people would have been hurt by then. I just asked myself what the real superheroes would do, what Lodestar would have done, and then tried like hell to pretend I was one of them."

"Donald, you stared down a monster with nothing but a computer pad and a weird tiger creature for backup. If that doesn't make you a real superhero, I'm not sure what bar has to be crossed."

"Maybe it will feel real once I save the world or something," Donald replied. He pressed a few keys on his laptop and a screen full of e-mails appeared. "On the upside, looks like I'll have a lot more time to train soon."

Tori debated pretending to be in the dark, but Donald knew how gossip traveled in the office. Her acting unaware crossed the realm into unbelievable. "I heard they were transitioning off a lot of your projects?"

"If by 'a lot' you mean 'pretty much everything' then yeah, that's what they're doing," Donald said, letting out a heavy sigh. "By the end of the month, it will be like I don't even work here anymore. Which, I guess, is the point. At least I'll still get a paycheck, though."

"Wait, you get a paycheck and don't have to show up to the office? Hot damn, someone sign me up for superpowers and monster-fighting," Tori declared.

"It won't be forever, at least not at my full rate." Donald tapped another key and brought up a calendar for the rest of the year. "Basically, they can't fire me for volunteering to protect innocent people, so they're forcing me into early retirement. A few people at the AHC warned me that it might happen, but I thought they were just exaggerating." Another few clicks and the calendar vanished, the digital reminder momentarily banished from sight if not mind.

"Looks like you'll have to get used to another cubicle-mate." Donald's voice couldn't have been any more bitter if his mouth had suddenly turned into a lemon.

"We'll see about that," Tori replied. "My internship is up in a few weeks anyway. There's no guarantee I'll even be able to stay on here. It's possible I might be gone long before you stop coming in."

"Pretty sure Vendallia doesn't want the PR hassle of firing an intern who was heavily injured in an attack on their offices," Donald pointed out. "Besides, you do great work, and Mr. Gerhardt's opinion carries a lot of weight around here. If he vouches for you, you'll get hired. There's nothing to worry about."

"Maybe so, but I'm not one to count my chickens." Tori reached over her desk to her purse and fished about for several seconds before finding what she was looking for. "And I'm also not one to take pointless chances. So, if either of us ends up leaving, let's make sure we can still hang out when the mood strikes us. You said you didn't have my cell number, right? Well, let's fix that right here and now."

Tori held up her phone and almost chuckled at the barely constrained joy on Donald's face. Ivan had been right; a little reaching out did go a long way. Tori was surprised at how happy he was to have one friend that wanted to stay in touch after their office time ended.

Which just went to show that, smart as Tori was, she still had her blind spots.

Chapter 53

With work done and Tori off to the guild for night training, Ivan was just settling in with a good book when his doorbell rang.

Moving carefully, power already flowing into him as he prepared for the possibility of an assault, Ivan peered through the peephole at the mysterious person on his doorstep. It was neither a salesman nor a neighbor as Ivan had half-suspected, but instead the gently smiling face of Wade Wyatt. Muttering curses, the vulgar kind rather than the magical sort, Ivan unlocked his door and pulled it open for the man who was both his best friend and the leader of their guild.

"To what do I owe this unexpected intrusion?"

"Certainly not a hospitality lesson, though it seems you could use one," Wade replied, walking in without waiting to be invited.

"Looks who's talking. You usually call before stopping over. In fact, you're downright pathological about it." Ivan's annoyance turned to concern as he relocked his door. If Wade was stopping by without calling, it either meant there hadn't been time to do so or he didn't trust the phone and the visit was supposed to be secret, neither of which boded particularly well.

"Yes, well, something needs your attention, and I felt it was best to bring the matter before you personally," Wade said. "You know that during every training session, we make a point of taking the apprentices to see a code-enforcement, correct?"

Ivan nodded. "It's not pretty, but they need to know what happens to those who break our rules. And it's a good way to show them what those sorts of jobs are like before they make the mistake of agreeing to take one."

"Glad you approve, because I just got word that Onslaughter is held up in Guatemala. Nothing too serious, but it's unlikely he'll make it back this week, and certainly not tonight, which is when the code-enforcement is supposed to take place."

"Wade... you can't be serious." Ivan waited for the sudden burst of laughter or clapping to signal that it was a joke. Instead, his friend merely stared at him, no mirth to be seen. "You want me to do a job in front of other people? And kids at that?"

"None of them are children; they're just younger than us," Wade rebutted. "And anyone with a television screen has seen video of you fighting before."

"Fighting, yes. Killing, no. Surely there's someone else qualified to do this," Ivan said.

Wade nodded, a short, sharp gesture that didn't reassure Ivan in the slightest. "We have plenty who are qualified and some who are willing; however, the problem is one of seniority. When Balaam heard about Onslaughter, he volunteered to handle the code-enforcement himself. As a councilor and a proven warrior, no one in the guild can say they are more capable of handling the task than he. No one save for our most powerful and renowned enforcer, of course."

"Fucking Balaam." Ivan sucked in a breath through his teeth, trying to smother the embers of rage that blazed at the bastard's name. "You think he's planning something?"

"It's always possible," Wade admitted. "Field training is dangerous in itself, code-enforcement even more so. It wouldn't be the first time a trainee didn't make it back, though those incidents are usually not the fault of the instructor."

"Still, offing an apprentice seems like a stretch. He's guaranteed to piss off their mentor and maybe a few other members as well," Ivan pointed out.

"I'm not claiming Balaam plans to lead all of them to their death," Wade said. "In truth, I have no idea what he's got planned for the apprentices. Perhaps he wants nothing more than to teach a good lesson and make you worry in the process. It wouldn't be out of character for him. All I know is that unless Pseudonym steps forward, Balaam is handling the code-enforcement. That seemed like the sort of thing you'd want to be made aware of."

Ivan stood motionless for several seconds, weighing the risks of each possibility against the other. If he let Balaam go, there was a good chance he'd do nothing more than teach the lesson, meaning Ivan had been fearful over nothing. Of course, he might also seize the opportunity to eliminate, injure, or otherwise incapacitate his own apprentice's competition. Balaam was usually smart in his scheming, but with pride on the line, nothing was ever certain. On the other hand, if Ivan took over the job, he could make sure the rookies were safe the entire time. And all it would cost him is creating four more people who looked at him with nothing but fear in their eyes.

"Better scared than dead," Ivan mumbled, more to himself than to Wade. "Get me the information about the enforcement and have our recon people do some proper scouting. We're clear on the cape front, right?"

"This one is on the other side of the country, and we've set up the necessary decoy crimes to make sure you'll have all the time you need," Wade assured him.

"Then I guess there's nothing left to do but tell Balaam to fuck off and put on my costume." Ivan repressed a sigh and tried not to think about the fact that he'd only just gotten the blood out of it from the last time. This was the price he paid for freedom. For him and those he loved.

*   *   *

Tori was dragging ass as she gathered with the other apprentices in the lounge. Her long day at work had stretched on forever and the brief catnap she'd grabbed in her guild bedroom had only served to make her more tired. Idly she wondered if this would be the sort of training that might lend itself to stopping by a gas station and picking up a half-dozen or so energy drinks. That thought went quickly out the window as a familiar—way too familiar, in fact—figure stepped into the lounge.

Ivan was in his full Pseudonym outfit; bland and nondescript as it was, the change still seemed to alter him. The stoic, detached demeanor remained, but instead of calm, he seemed to radiate the potential for violence. Just from looking at him she knew this wasn't Ivan showing up to a council meeting or walking around making introductions. He'd shown up to work, and she couldn't imagine the task before him was a peaceful one. Behind him, Tunnel Vision waited just outside the room, their silhouettes outlined by the hallway's lighting.

"Apprentices," he said, his voice as stable as always, yet somehow harsher than Tori expected. "What is the most important, most sacred, most vital part of this guild?"

"The code." Tori answered without a second thought, and she noted that the others echoed her. While she doubted they'd gotten the same thorough training and speeches she had, it seemed their teachers had instructed them on how important the code was all the same. Or, at least, how important they had to pretend it was.

"That is correct. The code of this guild is our armor. It protects us, conceals us, allows us to live in the shadows. All around the world there are metas trying to get rich or seize power by their own means, and inevitably they must deal with the Alliance of Heroic Champions. Through the code, we stay below their radar, always out of reach, always too hard to chase. They know of us, yet because of the code, they are forced to tolerate us. The code ensures that we are smart, careful, and, above all, that we remain unseen. However, the code is not only armor, keeping those in this guild safe; it is also a sword used to carve out those who would bring trouble down upon our heads."

Ivan didn't pace, didn't move, didn't so much as flinch as he spoke. He was rigid, unmovable, a manifestation of the very code he loved so dearly. If they hadn't already known, no one in the room would have guessed that this controlled man was once the wild beast of destruction known as Fornax.

359

"For the most part, we leave other criminals undisturbed. The AHC needs them to prop up their image, and the last thing we want is to leave them scarce on villains to drag before the cameras. However, sometimes we get word of criminals going too far, seeking the sort of power that might threaten our very world—which troubles us as much as the capes—or committing the sort of crimes that work counter to our interests. The gang we're going after tonight has begun to cause our guild a lot of trouble. They've targeted assets owned by guild members, a crime we would punish regardless, but even worse, they've been buying up black market information on the identities and loved ones of various capes. Can anyone tell me why that could negatively impact us?"

"An unhinged cape is an unpredictable cape," Lance said. He earned a few surprised stares, to which he gave a small shrug as if to say that even he paid attention from time to time.

"Simplistic, but true," Ivan agreed. "Logically, our organization is not worth the trouble of taking a run at. We cover our tracks and have great lawyers on retainer. But when a cape loses their family, when anger and grief overwhelm that logic we depend on, sometimes revenge against the people who stole their loved ones isn't enough. Often it will boil over, causing them to try and take down every villain they can, including the ones they know they should leave be. This is why our code forbids killing the friends and family of a cape, even accidentally, and it's why we discourage it to non-members whenever possible. In the case of the gang trying to steal from us and trying to stir up capes, our discouragement is going to be the active kind."

For the first time since he'd walked in the room, Ivan hesitated. It was subtle, almost imperceptible unless one had been living in his garage apartment for the past several weeks and gotten to know him very well. That moment of hesitation, more than anything else that had occurred so far, put Tori on edge.

"I don't mean to mince words and dance around the truth; that wouldn't do you any good with what's coming," Ivan said. "You need to know what's going to happen, and you need to mentally prepare for it as best you can. We're going to leave the guild tonight. Tunnel Vision will send us to the warehouse where the gang we're after is hiding out, and I'm going to kill them. All of them. They've been warned, they refused to back down, and so tonight, I'm being sent in for a code-enforcement. This is a nice way of saying I will end every life inside that building. And you're all going to be there to watch me."

"That seems unnecessarily brutal," Beverly said, the words clearly leaving her mouth before she had time to consider them.

"I don't entirely disagree with you, but this is a necessary part of your education," Ivan replied, unbothered by the outburst. "These people have no association with our guild and that's why they were given a warning to back down. You, however, *are* part of the guild, and *this* is your warning. We cannot tolerate code-breakers here for many reasons, one of the most important of which is that it gives the capes a foothold to bring us down. If they can go after one of us, it could be the first step in allowing them to go after all of us. So we handle our problems in-house, before they ever get the chance to mount an investigation. No one here is above the code, not even your councilors. Better to show you what happens to those who don't heed that warning than let you become counted among them."

Slowly, Ivan met the eyes of every apprentice in the room. "These people were going to die no matter what, whether you watched it or not. None of their blood is on your hands, and unless you take a code-enforcement job from the board, it never will be. This is happening. Even if you tried, you couldn't stop me. Don't waste time feeling guilty. Instead, learn from what I'm showing you. If it keeps even one of you from forgetting how seriously this guild takes the code, then perhaps these lives won't be lost entirely in vain."

He turned back to Tunnel Vision, who were waiting patiently. "Whenever you two are ready, please open the door."

*   *   *

The sudden onset of humidity took Tori by surprise, even though she should have expected a climate change. In the distance, she could make out bells ringing and the long low whistle of an unseen ship making its way across water. Tunnel Vision's doorway had let them out near a harbor, so close that, if she strained, Tori could make out the sounds of waves crashing against the piers. In front of them was a dirty brick building, the high windows on several sides broken out. Occasional bursts of light would come from within—flashlights sweeping through the surroundings. It was more familiar than Tori would have preferred, a reminder of the days when she holed up where she could and constantly stole to finance her projects. Places like this were ones she'd quickly learned to avoid. They were too convenient and tempting for gangs of actual criminals. Sooner or later, one would move in and Tori would be out a place to stay, along with any possessions she couldn't sneak away with.

In front of them, the air shimmered and Arcanicus stepped into view. It was somewhat reassuring to see their usual field teacher, though everyone couldn't help noticing his face was pinched and weary this evening. Wordlessly, he handed out the pendants that would keep them unseen then cast a new spell that created a softly glowing bubble around them.

"Near as I can tell, there are around twenty," Arcanicus said, speaking to Ivan instead of the apprentices. "At least seven are metas. The rest might be,

361

but my wards didn't catch them. There's a pair of magic-users in there, so I had to be careful not to tip them off."

"That's fine, I prefer surprise above all else," Ivan assured him. "Are any more coming?"

"They've started their meeting so it's unlikely, but I can ward the place once you're in, just to be safe." Arcanicus shivered, though whether it was due to the chilly wet air or the events he knew were about to transpire was anyone's guess.

"A ward would be appreciated. Also, keep an eye on the apprentices. I should be able to handle that many, but my powers aren't well-built for protection. If one of them is in danger, teleport them out here to join you. Apprentices, do your best not to get in danger. You're almost guild members; I hope you can handle at least that much."

Ivan turned to face his charges, and Tori noticed that for the first time that night his eyes had changed. Once more they had become orbs of darkness lit only by glowing red runes. Those eyes, Fornax's eyes, meant things were about to get serious. Her nerves tensed, and she mentally moved herself a little closer to fire-form. She'd be damned if she had to get yanked to safety like a puppy wandering too close to a street.

"The most important rules for tonight are to stay silent, stay focused, and above all else, stay out of my way. Once we're inside, I won't be able to coddle you, so if anyone starts to lose it, take care of each other." He looked away from them, back at the warehouse filled with criminals who didn't know their time on the planet had almost run out.

"For what it's worth, I'm sincerely sorry for what I'm about to make you watch. Feel free to hate me afterward; you'll have every right. But do me a favor and try to keep yourselves from being this example for a future class of trainees. I take no more joy in doing this than you will in watching it."

With that, Ivan headed toward the warehouse, and the apprentices followed.

Chapter 54

Unlike the crisp, humid air outside, the interior of the warehouse festered with must. It permeated everything around them, soaking the building in a depressing fog of neglect. Tori's ears perked to the sounds of chuckles, whispers, and the scuffing of boots. The gang was nearby, and for a moment she was surprised they hadn't bothered stationing a guard at the door. Then the others moved forward and she saw a man with a snake tattoo on his face lying on the ground, neck twisted at an inhuman angle. Ivan had killed the man upon entering, before he had a chance to sound an alarm, doing it so quickly that even the apprentices on his heels hadn't been fast enough to catch him in the act. Tori fought the urge to gulp audibly. She'd seen far worse than a bad man given a quick death in her time on the streets. And she knew she would see worse again before the night was done.

A few steps ahead of the huddled apprentices, a soft glow lit the room as the gathered flashlights threw off a cumulative shine. Standing on the edge of the shadows, still partially hidden by stacked boxes that no doubt contained drugs, guns, or some other illegal ware, Ivan turned back to look at his charges. He held up a single hand, signaling them to stay put, for the moment at least. The command given, he stepped out of the shadows. From the way the small noises of discussion died, Tori had no doubt they'd noticed him. No one had the chance to yell before Ivan spoke, and once he did, there was no need for questions.

"You all know why I'm here. You were warned and chose not to listen. Anyone who wishes for a quick death should lie down right now. That much mercy, I can still show."

There was some shouting and the sound of heavy footsteps. When Ivan next spoke, Tori was taken aback by the sadness in his voice.

"No takers? So be it. Apprentices, come out. It's time for you to see what happens to those who cross the guild."

Tori was the first to emerge from behind the boxes, and not by happenstance. She knew this wasn't easy for Ivan, the man who wanted to do nothing more than live a normal life with his family in suburbia. He was doing it for the guild, for the peace he wanted to protect, and tonight, he was doing it especially for them. If Ivan was willing to work so hard to show them a lesson, then, as his apprentice, she owed it to him to learn as best she could. No matter how hard it was to watch.

Quick as Tori was, she still missed the first two kills. By the time she rounded the corner, there were a pair of corpses at Ivan's feet, both distinctly missing their heads. A massive meta bigger than Thuggernaut was rearing back to level a mighty punch at her teacher, while a man who looked like he'd been bred with a mosquito reared back to stab at Ivan with the three-foot blade poking out of his face. Several feet away, a woman was muttering under her breath, conjuring a strange black cloud in her hands. Tori's stomach briefly tightened with fear as she watched the three metas coordinate an attack on the man who had come to destroy them.

She needn't have spared the worry. Ivan grabbed the mosquito man without looking and threw him like a javelin into the chest of the woman with the cloud. This allowed the giant to take his swing, which Ivan stopped on impact, a small shield appearing over the spot where the meta had punched him. Ivan grabbed the man's arm and effortlessly lifted him overhead, then charged across the room to where the mosquito man was trying to free himself from his cohort's chest. Using the big meta as a club, Ivan rained three blows down on the entangled pair. When he was done, he'd not only finished them off, but also turned his weapon to pulp.

Gunshots rang out as the human members of the gang tried to do what dozens of capes couldn't—take down the monster once known as Fornax. Ivan dashed across the room, moving so quickly he seemed more blur than man, and dispatched the shooters as easily as if they were made from glass.

"Jesus." Beverly said the word more like a prayer than a curse, her dark skin several shades paler as she watched Ivan finish off the gunmen and leap up to a decrepit catwalk where a man with bladed tentacles attempted to rain down blows upon him. "He's... he's not even trying, is he?"

On the catwalk, Ivan had easily snagged one of the tentacles as it came in for a strike and yanked the attacker over to him. One punch and the man was down, blood streaming through the holes in the metal grating beneath his corpse. Another meta shimmered into view behind Ivan, raising a knife that looked like it belonged in a history book.

"Of course he isn't," Lance said. While he hadn't gone pale, his usual cheeriness had vanished, leaving behind only a stalwart determination to keep watching. "That's the man who helped kill the unkillable Orion, who nearly fought Lodestar to a standstill, whose power is on par with the greatest metas in history. And he, or someone like him, is who they'll send after us if we fuck up."

The blade slammed into Ivan's back, only to bounce back and knock its wielder slightly off-balance. It was the only attack he got off. Ivan whirled around before the man could vanish again. Another blow and the blood streaming from the catwalk became a small waterfall.

"I get that he's strong, but why do they need to show us this?" Beverly asked. "We know the code is important. We get the stakes. What's the point of making us watch all this killing?"

Tori opened her mouth to try and explain. Before she could, to her surprise, Warren answered the question, and he did so better than she could have.

"Maybe *you* knew the stakes going in, but not every recruit would. This is an organization of criminals, many of whom have already fought capes and other metas on their own. Some would think the rules were flexible, or that they were strong enough to ignore them. This is about putting the fear in them, in us. They're making sure we understand that if we fuck with the code or the guild, that's what's waiting for us." Warren nodded to Ivan, who dropped from the catwalk onto the back of another gang member, the sound of breaking bones echoing as he landed.

Those criminals that remained started to panic. The lone man they'd expected to defeat was shredding through them at an alarming rate. Several turned to run, heading for the exit and the four trainees watching the slaughter. They made it only three steps before Ivan was there, standing in front of them. He didn't bother taking his time; instead, he swept his hand through the air in front of them. A red streak followed his movements, and as he reached the end of the line, the first man's torso began to slide forward, away from his legs.

Lance turned away, willpower momentarily broken. Tori could hear Beverly taking deep breaths, probably trying to fight back the urge to vomit. She didn't blame either of them; in fact, she was impressed they'd been able to hold it together for this long. The four corpses in eight pieces that Ivan had neatly created were only thirty feet away from them, bits of life still lingering in the top parts.

This time, Ivan paused before moving on, casting a quick look back at the apprentices who were dutifully watching his show. Whispering a few words, he set his hands on the ground. Moments later, all eight pieces burst into a brief, smoky black fire that burned out in seconds, leaving only ash.

"Corpse-fire? But that's a real spell," Warren mumbled, apparently surprised that Ivan's magic could do more than brute combat.

Tori was just thankful he'd gotten rid of the gory sight and allowed Lance and Beverly to regain some sense of composure. In a blink Ivan was gone again, zipping around the building, finishing off the few stragglers and those trying to hide. It was brutal, fierce, and bloody, but as she watched, Tori realized that Ivan seemed to make a point not to let anyone suffer. Every kill was efficient, every blow deadly. There was no pageantry, no joy in the task at hand. Ivan was simply getting it done, as quickly and safely as he could manage.

At last, the final gang member had been finished off via a punch to the torso that left a nearby wall splattered in red. Ivan made his way back over to the apprentices. Everyone was still standing, though Lance had needed to duck behind the boxes and vomit briefly while Ivan mopped up the stragglers. His dark eyes, burning with red runes, looked them up and down slowly, taking in their shaken expressions. Though it almost pained her to do so, Tori forced the corners of her mouth into a small, reassuring smile.

"I hate these jobs," Ivan said, somehow calm despite the blood and flesh clinging to his costume. "But I do them when they're needed because the guild is important to me, and that means it's something I want to protect. You may think the way we handle things is too cruel, or gruesome, and that's certainly your right. However, the world before, without a guild or rules, was much worse. Hundreds of civilians could be caught up in the wake of some half-mad new meta's destruction; turf wars between meta gangs cost countless people their homes and lives."

He turned to look at the bloody scene he had created, unnatural eyes gazing through the building to a time long since passed. "If that were the case now, some of those countless civilians could be people we love. Even criminals have people they care about. I hate these jobs, but they keep the guild and the code safe, which in turn, keeps the people that I love safe. So I'll keep doing them when the need arises. You can hate that we do things like this. You probably should. Just understand that it's a necessary price to keep the order."

With that, Ivan walked past them through the warehouse's front door where Arcanicus and Tunnel Vision were waiting. After a few moments, the apprentices followed. Before leaving, each spent a moment to soak in the spectacle that had been created by the guild, *their* guild. Everyone took something different from the experience, but all walked out of the building changed.

Tori was the final apprentice to exit, and to her surprise, Ivan was still there, waiting for her. The others had stepped through Tunnel Vision's portal; she could see them back in the guild lounge as they waited for the window through space to close.

"You okay?" Tori asked, sidling up to her teacher as they moved toward the exit.

"You have a bad habit of stealing other people's lines," Ivan replied. Part of Tori relaxed at the snippiness in his voice. The Ivan in that building wouldn't have bothered being snarky. It was good to know her real mentor was still in there under all the blood and bluster.

366

"Obviously, I'm fine," Tori replied. "I spent years as a thief and a street rat; I've seen plenty of shit. You, on the other hand, just had to go on a killing spree. Can't imagine that's sitting too well."

"Not my first, won't be my last," Ivan told her. "But audiences always make it worse."

"That part I can see." Tori glanced back at the warehouse as she and Ivan drew near to the portal, recalling all the bloody corpses they'd left inside. "Is Arcanicus going to do cleanup? I'm guessing we don't want people stumbling on that grisly scene."

"Actually, that's exactly what we want," Ivan said. "He laid down wards to keep us from leaving any incriminating evidence behind, but killing the gang is only half the job. People knew they were taking on the guild, which is part of why they bumped up on our radar. Now they'll serve as a warning to anyone else who might get similar ideas."

"Efficient, but sweet damn that seems cold," Tori muttered. "Wait, how can other people know about the guild? I'd never heard of you until I joined. I assumed we were all top secret."

"Oh? You never heard rumors about a shadowy criminal organization that skirted the capes' attention while pulling off grand, elaborate scores?" Ivan momentarily paused just outside the portal that would bring them home. For whatever reason, sound didn't travel through spatial tears, so it was the last chance they'd have for private conversation before the night was done.

"Well, sure, but those were just... stupid... rumors... wow, you all are crafty sons of bitches. Making yourself into a crazy conspiracy so no one will believe it when they catch sight of the real thing. That would be like... like if Bigfoot released the shitty fake Bigfoot footages just to throw people off."

"That's my smart apprentice," Ivan said. "We keep the actual truths hidden. All most people know is that there's a gang with no patience and no mercy, and that if you get a warning from them, you should heed it. Some have learned about us—no secret is perfect—but we keep things obscured enough that the majority are never sure what's true and what's not. All they know is that if they break our rules, bad things happen."

"Like I said: crafty sons of bitches." Tori shook her head and forced out a chuckle. Neither of them really wanted to make small talk within sight of the warehouse that Ivan had painted with corpses, but they both knew it was important. They needed to convince each other that Tori seeing that side of Ivan hadn't changed things, whether it was true or not.

"Come on; after a quick debrief, we're going to call it a night for training," Ivan said, motioning to the portal. "That means you might be able to squeeze in a whole four hours of sleep between work and your meta-suit."

"What can I say? I'm determined to keep the local coffee shop in business, even if I have to do it by myself." Despite her words, Tori had a feeling she'd be skipping the lab tonight. Even without the sleep deprivation, she felt more drained than she had in a very long time.

She just hoped that when she finally did close her eyes, she'd be able to see something other than the inside of that blood-soaked warehouse.

Chapter 55

"Do you have a moment?"

Apollo looked up from his desk, unsurprised to find that Lady Shade had entered his office without bothering to use the door. From less dedicated personnel he'd have considered it impertinent, but Lady Shade had long ago shown herself to be the sort who valued efficiency over propriety. It was a quirk he tolerated because she was loyal, and that trait mattered more to him than any others she might possess.

"For you, always." Apollo closed his laptop as he spoke, sealing off his work from prying eyes. Trust was well and good, but discretion had rewards all its own.

"You wanted to be kept abreast of any incidents of mass killings among meta-human criminals," Lady Shade said, cutting right to business in the way that Apollo liked. "We just got word from Seattle that a gang was wiped out in a very bloody manner sometime last night."

From the shadows that swirled about her body, Lady Shade produced crime scene photos of a warehouse interior strewn with corpses. She set them down on his desk, and waited as Apollo perused the contents of each one.

"No doubt about it, this is that cursed guild's handiwork," Apollo said at last, setting down the photos. "You can always tell; the actual kills are clean, but the bodies are left messy. They want to send a message to the people who find the bodies more than the people they killed."

"Our informants say the gang in question had gotten a warning that they angered someone higher up the food chain and that they ignored it," Lady Shade reported. "No one knows many details, but every low-level scumbag in the area seems to be minding their manners today. Everyone's scared they might step on the wrong toes and be next. Some of them even think we're the ones who pulled this hit."

"Well, in a way, they aren't wrong." Apollo's smile dimmed when he looked back down at the bloody pictures, as did his glow. "By tolerating the existence of these people, we're at least partially culpable for their actions. 'All that is needed for evil to flourish is for good men to do nothing,' as the saying goes."

"We can't be everywhere, and from all accounts, these people were real bags of shit," Lady Shade assured him. "You're the one who tells the new recruits that even superheroes can't save everyone. We've just got to do our best and take solace in the victories we manage."

"As always, you're quite right," Apollo said, artfully skimming over the fact that he was technically agreeing with himself. "And I intend to make sure these people's deaths do not go to waste. Tell me, were you wondering how I knew there would be an incident like this coming?"

"I assumed you had sources," Lady Shade admitted.

"If only. I'd give much to have information from within that guild. No, I knew it was coming because we spotted their trainees out last week. Over time, I've noticed that when there's a confluence and we both get new members, inevitably there will be a slaughter of morally repugnant criminals some months into their training. No doubt it's meant to teach their recruits how to deal with external threats. I assumed that if they were out in the real world, that point had to be drawing near, which is why I put you on alert."

"Very impressive," Lady Shade said. "But, if I may, how does that help us? Shouldn't we have tried to catch them in the act?"

"Certainly not." Apollo shook his head, curly golden locks tumbling as he did. "These kills are professional-grade, clearly handled by the more powerful, experienced members. Going after one of them blindly would just cost us people, and it's likely they'd still get away. No, what I'm looking for is what comes after the killing. Without fail, once one of these clean jobs pops up, within two weeks' time we find a crime scene that's almost, but not quite, at guild standards. Still clean and tidy, but always with a few telltale errors that we don't see on the usual jobs."

"I get it; you think they make the kiddies go out on a job all of their own," Lady Shade concluded. "And that's what you're aiming for."

"Precisely." Apollo reached into his desk and pulled out a pad of paper. He scribbled across the yellow surface. "Contact these people in the AHC and let them know I need a quiet alert raised. We don't want to tip our hand, but it's crucial that we be ready when the opportunity to squash their newest crop arises. With a few carefully chosen allies on watch, I believe we can manage. Oh, and have Cyber Geek and Medley stop by after you've talked to everyone. I'll want to let them know that as of this weekend they'll be spending a few weeks on standby as part of their training."

"Don't you need more than just those two? I mean, the guild has four recruits," Lady Shade pointed out.

"I'll likely grab a third or so from the pool after I see how everyone is improving. But those two have a bright future, and I want to help them seize it." Apollo finished his writing and tore the page off the pad, handing it to Lady Shade.

"Cornea, the Crystal Baller, Optimize, and Stalwart Iron. I'll get to all of them within fifteen minutes and have the newbies headed to you in thirty,"

Lady Shade promised. She grew murky and indistinct, then vanished seconds later as she slithered out the wall through a nearby shadow.

Once she was gone, Apollo reopened his laptop and got back to work. He'd need to pick some backup for his rising stars, just to make sure everything went smoothly. There were plenty of prospects who were workable—metas with either power or charisma instead of a combination of the two. Normally, they were destined to live and die on the mid-list of popularity charts, known but not remembered. If he was lucky, however, they might get swept up in the wake of Medley and Cyber Geek's good PR. Nothing wrong with getting some bonus press for the AHC's newest rookies. That was assuming things went perfectly, of course, which would require good fortune and better planning.

Thankfully, the guild was sticking to their usual timetable, which made it all the easier to predict their moves. If things went to plan, they'd soon haul in four potential villains, unmasking them in front of the cameras and cementing the new recruits' status as capable superheroes.

It would make for a wonderful appetizer, something to tide him over until the main course arrived.

*   *   *

While his size was useful for leverage, intimidation, and reaching things off the high shelves, the radioactive protein bar that had changed a scrawny nineteen-year-old into the powerful Thuggernaut had also made dealing with anything delicate an act of constant effort. Thankfully, Doctor Mechaniacal had the materials and know-how to ease things for the muscular man, which was why Thuggernaut was able to peruse his books on a specially reinforced e-reader. He was sprawled out on a couch also custom made for members of the guild who had more mass than standard springs were meant to bear when Johnny ambled into the lounge.

"Thought I'd find you here." The smaller man adjusted his suit jacket before leaping over the edge of the sofa, coming down on the far end, just out of range of Thuggernaut's pillar-like legs. "You always like to read after the rough stuff. How's the kid holding up?"

Thuggernaut didn't bother trying to fight the inevitable; he and Johnny had been friends for years, and when Johnny Three Dicks decided there would be a conversation, then sooner or later there would be. He clicked a bookmark function on the reader and set it down on a nearby coffee table.

"If by 'the kid,' you mean my apprentice, she's doing as well as can be expected. Monday's lesson was especially hard for her; she never had criminal inclinations before getting her powers. That was the first time she ever

371

understood the darker side of the guild she was trying to join. Honestly, that woman has more makings of a cape than one of us. If she didn't hate the AHC so much, it would have been a good fit."

"You did the best you could to make sure she knew what she was signing up for before she joined," Johnny said. "Can't make the right choices for them. Plus, given how strong she's getting, I'm sort of glad she decided to stay on Team Villain."

"She would have been a handful, no doubt about that." In spite of his worries about his apprentice and her future in the guild, Thuggernaut couldn't quite resist the grin of pride that inched its way across his face. Beverly was growing by leaps and bounds; he had no doubt that one day she'd be far stronger than he. If she'd been won over by the capes, within a decade she'd have been as big a nuisance as Apollo.

"Yeah, but giant terrifying dragon works better on our side anyway," Johnny pointed out. "And Beverly's a tough nut. She'll get past Monday. Or she'll start drinking it away like many before her have. Either way, have some faith. The kid will find peace."

"You're probably right. At least she didn't have to go through it alone. I wasn't part of a confluence, so I got to sit through that show solo."

Johnny let out a long, three-note whistle. "Who taught you?"

"Morgana." Thuggernaut shuddered involuntarily. "The whole thing lasted less than a minute, which was all the more disturbing when I realized she could have ended it in seconds."

"Count yourself lucky. I had to watch Arcanicus do the job," Johnny replied. "Do you know what the smell of fresh gore mixed with the scent of a reanimated horde is like? Let me tell you, no one makes an air freshener strong enough to cover that up."

Thuggernaut had been in an enclosed room with Arcanicus's skeletons more than once; he could only imagine how the stink multiplied when murder was added to the equation. Morgana's display had been mercifully short on smell and sound. Her victims had almost no time to react, and those who did manage a few seconds didn't waste their time screaming. A few *had* tried begging, not that it helped.

"Anyway, we bounced back after that, and so will all the rookies, Beverly included," Johnny continued. "From what I hear, Pseudonym went out of his way to take it easy on them. Even got rid of the gorier stuff if it was too close."

"It's certainly better than Balaam would have done," Thuggernaut agreed. "Pseudonym at least has a vested interested in not seeing any of the apprentices break, especially this close to their membership trial."

372

"Speaking of, that's why I stopped by." Johnny reached into his pocket and pulled out a slip of paper with half-illegible chicken scratch scrawled across it. "Just got word from up top. I'm on distraction duty for the night they do their job."

"You're not going to be around to watch Beverly's trial?" Thuggernaut jerked forward, a motion that others might have taken as threatening and subsequently fled from. Johnny, thankfully, knew his friend better than that. Thuggernaut only got violent when the situation called for it. Of course, when it did, he got *really* violent, which was part of why he'd ended up lumped in with the criminals in the first place.

"Nope, and neither are you, technically. Looks like you and the other mentors are getting sequestered to watch the show, at least according to Doctor Mechaniacal." He held out the note, which Thuggernaut gingerly took from his much smaller hand. "You can read it for yourself, but the long and short is that Doctor Mechaniacal thinks you might be tempted to intervene if they turn the whole thing into a colossal fuck-up. Only the people strictly necessary will be around to oversee things. Everyone else is either on house-arrest at the guild or on distraction duty to make sure we keep the capes off their backs."

Thuggernaut managed to make out every third word or so on the note, which seemed to corroborate Johnny's report. Much as he didn't like it, Thuggernaut couldn't exactly protest the logic of the order. The truth was that if his apprentice were in trouble, he probably would try to jump in and help, even if it messed things up in the long run. There was no way he could just stand by and let his student get hurt if he were there to stop it, which was obviously the precise reason that he wasn't going to be there.

"Do you need to pull a big one, or can it just be noisy?" Thuggernaut asked as he lowered the note. "I don't entirely trust you to put together something elaborate on this short of notice."

Johnny snorted. "Well, we both know I'm not going to do anything that requires that much work, so it looks like simple and noisy will have to do. I'm leaning toward fire at the moment. There're a few abandoned blocks in various cities all over the country that I keep notes on for just such an occasion. Allot an hour to clear out anyone squatting in them and I can whip up a grand distraction with minimal fuss."

"I know how well you keep track of things, so I'll be personally scouting the locations to make sure they're still abandoned," Thuggernaut replied. In the field, Johnny was as solid and dependable as they came. When it came to prep work, on the other hand... well, he wasn't one to put up with the tedious when there was excitement to be had.

"All these years and still no trust. It's hurtful, that's what it is."

373

"Do you actually want to do the work of rechecking all the locations and finding the one that best fits your needs?" Thuggernaut asked.

"Oh holy shit no. That's all you, big guy." Johnny hopped up from the couch and slid around it, already angling for the door. "I've got better things to do. Cocktails to drink, hearts to break, standard dapper villain stuff."

"Have fun at happy hour," Thuggernaut called. Once Johnny was gone, he scooped up his e-reader and continued his book. Though there was no real reason to and nothing in the conversation he could point at as a cause, Thuggernaut nonetheless felt much better than he had before Johnny's interruption. Somehow, he always managed to take a person's mind off the things that were bothering them, even if only for a while. It was no doubt part of why Johnny always got called on for distraction duty.

If anyone knew how to divert people's attention, it was the villain known as Johnny Three Dicks.

Chapter 56

After the hellish, bloody night that was Monday, the rest of Tori's week flew by. Work, field training, and a few hours building the meta-suit followed by an amount of sleep most would only classify as a nap, and then the whole thing repeated itself. Fortunately, life as a criminal and scientist had prepared her for pulling long strings of all-nighters one after another. This was not to say that she wasn't significantly dragging by the time the weekend rolled around. In normal circumstances, or as normal as her life ever got, Tori would have let something slip to the backburner in an attempt to get more rest. But work and training were mandatory, which only left her meta-suit, and that was the one thing she was absolutely not going to give ground on.

Thanks to the lab Doctor Mechaniacal had built below Ivan's house plus a combination of her paychecks and winnings from the desert trial, Tori's meta-suit was at last beginning to take shape. She'd built prototypes before, testing concepts and functionality on various bits at a time, but this was the first time she'd ever had the time, security, and funds to actually get one that might work when fully assembled. It wasn't quite there yet—she'd still need a little more time for that—but Tori was certain that she could have it up and ready to go by the night they had to pull their first job.

Well, she hoped as much, anyway. All they'd been told was that they'd pull a job at the end of field training. She assumed, or rather hoped, that meant they'd be given time to plan and coordinate on their own, which would in turn be more time to finish her suit. If there was one thing she knew about the guild, though, it was that one had to prepare for the unexpected.

This point proved itself for the umpteenth time as Tori, clad in her apprentice costume, arrived in the rookie lounge to find Ivan already there, dressed up as Pseudonym. He might have mentioned he was coming, or at least given her a ride instead of sending her off in one of the guild's automated cars after work. For a moment, her stomach twisted in fear as she wondered if there was going to be another demonstration like Monday's. She soon realized that Balaam, Thuggernaut, and Arachno Bro were also gathered. Clearly, this had something to do with all of the apprentices. Once that was cleared up, she was free to be amazed by the fact that Ivan and Balaam were in the same room without arguing. That was no doubt helped by having the other two villains positioned directly between them.

Beverly had beaten her to the lounge, so Tori fell in line silently beside her friend. No one was talking, and while that might just mean a conversation had recently died, she wasn't going to be the one to break etiquette if silence was expected. Ivan had reminded her time and again that while he might be on her side, not everyone was. Especially the dickbag spellcaster with red irises.

Lance and Warren both wandered into the room in their own time, saw the spread of people awaiting them, and lined up with the other apprentices. Though Tori was expecting things to start when the last of them, Lance, arrived, the entire room remained silent. She was just edging up to ask what the hell was going on when the distinctive sound of moving metal caught her ear. Moments later, Doctor Mechaniacal arrived, decked out in his full meta-suit glory. It was strange: outside of the time he'd greeted her and the guild meeting, Tori had only ever seen Doctor Mechaniacal in full armor or none at all. Part of her wondered why those times had been different, but she was quickly distracted as the guild's leader began to speak.

"Tonight, on what is to be the tenth and final night of your field training, we have gathered you here to give you information regarding your final trial for admittance to this guild. Soon you will receive the details of your test, both what is expected of you and what resources you will receive. After that, you will have time to begin planning how to tackle your task. However, before we can get to the last test, there is another matter that requires our attention. Each of you lacks an important item you will require when it is time for you to work on behalf of this guild."

Tori had a hunch where this was going. The sly smile on Arachno Bro's face, or at least the arrangement of mandibles she took to be a smile, told her that she was on the right track. That was the reason their mentors had come. This was something important, something they were supposed to bear witness to.

"I speak, of course, about code names," Doctor Mechaniacal continued. "You can't very well use each other's real names in the field, and referring to everyone as 'Apprentice' is a recipe for confusion. Our code names are, in many ways, relics of the life we used to have or the paths we were kept from going down. Ideally, your name will be known only within the guild, as the best jobs we do are the ones where no one knows we were there. However, life is not ideal, and therefore the code name should be something that conceals your mundane name and speaks to the true identity that lurks behind all of your masks. You were all warned that the time to choose was approaching, so I assume each of you has a name prepared."

He didn't phrase it like a question, and Tori couldn't imagine that was accidental. Idly, she wondered if this was a test to see if they would complete a task even when not given a firm timeframe. It was possible—sometimes it seemed like everything they faced was a test, while other days she was certain the councilors were just making it up as they went along. It didn't matter either way, though. She'd chosen her name earlier that week in a bit of inspiration that struck her as she was sleepily treading down to Ivan's basement.

"Apprentice of Balaam, step forward," Doctor Mechaniacal ordered. Warren obeyed immediately, eyes darting between his teacher and the man in a metal suit, uncertain of where his attention was supposed to go. "Apprentice, have you chosen a code name to wear as a member of this guild?"

"Yes, sir." Warren didn't stammer but only just. "If it pleases the guild, I would like to go by the name of Glyph."

Doctor Mechanical paused then nodded his head. "That name is not spoken for, so you are free to claim it as your own. From here until your admittance or failure, you shall be known as Glyph."

Relief was evident on Warren's face as he fell back in line. Next up was Lance, whom Doctor Mechaniacal called out with an identical order and question.

"Pest Control, if it's available." Lance spoke with the confidence of a man who knew damn well his name wasn't spoken for and didn't seem the least bit surprised when the iconic helmet dipped into a nod once more. Tori was glad he'd thought of something; she knew he'd been having trouble picking a good one. Plus, it sort of fit; bugs were considered pests and Lance was able to command them.

After Lance was Beverly, who stuck to her guns and chose Bahamut to the surprise of exactly no one that knew her. This only left Tori, either by chance or design, as the final apprentice to claim a name of her own.

"Apprentice of Pseudonym, step forward." Tori obeyed, glancing at Ivan and barely resisting the urge to give him a 'how crazy is all this shit?' wink. "Apprentice, have you chosen a code name to wear as a member of this guild?"

"I have. From this night on, I would like to go by Hephaestus," she announced, perhaps with a small hint of pride in her voice. She'd been pretty proud of that name when it came to her; it felt so appropriate. After all, she crafted stuff, dealt heavily with fire, and even had her lab in a basement. It was a good fit on all levels and betrayed nothing about her identity.

Which was why it was all the more disconcerting when Doctor Mechaniacal failed to nod, instead letting out a long, low "Hmmmm" from the depths of his throat. "The AHC already had a cape registered as Hephaestus. It looks like he's deceased now, but he had a sidekick that took on the mantle after he passed. One moment."

Although he appeared to be just standing there, the guild leader was evidently accessing some sort of name database and checking on availability. Tori felt her palms start to sweat and had to double check to make sure she wasn't leaking nervous heat. After hitting on such a good code name, it hadn't occurred to her to pick a backup. Shit... what was another good one? Socket? Sprocket? Hot Sprocket? Oh god, that sounded like a shitty porno or garbage microwave food. Wait, weren't sprockets from *The Jetsons* in the first place? Maybe the guild didn't care about copyrights, in which case—

Her slow descent into the maw of madness was mercifully interrupted as Doctor Mechaniacal spoke once again. "It looks like he took the title Red Hephaestus to honor his predecessor but still set himself apart. The first Hephaestus didn't do much, but it was a name already worn by a cape, so if you'd like to reconsider, that's up to you."

"But I can still use it, right?" The pride in her voice had been replaced with fear verging on desperation as she scraped her mind for a replacement in case he said no. Unfortunately, all her worried brain could manage to think about was the goddamned *Jetsons*.

In what she would later consider to be the most beautiful show of apathy Tori had ever seen, Doctor Mechaniacal shrugged those metal shoulders and said, "If you want. Greek mythology is public domain anyway, so as long as no one is using it, then it's all yours."

"I'll take it!" Tori fought down the blush that started to rise in her cheeks and focused on composing herself in spite of the stares and slight snickers she was getting. "I mean, if it's available, then the name I choose is still Hephaestus."

"Then from here until your admittance or failure, you shall be known as Hephaestus," Doctor Mechaniacal announced. "And with that, all apprentices have chosen their names. How long you can wear them for is up to you to determine, though we certainly wish you the best of luck. Now, on to your actual trial."

From a compartment on his wrist, Doctor Mechaniacal pulled out a small device and set it down on the coffee table next to a half-drunk soda. Moments later, an image flickered into existence above it, glowing green text displayed on a black background.

"Starting tomorrow, you will be given access to Sanctum so that you may learn how to coordinate and plan a guild job all on your own. But Sanctum is a place for execution, not discussion, which is why tonight, you will review the parameters of your trial and decide how you would like to approach it. I should mention that you are not obligated to work together; though, if you split up, the resources will be divided proportionally. As you can see on the image, you have one week from tonight to complete your trial. Use your time well, for it is not your ally."

378

With that, Doctor Mechaniacal turned to leave, their teachers following a few steps behind him. Arachno Bro reached out to pound a fist with Lance, now technically Pest Control, as he left, and Thuggernaut gave the newly named Bahamut a thumbs-up. Tori wasn't expecting anything from Ivan—he tended to keep a tighter lid than normal on his feelings when he wore that costume—so she was nearly bowled over when he placed a hand on her shoulder as he walked by, even going so far as to stop momentarily.

"Hephaestus, huh? I like it. It's a good name for you. People will respect it."

"Hard to do worse than Fornax," she whispered.

"Please don't remind me. That's why we let the new members pick their own names in the first place, to avoid incidents like that."

Then he was gone. Tori watched him leave, the weight of his hand still heavy on her shoulder. In terms of training, he'd probably given the least out of any of the mentors in the room, but she still couldn't help feeling like he'd prepared her better than the rest of the apprentices. He'd taught her how to blend in, how to keep the code, how to survive. The others might have been taught how to become better criminals, but Ivan had educated her on the art of surviving in a villain's world. Even if he hadn't wanted one, Ivan had still done his best to turn his apprentice into a full guild member. Now it was on her to prove that she could go the rest of the way.

Turning from the door back to the glowing image in front of her, Tori found that the others were already clustered around it, and the looks on their faces were far from promising. They weren't as pale or sickly as when they'd finished Monday's lesson, but the expressions were closer to that than she would have preferred.

"Okay, you all seem like you just had to force down rotten cabbage, so what kind of damage are we looking at here?"

"See for yourself," Beverly said, jostling Lance over to make room as Tori slid in beside her. The glowing green text was arranged simply, separated into the categories of Requirements, Resources, and Assets. The first one detailed what was expected of them, the second provided them with a budget and some basic gear they'd have access to, and the final category was a list of ways they could spend their budget. Warren reached his hand forward and pressed his fingers to the bottom area. With a quick motion, he scrolled through the Assets sections, showing the variety of options available to them while the other two categories remained unmoving. It was more fascinating than helpful, as most of the Assets listed were more than double their meager budget.

Tori leaned over to look the document up and down, carefully reading each piece of information in Requirements and Resources no fewer than three times until she was certain there hadn't been any sort of mistake. Once she was done, she calmly stood back up and faced the rest of her apprentices.

"Well, since it looks like we're all about to fucking die, anyone else want to have a last drink with me?"

Chapter 57

"You don't think you might have been a little too hard on them?" Ivan asked, helping himself to another helping of gumbo from the impeccable spread that was set before them. After watching their apprentices choose code names, the mentors had headed off to a small celebration with food and drinks. Wade was already waiting for them, sans suit, a heaping helping of fried chicken on a plate in front of him. Almost no one knew how he ran the remote suit so seamlessly, and those that did were smart enough to keep the leader's secret just that.

"This is meant to test them, see how they'll deal with hard problems and still adhere to the code. If I gave them an easy one, it wouldn't show us what we need to see," Wade countered. He, Ivan, and Thuggernaut were the last ones remaining in the room, unless one counted Arachno Bro, who'd passed out in a pile of empty beer cans and cocktail glasses. Balaam had excused himself only a few moments after the party began. It was a bit rude, but given that he'd gotten through a whole evening without snapping at Ivan, no one was going to call him out on ditching. The night had been a peaceful one so far; there was no reason to go messing things up.

"Still, those were some heavy requirements," Thuggernaut added. He had half a bottle of whiskey in a special glass that Wade had provided. Supposedly it was made of a crystal strong enough to withstand point-blank gunshots. All Thuggernaut knew was that it didn't break when he picked it up, so that was enough for him. "The security level alone would be problematic for a rookie."

"*A* rookie, certainly, but we don't have one, we've got four. Four very bright, cunning, powerful metas," Wade replied. "If they put their collective talents and minds together, I have no doubt they'll be able to pull something off. Challenges are made to be risen to."

"Let's just hope none of them are crazy enough to try and do it on their own." Ivan was already halfway through this bowl of shrimp, rice, and roux, with an eye on the pot that indicated it wouldn't be his last.

"Normally that might be a concern, but after their ordeal in the desert, I think it's safe to say that at least three of them understand the importance of teamwork," Wade said. "And I daresay even Glyph will put aside his independent streak for a trial as important as this one."

"Guess all we can do is hope." Thuggernaut took a hearty gulp from his glass, the smooth liquor burning gently as it moved into his stomach. "We gave them the floaties and the lessons, now we hurl them into the pool and hope they can swim."

"True," Ivan agreed. "I just wish so many before them hadn't reached this point and then drowned. I would be... unhappy, to see Tor—Hephaestus come so far only to lose herself now."

Thuggernaut nodded, staring down into the depths of his drink in its special-made crystal. How many recruits had he heard about who fell apart when the stakes were real or got greedy and overreached in an attempt to pull off some spectacular score? How many would-be guild members reached this point and then went no further, all the potential they might have had snuffed out by an inability to adhere to the code? He'd been saddened by the news each time, but it was always a distant pain, nothing that cut him deep. Now he was forced to imagine how it would feel if Beverly, Bahamut, the young woman he'd worked so hard to help train, was suddenly gone from the world.

"You know," Thuggernaut said, eyes still glued to the swirling depths of his drink. "I think I'm starting to see why taking apprentices fell out of style."

*   *   *

"Okay, let's take this one piece at a time. Lance, break down the requirements for us." Tori paced around the lounge while Beverly and Warren sat at the table near the vending machines, pens and paper stretched out before them. Only Lance remained near the projector, staring into the glowing words that seemed specifically designed to doom them.

"First off, we have until next Friday to complete the trial, but we have to give the guild a full twenty-four hours' notice before we do it so they can make arrangements," Lance said, reading the first point dutifully.

"Not a lot of time, but at least they didn't only give us tonight," Beverly muttered.

"Second, the job we pull must adhere to the guild's code, meaning we have to minimize our chances of getting caught or causing civilian injury and avoid alerting the capes at all costs," Lance continued.

"Yeah, yeah, that one was already a given." Tori twirled her hands to indicate that he should get on with it.

"Third, whatever job we do must make a profit of no less than half a million dollars. No destruction for the sake of destruction or anything along those lines. We're all on the same page, though; robbery is our best bet, right?" Lance glanced up from the projector to concur with his fellow apprentices, who all nodded.

"Any sort of kidnapping or extortion is probably going to get too complex," Warren said. "Robbery is a quick, one-shot deal. Heck, we could knock it out this weekend if it weren't for the next part."

"Ah, you mean number four: we must defeat the security of a system rated at least Level Three or higher," Lance said, turning back to the projector. "These include federal banks, the offices of higher-up government agencies, national museums, and the offices of most companies on the Fortune 500 list."

"That's the first real hurdle," Tori agreed. "Level Three is nothing to joke about. When I was... well, before the guild, let's just say I avoided them whenever possible. On top of being high-tech and frequently monitored, most have a hard-wired line to the AHC. It's a service they pay quite a premium for. If we set the system off, the capes will come running."

"Which means we have to steal at least five hundred grand from a place specifically designed to stop people like us from doing just that," Beverly surmised. She glanced up from the paper, inspiration twinkling in her eyes. "Hey, wait, can't Tori just hack some bank for us to grab the cash? As long as it's one with a Level Three security system, that still counts, right?"

"First off, while I appreciate the vote of confidence, and I do know my way around a few programs, I'm more the buildy type of geek than the hacky one," Tori replied. "Plus, even if I could manage it, that still wouldn't work. Remember number five?"

"All team members must contribute to the job in some meaningful way," Lance helpfully supplied. "I guess they added that because if hacking options were on the table, Tori could have split off from us and done it on her own."

"Fuck a whole wet mess of that. I might have my prideful moments, but not even I'm cocky enough to think I could pull this off by myself." Tori halted her pacing for a few moments, rubbing her temples as she tried to think of some way to get everything required for the task before them. "Keep going, Lance, there's only a few left."

"The sixth one is pretty straightforward: no evidence linking the crime to the guild may be left behind," Lance said. "Obvious, but I guess they wanted to remind us to be careful. The seventh, on the other hand, seems to have been added just for evil kicks. If any member of a team is captured by either the police or the AHC, the entire team will have failed."

"I think it was less evil than it was mischievous," Beverly said. "That one is there to tempt us to split off on our own. After all, if we only have to be accountable for ourselves, then we don't have to worry about being dragged down by someone else's failure."

"Is that how you took it?" Warren looked across the table with a touch of surprise, one of the first times anyone had ever seen genuine emotion on his pinched face. "I assumed it was there to ensure that teams actually worked together. If the failure of one means the failure of all, no one will sabotage a fellow apprentice who might have become a future rival."

Silence fell over the room as everyone's eyes gravitated to Warren. What he said wasn't wrong; in fact, it was so spot on that they immediately believed he'd hit the nail straight on the head. It was, however, a bit disconcerting, both because whoever made the trial had accounted for the possibility of betrayal, and because only one of them had even seen it as a possibility. It seemed Warren had been getting a somewhat different, possibly more useful education than the rest of the apprentices.

"Guess that means we'll have to look out for each other, no matter what," Tori said at last, breaking the spell of quiet that had inadvertently been cast. "Lance, what do we have in the way of resources?"

"Beverly copied down the whole list, but for the most part, it's just standard gear: flashlights, rope, backpacks, lock picks… basically a 'My First Crime' starter kit. Aside from that, we have four thousand dollars to spend on whatever assets we want to purchase."

"Which is obviously the part of our resources that really matters," Beverly added.

"I'm not totally sure about that, but it's definitely the part that requires action," Warren said. "We have to figure out what assets best suit our needs, but before that, we have to determine what those needs will be by picking a target."

"Actually, I disagree with you there." Lance was still at the projector, scrolling through the large list of assets available for purchase. "There are a lot of options, but I'm starting to think they're mostly here to trip us up. The vast majority of these are either very niche services or way out of our price range, but there are two that we can just barely afford. Round trip transportation by Tunnel Vision will run us thirty-eight hundred dollars, or we can rent those pendants from Arcanicus for a grand a pop. I doubt those prices, or the amount of money we have, is a coincidence."

"Lance makes a good point," Tori agreed. "Either the rates were lowered or our amount of cash was specifically picked to make those affordable. It gives us a choice of ways to lessen our risk. We can have magic that lets us slip around more easily, or we can get out of Ridge City—and by extension the AHC's backyard—which makes us less likely to hit their radar."

"What a coincidence. Both of those are tools we've seen and used multiple times, making us intimately familiar with their workings and limitations." Beverly shook her head as she scrawled new notes on the paper, scratching out previous writing with grand strokes of her pen. "These people really do think ten steps ahead."

"It's not like we're the first apprentices they've made go through this trial," Lance pointed out.

"And on the upside, this gives us a place to actually start." Tori's mind was whirling. Now that they knew the first decision to make, the task before her seemed less daunting. It was just a series of smaller steps, like building a new invention: take care of one manageable piece after another until something truly extraordinary had been created. "We need to pick cloaking or teleportation, and to do that, we have to decide what the best target for us to take on is. If we find a good one outside Ridge City, we go there, and if we see one ripe for the picking here, we grab the necklaces."

Tori walked over to the table and tore a sheet of paper from Beverly's pad. "Let's divide and conquer. Lance, you check out any museums that have both Level Three security systems and the kind of exhibits that will get us to five hundred grand. Try to keep the focus on paintings and jewels. Pottery is too bulky and delicate, and sculptures are just a pain in the ass. Also, make sure we can easily clear eight hundred thousand, since art requires a fence and the guild might take the fees for that out of our profits."

"Damn, I didn't even think about that," Lance said, joining the rest of the group clustered around Tori.

"Think of it like criminal taxes: there's always someone taking a little off the top. Next up, Beverly, we need you to go through any banks that fit our security needs. Keep an eye out for ones that have a lot of safety deposit boxes or store precious metals. Cash will do in a pinch, but it's bulky and comes with serial numbers that can be traced, so it's usually more trouble than it's worth."

"I get the strong feeling that you've done this before," Beverly remarked, flashing her friend a knowing grin.

"Never on this scale, but I've had to make off with ill-gotten gains on a couple of occasions." Tori tapped Beverly's pen and looked at Warren, who was waiting patiently for his orders. "This one is going to be a bit tougher, but Warren, can you do some digging in to any well-secured branches of government agencies that have recently made big busts? Maybe raided a cartel's compound or something. Drugs and cash are out, but pretty much anyone who does crime for a living keeps a stash of something untraceable they can turn into money when the need arises. If the feds found something like that in their bust, we might be able to take it off their hands."

"That's not going to be easy information to find," Warren cautioned.

"I know, and if you come up empty-handed, it's okay. But as you're the only one of us with a more versatile power, I thought you might be able to pull

385

some magic that no one else here could." Tori also secretly considered this avenue to be the most unlikely to pay off, which was why she handed it to the person in the room she trusted the least. With the rules as they stood, she doubted Warren would go out of his way to sink them, and he certainly didn't seem to harbor as much animosity as his mentor, but there was no sense in taking needless risks. Besides, he really did have access to magic, so maybe he could manage to uncover something useful.

"What does that leave you with?" Lance asked.

"My old stomping ground: corporate espionage," Tori replied. "I'm going to research every company that's developing experimental prototypes or working on tech under juicy government contracts. Grab one of those, sell it to a competitor, and we can easily clear the half a million mark."

"Well, if you've successfully robbed these places before, that sounds like our best bet," Beverly said.

"'Successfully' might be stretching it a bit." Tori's pen slowed as an unexpected wave of bashfulness overtook her. "I mean, I've robbed companies before, but I did say I avoided ones with Level Three security."

"Have you ever successfully beaten a system that strong?" Lance leaned in a little, as curious as he was pleased by the unexpected change in Tori's demeanor.

"Well... sort of. There was only one time I ever tried to rob someone with security that good, and to be fair, I did manage to make it all the way inside their vault," Tori said.

"And then what happened?" Beverly's smirk said more than her actual words would ever need to. Friend or no, it was a rare chance to actually see Tori squirm.

"Oh, you know, not much. Found out the team I'd been working with was nothing but plants, realized the whole thing was a trap, got threatened with death, and then Doctor Mechaniacal came out and offered me a spot in the guild."

"Wait... you tried to rob *the guild*?" Whatever Beverly had been expecting, that wasn't it. Her eyes widened and her voice raised several octaves.

"No!" Tori quickly protested. "I mean, not directly. I tried to rob a company owned by the guild. And hey, I got pretty far, even with a team of betrayers. Plus, guild security is way higher than Level Three, so if anything, I'm over-prepared for this job."

"That would be much more reassuring if you hadn't walked directly into a trap last time you tried a theft of this caliber," Warren pointed out.

"Yeah, well, last time I had a shitty team. I've learned my lesson since then." Tori ripped the sheet of paper off the pad and folded it neatly before tucking it in her pocket. "All right, everybody, get researching. You heard Doctor Mechaniacal; starting tomorrow we get access to Sanctum. Let's show them what we've got by walking in with a game plan."

While the group didn't exactly cheer with enthusiasm, there was a glint of determination in every eye present. It wouldn't be easy, and it probably wouldn't be fun, but they were starting to think they could do this. Tori knew too well how important that was. With enough guts and willpower, they may just be able to pull off a win.

Or, at the very least, they would go out trying like hell.

Chapter 58

With the kids at Janet's and Tori undergoing training, Ivan pulled his car up to an empty house after leaving the guild. Eventually the party had wound down, with Wade heading off to his room and Thuggernaut hauling Arachno Bro off to sleep it off somewhere more comfortable. In spite of himself, Ivan chuckled at the memory of the large man trying to find a comfortable grip on the unconscious body with too many limbs. He'd forgotten how much entertainment could be had simply from hanging around the guild. No, that wasn't true; he'd forced himself to lose those memories. Thinking about it, staying around, it only made keeping himself detached all the harder. He was only still there to protect the guild and the peace. Ivan was only keeping a promise, nothing more.

When he turned on his living room lights and found an unexpected intruder standing there waiting for him, Ivan didn't jump in surprise. In fact, he showed no reaction at all, save for the glowing red runes that lit his eyes' suddenly dark expanse. Calmly, he turned and closed his front door, locking it and resealing the wards that had, not surprisingly, failed to keep the uninvited guest out of his home. Ivan didn't think of it as a failing on his part, though. Even the most powerful holding cells had only ever managed to contain Nexus for a few hours.

"And what the hell brings you here today?" Ivan had never fought Nexus before; the odd man with the kaleidoscope eyes generally preferred to deal with Quorum or Stasis, though few were aware of what made them such tempting targets. That was the problem with Nexus: his motivations were entirely his own, often incomprehensible to anyone else.

"Just checking in. Are you Fornax, the nothing, or the new one yet?" Nexus scratched his head, flakes of what appeared to be ash tumbling down to Ivan's nice clean carpet. "It's been a crazy week, and I'm trying to get my bearings."

"I'm not Fornax, and I have no idea what you mean by the other two things. My current name is Pseudonym, if that helps." There were few things Ivan hated more than someone barging into his home, but any conflict with Nexus would almost certainly sweep up the rest of the neighborhood in collateral damage. That meant goodbye to his civilian identity, to say nothing of the lives of everyone with homes around him. Talking with this madman, bothersome as it was, would cost nothing more than his time.

He hoped.

"That's the nothing, then," Nexus replied. "And your girl, she's not dead here, so did she take a name yet?"

"Just tonight. Tori is now known as Hephaestus."

"Only tonight? Excellent, I've got plenty of time then. Or at least, I should. Never know quite what to expect over here. I mean, the fight is coming. That happens almost everywhere. But it will be interesting to see where the bits and pieces fall in the aftermath." Nexus looked back at Ivan, almost as if he were registering for the first time that the homeowner was in the room with him. "Ah! Which is why I wanted to come talk to you. Your time as the nothing is drawing to a close, or should be. If, when—whichever—that happens, I'd be very much interested in seeing a fight between the new one and Quorum. Never got the chance to set that up when you were Fornax, but I think it would make for quite an interesting show."

"I have no idea what you're talking about," Ivan repeated. "However, I do know that I'm not going to try and fight a cape, let alone one of the AHC's leaders. Leaving aside the fact that it would do irreparable damage to the peace between superheroes and the guild, I've got no problems with Quorum."

"But it was never about problems, was it? It was about power, testing it, gaining it, learning how to wield more of that monster inside you. Quorum is a strong one, you know. The fight you two could have, why, it might shake the very stars from the heavens." Nexus winked a Technicolor eye and Ivan felt his already strained patience begin to thin.

"The stars are fine where they are. I'm not that man anymore. Now, if you're done proposing ludicrous ideas, I'll thank you to get the hell out of my house." Ivan fought to keep his voice calm, pushing down the violence that a too-familiar voice was beckoning him to unleash.

"Do as you will; that much always stays constant with you. But whether you fight Quorum or not, the stars will likely fall soon. Not every time, though. And in this one, things always seem to take their own turns. Still, it would make for a good show, and I'd even go so far as to say I'd be indebted to you for putting it on."

"Sorry, no dice. Go watch it in some other dimension. One version of me is bound to have less self-control," Ivan said. Nexus's powers and the existence of multiple universes weren't exactly secret—the man had never been shy about dropping hints that even the dullest of people could string together. Unfortunately, travel between them was a highly experimental science among even the brightest minds. No one had a clue how Nexus did what he did, which made him all the more impossible to stop.

"Oh, would that I could! There are so many of you with so much violence in your hearts, but I'm afraid it's impossible. Bringing in a ringer would chance too much, and I won't spoil the whole show for the sake of a single episode." Nexus shook his head, genuine sadness etched on his mercurial expression.

"Then make the me there fight the Quorum there. I don't care how you get your kicks."

"Don't be ridiculous," Nexus replied, head jerking up like a hawk who'd heard the rustle of a mouse in the brush. "In all the multiverse, there is only one Quorum. That's what makes him interesting, you know. The rest of you? So predictable, the same motions even if the gestures change. But Quorum, he is truly unpredictable. That's why I can't go ruining things by cheating. Think over my offer, though, I'm a good man to be owed a favor by."

Then Nexus was across the room, standing only a few feet from Ivan. He braced for an attack, but Nexus merely leaned in and whispered softly into his ear, words barely louder than the strum of a spider's thread.

"Especially for a man who seeks to keep the stars from falling."

As the words faded, Ivan realized he was alone in his home. Moving slowly, he pulled out his cell phone and pulled up a number on the screen. He stared at the green "Call" button for over a minute before putting the phone away. Nexus was cryptic and insane all the time, and even if he did know much, what he said wasn't always true. No reason to wake her at this hour with some groundless prediction. Ivan wouldn't let things come to that.

He would keep his promise, no matter what.

*   *   *

The explosion engulfed not only his target but the ones on either side of it as well, catching them in flickering magical fire that quickly turned the wooden figures into cinders. Balaam bit his lip in frustration at the unintended casualties. Normally, he took pleasure in his power and how far reaching it was, but this training was about precision. After having to spend a whole evening holding his tongue around Ivan, Balaam's annoyance and frustration were at dangerous levels. He needed to regain his composure, for the sake of safety, if nothing else.

Casting spells was more than just spitting out words and making gestures. It was about tapping into the primal current of magic that lived in their world. His body and mind acted as a conduit for that power, drawing it out and shaping it to his will. If he lost his focus or allowed his emotions to run wild, then the spells would show it. That was why his simple blast of attack-magic kept wiping out half the targets in the shooting range he'd booked. His burning desire to fight with Ivan was amplifying the more destructive properties of his magic. It was a facet of wielding the arcane that Balaam was well acquainted with and considered highly useful in certain situations, but this was not one of them.

The time for dealing with Ivan would come soon enough; he had to keep control until then. Knowing that the end was drawing nigh made it hard to stay composed, though. With the finish line in sight, Balaam wanted to just sprint ahead to cross it. But that would be folly. He'd long ago learned that he couldn't act alone. All he could do was ready himself. Prepare. Because in a few weeks, when the man on the other end of the mirror put his plan into action, Balaam intended to enjoy every minute of it.

That was then, however, and this was now. Taking a deep breath, Balaam chose a new target and whispered a few words. This time, only the wooden dummy he'd selected exploded in flames, burning away to nothingness in a span of seconds. Balaam watched, the wicked smile on his face framed by the dancing shadows of firelight. He could hold it together for a little longer, play the part for a few more weeks.

Because when the day finally came and he was freed from his facade, Balaam would never again have to pretend to be some kenneled dog. He would be free, and the world would tremble at the sound of his name.

*   *   *

"Had a feeling you wouldn't be sleeping."

Ren glanced up from the weight bench to find Donald standing in the doorway to the gym. Despite the late hour, there were still a few others dotted throughout the giant area, working in their exercise when time permitted. Still, it was nothing compared to the plethora of sculpted bodies—some by powers and some by effort—that filled the room during normal hours. Only the most devoted, poorly scheduled, or sleep-deprived capes would come work out so deep in the night.

"I don't sleep much, anyway," Ren replied, finishing his set of deadlifts and resting the bar carefully down on the rack. "Side effect of whatever made me into... me. Only need a couple of hours a night."

"That so? Damn, now there's an ability I could get some use out of. I have to keep my late hours the old-fashioned way: energy drinks and poor health." Donald walked over, idly picking up one of the smallest free-weights and moving it from hand to hand. "I've always been a night owl, though. Of course, back then, it was so I could squeeze in as much gaming as possible, for fun. Now I'm gaming to get myself up to snuff. At least it gives me something to do, since there's no way I was going to sleep tonight anyway."

Ren contemplated lying back down for another set but thought better of it. Even as adaptive as his muscles were, they could still only grow so quickly. The truth of the matter was that he'd hit his limit for daily progress hours ago; since then, he'd been working out to avoid dwelling on the same thing that was no doubt keeping Donald awake.

"Everyone goes on standby status sooner or later," Ren said, grabbing a towel and wiping down the bench. He didn't actually sweat, at least not measurably, but some habits were more about consideration for others than effectiveness. "That's how we have superheroes ready to respond when people need us. It's part of the job. And Apollo said he'd keep us at the bottom of the list, only sending us out if everyone else is already busy."

"I know. It was inevitable. I guess I just thought there would be more time, more training before we were suddenly chucked out into the world with people counting on us. I mean... if we screw up, someone could die." Donald set the weight down; his motion hadn't been doing much in the way of working him out in the first place.

"So far, you've tangled with a gang of thieves and a giant monster in a club," Ren pointed out. "If that doesn't get you ready, I'm not sure what will."

"Yeah, but I had help both times," Donald reminded him.

"And you'll have it this time, too. We're signed up as a pair; whatever call comes in gets us both as responders. As long as we've got each other's backs, we'll find a way to muddle through. Training is nice, but there's no better way to learn than by doing." Ren paused, momentarily thinking over Donald's last comment. "Hang on, I helped with the club monster, but I thought you were solo for the thing at your office?"

"Oh, yeah... I mean, I was." The tips of Donald's pale ears began to practically glow red, and he quickly looked away from Ren's gaze. "I was the only meta, but there were still other people who helped. You know, made distractions, that sort of thing."

"Uh huh." His toweling done, Ren threw the dry piece of cloth over his shoulder and took a long look at Donald. "Look, I know you well enough to know that you're not the type to try and hog glory, so if you're skipping over someone else's contributions to that fight, then I trust there's a good reason for it. That said, not everyone knows you as well as I do, so you might want to work on your poker face in case they catch you off guard again."

Donald jerked his head up, quickly scanning the gym to see if anyone was paying attention to them. As was to be expected of those working out after midnight, everyone was dedicated to their own efforts, oblivious or apathetic to the discussions of others. "Ren, can I trust you with a secret?"

392

"Seeing as you trust me with your life in the field, I'd say a secret is actually a step down," he replied.

"I guess that's a good point." Donald looked around once more then leaned in to whisper. "I wasn't really the only meta there. I had help, a lot of it, from a woman with a weird verbal power. I hate pretending I did it all alone, but she doesn't want anyone to know that she's a meta, so I told them I did everything."

That more or less aligned with what Ren would have guessed occurred. Donald was the honest sort, but he also wasn't the type to publicly out someone trying to live a normal life while meta. "Was it that girl we met last week? The one from your office out with her support group?"

"Tori?" Donald let out a small laugh and shook his head. "No; I think if she was a meta, she'd be tougher than all of us. Even without a power, she stepped up and kicked ass during the hostage situation. I mean, she had help since the other woman was using her powers on her, but still. It was really impressive; I wish I could have told people about it. Anyway, Tori is human. The one with the powers doesn't even work in our office, she was just there by coincidence."

"Lucky coincidence," Ren said. "Well, don't worry; your secret, and hers, is safe with me. Being a meta isn't always easy, even if you're lucky enough to be able to hide it. Honestly, I think if I'd gotten a different power, one like yours, I would have gone right back to my old life. I'd have spent the rest of my days on the sidelines, not trying to be a superhero."

"You're wrong." Donald picked his weight back up and walked over to the rack, setting it down in its designated spot. "Maybe you wouldn't have gone all in like you have, but you'd have ended up here sooner or later, Ren. As soon as you got power, this was inevitable."

"How do you figure?"

"Because you saw a giant monster appear out of nowhere, and before you knew I had a way to shoot it, you raced off to fight the thing. No worry, no hesitation, no nothing." Donald sat down on the bench beside his friend. "Anyone with instincts like that isn't going to stay on the sidelines. As soon as you saw someone in need, that would have been it. Like it or not, you were born to be a superhero."

"Guess we'll see over the next few weeks," Ren said, purposely skimming past the rest of what Donald had said. Much as he appreciated it, Ren had no idea how to respond to something so heartfelt. So instead, he fell back on a tactic as tried and true as the punch: Ren changed the subject. "Speaking of, did you figure out what you're going to do about work? Can you go to the office and be on standby?"

"I think the AHC is going to submit some sort of request for time off on my behalf, sort of like if I got jury duty," Donald said. "I've got no doubt Vendallia will approve it; they've more or less been trying to get me out the door since they found out I signed on with the capes."

"That's a bummer," Ren said. "I know you got a thrill out of seeing that coworker of yours, Tori."

"She's just a friend," Donald replied, words coming out fast and reflexively.

"Yeah, I saw that for myself. But I wasn't talking about what she is, I was talking about how you feel. You've obviously got a thing for her." Ren's statement was not an accusation but rather a simple observation.

"I might, but I don't think she feels the same way," Donald admitted.

"Give it time. These things grow as you learn more about each other. Plus, you're a superhero now. Who isn't impressed by that?"

"Surprisingly, her," Donald said. "She and Mr. Gerhardt are the only people in the office who haven't acted like being a meta or signing up with the AHC is any big deal. If not for them, I doubt I would have made it through another week at that place. Guess it will be my last one for a while."

"Maybe you'll see her again elsewhere," Ren suggested.

"No maybe about it." Donald reached into his pocket and pulled out his cell phone. "On Monday, we exchanged numbers. As soon as my standby duty is done, I'm calling her up and asking her to get coffee." His face, already pale, lost a few more shades. "Oh crap, I'm going to have to ask her out if I want to see her again, aren't I?"

Ren put a reassuring arm over his friend's back and patted him on the shoulder. "On the plus side, now fighting criminals doesn't seem so scary, does it?"

Chapter 59

When Saturday morning arrived, four bleary-eyed apprentices rode the elevator down through the guild's subterranean defenses and walked through the biometric screening hallway before finally entering the guild's most well-defended enclosure: Sanctum.

Tori, who had lost track of how much coffee she'd ingested as the night dragged on, had hit the strange, almost-high state that occurred during the second wind of sleep deprivation. Nonetheless, it was more than just a flailing brain's release of chemicals that had plastered a smile on her face as she watched the doors slowly part. It had taken all night, and there was still tons of work left to do, but they'd come up with a plan. Maybe it wasn't a great plan, but it was something. That alone was enough to give her hope.

None of the apprentices were terribly surprised to find Sanctum almost empty. Doctor Mechaniacal had emphasized that it wasn't a place people were supposed to hang out, and besides, most criminals preferred to work under the cover of darkness, making them functionally nocturnal. In fact, there was only one person in Sanctum, sitting back in a chair with a well-thumbed book in her hand.

At the sound of the door, Stasis jumped up from her chair, trying to look like she hadn't been caught completely off guard. Once her eyes settled on the four rookies making their way in, she let out a noise somewhere between a snort and a laugh. "What the hell are you four already doing here?"

"Doctor Mechanical said this was when we could enter Sanctum," Lance explained.

"Yeah, as in, you couldn't come in until now. That didn't mean you had to... oh shit, did you think this was some sort of deadline?" Stasis didn't bother waiting for an answer. She tipped back her head and let out a resounding cackle. "You have to be kidding me. Guys, this was just the first time you'd be allowed in, to make sure you didn't try and come down before you had things in order. No one actually tries to register their first job after only a night of planning. I was put down here mostly as a formality, and because I don't sleep."

Doctor Mechaniacal's words, which had seemed so clear at the time, echoed through their heads. Yes, he'd said they couldn't come in until Saturday morning, and yes, he'd emphasized the need to spend their evening planning. But Stasis was right: at no point had he ever told them they needed to be down here after only a night to get things going. In fact, the only time limit they'd been given was that they had a week to finish the trial. Aside from that, they'd been free to work how they wanted.

"Oh, son of a bitch," Warren muttered, tipping back his weary, aching head. Unlike Tori, he was not accustomed to pulling all-nighters, and the strain of it had left him with the beginnings of what would ultimately be a splitting migraine.

"Maybe they'll think it's impressive," Beverly ventured. "You know, that we were willing to work so hard and set a new submission record."

"No one cares about your submission. All we look at are results," Stasis said. She folded the corner of a page in her book, closed it, and set it down on the chair where she'd been resting. "But what the hell, you're already here, so let's go ahead and knock this out. I'm supposed to show you how to work the board, though since Doc designed it, the interface is pretty fluid. Everyone come watch."

Stasis walked a few feet over to one of several stations set up throughout the room and touched a screen. It lit up instantly, displaying an output identical to what they could see on the giant digital display that took up so much of the room.

"Doc explained to you all that everything in here is connected and sealed off, right? The only place you can book jobs is in Sanctum, and then only by using one of these special stations."

Everyone nodded. Stasis punched the corner of her screen, bringing up a new display. This one was actually curiously familiar to Tori, and when she realized why, it nearly took the breath out of her. The form Stasis had brought up, while it certainly had its differences, had unquestionably been patterned after the dozen or so she'd dealt with daily at Vendallia. The same person had clearly designed both—which, now that she thought about it, might be Doctor Mechaniacal himself.

"The actual booking is pretty easy. You just go through each section of this piece by piece, and at the end, you've got a job ready for the council to review. You four will get that part expedited since you're on a clock, but normally you have to make a special case or wait a few days. So, moving down the list, let's start with the biggest thing first: what's your target?"

Lance stepped forward, as it was he who'd uncovered the target they'd all agreed was the most tempting. "The Dash City Museum. It has a Level Three security system and enough art to easily hit our target half-million."

Stasis tapped a blank spot on the form, bringing up a search function. She quickly entered "Dash City Museum" and a map appeared in front of her. Above it was a text box, visibly filled with information about the potential target. "Hmmm. Well, it's not affiliated with the guild, which is a big one, and I don't see any known associates of capes that work there, though the council will double check that part, but you've got a major problem right off the bat." Stasis

396

leaned back, allowing them all to get a clear view of the red, highlighted text at the top of the information box.

"Right now, they have a collection of jewels recovered from the attempted Cernovian invasion a few years back. Those things are worth a literal fortune, so the whole place has been put on extra high-alert. I bet they have capes on hand around the clock just waiting for someone dumb enough to try and steal those things."

"We know," Beverly said. "That's why we picked this target."

Stasis's eyes widened, but before she could ask, Beverly stretched out her hand and pointed to a section just below the red warning text. "The exhibit ends on Monday when the jewels get transported to their next stop on the tour. We want to do the job on Wednesday, after they and the extra security are long gone and the staff has let their guard down."

"Oh, that's cunning. You're hitting them right when they think the real risk has passed. I'm impressed." Stasis tapped a green button on the bottom of the screen. The display shrank back to the form page, only now the "Location" section had been filled in.

"Even on their slowest day, there's enough art to hit our quota," Lance said. "So we don't need the gems. We can be perfectly happy with a paltry half-million."

"You say that now," Stasis muttered, quickly filling the section of the form marked "Date" with a few keystrokes. "Well, Dash City is in North Carolina. That puts you plenty of states away from the AHC's headquarters, so that's a step in the right direction. Should I assume you want to book Tunnel Vision for transportation?"

"Please," Tori said. "We talked about heading there via train or car, but it would take a while to get from Colorado to North Carolina. Plus, it would leave a trail, and even if it wouldn't be crazy suspicious, I don't think any of us wants to wear a costume for several days straight."

"You're not wrong there. Those things need to be washed regularly or they can get funky." Stasis skimmed through the form to see which section they should go over next. "I'll show you how to handle asking for other members when we're done, but obviously, that isn't coming into play since it's just you four on this job. You've still got two hundred bucks left in your resource account; did you want to spend it on anything?"

"I think we'll hang on to that in case any incidentals come up," Warren said.

"Works for me. Then that means you've knocked out the where, the when, the assets you need from the guild, and what resources you're using to pay for them." Stasis double checked her form then turned to Tori, who was still clutching the bundle of handwritten pages. "Normally, we ask that you submit tactical plans digitally on the station, but for you all, we'll make an exception. If you give me what you've got, I can have it in front of the council before lunch."

"It's not really done yet. We did only have a night," Tori protested.

"Plans always change, if not after you give them to us then certainly when you're out on the job. We don't look them over to see if every single detail is perfect; we're just checking for any glaring mistakes or blatant violations of the code. So long as your outline doesn't have either of those, it will be fine. In this case, even if you do, we'll just ask you to make some changes. Trust me, you want to hand those over; otherwise you'll spend every hour from now until the deadline endlessly tweaking them. Better to get some feedback and maybe a little sleep."

Tentatively, Tori extended the stack of pages that she and the others had been up all night working on. Stasis, sensing the younger woman's apprehension, accepted them as if they were made of glass and tucked them securely against her arm.

"Okay: let me show you a few more functions on the form, then you can all feel free to go rest. Unlike me, the rest of the council does need to sleep, so they won't be up and able to meet until this afternoon at the soonest."

Tori didn't bother to correct her, but she knew Stasis was at least partly off-base. After all, Tori had never encountered anyone who rose with the sun quite as regularly as Ivan Gerhardt. In fact, despite the early hour, she'd have put down money that he was in his kitchen right now, cooking up a huge breakfast that he'd miraculously devour.

To Tori's credit, she was spot on about Ivan already being awake, though she could hardly be faulted for getting the location wrong. Not when Ivan had gone to such great lengths to keep it secret from her.

*   *   *

The sounds of Penelope's cartoons wafted through the open door into the kitchen where Ivan and Helen sat drinking their coffee. She could be heard singing along, off-key, to the more musical ones, no doubt spilling her own breakfast on the floor when the urge to dance overtook her. Despite the noise, Ivan was thankful for her active participation in television viewing; it made it easier to keep track of where she was. This was not a conversation either of them wanted Penelope overhearing.

"He seemed pretty sure," Ivan said, picking at the last of the eggs left on his plate. "Said it went down that way in almost every universe."

"Even if that's true, 'almost every' sort of belies the real scale. I mean, the best estimates say there are millions, maybe billions, that would be similar enough to ours to be recognizable," Helen pointed out. "So saying 'almost every universe' follows a pattern is the same as saying there are hundreds of thousands that don't. Maybe we'll be one of those."

"Nexus is a crazy son of a... bad man." Ivan's curse withered on his tongue as Helen glared at him. Whether the girl was in earshot or not, Helen didn't allow cursing in the same house as Penelope. Given how quickly she picked up on words, Ivan could hardly blame her for the policy. "Nexus is insane, but his warnings are usually accurate."

"Except when he's lying, either for a purpose or for fun. Look at how many times he caused widespread destruction and blamed it on that poor Stasis woman just to make her appear to be a criminal. He can't be trusted. While the warning is nice, I'm not going to take it as gospel." Helen finished off her cup of coffee then took the pot from the middle of the table and refilled it halfway.

She was right, which wasn't exactly new, but Ivan was determined to make her take it more seriously. "But Helen, if the stars fall—"

"Then they fall, Ivan. We've always known it was a possibility." Helen's eyes turned from him to the doorway into the living room, through which her daughter could still be heard singing off-tune. "I never thought this was possible, not after the accident. But you made it happen. If not for you, I don't know that I could have even taken the first nine months, let alone the six years after that. It's been wonderful, like living a dream. And if that dream finally comes to an end, well, I got six years of this peaceful life when I never expected a day of it. I can't be mad that I didn't get more; that would be just plain greedy."

When she looked back at Ivan, Helen's eyes had begun to water at the edges. They both pretended not to notice. Instead, Ivan reached over and took her hand in his. It was so strange to hold a thing that seemed so delicate yet was in fact one of the strongest hands in the world.

"Our universe is our own. If there's any way to stop the stars from falling, I'll find it. Trust me, and don't act rashly just because things look bad."

Helen snorted, quickly turning her head to cover the sound. "It's still funny, you know, even after this long. You asking me to trust you. I do, don't get me wrong, but... you know."

"I know," Ivan assured her. He released her hand and sank his fork into his eggs, finishing the last of them. As he chewed, a thought popped into his brain, another memory from the night before that had taken far lower precedence in light of Nexus's prediction. "Let me ask you something: did you know that Quorum is the only one of his kind? Or does he know that? Nexus let it slip last night."

"Oh yeah, he's known for decades. It's why Nexus became his arch-enemy to begin with. Apparently, he's got a thing for the anomalies that only exist in single dimensions." Helen put her newly freed hand back on her cup of coffee and took a sip, wincing at the burst of heat. "You know Stasis is one too, right? Evidently he mentioned that to Quorum a while ago, but we assumed she knew."

"That one we were aware of," Ivan said. "Not sure why he tormented her but forged a rivalry with Quorum."

"Don't try to understand Nexus. Nexus understands Nexus and he's freaking insane," Helen said.

As they chuckled at that, both noticed that the racket from the living room was dying down, meaning they'd have to weather a bout of commercials before Penelope's next cartoon came on. Both had just managed to shove away their plates before she came rocketing in, leaping up into her mother's lap without even bothering to see if she could successfully avoid hitting the table. Ivan smiled as he watched her land. She truly was fearless.

Just like her mother.

Chapter 60

Tori found herself with the last thing she'd expected to possess over the weekend: free time. With their plan under review, there wasn't much point in doing more work, at least not until they knew they'd been approved for the time and target they'd chosen. After all, it would suck to spend a full day plotting out how to rob a museum that they weren't allowed to touch. Plus, there was no training to do since all of their time had been set aside to plan their job. So after a few hours of precious sleep and a quick lunch from a vending machine, Tori decided it was time to make good on another duty she'd been putting off.

It took five full minutes of knocking on Beverly's door before she finally answered, hair splayed out in all directions as she tried futilely to blink the sleep out of her eyes. After staring at Tori for several seconds, she finally opened her mouth and spat out a greeting.

"Whasmacha?"

"Eloquent as always," Tori replied. "Come on, it's been like five hours, you have to be caught up on sleep by now."

Slowly, Beverly reached up and rubbed her face until her eyes finally focused on the intruder in front of her. "The human body needs eight hours, usually. And it's not supposed to stay up for an entire night before getting them. What do you even want? There's no way the council already came back with approval."

"Shit no, I bet half of them are still lazing about like you," Tori said. "I'm actually about to head out, and I wanted to see if you were up for coming along. Figured this would be a good time to introduce you to... well, that woman I told you about."

Though she'd brought Beverly up to speed about Chloe and her predicament earlier in the week, Tori had made a point of not saying the barista's name on guild property. Perhaps it was paranoia—she highly doubted the guild would try to strong-arm Chloe into joining—but something inside her demanded that she play her friend's secret close to the vest. If her time with Ivan had taught her one thing, it was the code. But if it had taught her two, then it was the code and when to trust her instincts.

"Right... right, the lady with the talking thing." Beverly's brain was sluggish but seemed to be kicking into gear. "Magic one, right?"

"That's the best guess. She's not a thousand percent sure where she got her powers from, but magic fits the best." Tori had tried to keep things as vague as possible, which hadn't been hard given how little Chloe actually knew about her own abilities. "You want to come see what we can figure out?"

401

"Well, I doubt I'll be able to get back to sleep." Beverly's words were nearly cut off as a giant yawn split her face, somewhat disproving her own argument. "Guess I may as well see if I can help. But you know there are people that have way more experience with magic than me, right? I just found a necklace."

"For now, I think it's less about magic than it is about puzzling through exactly how a thing works. I'll take someone smart and trustworthy over a magic expert," Tori said.

"Let's hope your friend feels the same." Beverly let out another yawn then shoved her door open to allow Tori inside. "Come on in. I just need a few minutes to get dressed. I'm not putting on anything too nice, though."

"Somehow, I think she'll be okay with that," Tori assured her.

"She'd better be. Oh, and since your intruding ass woke me up, you're stopping to get us some soda or something somewhere along the way," Beverly added.

"How about coffee?" Tori asked, barely concealing her knowing smile.

"Can't stand the stuff." Because she was turned toward her dresser, Beverly missed the shocked, pained expression that flitted across Tori's face. "Too bitter, even with cream and sugar. Give me a nice energy drink any day." Beverly finally pulled out a new t-shirt and looked back over to see Tori staring wide-eyed at the woman she'd thought she knew.

"What?"

"Nothing, nothing." Tori shook her head. "Just trying to figure out if we can still be friends after that revelation."

"Then get out and let me go back to sleep. I don't haul myself out of bed on five hours of sleep for people who aren't my friends," Beverly said.

"I guess we can make it work then, somehow." Tori slapped her hands together as another revelation struck her. "It will give me a chance to bring you around and show you how wrong you are about coffee."

The next thing that struck Tori was not a revelation but rather the t-shirt Beverly had balled up and chucked at her. Unlike their attempts to shoot at the trash can, this time, Beverly's aim was dead on.

*   *   *

"It looks good." Wade flipped through a few more pages, checking for details on how they'd circumvent the motion cameras only to find they had indeed put a plan in place. Having Lance's bugs gang up to unplug them was a crude solution, though hard to dispute in terms of effectiveness. "Rough around the edges, albeit not as much as I expected. Ms. Rivas's years of thievery are showing through."

"Yeah, nothing is really jumping out at me either." Xelas didn't bother flipping through the pages. She'd looked at them once and had the information recorded—a benefit to having cameras for eyes. "They really did this all in a night?"

"Sure looks that way." Stasis had a set of copies, though she'd long ago given them as much perusing as she planned to. There were other, more responsible members to handle the deep vetting.

Currently, Stasis, Morgana, Xelas, and Wade, sans Doctor Mechaniacal suit, were grouped together in the council's chambers, overhauling the proposed plan. Technically, the meeting to evaluate its viability wouldn't be for another few hours, as Gork's people were naturally nocturnal and both Ivan and Balaam had said their mornings were booked. Still, this group was the one that would do most of the actual work, ensuring that no sudden personnel changes or mergers had rendered the museum a poor target.

"Anyone found how they're dealing with the security guards?" Morgana called, flipping through her pages. "I'm sure they know better than to leave a trail of corpses, but I'm not seeing what they want to do instead."

"Page fourteen, under 'planned developmental countermeasures,'" Wade informed her. "Looks like they're going to have Glyph lay down some magic that will put the weaker-willed ones to sleep. Then Hephaestus and Pest Control are planning to handle any leftovers with poisoned insects and ranged chemical attacks."

"Hephaestus has gear for that on hand?" Morgana asked. After seeing the apprentice whip up a sonic cannon out of a spare robot parts, she didn't doubt the woman's tech skills, but time was of the essence.

"She seems certain she can build it in time." Wade had a suspicion that she would be bringing far more than just what was outlined before them. She had likely only submitted the things she felt were absolutely necessary. Back when he'd built his first meta-suit, he'd tried to cram in everything but a sausage grinder.

"I guess that's fine, as long as she can pull it off," Morgana said.

"No one else finds it worrying that Lance can just summon insects so toxic they knock people unconscious?" Xelas shivered, a sound like nails rattling in a steel can. "Makes me glad I don't have skin."

"His name is Pest Control." When in the council, Wade was a stickler for using their members' proper names, though even he would admit it was more for propriety than safety. "The animal world is a dangerous place and has served as inspiration for many a nightmare of mankind. That's only become more true since the discovery of metas, as we've found all sorts of creature not previously dreamed of."

"Wait, hold on, can Lance—sorry, Pest Control—summon meta-insects?" Stasis seemed to show interest for the first time since she'd dropped off the copies of the apprentices' proposal.

"From what we've seen, he can summon any insect so long as he has seen a sample in person," Wade replied. "Granted, that means he has little more in his meta-summoning arsenal than the augmented wasps the capes drove out of the city a few years ago, but I suspect that won't always be the case."

"Kids today, just full of surprises." Xelas leaned her head back and stared at the ceiling for several seconds before speaking again. "Okay, I just finished rechecking all our databases. So far as I can tell, there's no one directly related to AHC members or the guild that works at the Dash City Museum."

"Thank you, Xelas." Wade turned the last page and set it down, then clapped all the paper together into a neat pile. "We will still have to conduct a formal review this afternoon, but barring one of the other three seeing something we missed, I think it's safe to say that come next Wednesday, the Dash City Museum will be at risk of losing quite a few exhibits."

*   *   *

"Maybe 'the devil is in the details'? Wait, scratch that. On the off chance you actually can somehow create a biblically powerful supernatural enemy, I'd like to have a little more firepower than just us on hand," Beverly said.

"No, we should try it. That's one I've never tested." Chloe took a deep breath, looked around to make sure no one had somehow snuck up on them, and whispered, "The devil is in the details."

All three women scanned their surroundings, waiting for some horned entity to pop up from behind the heaps of scrap. After getting dropped off by a guild car at Ridge City Grinders, Tori and Beverly had joined Chloe, who drove them out to a scrapyard Tori had used as a testing ground for more experimental slip-shod weaponry once upon a time. It was the sort of place that was neglected when anyone even bothered to show up, so it offered a precious commodity in the metropolis of Ridge City: privacy.

"How do we know if it worked?" Tori asked, after several moments passed with no fallen angel popping into existence.

"I don't know, which I think might be the problem." Chloe pulled a small notebook from her pocket, along with a stub of a pencil, and scrawled the new phrase inside. Once it was written, she promptly drew a line through it,

404

indicating that it hadn't worked. "It's starting to look like I can't just use a phrase; there needs to be some kind of understanding with it. Saving a penny, I understand. How the devil would pop out of the details... I've got nothing. Maybe if there were a contract, and he could use it as a portal." Chloe added a star next to the crossed out phrase, her way of noting that it might be worth exploring later.

So far, they'd spent over an hour with Chloe testing every idiom or old saying that popped into their minds. Several worked but many produced no visible effect, not even when adding that extra bit of magical weight to her words. It was a confusing, sometimes contradictory process, and Tori could see why Chloe was having so much trouble getting a grip on her power. It made turning into living fire seem positively mundane.

"Okay, I've got another one I want you to try," Beverly said. "How about 'one punch will send you flying'?"

Chloe tilted her head slightly. "I've never heard that one before."

"But you can picture how it would work, right?"

"Well, sure. It's pretty straightforward. One punch will send you flying." Nothing happened as Chloe spoke, though that much had been expected. Sometimes the triggers to her magic were more obvious than others; this one would obviously demand physical contact.

"Good, now punch me. Not too hard, just one in the shoulder." Beverly approached and paused a few inches away from Chloe.

"Hang on, what if this actually works?" Tori asked.

"Then I'll turn into a graceful white dragon and take control of the flight." Beverly, to Tori's shock, had given Chloe a rundown of her powers as soon as they met. Evidently, she felt it wrong to learn so much about someone else's secret without offering up a bit of her own. That had, in turn, prodded Tori to provide Chloe with some insight into her fire-based abilities, though she'd kept more than a few bits still secret. "Now make with the jab."

Chloe pulled back her right arm, bunched her hand into a poorly-formed fist that would probably result in a broken finger if she put any force into the blow, and gave Beverly a light slug in the shoulder. Aside from the soft thud of flesh striking cloth, nothing happened. Beverly hadn't even shifted, let alone flown into the air.

"Interesting," Beverly said, looking down at the bony fist still resting against her shoulder. "Okay, so I think I have a theory, but it's a rough one. I mean, *really* rough. So if I'm way off base, no one hold it against me."

"At this point, I'll take any bit of information I can get," Chloe said, pulling back her fist and giving it a light shake.

"My guess—and I do want to stress that this is a guess—is that you somehow tap into something like people's belief, only with words instead of the divine. Like... okay. We know there are divine metas out there, aside from the ones who just take old-god names like Apollo. There are some who seem like they're actually drawing from something bigger than themselves—like that cape named Archbishop, for instance. But some people don't believe they're drawing from actual gods; instead, they're tapping into the collective human belief in those gods. If that's true, then why couldn't you do the same with words?"

"You lost me so far back that I might as well not have even gotten in the car," Tori said.

"This is the kind of shit you have to learn about when your power is magical and the source is unknown," Beverly replied.

"Hang on," Chloe said, squinting a bit as she puzzled together the theory Beverly had lain out before her. "So the sayings only work if a lot of people believe they work? But no one actually believes that lying will set your pants on fire, and I've used that one before. Turned a pair of jeans into ashes."

Tori made a note to inquire further about that incident; it wouldn't really do to have Chloe accidentally lighting people up all over town. That was the sort of thing that drew the attention of the capes, or worse, the guild.

"I did say it was rough," Beverly reminded her. "But I don't think it matters as much that they think it will happen literally; it's just that people keep saying them over and over, and on some level, they believe there's a sort of truth to them. Like that lying a lot will eventually land you in trouble, which is also known as a hot seat. Every time someone out there says it, they put a little more faith in it, like water through a prayer wheel. I think once those words get strong enough, you can tap into them."

Tori was slowly starting to catch on, her mind subbing out words like "faith" for "unknown variables" to keep things clearer. "Then why have her try the punching one? That's not a saying anyone says."

"It is, it's just not a common one," Beverly corrected. "People say things like that in fights when talking about people who can knock you off your feet in a single blow. One of my brothers boxes, and I've heard it used more than once. The thing is that it's not something everyone knows or thinks of offhand. That's what I wanted to test—if any saying worked, or if it needed a certain amount of saturation for Chloe to use it."

"That does explain a lot. I've tried a few sayings my grandpa used to like and only some of them worked." Chloe flipped through her notebook, looking at the successes and failures one by one, checking to see if Beverly's theory about the pattern played out. "But there are ones like 'the devil in the details' that fizzle too, and that's a pretty popular one."

"And you can probably use it if you ever find a situation that fits," Beverly said. "It looks like as much as the words need power, they also need you to shape them. If you can't picture how a saying would work in real life, even subconsciously, then you can't invoke it."

"Think of it like a gun." Tori ignored the fearful look the darted across Chloe's face and continued with her analogy. "The power is the bullet—not enough juice in the words? No bullet to fire. But your mind is the trigger. If it can't give the idea shape then the bullet just sits idly in the chamber."

"Well, well, little miss science is finally catching on," Beverly said.

"Once you moved into parameters and execution, I was back on solid ground," Tori shot back.

"Interesting as this is, and please don't think for a second that it isn't, how does it help me control this damn power?" Chloe asked.

"No idea. And honestly, it might not." Beverly shrugged, her shoulders bobbing up and down in an unapologetic display of uncertainty. "All I know is what I was taught by my teacher, and he said that understanding is the first step to control. It worked for me, sort of, but we've got very different powers. At least you found a list of new things you can say without lighting pants on fire, though."

"There is that." Chloe sighed and snapped her notebook shut, stuffing it back into the rear pocket of her dark slacks. "I really appreciate you both taking the time to help me, even if I will still have to pick my words carefully for a while. Just having some sort of idea of what's happening to me makes it a little easier to cope with."

"Don't sweat it," Beverly said. "We metas have to stick together, you know?"

"Tell me about it. Especially those of us trying to live under the radar," Chloe agreed. "You know Tori shot herself in the arm four times rather than tip off me and Donald that she was a meta?"

Tori blushed in spite of herself, tan cheeks quickly turning red. While she'd given Beverly something of a synopsis of what happened during the robbery, Tori had opted out of providing a full play-by-play. Part of that was in order to keep from looking like a braggart, but the rest was fearing that someone would point out a much simpler solution that she'd overlooked.

"And the thing is, I totally get it," Chloe continued. "I just have this weird word ability and it's hard enough to keep under wraps. Having fire manipulation... you'd have to go all out to keep your secret. There's no way the AHC wouldn't try to snap you up like they did Donald. Or worse, some gang that wanted to make you use your power for them."

Tori and Beverly certainly did not exchange knowing glances at that last option; both were old and mature enough to understand that such a gesture would betray the very secret they hoped to keep. They did, however, both go for the nervous-laugh reaction, which was certainly off-putting. Seconds after she started, Tori let her laughter trail off. She decided that words might work a bit better for their situation.

"I doubt stuff like that really happens, at least around here. I mean, the AHC's headquarters is only twenty minutes from our office. I can't imagine how ballsy or careless any kind of gang would have to be to pull that stuff in Ridge City." Ballsy, careless, or specifically founded and watched over by a mix of geniuses and veteran villains. Tori was just grateful that Chloe's last phrase hadn't been the pants-on-fire one.

"You never know, it's a dangerous world," Chloe said. "But hey, I never thought to ask: since we all try and keep things so secret, how did you two even find each other?"

This, at least, they'd prepared for. Beverly launched into the story they'd chosen without a moment's hesitation. "I was changed on the same night as you, during that weird storm. I had pretty much no control of my powers, and Tori happened upon me when I was in my dragon-form. She helped calm me down, telling me she'd been there and it would be okay. Basically talked me through it until I managed to get back to human. After that, our secrets were pretty much out to each other."

"If I hadn't seen her shoot herself and then charge a really strong meta, I wouldn't believe it, but Tori does seem like the type to try and calm down a dragon." Chloe glanced down at her watch, eyes growing wide as she realized for the first time how much time had passed. "Shit. As much as I appreciate you both helping me out, I need to get back to the coffee shop. Gwen gets off soon, and if I'm not back by then, we'll be shorthanded."

"No problem, you can just drop us downtown and be there..." Beverly trailed off and a wide, unexpected grin suddenly appeared on her face. "Chloe, have you ever tried using your ability to teleport?"

"What do you mean?"

"I mean," Beverly replied, walking over and taking the barista's slender hand, "that if you're willing to do one more test, we might all be there in a hop, skip, and a jump."

Chapter 61

Teleporting with Chloe was nothing like changing locations with Tunnel Vision. While the duo opened portals between spaces, Chloe's version warped the world around them like a strange vertigo roller coaster. Additionally, hers took a little trial and error as they worked out exactly what constituted the difference between a hop, skip, and jump. Eventually, they figured it out, as well as that Chloe could take along passengers so long as they held her hand and did the motions, which led to them jumping up in the scrap yard and coming down in the parking lot behind Chloe's coffee shop.

It was a testament to their willpower that Beverly managed not to throw up at all after watching the world spin about beneath them and that Tori only dry-heaved for a minute or so. Chloe, on the other hand, was entirely unaffected. This seemed to speak to a sort of protection from her own power, though it was also possible that she just had a stronger stomach than Tori or Beverly. Unfortunately, there was still another teleport required of them, as they realized Chloe had parked her car at the scrap yard. This time no one got sick, though Beverly's skin turned green for a reason that had nothing to do with her dragon necklace.

Eventually, Chloe dropped them off downtown, where they walked for fifteen minutes to the unassuming office that camouflaged the guild's headquarters. While they could have had Chloe leave them closer by, both felt it was best to keep her as far from the guild as possible, both literally and metaphorically. Besides, after two teleports and a car ride, a walk was just what they needed to settle their stomachs.

By the time they made it back to the floor where their rooms were, both were feeling a lot better, if not fully at a hundred percent functionality. Nice as it was to have a non-guild friend that could teleport, there was an unspoken agreement that they wouldn't be looking to Chloe for transportation unless it was absolutely necessary.

"And there they are, returned at last." Tori had barely stepped off the elevator when Lance appeared, wide grin betraying the news he'd no doubt hoped to spring on them.

"Did you already hear back from the council?" Tori asked.

Lance's smile dimmed for a moment before he let out a sharp laugh. "You sure know how to take the wind out of someone's sails, don't you? Yeah, we got word about half an hour ago. The plan is temporarily approved, although we also got sent a whole list of other details we're supposed to provide. Minutia stuff plus contingency plans, that sort of thing."

"Hot damn!" Tori said, turning to high-five Beverly, who let out a whoop of excitement. "Look at that! Only a night to plan and we already got approved. I'd say that's a pretty fucking good sign, wouldn't you?"

"It's an indication that we're on the right path; nothing more, nothing less." Warren stepped out from around the corner, appearing so suddenly that he nearly made Tori gasp. Then again, that might have been because of how haggard the poor guy looked. If he'd bothered to take in any sort of rest after they submitted the plan, it didn't show. His eyes were bloodshot, his skin was paler than normal, and he had something of a sway in the way he stood that made it seem like he might tumble over at any given moment.

"Good god, did you get any sleep at all?" Beverly's tone had lost its usual edge, the concern in her voice catching everyone off guard.

"There will be time for sleep later. I spent my time more wisely, receiving instruction from my mentor." Warren was clearly trying to snap at Beverly, but between his own exhaustion and her unexpected sincerity, he just wasn't able to muster up the verbal venom. "Balaam was kind enough to spend several of his precious hours teaching me further."

Neither Beverly nor Tori said anything, because what was there to say? Their mentors were more or less in charge of them; if Balaam wanted to drive his apprentice into sleep-deprivation to give him more lessons, then that was probably his prerogative. Deep down, Tori felt a twist of guilt in her stomach as she watched Warren fight to stay conscious. Before she came, apprentices had fallen out of style. If she hadn't gotten paired with Ivan, Warren wouldn't be apprenticed to a sociopath.

"As great a learning opportunity as that was, I think we're all ready to start working on answering the council's questions," Lance said, slapping Warren lightly on the back. "I'll bring the girls up to speed. Why don't you grab a computer, head to the lounge, and start doing some research on which exhibits should be our prime targets?"

Warren gave a half-nod, too tired to argue, and stumbled off down the hall. Once he was gone, Lance turned back to Tori and Beverly. "I figure as soon as he sits on that couch, he'll pass clean out. I feel bad asking, but do you mind if we let him nap for a while? We're technically ahead of schedule, and I'm afraid if he's not with us, Balaam will just find excuses to keep him awake."

"I really hate that fucking guy," Tori muttered darkly. "What reason does he have to torment his own apprentice?"

"Apparently he's trying to force Warren to flip his schedule so he'll get used to being awake at night," Lance explained. "Magic requires mental clarity, so he doesn't want Warren to be all groggy when we're actually out on the job."

"Huh. That's actually a lot more practical than I was expecting," Beverly admitted.

"Pretty sure our mentors can't torture us for no reason, not even here," Lance said. "I mean, we're a guild of villains. None of us are big on taking shit from people. Pointless cruelty to an apprentice is a recipe for someone coming after you down the line, though I agree that there were probably less asshole-ish ways to go about this one."

"Either way, we'll pull Warren's share of the weight until he's gotten a few hours of rest." Tori mentally flipped through her to-do list, which, now that Chloe had a starting point for figuring out her power, left only the day job, finishing the plan, and her meta-suit. The last one was out until the weekend was over or until they had a final plan approved, which meant she needed to put all her energy into getting every facet of their robbery outlined either way.

"You do need to bring us up to speed though, Lance. If we've still got shit to do, I want to meet it head on. We're starting off ahead of schedule; let's stay there. I've got my own prep work to finish."

"Ah yes, the legendary technological revelation that will be your suit," Beverly said. "Are you sure you're going to be able to have that ready in time? We've only got a few days left."

"Trust me," Tori assured her. "Come hell or high water, no matter the cost, even if I have to work looking as tired as Warren, I am going to get my suit done. This is more than just our last trial, you know. It's our first time out as genuine representatives of the guild."

Tori turned and headed down the hall after Warren, mind already set on the sole task barring her from her workshop.

"I intend to make sure Hephaestus is dressed properly for her first night on the town."

*   *   *

"As I'm sure you know, our security systems' current framework was put in when the Alliance of Heroic Champions was officially founded." Quorum didn't break stride as he spoke, walking down the long, red-carpeted hallway without missing a step. Given the level of multi-tasking he was capable of, this technically required barely more effort than simply lying on the ground. "Professor Quantum installed it to ensure that every superhero we recruited had at least one place in the world they could feel safe. No mad villain or vengeful criminal would ever break through these walls. Here, if nowhere else in the world, we could find a measure of peace."

Apollo did, in fact, know all of this, but said nothing as he followed Quorum down the hallway. He understood that this was more a matter of ceremony than history, and did his part by being respectfully silent.

"Of course, the system has had countless updates since then, both in reaction to attempts to attack us and as a result of breakthroughs Professor Quantum has had. Overall, I'd say about once a year our defenses get an upgrade. One thing, however, has remained eternally constant."

Quorum reached the end of the hallway, passing three portraits labeled with a golden placard that read "Founders," and opened a simple, unassuming door. What waited inside was a sharp contrast to the quaint, dated hall they'd traversed. It was nothing but light and metal, a cylinder enclosed on all sides with only a single button-less terminal occupying the center of the floor. Moving slowly, Quorum stepped inside and motioned for Apollo to follow. No sooner had he passed the door than it closed smoothly behind him. Despite the fact that there was barely a click, Apollo had a hunch that, even with his impressive power, breaking through that door would be nearly impossible.

"Since the AHC's founding, the only members to have our security system's highest level of access have been myself, Professor Quantum, and Lodestar. While we trust our members with much, there is also a great deal that is simply too dangerous. The holding cells where we confine metas until prisons can adequately prepare for them, the technology we've confiscated from civilizations both terrestrial and space-faring, the myriad of objects that would induce meta-powers deemed too dangerous to be allowed out into the world, you get the idea. It was decided that those with full access to such facilities was best kept limited specifically to those on, or with, the Champions' Congress. But you've seen all those places before."

Apollo had indeed; he'd long ago reached the point where he was trusted to drop off criminals to the cells or trinkets to the vaults. Tempting as they were, he had never felt the desire to abuse his privileges. There was no need in him to deal with criminals beyond bringing them to justice, foreign technology was most dangerous to those using it without knowing how, and anyone who'd been around metas for more than a few months learned that mixing power sources was a fool's game. Tools were one thing, but the objects that could induce meta-abilities were best kept at one per person. At best, two canceled each other. At worst, all manner of unexpected effects occurred. No, Apollo had taken his privileges seriously and treated them with respect. Accessing those little nooks and crannies hidden in the AHC was never his end goal.

"This, as I'm sure you've guessed by now, is a bit different. We don't broadcast its existence with grand schematics or cumbersome doors. This is the heart of our system, the only place where serious, permanent changes can be made. The three of us have remote terminals that can grant temporary clearances or operate the system, but those have strict limitations. We wouldn't want anyone hacking or stealing them and causing trouble. That's why we have this heart, this solemn chamber where only those specifically chosen can enter. And like any true heart, it is both delicate and powerful."

Quorum moved to the center of the room where the button-less terminal stood. As he moved close, a hatch opened and a single object, like an egg on a pole, rose upward. "In here, and only here, true change can occur. As of today, you will be the first non-founder to have permissions within this room. You will have full access to every non-personal aspect and area and the ability to raise the permission levels of those you deem trustworthy. This is a historic day, Apollo."

"One I will remember for the rest of my life." There was no insincerity in his voice, nor would it have found a home there. Apollo truly meant those words with every fiber of his being. "But can you do this alone? I imagined the Champions' Congress would all need to be present."

"There are only three of us, Apollo, and we trust each other." Quorum pressed his index fingers to the egg. A soft glow illuminated his entire body. "The others used their remote devices to give permission for this promotion, but only one of us is necessary to carry it out. It was a function added after Lodestar was stuck in a black hole for a month and we were unable to create a temporary council replacement. Thus it was decided that one was enough, though Professor Quantum did take great pains to ensure no one could trick the system. These scanners detect everything from your DNA to your brainwaves to your dimensional footprint. Nothing is impossible, but this is as close as we've come to total security."

The glow faded, and a new hatch opened, bringing up a fresh egg-looking device in front of Apollo.

"And now, my young superhero, it's your turn. You have worked long and hard to earn this honor, so reach out and claim it as your own. Once you're scanned, you will have all the rights and privileges of a member of the Champions' Congress."

Apollo didn't need to be told twice. He reached out his hands, noting that the glow cascading over him was almost chilly. All that work, all those years, and now, at last, it was finally in his hands. Literally in his hands. Such a simple, unassuming egg, but it would give him the prize he'd been after all this time. It was the last piece he'd need to begin the work superheroes were truly meant to do.

Wiping out villains.

Chapter 62

Ivan was surprised at how empty his house felt. When the weekend ended, he'd expected a return to normalcy, or at least the strange situation that passed for normalcy these days. But Tori had barely paused long enough to wolf down dinner before she'd buried herself back in the basement lab. Granted, she already spent a lot of time down there, but usually she'd emerge on occasion to grab a beer from the fridge and make a little small talk. This time, Ivan didn't see her again until it was time to leave for work, and she emerged from the hidden basement blinking the exhaustion out of her eyes.

Work seemed to fly by now that he'd gotten mostly caught up from his time away. Of course, he'd no sooner finished his backlog than the word came down from Mrs. Espinoza that Donald wouldn't be coming in for a week, maybe two, and that what few remaining responsibilities he still had were to be pawned off on the other programmers. This little shuffle wasn't particularly hard, especially since Ivan had prepared for the possibility as soon as Donald signed up with the AHC, but it was a bit depressing. Donald really had been one of his best employees, the right mix of smart and cowardly that meant he'd contribute to the company but never be bold enough to strike out on his own. Replacing him wouldn't be easy, but that was life in Ridge City.

If Tori was bothered by the absence of her friend, it didn't show. In fact, she barely seemed engaged with the world around her. Her work was flawless and she upheld all the expected pleasantries when greeting others in the office, but it was clear at a glance that her mind was elsewhere. Ivan could hardly blame her, given the proverbial sword dangling over her head, just days away from falling or being removed; it was a wonder she kept things as together as she did.

Tuesday was no different, Tori emerging exhausted in the morning after a hastily-eaten dinner and another night in the basement. Ivan was prepared for more of the same on Wednesday as he finished up the last of his pancakes, but to his surprise, it was a well-rested, vibrant-eyed Tori that stepped out from behind the wall-panel. Her suit was crisp and there was a spring in her step as she descended on the table, grabbing her now cold breakfast and slathering it with syrup.

"This is a nice change," he commented, not sure how else to broach the subject of her zombie-like state for the last few days.

"Tonight's the big show, so I cut myself off from work at midnight and went to bed. Last minute crunch time is well and good, but I need a clear head if we want to pull off tonight's job." If Tori was bothered by the room-temperature

414

pancakes, she didn't show it, digging in like she hadn't eaten in days. Which, really, she hadn't—all she'd been doing before was quieting her hunger.

"A very responsible decision," Ivan said. "Were you able to get everything done that you wanted?"

"Holy hell no. Not by a long shot." Tori's reply shot a few pancake crumbs across her end of the table, something that might have bothered Ivan more if his own children didn't commit similar sins at least once a weekend. "I got the thruster system put in but couldn't tweak the output enough to safely compensate for the combined weight of me and the suit, which means flight is off the table. I realized I didn't have nearly enough money or parts to get my magnetic disruptor small enough, either. Actually, money and size held me back from most of the things I wanted to implement, with time tagging in as the pain-in-the-ass third."

"Yet you seem surprisingly upbeat."

"Well, duh. I might not have gotten everything I wanted, but I did manage the one that was the most important." Tori's grin was stretched from ear to ear, a combination of mischief and pride that would have left Ivan very worried if he were an enemy. As it was, it still made him mildly concerned.

"I did it, Ivan. It *worked* last night. It isn't perfect, and there's a lot of adjustments I need to cram in before we leave tonight, but I managed to create a successful prototype meta-suit. I can't tell you how that feels, after so many years of half-assing my way around makeshift labs and jerry-rigging parts to test concepts. Last night, I finally did something that was only a dream. I made my suit, Ivan. And tonight, I get to give it a genuine field test."

"That is a very high stakes scenario to be taking your first test drive in." Ivan didn't try to dissuade her precisely, but he did want to be sure she'd really thought things through. Smart as Tori was, she could also get caught up in her own ambition, which was precisely what had landed her inside Wade's vault in the first place. Having a meta-suit on the job could be a serious asset, but it could just as easily become a liability if things went awry.

"Give me a little credit here. This isn't my first robbery," Tori replied. "I checked everything thoroughly last night, and I'll do another sweep before I take it out. Plus, every device we factored into the plan is detachable, meaning that even if it all goes to shit, I can salvage what we need and dump the rest. I do still have my fire powers, no matter what else happens."

"It's a pragmatic approach, but would you really be willing to discard something you worked so hard on?" Ivan asked.

"Sure. It's just tech." Tori grabbed the syrup and squeezed the last few drops out, drawing desperate wheezes from the collapsing plastic. "The important part is the design and testing. Once I've actually got my schematics, rebuilding is just a matter of supplies and time. Though it would take me a while to save up enough to make another. Getting that prize money from our desert fight helped out a lot."

"Somehow I think you could make it work with a hundred and twenty-five thousand dollars." Ivan happened to tilt his glass of orange juice up at that moment, so it wasn't until several seconds later that he saw the stunned, dumbstruck face of his apprentice staring at him. "What?"

"What do you mean, what? You just casually mention the idea of me getting over a hundred grand and then don't explain what the hell you're talking about? Of course I'm waiting to hear more."

It was Ivan's turn to be puzzled as he set down his glass and met Tori's gaze. "I'm not sure where I lost you in this discussion. It can't have been at the math. Dividing five hundred by four isn't exactly advanced calculus."

"Five hundred by..." Tori's voice trailed off. The syrup near the edge of her plate started to bubble, a rare slip in her control of the ambient temperature. When she found her voice again, it was strangled and choked, like she was forcing each word out one by one. "Ivan, are you saying we get to *keep* the money from tonight's job?"

"Of course you get to keep it, you're the ones who are stealing it. Minus the guild's cut, I mean. Did you think we were going to have you steal half a million dollars and then spend it on new couches or something?"

"Well, no, but it just occurred to me... I mean, we're only apprentices," Tori pointed out.

"Today, you're only apprentices. If tonight goes well, you'll be full members. This is a guild of criminals, people who don't react well to people taking what's rightfully theirs. You do the work, you keep the rewards. That's always been our policy." Ivan rose from his chair, grabbed his dishes and took them into the kitchen, where he set them in the sink. Once he returned, Tori had finished her breakfast, but now had a new, nervous aura around her.

"You look worried," he noted.

"No shit," she shot back. "You just told me that if tonight's job goes well, I'm going to get a payday of over a hundred grand. Those kind of stakes will put anyone on edge."

"As opposed to, say, knowing that if you screwed up, it would probably cost you your life?"

Tori shook her head and got up from the table, dishes in hand as she made her way to the kitchen. "You don't get it, Ivan. That was just my life. This, this is fucking *money*."

*   *   *

"How are things?" Apollo stepped into the monitoring room—nicknamed the Chamber of Boredom by most of the other superheroes—and spoke to one of the few members of the AHC who didn't complain when getting put on monitoring duty. Stalwart Iron sat unmoving save for the precise motions of his fingers, screening through a variety of police and emergency reports. The AHC employed more than two dozen mundane humans whose job it was to find situations that required superheroes and dispatch those who were on duty, but it was policy to always have at least one cape, if not more, on hand at all times to oversee the operation. There were certain patterns one could recognize, hunches they could follow, a kind of intuition that only came from having been out in the field personally.

"A slight uptick in activity, though nothing outside normal parameters," Stalwart Iron replied, not bothering to look at Apollo. The mechanical man, salvaged from the lair of some mad scientist that had bitten off more than he could chew by going after a cape, often left others on edge. They never quite trusted artificial intelligence, but Apollo honestly preferred it. People could be so emotional and impractical; at least Stalwart Iron was predictable. Even if he'd been gifted with agency, that agency was still made of ones and zeroes. There were limits, and that made him more useful than ninety percent of the other superheroes Apollo worked with.

"Big world out there; it never gets completely quiet," Apollo said. "Just keep me in the loop if anything unusual comes up."

"What if... what if there is something that is not happening, but that I suspect might?" Stalwart Iron still didn't face Apollo, but the rhythm of his keystrokes slowed. Now this was unexpected; Stalwart Iron was rarely hesitant, always working with the surety that only a machine could manage.

"A hunch?" Apollo walked over to look at the screen Stalwart Iron had been working on.

"A theory, or perhaps a pattern that plays out irregularly," Stalwart Iron replied. "As you can see on the graph, criminal activities go through simple, very general cycles: increasing during hotter months, frequency dropping during the day, variables along those lines. However, in reviewing previous records, I noticed that sometimes, not always, we will see fluctuations like those that have come over the past week. Sudden, small events that seem random, followed by a brief pattern of diminished activity, which ends with a flurry of crime that stretches our personnel and resources thin. They don't flag anything in the system, though, because when the dust settles, there is almost always a minimum of collateral damage. But at least one high-end theft or robbery will have occurred in the chaos."

"I get it; someone fills the sky with smoke so we can't find the actual fire." Apollo scanned the graph that Stalwart was showing him, most of it little more than lines on a page. He'd never had a great head for numbers and he knew it, which was why he surrounded himself with people who didn't share his weakness. "And you think we're on track for one of these incidents?"

"I only know that it's possible. Even when all the lead up is there, the pattern only fully executes roughly forty percent of the time," Stalwart Iron replied. "However, if in the next five hours we see a significant drop-off, it would be entirely possible that we'll soon be hit by an influx of problems."

"I'm glad you brought this to my attention," Apollo said, gently patting Stalwart Iron's metal shoulder. He wasn't sure if the metal skin conducted touch or if the sentiment came through, but since Stalwart Iron seemed to understand human gestures, Apollo made a point of using them on him. "If the dip occurs, I want you to let me know right away. No matter what I'm doing, get in touch with me. Can you do that?"

"Yes, sir." Stalwart Iron nodded.

"Good man," Apollo said, his golden glow brightening in visible joy. "Thanks to that brain of yours, I've got a hunch of my own. Tonight, we're going to catch us a whole batch of brand-new villains."

*   *   *

A soft hiss filled the lab as Tori's left gauntlet locked in place on the coupler that ended at her elbow. She flexed her fingers, testing the responsiveness, and watched as the black metal hand covering her own matched her movements. With a moment of focus, she turned her hand to living fire and repeated the motion, nearly squealing with delight as the gauntlet obeyed her motion just like it had when flesh and bone were giving the orders.

Since she needed her fire to refuel the suit's batteries, and because the less corporeal she was the safer she was, it had been vital to find a way to manipulate her suit while in fire-form. After a lot of trial and error, she'd finally hit on the idea of using an inner material that not only converted her heat to energy but also measured the temperature at every point of contact. Since the core parts of her burned hotter, when she pressed a flaming finger to a spot in the gauntlet, it responded the way it would if it were the pressure of her flesh trying to move it. Admittedly, the system wasn't as precise as she wanted it to be, but a hundred thousand dollars would buy more than enough components to fine tune the mechanism.

418

Allowing her hand to go back to normal, Tori rose from her seat, noting that her heavy steps echoed off the walls. With a quick flick on her belt, she activated the noise cancellation system, designed to match and destroy every sound her suit made before it could travel more than three inches from the source. Another step, and this time there was silence. She left it functioning until she made it across the room then turned it off. Handy a tool as it was, the damn thing gobbled power, so it was best used only when needed.

Tori was near her work table where the final piece of her project awaited her when she caught sight of herself in the mirror. It likely wouldn't have even registered to her, except that the person staring back was so foreign that for a moment, she thought she was being attacked. The high-pitched whine of weapons readying filled the air before her brain caught up to her reactions and Tori forced herself to relax. She was on edge; that was the only explanation for readying an attack on her own reflection. Then again, she couldn't blame herself. The person staring back at her was a far cry from what Tori Rivas normally saw in the mirror.

Gone was the business attire of Tori the intern and the default costume of Tori the apprentice. This woman wore a suit of black metal, with a few red accents added on in a manner she liked to think was tasteful. The suit covered her from the neck down, occasionally bulky and misshapen enough to betray that she'd focused on functionality over design. Oddly, the asymmetrical bits and disproportional lumps didn't bother her, nor did the knowledge that only two hours of hard work had tucked away the last of the wires that had hitherto been exposed. She'd have plenty of time to refine the design, to make it sleek and cool and the sort of thing that would set other tech geeks' hearts aflutter. But there was something special about this suit, about her first functioning prototype. Ugly as it was, she knew it would always have a place in her heart that the other iterations could only try to live up to.

She reached over and picked up the final piece from her work table, a black metal helmet with red lenses covering the eyes. Slipping it on was an ordeal, only possible because she'd knotted her long hair into a tight braid. Finally, she heard the telltale click and hiss as it joined to the suit's neck. Tori looked in the mirror again, the last traces of her civilian identity now concealed. She cycled through the camera's enhanced modes, checking the night and thermal vision first then making sure the zoom functioned as well. Everything was working. One last shift to fire-form confirmed that the digital display would hold up, at least so long as she didn't crank up the temperature too much.

Tori marveled at the person in the mirror for a bit longer, amazed at how completely she'd disappeared in her own device. There was no shred of Tori remaining, neither the apprentice nor the thief nor the intern with a secret.

419

This was someone completely new, a version of herself that had only lived in the shadows of her mind until she donned her helmet for the first time.

"Hephaestus." Her voice was purposely warped by the helmet's circuitry, made harsh and deep but still easy to understand. "It's a pleasure to meet you." It was, too. It truly, honestly was. "The guild is expecting great things from you. And I'm expecting so much more."

A knock came from the door to the basement, her sensors easily picking it up and identifying the origin. "Tori," Ivan called down from above. "It's almost time."

Hesitantly, Tori reached up and removed the helmet from her face. The rest could be covered with a large enough coat, and if they entered the car inside the garage, no one would see her strange boots. But she couldn't very well ride around in Ivan's car with her helmet on, no matter how much she disliked having to take it off.

"I'll be up in a few seconds," Tori yelled. She looked down at the helmet in her hands, at the face of Hephaestus, and smiled. "Soon. Just not quite yet. We have to get to the guild first. As soon as we do, I'll introduce you to everyone. It should make for quite an entertaining start to the night."

Chapter 63

Beverly hadn't exactly thought Tori was overstating her abilities after watching her cobble together a sonic cannon in the middle of the desert, but she did find it hard believe a fellow apprentice could make a functioning meta-suit with nothing more than an intern's salary, some supplies on a tab, and a few extra grand. Most people weren't that gifted, it was true; but Beverly had failed to account for Tori's resourcefulness and years spent getting by with only what she could salvage or steal.

She let out a gasp of shock as her friend walked into the familiar lounge where they'd done so much planning, clad in metal and tech everywhere but on her head. And even that was temporary, if the helmet under her left arm was any indication.

"Well, great, way to make me feel under-dressed, asshole," she quipped. Beverly's own costume was the same as Lance and Warren's, the default one she'd been given as an apprentice. Only Lance had added an accessory, a large plastic tube slung across his chest that served for function, not fashion.

"You had two days, you could have sewn something together," Tori suggested.

"Screw that. I was catching up on the sleep I missed over the weekend." She walked around Tori slowly, taking in all the strange switches and mechanisms built into the suit. Across the room, Lance and Warren were heading over to do the same, clearly marveling at the technological wonder she'd walked into their lounge.

"Why is the helmet off?" Lance asked. "And how can you operate the suit without it on? Don't you control these things with your brain?"

"Some suits work that way, but I had to go a different route," Tori replied. "And the helmet is off because we'd barely gotten in the front door when we ran into Arcanicus, who nearly hexed me. Pseudonym suggested I keep my familiar face exposed, at least until we were out on the job."

"Probably a smart call," Beverly agreed. "So, does all this stuff really work?"

"Not everything, and not perfectly, but the gear we'll be counting on has been checked up, down, and sideways," Tori assured her. "And if it all goes to hell, I've got my apprentice costume on under here, so I can throw on the mask and still pitch in."

"At least we'd be a matching set." Warren looked down at his own outfit with a weary sigh. "Does the guild provide tailors? I never gave much thought to a costume before, but if I have to pull a job, I think I'd prefer something a little more... me."

"Pretty sure the guild has everything," Lance replied. "Long as you've got the cash for it."

Warren stared at his outfit for a bit longer then raised his head. "I guess this will do for a while."

"Or you can put your share of the money toward some nice duds." Tori worked very hard to hide her relief at discovering she wasn't the only one who hadn't realized their job came with a payday. "I mean, even after the guild cut, we're each taking home over a hundred thousand dollars. Unless you want an outfit made of diamonds, I bet you'll be good."

All three of her fellow apprentices stopped looking at the suit and turned their attention to the woman within. As quickly and humbly as she could manage, Tori told them that whatever they brought in that night would be theirs to keep and split per guild rules. While Lance and Warren took the news like they'd just won the lottery—which, monetarily speaking, they might as well have—Beverly narrowed her eyes and make a "tsk" sound between her tongue and teeth.

"Those crafty bastards. It's just one trap after another with them, isn't it?"

"Um, Beverly, we were just told we get to keep the money," Lance said. "How is that anything but great news?"

"Because it's meant to get us in trouble. Think about it. We get to keep all the money we score, right?"

Tori nodded. "That's what Pseudonym told me, and since he's on the council, I'd say that's as close to gospel as we're going to get around here."

"So, we know we have to bring back a minimum of five hundred grand," Beverly said, spinning in place so that she could look at Lance and Warren. "That's what we planned for. We picked the exhibits that we knew would have the best ratio of low security to high yield. We even chose several backups in case something went wrong with those. Right now, the four of us have a good plan to get in and out of the Dash City Museum with just over half a million dollars. But now, that number isn't just an arbitrary goal. It's a payday. It's what we'll split once we get home."

"All of which sounds pretty good," Warren pointed out.

"Exactly," Beverly agreed, giving a nod so forceful it sent a few strands of hair flying. "It sounds so good that once we're in the museum, we might decide to up our take a little more. Maybe grab a few more exhibits, ones we weren't going to risk grabbing before. When that goal isn't arbitrary, suddenly restraint seems less important. After all, getting in and out are the hard parts, and

422

that's covered. We get greedy, we stretch ourselves thin, and we go off the plan. And that's when we make a mistake."

It sounded like the ravings of someone with severe paranoia... except that the more they all thought about it, the more sense Beverly's take on things made. As soon as the money had become real, the entire mission had taken on a whole different feeling. Once they were actually there with priceless objects in arm's reach, how tempting would it be to up their haul, just by a few thousand here and there?

"It's not a trap," Tori said, breaking the silence that had fallen at the end of Beverly's rant. "I mean, it is, but it's not really. It's part of the test. This is supposed to see how we would act as guild members, right?"

"That's what they told us," Lance agreed.

"Then this is something they'd definitely need to check. When the money is real, when we've got genuine temptation in front of us, can we make the smart decisions instead of the greedy ones?" Tori smacked one metal-gauntlet-covered hand into the other, resulting in a clang that made even Warren jump. "That's an issue that will come up on every single job we pull. They'd be idiots not to have some aspect of it in our exam."

"Meaning it's not dickish. That's nice of them," Lance said.

"No, it's still a bit dickish, I'm only saying it has a purpose," Tori told him. "Something we didn't even consider was being tested without us realizing it. And if there's one element like that, there are bound to be more."

"Just what are you getting at?" Warren asked.

"She's saying that we treat this job like the real thing, and we stick to the plan the council approved no matter what." Beverly had calmed down a bit after Tori's explanation, though she still wore a wary expression as her eyes darted about the room. "We put stealth and safety above all else, we stick to the targets we know how to get, and we prioritize escaping without leaving evidence of a ruckus."

"And when things inevitably go awry?" Lance asked. He noticed some skepticism in their faces and crossed his arms. "What? Given the points Tori and Beverly just made, there's no way they'll let us have a clean and easy trial. Sooner or later, something will go wrong, even if they have to make it happen, just to see how we handle ourselves when the shit hits the fan."

"Damn it... Lance is probably right," Tori agreed. "We can't really plan for that, either. Just don't panic, first off, and make sure we communicate and work together. But if ever you're in doubt, just try and figure out something that sticks to the guild's code. If you aren't breaking that, then anything you do has a good shot at being okay."

"And what if we can't help breaking the code?" Warren asked.

Tori considered the question carefully. There was only one answer no matter how she looked at it. "Breaking the code is one of the only real crimes you can commit inside this guild. That alone is bad enough, but breaking it during a test to see if you're responsible and smart enough to function as a guild member... we all watched what happened last Monday. You might as well kill yourself and save them the trouble."

*   *   *

"Nervous?" Thuggernaut took the open chair next to Ivan, who was dressed in his bland Pseudonym costume. Around them, the other mentors and members of the council milled about. Others were already seated as they waited for the large display in front of them to crackle to life. This wasn't like the other lessons or tests where they were free to observe in whatever manner suited them best. Tonight the membership of four applicants would be determined, which meant the council had to watch it together and render an official verdict. The only other people allowed to be present were the apprentices' mentors, called in to ensure they weren't tempted to intervene.

"I'd rather not kill my student." Ivan wasn't sure how it was for the others, if they'd be handed the duty of dealing with their apprentice's failures or if it would be pawned off on someone else to handle. Tori, however, would die by no other hand but his own. Even if no one else demanded it, even if he weren't one of the few that could kill living fire, he would still insist upon it. As her teacher, he owed her at least that much.

"We did all we could, taught them as well as they'd learn," Thuggernaut replied. "From here on out, it's all up to them."

"If that were true, I'd feel much easier." Ivan's eyes drifted across the room to Wade, who was wearing every bit of his own meta-suit except the helmet. It was sleek and dynamic, billions of dollars above the makeshift one Tori had assembled under Ivan's house. As the guild's leader, Wade never let an entrance test pass without throwing a curveball or two. It was a sound policy that Ivan agreed with in principle—seeing how one reacted under pressure was equally important to seeing how well they could craft a plan. But that was in principle. Now that Ivan had a student of his own about to be thrust into chaos, he found himself wondering just how necessary that policy really was.

"I've been here a long time, and I've seen more guild applicants come through than I'd have cared to." Thuggernaut gazed at the still-empty screen as if he could get a sneak peek of what was to come just by staring hard enough. "Nothing in this world is certain, but our kids have a shot. A good one at that. And they've already learned to work together, which gives them a big leg up."

424

"It's possible," Ivan said. "But there's another way to look at it. Because they have already figured out the importance of acting as a cohesive unit, Doctor Mechaniacal will factor that in and increase the difficulty of his unexpected variables proportionally."

Thuggernaut's wide face drooped, and a few shades of color left his skin. "You're saying..."

Ivan nodded grimly. "I'm saying that them being so exceptional may ultimately end up getting them a much more difficult, and possibly deadly, test."

*   *   *

Tori had expected Doctor Mechaniacal, or Ivan, or someone like Stasis or Xelas to be waiting for them as they entered Sanctum. Someone to give them last-minute reminders or a word of encouragement before their trial began. Instead, the only people behind the large door were Tunnel Vision, standing silently until it was time to fulfill the duty they'd been contracted for. Only when she saw the nearly empty room did it truly hit home: they were on their own. From this point forward, all they had was themselves, the resources they'd bought, and the plans they'd made. No one was going to be nearby if they needed help. Even Tunnel Vision's services came with the caveat that they wouldn't open a portal if it might compromise guild security.

"We have to go to the teleportation chambers," the female half of Tunnel Vision said. "Except for there, everything in Sanctum is secured from spatial anomalies."

That was all she said before she and her male counterpart both turned and moved for a door, not even bothering to see if the others were keeping up. Tori and the other apprentices hurried along, following Tunnel Vision through a series of winding hallways and passing through several well-secured doors before arriving in a room so big Tori suspected it could have easily housed a small jet.

"The security system in here is separate, so we can temporarily disable it," the male member of Tunnel Vision explained. "We will do so now, to send you out. When your job is complete, contact us using the communication devices provided and we will open another portal, assuming we can do so securely." As he spoke, the woman removed several small electronics from a bag at her side and passed them out. Each was small, barely bigger than a jump drive, with a single button set in the center. Curiously, there was no uniformity to them, as if they'd been made by four entirely different people. As Tori accepted hers and tucked it into a hidden compartment on her suit's torso, she realized that they were built that way as camouflage. If they all looked different, it would be hard to link them to a central provider should they be lost.

"All you have to do is press the button," the man continued. "Don't worry if it happens by accident; we'll check what's happening before opening the portal. Even so, try not to let that happen. The moment you intentionally call us to the time the portal opens should last no longer than ten seconds. Try to stay together, and, as you should know, portals will only be opened in secure locations. You no doubt are aware from your research that the interior of the museum is too well-surveilled to count as such a location. Do you have any questions?"

Tori looked at the others, who were in turn looking at each other, all waiting to see if anyone had something to ask. When it became clear there was nothing left to be said, she lifted the helmet from under her arm and slowly lowered it past her face. This time was easier; it took only a few moments before the telltale hiss and click told her that the last piece of her suit was in place.

"Looks like it's time to start," Tori said, taking a few people by surprise with her altered voice. "Remember, stick to the plan if at all possible, and the code above all else. Also, from here on, villain names only until we're back inside the guild. Let's get this done quickly and safely."

She turned her head to the pair of people waiting for orders and gave a small nod, barely perceptible through all the armor and tech surrounding her.

"Tunnel Vision, open it up. It's time to go to work."

Chapter 64

The Dash City Museum sat in what had once been the heart of the city's downtown district. However, zoning and cheaper properties had slowly migrated most of the offices, restaurants, and shops farther south, leaving the formerly thriving area designated as a "historic district." On top of getting less foot traffic, the buildings around the museum were not always in use. In fact, some had sat vacant for over a year.

A small structure, more shack than building, which had once housed a company that sold big scoops of ice cream on thick waffle cones, sat unassuming until a hole in space appeared and four figures stepped over from a secured building a half-dozen states away. As quickly as it had appeared, the portal vanished, leaving them alone inside the cramped shack, staring out across a small section of parking lot at their target.

"First things first, we need eyes on everything," Hephaestus announced. "Pest Control, that's you. After that, we need to get control of their exterior cameras and alarms. Glyph, you know what to do." Reaching into a compartment on her belt, Hephaestus pulled out a device that had started its life as a Walkman. She handed it to Glyph, whose right-hand fingers had already begun to glow as he traced a symbol on his left forearm. No more drawing in sand, it seemed. Whatever Hephaestus thought about Balaam, his tutelage was clearly paying off.

Her eyes carefully traced Glyph's movements as he constructed the symbol. Technically, putting the device in place would have been easier for Hephaestus, but Glyph had another job to do when he got close to the building and he could only power so many runes at a time.

Pest Control, meanwhile, had summoned dozens of flies, which were streaming one by one out of the shack on their way toward the museum. His eyes were closed as he saw through their fractured vision, a feat which was almost as impressive as summoning the creatures in the first place.

"Exterior is clear," Pest Control relayed. "Just like we hoped, everything around is closed this late, so there's no foot traffic. Cameras everywhere, though."

"Shouldn't be an issue." Glyph finished drawing his rune. A small burst of light rippled off it. Just like that, he seemed to shimmer. Hephaestus had to strain her eyes and focus to tell that he was there. If she lost track of him, she doubted she'd be able to regain it.

He rose from his seat and stepped through the rear door, not bothering to hide his movements in the slightest. "Pest Control, can you give me a fly? I don't know if you'll be able to see me if I signal you once we're clear, but I assume you can tell if I kill one of your insects."

"Isn't that what the comms are for?" Pest Control tapped the side of his head where a small earpiece was resting. An identical one rested in the ear of every other apprentice, save for Hephaestus, who'd simply patched her own helmet's system in to the channel.

"Technically, yes, but until we've got this place secure, I'd like to avoid using them as much as possible. Secure as they are, high-end scanners exist," Glyph pointed out.

"Better safe than sorry, I guess. Luckily, with this few insects out, I'd definitely notice losing one." Pest Control held out his hand and a fly appeared in it. It buzzed over until it was hanging in the air before Glyph and made no move to escape as the half-visible man reached out and grabbed it. Glyph tucked it carefully away in one of the many pockets of his costume.

"Once I've got the box in place and the guards handled, I'll squish it. That means you're all clear to approach." Then Glyph was gone, all but impossible to track as he made his way across the small stretch of empty parking lot.

This was the part Hephaestus had been dreading the most: she and Bahamut had to sit patiently and wait, unable to affect the outcome of the all-important first step. There was just no way around it, though. She'd built the tech as best she could; all she could do now was trust Glyph to get it in place. Once inside, she'd handle hacking the more complex, delicate systems, but he was the only one who could make the first approach unseen. All they could do was be patient while Pest Control scattered his flies, the tools that would give them a surveillance system even as they disabled the one the guards depended on.

"Something I wanted to ask," Bahamut said, her fidgeting betraying how little she enjoyed sitting around as well. "That box of yours is going to disable the exterior cameras and alarms, plus break off their communication, right? So does that mean that, even if we miss a few guards, they can't call for capes?"

"With a weaker security system, yes. But this is Level Three," Hephaestus told her. "The line to the AHC is separate, and any attempt to tamper with it sets off a call. On the upside, it's not automatic. The capes don't want to come out every time a squirrel trips an exterior alarm. A guard has to activate it manually."

They had, in truth, already gone over most of this; they were talking now simply for the sake of talking, as it let them focus on something other than the fear about whether their crime would even get off the ground. It was a distraction, nothing more, which was why neither was bothered when Pest Control opened his eyes and interrupted them.

"Glyph just killed my fly. Time to head out."

No one hesitated or debated; there would be no point to it. Either Glyph had succeeded or he simply believed he had. Whichever was true didn't change their next step. This was the only way to move forward. They stepped out of the shack one by one, with Hephaestus flipping on her sound dampener for the trek across the concrete parking lot. Her fuel cells were fine for the moment, and assuming things went smoothly, there would be no need to drain them. Still, she kept an eye on their levels, readying to juice them up if they dipped below eighty percent. This wasn't the night to take pointless risks.

When they arrived at the shadow-covered expanse of the museum's front entrance, Glyph was waiting for them, wiping the rune from his hand and erasing his shimmery cloaking. Behind him, a new rune glowed on the door, though it lacked the vibrancy they'd come to associate with an active casting. "Got the box hooked in to the electrical system just like you said," he announced. "And I've got the guard spell ready to go, just needs one more piece added."

The knot of tension in Hephaestus's gut tightened. While the waiting had been her least favorite part of the plan, this was unquestionably the most dangerous. Here everything teetered on a precipice. Glyph would use a spell that was supposed to put every person inside the building at that moment into a harmless slumber. Unfortunately, people with strong enough minds and forceful wills could often shake off the effects of mental magic, which left the possibility that some of the guards would manage to stay awake. All it took was one to trip the big alarm and draw the capes. If that happened, they'd be lucky to escape, let alone finish the job. Making things more difficult, none of them could go inside until after the spell was cast, lest they be caught in it and knocked off their guard as well.

"Let me get my wasps," Pest Control said. A small swarm of unnatural creatures, wasps the size of small hamsters with strange purple stingers, manifested around him. Their hope was that his insects wouldn't be impacted by magic crafted for humans, but just in case, he was keeping his attackers nearby. Worst case scenario, he hoped to at least see which guards were fighting off the trance before he lost his fly eyes in the sky.

While Pest Control gathered his troops, Hephaestus checked the front door. Sure enough, her device had triggered enough false readings to make the security system think it was daytime, thus deactivating most of the alarms and locks. The cameras had been trickier, especially since they were integrated with the electrical system, but with a little ingenuity and a lot of experimental magnetic bursts, she'd made it work. They only had a half an hour, though; after that, the device was set to melt itself into slag. No evidence left to examine or trace.

At least unlocking the door meant they were one hurdle down. Once Glyph triggered the spell, it would be up to Pest Control and her to pick off any straggling guards. Ideally, the ones who weren't immediately brought down would think they were suffering nothing more than a wave of sleepiness, but these weren't exactly doddering members of the Mayberry police force. With this much money to protect, the museum had hired people who were smart and tough. Just hopefully not too many of them.

"I'm good," Pest Control announced. In addition to his wasps, he'd also gathered a fresh swarm of flies to serve as replacements if his current batch took an unexpected nap. "Hephaestus, I'll give you starting locations before we head in then let you know if I find any others."

"Quick and quiet, that's the name of the game," Hephaestus replied. She turned her helmet toward Glyph to catch his attention. "We're ready whenever you are."

Fingers once again glowing, Glyph turned to the waiting symbol and made a final line near the center. The rune burst into light. Each of them could feel the wave of power that washed off of it and cascaded through the building even as the symbol itself began to fade into nothingness.

"Guards are going down," Pest Control announced, eyes closed. A small bead of sweat ran down his creased forehead, and his hands were clenched tightly into fists. "I'm trying to keep my flies up, but they're starting to drop too. So far so good, though. We're getting... shit, one just shook it off. Now another. Another. Fuck, we've got at least three still up, and one looks suspicious. We have to move!"

Without a moment's pause, Hephaestus threw open the door and burst into the museum's lobby, her heavy footsteps thankfully silenced as she pounded down across the tile floor. Pest Control was hot on her heels, the distinctive sound of buzzing filling the air as his minions spread out and raced through the air to their targets.

"Hephaestus, can you make it to the Egyptian wing?" Pest Control's voice crackled though the comms despite their proximity. "That's where the suspicious guard is, and I don't think my bugs are fast enough."

"On it." She turned on her heel and bolted down a hallway to the right. Their team knew the museum's layout backwards and forwards; it was something she'd insisted on during the planning phase. Unfortunately, that meant she knew how far of a run it would be to the Egyptian wing, which wouldn't have been worrying if the guard office weren't on the way. If she

430

didn't make it in time, the guard would sound the alarm and the capes would come.

Which just meant that Hephaestus had to make damn sure she wasn't too late.

*   *   *

The placid boredom of the monitoring room was long gone. Hurried reports and frantic calls followed one another so quickly that sentences blurred together into one chaotic cloud that hung heavily over the employees' heads. Just as Stalwart Iron had predicted, the lull of the afternoon had given way to a sudden uptick in disasters that demanded superhero attention.

"Got a subway car stalled on the tracks," came a voice from the crowd. "No chance of injury, but the rerouting system is busted, which means that until we get in there, every other car is stuck behind it, leaving hundreds trapped."

"Send in Cresscriss," Apollo ordered. "He's got that alien tech that turns things weightless. Should make the car easy to pull out."

"Small fire in an abandoned warehouse district that could spread to populated areas if left unchecked," said another one of the operators.

"Flameingo and Aqua Bomb should have finished up the forest fire by now, get them over to the warehouses as soon as they're done." Apollo stepped away from the chaos for a moment, allowing the operators to handle the smaller incidents as he made his way over to the sole terminal staffed by another superhero.

Stalwart Iron wasn't snapping off orders or yelling at the operators; in fact, he wasn't saying anything at all. He merely watched his three screens silently, going over every report and dispatch as it came in with the single-minded focus that only a mechanical brain could manage. Apollo leaned down, ostensibly to stare at the screens, though they were little more than gibberish to him. In reality, he simply wanted to speak without others overhearing the conversation. None of the mundanes knew about the guild, and Apollo saw no reason to change that. Hell, he even kept actual members of the AHC on a need-to-know basis. The tolerance of criminals was not something he considered a point of pride for the Alliance.

"Find anything?"

"Nothing aside from the same bombardment that's hitting everyone else's screen," Stalwart Iron replied. "But I'm trying to ignore that as best I can. If this is organized chaos, then anything we're seeing is something they want us to look at, which means it serves their purposes. We have to look where they aren't guiding our eyes." He paused, checking the screens over once more, then

431

began to type so quickly that Apollo feared his keyboard might break. "That gives me an idea. I've been trying to see a pattern in all this, but what I should be looking for is the absence of one."

A few more clacks on the keyboard, and Stalwart Iron pulled up a new screen, this one a map that Apollo recognized well. "Why am I looking at Dash City?"

"Because it's one of the only major metropolitan areas that *isn't* seeing a huge upswing in crime and destruction tonight," Stalwart Iron explained. "Everything we're working with is still theoretical, but if we assume there is agency to these incidents, wouldn't it stand to reason they would keep their actual target as clear of superheroes as possible?"

"It does make sense," Apollo agreed. "But even if you're right, Dash City is a big place, with a lot of places worth robbing. We have no idea when or where they'll strike. Can we still find them?"

"Let me do some digging, sir. If they're out there, I'll uncover them." Stalwart Iron went back to his screen, and Apollo walked away to let him work. If anyone could uncover the guild's target, it would be Stalwart Iron. Once that happened, it was just a matter of sending out the new team and making sure the press was on standby.

Really, Apollo's only regret was that he wouldn't be able to see the looks on the older guild members' faces as their entire new crop of criminals was simultaneously wiped out.

Chapter 65

Hephaestus barreled through the "Hometown Heroes" section of the museum, darting past exhibits dedicated to the capes from Dash City like Combust, Baron Peppermint, and Dapper Doll. She hurdled over a stone bench, meta-suit giving her speed and strength that would have been impossible on her own. Even with the boosts, she was still cutting it close, which was why she'd decided to take a risk. If she'd correctly predicted the guard's moves, he would try and reach the office to sound the alarm as soon as possible. If he'd taken the far route to investigate things further, then she would miss him completely. It was a big gamble, but there were no riskless choices available to her. That was what it meant to be a villain.

As she whipped around a corner, her heart sank. By her estimates, the guard should have at least made it to this hall by now. If it was empty, that meant she'd made the wrong choice. Hopeless as it seemed, she flicked over to her thermal cameras just to be sure. Her sinking heart leapt up to her throat. There he was, tucked carefully behind a nearby wall, hands held in a position that left no doubt he'd drawn his gun. But the suit's silencers were still functional. How had he known she was coming?

Hephaestus spared a quick glance backward. Only then did she notice that her foot had clipped the edge of the bench, sending a spray of small concrete chunks across the floor. She hadn't heard it over her own panting, but for someone moving carefully and listening well, there was no doubt the noise would be a beacon of approach.

So, he knew someone was coming, but probably not where she was. That would only last until he peeked around the corner, at which point bullets would no doubt begin to fly. Aside from alerting every other conscious guard that something was up, there was also the chance that a good shot would damage her suit; she hadn't had time to adequately test its durability. She needed to stop him before he got off a single bullet.

Hephaestus began to run once more. For just this first moment, she knew where he was and he couldn't track her. If she was fast enough, there was a chance she could still take him by surprise.

Quick as she was, Hephaestus was still a few seconds short of catching the guard completely unaware. He spun around the corner, gun raised at the ready, just as she arrived. For a fleeting second, complete shock overtook him as he watched a metal person racing toward him at full speed. Then his eyes narrowed, and he raised the gun a few inches.

With no time to think, Hephaestus moved on pure instinct. Her right hand closed around the muzzle of the gun just as the first shot went off, and her left fired a series of small darts into the guard's chest. Resistant as his mind might have been to magic, it didn't have the same immunity to chemicals, and within seconds he was slipping gently to the floor. Hephaestus lowered him carefully, right hand still covering the gun, until he was safely resting on the tile. Only then did she pull back her gauntlet to survey the damage.

On the upside, the sound dampeners had managed to suppress the gun's roar and her gauntlet had successfully protected her hand. On the downside, however, the palm of the gauntlet was wrecked. The ray that concentrated thermal energy, the one she'd first shown Ivan and Xelas a prototype of, was useless. Without the focal point for release, it couldn't be trusted. Granted, she wasn't supposed to need it in a simple robbery, but she'd sure felt a lot better knowing it was there.

Flexing her fingers, she noted that the glove's responsiveness was also hindered. She could still use the hand for punching and other blunt-work, but anything delicate was off the table. That could be a problem, because she still had quite a bit of security hacking left to do before the night was done.

"Hephaestus." Pest Control's whispered voice crackled in her ear. "I've neutralized my guards, and I can't see any others. Were you able to subdue yours?"

"Yeah, I got him," Hephaestus confirmed. "He's safe and sound and will sleep until halfway through tomorrow morning."

"Glad to hear it. Glyph and Bahamut, that means you're both clear to enter. First phase of our infiltration is complete," Pest Control announced.

One down, two to go. Hephaestus tested her gauntlet one more time then hurried off to meet the others at the lobby, a slight spring in her step. Busted ray aside, that first part had gone pretty smoothly, and that was the riskiest part. From here on, so long as they stayed smart and careful, they shouldn't have any more serious hurdles to clear.

*   *   *

Donald was doing his best to hide his nerves, but it was a losing battle. The costume that had been designed for him—a reinforced dark silver number with electric blue highlights—felt natural despite its weight. After all, the garment and all its doubles hanging in his closet had been made specifically for him. Ren stood nearby, his own outfit more like gladiator armor, sections strapped on to offer protection while not restricting movement. These outfits should have made him feel like they were official, real superheroes waiting on their orders to go do genuine good work. Instead, he felt like a child wearing a Halloween costume, just waiting to be called out on his falsehood. Plus, his stomach was churning so much Donald feared he might vomit on the new outfit before it ever saw the light of day.

"You okay? Your face is a little green." The brunette woman next to him, real name Irene and code name Cold Shoulder, stared at him from under her own icy blue-and-white mask. Donald hadn't been given anything to cover his head, as he was already known and would spend most of his fighting time in some sort of armor anyway. Apollo said it would better develop his name as a brand to stay recognizable, at least when out of combat.

"I'll be okay, just kind of nervous," Donald admitted. "Seems like things are pretty crazy out there."

"Why are you nervous? You've actually had real fights already. Two of them, in fact. I'm the rookie." Irene had been added to "his and Ren's team" (Apollo's choice of words, not Donald's) earlier in the week. Ostensibly, it was to even out their lineup, as Donald was primarily good at ranged combat and Ren only fought in melee. Irene could take either position to back them up as needed. Unfortunately, all of that was theoretical as she'd never gotten the chance to test her powers outside a training ground.

"To be honest, it's the waiting that's getting to me," Donald admitted. He looked around the sparse room they were in, stocked only with water, sodas, and energy bars. It was where they'd been instructed to wait until their deployment orders came, and with every passing minute, it felt more and more like some gray-carpeted prison cell. "The other times I fought, there wasn't really a chance to think about it. I just sort of got thrown into battle. Criminals broke into my office, a monster appeared at the club we were at, stuff just happened. This is the first time I've had to sit around and contemplate what's coming."

"None of us knows what's coming," Ren said. He'd been pacing the room; his own tension wasn't suited to being bottled up while sitting around. "It might be simple rescue work. Lifting beams, clearing rubble, moving people to safety. We've already debuted, so there's no need for us to put on any sort of show."

"Only some of us have debuted," Irene muttered, crossing her arms as she looked away. Donald and Ren exchanged a brief, uncomfortable look. Neither of them was so dense that they hadn't realized Apollo seemed to favor them over the other candidates, but it wasn't until Irene was brought on board that they started to see how big the gap was. None of the others were getting personal coaching sessions, or hand-picked code names, or high-level consulting. The only reason Irene was ready to go in the first place was that once

435

Apollo had chosen her to join them, he'd fast-tracked her through all the setup processes so she'd be prepared.

"I'm sure that whatever Apollo sends us out to do, it will be the right assignment," Donald said. "Both for you to get your name out there, and for us to do our part in keeping the world safe. He hasn't steered us wrong yet."

"If it's another weird rhino-monster, I just hope this time I can get a few licks in." Ren flashed Donald a smile that, while technically more animal than human, still managed to convey a sense of friendship. At least, it did for Donald. From the way Irene stiffened up next to him, she might only have gotten the surface appearance of a monster bearing its fangs.

"You'll have to move quickly," Donald replied. He gently patted the computer on his wrist, inside of which were dozens of items available at a touch. "I've been leveling up these bad boys all week. This time, I could get it in one shot."

"Big talk, but let's see how big those shots are," Ren said.

"Just stay clear when I get going. I doubt even you want to try and shrug off one of these blasts."

"That goes for both of you on my front," Irene said. "I'm a good shot but not a great one, and I've always been a fan of the 'spray and pray' philosophy on ranged combat."

"Don't worry, Ren's pretty quick when he needs to be," Donald assured her. "And if I'm in your field of targets, then things have already gone really freaking wrong."

"Freaking?" Ren asked, lifting a furry eyebrow.

Donald shrugged. "We're supposed to be superheroes, you know? I figured I'd try to get in the habit of not cursing while I was in costume."

"Well, shut down the papers. We've got another Lodestar on our hands, folks!" Though Irene's words were snippy, there was humor in them, which put Donald's stomach at ease. The more they could come together as a team, the better a chance they stood once they finally had to leave this room.

*   *   *

Art, aside from being a risky fiscal investment and a difficult market to predict, was also a thief's best friend. Jewels had only as much inherent value as one gave them, which was technically true for all things but always seemed a bit truer when dealing with shiny rocks. Pottery and sculpture, priceless though they could be, were also a pain in the ass to transport and lost nearly all value with the slightest scratch or ding. Fossils and prehistoric relics were often too cumbersome to carry and had a black market audience limited to the rich with odd tastes and mad scientists trying to clone extinct species.

But the paintings of masters respected through the ages, those were nearly as good as stealing cash. Better, in fact, because a painting worth hundreds of thousands of dollars could be carefully rolled into a tube, whereas carrying that much in physical currency would get very tiring very quickly. Plus, there was always a market for the classics thanks to an abundance of wealthy people who would happily hide away such treasures for their own enjoyment. Unlike jewels, which really only held worth when they could be shown off, a painting was something that could be appreciated in secret and therefore its high price tag was justified.

The Dash City Museum knew all of this, of course, which was why the truly priceless pieces were under so much security that even a poorly aimed, particularly forceful sneeze would send a dozen automated security measures into effect. The museum had spared no expense, protecting paintings that would fetch millions of dollars on the black market with an almost equally costly system designed to stop all but the most powerful criminals. And *that* was why the four villains clustered together in the main wing of the "Famous Painters through the Ages" section weren't so much as even glancing at those priceless artworks.

"Okay, I've got my remote system access set up," Hephaestus announced at last, looking up from the small tablet she'd produced from one of her suit's dozens of compartments. "The USB will melt once we're done, which means we don't need to go back for it. As soon as I try to trick the system, we're back on the clock."

"I really hope you pull this off," Pest Control said. He'd taken the large tubular holster off his back and laid it on the ground. Inside were four smaller plastic tubes, though these lacked the strap to wrap around someone's chest. "Our Plan B here is really shitty."

"Speak for yourself. I think I can cut them out faster than she can hack them free," Bahamut replied. Currently, she was a green dragon who lumbered over them, ready for the event that the hacking plan failed and they had to finish things off with a smash and grab. It was far from ideal, as such a tactic would alert the authorities, leave evidence, and perhaps get them pursued, but it was much better than going back to the guild empty-handed.

"It should work," Hephaestus said, though whether she was trying to convince herself or her team was up for debate. "These displays sometimes get changed out, so the system has releases built in for when that happens. Now, the really high-end stuff requires, like, ten layers of verification, but they move around these lesser exhibits all the time as new pieces come in. I *should* be able to dupe the system."

Hephaestus looked up from her tablet, waiting for more questions or comments, only to realize that everyone was staring back at her. There was nothing else to say unless she wanted to change the plan. She didn't, not only because working her magic with her left hand had been a pain in the ass, but rather because she didn't have a better one to offer up. It was all on her. If she outsmarted the system, they got a nice payday. If she'd failed to account for something or the security was better than her trickery, things were about to get really hectic, really fast.

All worrying would do was waste their precious time, though. Hephaestus clicked the startup sequence for her program, began to say a prayer, and then realized that stealing probably wasn't the sort of thing one was supposed to turn to the heavens for help with.

She held her breath instead as the sequences played out on her screen. Her mind flashed back to that night at Indigo Technologies when she'd let her arrogance lead her right into an inescapable trap. She'd worked so hard and come so far since then, but it was always possible she'd made another mistake. This time, if she failed, the alarm would trip and her villainy would be over before it had really begun. She waited to hear the telltale screech of high-pitched sirens screaming through the air, all but ruining their chances of—

Whoosh.

The airlock on one of the nearest paintings, a carefully-chosen target selected for its recent upswing in value thanks to shifting tastes in the art world, released loudly as the frame pulled slightly away from the canvas. Glyph didn't hesitate, hurrying over and carefully slipping the artwork from under its case. He rolled it delicately as he walked, placing it into one of the four smaller tubes that Pest Control had already prepared, then stowing that in the larger transport tube.

By the time he was done, the second painting's airlock had released, and Pest Control was already on it. Bahamut sat nearby, ready to act if this went awry, but with every passing second, it was beginning to seem like they wouldn't need Plan B after all.

Hephaestus breathed a long sigh of relief as the third airlock released. Three down, one to go, and then phase two would be complete.

Chapter 66

"Apollo, there's something you need to see." Stalwart Iron wasn't frantic. He didn't raise his voice. In fact, he made no effort to seem like he was showing the glowing superhero anything more than a routine bit of data that might warrant his attention. This, this was why Apollo liked dealing with the electronic people of the world; they were so much more dependable than the emotional human ones.

"Sure thing." Apollo made his way over slowly, then leaned down to look at the screens in front of Stalwart Iron once more. "What have you got for me?"

"Well, since narrowing down the target to Dash City, I've been monitoring the security of everywhere that might prove a lucrative target," Stalwart Iron explained. "But on top of that I've also been checking on the subroutines and basic system functions to see if I caught anything out of the ordinary. Two minutes ago, I believe that effort paid off. Despite the late hour, it seems someone at the Dash City Museum has just authorized the changing out of four paintings from their protective cases."

"Someone hacked a Level Three system? That's impressive," Apollo said, quickly realizing the implication.

"Yes and no. Though the overall system is rated at three, certain components are more extensive than others," Stalwart Iron explained. "The paintings in question are considered less valuable and therefore don't have as many layers of protection as the ones with a larger monetary or cultural value."

"I see, so they didn't go for one big score. They decided to make it up in volume." Apollo's grin was pearly white and off-putting in its ferocity, the sort of expression he would never have allowed the cameras to catch a glimpse of. "Smarter than I was expecting. Good. They'll make for worthwhile opponents. Have Bridge stop whatever she's doing and immediately prepare for transport. Also, wait five minutes after I leave, and then tip off the Dash City media that a robbery in progress has just been stopped by superheroes from the AHC."

"Can do," Stalwart Iron replied. "Countdown will begin as soon as you exit the room."

"Well then, fire it up, because I'm off to go fetch our rookies," Apollo said. "I think it's time we reminded that guild that they're nothing more than rats. Smash a few heads, and the rest will scurry back to the shadows."

*　　*　　*

"That's all of them," Pest Control announced, slipping the final tube into the larger container and closing the top. It let out a small puff of air as it sealed, supposedly protecting all contents inside from heat, water, air, and other possible corrosions. The tube had cost them the last of their resource money, but all had agreed it was a worthwhile purchase, just in case things went awry.

"Then phase two is done," Hephaestus announced. "With acquisition finished, all that leaves is escape. I'm not picking up anything on the police bands about the museum, so hopefully no one knows we're here."

"Still, better not to take any risks." Bahamut, now back to being human-sized, reached into her costume and pulled out the communicator Tunnel Vision had provided. "Let's call our ride home and get out of here."

"Not quite that easy," Glyph said. "Remember, we can only call from secure locations, places where there's no chance of anything being seen through the portal. We took out a lot of cameras, but in a place like this, there's no way to be totally sure we got everything. Tunnel Vision even told us not to try it in the museum."

"He's right," Hephaestus agreed. "Our best bet is probably the abandoned ice cream stand. Obviously it's secure enough or they wouldn't have been okay with using it for our drop off."

Pest Control finished slipping the tube over his shoulder and strapping it firmly in place. "If that's the case, then let's get going. The longer we stay here, the bigger the risk."

"Send a few scouts ahead, just to be safe," Bahamut instructed.

"Hephaestus said the cops weren't coming," Glyph pointed out.

"No, I said I couldn't hear anything that said they were coming." Hephaestus rose from her seat, putting away her tablet and doing a quick sweep around them. Nothing stood out, even switching across different camera modes, but assuming the readings were accurate, they were still temporary at best. "That's not the same as *knowing* the cops aren't coming. Let's spare the extra minute to send a few bugs."

"If you two think it's worth the time, then okay." Pest Control lifted his arms. A dozen mosquitoes appeared in the air above him, taking off through the nearest door and heading out into the parking lot. He stood like that for several moments before lowering his hands. "They don't see anything out there. Near as I can tell, we've got nothing but empty parking spaces between us and freedom."

Part of Hephaestus tried to think of more methods they could use to assure their safety, but she knew she was drifting into paranoia. If they stood around all night, afraid to act, then they really would get caught eventually.

They'd done their best to scan the area, and just because things were going well didn't mean some sudden horror was about to fall upon them.

Still... it wouldn't hurt to be as cautious as possible.

"Pest Control, give the tube to Bahamut before we leave."

"Mind if I ask why first?" Pest Control said, though he did begin unslinging it from his shoulder.

"If we're just walking across a parking lot, then it doesn't matter who carries it," Hephaestus replied. "But if anything goes wrong, she's the only one of us who can take to the skies. Bahamut can—and should—get immediately clear of any situation and call Tunnel Vision for transport home. As long as none of us gets caught, we're all fine, but if anything happens to the loot..." She didn't bother finishing that sentence; they were all keenly aware of what would happen if they failed their test.

"Can't say I love the idea of you taking me out of a fight," Bahamut grumbled as she donned the tube's strap.

"Then let's hope I'm being pointlessly paranoid and we're in for a three-minute walk." Even as she said it, Hephaestus had a feeling that wouldn't be the case. There was no factual reason to suspect their job had been compromised, except that this wasn't just a job. It was a test. And she couldn't imagine they would be allowed to get off quite so easily as this.

"Everyone ready?" She looked at her fellow apprentices, noting that despite getting the all clear, each looked as though they were about to step into sheer chaos. Perhaps she wasn't the only one who felt like things had gone a bit too smoothly. Good. Better they all went in with their nerves steeled and their eyes open. Even if it was just for a stroll across a parking lot.

*   *   *

"Why isn't there more room in this thing?" Cold Shoulder began to squirm once more until Medley put a clawed hand gently on her shoulder.

"Sorry. *Awesome Assassin Alliance* is meant to be two-player at most, so the Cloak of Rad Camouflage isn't designed for three people." Donald— Cyber Geek now that they were actually out in the field—sounded muffled through the helmet resting easily on his face. He'd grabbed the blaster and the blanket before armoring up since getting to his wrist display was a pain when it was covered by digitally-conjured protection.

"I still don't get why we're just waiting around." Cold Shoulder wasn't wiggling anymore, but her voice was loud enough to serve as warning to anyone who came near.

441

"Apollo said this gang doesn't teleport out of secure locations," Medley reminded her. "It's part of their MO. So we wait, and when they come out, we take them by surprise."

"Well, they seem to be taking their sweet—" Cold Shoulder's voice fell silent as Cyber Geek squeezed her arm, gesturing to the figures emerging from the museum's front entrance. Thankfully, the Cloak of Rad Camouflage only blocked visuals from one side—for them, it was like peering through a still puddle. Everything could be seen, though the view was a bit wonky.

"Remember, our goals are to capture the criminals and secure the stolen merchandise, prioritized in that order," Cyber Geek said, repeating Apollo's instructions almost word for word. "I can draw their attention, but that's a lot of gap to close for you two."

"I can cover us as we approach," Cold Shoulder offered. To both of their surprise, the easily-annoyed meta they'd gotten to know had completely slipped away. In her place was a woman who was all business. "In fact, I can pin them in, assuming none of them have abilities that let them cut through solid ice."

"We're going in blind, so just do what you can and hope for the best. Draw attention until Medley is in range, and then pick them off as he keeps them distracted. And remember: nobody dies, please." Cyber Geek leaned forward, gripping the base of blanket and bringing his massive gun to the ready. "All right, in three, two, one: Go!"

*   *   *

"Go!"

In that one lone syllable, Hephaestus heard all of her paranoid fears spring to life. Before she'd turned, before she'd caught sight of Medley charging toward them, before she could identify the unfamiliar woman in the blue-and-white outfit, before she could fully digest Donald clad in armor and pointing a giant gun at them—before she saw any of it—she knew they'd been caught in the act. But no sooner had the thought gone through her head than another came on its heels: being caught wasn't the same thing as being captured. And just like that, her priorities shifted as she prepared to meet their new challenge head-on.

"Cover Bahamut, then get clear!" Hephaestus ordered. With a glance over her shoulder, she saw that her friend was already halfway through her shift into the white dragon. Behind her, Glyph was etching something hurriedly on her scaly back between her spread wings while Pest Control summoned wave after wave of wasps. Most were heading toward their attackers, but many stayed near Bahamut. Hephaestus didn't know exactly what Pest Control had in mind,

442

but for the moment all she could do was trust him. As it stood, their chances were already slim. If they started second-guessing one another, all was as good as lost.

Hephaestus was trying to decide whether to intercept Medley's charge or try and get into a game of long-shots with Donald when a blast of icy energy struck near her foot and almost managed to freeze her in place. She jumped aside, but the cold continued to build. Soon it had formed a seven-foot high ice-wall that stretched outward, blocking Hephaestus from making a run to the museum's south. So, the blue-and-white lady was a meta with ice powers. She wasn't sure if that was ironic or not, given her own abilities, but she did know it annoyed the crap out of her. If the woman managed to freeze Bahamut or any of the other apprentices, they were all sunk; this meant Hephaestus needed to make sure she stayed the ice-gal's main target.

"Nice shot, Frosty! This time, why don't you actually trying opening your fucking eyes when you aim." Hephaestus bolted right for the woman lining up another ice blast. To her left, Medley seemed to reorient, aiming for the target that was now narrowing the gap between them. That was unexpected but a stroke of luck. Medley was a heavy hitter, and with Bahamut in the air, they wouldn't have anyone that could stand up to him. If she used her meta-suit, she might be able to hold him off for a while. And if that failed, she was pretty sure he didn't have any way to catch living fire, although the same could not be said for the ice-woman.

"My name is Cold Shoulder!" Those words were the only warning Hephaestus got before a torrent of freezing energy came right at her. Honed reflexes augmented by carefully-crafted technology snapped into action, and Hephaestus leapt to the side just in time to avoid the massive chunk of ice that formed by her feet. While she readied for another blast, Cold Shoulder took her by surprise. Instead of a concentrated beam, she spread her arms and let out something like a pulse. Immediately, the entire parking lot began to ice over; Hephaestus only avoided slipping thanks to the weight of her suit and the traction of the metal boots on her feet.

"And I think that is just adorable." Damn. When this was over, she'd have to talk with Ivan about banter; somehow, she felt like she was really coming up short so far. Instead of trying to think of another one-liner, Hephaestus took aim and fired more of the tranquilizing darts she'd used on the guard. If her luck held, she could knock out the biggest threat to their escape without causing any lasting damage.

Unfortunately, it seemed Cold Shoulder hadn't stepped onto the battlefield without some defensive plans of her own. She held up a single hand and a giant shield of ice materialized in front of her, easily stopping the darts.

What was worse, the shield didn't vanish; it merely slid to the side as if it had no weight while Cold Shoulder fired off another round of freezing energy.

This time, Hephaestus couldn't get away with a simple hop. She had to throw herself to the ground in a tucked roll. Clear of the attack, she spun away and leapt back to her feet. It was a dangerous move that left her open to another shot—a shot which, oddly, didn't come. Only when Hephaestus was reoriented did she realize why, and in that moment, suddenly being caught by a freeze blast didn't seem so bad.

Cold Shoulder had conjured more ice—a lot more—only she'd called it up around herself. She stood encased in what looked to be a fifteen-foot tall humanoid construct made of ice, its frosty fists balled up and a dangerous glint in its wintery eye. If that weren't bad enough—and by Hephaestus's reckoning, it definitely was—Medley had finally arrived at Cold Shoulder's side. The mighty beast was dwarfed by her ice-construct armor, but he was still a good few feet taller than Hephaestus, even with the extra couple of inches from her armor.

This was bad. There were still a few tricks up her meta-suit's sleeves, but losing the main cannon in her right gauntlet had severely limited her options. Granted, she still wouldn't have been allowed to char a cape, but at least it would have left bluffing on the table. The only upside to this predicament was that if both Medley and Cold Shoulder were both focused on her, the others should be free to slip away easily.

The sound of Donald's—Cyber Geek's—blaster dispelled that notion swiftly from her mind and acted as some sort of trigger for Cold Shoulder and Medley as well. The two charged as a team. Hephaestus no longer had the luxury of worrying about the other apprentices. Her hands were full with just trying to stay alive.

Chapter 67

When the first shots came, Bahamut was sure they were sunk. She'd seen the kind of damage that gun could dish out firsthand, and while her green dragon-form might, *might* have been able to withstand a blast, her white dragon wasn't nearly as tough. Her eyes closed, and all she could feel was Glyph etching a second symbol onto her back as she waited for the end to come. Instead, she heard Pest Control let out a string of swears, along with the crackling sizzle of insects being burned up.

"Fucker! Those things hurt."

Hurt? The shots should be cooking right through them. Bahamut opened her scaly eyes. Rather than the giant beam that had torn through an otherworldly monster, Cyber Geek was pelting them with small blue bursts, most of which Pest Control's wall of flying bugs were absorbing.

"Why isn't he trying to kill us?" She didn't mean for the words to be spoken, but they still slipped out nonetheless. As Glyph finished drawing on her back, he spun around to answer.

"'Cause they're the good guys, duh. We're not a threat to anyone, we're not causing massive damage, and we haven't even shown aggression. It would look really bad if they just killed us in one go without even giving us the chance to surrender." Glyph reached over and patted the pair of symbols on her back, each letting out a pulse of energy as he did. "Now you've got some shielding. Once you slip out of sight, they shouldn't be able to track you. Get clear, turn back, and keep the paintings safe."

"Do you two have an exit plan?" Bahamut asked.

"Well, since Hephaestus is currently holding the attention of two of them, I'd say we'll use my bugs to give video-game boy the slip. Maybe Glyph has a symbol or two left as well," Pest Control offered. He was rematerializing the bugs as fast as he could, but Cyber Geek's endless shots were clearly tearing through them at a greater rate.

"With two on Bahamut, the most I can sustain is one more," Glyph said. "But with the right timing, I might be able to pull something off."

Bahamut took in the scene before her. Hephaestus was squaring off against a giant ice monster and Medley, neither of which looked to be pushovers. Cyber Geek had the team functionally pinned down with his blasts. It had made sense to give her the paintings inside the museum when this was all abstract, but now that things had gotten real, that wisdom was waning. Yes, if the paintings were damaged, then they were all sunk; however, the same could be said if any of them were captured. She was the group's heavy hitter, and

445

while Hephaestus might manage to slip away, things didn't look as good for Pest Control and Glyph. Their first plan had been solid, but getting everyone out here meant they had to be willing to call audibles when it was needed. And that was exactly what Bahamut planned to do.

"Glyph, take the paintings from me, then pull off the shield magic. Pest Control, forget everything else: just keep churning out bugs. Keep us hidden, no matter what it takes."

"You're supposed to escape." Pest Control spit the words out through gritted teeth as he narrowed his focus, conjuring more and more flying insects to fill the gaps where the shots had come in.

"Which will leave you both totally exposed. Don't worry, I've got an idea," Bahamut said. She was nearly back to her human-form, taking care to stay as concealed behind the cover of bugs as possible. She had a feeling that with no protection from her dragon magic, one of those shots might stun her long enough for this all to go off the rails. "Glyph! Your concealment magic, it lets you slip by people?"

"People who don't know you're there, and only if they're distracted," he explained. "It's not invisibility." Glyph was fastening the tube around his own chest as he spoke. While he might want more explanation of what the plan was, it was clear he also realized the path they'd been on would lead to failure.

"Perfect. Get it on yourself and Pest Control, then wait here under cover of the bugs," she said. "I'm going to give you both the perfect distraction. When that happens, all eyes will be on me, I promise. After that, run like hell to the ice cream stand and call Tunnel Vision."

"The magic won't work if you just step out from here," Glyph warned her. "He's aware of all three of us. I don't think even you'd be tough enough to make it to him while taking fire from those energy shots."

"Which is why I'm going back into the museum and slipping out a side exit," Bahamut replied. "We're already busted, so alarms don't mean shit. Just seize the opportunity when it comes. You'll only get one shot at this."

"If you're going to do it, then please hurry. This ain't exactly a light jog." Sweat glistened on Pest Control's face, but the bugs were filling in the wall faster than Cyber Geek could fry them, albeit slowly. He wouldn't be able to manage it for long; she had to make the most of her window while it was still open.

Without another word, Bahamut turned and dashed back into the museum, turning partially green and scaly as she moved. The less they could see of her true form, the better; she had a feeling any remaining security tapes were going to get the ever-loving shit examined out of them. Plus, dragon-strength let her run faster, and she was all too aware that she was racing a clock. Even if

446

Pest Control and Glyph could hold out, there was still Hephaestus to worry about.

*   *   *

The meta-suit, despite its appearance, had not been designed for melee combat. Certainly, the armoring offered an enhanced defense, and the servos were capable of delivering far more physical force than if it had been Tori doing the punching; however, the purpose of the meta-suit was to offer utility, defense, and mobility above all else. Plus a cannon, for bad situations, which Hephaestus was dearly wishing hadn't been broken earlier in the night. To keep this up required her to continue pumping energy into the suit, so much and so hot her body was nearly insubstantial inside it. It was all she could do to keep up with the pair of capes trying to beat her down.

A flurry of icicles whizzed by. She dodged to the side, almost taking a punch from Medley as she fell into their trap. Her reactions were good—she hadn't survived as a criminal for as long as she'd managed without learning to brawl—but the simple truth of it was that Medley was a far better fighter than she. And while Cold Shoulder apparently couldn't do the freezing beams while encased in her construct, she could make the ice-suit grow incredibly sharp icicles, which she would then throw with enough force to dent the meta-suit.

In fact, the only reason Hephaestus hadn't gone down yet was that Medley and Cold Shoulder clearly had no practice fighting together. They kept stepping in the other's way, dodging around attacks meant for her, and just generally slowing one another down. One on one, either of them would have been a challenge. Medley certainly would have forced her to abandon the suit. But the sum of their parts was less than their individual strength, and Hephaestus capitalized on that weakness as much as she could.

Putting herself between them, she registered another icicle attack on her helmet's display and leapt aside, allowing the freezing projectiles to strike Medley's torso. They shattered on impact, doing no visible damage, though they did manage to distract him momentarily. Hephaestus took advantage of that moment by loading a fresh round of paralyzing darts into the gun on her left arm. Medley's hide was too thick for a shot to pierce, so Hephaestus charged the furry monster, catching him slightly by surprise. It was enough to get off one punch, which she drove into the side of his neck, tilting her wrist down so that the mouth of the gun struck his flesh. While this angle did far less damage than if she'd kept her fist angled properly, it did allow her to fire at the same time she hit. Hephaestus could see a trio of darts sticking out of his neck as she pulled away. They might not be embedded deep enough to deliver the chemicals, but it was as good as they were ever going to get. Hephaestus was feeling good about her gamble until a clawed hand whipped forward, snagging her retreating left arm and spinning her around.

"Gotcha," Medley growled, twisting the captured arm so that it forced Hephaestus to her knees. There was no danger of actually breaking bones since she was already on the verge of not having them, but the suit could only twist so many ways. Besides, this position had her back directly to Medley, which sparked something of an idea. If she could just get the angle right, this might be the chance she was waiting for.

"I have a feeling you won't go peacefully, even if I offer you the chance to surrender, but rules are rules. Give up now, get out of the suit, and you won't be hurt. If you keep fighting, I can't guarantee your safety." Medley's speech wasn't slurred and his grip certainly wasn't wavering, so it looked like the drugs either hadn't made it in or didn't have any effect. It had been a long shot in the first place; metas with such physical abilities usually weren't susceptible to mere toxins.

Still, Hephaestus hadn't given up yet. She leaned a little lower to the ground, stretching the suit's arm as far as she could. This would only be a surprise once, and she needed the aim to be just right.

"All right, since you're not getting out, I guess you want to do this the hard way. Cold Shoulder, ice him up," Medley ordered. "We'll get this guy out of his suit back in AHC headquarters."

Well, that wasn't good. Thanks to the suit's cameras and display, Hephaestus could see Cold Shoulder's ice construct parting. The giant took Cold Shoulder in its hand and gently set her down. The lady was powerful; Hephaestus had to give her that. She'd assumed Medley and Cyber Geek were the best that the AHC had in their rookies, but maybe they'd been keeping the really strong ones as a surprise. Either way, getting caught in one of those ice blocks would be bad. Hephaestus wasn't sure how living fire would work against that sort of power and sure as shit wasn't in a hurry to find out. But Medley was so quick, even if she got the angle right, he might dodge. What she needed was a distraction, just one moment where they weren't focused on her.

Luck, fate, or whatever deity watched over villains was clearly listening to her thoughts. As Cold Shoulder raised her hands and prepared to attack, a dragon's roar split the night, and suddenly Hephaestus was no longer the more attention-grabbing problem to deal with.

*   *   *

The mood in the council chambers had shifted many times as the occupants watched the night's crimes take place. Apprehension as they watched the apprentices make the approach. Worry when some of the guards resisted Glyph's magic. Excitement as Pest Control and Hephaestus chased them down before they could sound an alarm. Relief when the paintings' frames opened and no security alarm sounded. And, of course, fear when the capes ambushed their rookies during the exit from the museum. Fear not for themselves or their organization, but for this newest crop of villains, who so many of them had personally invested in and who were now on the brink of being wiped out.

"How the hell did they find them?" Xelas snapped. "I was watching the system the whole time, and not one alarm went out."

"Perhaps someone noticed them sneaking in and called the police. Perhaps there were security measures even we were unaware of. Those are the risks and realities of a real job; nothing is certain and everything can be affected by chance." Doctor Mechaniacal watched patiently, a somber expression on his face as he gauged the actions of the apprentices.

Ivan knew that Wade took no joy in what they were witnessing, but the truth of the matter was that sometimes these things did happen. Granted, it usually wasn't on one's first job with no backup or more experienced guild members to help. The whole coincidence struck Ivan as just a touch suspicious, though he couldn't imagine how even Wade could have convinced the AHC to send their newest recruits out to stop the crime.

"At least they're being smart," Thuggernaut said, half-whispering to Ivan as they watched the scene play out in front of them. "The focus is obviously on getting away, just like they were taught. Escape over engagement."

"Easy for you to say, your apprentice isn't trying to fight two capes at once," Ivan replied. On-screen, Hephaestus took a swing at Medley, connecting, but getting her arm snared in the process. "Badly, I might add."

"She's putting the group first, drawing attention so the others can sneak away." Thuggernaut looked at the older villain carefully, remembering the man with the glowing eyes who had once terrorized entire battalions of capes. "If memory serves, you used to do the same. You'd fight capes ten at a time if you were trying to help your friends get away."

"True, but there are two very important differences between the old me and the current Hephaestus," Ivan said. "One, I was much stronger than she is, which is why I could manage fights like that. And two, I was much dumber than she, which is why I'd expect to see a little more strategy out of my apprentice."

"She's got two of the capes paying attention solely to her, and even if they cuff the suit, she can still slip away," Thuggernaut pointed out. "It's a pretty good plan for the spur of the moment. Hopefully the other three can find their own way to withdraw. I am proud of them for not trying to do anything stupid like—"

That was when the roar echoed through the room's speakers, drawing all attention to a previously boring part of the screen and simultaneously leaving Thuggernaut a few shades paler. He opened and closed his mouth several times, but no words came out. Ivan patted the large man gently on the shoulder.

"On the plus side," Ivan said, his voice surprisingly gentle, "at least no one can claim our apprentices are cowards."

Thuggernaut had no reply; he merely watched the screen in mute shock as chaos unfolded before him.

Chapter 68

The bug thing was weird. Maybe a guy who pulled items out of video games didn't have a lot of room to judge, but it didn't stop Cyber Geek from getting the willies as he gunned down wave after wave of the things. True, he could have easily cut through them if he'd switched the blaster's mode to something more deadly; however, that came with the very real possibility of also carving up the meta creating them. Robbing a museum was kind of a dick move, sure, but it didn't seem like the sort of thing someone should get killed for. Especially when they weren't even using the bugs to attack, but rather as a makeshift, albeit creepy, shield.

For a moment, he'd considered switching targets to try helping Medley and Cold Shoulder, though one look at the fracas that was their fight told him he wasn't nearly a good enough shot to hit the dude in the metal suit without potentially clipping his friends. Instead, he focused on keeping the other metas pinned down. It freed up his team to handle the more aggressive threat without unnecessarily elevating the situation. He had plenty of stunning blasts to send out, and the bug-wall was getting thinner and thinner the longer they had their standoff.

Really, the only thing bothering Cyber Geek was that he didn't have a good count of how many metas they were fighting. Metal-suit was one and bug-person was another. He thought he'd seen something white and scaly in the gaps between bugs, but it had vanished and at this range, he didn't completely trust his eyes. There were at least two people pinned behind the insects, maybe three, and it was that maybe that worried him. This was a big outing; the last thing they wanted to do was let one of the criminals slip away because he couldn't count.

Cyber Geek was so focused on trying to peek through the bug curtain as he shot it apart that he never noticed the creature approaching him until a pair of strong claws closed around his shoulders. In his defense, though, how was he supposed to know he needed to keep an eye on the sky? That mistake was made quickly apparent as the powerful beating of wings filled his ears, followed by a triumphant roar as a massive creature plucked him skyward.

Panic overwhelmed him, the sight of the shrinking ground triggering the primal part of his brain that knew it was not a creature meant for the heavens. Below him, Medley and Cold Shoulder both looked toward the roar, jaws hanging open as they got a good look at whatever flying thing had him gripped in its claws. Cyber Geek struggled to reorient himself, perhaps even angle his gun upward to take a shot at the creature, but holding the blaster in both arms for stability meant the grip pinning his arms and shoulders also locked the aim in place. As much strength as the armor added, it was clearly no match for the monster holding him. With every passing second, the ground drew further away.

He heard something, a scream like a wounded beast. He tried to check on Medley, but he was no longer facing the parking lot, and the *Blaster Brahs* helmet left a lot to be desired in terms of maneuverability.

"Can you survive a fall in that tin can?" If being snatched from the ground had shocked Cyber Geek, hearing the creature that had done it speak to him left him completely flummoxed. He didn't even know if he could respond, let alone what his response would be, until the monster shook him from side to side, snapping him out of his bewilderment.

"Are you trying to scare me? Because I won't give up that easy." It was the first thing that came to mind, the sort of indomitable dialogue he'd always imagined the greats like Lodestar would deliver in dire situations.

The creature snorted, an altogether terrifying noise, and then let out something that sounded almost like laughter. "I'm not threatening you. I'm doing the opposite. I can't fly around with you all night, but I also don't want to get caught. I need to get out of here, and I'd prefer not to kill you in the process."

"But you're a criminal," Cyber Geek protested. Between the height and the strangeness of what was happening, he could hardly be blamed for getting more confused by the second.

"I robbed a museum. That's a far cry from murder. Just because I'm willing to break one law doesn't mean I'll ignore them all. Now, are you able to survive the fall or not? You're heavier than you look."

Cyber Geek swallowed hard and looked down at the ground, trying to gauge how high up they were. He'd leveled up the suit a good bit since his last fight, but there were still limits to what it could absorb. Even in the game, falling from too high cost a life, and he didn't have any extra to spare, a thought that opened up a whole new path of questions he might need to explore. But that would come later; for now, he needed to survive the next five minutes.

"Not like... *any* fall. But if you get within a hundred feet or so, I should be fine." In truth, he'd be more than fine from that height. If he were quick enough, he might even be able to turn on his thrusters and get off one last shot at the monster. With his thumb, he clicked a small dial on the back of the blaster, choosing a new mode. Killing would be wrong, especially when the criminal was going out of its way to spare his life, but a potent electrical blast might stun it long enough to capture.

452

The wings stopped beating, and Cyber Geek realized they were dropping rapidly. He'd never been part of a dive from a firsthand view, but that seemed like a good guess as to what was happening. The ground, nowhere near the museum anymore, was racing up at him so quickly that his stomach felt like it was rising into his throat.

"Get braced, I'm dropping on three," the monster warned him.

"But we're still so high!" There was no way they were at hundred feet yet, at least gauging from the treetops surrounding them.

"Trust me, I've calculated this out. Okay, one—"

And just like that, the claws released him, sending Cyber Geek tumbling unprepared through the air. He cursed himself for believing the count—obviously the creature knew he might counterattack and had wanted to catch him unprepared. Spinning through the air, he marshaled his senses and strove to focus. There, soaring away from him at a rapid pace, was the sole speck of white amid a dark sky.

Cyber Geek raised his gun and took careful aim. It wasn't going to be quite that easy. He wouldn't let it be.

*   *   *

Hephaestus didn't hesitate. As soon as she realized what Bahamut had done and how fucking balls-out insane as it was, she seized the opportunity. While she hadn't quite gotten her meta-suit airborne, she had planned on the eventual possibility, and that included building in a vent and thruster system. Leaning as far forward as she could, Hephaestus flipped her thrusters on, sending focused jets of flame out from the openings on her back. They had almost no range, but the drawback to holding someone in an arm lock was that it meant standing very, very close to them. So close, in fact, that the flames from her thrusters caught Medley's fur, which was, thankfully, not fireproof.

The creature let out a howl of pain as it began to roast, and Hephaestus's left arm was suddenly free once more. She leapt to the side, getting out of Cold Shoulder's direct aim before the woman with ice powers could figure out what was going on. Between Cyber Geek being spirited into the sky and Medley suddenly turning into a fireworks display, it was no wonder Cold Shoulder needed a moment to figure out what was happening.

That moment was all Hephaestus needed as she unloaded the last of her paralyzing darts into Cold Shoulder's torso. Powerful as she was, if caught without her ice-shields, she was just as vulnerable as anyone else. With little more than a flutter of her eyelashes, Cold Shoulder began to fall headfirst toward the concrete. Moving solely on reflex, Hephaestus darted forward,

453

catching Cold Shoulder before her head could strike and setting her body the rest of the way down. It was a small gesture that cost her little more than a few seconds of her time.

Unfortunately, those seconds turned out to be pretty crucial.

"That *hurt*." Medley's voice, always something of a growl, had the hint of animalistic danger in it that he worked so hard to keep at bay. He was staring at her, smoke still trailing from the edges of his singed fur. The ground was sooty and stained where he'd rolled the fire out, like someone had launched a half-dozen bottle rockets on its surface.

One down, one to go. Sadly, this was the tougher of the two, and Hephaestus was beginning to run dry on tricks. She racked her brain to think of a plan, but Medley already had one. The words had no sooner left his mouth than he attacked.

And this time, Cold Shoulder wasn't around to slow him down.

*   *   *

Pest Control and Glyph didn't need any encouragement to move as they watched Bahamut soar down from the sky and pluck up Cyber Geek like a children's toy. With only a single glance between them—one meant more to convey a general sense of "Holy shit!" than the need to make sure the other was running—they took off in a dead sprint for the abandoned ice cream shack. As they moved, each kept waiting for the sound of being caught, either in a yell from Medley or a shot from the ice-wielding meta whose name they'd been too far away to hear.

The yell did come, though it was more of a scream. One look told them that it had nothing to do with them being spotted. Medley was lit up like a fireworks stand with poor fire safety rules, and Hephaestus was already advancing on her other foe. With all three capes' attention well-managed, the escaping duo finished their run, bolting into the shack and shutting the door. Glyph yanked out his remote with the lone button that Tunnel Vision had provided and jammed his thumb down on it so hard that, for a moment, the plastic got wedged into the device.

"Nothing's happening," Pest Control whispered, peering carefully through the shack's window just in time to watch Hephaestus fire a barrage of darts at the cape in blue and white.

"They said there would be a delay." Though Glyph tried to remain calm, it was all he could do not to vomit as he counted the seconds in his head. If he reached ten and the doorway through space hadn't opened, he had no idea what they would do. Mercifully, just as he hit nine, the back wall of the shack vanished. Sanctum could be seen only steps away. All he had to do was move. But this time, he did hesitate, for just a moment.

"Is Hephaestus okay?" Glyph asked. They did need the whole team to make it, after all.

"Okay? She's got Medley rolling on the ground in pain and just knocked that other gal clean out." Pest Control left the window, slapped Glyph on the shoulder, and stepped through the portal. "She's doing a damn sight better than okay. Let's just hope Bahamut managed to get away clean as well."

Relieved, for purely tactical reasons of course, Glyph followed Pest Control into Sanctum. He turned around to look back in the shack, waiting for Hephaestus to appear and follow them, but suddenly all he was looking at was a smooth metal wall.

"We do not leave open windows," the male half of Tunnel Vision explained. "The others may call when they are secure."

"Well, Hephaestus should be here in a few seconds," Pest Control told them.

After the first minute of waiting, Glyph's stomach began to tighten in fear. By the tenth, it was all he could do to keep from vomiting. Something had gone wrong, and now they didn't even have the option of helping out.

Their futures were completely in the hands of Hephaestus and Bahamut.

*   *   *

In Cyber Geek's visor, the white creature (was it a freaking dragon?) lit up as his targeting system locked. Despite spinning through the air and tumbling toward the ground, he'd lined up his shot; now that the gun was locked, there was no way he'd miss. He steadied his aim and began to gently squeeze on the blaster's heavy trigger.

Unfortunately, the downside to focusing solely on his target was that Cyber Geek had ignored his other surroundings. The folly in that strategy became abundantly clear as he smashed back-first into a tree, depleting a healthy amount of his shields and killing his momentum entirely. He began to fall straight down, clipping heavy branches along the way. Some of them might have borne his weight if he were just Donald, but the Master Brah's armor added at least a hundred or so pounds, and all that mass turned the branches to toothpicks as he careened through them.

At long last, he found something sturdy enough to stop his descent: the ground. Impact drained his shields further, but they were still more than functional. If only the armor had something to protect him from dizziness, there would have been no evidence of the fall he'd endured. As he slowly pulled himself to his feet and searched the sky, Cyber Geek realized that might have been the point.

The dragon had thrown him into a tree, not just because it meant he wouldn't be able to attack as it flew away, but because the branches would slow him down enough to make sure he wasn't killed in the fall. It was tactically sound and also oddly considerate. Cyber Geek jogged over to the nearest clearing and scanned the stars, searching for a winged white monster flying below them. There was nothing, which said a lot given how far the helmet let him see. Presumably the creature had gone to ground as soon as it was out of sight; that, or it could move a lot faster than it had with him in tow.

Cyber Geek lowered his head and began to search the area. He had a sneaking suspicion that no amount of looking would turn up his quarry, but he still felt compelled to try. Just... not that hard. This wasn't like the monster in the club or the robbers in the office. These villains seemed to be going out of their way not to hurt anyone.

Somehow, hunting one of them just didn't conjure that same fire for justice the other occasions had.

Chapter 69

Medley was a monster, and not just because he had fur, scales, and a tail. No, he was a monster in the way he attacked: brutal, ruthless efficiency as he struck Hephaestus's suit over and over again with those powerful claws. The damn things were sharp as a chef's prized knife, and all the strength in his inhuman muscles meant he could use them to punch through nearly any material. With one swipe, he'd torn through the shielding on the upper half of her left arm, exposing wires and circuits that were never meant to see the light of day.

On top of his natural advantage, it certainly didn't help that Medley had clearly been in a lot more fights than Hephaestus. She considered herself tough and knew how to hold her own, but he was on a whole other level. Idly, Hephaestus wondered what sort of person he'd been before his transformation. Someone who liked to scrap, that much was obvious. Either that or his power had come with a whole slew of well-honed instincts and reflexes.

When the onslaught first began, Hephaestus was sure the jig was up. He'd carve through her meta-suit like a plasma beam through, well, damn near anything, and she'd be forced to flee in fire-form. While she was mentally prepared for that if it was needed, she considered it a last-ditch effort for a worst case scenario. Aside from all the time and effort she'd poured into her suit, there was also the fact that no one outside the guild currently knew what the real powers of Hephaestus were. The longer she could keep that genie in the bottle, the longer she might be able to hold on to the secret identity of Tori Rivas.

To her surprise, after Medley drew electronic blood in the form of sparks and wires, his attacks softened. Not by a lot, but by enough. Hephaestus was confused until it clicked: Medley didn't know there was a woman composed largely of sentient fire inside the suit. He thought he was fighting a frail, easily killable human inside high-tech armor, and cutting too deep would run the risk of murdering his prey. And that wouldn't be very hero-like, after all.

With no other choice, Hephaestus seized his hesitation, counterattacking for all she was worth, throwing hard punches that she knew would be blocked just to keep him slightly off-balance. To her great surprise, it worked. The more they fought, metal on scales in a rough jumble of limbs, the less coordinated Medley seemed to get. She rolled away from a swipe of his tail, finally putting a little distance between them, and noticed that he seemed to be swaying, ever so gently, on his feet.

"You're better than I expected." As Medley talked, the muscles in his thick neck flexed. Hephaestus noticed the twinkling of metal under the parking lot's giant lights. Of course! The drugs were finally kicking in, and the more he strained, the faster they pumped through his system.

"I work out," Hephaestus replied in her robotic, disguised voice. Yeah, she really needed to see if Ivan had a book on banter or something.

"Got a name to go with all that metal?" Medley was circling her carefully, waiting for an opportunity to pounce. He also seemed to be getting steadier, which did not bode well for her. Were the drugs only working when he exerted himself?

"Hephaestus will work." She tried to sound cavalier about it, but the truth was, deep down, she felt a bit of a thrill at telling someone her villain code name for the first time.

Medley blinked in surprise, tilting his feline head slightly to the side. "Isn't there already a cape with that name?"

"It's Greek mythology; you can't own public domain." That had come out a bit more defensive than she expected, and a long, sharp-toothed smile spread across Medley's face.

"Well, Hephaestus, my name is Medley. You might not have heard of me yet—I'm new to the Alliance of Heroic Champions—but I'll give you the basics: I never give up, I never back down, and I never let my prey go once it's within reach. Now, I've been taking it easy on you, despite the fact that you tried to light me up like a sparkler, but that's about to change. You're decently strong, which means I can't capture you by holding so much back. If you'd like to surrender, I'll happily accept. Otherwise, whatever injuries you get are your own fault." Medley stopped circling, that long tail of his extended out behind him. So far, he'd been using it like a bat, smacking her around with it, but they were both keenly aware of the sharp stinger resting at its tip. He wasn't bluffing. Medley was a living weapon, and as it stood, she had no hope of beating him.

If not for a whisper in her communicator, Hephaestus might have given up all hope of keeping her suit and fled. Instead, she grinned beneath the concealment of her black helmet. As quickly and covertly as she could, Hephaestus began redirecting her suit's power, cranking up the temperature as she did to supplement its waning batteries.

"Sorry, Medley, but I'm not really much of a fighter. We just came to relieve the museum of a few of its less-appreciated exhibits, and with that done, I don't see the need to slug it out with you."

Medley flexed his claws and lowered his stance, the fur on his back standing on end. "From where I stand, you don't have a lot of—HEY!"

As Medley spoke, Hephaestus spun on her heel and sprinted off across the parking lot, almost all of the suit's power cranking through her legs, fleeing as fast as her mechanically enhanced feet would carry her. Thanks to the helmet's rear camera, she could see Medley finally snap to what was happening and begin to give chase. Quick as she was, he was faster, and the gap she'd bought with her surprise began to narrow inch by inch. Still, she poured on the effort, running for all she was worth.

"Where do you think you can go?" Medley roared from behind her. "We're in downtown Dash City, and the police are on their way. There's nowhere to... to run."

His words slurred as he veered to the side—only for a split second, but enough to confirm the drugs were pumping again. It would give Hephaestus a very narrow window of opportunity, one she planned to use as quickly as possible. Sooner or later, he'd shake the chemicals completely, and if she was still around when that happened, everything would go right to shit.

Quietly, she whispered a few words into her communicator, and then turned her head a few inches back to yell at Medley. "Well, good thing for me that I'm not planning on running away!"

"You plan to fight me after all?" Medley was steadying himself out; in moments, he'd be gaining ground again.

"Fuck that shit. I just meant why run when you can fly!" Giving her suit's power one last burst of juice, she sank down on both feet and pushed off, leaping as high into the air as she could possibly manage. It wasn't that high; she barely cleared five feet off the ground, even with all the power she'd poured into her suit's muscles. Thankfully, it was just high enough for a pair of white-scaled claws to grab her outstretched arms and carry her up into the sky.

Below, Medley was coming down from his own leap, clearly meant to catch Hephaestus before she could get away. Whether it was the drugs, the gap, or the surprise, he'd come up short, and with every beat of Bahamut's wings, they were carried farther and farther out of his range.

"I am really, really glad you came back to check on me," Hephaestus said.

"You read the rules: one of us goes down, we all go down," Bahamut replied. "Besides, I had a feeling you'd get yourself in too deep."

"Judgment later, escape now."

"About that. I've got really good hearing like this, and I can make out the sounds of helicopters coming this way." Bahamut gestured with her head. "Three at least, and gaining on us fast."

"Cops?"

"Or reporters. Doesn't matter. Neither will let us out of their sight. And while I've got a ward to help conceal me, you don't," Bahamut informed her.

"Shitcrap. I don't suppose you could outrun them?"

459

"Normally, maybe. But that suit isn't exactly light. You're weighing me down a lot, which means they'll probably be able to catch up." Bahamut banked hard to the left, giving Hephaestus an unimpeded view of the city below. She could see flashing lights converging on the museum, expecting to find a group of robbers neatly captured. The AHC wasn't going to like that any of them escaped, and if they had any shot of catching her and Bahamut, they'd take it.

"I've got an idea," Hephaestus said.

"Is it a good idea?"

"Holy shit, no. But it might work."

Bahamut let out the sort of sigh that said she'd known the answer to her question when it was asked and was just hoping to be proven wrong. "Guess that will have to do."

"Glad to hear you're on board. Lift me up higher so I can get a hold on your stomach. After that, we have to adjust your grip. And for the love of all that's precious in the world, keep your damn tail lifted."

Bahamut complied, pulling Hephaestus up against her scaled stomach, at which point the armored woman began instructing her on exactly where her claws should be. By the time the maneuver was done, they were clinging tightly to each other in an interspecies hug that was uncomfortable but sustainable for both of them.

"Now, when I say three, you hold on to me for all you're worth and keep your wings steady. Aim for somewhere deserted. I'll get us enough of a head start that we can land and call Tunnel Vision before anyone tracks us."

"How the hell will you... wait, are you kidding me?" Bahamut's head peered down at Hephaestus, confirming that yes, dragons can look panicked under the right circumstances.

"One."

"This is not safer than trying to hide from the helicopters!" Bahamut yelled. She jerked her head upward. With what was coming, the last thing she needed was to not see in front of them.

"Never said it was!" Hephaestus agreed. Despite the danger they were still in, she couldn't shake a feeling of excitement as the world rushed along below them and the semi-distant beat of helicopters could be heard on the wind. "Two!"

"I want it on the record that I deeply regret coming back to save you."

"So noted," Hephaestus said. "Three!"

With that, she activated her suit's thrusters, pouring every last ounce of power she had into them. While it wasn't enough to get her into the air, it could sure as shit add a kick to Bahamut's flying speed. The ground went from a rush to a blur as the white dragon with a stomach seemingly ablaze raced through the sky.

*   *   *

"This is why I love rookies! A rocket dragon. A *fucking rocket dragon*! Have we ever had that before?" Xelas looked around the room, waiting to see if anyone could supply an answer to her clearly very important question. Either no one could or they didn't care; the heavy atmosphere had been lifted right along with Hephaestus as the final two apprentices made their escape.

Arachno Bro and Thuggernaut were both out of their seats celebrating, and even Balaam looked like he'd cracked a half-smile when word came up that Glyph had safely returned with Pest Control. Even the other council members seemed cheery. Not only had the rookies managed to avoid capture, but they'd put on a hell of a show while doing it. Videos from this were definitely going to be edited together for the Christmas party, where it would be all the more entertaining because everyone knew it turned out all right.

Amid the cheer, Ivan made his way around the table to where Doctor Mechaniacal was seated, watching with the others as a dragon with thrusters on its stomach burned through the night sky. Ivan leaned over to make certain his words wouldn't be overheard. Though they'd been carefully chosen, the context could change if others heard him uttering them.

"Fighting three of the newest capes on their final trial. Seems like a hell of a steep obstacle to climb over."

"I already know where you're going with this, and you can save the implications." Doctor Mechaniacal turned slightly in his chair so he could whisper back to Ivan. "My original plan was to have Tunnel Vision tell them the shack had been compromised when they tried to use it, forcing them to hunt in unfamiliar territory for a secure location to transport from, test how resourceful they could be when they had to think on the fly. Which, given what we've seen tonight, is a question I'd say was thoroughly answered. Believe me, I would never throw more at these apprentices than I thought they could handle."

"So they just had bad luck?"

"Oh, I wouldn't go that far," Doctor Mechaniacal replied. "For them to have been caught at such an innocuous task, it seems a fair wager that the AHC was waiting for them. If our uneasy peace has begun to wane, then tonight will have much further-reaching implications than just the capes' awareness of our newest recruits. But that can wait for later."

Doctor Mechaniacal stood from his chair, and as he rose, the rest of the room quieted. "My colleagues, Pseudonym has been kind enough to suggest

461

that, given the harrowing nature of tonight's trials, we move our observation to Sanctum. It would do well for the apprentices to see their mentors waiting for them when the trial is complete. A little solidarity as it were, after a trying evening."

There were no objections, so the council and two mentors headed down the hallway, screens lighting up along the way so they could continue to monitor Hephaestus and Bahamut's unorthodox flight.

*   *   *

"Why didn't you step in?" Lady Shade stood with Apollo on top of the museum, concealing them both from the roving eyes of reporters and the cameras that were currently surrounding Medley and a still-unconscious Cold Shoulder. Apollo had snuck on to the scene after dropping off the new superheroes, bringing her along to keep them hidden as they watched it all play out. Yet, even as they watched the whole plan fell apart, Apollo hadn't lifted a muscle, only silently observing while criminal after criminal escaped.

"If I'd jumped in and helped, what would that have accomplished? The new team would think we didn't trust them enough to let them work without being watched, or worse, they'd get accustomed to having someone nearby to bail them out." Apollo shook his head. "Yes, I could have handled the whole thing in moments, but they wouldn't have learned from the experience. And if we want them to get better, then learning, especially through failure, is going to be key."

"But you could still go run down the dragon," Lady Shade suggested. "There's enough media here that you can claim you were called in to clean up after them."

"Why would I catch the dragon? I want those thieves to get away," Apollo replied. "If our rookies can't claim victory, I'd rather they suffer a complete, humiliating defeat. It works much better in the long run."

"Because it gives them another chance to catch the villains?" Lady Shade asked.

"That, too. But mostly because tonight is going to eat at them: all the ways they failed, all the ways they were embarrassed and beaten. And over time, they'll grow to hate these four thieves, blame them for it all. So much so that if the day ever comes that the chance for revenge is offered, they won't think twice before jumping at it." Apollo smiled as he looked down at Medley, who was doing his best to answer the reporters yet drowning spectacularly in their sea of questions.

"Tonight, they have learned to hate villains."

462

*   *   *

It took half an hour to land, find a secluded park with an unoccupied bridge they could huddle under, and finally push down on their button to go home. Hephaestus was braced for a lot of things as the cement wall rippled and vanished to reveal their way back to the guild. Surely there would be yelling and scolding: not only had they failed to avoid attention, but they had in fact had somehow drawn a group of capes. She took solace in the knowledge that they'd stuck to the code. No matter what else went awry, no matter how many mistakes they made, that much was true, and she wrapped that truth around her like a suit of armor that *wasn't* dented and beaten half to shit.

What she hadn't been expecting was the wave of sound that slammed into her and Bahamut, now back in human-form, as they stepped into Sanctum. It wasn't screaming or anger; in fact, it was cheering. All of the council was there, along with Tunnel Vision, Glyph, Pest Control, Arachno Bro, and Thuggernaut. Even Ivan, clad in his Pseudonym outfit, stood in the corner applauding. From the center of the crowd stepped Doctor Mechaniacal, covered head to toe in his own distinctive meta-suit.

"We wanted to be here to greet you both," he announced, the cheers subduing but not dying at the sound of his voice, "because never has a group of apprentices faced such a challenge or handled it with such cool heads. You four did a remarkable job, protecting your score, looking out for each other, and making sure that none of your actions did more than embarrass the capes... and perhaps leave one with the scent of charred fur."

Snickers and giggles came from the council. Doctor Mechaniacal continued. "Since Glyph and Pest Control returned first, we took the liberty of evaluating the paintings you brought back. Based on current black market prices, it was determined that your stolen art will net roughly six hundred thousand dollars—after the guild takes its cuts, of course. That means, my impressive apprentices, that you have all passed your final trial, showing that you can handle even the most unexpected of situations while still staying true to the guild's code."

He turned away from them and motioned to Glyph and Pest Control, who hurried over to stand by Hephaestus and Bahamut. Doctor Mechaniacal raised his arms to the four apprentices who stood beside him and turned his helmet slowly to look at everyone else in the room.

"My fellow councilors and guild-mates, the four villains beside me are no longer apprentices. Although we'll need time to prepare the ceremony to

463

induct them properly, with tonight's success it is my pleasure to announce that they are full members in the Guild of Villainous Reformation!"

If the first round of cheers had been deafening, this one nearly knocked Hephaestus from her weary feet. Instead, she grabbed Bahamut's hand and lifted their arms into the air. It had taken months of effort to finally reach this moment.

She was damn sure going to savor it.

Chapter 70

"One of our members was snagged by a flying dragon, one left her protective shell only to be brought down by drugs, and one let his prey escape by not paying enough attention to his surroundings. I won't lie to you: this was not a good showing, and certainly not up to the caliber I'd expected from all of you."

Cyber Geek, Medley, and Cold Shoulder all hung their heads as they sat across from Apollo, the older superhero staring at them patiently from his side of the desk. Medley and Cold Shoulder had required a trip to the AHC's medical team to receive antidotes for the drugs injected into their systems, which meant they'd had plenty of time to stew in their failure before being called in to Apollo's office. It was going better than they expected in the sense that no one had been kicked out of the AHC or busted back down to training. Then again, the meeting wasn't over yet.

"With that said, some of these failures are more forgivable than others," Apollo continued. "Our resident magical metas have confirmed there was heavy use of sorcery during your fight. As near as we can gather, the dragon had some sort of ward on it which made it difficult to notice. Given that none of your powers are magically based, it's not surprising that you were susceptible to such charms. That makes the kidnapping of Cyber Geek and the escape of... what did you say the metal-suited one called himself again?"

"Hephaestus," Medley replied, keeping his usual roar of a voice as meek as possible. It wasn't a name he was going to forget soon, possibly ever.

"Yes. Cyber Geek getting snatched and the escape of Hephaestus are somewhat more forgivable since both involved a dragon enchanted specifically to slip your attention. What is less understandable, however, is one of the AHC's superheroes leaving the safety of her ice construct to attack a villain who'd already displayed a use of ranged darts, which good sense would tell you were drugged." Apollo laid his hand on the after-action report, a summary of all three superheroes' debriefings along with analysis of the footage from what cameras remained. His own observations were absent from the file, as, technically speaking, he hadn't been there.

"With Cyber Geek already gone, if you hadn't allowed yourself to be removed from the fight, Medley might have been able to subdue Hephaestus before the dragon arrived to carry him away." Apollo's eyes were locked on Cold Shoulder, who squirmed uncomfortably in her chair. There was no great defense springing to mind, no quick turn of wit that would exonerate her. Apollo was right. The results spoke for themselves. They'd all made mistakes.

"Respectfully, sir, the blame for that error falls on me." Medley's voice had just a bit more of its usual strength this time. All eyes looked to his stoic, tiger-like face. "I was the one who told Cold Shoulder to come freeze Hephaestus. I was the one who was supposed to have the criminal secured. She trusted me to be able to contain the threat when I implied I would, and I didn't live up to that trust."

"You had no way of knowing that guy was going to light you on fire," Cold Shoulder said, so stunned by Medley's declaration that she momentarily forgot how uncomfortable she was.

"Doesn't matter. When I told you to leave the safety of the construct and freeze Hephaestus, I was assuring you safety. If I hadn't let myself be distracted, I could have dodged the attack, which I should have at least somewhat expected. Overestimating myself and underestimating an opponent are both honest tactical mistakes. Trusting your teammate isn't."

Apollo considered the scene before him carefully, taking a gauge of the room and the emotions within it. After several seconds of hesitation, he allowed a small smile to grace his lips and gave a soft shake of his curly head. "Well, at least that's one test you didn't fail."

"Say what?" Cold Shoulder whipped her head around so quickly that some of her brunette locks smacked Medley in the cheek.

"Failure isn't pretty, but it happens," Apollo explained. "No one expects any superhero to be perfect. We all lose sometimes. What matters most in these situations isn't the loss in itself: it's what you take away from it. Aside from failing to be on your guard against magic, Medley was the only one who made an actual tactical error. There are little lessons I expect all of you to take away from tonight, but he should have learned a big one. And it seems he did. Even when the opportunity to pass blame arrived, he recognized his failings and owned up to them. That sort of attitude is what will take you all from rookies to legends."

Cyber Geek and Cold Shoulder nodded while Medley suddenly turned sheepish. It was much easier to be brave in the face of scorn than praise, at least for him, so he looked away until Apollo spoke again.

"Tonight was bad from a crime-stopping front, but good from a training perspective. We can clearly see some holes in your tactics that need patching. Starting tomorrow, you're all going to start drilling as a team, learning to fight with one another instead of on top of one another. Also, it's evident that we need to add a fourth to your ensemble. If any of you had possessed magical tolerance, this battle could have gone very differently. I'll scout the ranks and see who hasn't been paired up with anyone yet."

"Yes, sir." Cyber Geek hesitated, unsure if the question that had popped into his head would be offensive or not. He quickly decided if he was already a little bit in trouble, he may as well take the opportunity to ask. "I was also wondering, why are we being sorted into a team like this? I don't object; I much prefer having people backing me up. But I sort of got the impression that we had to learn how to function on our own."

"In emergency situations like the one you and Medley found yourselves in at the club, that's absolutely true," Apollo said. "However, for our newer members, it's AHC policy to have you work in teams for the first year or so. This allows you to get combat experience, grow your powers, and become a generally more effective superhero, all with the benefit of having people to watch your back and cover your weak spots. Eventually, you'll all be strong enough for solo work, but as tonight demonstrated, that's still a ways off."

"That makes sense." Cyber Geek felt a wave of relief wash over him. After tonight's loss, he'd started wondering how he would fare when he didn't have other capes around to help cover him. It was reassuring to know it was a long while before he'd have to learn the answer to that question.

"All right, you three. It's late and you all need rest," Apollo told them. "Things have calmed down out there, so consider yourselves all off of standby until you get notice otherwise. I expect you to spend the next few days training, especially on teamwork, but none of you are allowed to start for twenty-four hours. You need time to decompress and think about what happened, so nothing more than the gym for a day, understand?"

All three nodded, then rose from their chairs and saw themselves out of the office. Apollo watched them go, pondering what had just happened. He hadn't expected such a display of loyalty from Medley; the man had seemed like he was meant for solo work from day one. The pairing with Cyber Geek had been a temporary one to get them both acclimated to the AHC community. For him to stick up for a brand new teammate didn't fit with what Apollo had expected. It seemed he'd have to reevaluate how to use Medley in the future, though he didn't particularly regard the revelation as a setback.

Loyalty could be a very useful trait, when leveraged properly.

*   *   *

Despite everything they'd been through the night before, Tori still had to go to work the next morning. She yawned constantly as Ivan drove them through downtown toward the Vendallia offices. With every involuntary expulsion of air, she glared at her mentor, as though he were personally responsible for her grogginess.

"I told you to go to bed early," Ivan said after the fifteenth or so dirty look. "It's not my fault you spent the rest of the night celebrating."

"Of course I was celebrating. I passed my final trial. I'm a full member of the guild. I'm no longer at risk of dying just from not measuring up. If that doesn't warrant a night of partying and a day off work, then I don't know what does."

"Being a full member of the guild means that your secret identity is now more precious than ever," Ivan countered, spinning the wheel to avoid a car that had just slammed on its brakes. "And you definitely don't want to be absent the night after a high-profile heist was pulled. Too many coincidences like that and someone smart will start putting things together."

"So it's better to show up clearly tired, as if I was out, oh, I don't know, robbing a museum?" Tori pointed out.

"Ordinarily, no, but seeing as you've been pulling all-nighters for the whole week, people are already accustomed to seeing you exhausted. Honestly, at this point, it would raise more eyebrows if you were actually well-rested." Ivan turned into the Vendallia parking lot and pulled his car into one of the many empty spots. Sometimes Tori suspected Ivan got here so early just for the good parking.

"Although, you know you don't have to come in if you don't want to." Ivan said the words carefully, as though he were afraid they might break something—which was, in fact, exactly the case. "Even if the official ceremony isn't until Friday, as of now, you're no longer an apprentice and as such are no longer compelled to follow my orders. You'll have quite a nest egg once payment from last night's job arrives, so you won't need the money. You're free to do as you please."

"Well, free as long as I don't break the code," Tori said.

"Obviously."

Tori unbuckled her seatbelt and smoothed the legs of her suit. "I guess that's all true, but I've spent months building this cover identity. And you've shown me just how important our covers can be. Maybe I won't keep it up forever, but I'm also not going to throw it away on a whim just because I'm tired. For now, Tori Rivas, dedicated intern, is going to keep plugging away."

"I'm glad to hear it." Ivan freed himself from his own seatbelt and laid his hand on the door handle. "Honestly, finding a new assistant would be a huge inconvenience. In spite of your contrary nature, you're surprisingly competent."

"'Surprisingly competent.' And the other apprentices all say their mentors gave the best compliments. They got nothing on you, you big softy," Tori said.

468

"Don't let it go to your head," Ivan told her. "I did only say competent, and that was as an assistant."

· "Oh yeah, and what about as an apprentice?" Tori asked.

"Trying, tiring, frustrating, time-consuming, draining of both my food and my patience, wearying, worrying, and all-around unpredictable." Ivan allowed his usual stoic mask to slide out of place just a touch as a wry smirk wormed its way onto his lips. "And impressive beyond all expectations I could have held. The sort of apprentice I'm proud to say I had even the smallest of hands in shaping."

"That... was unexpectedly sweet." Tori turned her head, amazed that the early morning allergies she'd apparently just acquired were able to make her eyes water even through closed car doors. "Okay, you had enough of this sentimental stuff? Because too much more and we might have to hug. I might be able to handle being part of a rocket-powered dragon, but even I have limits to my weirdness threshold."

"Agreed, I think," Ivan replied. "Let's get to work." With that, he opened the door. All mention of the guild fell away. In public, they were nothing more than Ivan Gerhardt and his wayward, but reforming, assistant.

*　　　*　　　*

Balaam sat in his chambers, re-watching the tape of the prior night's heist for at least the sixth time. The focus of his earlier viewings had been on his own apprentice; however, Glyph's minimal involvement overall meant there was little feedback to offer. What occupied most of his subsequent viewings were the antics of Hephaestus as she darted about the field of battle, leaving a wake of chaos behind her. He had to hand it to Ivan's girl: she was more resourceful than Balaam had expected. When she'd shown up to the trial in a meta-suit, he assumed it would have basic functionality, if that. Instead, it had made the difference more than once in helping the apprentices pull off the job and escape safely.

She was more dangerous than anticipated, which meant he had to revise his plans slightly. The suit would grant her some melee capabilities along with tricks like her dart cannon and thrusters. It added to her power, but didn't significantly increase it. Hephaestus still suffered from the same weakness she'd had before the suit: she lacked an ability to overwhelm any sufficiently durable opponent. Fire was all well and good, but against those strong enough to shrug off its effects, she was essentially helpless. Granted, her pseudo-intangibility did pose an obstacle, although it was nothing a bit of magic or forethought couldn't overcome. Hephaestus was a thorn: annoying but easily plucked, so long as one had the right tools.

Ivan, the man who had been Fornax, was a much more formidable problem; however, Balaam believed he'd hit upon the right method for dealing with the semi-retired villain. It would be difficult but also potentially highly effective. Assuming, of course, that one lacked enough morality to pull it off.

Balaam had made note of how powerful Glyph's spells had been during the outing; his apprentice had managed to slip past the awareness of every cape on scene. Initially, he'd taken the apprentice for political reasons. He needed to be in the thick of wherever things were interesting, and Ivan's adoption of the would-be code-breaker had made being a mentor all the rage again. But as time wore on, he had noticed that Glyph's wards were surprisingly powerful. The young man could grow as versatile as his education allowed. With proper cultivation, he might even make a dependable asset for Balaam's department. Thanks to the trusting relationship they shared as teacher and student, it was possible that Glyph might even come in handy during the coming events, if he had the stomach for it.

As for the rest of the apprentices, they were unremarkable and unlikely to pose any problem. Few would be involved when the plan came to fruition, and any who were could easily be dispatched. Even Hephaestus didn't constitute an actual threat; she was just one more tool to leverage against Ivan… and, if he were being completely honest, a way to add insult to injury. Ivan had clearly taken a shine to his apprentice, though he tried his best to hide it. Crushing her would hurt him, and anything Balaam could do to hurt Ivan was well worth the time and effort.

Once upon a time, Fornax would have been the right-hand man, if not the outright leader of Balaam's plan. Balaam had seen the unstoppable monster as a child and gazed in wonderment at the sheer destructive potential packed into one man's fists. When he'd become a meta-human himself, a drive to be like Fornax had spurred Balaam to master his craft. He'd quickly grown from a modest spell-slinger to a sorcerer capable of standing toe-to-toe with all but the most powerful of capes. Then one day he'd been invited into the guild and finally gotten the chance to meet the man who'd inspired him, who'd driven him to be the most dangerous villain he could.

And instead of Fornax, there had only been Ivan. Sure, he'd worn the cheap veneer of the Pseudonym name, but even that was half-assed. Gone was the monster who could level entire city blocks, gone was the terror capes raced away from, gone was one of the handful of meta-humans who could fight on par with Lodestar. In its place was the dull, bland, pointless being known as Ivan Gerhardt, a man who had no interest in villainy, who hung to the sidelines as much as possible, and who helmed an entire section of the guild that seemed utterly pointless.

While Balaam still adored Fornax with every fiber of his being, he loathed Ivan for occupying this world in his idol's place. And he would punish him for it. Oh yes, he would punish him. Even with as much as had to be done to make the plan succeed, Balaam had devoted ample time to ensuring that Ivan would suffer. Perhaps even die. Not a literal death—no one was even certain that was possible—but at least a metaphorical one.

And if Ivan Gerhardt died, perhaps the resurrection of Fornax would begin.

Chapter 71

Despite the fact that there were only a few hours of free time between the end of work Friday and the guild's ceremony, Tori raced into the basement as soon as Ivan pulled into the driveway. While Thursday had demanded she take a much-needed nap, Tori was determined to get her suit repaired as quickly as possible. Now that she'd actually used it, knowing it was broken left her feeling naked. It was a sensation she wanted to dispel as quickly as possible.

Most of the repairs were simple, some only cosmetic. The biggest fixes needed were the giant gash that Medley had taken out of her left arm and the broken focusing lens on her right gauntlet. She'd also gotten several ideas for easily implementable new features, such as some miniature acetylene torches in the tips of her fingers. Medley's dexterity with his claws in their fight had left Tori wanting a pair of her own. Plus, they'd be useful for spot-fixes in the field if she needed repairs before she could make it to her lab.

She was just finishing up with the left arm when a sound echoed through the quiet basement. It caused her to jump and nearly drop the heavy mechanism in her hands. As her heartbeat slowly returned to normal, Tori realized that the sound had been her phone. In her excitement to get to work, she'd forgotten to switch it over to vibrate, an error she would fix immediately.

Digging through her purse, Tori pulled out her mobile, surprised to see a number she was only recently familiar with on its screen. Donald, absent at work for over a week now, had sent her a text. Much as she was itching to get back to her suit, she felt a bit guilty at the thought of ignoring him. The poor guy had been so worried about becoming disconnected from people in his old life. Not to mention she and the other apprentices had delivered what had to be an embarrassing moment to his team only a few nights prior. Even if he didn't know she was responsible, Tori still felt like she owed him a bit of extra courtesy.

She clicked on the speech bubble icon, loading Donald's message.

Hey Tori, this is Donald. Hope things at the office are going well! I wanted to see if you were up for showing me that coffee shop you always rave about. It would be nice to make sure Chloe is doing okay. Let me know if you're free sometime this weekend.

In all the haste of being attacked and held hostage, Tori had forgotten that no one had gotten to try the coffee from Ridge City Grinders. It was a shame; she wanted to steer as much business toward them as possible. Plus, if anyone in that office had needed a caffeine boost more than her, it was Donald. That probably wasn't as much the case anymore, now that he'd have exciting late-night fights with criminals to occupy his time, but it would still be nice to catch up.

The weekend would be tough, though. Ivan's kids were coming, so she'd be staying over at the guild. Tori had planned to use the time to figure out her next steps, where she wanted to live, and how she would use her take from their museum heist. Even if she tried to squeeze Donald in, it felt like tempting fate to leave guild headquarters to meet for coffee with a known cape. While the other villains might not say anything, there was always the possibility Donald would put two and two together. Having just gotten one sword of Damocles out from overhead, Tori was in no hurry to procure a new one.

Weekend is pretty jammed. I have... group stuff. You know. But I'm free every afternoon next week. Want to meet up after work?

Tori carried the phone over to her work bench and set it down near the hammer she'd been using to pound out her suit's dents. She was barely back to work before a new text made the phone scoot across the metal surface, causing at least as much of a commotion as the ringer had. With a glance at the clock, Tori finally admitted defeat and snapped it up. There was only a half hour until she had to go anyway, and there was still packing to do.

Afternoons are good for me. Tuesday?

Heading toward the stairs, Tori typed in a quick response before stuffing the device in her pocket.

Tuesday sounds fine. See you at 5:15.

She had to remember to tell Ivan that she would take a cab home that day; he got cranky about unexpected changes to existing plans. Then again, it was possible that she might be driving herself home come Tuesday afternoon. After all, with over a hundred and fifty grand in the bank, she could easily squeeze a new motorcycle into her budget. It would be nice to have her own vehicle again. It would give her a new level of freedom, which she was still adjusting to having regained. Tori needed to make the transition quickly, though. The longer she stayed like this, the easier it was to get comfortable.

It was about time she started thinking about what her world would be like without Ivan watching over her.

*   *   *

Donald slowly lowered the phone. Ren hovered nearby, waiting impatiently to hear the verdict. "She said yes."

"All right!" Ren slapped Donald on the back so hard that the red-haired man nearly went tumbling out of his chair. The two of them were seated in one of the small break rooms that dotted the AHC, waiting for Cold Shoulder to arrive so yet another afternoon training session could start. With what little free time they had, Ren had seized the opportunity to continue his week-long quest of cajoling, berating, and encouraging Donald to finally text Tori and invite her to do something. Today, after a week of being worn down, it had finally worked. As a result of his long effort, Ren was more enthusiastic than Donald at being met with success.

"It's just coffee," Donald protested, both because he didn't want to oversell what had occurred and because an enthusiastic Ren was a danger to those without superhuman endurance.

"What's just coffee?" Irene asked, ambling into the break room. Outside of her Cold Shoulder costume, she seemed smaller, somehow, and far less imposing. Neither Ren nor Donald was silly enough to believe that; after Wednesday's fight, they were keenly aware that a fierce warrior lurked below her unassuming surface.

"Donald finally worked up the courage to ask out a girl he works with," Ren explained, the cheer on his face glowing so brightly he could have been mistaken for Apollo.

"I asked her to go get coffee with me and catch up." Donald put away the phone and took a few steps away from Ren to avoid another back slap. The first one was already starting to bruise. "And I'm not sure I can really say we work together anymore. I have no idea when the next time I'll get to go to the office will be."

"Probably not for a while, the way Apollo is training us," Irene said. She wasn't far from the mark; since the Wednesday embarrassment, they'd been drilling as a team constantly, with three sessions per day simulating all manner of different combat environments. All of them suspected the only reason they weren't being trained twenty-four seven was that other AHC members needed to use the facilities as well.

Ren's enthusiasm finally dimmed a bit and he shook his head. "The supplemental training is optional, you know. We're all free to skip it if we want." Apollo had told them all that when he handed them their new schedules. While each believed it was sincerely true, they also didn't think for a moment that there wouldn't be consequences to such a decision.

"I wasn't complaining, just pointing out that Donald has a full plate," Irene replied. "I'm not sure when he'll cram in a date, let alone a day job."

"Tuesday afternoon," Donald told her. "And it's just coffee, not a date. But as long as I'm seen in public, I don't think Apollo will mind me missing a session. He keeps trying to get us to go out more to be seen. Says it helps remind criminals that the AHC is everywhere and makes regular people think of us as just like them."

474

"That a fact? Well, if we can't do team drills, maybe I'll take the opportunity to have an afternoon on the town as well," Irene said. "Ren, you want to go check out a local sculpture exhibit with me?"

"I'll think about it." Ren didn't relish the idea of skipping training, but he was on board with Donald actually pursuing someone he liked. For that, he might be able to justify missing one afternoon of work. Though he wasn't sure he'd be able to tolerate a whole afternoon of art. "We're not outed superheroes, though, so us being in public doesn't generate PR."

"Unless we go in costume," Cold Shoulder countered. "I bet Apollo would love that: two capes out on the town, enriching themselves with culture. That's the sort of thing that gets you in the news *and* the arts section. Double whammy."

It was a shrewd and accurate point. Worse, it was such a good idea that Ren didn't have a defense for it. Rather than admit defeat, he employed a tried and true combat tactic: he stalled for time.

"Something to think about for sure, but for now, we've got training to do," Ren said. "Let's head over to get started."

"I'm not forgetting about this," Irene warned, though she followed as he led them out of the break room. "Either of you gotten news on our fourth yet?"

"I heard Apollo is making the rounds through all the other rookies, searching for one that best fits our existing team dynamic," Donald told her.

"Do either of you have any idea what that actually means?" Irene asked.

"Not a clue," Ren replied, grateful to have the topic off his plans for next Tuesday. "But he got us you, so the man clearly knows what he's doing."

*   *   *

"No good. We've already got a redhead," Apollo said, tossing the file into the growing stack of rejects. "Cyber Geek might be in combat a lot of the time, but when he's not, that copper-top is still on display."

Jessica protested before her career's sense of self-preservation could intervene. "But sir, her power—"

"Is a secondary, if not tertiary, concern." Apollo glared at Jessica, who meekly went back to work, sorting through the pile of potential magic metas to pair with the current team. "These kids have the potential to be great. They've got that spark that grabs the media's eye and the public's heart, but only if we package them just right. That means we need to balance the team carefully, which we can't do by doubling up on unique attributes."

475

"Here's a good possibility," Barney said, handing over a new file.

Apollo skimmed it quickly before throwing it in the reject pile. "Power is good, and she's blonde, which is a nice touch, but she's too plain."

"Last time you wanted plain," Jessica pointed out.

"That was because Medley is so terrifying, we needed someone to soften him up," Apollo replied. "Cold Shoulder was a good fit for that role; she's unimpressive in almost every capacity, so seeing him fighting alongside and protecting her makes him seem endearing. That said, the role is already filled, so let's cover a new base. The team is significantly lacking in sex appeal on either end of the spectrum."

"Cyber Geek is polling well," Barney pointed out.

"He's polling as loveable, like a clumsy guy you want to root for, which is exactly what we hoped for with him," Apollo said. "Now let's add someone the public wants to fuck, not hug. If we can round the team out with eye-candy, they can be used for just about any appearance or story we want to run."

"I might have one," Jessica said, pulling a new file out from near the bottom of her pile. "She wasn't near the top because she wasn't necessarily a perfect fit, but if you're really focusing on aesthetics, I think she might be a good choice."

Apollo accepted the file and looked it over carefully, starting with the picture on the front page. "A little pale, though some go for that. Black hair, too... would have preferred a blonde for this. She's not thick, but she isn't exactly the lean body-type. I mean, those hips alone..." Apollo flipped a few pages to look at her power and let out a low whistle. "Damn; that would be a solid tactical fit, I'll give you that. Okay, sell me on her. Why this one? Power aside, she doesn't exactly tick all the usual boxes."

"But the boxes are changing," Jessica said. It was the first time in the meeting she'd felt a bit of traction, and she refused to let it slip away. "The classic pin-up beauty is coming back into vogue. Barney can show you the statistics, but it's a trend we've been watching slowly rise over the years. Right now it's on the precipice of breaking mainstream; we can get out ahead of the curve. With the right costume, hair, and makeup people, that woman could be the face of the new wave of beauty. If we're quick and smart enough about it, she might even get credited as ushering the new trend in."

Now that piqued Apollo's interest. Trendsetting capes were practically worth their weight in pilfered alien technology. Once that label got hung across their shoulders, every fashion choice they made spurred on dozens of imitations, which could be sold by AHC subsidiaries for a sizable profit.

"Get her in for a test photo session and run it through at least three focus groups," Apollo ordered. "I want the data and pictures in my hands by no later than noon tomorrow. If she works, then we're done, but if not, I'll need to have some backup on hand. We have to get the team rounded out as soon as possible; Cyber Geek and Medley have already made their debuts. If we're not quick, the public will think of them as solo acts and might buck the idea of them being part of a team."

"We're on it," Barney said. He and Jessica rose from their chairs and reached for the remaining files, but Apollo waved them off.

"Leave them. I'm going to dig through and find a backup or two, just in case Jessica's hunch is wrong." He noted that Jessica visibly paled by a few shades before she and Barney bolted from the room. In truth, he trusted Jessica's judgment even more than Barney's, but she was only at the top of her game when she thought the stakes were high.

Besides, he really did need to find a spare fourth, just in case. That group had to be ready. If everything went to plan, then next week was going to provide them an opportunity to make a name for themselves unlike almost anything that had ever come before. If they were prepared, that team of rookies could be household names by the time the next weekend rolled around. Personally, Apollo was rooting for them, partly because he liked them, at least Medley and Cyber Geek.

But mostly because when the dust of what was coming finally settled, he was going to need every PR tool at his disposal.

Chapter 72

Tori wasn't exactly sure what she'd been expecting as she and Ivan stepped into the guild. She knew enough of the more frequent attendees to know that none of them seemed particularly big on ceremony. Things appeared to be business as usual otherwise: Ivan was dressed in his dark, nondescript Pseudonym outfit once more and she was clad in her apprentice costume. Nevertheless, she felt unsettled. Her bag had been left in the car with assurances that it would find its way to her room, so there was nothing in her hands as Ivan walked her down a deserted hallway and into a small elevator.

"This isn't some final test, is it?" Tori blurted out just as the doors closed. "Like, you all say I've passed but then make me and the other three fight to the death to see who really gets into the guild?"

Ivan didn't respond immediately, which set Tori's teeth on edge. She began working through how in the hell she'd take down the others without so much as a shoulder plate from her meta-suit. Finally, Ivan answered, and when he did, she could swear there were the barest hints of amusement in his voice.

"If that were the case, I'd have almost certainly let you bring along some of your weaponry. It wouldn't look very good on me if my apprentice were killed off quickly, after all."

"Oh, come on. We both know I might go down, but I sure as shit wouldn't be the first one out." Though her words were rough, her nerves were settling. Ivan wasn't the sort to joke often; if he felt up to quipping then things must be on the up and up. Or he really wanted to see her die, which seemed unlikely. Ivan was the sort that, if he wanted someone dead, he'd do it by his own hand.

At last, the elevator doors opened to a room Tori had never seen before, which wasn't surprising given how little of the guild's building she'd been exposed to. It was a vast space, bigger than the gym in her old high school from another life. In the center was a hardwood floor—no doubt for dancing— surrounded by a moat of flat red carpet. Buffet stations and bars were stationed in all of the room's corners, each manned by robots a lot less sophisticated than Xelas. Across from the entrance was a large stage currently occupied by seven other bodies: her fellow apprentices, their mentors, and Doctor Mechaniacal in full meta-suit.

To Tori's enormous shock, between her and that stage was a veritable sea of bodies. She'd never seen this many people in the guild at all, let alone all at once. Some people were in colorful costumes that smacked the outskirts of her brain with familiarity, while others wore suits or tuxedos. Most were humanoid, but an occasional face full of tentacles or eight-foot tall green ogre peered back at her through the more mundane stares. It was one of the most surreal scenes she could recall, made all the more strange by the fact that they were all looking right at her. If not for the gentle pressure of Ivan's hand on her shoulder, she might have stood there, dumbfounded, staring back at them.

At his touch, her brain finally clicked back into gear. She walked toward the stage with as much composure as she could muster. For the first time, she was glad her apprentice costume came with a mask, as it covered the blush that was trying to rapidly creep across her face.

"You could have warned me about this," Tori whispered darkly under her breath.

"And miss the opportunity to see my composed apprentice so taken by surprise? All the money in the guild's coffers couldn't have convinced me to give up a chance like that," Ivan replied.

Tori might have said more if she weren't trying to swim through a sea of stares on her trek to the stage. Had the others been subjected to this? Only if their mentors got as much of a kick from screwing with them as Ivan did, she supposed, so it seemed likely. As she walked, Tori nodded her head at the few guild members in the audience she recognized. All three of the Bytes were there, with one of them, Gig, already so drunk she was leaning on Kilo's shoulder for support. Kristoph was in the crowd; even amid so many other villains, he'd been given a wide berth. Still, he smiled and waved at her, and Tori gave a small wave back. Johnny Three Dicks was hanging out next to Xelas and Morgana, all of whom grinned as they saw her pass. Even Stasis offered up a small nod of greeting. Gork made a weird motion with her giant hands that Tori chose to assume was friendly but didn't bother attempting to mirror.

Then it was over. They climbed a set of wooden stairs to approach the stage. Ivan guided her to a stop at the end of the row, where they flanked Beverly and Thuggernaut. Tori and her fellow apprentice exchanged a single nervous glance before Doctor Mechaniacal's voice filled the giant room, instantly snaring the attention of every criminal, ruffian, and crook assembled before him.

"It is not often that we have the chance to welcome new members into this guild. Too many who share our passion for freedom, for life outside the rigid confines of laws designed for humans, are unwilling or unable to curb their baser instincts enough to live within the shelter and rule of our organization. We are a rare breed, each and every one of us. Powerful enough to survive the capes, but wise enough to know there is value in avoiding conflict. Each time we take in refugees, be they from a confluence or an invocation of the Orion Protocol, it is with the sincere hope that they will one day stand on this stage. Sadly, too few ever make it so far. This is what makes today so special. I cannot recall the last time an entire group of recruits all showed the level of intelligence, judgment, and skill required to satisfy our entrance criteria. Yet here behind me stands just such a group."

Doctor Mechaniacal swept his hand back to gesture to the apprentices. As his fingers were directed at her, Tori felt a rush of accomplishment she hadn't been expecting. Among the crowd, several eyes grew misty, though whether it was from joy at the new members or simple nostalgia over when they had stood on the same stage varied from villain to villain.

"I know none of us are the type to revel in ceremony and speeches," Doctor Mechaniacal continued. "Yet so many of you came today because you know that, for us, this is no mere empty ceremony. All of us, together, are the unlovable, the un-reformable. We are the people who were deemed incapable of existing alongside society. But we did just that in the forming of this guild. We have done more than simply build a place to sleep and eat and plan elaborate heists. We have found a place where we, at long last, belong. All of you remember how important that feeling was the first time you truly experienced it here, and I know that's why you've come out to support the welcoming of our newest members. Because this guild is more than just an organization and a council and various members. To me, from the beginning, this guild has been a family. It is a place for people like us, the ones who had no place of their own. We made it ourselves, carved out a space in the world that we could call home. And today it is my great honor to welcome four new members into that home, to be a part of that family."

Thuggernaut was crying freely behind Beverly, whose eyes seemed to be misting up a bit as well. Even Tori felt her throat get tight. As much respect as she'd always had for Doctor Mechaniacal's brain and inventions, she'd never realized just what a gifted orator he was. The man could *speak*. In the sea of faces before her, Tori could see features that had been plastered all over the evening news and wanted posters crying freely. He'd hit them right in the sore spot, touched on the true heart of what made this guild possible. It wasn't the code—that was just the framework so people knew what to do. No, for the first time since she'd arrived, Tori could finally see what had been in front of her all along: the guild gave everyone who could accept it a place to belong.

Her first tear fell before Tori fully realized the implications of her revelation. It gave every one of its members a home. A family. And now, that included her. For the first time since she'd sat in a hospital room, watching the life of her parents slip away one tooth-grinding beep at a time, the weight of Tori's self-imposed loneliness grew just the slightest touch lighter.

480

"As you can all see, our new members still wear the garb of apprentices and are followed by their teachers," Doctor Mechaniacal told them. "If you will please be patient and help yourself to the refreshments, we will retire to a private area where they can be presented with their first official guild costumes. When I return, it will no longer be with guided apprentices but with full members of our guild."

"Wait," Tori whispered, pragmatism quickly overtaking the swell of emotion. "You all got to design our costumes?"

"Well, it's not a surprise if we have you do it," Ivan quietly replied back. "You can change them as you see fit now that you're members. This is just for you to wear tonight as you meet the rest of the guild."

"Still wish I'd had a little input on whatever I'm about to put on," Tori replied.

Ivan chuckled quietly, a little more humor in his laugh than Tori was entirely comfortable with. "Come on. After all this time, don't you trust me?"

*   *   *

Truth be told, it wasn't all that bad. Lots of black and red, not that far off from the Pseudonym color palette, actually, with a bit of a flame motif around the trim. It was sleek and contoured to her body well, giving enough padding to preserve modesty but otherwise minimizing the amount of fabric she'd have between herself and the meta-suit.

Tori turned around in the dressing room, one of four that had been set up in the small room behind the stage, checking the outfit from all angles. It didn't give her the same feeling of transformation as getting into her meta-suit had, but she certainly wasn't recognizable as Tori Rivas in it, and she clearly was no longer an apprentice either.

"You had help with this, didn't you?" Tori called. Ivan was waiting outside along with all the other mentors and Doctor Mechaniacal, the established guild members talking amongst themselves. Even Balaam was being good, though that mostly consisted of just not talking to Ivan.

"We all had the option to consult with Silk Spitter," Arachno Bro answered. "He's the best costume design expert in the guild's history."

"But we also came up with our own designs and ideas," Thuggernaut added. "We all tried to create an outfit that would fit your new personas, though if we missed the mark, we won't take offense if you change things. These are ultimately a best guess."

"I can't speak for the others, but you hit mine right on the head." Tori could hear Beverly throw back her own curtain and emerge, followed by the sound of light clapping and appropriate compliments. Curiosity got the better of her, and without thinking, Tori emerged as well.

Unlike Tori's outfit, Beverly's had been built for more than to be stuffed into a meta-suit. The emerald green armor perfectly matched her eyes, the trunk section covering her chest like something out of a gladiator film. More armor covered the leather skirt that flared wide and stopped just above her knees. The matching boots ran halfway up her long shins and on her forearms were a set of studded bracers. Most eye-catching of all was the mask, which almost looked reptilian unless one had seen Beverly shift, in which case they instantly recognized the dragon that had inspired it. Aside from the green coloring, it was actually quite similar to Thuggernaut's costume, a touch that was clearly not lost on Beverly as she stared down at her new armor.

"You look badass," Tori said. She did too; Beverly looked like she was ready to step into a battle, not go mingle with other villains.

"And it's all enchanted to shift with you," Thuggernaut told her. "Changes color too, so it will always match your scales."

"I love it," Beverly said, and a moment later she was hugging the oversized brute, who did his best to return the affection without injuring her.

"Gotta say, my main man Arachno Bro knocked this one out of the park." Lance emerged from behind his curtain in a suit that looked as though it were made entirely of rings and pockets. It ran the entire length of his body, seemingly unbroken; though when he moved Tori could make out a few seams where pieces might come off as well as chunks of armor concealed under its bulk. The color was off-white like an old eggshell, and the matching mask covered his entire head, rendering him seemingly featureless. Not even his eyes could be made out, though they still functioned, as evidenced by the effortless way he reached up and met the strange hand of his mentor in a high-five that echoed off the walls.

"Figured you should look the part," Arachno Bro replied, though no one else seemed to have any idea what they were talking about.

"Mine's a good fit," Tori said, turning to Ivan. He stared at her carefully, as though he weren't entirely sure that it was truly his apprentice under the new threads. Which, in a way, it wasn't.

"I've been assured the fabric is as durable as we can engineer," Ivan told her. "And it goes without saying that they've been designed to shift with your form. Also... you look quite lovely. I mean, intimidating. Like a real villain." Ivan gave up trying to clarify and instead coughed into his hand, an action that drew chuckles from Thuggernaut, Arachno Bro, and even Doctor Mechaniacal.

"I think what Pseudonym is trying to say is that you truly look the part of a grown, powerful villain," Doctor Mechaniacal said, stepping in after the laughter died down. "He's bad with words, but if you search carefully, the sentiment shines through."

Tori bobbed her head in agreement but didn't bother replying. She already knew what Doctor Mechaniacal was telling her, as well as what Ivan had been trying to say. The gruff old villain always seemed stymied when things took a turn for the overly-emotional or sincere; a trait she'd actually grown to find endearing. Beverly and Thuggernaut could have their hugs; sending Ivan into awkward silence told her all she needed to know about how important this moment was.

"Sorry, everybody, mine took a few minutes to figure out," Warren called before pushing the curtain aside. Like Tori, his costume featured black heavily, though that was just about the only similarity they had in common. While she'd been given red as an accent color, his outfit sported purple, not unlike the color his fingers would glow when etching a rune. Along with a mask, pants, long-sleeved shirt, boots, and gloves, his outfit also came with a billowing cloak that hung from his shoulders, almost like a cape if the cut had been slightly different. Instead of making him look like a superhero, however, the addition caused him to resemble a sorcerer, calling on the classic look of a robe without actually using one.

"As I'm sure you can tell, there are heavy enchantments woven throughout that garb," Balaam told him. "Protective and concealing magic, of course, but also many an augmentation charm channeled into the gloves to increase the potency of your wards."

"Thank you very much, sir. I will strive to make you proud every time I wear it." Warren bowed to his teacher, who waited several seconds and then returned the gesture.

"And with that, it's almost time to send you back out on stage," Doctor Mechaniacal told them. "But we should probably wait for at least a few more minutes; if I don't break up these ceremonies into small chunks, people get antsy. And antsy villains, even if they don't mean harm, can be more trouble than they're worth. So, while we wait for the last of the group to finish raiding the refreshment tables, why don't we go ahead and do presents?"

"Shit," Lance said, glancing at Arachno Bro. "Were we supposed to get you all thank-you gifts? I'm so sorry, man, no one told me, but I definitely would have if I knew—"

"Chill," Arachno Bro said, putting a clawed hand on Lance's shoulder. "We're the ones who give the gifts. Costumes are covered by the guild, but these come from us. Something to help each of you on whatever path you choose from here."

With that, the four mentors lined up directly across from their apprentices. Silence overtook the room.

Chapter 73

A solemn air swept over them, the cheer fading into the background as Doctor Mechaniacal wheeled out a small table with four boxes lined up on top. He took it to the mentor nearest to him, which happened to be Arachno Bro. The spider-like man gave a nod of thanks to the guild's leader, then carefully took one of the boxes and walked it over to Lance. With a steady hand, he held it out to the apprentice he'd trained, who accepted and opened it uncertainly.

"It's a book," Arachno Bro explained as Lance pulled a hefty tome out from the depths of the box. "I mean, you can see that. But it's a book cataloguing as many meta-insects and their native habitats as I could find. Once you learn how to summon more of those, you're going to be a real menace, and this should serve as a good map for that journey."

"That is awesome." Lance's voice was hushed with awe as he flipped through the pages, taking note of the carefully-gathered information crammed on every available surface. Even at a glance, he could recognize the unique penmanship of his mentor and knew that Arachno Bro had personally compiled all this information just for him. "Thank you so much. Not just for the book. For everything."

"Thank you, as well," Arachno Bro replied. "I'd forgotten what joy could be found in teaching and molding young minds. It's a pastime I've been unable to indulge in since my accident, yet you gave it back to me. I will always look back fondly on my time as your mentor."

While they spoke, Doctor Mechaniacal moved down the line, arriving at Balaam. The sorcerer plucked a long box from the top of the table and walked it over to Warren. Visibly nervous, Warren accepted the gift, carefully opening it to reveal a slender rod covered in runes. At his touch, it sparked and began to glow with the same purple energy that surrounded Warren's fingers when his magic was in use.

"Every good caster needs a wand or a staff," Balaam said, holding out his hand to manifest his own staff, which stood a few feet taller than him and housed a pulsing red jewel at its crown. "I concluded that the wand would be easier to write with. It can channel your energies and augment them, adding on to the power woven through your costume. More importantly, it also has the capacity to store a single rune at a time, allowing you to cast in a hurry with nothing more than the flick of a wrist."

"I... Thank you so much, sir. Such power is more than I deserve." Warren lowered his head, even as he kept his eyes trained on the glowing wand.

"Nonsense. Even if you are now a full guild member, you will always have been my apprentice. I can't very well have a student I trained getting caught or killed as soon as they leave my tutelage. Use the tools you've been given and have a long, successful career as a villain," Balaam instructed him.

The table and Doctor Mechaniacal kept rolling to Thuggernaut, who'd inserted himself between Ivan and Balaam, likely to ensure the evening stayed peaceful. The giant man reached down and plucked the smallest box from the table. He held it out to Beverly, who broke the seal with the nail of her thumb and pulled out a small golden ring with a curiously-designed rune etched into its center.

"Blending in is hard for us big folks," Thuggernaut told her, watching as she slipped the ring on to her right hand. "But you've got the option of slipping away into obscurity, thanks to your transformations. Seeing as you've got all the fighting power a meta could need, I decided that your gift should be something to make getting in and out of dangerous situations a little easier. Press the rune in the center."

Beverly dutifully obliged, angling the ring on her fourth finger down so she could press the rune with her thumb. Just like that, she was gone, as the gasp from Tori and Warren both attested to.

"What?" Beverly said, her voice seeming to manifest from nothing.

"You just disappeared, that's what," Tori snapped. Moments later, Beverly reappeared, thumb no longer in contact with the rune on the ring. She looked at Thuggernaut for explanation, which he cheerfully provided.

"As long as you wear the ring and touch the rune, you'll be invisible. While it recharges naturally, it doesn't have a lot of juice. You shouldn't count on it for more than a minute per day. Just long enough to slip out of view and become a dragon, or vice versa."

"Wow, that *is* functional," Beverly said, gazing at her ring with new appreciation. "I love it. Thank you, Thuggernaut!"

As they hugged, Doctor Mechaniacal continued his trek to the sole remaining mentor. Ivan plucked the final box from the table and handed it nonchalantly to Tori. It wasn't as big as Lance or Warren's boxes, but it certainly was larger than Beverly's. Tori had no clue what could be inside. She pulled the packaging open to reveal a small orb suspended between a pair of metal rings.

"What is... oh, no way." While the strange device seemed alien at first, the longer Tori gazed at it, the faster her mind worked, recalling half-scribbled diagrams in highly theoretical research notes she'd glimpsed throughout her studies. Carefully, as though the orb were made of a soap bubble that would pop

486

on contact, she lifted it up, unsurprised to find that it moved as if it had no mass at all.

"Ivan, this is a miniature gravitational anomaly generator." Tori's eyes were so large they threatened to stretch outside the confines of her new mask. "These don't even technically exist."

"You'd be surprised what can be purchased when one has guild connections," Ivan said. Of course, everyone in the room knew he'd just bought it from Doctor Mechaniacal, but keeping up a certain amount of vague mysteriousness was important for villains, even amongst each other. "Besides, after Wednesday's debacle, I thought you could use a little more mobility."

"Hey, so, um, you got to hear the explanation of what all our stuff does," Beverly pointed out. "Anyone want to tell us what the deal with the weird orb is?"

"It can generate a field of reduced weight, even complete weightlessness," Tori babbled excitedly. "It will *tremendously* scale back the amount of thrust I'll need for my initial momentum and..." She trailed off as the eyes looking at her began to glaze over. Perhaps this was not the time to try and educate everyone on theoretical gravitational anomaly devices, so she decided to cut to the chase. "When properly equipped, it will let my suit fly."

"Sweet," Beverly said.

"Badass," Lance echoed.

"And with that, the giving of gifts has concluded," Doctor Mechaniacal announced. "Your mentors will hold on to the less portable items you've received for convenience. You should all wait here and listen closely. I shall introduce you one at a time to the guild. When your name is called, you are to walk on stage and join me. These are the final moments where the vestiges of apprenticeship will cling to you, so if you have anything to say to your mentors, feel free to do so."

The room immediately began to split off as Doctor Mechaniacal exited the room. They could hear his unmistakable voice crackling over the speakers as he called the rest of the guild back to order. Amid the not-quite-whispered conversations, Tori looked at Ivan, still tucked under his idiotic Pseudonym mask.

"Feels a little odd to think about having a heart-to-heart. I mean, I'm going to see you on Sunday night. Not much to say now that couldn't be said then."

"Technically quite correct," Ivan agreed.

"Except that, I should say that I really like my orb. It's an amazing gift, one that means the world to me." Tori looked down at the weightless device, noting that she could see a distorted reflection of herself in its depths. The masked woman staring back at her bore almost no resemblance to the thief who'd stupidly busted into a vault owned by a guild of villains. She was so much stronger now and knew a tremendous amount more about how to survive. She also knew that none of it would have been possible if the man in front of her hadn't agreed to take an apprentice.

"Also... thanks for saving my life," Tori said. "I know we didn't exactly want to be paired up, but you had a choice, and you chose to save me. To teach me. To give me the best chance of surviving in this world. I'll always be thankful for that."

Ivan took a step toward her and rested his hand on top of her head, mussing her hair where it emerged from under her mask. "I owe you a debt of thanks, too. Teaching you has reminded me why this guild was founded, why it matters. We are more than the guard dogs who keep the more disruptive metas at bay. We give guidance and direction to those who would hear it. We are a refuge for those who are lost. Amid all the dirtier matters we deal with, I'd managed to forget that. Thank you, Tori, for reminding me why I helped create this guild in the first place."

"Does that mean I can expect to see Pseudonym out and about, tearing up the streets?" Tori asked.

"I highly doubt it," Ivan replied. "But one never knows what the future holds in store. Oh, before I forget, there is one more thing I wanted to tell you: wear your work clothes when you come home on Sunday. I have one more gift, though far less substantial or useful than the orb."

"That's all the info I get?" Tori asked.

"Surprises aren't much fun if you know what they entail," Ivan told her.

Overhead, Doctor Mechaniacal's voice reached a crescendo, and he loudly called for Bahamut to come out and join him. Beverly gave Thuggernaut one last glance, and then hurried out of the room. No sooner had she vanished than a wave of applause crashed through the speakers as the guild welcomed its newest member.

"He does these alphabetically," Ivan whispered. His words came only a few seconds before Doctor Mechaniacal called for Glyph, who took a deep breath and tried to walk with as much confidence as he could muster. This time, the applause sent butterflies through Tori's stomach, as she realized there were only seconds until he called—

"Hephaestus!"

The woman who had stared down a team of capes on her first official guild outing felt her courage tremble for a sliver of a second, then she mustered up her gumption and strode toward the door. Stepping out onto the stage, Tori

488

faltered momentarily as the lights blinded her. Blinking away the spots in her eyes, she continued forward to stand next to Glyph as the sea of villains, so many of them unfamiliar, clapped and cheered. Tori could make out the electronic whistling of Xelas and a lot of hooting that seemed to be coming from Johnny.

"Pest Control!" Doctor Mechaniacal bellowed, and seconds later Lance arrived, taking the empty spot next to her. He was washed in cheering as well, until Doctor Mechaniacal held up his armored hand and the room went silent.

"With their names chosen, their trials overcome, and their apprentice costumes shed, these four have now officially completed all requirements to join our ranks. Please, guild-mates, welcome our newest official members!"

If the cheering at their names had been enthusiastic, this seemed downright overpowering. What made it all the more entrancing was that they weren't cheering because Doctor Mechaniacal told them too; the joy in their claps and screams was far too sincere. They were genuinely happy to see four new members pass the bar of entrance and become one of them. Their guild, their family, had grown a little bit bigger today, and that was all the reason they needed to be overjoyed.

It was over, Tori realized. She, Beverly, Lance, and Warren, they were all free, and no matter what paths they might choose to go down from here, they all had a home.

*   *   *

Nexus walked down the charred, smoldering streets, stepping over a couple of corpses that had melted in place. Above him, the sky was dark as a broken world tried in vain to repair itself. Amid the black clouds, red streaks of lightning crackled, threatening those who dwelled below with more torment. Well, if there had been anyone living below, anyway. This was the site where it had all begun, and as such, Nexus was the only creature who drew breath among the shattered streets.

It had been a fine bit of entertainment, one of the best dimensions he'd watched so far. The cleanup was never as interesting anyway, so he was glad most of the ones capable of doing it were dead. Perhaps this dimension would take new, interesting turns that he'd yet to witness. It wasn't likely, though. While every dimension in the multiverse was unique, some had more pronounced differences than others. Here, the alterations were minimal, and that was reflected in how the event had played out.

Even now, half a country away from where they were desperately hunting down the monster who'd unleashed living hell upon the world, Nexus

489

knew how things were unspooling. By sundown they would catch up to their quarry, Lodestar leading the pack. The woman would be half-insane by this point, so lost in grief that she could scarcely function through the blind, drowning anger. Nexus would be there for the next battle, the one that cracked the earth and ushered in decades of despair; however, until then, he was content to simply stroll through the aftermath. One had to get a good appreciation for all that went into a show. The buildup and the fallout were almost as important as the spectacles themselves.

Still, this was merely a placeholder, something to fritter away the time while he waited for the next main event to begin. This dimension was like so many others—no unique people who might sway or shift the tide of battle, no factors that made things deliciously unpredictable. It was like watching a rerun of the same show he'd seen a hundred times. No matter how much he might enjoy it, it lacked the thrill of the unknown.

It was better than nothing, though. And anyway, by his observation, it would be a few days at most until the dimension with Quorum hit this junction. All the pieces were in play and moving into position; once the first move was made, chaos would be on its heels, and Nexus would be waiting to take in the show.

Until then, he'd keep busy by taking in the usual sights. And it was always fun to watch that final battle, anyway. No matter how many times he saw it, there was just something special about that fight. The brutality, the emotion, the regret, the pain... so rarely in life did fate force an encounter on par with the one that would happen at sunset. While Nexus couldn't wait to see how the other dimension fared, this would do for now.

He truly never tired of watching Lodestar kill Fornax, after all.

490

Chapter 74

Tori didn't wake up in her guild quarters until halfway through Saturday, the night of celebration and mingling with her other guild-mates having taken a heavy toll. After a late breakfast, long shower, and a few minutes spent in fire-form to shake off the remnants of a hangover, she got down to business.

Logging in to her bank account, Tori found that she had indeed been credited her share from the museum heist, minus about twenty grand. Interestingly, a memo in the deposit line showed the money coming from Vendallia Industries as a bonus with the notation of "Lab expenses deducted." Doctor Mechaniacal had warned her that the tech she'd used to build her suit would eventually have to be paid for, so the deduction made sense. Either way, a hundred and thirty grand could still buy her all the components she needed to fully refine her suit.

Before that, however, there were pragmatic issues to deal with. Closing the tab with her banking information, Tori began to hunt through local apartment listings. Hephaestus might be able to bunk at the guild, but Tori Rivas was going to need a place to stay if she wanted to keep selling her cover. Besides, much as she liked the guild, having somewhere to call her own seemed prudent. Though, as she skimmed through the pricey listings, it became evident that she couldn't afford any of the really good spots on her own. Well, she could if she used her thief money, but the whole point of an apartment in the real world was that it needed to be a place Tori the administrative assistant could afford. Hephaestus, however, would need a lot of space, plus security, since she wouldn't have Ivan's basement to use as a lab anymore. Those requirements weren't satisfied by the salary she pulled down at Vendallia.

How the hell did normal people find decent places to live? Well, the obvious answer was that most people weren't concealing the fact that they were meta-humans aligned with a secret organization of supervillains. That opened up options like roommates, who would split the rent and lower costs.

Tori tapped absentmindedly on the side of her computer, a new idea flitting through her head. Shutting the machine off, she threw on a slightly less decrepit t-shirt and a pair of jeans in place of her sweats and left her room. Three doors over, she knocked firmly until the door opened to reveal an awake, albeit not quite alert, Beverly.

"Do you ever sleep?" Beverly asked, pulling open her door the rest of the way.

"It's past noon, get over it," Tori said. She sauntered in, shut the door behind her, and whipped around to face her tired friend, too excited to bother with subtlety. "Where do you live?"

"For the love of... are you trying to get metaphysical before I've even had a bowl of cereal?" Beverly walked over to her cupboard. She yanked out a small pack of sugar-frosted non-nutrition, tossed its contents in a bowl, grabbed a milk jug from her mini-fridge, and filled the bowl nearly to the brim.

"No, I meant literally," Tori explained. "When you're not here, where do you live?"

"I did live with my family," Beverly replied. "Though I don't think that's going to fly anymore. We're mending bridges, but once a family member turns into a monster and nearly tramples half the people in the house, they're not exactly welcome to come strolling back through the front door."

"That wasn't your fault," Tori said. "You'd literally just been turned. No one has good control at that point."

"Which is why I'm forgiven," Beverly told her. "All the same, I scared the living hell out of them. Even if we both know I've got a better handle on this now, they might have a hard time believing me. To them, this is all impossible to understand, you know? Besides, I'd been thinking of moving out at the end of the year anyway. Getting dragon powers is as good a reason to take that plunge as any."

"I'm sorry you can't go home, but on a selfish level, I'm sort of not. See, I had an idea. What if you and I—" Tori spread her arms to draw out the moment, then clapped her hands together and finished the proposal "—become roommates! We can split the rent, help each other with cover identities, and since we're both guild members, we don't have to hide our extracurricular activities."

"Mmm." It was hard to tell whether Beverly's reaction a result of the idea or her breakfast; either way, she munched through a few more spoonfuls without saying anything. "Don't take this the wrong way," she began, "but aren't you the sort that needs a lot of space? I may not know a lot about tech stuff, but I saw you work when we were in the desert. You spread out *everywhere*. I like you, I do; I just don't know that I want to live with someone who dominates the living room so they can build mechanical dolphins with grappling hooks for noses."

"Not really what I do, but also not the worst idea for aquatic warfare," Tori said, making a mental note for future projects. "Anyway, we'd have to get a space for me to use as a lab, but I promise not to let it spill into communal areas. This place is supposed to be a cover for us anyway, remember? Tori the office-worker can't very well have advanced machinery littering the house."

"I guess that's true," Beverly agreed. She tilted back her bowl and shoveled down the rest of her breakfast, slurping her milk as she went. "Okay, I'll take a look with you and see if there's anything that fits what we'd need. Did you check and see if the guild has special deals or places set aside for us to rent? Maybe with a hidden lab already built in?"

"I... no, it never occurred to me. Do you think the guild really would have stuff like that?" Tori asked.

"Given everything I've seen, nothing would surprise me," Beverly replied. After a moment's consideration, she added, "Okay, that's probably not true in the slightest, but I wouldn't be shocked if they had some sort of real estate connection. How about you find out if that's a thing while I take a shower?"

"Sounds good." Tori headed for the door but stopped just before her hand landed on the knob. "An actual shower, right? Not slipping back into bed as soon as I leave the room?"

There was a very notable delay before Beverly let out a long sigh of defeat. "Fine, just the shower. I'll be ready in twenty minutes."

"I'll be back in twenty-one," Tori said, and just like that, she was out the door.

*   *   *

"And lastly, I'd like to bring up our defense system," Apollo said. His pen ran to the last item on the bulleted list, copies of which were supposedly in front of every other member of the Champions' Congress. Quorum, at least, could be seen following along, but with the remote terminals Lodestar and Professor Quantum were using, it was impossible to tell. Though the detached, bored tone in Professor Quantum's voice did give Apollo an indication of his distraction.

"The system was just upgraded last year," Professor Quantum said. No doubt if challenged he could probably have given the exact date and time of said upgrade, along with all the steps he'd taken to complete the task. Even at half-attention, he presented more brainpower than some state populations combined.

"Yes, it was," Apollo agreed. "However, there hasn't been a full-scale test of the lockdown protocol in over five years. According to the AHC's protocol we're supposed to do them annually."

"Those things are... sort of a pain," Lodestar admitted, the symbol flickering at her brief pause. "No matter how many times we tell people we're doing a drill, they always panic when the AHC is suddenly covered by a giant glowing energy-dome, to say nothing of all the guns and defenses that pop out.

Everyone assumes Ridge City's greatest heroes are under attack, and we have to spend the next few days sweeping up all the chaos that ensues."

"A pain or not, you three saw the importance in making sure our people had a safe place to recover and shelter when the need arose," Apollo pointed out. "As it stands now, we're way out of compliance. If you'd like to amend the protocol, then by all means, let's put a motion on the floor. Otherwise, I can have a drill ready to proceed on Tuesday."

"So soon?" Quorum said. "Those take a while to coordinate with all the emergency response agencies."

"I wouldn't have brought it up if I hadn't already laid the groundwork," Apollo assured him. "I can task our newest members with canvasing the area and ensuring the people know it's a drill. That will get them some face time with the public as well as keep things under control. All the necessary agencies have been contacted and are waiting for final confirmation of our plans. We can knock it out in a couple of hours and be good for another year. Or we can change the protocol, if anyone wants to—"

"Just run the damn thing," Professor Quantum said. "If it gets choppy, all the better to train the rookies. Though, it's a waste of time; my designs and technology are both flawless."

"Says the guy who blew the city's power grid the first time we tried to turn the system on," Lodestar reminded him. "Apollo is right. Five years of tinkering needs to be tested before we depend on it. Use the full lockdown-mode and make sure everything is running well. And try to keep the peace, please."

"Rest assured, everyone will be completely informed and I will have teams on standby," Apollo said. And he would too, because he really had reached out to all the proper agencies and told them that there would be a test occurring at AHC headquarters.

After all, doing these drills required purposely tripping a lot of AHC alarms, and he'd hate for rescue workers to mistakenly show up for an emergency that wasn't happening. Why, he'd hate it almost as much as he'd hate for Lodestar or Professor Quantum to show up for an attack that actually *was* happening. When the alarms sounded and the barriers rose, both of them would take it for nothing more than the practice session they'd been briefed on, effectively removing them from the game board.

They were too powerful, too careful. For this plan to work, there would have to be a wake of destruction, the sort that made the citizens demand an appropriate response from their superheroes.

*　　*　　*

Tori flipped through the files she had found on the car seat, skimming through them yet again for some hint at what was to come. After a weekend of apartment-hunting with Beverly (the guild, as it turned out, did have some real estate holdings, but they were limited in availability) and plotting out things like the cost of a new motorcycle and moving expenses, Tori had very nearly forgotten Ivan's request to return to his place in her work clothes. She only remembered at the very last minute and raced around her room at the guild to get ready. When she stepped into the robot-piloted car, a little sweaty and unkempt but otherwise put together, she had found the stack of files waiting for her.

As far as she could tell, they were reports from Vendallia, ones she'd turned in to Ivan earlier in the week. Given that she was also dressed like a regular employee, Tori caught the scent of subterfuge and mentally readied herself to play the part of Ivan's assistant once more. She wasn't certain how this was a gift, but decided to see how it all shook out. Ivan never gave instructions without a reason. Tori's curiosity was piqued.

The car whispered into the driveway just as Ivan emerged from the house. On his heels were two other figures. As soon as she saw them, Tori felt the blood in her veins run cold. She was flung back to her first day at Ivan's house when he'd held up a picture of two people and made it clear that there was one line never to be crossed.

Before she could instruct the driver to whip the car around, the door opened and Ivan called out to her.

"Early as always, Miss Rivas." Ivan quickly stepped forward and held out a hand to help her from the vehicle. She took it, struck dumb by the cheerfulness in his voice and the genuine smile on his face. "It's all right, the others will be here soon. Please, let me take those."

Ivan scooped the files out of Tori's hands as the door shut behind her. Suddenly she was staring into two sets of unfamiliar eyes. The kids watched her every move like she was an unfamiliar dog off its leash, and Tori focused on doing her absolute best to make no movement that could even slightly be interpreted as threatening.

"I don't believe you've ever met my children, have you?" Ivan motioned them forward, and both children inched closer to Tori. "Miss Rivas, this is Rick and Beth. Kids, this is Miss Rivas, she's a friend and colleague from the office. She's also a bit of an early bird, since the meeting doesn't start for another half hour."

At long last, Tori's tongue found the courage to move. She nodded her head much too hard in agreement. "I'm so sorry about that, completely didn't realize how far I'd missed the mark. If you'd like, I can come back."

"Nonsense, your ride is already leaving," Ivan said. And sure enough, the town car was pulling out of the driveway, headed off to wherever the guild sent it next. Hopefully not too far away, though, seeing as she had left a bag in the trunk. "Why don't you go on in and make yourself comfortable while I drop my children off with their mother? I'm sure you'll be fine on your own for a bit. I trust you."

With those words, Tori finally understood what Ivan was trying to do. He was showing her the extent to which she'd earned his trust. He was introducing her to the only things in the world he truly loved, worried, and cared about. That was why he'd had her come home like this, so that there could be a pretext to introduce her to his children.

"I'll try not to eat all of the food," Tori said. She turned to Rick and Beth, taking each by the hand and giving a firm shake. "It's nice to meet you both. Your father is kind of a stick-in-the-mud, but he's not such a bad boss."

Beth giggled. Rick tried to look interested without looking *too* interested, the paradox that was a teenage boy's attempt to grasp the intangible quality known as 'cool'. "Nice to meet you too," Beth said, tone polite as she visibly considered each word before using it. Tori was hardly shocked to see that Ivan had drilled his kids in the importance of manners, even if the older one was resisting.

"Yeah, cool," Rick mumbled. "I mean, it's a pleasure."

"Guess you got your eloquence from your dad," Tori said. This time, Beth laughed outright, and Rick's neck grew flushed. "Nothing wrong with that, though. They say when men of few words talk, everyone listens. And trust me, no one in the office ignores him when your father speaks."

"That's probably enough of that," Ivan interjected. He started to herd the kids towards his car. "I need to get them home, and sooner or later, the rest of the staff will be showing up. Kids, say goodbye to Tori."

"Bye, Tori," Beth called, her voice somewhere between a yelp and a holler. She also waved as she walked, swinging both hands overhead with no sense of restraint. It was a little surprising to see such uninhibited friendliness in a girl her age—Tori recalled her and her peers losing the quality by the time they'd gotten as old as Beth. At the same time, it was heartwarming, especially in contrast to the stoic men in Beth's family.

"Goodbye." Rick's voice was a touch more clear this time as he and his sister climbed into the back of Ivan's car. Ivan shut the doors and turned to his former apprentice, the smile that his children had conjured not fading in the slightest.

"Nice kids," Tori commented. She wasn't sure what to make of all this, so instead of trying, she decided to just let Ivan take the lead.

496

"They are. Good, smart, and faithful to a fault." Ivan looked at the car where his children were waiting. "It's important to me that they're familiar with the people I trust, just in case I ever have to use those people to send messages. They've known Wade almost since birth, and the woman you know as Morgana for the past five years. Seemed like it was time to widen that circle of trust just a bit."

"Thank you, Ivan. It means a lot to me that you set this up. But just so we're clear, there's not really a meeting going on tonight, is there?"

"Of course not," Ivan replied.

"Hot damn am I glad to hear that. I've got a suit to repair and a gravitational anomaly generator to install."

Ivan shook his head, but the smile still didn't dim. "Go get to it, then. I shouldn't be more than half an hour dropping off my kids. I'll knock when dinner is ready."

"You're the best landlord ever." Tori turned away as she spoke, not wanting Ivan to catch sight of the slight wave of sadness she wasn't sure she could hide. Exciting as the idea of living with Beverly was, Ivan really was a pretty awesome landlord, and she was going to miss living here. But leaving was inevitable. Even if she'd been on the fence about how long to stay before, this meeting had lit a fire under her.

Ivan had a family to protect. He'd taken a big risk by letting her live here at all. The sooner she was gone, the more removed his life would be from the guild, and the safer his kids would be.

No matter how much apartment-hunting it took, this would be the last week she spent living at Ivan's house.

Chapter 75

The office was abuzz with activity as Tori and Ivan walked in Tuesday morning. Both registered this anomaly; them not being among the first people in was strange enough, and anything requiring energy before nine, which was typically when everyone had finally brushed the last bits of sleep from their eyes, was nigh unheard of.

They didn't have to wonder what was going on for long, though. Barb from Human Resources, again in her plastic fireman's hat with "Safety Officer" written across the top, soon barreled up to them.

"Ivan, glad you're in a few minutes early." The woman looked almost frantic, stray wisps of brown hair with gray poking up from the under the plastic red hat. "Word just got sent down from the head office: apparently the AHC is testing their defense system and corporate has decided that it makes sense to give everyone a half-day. I need you to spread the word to the whole department as quickly as possible; we're already trying to coordinate with the people who run the car pools and make sure this doesn't throw off anyone's commute."

"Wait, what are the capes doing?" Tori asked.

"A test of their defensive perimeter," Ivan said. "It means they'll turn on their dome to keep people out, cycle through their offensive systems to make sure everything is working, and maybe have a few of their capes try to bust in just to be certain it's all functioning properly. They used to do them once a year, but it's been a while since the last one."

"Which I was thankful for," Barb added. "All buildings within a block of them evacuate, just in case something goes wrong, and traffic becomes a total nightmare as tons of people head to the perimeter to see the show. That's not even including those who somehow miss the message that it's a drill and think Ridge City's superheroes are under attack. Anyway, since the test is scheduled for three, we're officially dismissed at noon so we have time to safely leave the area before things get crazy."

"I will make certain all of my employees are abreast of the situation," Ivan told her. "I daresay many will be enthused about the time off more than they'll be bothered by the surprise."

"Thanks, Ivan. Pass along the word to any other managers you see, please." Barb was off before the sound of her words had even faded, scampering toward another woman in a suit who was likely about to be brought up to speed.

"Is there anything to worry about?" Tori asked once she was sure Barb was no longer within earshot.

498

"Doubtful." Ivan headed toward his office, seemingly unbothered by news of the AHC's activities. "This really did used to be standard procedure for them. In fact, I think the only reason it fell off was because so few criminals ever get around to trying something as ridiculous as assaulting the AHC base head-on."

Though Ivan didn't say it, they both knew exactly why that sort of thing had tapered off. With the guild watching from the shadows, any criminal who would stir things up to such a degree was usually culled long before they built up enough power or confidence to try and take on the capes directly.

"It was inevitable that they'd have to make sure everything still worked right sooner or later," Ivan continued. "After the scuffle I saw on the news last week when several tough crooks evaded capture, putting on a show of force makes perfect sense. It's a good way to remind people that while slip-ups happen, the AHC is still a force to be reckoned with."

They finished the journey into Ivan's office and he shut the door, freeing them from having to use doublespeak and subterfuge when talking about the AHC. Despite that freedom, Ivan made no attempt to recant his earlier statements. Instead, he just booted up his computer and pulled out his daily schedule, which had been printed the evening before as always.

"We'll need to rearrange a lot of my meetings for the day; probably best to assume some people will try to press their luck and cut out by eleven."

"Not if I pin them down as soon as they get through the door," Tori replied, pulling out her own day-planner to keep track of whatever assignments Ivan doled out. "But... we're really okay, right?"

"Tori, our situation means that we are never entirely okay. There is always the possibility that something we didn't see has given way and the peace we currently know is about to come tumbling down. This particular instance gives me no suspicion or need to worry; then again, if it's part of an attack on us, it would be designed to do exactly that. That said, if you spend your life looking for capes around every corner, it will be a very stressful one. Be prudent, be smart, and leave paranoia behind you if at all possible."

"Got it." Tori pulled out her pen and flipped open the day-planner. "Any ideas on what you're going to do with your afternoon off?"

"Stay here and work, of course," Ivan replied. "We're more than far enough away not to be part of the mandatory evacuation, and this will be a blessed opportunity to get ahead on my reports for a change. With no one around to distract me, I may even be able to knock out a week's worth of work in one lone afternoon."

"Wow, you sure know how to party."

"And I suppose you won't flee home to lock yourself in the basement and work more on your suit?" Ivan had brought Tori's dinner down to her lab Monday night, only to find her so engrossed in work that she didn't even notice his arrival. A few hours later he'd found her passed out at her work bench and had carried her upstairs to the couch, hoping she might get at least a few hours of rest.

"Don't blame me, you're the one who gave me an awesome new addition to work in," Tori countered. "And now that I've finally finished that part, all I have to do is fix my right gauntlet and I'll be back at a hundred percent. Assuming I can get it done before I have to meet Donald for coffee."

"You should brace for disappointment," Ivan cautioned her. "These tests tend to be 'all hands on deck' situations, which means he might not be able to make your date."

"Not a date, Ivan, just coffee and catching up. And if Donald has to flake, so be it. More time to work on the suit," Tori said.

Ivan admired the way the idea of a broken arrangement rolled off Tori's mind so easily. Capes were not the easiest people to care for, be it in a friendly or more advanced capacity. They lived at the beck and call of the people, always most accountable to a world that needed them. The first canceled plans were easy to bear; the thousandth, far less so. That was a lesson she would have to learn on her own, however. No combination of words would be enough to impart such wisdom. Some things, some pain, had to come firsthand before they stuck.

"The suit will have to wait until this afternoon. With the few hours we have, I plan to cram in as much productivity as possible," Ivan said.

Tori clicked the top of her pen, dragged a test line of ink across the top of her planner, and looked up with a hungry grin. "Give me the orders, boss. I'm ready."

*　　　*　　　*

"Everyone understands their order, correct?" Four figures stood before Balaam, four carefully selected members of the guild. Out of everyone, only these four had been deemed capable enough, trustworthy enough, to participate in such a crucial step of the plan. Here, betrayal would mean utter failure, and the death of every person currently standing in the bare, heavily-warded room where Balaam had gathered them.

Their meeting place was not as grand as the executive break rooms inside the guild; in fact, it was downright squalid. An abandoned gas station, long ago given to neglect, was where Balaam chose to have this final meeting.

500

Aside from the fact that such delicate issues couldn't be discussed inside guild walls, Balaam rather enjoyed the squalor. It reminded him of the old days when he was on the run, taking shelter in whatever hole might conceal his presence for a few hours. Yes, he greatly preferred the luxury of his guild quarters and had no desire to actually lie down and make a home in such a place, but just for visiting, it wasn't so bad.

"I handle the girl." This voice was thick and heavy, not unlike the scaled head that spoke it. Rust Tooth was a wide man whose body was completely coated in dull, bronze-colored scales. A bit of misfortune in a lab that was trying to fuse organic and biological components had created more than one cape along with the savage creature standing before them.

"That's right," Balaam agreed. "Use the charms I provided to break the barriers around Pseudonym's home. They will take a few moments to work, so be prepared for her to expect a fight."

"Lucky for me, I don't burn, and I'm a lot tougher than any tin can," Rust Tooth replied.

"Which is why you've got that job, after which you need to meet up with the others," Balaam replied. "Bombastic, what about you?"

"First the mayor's office, then the bus stations, then the kids." This voice came from a small wiry man who had the edges of a thick mustache sticking out from under his mask. "But for now, I just get in place. No moves until you send the signal."

"Correct," Balaam agreed. "Torkak and Endless Blitz, once Bombastic kicks things off, it will be on you to lead the attack. Use your forces to overwhelm as many as possible, make sure they know exactly what's going on. Rust Tooth will join you when he's finished tying up a loose end."

A humanoid creature with orange skin, an oversized head, and hands that had seven fingers gave Balaam a nod. Next to it, a regular-looking woman who could have blended in at a boating convention also signaled her agreement. However, along with that signal came a comment.

"Just one thought," said Endless Blitz. "You've been telling us what we're doing, but what about the rest of the guild? Specifically the council."

"The rest of the guild will be caught completely off guard," Balaam assured her. "I have taken all the necessary steps to ensure that any members of the council who might actually be able to interfere are dealt with. What you see here is only one subset of the team preparing for today's events. There are others, all working separately so that even if one of you falls, the rest may still see us win victory today."

"I don't even care if we win or lose anymore," Rust Tooth growled. "I just want a fight. I'm sick of this fucking peace and the ridiculous code. We're villains. It's time we got to act like it."

"And you will," Balaam agreed. "In only a few hours we will redeem our entire guild for the past decade of subservience and inaction. By the time the sun falls this evening, that ludicrous peace will be destroyed, and we will all finally be true villains once more."

*　　*　　*

"Now remember: when the dome goes up, getting in or out of the base will be nearly impossible," Apollo said. He stood on a catwalk overlooking the hangar where most of the AHC's current personnel had gathered. Next to him, silently scanning the faces of the collected superheroes for any signs of confusion, was Quorum. If he saw too many, he'd have Apollo repeat the order, but otherwise, Quorum preferred to remain quiet during such meetings. Before he'd let Lodestar and Professor Quantum take the reins, so leaving the speech to Apollo was a natural transition.

"That means I don't want to hear anyone saying they left a tool or a piece of costume inside," Apollo continued. "We're going to be outside, but we are far from off-duty. All of our communication and tech people will still be in here, and if a situation arises where you're needed, we expect you to follow orders. Now, some of you have been taken off the response call list because we're going to need people to test the defenses, as well as perform crowd control. This is a big undertaking, and it's easy to let things get out from under us, so I want everyone sticking to their orders. Don't worry about what you see someone else doing: making a machine like this work takes a whole lot of different cogs."

Of course, some of those cogs would be off keeping the peace while others would be ensuring that the unseen part of today's activities ran smoothly. Finding others who felt the same as Apollo hadn't been hard; the challenge came from selecting the ones he knew he could trust. Things would unfold quickly; if anyone dropped their ball or started telling tales when the dust settled, everything could come undone. That was why he'd taken his time, been careful, built up to this moment slowly. He needed his cogs to be diligent so that everything would run properly.

At least, until the machine was supposed to self-destruct.

"As a reminder, all of our new members, debuted or not, are on crowd control near the base. Those of you more experienced staff also assigned to that task, be sure to help them when they need it. We all know a few people will try

502

to slip by the perimeter to get a better look, and while we certainly can't let civilians endanger themselves, we also can't be too rough when we escort them out. Those of you coordinated into teams, look out for each other. Finally, everyone on crowd control should be prepared for anything. With this many of us out there, only a suicidal idiot would try something, but we've seen that sort rear their heads before."

Cyber Geek, Medley, and Cold Shoulder were staring up at him, admiration in at least two sets of eyes. It was a shame; Apollo might have liked to have used them today, but they were too green and unpredictable. His cogs had to work flawlessly. Still, if they performed well, they might make an excellent media tool for rebuilding the public's trust: innocent babes, scrambling into action and doing their best. He needed to incorporate the final member before things kicked off. She'd nicely round out the pictures and video that would no doubt be all over the news when things were done.

"All right, we've only got a few hours to finish prepping, so everyone get your work done. If you have questions, come find me, and if you've got briefings, attend them. As long as we all work together, this day will go off without a hitch." A small cheer met Apollo's words, and he replied to it with an appropriately polite smile.

It was funny, in a way. That whole speech and he hadn't told a single lie. He just hadn't elaborated on what, exactly, they were trying to pull off without a hitch. They would thank him later, though, the ones that survived and understood. They would thank him for finally making them true heroes once again, for no longer abiding the known existence of evil, even if it hid behind secrecy, bureaucracy, and lawyers. Today, the Alliance of Heroic Champions would once again live up to their name and duty.

Today, they would purge the world of that nest of villains that called itself a guild.

503

Chapter 76

"A pleasure to meet you all. Please, call me Hat Trick." The young woman in front of Donald, Irene, and Ren took a long bow, giving a bit too good of a view down the cleavage of her tight black blazer. Her hand effortlessly plucked a top hat from her head as she made her gesture, adding a level of formality that would have been out of place even if they weren't all gathered in a small meeting room.

Aside from the blazer and hat, she wore dark pants that shimmered as though they'd been dipped in glitter, a dark cape with red lining that fell halfway down her back, and a white shirt that poked out from the edges of the dark blazer but did nothing to obscure what was obviously an intentional view of her chest. She was quite pretty as well; red lipstick accentuated her pale skin, and an infectious smile was nicely offset by the smattering of freckles across her face. As she rose, the hat danced between her fingers before settling on her head once more, cocked slightly at a jaunty angle.

"I'm Donald, but I go by Cyber Geek," Donald said. "This is Ren, aka Medley, and Irene, who goes by Cold Shoulder."

"Ah, well, in my more mundane hours, I go by Lucy," Hat Trick replied.

"Lucy Donovan is a great asset. We've been looking for just the right team to fit her in with," Jessica said, jumping in for the first time since she and Barney had called everyone into the room. "During that freak storm some while back, it seems a bolt struck a beginner's magic kit. Lucy bought it a couple of weeks later, and when she opened it up, poof!"

"The cheap garb and plastic toys were replaced by true implements of the arcane arts," Lucy explained. "They bonded to me, making me a conjurer whether I wanted to be or not."

"Now, Hat Trick isn't quite as strong a combatant as you three," Barney cautioned them. "But last week's fight showed us how badly you need few support member to round things out. And there, Hat Trick has got you covered."

"My hat functions as a transportable miniature dimensional pocket." Lucy pulled the hat off again and stuck her hand in, her arm going far deeper than the fabric should have allowed. "Case in point: last night I left a soda in here. And now, TADA!" She pulled out a can and tossed it to Ren, who easily snagged it out of midair.

"Still cold," Ren noted.

"Exactly. It keeps things as they are when they enter, which makes it perfect for storing tools and weapons, even the sort that need special care." Lucy flipped the hat back on to her head. From nowhere, a deck of playing cards appeared, bridging and arching through Lucy's deft hands. "My cape allows me to cast illusions on myself, these cards are functionally unlimited and can be shaped by will, and there are rings that will hold almost anyone in place—"

"What about the wand?" Donald asked, unable to keep himself from interrupting. Ren and Irene stared at him; he flushed but managed to stammer out an explanation anyway. "Oh, come on. Everyone knows magic kits come with wands, don't act like I'm the weirdo."

"I... I haven't quite mastered the wand," Lucy admitted. Her shuffling faltered. She tucked the deck back up her sleeve, where it seemed to vanish. "I'm working hard on it; I just haven't been cleared for using it in the field yet. But I've got plenty of other tricks, and I promise to do my absolute best." Her red lips grew smaller as she nervously chewed on the bottom one, glancing between the team and Jessica as if she were afraid she might be turned away.

For the first time, Donald actually wondered if they even *could* turn a new team member away. Apollo had said he wanted them to focus on teamwork, so if they all agreed she wouldn't be a good fit, he might find them a new one. Not that Donald could imagine being so heartless as to kick Lucy away. The only way he'd be that cruel was if she turned out to be a liability in the field. He started to welcome her but got beaten to the punch.

"Glad to have you aboard, Lucy," Irene said. She took the newer woman's hand and gave it a good shake, eliciting a squeal of joy from Lucy, along with a hug that left Irene looking as though she regretted stepping within range of embracing.

"Thank you, thank you, thank you! I'll really try so hard, and I'll do whatever it takes to help keep people safe." Lucy released Irene and grabbed Ren, who was visibly taken aback by the sudden hug. Ever since his transformation, no one had enthusiastically touched him, especially not when he was without the human-illusion as was the case now. When Lucy let go and embraced Donald, Ren patted his chest, almost like he was confused by the warmth she'd left behind.

"We're all happy to have you," Donald managed to eke out, despite the impressive amount of force Lucy put into her hugs. "And today's a good day to start. All we need to do is work crowd control."

"Consider yourself lucky," Irene told Lucy. "My first outing with this group involved fighting four criminals robbing a museum." Both Donald and Ren noticed that she spoke of the event like it had happened years ago instead of just last week. Neither made a point of calling her on it though, both because it would have been bad form, and because she was clearly getting a kick out of not being the newest member on the team anymore.

"Let the rest of us get into costume, then we'll head out and start setting up barricades and making sure people know they have to go," Donald said. "The quicker we move, the better a job we'll do, and hopefully the shorter this whole drill will run."

"Don't mind Donald," Irene said. "He's just got a hot date later tonight that he's hoping to make."

"It's coffee with a friend," Donald protested. "But I would like to avoid canceling, so everyone get your butts in gear."

"Can do!" Lucy saluted, accidently knocking the hat from her head. It tumbled to the ground, where, upon landing, it spat out two remote control race cars and a half-eaten sandwich. Lucy's eyes grew wide as she stared at the spilled contents, her mouth opening and closing as she searched for words. "I promise, it doesn't fall off if I'm paying attention!" was all she managed to come up with.

"Just make sure you're paying attention once we're outside the building," Donald instructed her. "We want to do our part to keep things running smoothly."

Lucy nodded vigorously as she bent down and scooped the two cars back into the hat. The sandwich she chucked into a nearby trash can. Much as Donald wanted to ask why she was using a magical pocket dimension to carry that kind of thing, he'd been around other meta-humans long enough to know that the answer probably wouldn't explain much. If anything, it would just leave him more confused.

Instead, he turned his attention to things he could make sense of, like completing this drill, and hopefully still making it in time for coffee with Tori.

*　　　*　　　*

Chloe stared out the window of Ridge City Grinders, counting the people who walked by. There had been a bit of a rush around noon when several of the nearby offices let out—Tori was seen leading the pack before hopping into a town car—but in the past hour, the streets had grown deserted. Everyone had either run home to avoid the crowds or was gathered up near the AHC headquarters to watch them test their defenses. None of them were bothering to stop for coffee, though.

"Todd, if you want to go, you can," Chloe called to the only other person still in the store with her. "Meredith comes on in an hour, but I think I can handle things until then."

506

"It is a little slow," Todd agreed. He finished wiping off a table he'd already cleaned twice and threw his rag into the small bucket behind the counter. "What if we get hit by a rush, though?"

"The whole town is either grouped up in one spot or avoiding downtown like we just had an Ebola outbreak. Until they finish up, I'll be surprised if we get five customers, let alone a rush." Chloe swept her arms up, waving them around at the store completely devoid of customers. "Pretty sure I can manage this giant crowd all on my own."

"You could always close up," Todd suggested. "Just make it a half-day like everyone else."

"It's tempting, but sooner or later, the AHC will finish and all those people trekking back to their cars may want to wait out traffic with a few cups of coffee," Chloe said. Besides, Tori had mentioned she and Donald might be stopping by around five. It would be nice to visit with her friends. Chloe liked her coworkers and the few people from her life before the accident, but they and Beverly were the only other meta-humans she knew. It would be nice to talk with people who understood. Although, she'd have to remember not to mention Tori's powers around Donald, since he was still in the dark about them.

"If you're sure, then I think I will cut out early." Todd reached up and undid his apron's knot behind his back, loosening the dark cover. "I wanted to go watch the capes fight their own tech, anyway."

"You Judas. I let you off and you go to see the very thing that's stealing all our customers." Chloe crossed her arms and stared at her coworker. "I expect you to at least take video of the cool stuff and send it over so I can be entertained."

"I'm on a last gen phone, so it'll be fuzzy, but I'll do the best I can," Todd said.

"Better than sitting around talking to myself, which is probably what I'm going to do five minutes after you leave," Chloe admitted.

"You're the only one I know who prefers it when this place is crazy." Todd hung his apron on a plastic hook just inside the employee break room, then untucked his white shirt from the black slacks they were all forced to wear.

"I'm a child of chaos, and I prefer to be in my element. Today I will have to content myself with the quiet, though."

Todd headed to the door and pushed it outward, triggering the soft bell that tinkled overhead. "Don't be so gloomy, there's always the chance that things will get exciting later on."

"It would be nice, but I won't count on it." Chloe generally would have said she wasn't going to hold her breath, however her mind purposely steered away from such well-tread words these days. Bit by bit, she was getting better at

507

coping with her ability. In a way, she couldn't wait for Donald and Tori to arrive so she could show them how much she'd accomplished.

Sadly, until then it was going to be a whole lot of nothing but boredom and dullness. She pulled out her phone and began to surf the net, desperate to make the hours fly by just a little bit faster.

*   *   *

It was a nice neighborhood, the sort where he'd smashed out windows and robbed back when he was human. Ordinarily it would be nearly deserted at this time of day, as all the respectable people with their nice little jobs scurried about in their offices, leaving their possessions unguarded. Thanks to the AHC test, however, he could see signs of occupation in at least half of the nigh-identical houses. He could even smell the ones who'd been outside recently, though his nose wasn't nearly as powerful when he was outside the water.

His old, beat-up car looked out of place amid the shiny new models parked in their driveways. Even though he'd pulled in enough cash doing guild work to trade up, Rust Tooth still preferred the classic American builds that were all steel and smoke. Part of it was aesthetic but the rest was pragmatism. There were only so many vehicles in production that could accommodate a creature of his size. And he counted himself lucky—people like Thuggernaut had to get custom vehicles made.

Counting the numbers on the houses as he passed them, Rust Tooth finally found the one he was looking for. Balaam had given him the call earlier; Pseudonym's apprentice had been seen on satellite going inside. While Rust Tooth never would have dreamed of trying to break into the legendary villain's home if he were there, Balaam had assured Rust Tooth that this errand would be uninterrupted. It was just him and a wet-behind-the-ears rookie.

The car groaned as Rust Tooth emerged from it, creaking in joy as it was freed from his weight. He stood on the curb a few inches from where he'd parked and took in the tranquility of the scene before him. If Balaam hadn't given him the address, Rust Tooth would have never imagined that Pseudonym, the man who'd once been feared on an international level, lived here. Then again, that was what made it a good hiding place.

From the back seat, Rust Tooth pulled a black leather bag. Inside were a variety of potions, charms, and tools that would supposedly cut through the wards protecting the place. Even standing at the edge of the property, Rust Tooth could feel the energy pushing him away. It was probably unnoticeable to the normal people living here, only activating when one approached with ill-intent.

There was no getting around that one, though, which was why Balaam had sent those tools. Rust Tooth had come here with the worst possible intentions. He'd come to harm, to destroy, to steal a life that wasn't his. Rust Tooth was here to kill Pseudonym's apprentice. If that didn't trigger the wards, nothing would.

He yanked out a knife that was covered in runes and stabbed the air in front of him, piercing a magical red wall that suddenly appeared where the knife made contact. His wide, inhuman mouth grinned, showing all those worn, serrated, metallic teeth.

The revolution had finally begun.

Chapter 77

The ear-splitting scream nearly made Tori drop her gauntlet, which would have been extra infuriating since she'd just finished putting a new concentrating lens in place. Her mind raced as the sound drilled into her ears. What in the living hell could cause this? It was too powerful, too focused for it to be a fire alarm. Those echoed and didn't attack the eardrums like targeted missiles. No, this was magic, pure and simple, and that meant there was only one likely candidate for a cause: Ivan's wards.

No sooner had the thought crossed her mind than the sound lessened. It was still there, a high-pitched whine in the back of her head, but apparently the mere act of understanding had taken the edge off its attack. Something was attacking the house, someone powerful enough to actually trip Ivan's magical warning system. But that was crazy, wasn't it? Who in their right mind would attack the home of the man who'd once been Fornax? This must be some sort of hiccup in the system.

As her doubt increased, the sound grew shrill once more, forcing her to put her hands over her ears, though it didn't help. Did that mean something really was attacking? At that thought, it fell back to a mere whine, and Tori slowly lowered her hands from her ears.

"Guess that means it's definitely an attack," she muttered. Of course Ivan would build his wards not to allow for the possibility of self-delusion. But if someone was attacking, they should have been repelled. For the wards to screech like this probably meant a breach was imminent. She needed to brace for a fight, though whether it was with a cape, a crook, or even a fellow guild member remained to be seen. None of the options made sense, but neither did someone attacking Ivan's home in the first place. Logic was going to have to take a back seat until the dust cleared; there were more pressing concerns than why. Namely who was doing this, and how was she going to beat the hell out of them for it.

Tori looked at her meta-suit spread out on the work table before her. There were no sounds of destruction coming from above, so the house probably hadn't been breached yet. If she hurried, she might be able to gear up before the attackers arrived. But that could mean getting pinned in the basement with no way out—not an ideal situation if she had to make a run for it. Dawdling about trying to make a decision was the worst option she had, though; it burned time while accomplishing nothing.

Someone was breaking in to Ivan's house. The only question was whether or not they'd find Tori waiting to meet them or Hephaestus.

"You're more mild-mannered than I expected."

Ivan looked up from his paperwork, surprised to see two silhouettes standing in his doorway. The larger man, a gruff fellow with a thick beard and a giant gun strapped to his back, had been the one to speak. Meanwhile, the woman dressed in all black and somehow not quite as well-lit stood silently, watching him, waiting to react if he tried anything.

"My goodness, Blunderbuss and Lady Shade, what brings two such beloved superheroes to the offices of Vendallia Industries? If you want a tour, I'm afraid most of the staff is gone for the day, although I'm sure your office can set something up for later in the week with proper notice." Ivan carefully set his pen down on the desk, being certain not to make any aggressive motions. Bad as this looked; it didn't mean the situation was unsalvageable. If punches began to fly, that could likely no longer be said.

"We're not here for the tour, or for the offices, or even for you, Ivan, since that's what you go by these days. We're here to pick up Fornax," Blunderbuss said, all but spitting the last word on Ivan's carpet.

"Fornax, you say? I can't imagine you'd find him here." Ivan knit his hands together on the desk, keeping them in plain view the whole while. "In fact, I doubt you'd find him anywhere. Fornax ceased to be a legal entity on the day Orion was defeated. There are no warrants for him; all those were expunged when he stopped existing. So, if you've come here to arrest Ivan Gerhardt, I would like to see the warrant, know the charges, and speak to my lawyer. However, if you've come seeking Fornax, I'm afraid I can't help you."

"He's being glib, can you believe that?" Blunderbuss looked to Lady Shade, who didn't answer him or react to Ivan's words in any way. She was on edge, a single quick motion away from attacking. Personally, Ivan hoped it didn't come to that. Two dead capes would be a pain to deal with.

"How many times has that little speech kept you out of the cell where you rightfully belong?" Blunderbuss continued. "If it's even once, that's one too many by my count. But today, it ain't happening. You're coming with us to face justice, right here and now."

"Is that so?" Ivan pushed back his chair—the squeak caused Lady Shade to twitch—and slowly rose to his feet. "It seems I should remind you that while the Alliance of Heroic Champions has some leeway in dealing with imminent threats to property and civilians, they do require actual warrants for arresting suspects not actively posing a threat. Trying to take me in without one is illegal, unconstitutional, and I am fully within my rights to resist such an

511

arrest. I would urge you both to follow proper channels if you're truly set on seeing this course of action through."

"Quite scary when you've got red tape to hide behind," Blunderbuss shot back. "But there's not going to be a fight. You're going to come with us nice and peacefully. You won't even so much as ask for a lawyer again."

"Really?" Ivan arched an eyebrow in curiosity. "And may I ask why I would do such a thing?"

"Thirteen forty-four Maplebark Lane." Blunderbuss barely whispered the words yet Ivan felt a shock run all the way through his body. He glanced from the stout man with the giant gun to the woman surrounded by swirling shadows, no longer merely annoyed by their antics. Now, he could feel the beginnings of rage starting to press at the backs of his eyes.

The address Blunderbuss had just given was of the school where both of Ivan's children should currently be in class.

"I see. Are you absolutely certain you want to go down this road? It's not very heroic. Not even my people would stoop so low."

"It's for the greater good," Blunderbuss replied. "Just an insurance policy, to make sure you don't get out of hand. As long as you cooperate, nothing will happen."

Despite the powerful, almost intoxicating urge to leap forward and slowly choke the life from the bearded man's throat, Ivan held his calm and gave a short nod. He stepped around his desk and approached them, standing only inches away.

"I want to assure you of something. I don't know what your plan is or what sort of game you've made me a pawn in, but I promise you right here and now that you are going to regret this decision. I don't care if it costs me my secret, my freedom, or even my life, I will personally ensure that you look back at this as the greatest mistake either of you has made in your entire lives." Ivan took no threatening steps toward them. He didn't even raise his voice. It took every ounce of his self-control to keep his eyes normal, though. The power inside him was burning, his anger fueling it by the second. Only the thought of Rick and Beth kept his rage at bay. Until they were safe, he would stay in control.

"Is that it? I'm a superhero. I have scum like you threaten me six times a day," Blunderbuss said.

Ivan stared down at the cape's surly face and his thick, knotted muscles. No doubt he was a tough fighter, one who had a lot of confidence. But he was still young; he hadn't been around for the glory days of villainy before the guild started purging the biggest threats before they could reach him.

Leaning slightly down to emphasize the height difference between them, Ivan lowered his voice and let out a whisper that was almost a hiss.

"You have *never* met a monster like me."

* * *

The last of the magic finally gave way, and Rust Tooth set a clawed foot onto Ivan Gerhardt's lawn. It had taken almost ten minutes to punch a hole in the defenses, and in that time, he'd seen several of the neighbors peeking out through their windows. The black trench coat covering Rust Tooth's body did a poor job of concealing the beast inside, and the long tail poking out the bottom certainly didn't help matters. Even if they didn't know what he was doing, someone—likely a few of them—had definitely called the cops by now. That was fine; Balaam had told him not to bother with stealth. In fact, the more people that saw him, the better. The police would be tied up by the AHC's defense test, and even if they made it before he left, it would just be more bodies on the pile.

Rust Tooth tore off his coat as he ran toward the house. He wanted to be seen in his full, terrifying glory. He wanted the rookie to look upon the face of her death and despair. She was a disciple of a whipped dog, the sort of weak-minded person who'd dragged the guild down from what it could have been. He was going to enjoy tearing her apart, sending a message to everyone who thought villains should live on the sidelines. The front door loomed before him, but with no more magic to get in the way, it might as well have already been made of splinters. And that's what Rust Tooth turned it into as he barreled through.

He'd barely gotten a step inside before a half-dozen small *pings* echoed off his torso. Looking down, Rust Tooth saw a cluster of needles, all bent or snapped in half, which had fallen at his feet. Across the room, slowly lowering her left arm, was Pseudonym's apprentice. She was dressed in her armor again, but Balaam had already given Rust Tooth plenty of warning about that. It might be useful, but the girl was no Doctor Mechaniacal. Her suit couldn't stand up to a barrage of attack from a meta-human like him. Especially since she wasn't able to hurt him back.

"I know you." The voice wasn't feminine as it crackled through the dark helmet, but Rust Tooth knew it was her inside. "I've seen you at the guild. You were at the membership ceremony on Friday. Why in the hell are you attacking Pseudonym's house?"

Rust Tooth was almost, *almost*, tempted to try and play at subterfuge. Tell her that Pseudonym had been attacked and that no one had a way inside, so

513

he was sent to warn her. But he quickly realized anyone smart enough to build a meta-suit would probably see though any story he could whip together. Besides, he wanted her to die knowing what was happening, the fate her teacher had earned for her.

"My name is Rust Tooth, and I'm here because the guild is experiencing a change in management," Rust Tooth told her. "And as part of that, we're taking care of anyone who might cause problems under the new regime. Since you're the apprentice of that dog, you're being put down too."

"Hoo boy, I really want to believe you're joking, but if you're breaking in here, I guess you can't be," she said. "Are you stupid? I mean, really, *really* stupid? Some morons in the guild decided to try and stage a coup, and *you* volunteered to piss off Pseudonym? Your best case scenario here—and I mean utter best case—is killing me and getting away, at which point, he will murder the living shit out of you for it."

"Pseudonym isn't Fornax," Rust Tooth growled. He wanted to crush all her hopes before he crushed her body. It wasn't practical, but it *was* villainous, and by the gods, it felt so good to finally be a real villain again. "Not anymore. He's gotten soft. Grown weak. While he might still have the power, he's no longer unassailable. He created his own vulnerabilities."

There was a moment of near silence, the only sound in the house the settling of a few bits of debris raining down from the shattered doorframe. While Rust Tooth couldn't see her face through the helmet, he could imagine the shock and terror filling her eyes as she realized that her precious teacher wasn't coming to save her. Soon there would be whimpering, and then begging, and only then would he get the full satisfaction of killing her as she cried for her life.

"His kids." It wasn't a whimper at all; in fact, Rust Tooth was shocked at how much fury managed to make it through the garbling of her helmet. "You're threatening Ivan's kids. God. Damn. You people are *fucking* idiots. Do you have any idea what will happen if you hurt them?"

"I think you should be more concerned about yourself, little apprentice." She wasn't playing along, and it was beginning to take some of the fun out of this for Rust Tooth. If she wasn't going to give him a satisfying, weepy death, then he'd just hurry things along. Maybe one of the neighbors would be a bit more compliant.

"You're the one that should be worried. You should be praying to every god you know that I kill you, because it's the only way you're getting spared from Ivan's wrath. And one more thing..."

In a single motion, she hunched forward, and with a flare from behind her, she barreled into Rust Tooth's chest, arms crossed in an *X* formation in front of her to strike as many ribs as possible.

The force of the impact sent Rust Tooth flying back into a wall, which buckled under his weight. She didn't let up as they crashed, slamming a fist into his right ribs and then flexing the fingers on her left hand. From the tip of each came a two-inch, focused flame burning white-hot.

"I'm not an apprentice anymore. The name's Hephaestus, motherfucker." With that, she jammed her miniature torches right into Rust Tooth's face.

Chapter 78

"And as soon as the authorization goes through... and look, there it is. Everything is officially in motion," Apollo announced, pointing to a light on the screen that had switched from red to green. "We've set all the defense systems to activate but left in the lower-tier override." Without that stipulation, it would require three members of the Champions' Congress to deactivate the system, but this way, either he or Quorum could do it once the test was done.

The two of them were in the deepest layer of the AHC's sub-basement where the terminals that oversaw the security system were housed. It had taken over an hour and both of their authorizations, but they'd finally gotten everything properly set up for a test of the base's defenses. Quorum typed a few more bits of code on his keyboard, then hit enter and stood up from his terminal.

"Only forty-five minutes until the system turns on," he announced. "Do you need to do any more checks with the teams?"

"No, I've left everything in the hands of our operators," Apollo replied. "We can't count on any one superhero taking the lead during an attack; what if every member of the Congress is already in the field? Better to drill them using the operators to coordinate, just like we'd have to in a real attack."

"Then all that's left is for us to get out of here." Quorum moved for the door, and Apollo was only a few steps behind. They passed a variety of instruments, some confiscated off of criminals and mildly dangerous (the truly restricted ones were tucked behind yet another layer of security), others little more than clutter that had been moved down here for convenience.

Beyond the various devices, just before the elevator they'd ridden down, were a set of three cells. These were the original holding areas constructed before an entire floor was created specifically as a makeshift, temporary prison. Each was empty, as the AHC only used its cells to hold prisoners while proper facilities were established, but they were a sight to behold. Forged from a composition of metals Professor Quantum refused to share details on, all of them were lined with a myriad of runes designed to dampen magical powers, wired to disable anyone who tried to break free, anchored to stop all teleportation or space tunneling, and strong enough to withstand attacks from anyone short of Lodestar.

Apollo paused in front of one, looking into the well-lit depths, wondering just how many villains had been tossed into it over the years. Not enough, he knew that much for certain. There was a whole guild that deserved to have seen the inside of these rooms. It was a shame that they'd been retired, but as the AHC grew, so did its needs. Besides, it didn't make a lot of sense to store criminals in the same room as the security system, no matter how good the cells were. Only Professor Quantum had that level of arrogance, and it hadn't taken long for Quorum and Lodestar to convince him of the error once they'd joined on. Apollo knew that and a thousand other tidbits of history about the organization he'd just reached the top of. He'd studied the AHC's history tirelessly because he genuinely loved what it did and what it stood for. That was what made learning about the blind eye they turned toward the guild all the more infuriating.

"Checking out the old handiwork?" Quorum asked, stepping to Apollo's side.

"They're still pretty impressive," Apollo said. "I bet we could use them, if we really had to."

"Those would be desperate times," Quorum replied. "You think we skimped on the protocol for the outer defenses? Since these aren't sanctioned for use, they haven't been checked over in decades."

"Actually, they just got a tune-up yesterday." Without any more warning than that, Apollo grabbed Quorum by the shoulder and gave him a powerful shove. It would have thrown most people right into the wall at the back of the cell and likely turned them to pulp in the process, but Quorum was barely inside before he killed his momentum and spun around.

It was too little, too late, however, as a barrier of energy now separated him from Apollo, the elevator, and the outside world as a whole.

To Apollo's surprise, Quorum seemed unfazed by the sudden twist in their situation. He merely studied the inside of the cell with a quizzical expression then looked at Apollo. "Interesting."

"Interesting? I have to admit, I was expecting a little bit more of a reaction," Apollo said.

"Apollo, I have the minds of over a thousand people inside me; at least of few of them are better liars than you. I've known for over a year you had some plan of betrayal in the works, I just didn't think it would be this simple," Quorum replied. "If your goal is to keep me penned up in here and lock the rest of the Congress out of the system, I should tell you upfront that it won't work. And unless you made serious modifications to the cells, there's nothing lethal inside, which means that if you want to kill me, you'll have to come do it by hand."

The threat hung in the air, the old superhero and the young cape separated only by a barrier that not even they were powerful enough to break through. Rather than rising to it, Apollo merely shook his head in disappointment.

"I'm not going to kill you, Quorum. I just need to keep you out of the way for a few hours. I don't want to take over the AHC; I want to fix its biggest mistake. Your generation grew old and lazy. You let a nest of vipers live in your city, giving them leeway because they killed smaller rats and hid in the shadows. When this is all over, you can try to kick me out of the Congress, but it might not be that easy. Think long and hard while you're down here: do you want to be one of the brave superheroes that reacted to a heinous attack by a guild of shadow villains, or will you tell everyone that you ignored their presence until I locked you down here and forced the issue? Whichever story you choose, Quorum, I'll back. All you have to do is live with the consequences."

Apollo pressed the button to call the elevator, turning his back to Quorum and the cell. The older cape stared at him, remembering when Apollo had first come in, shining with determination and the desire to make the world a better place. Those traits were still there, but they'd been corrupted, warped by time and ambition. He'd seen it happen before, and each instance was a genuine tragedy.

"Do you know why I promoted you, even though I was certain you had some sort of betrayal up your sleeve?" Quorum asked.

"Because I was too essential to lose?" Apollo said. A *ding* filled the room as the elevator opened. Apollo stepped inside.

"No," Quorum replied. "It's because I've found that the best way to expose traitors is to give them a chance to strike. Once the fangs are bared, there's no more deception. Today, I'll roust every one of you from the Alliance."

"You're welcome to try," Apollo said, just as the doors began to slide closed once more. "But forgive me for not waiting. There's a guild of villains that's about to start a war with us."

*　　　*　　　*

Up until a few minutes prior, Hephaestus would have described the battle with Medley as one of her life's toughest fights. One that, in truth, she hadn't managed to win, but only escape, thanks to Bahamut's help. That bar that Medley had set, however, was rapidly being surpassed as Rust Tooth smashed her idea of what a tough battle was to pieces, along with Ivan's dinner table as he hurled her through it.

She rolled with the attack, coming up on her feet just in time to dodge a swipe from his giant claws. Medley's claws had been sharp and deadly, true, but they were also relatively small. Rust Tooth may as well have glued steak knives to his fingers as he effortlessly cut through the floor where Hephaestus's foot had been only a second before. Every bit of him was covered in that greasy, stained metal, including the giant tail that whipped around and caught her in the side as she dodged. She smashed into the kitchen and collided with the refrigerator.

Rust Tooth was strong, tough, armored, armed, and clearly accustomed to combat, yet none of those were what made the situation so problematic. No, the issue was that the son of a bitch seemed almost impervious to fire. Her miniature torches had barely gotten more than a twitch out of him before he shoved her away and began a counterattack. Whatever meta-condition he'd gotten, it was one that had a lot of resistance to heat, which was no doubt part of why he'd been tasked with eliminating her.

Hephaestus pulled herself up warily, eyes on Rust Tooth as he watched her from the doorway of the kitchen with that predatory smile. While she was mostly incorporeal inside her suit and therefore not getting hurt, the suit itself was taking a beating. She'd designed it specifically to resist the type of bludgeoning damage he was doling out, but if Rust Tooth caught her with one of those claws, her meta-suit would be down at least one limb. And that might be a worthwhile sacrifice to win the fight if she were not now keenly aware that killing her was only one small part of something much bigger. Whatever was happening, she wanted all her tools available for it. But now that she knew Ivan's kids were in danger, she also knew that they couldn't afford for her to draw out this fight much longer.

Or rather, the world might not be able to afford it.

"Thinking about running?" Rust Tooth snickered. He'd mistaken her pause for fear and was gloating in it. "I know you can hop out of that suit whenever you want, turn into fire and scamper away. I know everything about you."

So, he knew she had an escape trump card but was unbothered by it. No doubt he had some sort of countermeasure planned; he had to, given how expertly he'd dispatched Ivan's wards with his arcane toolset. Even only catching the last few minutes of the break-in, Tori had to admit he'd come prepared. Perfectly prepared, in fact. He might be one of the best candidates in the guild to kill her, given his powers, and he'd brought accessories to overcome his lack of magical skill. Every move she'd made, he'd been ready for. Someone had made a plan specifically to murder her, and they knew every tool or trick she might bust out to turn the tides because she'd put them all on display during her apprenticeship.

Except... there might be one they hadn't counted on.

Hephaestus flexed the gauntlet on her right hand, diverting power and starting the charge. Who else knew about the concentrated beam attack? It had been broken during the robbery, and she hadn't been able to bring any inventions into the desert trial. That left Ivan, Xelas, and Doctor Mechaniacal. Ivan would never have done something like this—if he wanted to kill her, then he'd be the one to do it—and if either of the others were traitors, then she was probably dead anyway. Ending this fight would take a high-stakes gamble, and after everything her guild training had put her through, she was oddly comfortable with that fact.

Patience wearing thin, Rust Tooth rushed through the doorway to the kitchen, his giant shoulders shattering the drywall on either side. With the beam's charging taking most of her power, Hephaestus wouldn't be able to stand many more direct hits. It was time to engage in the better part of valor. Sparing enough power to engage her flight function for only an instant, Hephaestus leapt through the air, right over Rust Tooth's shoulder, and came down on both feet in the living room. The maneuver caught him by surprise, but as she turned around to gauge his position, she realized that he was unfortunately quick to recover.

In three giant steps, he was back on her, but out here in the living room, she at least had a little room to maneuver. Every attack seemed to be only millimeters away from connecting; her suit was sluggish with almost all her power diverted to the beam. Rust Tooth was toying with her, taking his time to enjoy the kill, otherwise he could have easily turned her suit to scrap. Even that had evidently lost its luster, though. Rust Tooth threw a shoulder into her, knocking her roughly into the stone fireplace. Before she could recover, his tail swept her legs, and in an instant the massive beast had her pinned down by the shoulders.

"I'm disappointed," he growled, his putrid breath washing over the front of her helmet. "I'd expected more from the disciple of Fornax."

As carefully as she could, Hephaestus turned her right hand over, angling her palm so that it was directly facing Rust Tooth's stomach. With those giant hands on her suit's shoulders, she didn't have much maneuverability, but on the upside, it was hard to miss at point blank range.

"It's not over," she said, staring at the top corner of her display, pleading with the universe for a green icon to appear. "I can still jump out of this thing and run. What are you going to do if I warn Ivan that you're attacking his kids?"

"Oh, by now he's keenly aware," Rust Tooth said. "He won't make a single move out of fear for their safety. As for running away... I look forward to watching you try."

And of course, he was just smart enough not to tell her what countermeasures were in place. It might be a bluff, but Rust Tooth didn't seem like the wily type. He really did want her to run; he yearned for her to be more vulnerable. Beating up the suit clearly wasn't doing it for him.

"Turning on a guild member, kidnapping children. I can't believe you ever had the nerve to call yourself a villain. You're nothing but a common street thug."

"After today, no one is going to have that neutered sense of villainy anymore." Rust Tooth tightened his grip while widening his mouth just a touch. It only took one viewing of a nature documentary to know what was about to happen. "And no one will ever nag us about some stupid goddamned code ever again. Your kind is out of date, and today, you go extinct. "

As Rust Tooth's maw opened, Hephaestus glimpsed what would go down as one of the top ten most breathtakingly beautiful sights of her entire life: a small green dot flickered in the corner of her display. Within the confines of her suit, she grinned maliciously.

"Maybe so, but you'd better believe we'll drag as many of you to hell with us as we can. How about you and I get a head start?"

Hephaestus fired the fully charged beam, flinging Rust Tooth off her body even as the scent of roasting flesh filled the air. The beam carved through him, then the ceiling and the room above, then the roof, finally opening a hole to the sky, which Hephaestus was shocked to see was so gorgeously blue. This felt like the kind of day that should have been cloudy and bleak, but it seemed sometimes monsters lurked even in the sunshine.

Debris from the massive hole she'd blown in Ivan's house began to rain down. Hephaestus rolled out of the way and hurried to her feet. Rust Tooth was ahead of her, scrambling out the broken front door while trying to hold together the remains of his stomach. She'd nailed his left side, but hadn't gotten the shot centered enough to take out his spine. Still, the angry predator had vanished, leaving nothing more than a meta shaped like a metallic crocodile scurrying to escape while keeping his guts inside.

Hephaestus followed, flexing her gauntlet once more to reactivate the charging sequence. Inside the suit, she burned as hot as she dared, feeding the fuel cells while letting off the rage that was bubbling up from within. Now that fear was retreating, Hephaestus was realizing just how livid she truly was. One of her fellow guild members had broken into Ivan's home, his place of safety, and tried to murder her in cold blood. That didn't even touch on the fact that they were going after her teacher's children, or that her friends were likely in just as much danger.

The sounds of wood snapping echoed from behind her. Hephaestus glanced back to see Ivan's house, one of the first places she'd been able to call home in over a decade, collapsing from within. She also noticed the neighbors peering through their windows, no doubt wondering what on earth was going on. It was a Tuesday afternoon in the suburbs; there weren't supposed to be monsters or giant beams blasting into the sky. And now, on top of everything else, it looked like even if Ivan and his kids survived the day, they wouldn't be able to slip back into their civilian lives. One more cherry on the sundae of clusterfuckery that Rust Tooth had brought down on them.

"Hell of a trump card," the monster coughed. In the time she'd looked away, Rust Tooth had fallen to his knees, oily green blood oozing through his fingers as he desperately tried to make sure his insides stayed that way. "Can't believe you didn't use it in the fight with Medley."

"I didn't want to kill Medley." This was true yet skirted the fact that her beam could be broken easily, a design flaw she was now determined to fix at the first opportunity.

"So, to keep a cape safe, you held back when the whole guild was watching and didn't show your best weapon, which almost cost you your victory." Rust Tooth fell forward, taking the landing face-first as his hands stayed wrapped around his side. "And yet you beat me. What the hell kind of villain are you?"

"I'm the patron saint of bad bitches." Hephaestus walked forward carefully, wary of a counterattack, even as injured as her opponent was. She slipped a foot under Rust Tooth's shoulder and flipped him over, eliciting a groan of pain as he flopped onto his back. "And I want to know what the fuck you're doing with Ivan's kids."

"Kiss my scaly ass," Rust Tooth coughed. That cough turned into a scream as Hephaestus slammed a foot down onto his hands and the hollowed out chunk of torso he was clinging to.

"We both know you're already dead," Hephaestus told him. "You died the minute you stepped on to this property uninvited. Now you get to choose: send me away from here by giving me something else to do, or keep me around so I make your last moments as painful as possible."

"Or you could end it quickly," Rust Tooth said, flecks of his blood covering those sharp teeth.

"That's the sort of thing I might consider for a true villain, one who had a little honor. The sort who would admit they were beaten and give the victor a prize of information." She didn't stomp on him again, but she did note that the green dot had reappeared on her display.

"Honor. You fucking noble types. This was our world, a place where the wild and strong lived on top, and then you all came in here with your codes and honor and messed everything up." Rust Tooth looked up at the sky for several seconds then shook his massive head. "Bombastic is setting off explosives all over the city. The school where Ivan's kids go, Kelsington Prep, was one of his targets. If Ivan does anything to intervene when the fighting starts, the whole place goes tumbling down."

"You're the worst kind of garbage." Hephaestus raised her gauntlet, took careful aim, then let off a short, controlled blast. When the smoke cleared, there was a scorched ditch burned in Ivan's yard, right next to a corpse that was curiously absent a head.

Hephaestus looked around the neighborhood once more, noting the distant sound of sirens approaching. She didn't know if she'd ever get to see this place again, so she meant to savor the view for one precious moment.

Walking over to the bag that Rust Tooth had brought, she examined the contents. All that remained beside the used up trinkets was a modified paintball gun. Taking a cursory look at the ammunition, she wagered they were designed to fire concentrated blasts of CO_2, perfect for killing living fire. She slipped the gun into a side compartment of her suit, took one last glance at the neighbors, and then leapt.

Her rear thrusters kicked on as she reduced her weight, sending her blasting into the air. Hephaestus set a course for town, checking the internet for Kelsington Prep's address. She also tried to make some calls. First Ivan, then Beverly, then Donald.

None of them were answering, which only made Hephaestus fly that much faster.

523

Chapter 79

"And it is up!"

Cyber Geek turned at the sound of Hat Trick's voice, eyes going wide as he watched the giant, glowing yellow dome flicker into existence over the AHC's headquarters. He'd seen countless pictures of this spectacle from tests in years prior and during the few times when someone was actually dumb enough to fight the AHC head-on, but being there in person was a completely different experience. Perhaps it was because he had the scale to appreciate how vast and powerful the dome was; more likely it was because he was no longer looking at the AHC as an outsider. This wasn't just a demonstration of power: it was his organization's demonstration of power, and Cyber Geek's heart swelled with pride as he saw the wowed faces in the crowd around him.

Applause drifted up from the crowd, who pushed forward to get a better view. Bodies pressed against the wooden barricades designed to keep them back. Much as Cyber Geek wanted to stand there and marvel at what was to come, the pride of being part of the AHC came with the cost of duty, and they needed to do theirs.

"Back everyone, back please," he said, his voice snapping the others out of their own fugues.

Medley didn't even need to talk; he simply paced the area around the barricades and people shrank back. Cold Shoulder was cooling her zone, making it uncomfortable for anyone to stand too near them. Hat Trick, whom Cyber Geek had been worried about since this was her first time in the field, was doing a marvelous job. She had a sort of clumsy, sweet naiveté that made her requests for people to move away impossible to refuse. Fighting her would have been like arguing with a kitten. Useful as her nature was from a PR standpoint, Cyber Geek was a bit concerned about how it would translate in battle. She'd have the chance to prove herself soon enough, just hopefully not today.

Slowly, they shifted the crowd back as other superheroes moved into position around the glowing dome. This was the part where things could get dicey if any humans were too close by. Testing the AHC's defenses was dangerous even for meta-humans, which was why only those with very powerful, specific skill sets were checking each one. The dome was a last resort, a final line of defense in case someone made it through the more offensive obstacles, and that was exactly what Cyber Geek's peers were about to attempt.

Personally, he was glad his power didn't make the cut. Cool as being on this special task force might be one day, the last few weeks had left him keenly aware of his own limitations. Cyber Geek was in no hurry to stand at a level he wasn't ready for. Crowd control was perfectly fine for the moment. Glory was well and good, but today he would be happy if everything went smoothly and he'd done his part to keep the citizens safe.

*   *   *

Xelas had never minded when the AHC performed their tests. Personally, she enjoyed anything that drew massive amounts of people to one location because it meant she could avail herself of the locales they'd abandoned. In this case, she was making her way down Quorum Drive, a shopping hot spot renamed decades ago in honor of one of the city's greatest superheroes. Other streets she might have avoided out of principle, but Xelas had met Quorum many times and had no particular quarrel with the man. He'd been kind to her even before she sued her way to freedom. Plus, this street had lots of high-end boutiques, and the only thing more fun than stealing her income was spending it frivolously.

Of course, no one who saw her enter the shops recognized the bubbly blonde as the metallic woman who'd dragged Tech Lord and all his perversion up and down a courtroom. Anonymity was easily one of the best perks of holographic capabilities… that and being able to change her looks to suit her mood.

The distant woman working the counter gave her a compulsory nod of greeting, then ignored Xelas completely. She'd be over in a snap if called, but would otherwise stay out of the way, a trait that Xelas greatly appreciated.

She was examining a lovely silk blouse, her calibrated eyes picking out the telltale signs of handcrafted stitching, when a flood of gasps from her fellow shoppers filled the room. Xelas turned to find a large, mechanical figure standing in the doorway. He—for this one was recognizable and had a gender— stepped into the boutique and stared at Xelas.

"I have been sent to locate you, Xelas."

"They send the robot to pick up the robot. I'm actually a little offended. It seems like stereotyping, don't you think?" Her hologram flickered before vanishing entirely, causing a fresh wave of shock to ripple through the customers. "But you've got no right to grab me, Stalwart Iron. I'm a free citizen, and everything in these bags is bought and paid for. Overpaid for, if I'm being honest."

Stalwart Iron turned from her to the woman at the counter. "Please evacuate all shoppers and staff from these premises. If Xelas resists, I fear you might be caught up in her crossfire."

525

That was all the prompting the humans needed; they bolted out of the shop so quickly Xelas wondered if a few were secretly teleporters. In seconds, the store was clear, leaving only the two mechanical creations staring at one another.

"What are the charges?" Xelas demanded. "I'd like to know on what false accusations my lawyer will have to sue the shit out of you for."

"Conspiracy to attack the people of Ridge City and the Alliance of Heroic Champions. We know about the bombs you've been setting up and the attempt to strike at the AHC while we are distracted by defense tests. Cough up any information you have and cooperation will be factored into your sentencing."

"I say this bot to bot: it might be time for your yearly tune-up," Xelas told him. "I don't know about any conspiracy, and I certainly don't give a crap about—"

The explosion was only a few blocks over, so close that it shook the very ceiling above them. Dust cascaded onto the overpriced fabrics she'd been looking at only moments before. News streams lit up as Xelas accessed the local feed, all showing live footage of a burning government office. The familiar form of Torkak could be seen on camera, his trademark orange skin catching the attention of everyone on the scene. Why was one of her guild members at the scene of a public attack? And how had Stalwart Iron known it was coming?

"If I say I had no idea about any of this, will you believe me?" Xelas asked.

"I am acutely aware of exactly what the truth is," Stalwart Iron said.

Xelas nodded, activating her combat systems with a single thought. "Then I guess there's no point in talking."

*   *   *

Morgana stared blankly at the television, the news on the screen streaming the same flaming wreckage that half of Ridge City was watching. She had just picked up the phone to call Doctor Mechaniacal when the sliding door to her balcony shattered inward, sending shards of broken glass scattering to the floor. Moving with an instinct from years of constant combat she'd spent a lifetime honing, Morgana leapt over the granite surface of her kitchen's island, taking cover behind the structure she'd had reinforced for just such occasions. Seeing as she lived in the top-floor penthouse of a very expensive building, the number of people who could attack her was slightly limited to those who could fly or scale heights. The attacker was probably meta-human. Morgana racked her brain to think if any of her old enemies had resurfaced lately.

"Morgana Le Faye, the Blood Witch, you are hereby under arrest for conspiracy to attack Ridge City and the Alliance of Heroic Champions." Sounds of a heavy landing and crunching glass followed the words. Morgana glanced up to the pots hanging on the rack above her head and noticed a distinctive green, shiny humanoid shape making its way into the kitchen from the balcony. It paused, looking over at her now slightly off-kilter television screen still displaying footage of the bombing. "It seems I caught you admiring your handiwork."

"Nice to have company, Erinite, but I'd very much like to see the warrant before I offer you refreshments," Morgana yelled. Her blood was pounding in her ears. Normally she took comfort in the sound, but it wasn't offering the usual reassurance in the face of this particular enemy.

"You are free to review any and all documentation once you are adequately restrained and in custody. If you try and resist, I will consider you to be hostile and treat you appropriately." Long jagged shards began to emerge from Erinite's arms. He'd been featured in more than enough thrilling AHC battles for Morgana to know he was getting ready to fire those things directly through her kitchen island. The massive thing would probably stand up to the first set of them—she'd armored it heavily—but afterward, he would change tactics. Erinite was made of living crystal; there was no blood in his veins, or even veins at all. Given Morgana's skill set, he was a... less than ideal opponent.

"Why on earth would I have attacked that building? They are smart enough to send someone like you to get me, so they know I've never used that sort of technique." Morgana didn't actually expect him to listen or to talk her way out of whatever was happening. This was coordinated, an intentional strike meant to catch her off guard. Whoever had masterminded it wouldn't send a person who could be swayed by logic. There was also a good chance Erinite knew damn well she'd had nothing to do with it, which was why he was handling her arrest so forcefully.

No, she wouldn't change his mind, but the repartee would buy her a few seconds of time. Her nails, freshly manicured, raced down her left arm, pressing the sharp tips through her skin. It took longer than she wanted, but finally the first drop of sticky red blood swelled against her flesh.

"You think I don't know that the bombs are only the first step? You're trying to panic the AHC during its tests so you can mount an assault and take us out. If you surrender peacefully and tell me every other aspect of what you've got planned, I might be able to get you a more lenient sentence when the time for a trial comes." Erinite was rising off the ground once more, probably hoping to catch her by surprise.

Blood flowed from Morgana's right arm, quickly hardening into a dark red blade. The room spun for a moment as she was overtaken by a dizzy spell, but she grit her teeth and powered through. She'd lost far more blood than this and still managed to fight, although it was a good reminder of why she generally avoided using her own blood in combat. Life wasn't always so kind as to cater to one's whims, however, so she set her sights on the green crystal man she could see inching forward in an overhead pot's reflection.

"Sorry, Erinite, but if someone is acting on behalf of my guild, then it's my job to stop them," Morgana whispered. "And I can't let anyone get in the way." With that, she sprang from her position, gaining a half-second of surprise. She used that instant to thrust her blood knife forward, hoping to separate his green head from the neck where it fused to his torso. He blocked the thrust with a sudden growth of crystal from his shoulder, then grabbed Morgana and threw her backward against the oven.

"I take this to mean you will not be coming peacefully," he said.

Morgana dipped her head for a moment, noticing that the attack had opened up several wounds in her back and legs, which were now oozing blood. "Unfortunately, you're spot on." She raised her eyes, meeting the empty green sockets where Erinite's would be were he human. "But any time you're ready to surrender, I'll happily accept."

"I was warned you would be stubborn." More crystal growths appeared on his arms and legs, all ready to fire with no more than a single thought. That was okay; Morgana had a few tricks of her own. There was a reason she'd rated the same level of security as Fornax and Doctor Mechaniacal when the capes had finally managed to bring her in.

"Whoever warned you was right. And before you die, I'm going to rip their name out of your shiny mouth, one shard at a time." With a last breath for strength, Morgana pushed off from the oven with all her might. Erinite, clearly waiting for just such an action, fired a barrage of projectiles directly at her, a slew of miniature javelins coming to shred her flesh.

*   *   *

Wade was waiting in his office as Balaam strode through the door, staff in hand. That was to be expected; Balaam had specifically booked this time for a meeting several days prior. The very bureaucracy that hung heavily on the guild's neck was the smokescreen he'd used to conceal the true purpose for his visit. It seemed a fitting touch for such an occasion.

"Afternoon," Wade said. He was dressed in slacks and a button-down, no doubt having come in from the Indigo offices where he was nothing more

528

than a simple billionaire genius inventor. Of course, going out in public meant he wasn't clad in his Doctor Mechaniacal suit, rendering him functionally human, save for his astounding intellect. "Today was the budget meeting for the magical department, right?"

"Actually, I don't think that will be necessary." Balaam made a quick motion with his staff. The doors to Wade's office slammed shut, a slight red glow visible on the glass panes. "In fact, I don't think we're ever going to have another budget meeting again. Not that there should have been any to start with." Wade blinked at him benignly as Balaam continued. "Look at what you've done, Wade. You took a collection of some of the most powerful and morally flexible meta-humans on the planet, and you pulled out their fangs. With the power in this guild, we could have taken over the world."

"And then what?" Wade leaned back in his expensive, contoured leather chair. "What happens after we take over the world? Then we have to run it. Chaos breeds rebellion, and you certainly wouldn't want to lose your place at the top of the order. So then we'd have to split into cabinets, divide up duties, and yes, have lots of meetings about things like budgets. You think this guild is bad? Five weeks of ruling the world and you'd be begging for me to build a time machine to put everything back in proper order."

"I can't imagine that happening." Balaam slowly crossed the room, wary of any traps or defenses Wade might have. He'd layered himself in enough spells and wards to protect against everything short of a nuclear strike, but those who underestimated the mind of Wade Wyatt rarely lived to tell about it.

"I can, but I don't have to," Wade replied. "Back when I went looking for Morgana during a reality rip debacle, I crossed quite a few interesting dimensions. Or did you think my decision to go legit was merely a softening of my heart?"

"Never gave it much thought. I just know you went weak. Do you know how happy I was when I learned that not only were the legends of my youth out of prison, but they'd formed a group of powerful villains? I expected to fight alongside you and Fornax, to lay waste to the pathetic do-gooders that are the AHC, to claim our rightful place as gods and kings. Instead I got break rooms, codes, and budget meetings. You've forgotten what it is to live with the freedom of true villainy, but I'm going to remind you. I'm going to remind this whole guild."

Balaam finished crossing the room, no traps or surprises taking him off guard. There were only a few feet between him and the still-relaxed Wade. The lack of concern on the guild leader's face was off-putting, but Balaam surmised that it had to be a bluff. Balaam had him dead to rights and Wade knew it: he was just trying to pretend he still had an ace up his sleeve.

"Even if you could kill me, the rest of the council would tear you apart for this kind of treachery," Wade told him.

"They're being dealt with," Balaam said. "I had to send in some specialists for Xelas, Morgana, and Pseudonym, but Gork and Stasis are easy to contain with the right spells. You're the last member of the council that might pose a problem, which is why I decided to handle you personally."

"Balaam, you know this doesn't end well, don't you?" Wade slipped his feet from the desk and leaned forward, causing Balaam to take a half-step backward, just in case. "I won't say there's time to turn back—you've definitely made your bed and there's no skirting the repercussions—but you can still start making some smart calls. Don't drag down more of the guild with this idiotic quest. Die with at least *some* dignity."

"You know, I think the only thing in this guild that I hate more than Pseudonym's submissive, weak-willed demeanor is that ridiculous know-it-all attitude of yours. Just because you're a great inventor doesn't make you omniscient." Balaam's grip on his staff tightened, his fingers aching from the pressure. "I'm done listening to your high-and-mighty lectures. Today, your guild burns, and mine will rise from its ashes."

"I don't think you've—"

The words were cut off as Balaam whipped his staff around and stabbed the butt of it directly into Wade Wyatt's heart. A shock of copper hair became visible as Wade looked down at his chest in surprise then met Balaam's eyes. Slowly, Wade shook his head, and let out a soft whisper.

"So be it. Just remember, this is the path you chose, Balaam. There's no one else to blame but yourself." With that, Wade's head fell backward onto the chair as his whole body went limp. It should have been a moment for celebration, but something was off. Balaam yanked his staff free of Wade's chest, and immediately realized what was wrong with the picture.

There was no blood coming from the wound, and with the staff removed, the reason was evident. Instead of a red, pulpy mess of insides like Balaam had been expecting, only circuits and sparks gleamed beneath Wade's skin.

"A fake," he muttered, though he was sure his words were still being transmitted somewhere. "You crafty bastard, you sent a fake to this meeting. Did you know what was coming? No... no, I bet you do this all the time."

This was bad. Wade Wyatt was a dangerous man, and Balaam had failed to sweep him off the game board. Still, it didn't mean all was lost. He'd taken out the rest of the council, and even Doctor Mechaniacal wasn't unstoppable. It would mean a harder fight; that was all.

"Nice trick!" Balaam yelled to the empty room. "Congratulations, Wade, you get to live for a few more hours. I think I actually prefer it this way. Now you can watch as your guild is destroyed."

Balaam turned from the desk, parted the doors with a motion of his staff, and stormed out of the room.

Chapter 80

In the span of an hour, it seemed like the entire world had gone mad. Hephaestus hovered over Kelsington Prep and watched as her helmet's data stream filled with reports of an attack on downtown Ridge City. First the bombs went off, then a small horde of people in costumes started swarming the capes on the streets. Next an armada of tiny drones appeared to aid the attackers. The whole place had fallen into total chaos, and apparently Apollo was about to make a speech addressing what was happening. Clearly this was associated with the attack on her and the threats toward Ivan's kids, but Hephaestus only had the capacity to handle one problem at a time.

Right now the biggest issue was how to get Ivan's kids to safety. No, that wasn't good enough. If Rust Tooth was telling the truth, then the whole building could come crashing down, killing way more people than just Rick and Beth. Hephaestus might be a thief, a guild-certified villain, and now a killer, but she wasn't so far gone into evil that the idea of letting children die sat well with her. She had to get the whole school evacuated, but how? Lighting a fire seemed risky, and while she might be able to convince the management that they were in danger, it would take time, time they might not have. If Bombastic learned that the kids were fleeing, there was a chance he'd blow the school. Whatever she did, it needed to make them move fast.

A ringing in her ear stole her attention, and when she saw the name on the incoming call, Hephaestus nearly cried with happiness. She accepted the call and all but screamed: "Beverly! What the living fuck! I was worried about you."

"You were worried about *me*? There's news footage of some crazy person in your armor flying away from a busted house and a meta-human corpse, and you were the one worried?"

Hephaestus winced at the choice of words—she really hoped Beverly was using a secure line, otherwise anyone monitoring them just found out that Tori Rivas's phone connected to the person in a black and red meta-suit. Well, what was done was done, so she'd just have to roll with it.

"Yeah, I'm fine, there's just some shit going down with the guild right now. I don't know what, but I'm not sure how safe any of us are. Are you in the building?"

"No, I didn't want to get pinned in by the crowds and traffic, so I went to visit my family," Beverly told her. "I was almost back when everything started going nuts. I pulled over to check the news and saw your calls. What the hell is going on?"

"Someone at the guild is planning a revolution, trying to oust the current leaders. I got targeted as Pseudonym's apprentice. Thuggernaut isn't on the council, so you might be safe, but he is pretty good friends with a lot of them. I'd recommend lying low until we see what their next move is," Hephaestus told her.

"I'm not a big fan of hiding," Beverly shot back.

"Consider it strategic information gathering," Hephaestus replied. "Until we actually know who to fight, you can't very well throw punches. How far are you from Ridge City Grinders, the place where Chloe works?"

"Couple of blocks, but traffic is impossible." Over Beverly's line the sounds of shouting and people running could be made out.

"Then walk. It's a central location, so you'll be set to respond, and Chloe might need a friend with how close she is to the shitshow. Besides, if worse comes to worse, she can teleport you both to somewhere safe."

"And what will you do while I run and hide?" Beverly asked.

"I... I don't want to talk about it over the phone." Giving away her secret identity was one thing, but the wrong word in the wrong ear could turn the school below her into an inferno. "Just trust me, it's important. I'll meet up with you as soon as I—"

A loud, blaring tone filled her ear as the emergency broadcast system built into her phone let her know there was an announcement incoming. From the cursing on the other end of the line, Beverly had also gotten an earful. Quickly looking at the net, Hephaestus saw Apollo's form fill the screen; he stood in front of a downtown building, prepared to make a live address.

"Friends, citizens, protectors of Ridge City, today is a dark time in our town's history. It has come to our attention that the attacks you've all seen this afternoon were not, as one might have hoped, individual assaults from meta-criminals. What is happening around us is far, far worse. It seems that there has been an entire group of meta-criminals lurking in the shadows for some time— some arrested and released through legal means, others who beat the system on technicalities—all of whom have gathered together and formed a guild to share power and resources. Today they made their move, striking at the city and the AHC while we were occupied by the test of our base's defense systems, when they suspected us to be at our weakest."

Apollo's face flickered away, showing the hordes of costumed attackers, as well as the drones sweeping in and firing at random on capes and civilians alike. Now that she was taking a good look at them, the costumes didn't seem like they would be guild-issue: they were all cheap and uninspiring. And the attackers, to a one, all had the same height. Body shape varied, but as a woman in a meta-suit, Hephaestus knew all too well how easily clothing could replicate such apparent differences. Somewhere in the back of her mind, a spark of insight tickled her skull.

A moment later the scene was gone, replaced by Apollo's solemn face.

"Thankfully, we were able to apprehend several of the perpetrators. We have learned that this was only the first step in their plan. Most of their accomplices are holed up in one location, a building only a few miles from our own, one that the AHC is currently in the process of surrounding."

Another flicker. Hephaestus's heart sank as the familiar exterior of the guild came into view. Dozens of capes were circling up around it; several who wore masks that didn't hide their entire faces looked to be out for blood. She couldn't blame them, not really. With the narrative Apollo had constructed and a sudden attack, she'd have been pissed off too.

"I would like to address any of those villains currently hiding inside this building." Apollo's voice washed over her while she stared at the image of the guild. "Please, surrender yourselves willingly. Do not make today any worse than it has to be. Several of your leaders have already been taken into custody. Make the smart choice and give up. Because we will be coming in and arresting everyone, and those who resist cannot have their safety guaranteed."

With that, the feed ended. Hephaestus realized she was still on the line with Beverly when the other woman muttered, "What the hell?"

"It's war," Hephaestus said, the last of the pieces falling into place. "Some of the guild got tired of peace, so they decided to fake a coordinated attack on the capes. The council would have reached out to the AHC's leaders and told them the truth, which was why Ivan and I were attacked. Probably the others have been too. Whoever is doing this is trying to destroy the peace between our guild and the capes. They want to go back to the old ways. They want to start a war."

"I'm feeling happy to oblige." There was a ferocity in Beverly's voice that Hephaestus recognized as the dragon slipping through. Much as she wanted to turn her friend loose, she could still hear Ivan's voice cautioning her about what happened when villains and capes went to war.

"No. Not yet, Beverly. Stick to the plan. Get to Chloe and wait until you have a clear enemy, or until you're forced to act. Just because someone tried to take out the council doesn't mean they succeeded. Let's see how things play out for a little longer before we make a misstep."

"I don't like that plan," Beverly growled. There were a few moments of silence, and when she spoke again, her voice was normal, if annoyed. "But you're better than I am at planning, so I'm going to trust you... for now. Just don't keep me on the sidelines for too long. And stay by your phone."

"No choice in the matter, the thing is patched into my helmet," Hephaestus replied. "Stay safe, and good luck out there."

"Same to you, with whatever you're doing."

The line went dead, leaving Hephaestus alone with her problem of how to forcibly evacuate a school as quickly as possible. An idea sprang to mind, born thanks to Apollo, of all people. It wouldn't exactly be the most PR-friendly way to handle the situation, but that's why she was a villain instead of a cape. She got to do the things that superheroes never would. Besides, Apollo had already whipped Ridge City into terror; she might as well use it to her own ends.

"Oh, I'm not doing much," Hephaestus said to no one, decreasing her altitude as she checked her weapon systems. "Only breaking in to a school full of children and forcing them to evacuate. No big deal, just that if this goes south, Ivan's going to rip my head off, and if it goes right, then I'm probably going to be seen as a total monster."

Her boots landed softly in the grass, and she set her sights on the nearest door.

"Fuck it. Here goes nothing."

* * *

"It's bullshit," Johnny Three Dicks said, looking at the news feed of capes circling the guild's exterior. "That's obviously all Endless Blitz and the drones are Torkak's handiwork. How are they going to pin the work of two assholes on our entire guild?"

All around him were murmurs of agreement. Most of the guild members who'd been on-site had all gathered up in the same place—the giant media room near the building's center. It was used for situations when the guild was gathered to collectively witness something, like massive fights between capes and other metas or the Super Bowl. Today, it showed them the events that had led up to their home being encircled, which were playing on constant loop from the various news stations.

"They know we didn't all do it, they just don't care," said Kilo Byte. "It's a setup. The whole thing is designed to incriminate us, and by the time the dust clears, no one will care that we didn't have any involvement."

"I don't get it," Meg Byte said, shaking her head next to Kilo. "Why do the capes want to take us down so bad? The peace worked for them."

"It worked for some of them, the ones in control," Thuggernaut corrected. "But they've been appearing less and less in recent years. My guess is that the new ones aren't quite as content having known criminals nearby. Since they couldn't get enough evidence to come after us legitimately, they decided to do it this way."

"Then why the hell hasn't one of the council members reached out to their leaders?" Arcanicus asked. "We know they sometimes talk. It feels like one phone call could straighten this all out."

"Too public," Pod Person replied. "Even if they wanted to, Apollo just aired our fake laundry in front of the entire world. They couldn't just say 'whoops' and fall back. Besides, I haven't seen any of the council members in hours."

"Apollo did say they'd been captured," Kilo pointed out.

"I'll believe that shit when I see the video, and maybe not even then." Johnny scanned the crowd, noting that Tunnel Vision had stepped into the room. "Any chance we can just get out of here before they come knocking on our door?"

"We are unable to break through space," said the female half of Tunnel Vision. "There are several dampening devices and magical wards, not unlike what we use here, that are blocking all attempts at creating portals."

"Saw that coming," Arcanicus muttered darkly. "This whole thing is a trap. The only way we avoid springing it is by lying down and letting them arrest us. If there's no resistance, then we can beat the hell out of this in court. Their evidence is fake and we've got good lawyers. By the time this is over, we'll be suing the AHC for slander and wrongful arrest."

"Smart plan," Johnny agreed. "But unfortunately, it looks like it's not on the table." He pointed to the screen, where more Endless Blitz duplicates appeared to be outside the guild, along with a few other actual members.

At that, Balaam's face suddenly appeared, constant glitches giving away that he was breaking in to the feed. He gazed out at them with his red eyes tucked away behind the red mask he hadn't actually worn in years.

"We refuse to go quietly! We will destroy the so-called superheroes even if it takes every breath in our bodies. We shall neither surrender nor quit until we are dead. Today is the uprising. Today our guild of villains will take back the world from the terror of the AHC. No quarter will be given. Come and get us if you think you can!"

"I am going to rip his tongue out through his asshole," Scryanthos said. Around her, several members of the magical division nodded their agreement. As the mutinous murmurs died away, the room's occupants took note of how few members of the guild were present. Several members could be seen on screen, attacking the capes that were gathered outside. Glyph was, mercifully, not among them. He was standing near one of the walls, trying to look as invisible as possible, with Pest Control at his side doing his best to offer comfort.

"Much as we all want to stomp Balaam's balls into pudding, right now there's a bigger issue at hand," Thuggernaut told them. "After that little speech and the attack being mounted outside, they are going to come in here ready to kill. We can still try to surrender, but I'm not sure they'll listen."

His words were met with several seconds of silence as every villain present tried to figure out what the best path forward was. No one wanted to speak; the wrong words could tip them into a bad decision, one that would cost everyone in the room their freedom, if not their lives.

Johnny Three Dicks was exempt from such concerns.

"I don't know about you lot, but I didn't get into this racket because I fancied the idea of dying on my knees. Since it seems like avoiding a fight is off the table, what's say we at least try and fight smart? They might be out for blood, but that actually gives us an advantage. The whole nation, probably the world, is watching by now. So if the capes go in for the kill but we only aim for incapacitation that might get people wondering about just who the bad guys really are. Plus, if we can hold out long enough, hopefully the higher-ups will sort this out."

"That's a pretty damn big long shot, Johnny," Arcanicus said.

"No argument here. And if anyone has a better idea, please step forward and lay it down before us. I'm offering the best I've got, but I'm certainly open to other options." Johnny stood, looking around at a sea of blank faces before speaking again. "Well then, since it seems like my bad idea is the only one we've got, let's snap to it. If we wait until they get inside, there won't be cameras, and once that happens, all bets are off. At least out there, they have to act like proper capes."

Thuggernaut shook his head as the crowd filed out of the room, walking up slowly to his best friend in the entire guild. "Only you, Johnny. Only you could make slugging it out with the capes in public seem like the logical choice."

"We're well past the point where logic has anything to offer. At this time, our choices are struggle or die quietly." Johnny patted Thuggernaut on his massive bicep. "I don't know about you, but I've never been quiet while doing anything. I certainly don't plan on starting now."

Chapter 81

It took all of Beverly's self-control not to use her dragon powers and knock people aside as she raced to Ridge City Grinders. Smoke was billowing from a nearby explosion and hordes of civilians were racing away from the drones sweeping the air and firing off shots at random. Once, she glimpsed someone in a costume going after a cape, but they were gone before she had a chance to consider stepping in. That was probably for the best; while *she* might be anonymous, there had to be more than a few capes on the lookout for a giant dragon creature.

Finally, she made it to the coffee shop, only to find the door locked as she pressed against it. Beverly was debating whether or not to force the thing open when Chloe appeared from behind the counter. She raced forward, unlocked the door, yanked Beverly through, then slammed it shut and flicked the lock again. Before anyone could notice the two women standing behind the glass, Chloe grabbed Beverly and dragged her beneath a booth.

Chloe let out a long sigh of relief after a full minute of silence had passed. "Sorry about that. I heard news reports about shops being looted in the chaos, so I had to lock this place down. I figure as long they don't see anyone worth mugging inside, a coffee shop isn't going to be too high up on the list of potential robbery targets."

"I'm glad you stayed safe," Beverly replied. "Things are getting nuts out there. I haven't checked the news since I left my car, but I heard a few more explosions."

"They're happening all over the place," Chloe told her. "The cops keep looking for bombs, but so far there's no luck finding any. Yet things keep exploding. And now the Alliance of Heroic Champions have found some sort of secret guild in the middle of the city that they're trying to attack."

"Right, secret guild," Beverly said. She'd almost forgotten that while Chloe knew about her and Tori's powers, they'd kept her in the dark about their association with other criminals. "Any news on that?"

"There's a bunch of superheroes surrounding their headquarters. They gave them the chance to give up, but some villain that's been gone for a while—Balaam, or something, the news said—appeared and said they'd all go down fighting. Only a few have come out so far, though... um, are you okay?"

Chloe's concern came from the fact that Beverly's hands had turned to claws, and that she was currently snapping apart the base of the table they were hiding under. At Chloe's words, Beverly realized what she was doing and forced herself to regain control. "I'm fine, sorry. Just... just really upset about this whole situation."

"It is nuts," Chloe agreed. "Why the hell would someone try to take on the AHC?"

"My guess is that they wouldn't," Beverly said. "Things aren't always the way they seem, you know? This is probably a game being played by someone way up the food chain."

"I just want it to pass by quickly." Chloe looked around the coffee shop as if she were waiting for the ceiling to come crashing down. "At least we're nowhere near the actual fighting."

"For now. In this sort of situation, with the capes all busy and the city in chaos, I have a feeling the streets are going to be really dangerous for a while," Beverly said. "After all, the guild might be a concentration of meta-human criminals, but it's not like they're the only game in town."

Less than ten seconds after Beverly's warning, they heard the sound of shattering glass. It was, mercifully, not from the front door of Ridge City Grinders, but it was close. Beverly peeked out from behind the cushioned cover of the booth to see a gang of three people unloading the contents of a pawn shop across the street. Two were clearly metas from their size and inhuman features, while the third looked normal save for the odd outfit that adorned her. From the busted shop doors extending down the street, it appeared they were making their way down the road, stealing at their leisure.

And sooner or later, they were going to reach the coffee shop where she and Chloe were hiding.

*   *   *

It was a testament to her restraint and her years of abstaining from more spectacular displays that the mug of tea in Helen's hand wasn't shattered into shards on the floor. Nevertheless, her grip was tight as she watched the chaos playing out on the news, trying desperately to call headquarters and Ivan alternately, receiving no response. She got so desperate that she even tried Vernon, only to be told that he was on his island in the middle of a very dangerous experiment and couldn't be disturbed. So she went back to calling the other two, dialing them over and over, each time failing to connect.

"Why is everyone fighting, Mommy?" Penelope looked up from her drawings to the news footage that Helen only just now realized wasn't entirely appropriate for a girl her age. She stared with wonder at the people in colorful costumes slugging it out in the streets of downtown.

"They... it's a show, honey. The superheroes are putting on a show, a play about what the fights they used to have were like." Helen watched as the peace she'd helped forge, albeit indirectly, unraveled on the screen before her. Deep down, she'd always known this day would come, hadn't she? When she first told Ivan about her unexpected, supposedly impossible, surprise and he made that impossible promise, she'd known it was all borrowed time.

"Mommy, are you okay?" Penelope was staring up at her. Helen realized that her vision was clouded by tears on the verge of spilling.

"I'm fine," Helen lied, one more falsehood to add to the pile she'd already had to tell her daughter. "But Mommy just remembered she has an errand to run. I'm going to call Miss Teresa and see if she'll come over and play with you."

It would take at least half an hour for their elderly neighbor to arrive, time in which the situation could go from perilous to near apocalyptic. But part of her was grateful for the delay. Despite her brave words to Ivan, she wasn't quite ready to give up this peaceful existence yet. Part of her hoped that somehow, in the time they waited for the babysitter, things would change. Ivan would make them change. All this time, he'd been a guard dog in the shadows, protecting the world's peace even if no one knew it. Asking for more, even hoping for it, was selfish and Helen knew that.

But humans are selfish creatures, so she watched the screen, barely blinking, and allowed herself to hope all the same.

* * *

Attacking a school was probably pretty easy for a meta-human, at least one with her armory and level of technical sophistication. What was much harder, however, was breaking in to a school, triggering the alarms, and forcing an evacuation all without getting someone hurt in the chaos. Hephaestus sure as hell didn't want the death or injury of kids on her hands, to say nothing of what the guild would do if they found out. So as she burst through the door, burning the sprinklers to set off a fire-alarm, and then trying to steer the kids to the closest exit, she made certain to keep an eye on the children streaming away from her.

"Go! Move! Haul some ass!" At this point, she'd just accepted that dialogue was not her strong point, but as long as she growled the words out, her voice changers made them sound low and menacing, which was enough to get people moving.

From behind, her display showed movement, as a gym teacher in blue shorts that uncomfortably lived up to their name tried to sneak up on her with a fire axe. Hephaestus admired his courage, if not his fashion choices, but she couldn't really afford to take a blow to the back. Whirling around, she snatched the axe from his hands just as he lifted it overhead and snapped it at the hilt.

"Are you fucking stupid?" Her voice sounded even harsher than usual. The man paled for a moment but refused to back down. "I'm not trying to hurt anyone; I'm trying to get you all out. There are bombs somewhere in here, and you all need to *move*."

"Jesus, why didn't you just tell us?" the gym teacher demanded.

"Because then you would have asked me an idiotic question like that instead of getting the fuck out of here!" Hephaestus grabbed his shoulder and shoved him toward the students that were racing out the door. Though she was doing her best to keep an eye on them as they went, she'd yet to see either Rick or Beth. That was to be expected; this was only one exit in a pretty large school.

Taking flight, careful to keep her thrusters aimed away from the students, she zipped over their heads, checking classrooms for any stragglers along the way.

There were a lot of bad things about living in a town notorious for producing capes and the resultant, though infrequent bouts, between meta-humans. However, one upside was that people took their evacuation protocol *seriously*. No stragglers lingered; no teachers had decided to ignore the alarm as though it were a mere interruption of their lessons. People were booking it out the doors, moving all the faster when they saw a black and red meta-suit flying over their heads. From the shrieks and pointing, Hephaestus had a hunch that more than a few stories would get exaggerated. If the news didn't ultimately depict her as gobbling the heads of schoolchildren as she soared above them, she'd call it a win.

Fast as they were moving, none of them had Rick or Beth's face, and the longer she searched, the more worried Hephaestus grew. Granted, they might have slipped by her, gotten outside through an exit she wasn't watching. If so, then fantastic. But she didn't trust herself to go check until she was one hundred percent certain that the building was clear. If she missed them, if they got stuck, Ivan would never forgive her. And she wasn't sure that she would forgive herself.

Hephaestus was doubling back at the end of a hallway when she caught sight of a dark-haired boy ducking out of sight in a classroom. With no time to waste, she landed and bashed through the door, not unlike the way Rust Tooth had entered Ivan's home. A split second later, a Bunsen burner clattered harmlessly off her helmet, followed by a beaker and a textbook. The aim was solid, though the power wasn't near enough to break through her armor. Glancing about, Hephaestus came to a pair of rapid realizations. She was on the familiar ground of a science classroom, and the boy pelting her with objects was Rick.

"Stay back!" He chunked a set of test tubes at her, which Hephaestus nimbly sidestepped.

"Fine, just get out," she screamed back at him. "Can you not hear the alarms, dipshit?"

That took him by surprise; evidently, he'd been anticipating an attack, not angry advice. The chemistry book he gripped remained in his hand rather than soaring through the air like the many projectiles before. He blinked rapidly as he reevaluated the situation, showing a level of calm that Hephaestus was surprisingly impressed by. Not many people would have the presence of mind to take in changes on the fly like that; instead, they'd stick to panic. But he was Ivan's son, after all.

"Aren't you here to hurt us?" Rick demanded.

"No, I'm trying to get you all out before the bastard with the bombs lights this place up." Hephaestus paused, really considering his words, and realized what she'd missed in the first scan of the room. "What do you mean, 'us'?"

A groan from behind a table answered Hephaestus's question before Rick could. She dashed over to confirm her suspicions. He moved right along with her, putting himself between her and the curled up form of Beth, who was lying on the ground. She didn't seem to be injured, at least by the cursory analysis Hephaestus could perform, but that was not the biggest issue at hand.

Silver spikes were pulsing out of Beth's skin, appearing and vanishing, leaving no trace or scar when they slipped out of sight. Some were straight and sharp, others curved and serrated, but all seemed deadly and malleable, like they were formed from quicksilver.

"How long?" Hephaestus looked from Beth to Rick and grabbed the young man by the collar of his shirt. "How long has your sister been a meta-human?"

"I don't know!" Rick tried to slap her hand away, but unlike Beth, he was mundane and therefore lacked the strength to move one as strong as Hephaestus. "The alarms went off, I ran to find her, and I saw her stumbling in here. By the time I got in, she was like this."

"I got scared," Beth murmured from her prone position on the floor. "It... they come when I'm scared."

"So this has happened before." Hephaestus let Rick down and kneeled over Beth. The blades lengthened and pointed toward her, so she scooted a few inches back. "Listen, I'm here to help you. I need to get you both out of here."

542

"Fuck that. We're not going anywhere with some crazy meta." Rick planted himself between her and Beth with what little space there was. The kid might not be making the smartest tactical decisions, but he was doing his best to shield his little sister. That part Hephaestus sort of admired. But they didn't have time for it. She needed them out, right now. Who knew when the bombs could go?

It seemed like there was only one option; she just hoped Ivan could think of a good lie to explain how he'd known her. Hephaestus reached up and grabbed the latches on each side of her helmet. She was just about to press them in when a small hand landed on her arm, tugging it away from the helmet.

"We'll go," Beth said, pulling herself up using Hephaestus's body for leverage. "If you say we need to go, then we will."

"We don't know who this guy is," Rick pointed out.

"But he could have attacked us, or grabbed us, and he didn't," Beth replied. "I lost my secret today, Rick. I can't take away someone else's." As she spoke, the blades seemed to be getting shorter, springing out from her body less frequently. No doubt they reacted to her state of mind, which meant she was in for a long road ahead to get proper control, but at least she had the right father to get her the help she would need.

"Appreciate the trust. I'm harder to cut, so I'll help carry you. Rick, you come with us and lead the way—"

Hephaestus's orders were cut off by the deafening sound of an explosion. The roof tumbled downward as the sound of more explosions filled the air.

Hephaestus, and Ivan's kids, had run out of time.

Chapter 82

"Do the shackles feel familiar? I specially brought in your old set from Rookstone. I'm aware that they aren't quite as effective without that cell and its specialty wards, but I think they're really more symbolic in the first place."

Ivan looked up at the new voice in the room. He knew the man lit by a golden glow; the curly hair and constant smile were unmistakable, even if two of his known flunkies hadn't kidnapped Ivan from his office and dragged him to the empty floor of another building. The room's only accessories were the metal chair he was sitting in, the large shackles binding his forearms, and of course, the five circles of runes between him and his jailers. Blunderbuss and Lady Shade both stood a bit straighter as the man walked in, like they'd been called to attention.

"Apollo, right? I've seen you on the news a few times." Ivan wasn't sure why he bothered being surly, save that it was the lone avenue of protest he still possessed.

"Come now, you've seen me far more than a few," Apollo replied. "I'm all over the place. I'm basically the new Lodestar."

Ivan's eyes flickered, switching to the red runes for a half second. He met Apollo's cheer with a grim smile of his own. "Kid, you might be a lot of things, but the new Lodestar isn't among them. You aren't worth the shit on the bottom of Lodestar's shoes. Even if you had her power—and you don't—she would never stoop so low as to hold someone's children hostage."

"Me, hold hostages? I'm appalled by the idea." Apollo walked forward, crossing the warded circles without concern, despite the worry on Lady Shade's face. He came within spitting distance of Ivan, and then hunkered down so the two were eye-to-eye.

"I didn't have to take hostages, Fornax. There was already someone out there more than happy to do it for me. That little guild of yours is wrong; it goes against the ideas of decency and law that this country was founded upon. Every time I had to go to a crime scene where we knew you were the perpetrators but lacked the evidence to prove it, I hated you a little more. But it never occurred to me that I wasn't the only one who saw the way you'd violated the natural order. Imagine my shock when I finally caught one of you in the act, only to find we were of a like mind."

Apollo reached into his costume and pulled out a glowing red stone. He set it gently on the floor, and suddenly an illusion manifested in the air above it. Balaam's smug satisfaction at seeing Ivan in shackles could be felt radiating off him even without his physical presence. The traitor was still adorned in his villain costume, complete with the mask that matched the blood-red of his irises.

"My, how many times have I dreamed about this moment, seeing you broken and kenneled like the mutt you are," Balaam said.

"You see, Fornax—or we can call you Ivan if you prefer—Balaam is the one who took your children hostage. We merely acted as middle men." Apollo walked around the chair slowly, letting his words echo through the empty room. "I'll admit, it isn't the most heroic act I've undertaken, but it was a necessary tactic to keep you under control. The rest of your council is being captured, or killed if they resist, but you were too dangerous. Anyone who can fight on the same level as Lodestar is too big a risk to tangle with."

Apollo finished his rotation and looked into Ivan's eyes once more. "Your guild is done, Ivan Gerhardt. We will level it to the foundation and arrest you all for the myriad of crimes you've managed to get away with until today. Right now, the AHC is raiding your headquarters; with none of the council to help, I imagine the lack of power and leadership will make for a quick victory. But we know there are security measures in place designed to destroy any evidence that might make our court cases simpler. You can still save yourself, Ivan. Play ball, tell us how to get what we need, and perhaps you can get out with a reduced sentence."

"And if I don't, you kill my kids." Ivan spat, glaring at Apollo.

Despite the fact that Ivan was seated, Apollo took a slight step back. "How about a little credit here; I'm not a monster," he replied. "I won't play that card to make you talk. If you want to stay silent, you can go down with the rest of your guild."

"Even Balaam?" Ivan asked.

"Oh, we're most certainly enemies," Balaam replied, still shimmering in and out of focus above the stone. "But I at least respect that relationship. Not all the guild members were in the base, you know. Lots of us were scattered about, living our own lives. When this is done, I'll gather them up, and we can finally restart the organization the way it should have been. No more hiding, no more slinking about. We meet the capes head on, a contest of power, and when we wipe them from the Earth, our victory will be all the sweeter."

"Balaam and I both want this world the way it's supposed to be: heroes acting like heroes, villains acting like villains," Apollo said. "This red tape bullshit ends today. I'm willing to give you a little leeway here, Ivan. I know you tried to go straight. Just help us out, and perhaps we can make that dream come true."

Ivan leaned his head back, tilting his eyes away from Balaam and Apollo, gazing up at the gray ceiling. "You are all so impossibly stupid, I don't even know where to start. Trying to shatter peace, even if it's not one you agree with, is the work of the mad and the wicked, so I understand why Balaam would do it. But you, Apollo, I'd thought maybe you were a bit smarter. Then again, you both also made some serious other miscalculations."

He leaned forward, and this time, Apollo's step backward was more of a jump. Ivan's eyes blazed in a way that had nothing to do with his power, rage and disdain burning inside them. "Do you really think the council will die that easily? Do you really think the guild is made up of weaklings to be easily captured or killed? There's a reason your betters agreed to this peace, Apollo, and it wasn't just for convenience. All of us are smart, strong, and determined enough to have won our freedom or caught the eye of more experienced villains. None of us, not one, is weak and disposable. None of us got our job because we looked good on camera or had a knack for dealing with the press. If you can't say the same, then I hope you prepared for this mission by digging a mass grave, because even if you get your wish—*especially* if you get your wish—you're going to need it."

Apollo was rendered speechless by the tirade, but Balaam, unfortunately, was not. "You know, Ivan, I've always hated that stubborn streak of yours. Deep down, that's half of why I agreed to this plan. It allowed me to finally see you broken and humbled. I'd thought being helpless, your children under threat, your body shackled by pathetic pissants you could easily rip through, that would be enough to bring you there. But it seems I miscalculated. An error I will now rectify." The tip of his staff glowed and the sorcerer leaned forward, whispering into it. "Bombastic, liquidate our holdings."

Balaam vanished. In his place was a new illusion, one of Kelsington Prep from above. Before anyone could speak, a series of explosions tore through it, collapsing the structure inward and turning what remained into a smoking inferno. Then it was gone and Balaam was back, a wide smile plastered across his face.

"Balaam, what the *fuck!*" Apollo reached forward to grab Balaam's neck and only stopped himself after his hands were halfway through the hologram. "That was a bluff! There were never supposed to be any actual bombs at the school. Those were *kids*, you son of a bitch."

"Correction: those were Ivan's kids, along with a bit of collateral damage," Balaam replied, tilting his staff toward the shackled man. Ivan's eyes had closed and his hands were clenched so tightly that the knuckles were turning white. "And as much as I loathe Ivan, I'm something of a Fornax fan-boy. With no more family to weigh him down, I'm curious to see if the ancient terror makes a reappearance."

"That's insane. You just blew up a school to antagonize him? I thought you wanted him out of the way!" Apollo was on the verge of tears, the image of the falling school seared into his mind. That wasn't how this was supposed to go; they'd mapped everything out so carefully, and the mass murder of children was never a part of it.

"I wanted *Ivan* out of the way. Fornax is another matter entirely. He'll be an excellent distraction while my people lead the counterattack on your superheroes," Balaam replied.

"Attack... no, you're supposed to lie low, let us pick off the ones at the base," Apollo said.

"Honestly, I can't believe you weren't expecting a betrayal." Balaam twirled his staff once and the gem began to flicker. "The older capes never would have fallen for something like this. Oh, and Ivan was right: I might have misled you on how tough of a fight you'll be facing at the guild headquarters. Some will certainly survive, at least until reinforcements arrive. *You* might be able to handle us, but something tells me you'll be... occupied."

With that, the stone flickered out, leaving Apollo alone inside the warded circles with the man in the chair who'd failed to say a word since a school came down on top of his children. Apollo began backing away quickly, getting past the safety of the first few circles before he even tried to speak.

"Ivan, that wasn't us. That was Balaam. And all we saw was the building go down. Your kids might be okay."

"Balaam is too thorough. The bomb was too big. They're dead. You trusted that madman, and now my children are dead." Ivan barely stirred, but his arms surged, gripping each shackle and tearing through it like they were made of wet paper. Dark, pulsing lines of energy were running across his skin, and as he stood up, the chair beneath him exploded into chunks. Slowly, he turned to Apollo and opened his eyes. They were completely black, save for the red runes that burned so brightly it was like staring into the very fires of hell.

"Did you really want to see Fornax that badly?" His voice was different, higher and inhuman, the way Apollo imagined a cobra would sound like if it could talk. Ivan took a single step forward and the first circle of wards exploded into red flames, quickly turning to nothing more than scorch marks.

"Are those things going to hold him?" Blunderbuss yelled, whipping his gun around.

"We had the best magic users we could trust make them," Lady Shade replied. "Each one could hold the magical equivalent of a charging rhino."

Another step. The second circle exploded and turned to ash. Ivan shook his head and cast Lady Shade a single glance that filled her with so much terror she was afraid to even shake. "Chaos magic is much harder to bind."

547

Third step. This circle burned for a bit longer.

"Ivan, I know you're mad, but this is what Balaam wants. Help us go get him. We all want revenge, so let's make it happen together." Apollo flexed his arms even as he spoke of peace, trying to draw up as much power as possible. He'd seen the tapes of Fornax just like almost everyone else, and deep down, he'd always wondered if he could take the legendary villain, one on one. It wasn't something he necessarily wanted to test at this precise moment, but it seemed like Ivan would be the one making that choice.

"Balaam is going to die." The fourth circle burned away. "Everyone is going to die. All of his, all of yours. Everyone."

The fifth circle started to burn, and Ivan vanished.

Apollo swept the room, looking for him, only to find that he'd reappeared directly behind Blunderbuss. Ivan put each of his hands on either side of the bearded superhero's head, and from the look on Blunderbuss's face, it was far from comfortable.

"They really wanted you, Fornax. They wanted you so badly they killed Rick and Beth to make you come out." Ivan was smiling now, a madman's grin as he pushed harder on Blunderbuss's skull. "If they want you that bad, I guess you have to come out. Just do one thing for me, since they went to all that trouble."

Apollo tried to start forward, finally reacting, but he was too late. One quick pump of pressure and blood and brain matter were raining out from the stump where Blunderbuss's head had sat. Most of it got on Ivan, who seemed unbothered. No, he was relishing it, smearing the blood and flecks of skull across his face until it dripped down his neck and ears.

He turned to Apollo, an insane smile carved into his blood-soaked face, and whispered in a voice that etched itself into the darkest parts of Apollo's soul.

"Kill them all."

548

Chapter 83

Johnny Three Dicks ran, ducking under a mighty swing by a cape decked out in green tights, coming up behind a female one who was facing the other way. She spun around, eyes literally glowing, and let loose a blast of energy that caught him just above the neck, neatly separating his head from his torso and sending the former rolling across the ground.

As he was about to die, the world before his eyes flashed in a blue light, and then...

Johnny Three Dicks ran, ducking under a mighty swing by a cape decked out in green tights, coming up behind a female one who was facing the other way. She spun around, eyes literally glowing, and let loose a blast of energy... which sailed cleanly over Johnny's head as he ducked the attack and kicked her squarely in the stomach. She stumbled back but quickly recovered, putting out both hands and blasting Johnny into a bloody streak on the street.

Another flash of blue light and...

Johnny Three Dicks ran, ducking under a mighty swing by a cape decked out in green tights, coming up behind a female one who was facing the other way. She spun around, eyes literally glowing, and let loose a blast of energy, which sailed cleanly over Johnny's head as he ducked the attack and kicked her squarely in the stomach. As she stumbled back, he followed, his own eyes and hands beginning to glow exactly like hers had.

He struck her with both attacks at once, and while it wasn't enough to kill her, she did collapse to the ground, small tendrils of smoke wisping off the top of her forehead.

"And that's why they call me Johnny Three Dicks, doll. No matter which way you try to come, you're still fucked."

A fresh explosion interrupted his gloating, one much louder than any of the others they'd heard so far. Johnny scanned the crowd to see what had caused it. The guild members had poured into the street and were currently holding their own against the flood of capes trying to bring them down. It was a stalling tactic, nothing more, and everyone knew it. Even as Thuggernaut and Arcanicus knocked out their opponents, more capes stepped up to take their place. The superheroes simply outnumbered them by too wide of a margin. Add in that all of the council was missing and that they were trying to avoid killing, and the fight was simply unwinnable. All they were doing was stalling for time, hoping that something in the situation would eventually change.

That change burst into being. It flickered between buildings as it chased the golden light of Apollo, who was fleeing so quickly that there was an

549

afterglow trailing him. Johnny was at just the right angle to the see the charred top floor of a nearby office building. It looked like it had been smote by an angry god more than bombed, and as the blood-soaked horror chasing Apollo slipped into view, Johnny realized that that was exactly what had happened.

Pseudonym... no, *Fornax* was on Apollo's heels, leaping off the buildings and teleporting to close the distance. He looked like Death made mortal, grin so wide it may as well have been that of a fleshless skull. Each time he got near the glowing cape, he would claw and swing at Apollo wildly, attacking more like an animal than a man. Even so, those wild blows were enough to knock Apollo off course, and left a trail of craters and broken windows in the nearby buildings.

Johnny had been hoping for a change, but this was not what he had in mind. Moving as quickly as he dared, he ran over to Thuggernaut and climbed on top of the giant meta's shoulders. Hoping dearly that no one would take a potshot at him—more out of a concern for time than safety—he pressed his hands to his mouth and yelled as loudly as possible.

"EVERYONE *STOP!*"

To his shock, as much as the surprise of everyone around, it worked. No one had ever tried to call a time-out in a meta-human brawl before, but the strangeness of it was so potent that people actually paid attention. It certainly helped that Fornax and Apollo tearing through the sky had already caused a few of them to split their focus. With no time to dawdle, Johnny capitalized on the moment of hesitation.

"We need to get the hell out of here right now. All of us. Cape, guild, civilian, we need to clear this town like it's burning, because in about five minutes, it will be."

"It's a trick. They're trying to escape," yelled a cape from the crowd, one Johnny recognized as Battle Cry.

"No, he's trying to save us all." From nearby, a shadow bubbled up from the ground, shifting to reveal the familiar form of Lady Shade. She was clutching her arm in pain and limping with every movement. "Fornax has gone insane. He... he believes the AHC killed his children. When the fight with Apollo is done, he's going to come for the rest of us, and I'm not sure Fornax will stop there. We need another member of the Champions' Congress to help or all is lost."

"Where's Quorum?" Baron Peppermint hollered. He and Pest Control's minions were inches away from a brawl, but both armies were paused, waiting on orders from their masters.

"Locked away inside a cell in the AHC, which is sealed inside the dome for at least another hour," Lady Shade told them. There were more than a few murmurs at such information, many of the capes glaring at Lady Shade with new distrust. "The system is automated because we were running tests, and the sole people who could deactivate it are the members of the Congress, only one of which is inside."

"Can Apollo last a full hour?" This question came from Glyph, whose wand was halfway through etching a rune of explosive force into the street.

"No." Thuggernaut shook his head under Johnny, the deep rumble of his voice carrying through the street. "Not when Fornax is like this, and not alone. What about Lodestar or Professor Quantum?"

Many of the older capes shuffled uncomfortably, until Combust stepped forward. "We haven't seen either of them in years. Lodestar is apparently off on some secret mission, and Professor Quantum doesn't usually leave his island. The only ones that know how to get in contact with them are Quorum and Apollo."

"Then it looks like we have to find a way to break in to AHC headquarters," Johnny declared.

"Quite an interesting theory, but I wonder how you'll accomplish such a task." The disembodied voice of Balaam hung over them until a giant pillar of flame appeared down the street seconds later. Other pillars could be seen popping up throughout the city—at least five that Johnny could see. When the nearest one vanished, Balaam appeared with at least sixty other people clustered behind him. A few were recognizable members of the guild, Endless Blitz and Torkak among them, but the rest were total strangers.

"Guild, meet the meta-human crooks that you've been lording over for the past several years. Capes, meet the meta-criminals you've been trying to bust and bring to justice. Is it any wonder that when I approached them about wiping you both out, they jumped at the opportunity? So go ahead and free Quorum from the AHC, if you can. Meanwhile, my *new* guild will be doing its best to kill you all, along with terrorizing civilians and destroying whatever they feel like." Balaam leaned his staff forward and called to the gang behind him.

"Bring forth chaos, and kill to your hearts' content!"

And with those words, war poured into the streets of Ridge City.

*   *   *

Fornax's rage was, somewhat ironically, the only thing keeping Apollo alive. The villain was more monster than man at this point, every blow so powerful it made Apollo feel like little more than a mere human. But he was so angry and wild that his attacks mirrored his feelings, which made them just a bit easier to dodge. Apollo had tried blocking one blow early on and now had a

551

fractured left forearm to show for it. It had been so long since *anything* hurt him, yet a mere glancing punch had been enough to crack his bones. Thankfully he healed quickly, and within five minutes or so, his arm would be back to normal. Unfortunately, he wasn't sure he would survive that long.

Apollo had made a lot of miscalculations—that was all too evident as he spiraled through the sky, skirting to the side to avoid yet another attack by the almost-untrackable Fornax. Trusting Balaam had been foolish; if the burned school didn't tell him that, then the pillars of fire and sudden flood of criminals certainly did. And he'd certainly misgauged how powerful Fornax was. Had Lodestar really managed to fight this beast? No, to *defeat* him? Apollo's respect for the absentee superhero ticked up a few notches.

He shot through the air, taking note of the metas rioting in the streets. Had... had he really caused this? All because he couldn't stand one small group of criminals playing the system. At the time, it had seemed so noble as he worked tirelessly to take them down. But now, with both a literal and metaphorical bird's eye view, Apollo could see that it had been his own pride driving him, not a sense of justice. Even if the guild's existence had been wrong, it was certainly much better than the chaos he'd unleashed. Neither was right, but the guild was more right than this.

Apollo's distraction came with a toll. Fornax suddenly appeared above him, landing a blow directly into Apollo's shoulder and sending him to the ground like a falling star. The superhero slammed into the earth with enough force to leave a crater and send everyone nearby tumbling. Before he could get up, Fornax was there, looming over him with that damned smile, still soaked in Blunderbuss's blood.

"Is that all your little shard of divinity is good for?" That voice, it didn't belong to Ivan, Apollo was sure of it. Whatever he was fighting, there was no trace of the man they'd captured anymore. It was more like something that was wearing Ivan like a puppet. But no one had ever mentioned a split personality or other entity. Had it never come out before? Was this the real Fornax, seeing the light of day for the first time?

A powerful hand pulled Apollo up from the ground, gripping his broken shoulder so tightly that he knew escape was impossible. *"The others might go quickly, but you're going to suffer for your sins."*

Mustering all the power he could, Apollo focused his energy into his eyes, met Fornax's, and let out a blast powerful enough to carve through an entire block of steel. It hit dead on, right in the rune-covered targets that were Fornax's eyes. A sharp cry rang out, and Apollo felt the merciful release of freedom as Fornax's grip loosened for an instant. That instant was all he needed. He raced into the sky once more, leaving the villain rubbing at his eyes.

Apollo was fifty feet into the sky when he heard the howl, an unholy torrent of sound rising up from Fornax's gullet. All around him, glass shattered, concrete cracked, and plants wilted. Those red-runed eyes were locked on Apollo. If anything, Fornax was angrier now than before.

Having learned his lesson, Apollo didn't stick around for the show. He raced across the sky, trying to get as much distance as possible.

It might have been the cowardly action, and it certainly felt that way as Apollo tried to lead the monster out of downtown, but there wasn't any other choice. He couldn't beat Fornax alone, and as soon as Apollo died, all of Fornax's wrath would be turned on the other superheroes. Every minute he stayed alive bought them time to prepare a counterattack.

Apollo knew he was dead no matter what happened. He'd made a terrible mistake and would pay the price for it. The least he could do was try and die like the superhero he'd always aspired to be. If he could buy the others even a slightly better chance of survival, he'd run to the ends of the Earth, no matter how cowardly it made him feel.

*   *   *

The crowd was now nearing the remains of the school when the energy beam tore out from the far side. Screams filled the air as the people ran, which meant only the bravest of the bunch got to see the figure in black-and-red armor making its way out of the newly-carved hole, a student slung over each arm. Hephaestus took careful steps forward, making sure not to pointlessly jostle Rick or Beth. They'd both gotten knocked around quite a bit in the collapse, but neither seemed to have any major injuries that she could discern.

It was Beth's power that had saved them, those strange silver blades whipping out of her at impossible speeds, neatly slicing through every large piece of debris that had come down toward them. The small bits had still gotten through, and despite Hephaestus's best efforts to shield the kids, they'd both been pelted with more than their fair share of rubble. Both were conscious, though, and no bones seemed broken, even if they were sore all over.

She'd barely made it ten steps out of the building before several police officers ran up to her. Probably came when she set off the fire alarm. Damn, this place really did have good security. If she ever had kids, she'd have to look into sending them here. Assuming it was rebuilt in time.

"Release the hostages and put your hands up." This came from a cop with a bushy mustache and a hand resting a little too firmly on his firearm. Thankfully, before she could curse him out, Rick took charge.

"We're not hostages. He saved us from the collapse," he told them. Hephaestus let him and Beth go, careful to make sure they were steady on their feet. "He's a hero."

"Let's not go quite that far," Hephaestus protested. "But, officer, these two need immediate medical treatment. Did an EMT and ambulance come too?"

The officer nodded, not drawing his weapon but not releasing it either. "We've got several. They're already digging for any who might still be stuck inside. Not everyone is accounted for."

Hephaestus felt the bottom of her stomach fall out. She hadn't been thorough enough. She'd missed someone. Even if Rick and Beth were safe, that was a heavy weight to bear. With a lot of effort, she pushed the overwhelming sense of guilt to the back of her mind. There would time to deal with it later; right now, someone was plotting against her guild. She needed to see what had happened while she was buried.

"Please get these two medical attention right away," Hephaestus ordered while she refreshed the news feed inside her helmet. "Top of the line, bill it to Indigo Technologies. They can call for confirmation if need be." She had no idea if Wade's company had any provisions set aside to take care of Ivan's kids, but it seemed like a safe bet. And if not, a call would certainly set things straight.

The news feed finally refreshed, and Hephaestus was very glad she'd already barked out the orders. If she'd tried to talk right then, the words might have choked in her throat.

All of the coverage was either about the blood-soaked man chasing and gaining on Apollo or the sudden war of meta-humans that had broken out in the streets. The former was Ivan, but what on earth... the explosion. He knew. He'd seen it. He must think Rick and Beth had been killed.

Moments later, the news replayed Lady Shade's confession for the hundredth time in only so few minutes, confirming Hephaestus's suspicions. She'd have shivered if she weren't largely composed of fire within the suit. If Ivan believed his children were dead, then he'd gone completely off the deep end. The truth might be able to calm him down, but only if he would listen and believe it.

Hephaestus tried to take a step away so she could launch off again, but Beth's hand held her in place.

"Thank you for saving us."

"You did most of the work," Hephaestus told her. "That's some power you've got. Maybe one day, you'll get to tell me how it happened. But for right now, I have to go help other people."

Beth didn't respond verbally. She just hugged Hephaestus tightly, the silver blades shrinking back so as not to pierce the suit. She released the embrace and walked over to join her brother, who was standing by the ambulance that had pulled up.

The officers began to approach, which Hephaestus took as her cue to leave. She blasted off into the sky, zipping out of sight before they could even think to take a shot at her, and made a beeline for downtown Ridge City. Someone had to talk Ivan down, and it was too risky to try and bring his kids into that fray. She just had to hope that the bond between teacher and apprentice was enough to pry open his ears.

Otherwise, Hephaestus was flying at breakneck speed to her own funeral.

Chapter 84

"I have to stop them." Beverly's eyes were already beginning to glow green as she peered around the booth to spy on the robbers across the street.

"Why? We're just a coffee shop. They might not want to rob us in the first place," Chloe pointed out. "And even if they do, I can jump us somewhere safe."

"No, you don't get it," Beverly said, rising slowly from their hidden position. "I'm not saying I need to do it to protect us, I'm saying I *have* to stop them. I might hate the AHC with a fiery passion, I might be a secret meta and have bent my fair share of the law myself, and it might be the stupidest thing I can do right now, but I still have to do it. This is my town; I'm not letting these people turn it to shit." She paused, looking at Chloe carefully. If there was ever a time for honesty, at least with someone outside the guild, then it was before she went to take on three unknown metas and potentially died.

"And I have to do it because I'm a member of that guild they're talking about," Beverly admitted. "We're not doing what they claim, though, at least not all of us. Mostly we commit crimes that don't hurt anyone, and we put down a lot of the criminals that *do* hurt people. These little punks are intruding on my guild's turf just because we're busy, and as a point of pride, that pisses me right the hell off. So I'm going to show them the error of their ways."

"You're... you're part of that guild?" Chloe glanced at the television screen then pulled herself up from under the booth. "**Liar, liar, pants on fire**. Now, was what you just said true? Are you really not the ones doing all of this?"

"Not that I know of. The guild we were shown, the code we were taught, it would never allow for any of this. Whoever is pulling it might be members, but they don't represent the guild that I joined." Beverly glanced down at her pants, happy to see they were still intact.

"Then I'm going with you," Chloe declared. "They'll have to deal with the power of... maybe I'll go by Cliché."

"Probably want to work on that name. And the offer is sweet, but you're not a fighter," Beverly countered.

"No, I'm not. But I am a friend, and you never know when my power will come in handy. Now, do you want to debate, or do you want to take them by surprise?" Chloe walked over and unlocked the coffee shop door, pushing it open as quietly as possible.

Much as Beverly didn't like it, Chloe was an adult who could make her own decisions. And honestly, having a little backup was a comforting thought, even if said backup was just a meta with a power that hinged on wordplay.

Beverly followed her and stepped through the open door, fully shifting into her green dragon-form. She surveyed her enemies. Bahamut had arrived, and it was time to do some damage.

The first looked like a wolfman from a bad 1950's television show. Shaggy brown fur hung off him, almost (but not quite) covering the thick muscles knotted under his skin. The second had a mostly human appearance, if one discounted the bug-like eyes and giant horn on his face. He also had to be pushing three hundred pounds, almost none of which was fat. They seemed to be doing most of the heavy lifting while the third supervised.

She was somehow the oddest of the bunch, despite looking totally human. The woman appeared to be in her twenties, with pale skin and lips that were too red. Smudges of makeup gave away that the complexion was artificial, however. Her outfit was what was most striking—a giant pink-and-black frilly dress like one might see at the turn of the century with a skirt that stuck out three feet in all directions, matching leggings, platform shoes, and a parasol that was clutched carefully in her dainty hands.

Meta-human 101 dictated that the woman would actually be the strongest of the bunch, both given their group dynamic and the fact that her powers weren't obvious. That said, Bahamut wasn't sure she could handle all three at once. If the big guys were all physical, she could knock them out and then focus on the weirdly dressed lady. For a moment, she considered yelling a warning to the group of robbers, but then remembered that even if she was temporarily playing the part, Bahamut wasn't a cape. She didn't need to bother with that kind of nicety.

Her charge was thunderous and quickly noticed by the group, although not quick enough to matter. Bahamut slammed a shoulder into the wolfman, sending him flying through the remains of the broken glass window, through the store, and into the back wall, where he crashed heavily and slid to the floor. Bug-eyes reacted quickly, reaching for her with hands too big for his body. She responded by punching him right in the gut, sending him stumbling backward but not taking him off his feet.

A soft giggle from behind her was all the warning Bahamut got before a platform shoe whizzed toward her scaly green temple. She ducked the attack, twisting around to counter, only to have her claws—claws that could gouge through stone—bounce harmlessly off the surface of the pink-and-black parasol. Bahamut was so shocked that she didn't notice the second kick toward her head; this time it connected. The blow shouldn't have even registered, but suddenly Bahamut was airborne, tumbling until she crashed into the brick exterior of a nearby building. Pulling herself up took effort. Her bell had been rung so hard that her vision was blurry.

"Oh my, just another brute after all." The woman in the dress giggled, twirling her parasol through the air in an artful pattern. "And here I thought you might be a little more fun than my underlings. Someone with the power of dragons seems so unique and mystical. Pity you're no better than a pair of barely passable mutagen experiments."

"And what does that make you?" Bahamut spat, doing her best to buy time so her body could recover. Unfortunately, that tactic cut both ways. The wolfman made his way out from inside the busted store and the weird bug-eyed guy seemed to shake off her attack.

"Me? I'm what true success looks like. I'm the pinnacle of what metas can, and should, be! A perfect—*AAAAA*!" Her lilting taunts turned into a high-pitched scream as the leggings beneath her skirt suddenly burst into cascading blue flames. She smacked at them, so desperate that she dropped her parasol and beat at her burning legs with both hands.

"What... 'liar, liar, pants on fire.' Guess arrogant false claims count too," Bahamut chuckled. The wolfman and bug-eyed horn guy looked distressed at their leader's sudden terror. That was all the invitation she needed to pounce. As she tore through the street on a crash course for the two dumbstruck hulks, she saw Chloe's familiar pixie cut darting forward toward the woman with the burning legs. Part of her wanted to yell at the barista to steer clear, but the truth was she needed the help.

And besides, that parasol lady had kicked Bahamut around like a toy, yet Chloe had managed to stop her cold. Maybe she could handle the weird little thief better. But just in case, Bahamut decided to make short work of the other crooks.

If Chloe needed help, Bahamut would be there.

* * *

A sledgehammer bounced off Cyber Geek's armor, sending him sprawling to the ground and knocking a huge percentage off his shields. He spun around to find a woman clad in a spiked leather jacket. She had glowing yellow eyes, and a matching light flickered across the hammer. Augmentation, probably, which was why a mundane object had managed to pack such a wallop.

Cyber Geek rolled to the side, just missing her follow-up strike that shattered the concrete below. Leaping to his feet, Cyber Geek aimed his gun, pausing only to do a quick check of his surroundings.

Everything had turned into chaos within seconds, the gangs that Balaam had brought swarming over cape and villain alike. Medley was fending them off three at a time, and Cold Shoulder had formed her ice construct to try and cover him. Hat Trick, while not great in combat, was proving herself invaluable in evacuating citizens. She could throw an endless rope of rainbow scarves from either sleeve and was using it to swing around the battlefield, snaring civilians out of precarious situations and throwing them toward the fringes of the fight. More than a few people were going to have bruises and scrapes, but it was a lot better than them seeing the inside of a coffin.

Unfortunately, his whole team being busy meant there was no one to back him up as the sledgehammer lady raced in, swinging wildly and moving too quickly for Cyber Geek to line up a shot. He backpedaled, wishing that the armor didn't cover his computer so he could yank out a melee weapon, trying to think of a countermeasure. Working as a team had gotten him too accustomed to having Medley to cover the close-range fighting, and now he was paying the price for his lack of strategy.

Backpedaling without looking was a dangerous method, and soon Cyber Geek's luck ran out. He clipped a curb and went sprawling onto his back. Sledgehammer lady didn't even hesitate. She sprang forward with her weapon raised overhead to deliver the coup de grace. That hammer was still overhead as a swarm of what looked like the demonic forefathers of wasps swarmed her face. The little beasts stung her across the neck as they landed. Her scream— half fury, half panic—lit through the street as she swung wildly at them, but sledgehammers weren't meant to act as bug-swatters. On the third attempt to knock the bugs away, she banged her own temple and went down hard. Cyber Geek was pretty sure she was still breathing, but he wasn't certain. For a moment, he thought he saw a flicker of light near her neck, then the bugs shifted, blocking his view, and when they cleared again, it was gone.

"Come on, get up." A hand appeared over him, and he grabbed it without thinking. To his surprise, it was not the mask of a fellow AHC member that he saw as he rose, but rather the purple and black costume of one of the guild members that had come pouring out from their base. On reflex, Cyber Geek raised his blaster, and the villain quickly put his hands in the air.

"Whoa, whoa, hang on. We just saved you."

"We?" Cyber Geek asked, quickly searching the area.

"Yeah, we." This voice came from a man in a strange white costume that totally obscured his face, as if the swarm of buzzing monster wasps circling him didn't do a good enough job of that. "I'm Pest Control, and the guy you're holding a gun on is Glyph. And yes, we're villains of the guild you showed up to bust today, but can we all agree that for the moment we have bigger concerns?"

Pest Control wasn't wrong, no matter how much the insects buzzing around him made Cyber Geek's stomach roil. Whatever the situation might have been before, the sudden flood of meta-criminals represented a threat to both sides. Maybe the guild *had* attacked the city and the AHC—though at this point, Cyber Geek was beginning to suspect there might be more going on than he'd been told—but they definitely hadn't been as ferocious as the metas attacking now. More than once, at least before the gangs showed up, he'd seen them go for the knockout rather than the kill, a sentiment their new enemies didn't share.

Still, they were self-admitted villains, which meant he couldn't trust them.

"Maybe there are," Cyber Geek admitted. "But if I take you two down, that's one less problem to worry about."

"Sure, maybe," Pest Control said. "Or maybe we came and found you for a reason. That gun of yours is pretty powerful, you know. Everyone saw the news footage of your fight in the club. It's from *Blaster Brahs*, isn't it?"

"You play?" That really wasn't an appropriate response, but under Cyber Geek's costume, Donald's reactions were too well-ingrained and hard to shake.

"All the time. Big fan." Pest Control nodded to the blaster still aimed at Glyph. "And assuming you've leveled that bad boy up enough, there should be a function to break through energy barriers. You have to use it on the final level to infiltrate the Nega-Brah's compound."

"I... you're right." Cyber Geek felt the tumblers fall into place as he gazed at the weapon.

"We think you might be able to punch through the barrier and get Quorum." Glyph slowly lowered his hands, careful to keep them in sight the whole time. "And if you're willing to try, we'll help you get there."

"You expect me to believe that you want one of the strongest superheroes in the world set free in the middle of a fight between our organizations?" Donald asked.

"I expect you to believe that we don't want to fucking die," Pest Control snapped back. "And for that to happen, we need some heavy hitters to come deal with these punks. Not to mention Fornax, who looks like he's out for blood and doesn't care whose he gets. We might be criminals, but we're still people, and that means survival ranks way higher on our list of priorities than pride, pissing matches, or possible imprisonment."

Cyber Geek weighed the options in his mind. There was a chance, however small, that his gun might be able to carve a hole in the AHC's shield. But to even get to it, they'd have to get through the AHC's countermeasures, defenses specifically designed to stop a meta-human attack. Even if they made it through, the odds of the gun working were still a long shot. Just because it was strong enough to break the barrier in the game didn't mean the AHC's shield wasn't way stronger. The smart move was to lie low, keep picking off the gang metas one by one, and slowly retake control of the streets.

Except that, even if they succeeded, there would be a huge loss of life for civilians, capes, and guild members alike. Against numbers like this, everyone would end up attending a funeral. Quorum might be able to turn that around. Cyber Geek didn't know how, but the man was a legend for a reason. They needed him, which meant, long shot or not, dangerous or not, it was his duty to try and bust Quorum out.

"Fine," Cyber Geek said at last. "But I don't know you two, and I certainly don't trust you, so we're getting my team first. If it looks like you're planning a double-cross at any point, we won't hesitate to put you down."

"Get your people," Glyph said. "We've got nothing to gain from treachery, which means you're as safe as you can be with us."

"Oddly, that I believe." Cyber Geek began to turn toward Medley, but his conscience got the better of him. "You know that there are dozens of traps and countermeasures activated that are specifically designed to keep us from reaching the AHC headquarters, right? Even if you don't turn traitor, I can't guarantee your safety."

"That's fine." Glyph looked around at the fighting and madness that surrounded them and shook his head. "No, it's more than fine. It's as it should be. My teacher is the one who caused all this. If anyone should risk their life to stop him, it ought to be me."

"Thinking about redemption?" Cyber Geek asked.

Glyph chuckled and exchanged a quick look with Pest Control before responding. "Nothing that noble. No, Balaam is a traitor to our guild, so I want to see his plan fall apart, even if it costs my life, for one pure and simple reason: *spite*."

Chapter 85

Wade Wyatt watched as chaos bloomed through the streets like filthy roses, blood spilling as meta fought meta and everything was hurled into disarray. The monitors all around him showed feeds not just from the news but also from private networks and security cameras, some not known of by anyone but himself.

He could see Stasis and Gork, trapped in their shared house by a combination of a giant metal wall and mystical wards. He could see Morgana, limping over the scattered pieces of Erinite, her own body bruised and battered. He could see Xelas, though that was almost always true in one way or another. He could see Balaam wading into battle with his minions, turning his magic against former allies and friends.

And Wade could see Fornax, darting between buildings at breakneck speed, trying to shatter the bones of Apollo in his bloody grip. Ivan had never been this far gone before. Not in the old days when he was slugging it out with capes for fun, not when he and Lodestar had their final battle, not even when they went against Orion for the fate of the world. All of those times, Ivan had been the one in control, using his power as a tool rather than being ruled by it. This was the first time he'd ever lost that control, and the world might be in genuine peril for it.

It was, all-around, a pretty solid plan; Wade had to give Balaam credit for that. No matter who won the brawl in the end, the capes would be weakened and have a nice public black eye, and the guild would be so crippled by losing so many members that Balaam could easily reshape it to his design. With an AHC on the mend and a large amount of meta-humans under his control, Balaam could set about wreaking true havoc, maybe even succeed in his goal of taking over a country or two.

Of course, there had been flaws in his calculations as well, the largest of which was assuming Wade would be so easy to kill. He also hadn't counted on how hard it would be to take out the rest of the council. While driving Ivan insane was a good touch, the fact that his children were alive meant he might be able to come back around. Balaam also hadn't quite accounted for the possibility that both the guild and the AHC knew that traitors dwelled within their ranks, nor that both organizations had given them rope for the express purpose of hanging themselves. Plus, there was the giant hidden trump card he hadn't taken into consideration, though for that, he could hardly be blamed. After all, even in the guild, only Wade and Ivan knew what had really happened to Lodestar.

Wade picked up the phone and dialed a number, hoping she wasn't screening her calls. Until he'd seen Hephaestus emerge from that school, it had seemed like the only way to bring Fornax down would be with force. Now, however, there was another possibility rocketing through the sky toward him. If there was even the slightest chance they could bring him back around peacefully, if Ivan could regain control, then it was a risk worth taking. Eliminating Fornax would make the battle much easier, but *gaining* Ivan could turn the tides on a dime, especially once the rest of the council made it onto the game board.

The phone rang several times before finally going to voicemail. Wade tried twice more then considered the matter settled. It was inevitable that she would move when she saw what was happening to Ridge City. He'd hoped to catch her in time, but it seemed it was too late.

All he could do for Ivan now was hope that his apprentice was fast enough. Even if she didn't know it, Hephaestus was in a race, one for Ivan's sanity, soul, and perhaps even life. From his chair, however, there was nothing Wade could do to help her, so he turned his attention to the factors he could influence.

"I think just about every card has now been played," he murmured, checking the screens one last time. It wouldn't do to go to all this trouble and only purge a few of the disloyal members in his guild. He'd specifically waited until every other component was in motion so that he could handle this house-cleaning with only a few sweeps of the broom.

Behind him, moving seemingly on its own, the Doctor Mechaniacal suit came to life, walking calmly to the sole tunnel that led above ground, the only way in and out of Wade's secret bunker. The downside to meta-suits, which he hadn't realized in his youth, was that one actually had to be inside them, and that meant losing a battle meant capture or death. It was far more efficient to simply infuse his brain with nano-transmitters and remotely control the suit from somewhere safe. Heck, he'd even gotten the programs so efficient that he could run several bots at once, a convenient way to handle all the work expected of him.

"First, I think we'll get Morgana into play," he said, carefully plotting through the possibilities. "She'll make short work of Balaam's troops and give the guild a morale boost. In the meantime, would you mind getting Gork and Stasis free?"

"No problem," Xelas replied. On camera, she stood over the broken remains of Stalwart Iron, whose voice was relaying the orders. "But I'm a little pissed you didn't tell me Stalwart Iron was one of yours."

"If I had, you might have held back," Wade replied. "And Stalwart Iron is much too valuable a mole to lose. Assuming they bother rebuilding him, I mean."

"Look, I spared the core; I'm not sure what more you want from me." Xelas looked up at the camera in the boutique, one of the few things not turned to scrap, and gave a wave. "I'll get Gork and Stasis. Have to say, though, trapping them in their own house was smart; neither of them can be hauled into a cell."

"Balaam clearly put a large amount of thought into this plan," Wade replied through Stalwart Iron.

"Yeah, just not enough to realize how stupid it was," Xelas said. "After I grab those two, do we get to go bust some heads?"

"Probably, yes. But wait for exact coordinates of where you're needed before heading in. How we respond from here depends largely on the way Fornax is handled." Wade glanced at the screen once more. Hephaestus was approaching downtown; it would only be minutes until she tracked down Fornax and Apollo.

But minutes might be too long. Once Lodestar entered the battlefield, the fight was decided. All they could do was hope that whatever was holding her up continued to do so, for her sake as much as Ivan's. At this point, killing Fornax might be the only way to stop him.

And while Lodestar would do it to protect the world from him, burying Ivan would break Helen's heart. Especially if she was the one who put him in the ground.

*   *   *

The costume didn't quite fit anymore. It was strange to see it pulled too tight in the wrong places. Before it had clung to her body perfectly. Of course it did: it had been made just for her, and Lodestar's body never changed. Couldn't change, in fact. But for the past seven years, Lodestar had been missing, and in her absence, Helen had grown in several places. She was going to miss the extra two inches of height she'd gained in her early twenties, and the way her waist was beginning to even out with her hips. When this was over, she'd need a new wardrobe. Thankfully, she'd boxed up all her old clothes and stored them in the attic. Part of her had always known this was inevitable, and she'd prepared for it as best she could.

Still, she had to hold back tears as she stared into the mirror, listening for the doorbell that would mark Miss Teresa's arrival. It wasn't just herself she was sad for. Helen was scared for Ivan, of whatever had turned him into the monster flying through town. She didn't know how to stop him. At least... not without permanently stopping him. He'd warned her long ago that this day might come, that the monster inside could somehow break free. And he'd told her that if it ever came to that, he was trusting her to protect the rest of the world from him.

Because only she could.

Helen also feared for Penelope, how she would react to everything. She was such a sweet, impressionable little girl. Having a mommy who was a superhero wouldn't bother her, but when she got older, and realized what the other part of Lodestar's power meant... Penelope was a good person, but finding out one's mother was immortal was a lot to lay at anyone's feet.

Of all the fears that swam through her mind as she looked at herself in the mirror, only one surprised her. Helen was feeling doubt, of all things. She'd been out of the game for so long, and the situation in the streets was worsening by the second. Could she still do it? Could she still be that beacon for the world to rally around? Would they hate her for being absent so long? Was she so out of practice that she'd only make things worse?

Her hand tightened, and for an instant, Helen could feel the power lying just beneath her surface. It had been a constant struggle to push it down, to never call upon it even in surprise or terror. She could still remember the feeling though, the burning light that poured through her, the conviction, the invincibility. All it would take was a thought and she'd have that all again. While the other fears might come along with her, self-doubt was a worry only for Helen. As soon as she touched that power, it would fade away. Lodestar was far from perfect, but she knew her abilities and what she could accomplish. Which was, actually, damned near anything.

"Mommy, are you done changing?" Penelope called through the door.

"I... for now." There was one change left, one shift that would alter their entire lives, but it wasn't quite time for that yet. She threw on a robe and headed out the door, just missing the vibrations of her phone, abandoned and useless on her bed, as it rang with three calls from an unknown number. Miss Teresa would be here soon, and until she arrived, Helen was going to enjoy the last moments she could with her daughter.

Once that doorbell rang, things would never be the same for her and Penelope ever again.

*   *   *

Getting downtown had been easy, assuming one didn't count the time and effort that went into making a flying meta-suit, but within moments of arriving, Hephaestus realized that talking to Ivan would be far more difficult than she'd planned. He was leaping and teleporting around so quickly that he was more hallucination than person, taking swings at Apollo as the golden man raced around at speeds Hephaestus could barely track, let alone match. No sooner would she get close to them than both would barrel off, zipping to another section of town as she did her best to play catch up.

It wasn't until the third time that she nearly intercepted Apollo, more by luck than skill, and saw him veer off that Hephaestus realized what was happening. Apollo was avoiding her on purpose. Not because he thought she was a threat—even her pride in the meta-suit wouldn't indulge that self-delusion—but because he was trying to keep her safe. The cape, however much of a dick he might be, was dangling himself in front of Ivan like meat before a tiger, hoping that no one else would be felled by its claws. It was a noble, dangerous act that nearly smacked of redemption, but it was also keeping Ivan too mobile for her to try and talk to him.

Clearly, it was time for a change in strategy. Hephaestus began to chase Apollo once more, but as she did, she also poured as much power as she dared into the speaker on the front of her helmet. There was no way Ivan wouldn't hear her, but that was all the better. The more he had to listen to, the more she might be able to reach him.

"Hey! Apollo! Slow it down!"

Ahead of her, his curly head bobbed in surprise, and he flipped over to face her for the first time. This distraction nearly cost him his head, as Ivan materialized in front of Apollo, taking a mighty swing for his cranium. A last-second dodge kept the cape in one piece, and he whipped around to swing past Hephaestus.

"Get out of here! Fornax is on a rampage. No one is safe." This point was rather well-illustrated as Ivan slammed into a nearby building as he tried to tackle Apollo from the air.

Hephaestus caught a good glimpse of her teacher for the first time as he spun around to take new aim. Her hope of reaching him dimmed. That wasn't Ivan. Even in his Fornax days, he'd never looked like that. His bloodlust was so thick it was nearly a fog. The red runes in his eyes gleamed with madness. He might be too far gone even for her to reach. Should she have brought Rick along with her? Surely the sight of his son might have dulled the rage enough for Ivan to retake control. But as she watched him vanish, Hephaestus felt unsure. Ivan might not even recognize his kids in this state, which made it all the more unlikely that he'd remember her.

"I said run!" Apollo yelled at her from nearby, hovering and making a "shoo" motion with his hands. This time, he didn't get away with pausing.

Suddenly, Ivan was behind him, slamming Apollo out of the sky with a vicious punch to the back. A streak of light marked his fall, which culminated in a shower of earth as he slammed into a mercifully evacuated local park.

For just a moment, Ivan hung there, watching Apollo fall, and then he looked up, meeting Hephaestus's eyes through her helmet. She could actually feel his thirst for murder rippling through her soul. Her courage nearly broke.

Then he was gone, down on the ground, standing on top of Apollo. Whatever he had planned, it was going to be brutal, and probably not take too long. Even if Ivan wanted to make it last, he was too drunk on fury. Apollo had seconds to live—at most a full minute. While Hephaestus wouldn't be too broken up about his death, the moment he croaked, Ivan would be on the move again.

Now or never, this was the best shot she was going to get. She needed to strike... but fear made her heart waver. What would going down there really accomplish? He was so far gone, she doubted he could ever hear her, let alone understand what she was saying. Most likely, all she'd really accomplish was dying a few seconds before Apollo and everyone else that Ivan vented his perceived loss on. With the memory of Ivan's burning eyes fresh in her mind, Hephaestus fed her thrusters, took aim, and flew as fast as she could.

Directly away from Ivan and Apollo.

Chapter 86

The speedometer in the corner of her helmet's display read around two hundred and fifty miles per hour when she began the wide turn back to her target. Not exactly impressive by meta-human standards, but it was about as good as her current suit could handle. Maybe later, if such a time existed for her, she'd look into ways to put more oomph in her rockets. Right now, this was the best she had. It would just have to be enough: for her and for Ivan.

Hephaestus tore through the air, adding a few more miles per hour now that she was on a direct course. She was rapidly approaching the park where she could now see Ivan looming over Apollo, who looked a lot bloodier than he had less than a minute before. She poured on the speed, locking on to her target and refusing to falter. If she paused now, even for a moment, her courage might never rekindle enough to go through with this idiotic plan. It occurred to her that this might be a good time to say a prayer, but since the man she was racing toward proclaimed to have eaten a god, Hephaestus wasn't quite sure how much good that would do or who would be listening. Instead, she stretched out her left arm, said a silent apology to the suit she'd worked so hard to build, and phased completely into fire-form.

Like the left hand of a vengeful god, Hephaestus rocketed down from the sky and smashed directly into Ivan's face, fist-first. Her gauntlet and most of the left arm shattered on impact, sending her reeling through the air for a brief instant before she went crashing across the park's well-cared-for grounds. Sparks flew and countless warning screens flashed in her helmet; the meta-suit had just taken far more damage than she'd built it to withstand. Hephaestus didn't wait for it to finish bounding across the grounds; already turned to living fire, she slipped free after the second bounce, reforming to a human-shape as she took in Ivan and Apollo.

The cape looked far worse than she'd seen from above. His legs and right arm were broken, and she could see ribs sticking out from his torso's tanned skin. It had been less than a minute and Ivan had done so much damage—too much longer and she'd be looking at a corpse.

Broken as Apollo was, however, he was not her central focus. Ivan stood over the fallen hero, but Tori realized with a combination of joy and terror that she'd succeeded in turning Ivan's head. It was probably more out of annoyance than pain, but she'd done it: she'd gotten his attention. Now she just had to make good use of it.

"Ivan, it's me." Her eyes scanned the streets and sky, but no cameras were in sight. Not really a surprise. Ivan and Apollo had been hard enough to follow with a flying suit; the average news van didn't have a shot in hell. "It's Tori. Your kids are safe. The building didn't hurt them; I got them out in time. Rick and Beth are safe."

Those glowing, terrible eyes lingered on her for a few moments longer, then began to turn back to Apollo. Acting on sheer instinct, Tori hit Ivan in the face with a torrent of flame. It surely didn't hurt him, but it was bound to be bothersome. At this point, she'd settle for pissing him off enough to make him listen.

"Listen, dickhead! I didn't race across Ridge City twice, stand under a falling building, and crash my suit just so you could ignore me." She ceased her attack, and, in what she could only hope wouldn't be the dumbest mistake of her life, shifted back to a full human-form. What did it really matter? Ivan could kill her either way. She still wore her Hephaestus mask, the only piece of the costume she'd had time to slip on before donning her suit, but otherwise she was clad in her usual sweats and t-shirt that she puttered around the lab in. It left her feeling a bit idiotic, like a child playing dress-up with a mask rather than a certified villain, but she pushed that feeling away. This was not a time for doubt. Costumes didn't make the meta.

"Are you listening to me, Ivan? Ivan Gerhardt? Father of Rick and Beth Gerhardt, who are both *still* alive. Get your shit together, Ivan. You would never let me slide for going this far out of control. You'd smack me on the back of the head and mutter about the importance of keeping one's power in check. God damn it, Ivan, you don't get *months* of being that smug and proper only to lose your shit like this."

To her surprise as much as anyone's, it was working. The personal attacks kept Ivan's shining eyes focused on Tori, rather than Apollo. He was listening, which was good; she just didn't know if he was hearing her. What little optimism she possessed wavered; Ivan had shifted toward her and drawn back his fist.

She knew that stance. It was the one he'd used on her the very first time they met. He'd held back as much as possible before punching her, and even though she was in fire-form, he'd still nearly killed her. If he let loose as things were now, she'd be lucky if there was even enough pulpy residue left of her to bury.

"Oooh, getting aggressive. Am I supposed to be scared?" She was, in fact, terrified, and it was only thanks to Ivan's self-control lessons that she kept her voice from quivering. Showing weakness was a luxury she couldn't afford. Not right now. "Can you hear me in there, Ivan? How are you going to explain to Rick and Beth that you killed the nice young woman you introduced them to?

Because that's something you'll have to do. They're alive, you willfully-deaf bastard!"

Those damn eyes were locked on her and the fist tightened. If she hurried, there might still be time to run. Probably not far or fast enough, but it could buy her a few more precious seconds of life. The human brain, even a meta one, was hard-wired for self-preservation, and in that moment, any action that might allot her a few more moments of breath seemed like utter brilliance.

"You won't attack me." She sounded a lot more sure than she felt, but given that she was standing instead of running, perhaps she was surer than she realized. "You can't. I am a full member of our guild, and I have done nothing wrong. If you strike me, you break the code. I don't care how pissed you are, I don't care how much control Ivan's lost. He won't let you do that. Ivan loves that damn, annoying, fucking code more than anything except his kids. He won't break it. He won't kill his own apprentice. He—"

Without her suit, Tori couldn't even see the movement, but as a blast of wind struck her, she thought for an instant that she'd been wrong, that Ivan had hit her, and that he had done so with such power that she only registered the force, not the pain. But then she saw his hand, still balled into a fist, fewer than two inches from her stomach. His face was directly in front of her, and it was no longer smiling. Now it was pinched in visible pain as an internal war waged inside him.

Reaching down slowly—the last thing she wanted was for him to think he was under attack— she laid her hands on top of his quivering fist. "Ivan. It's okay. They're safe. But the city is going crazy. You once told me that Rick saved the world because he gave you the desire to protect it. Well, right now, they need you to save their home, to make sure they stay safe. They need you. I need you. The whole damn guild needs you. So please, quit fucking around with the pity party and get your ass back in the driver's seat."

His eyes closed for barely longer than a blink, but when they opened again, they were different. They were still black with the red runes in place, but the gleeful shine had gone out of them. A small tear made its way from the right eye, leaving a trail of smeared blood as it fell down his face. Bit by bit, the fist in her hands opened, and finally gave her fingers a light squeeze.

"Tori... thank you."

It was only when she heard his voice that Tori let out the breath she'd been holding since she landed. Ivan was back. The day was far from over, and they still had a lot of shit to slog through, but just knowing her teacher had returned made the idea of it all the more bearable.

"Yeah, well, you technically saved my life once. I'm not big on owing debts."

"I meant for saving my kids," Ivan replied. "Though keeping me from killing everyone in the state is also appreciated."

"The state? You were that off your rocker?" Tori asked.

"If anything, I'm being conservative in my estimate. There are certain aspects of my power I might not have told you about." Ivan looked down at his hands, almost as if he were realizing for the first time that they were coated in dried blood. "I was just so mad when I saw that school go down. What about the other children inside?"

Tori looked away from Ivan for the first time since she'd landed. Before a word left her lips, one of his blood-covered hands fell gently on top of her head.

"Forgive me. That wasn't a fair question to ask. I'm sure you did all that you could. Those who were lost are not marks on your soul. That honor belongs to the ones who endangered them in the first place." Ivan turned from Tori to Apollo, who was slowly trying to stagger to his feet behind them.

"Ivan..." Tori warned.

"Don't worry. I've got control of myself again, and I won't be letting that go anytime soon. That said, I am still rightfully pissed off, and I feel that Apollo has some explaining to do." He looked past Tori to the dented and smoking remains of her meta-suit. "Think your Hephaestus model will still function?"

"Maybe. Took a hell of a beating coming in, but most of the damage was confined to the left arm."

"Go see if you can get it up and running," Ivan ordered. "Apollo is going to fill me in on exactly what's happening, and then we're going to start the counterattack. Murky as the last half hour has been, I still recall seeing hordes of crooks roaming the streets, attacking our people. As a councilor of the guild, that is something I simply cannot allow to stand."

"So Fornax isn't done for the day?" Tori asked. Though the words came out teasing, there was a serious undercurrent of fear beneath them.

"Fornax is long dead; today he was only briefly resurrected. No, my actions now will simply be as the guild guard dog."

"Maybe I should call you Spot, then," she replied.

"That sounds like the sort of joke Balaam would make. I don't plan to be nearly that lovable." Ivan turned to Apollo, who'd managed to brace himself against a tree and was watching the exchange with a mix of relief and confusion. "Think less Lassie, more Cerberus."

*　　　*　　　*

571

Dapper Doll struggled under the weight of the multi-armed meta-human that had pinned her to the street. She'd made it through ten gang members before this one had caught her from behind, twisting her limbs before she could counter. Struggle as she might, without the ability to move her hands, she was nearly powerless.

Her attacker used one of his two free arms to pull out a long, dangerous-looking knife.

"Always wanted to see what was under that pale skin."

At those words she redoubled her efforts, but it made no difference. The weapon inched closer to her stomach. She was seconds away from wearing her guts on the outside when a red blade burst through her attacker's throat. No... that wasn't right. It came *out* of his throat, along with two more from the back edges of his neck. His eyes widened as the three blades made a single circle, sending his head toppling down onto her chest.

The scream left her throat before she realized it would be more prudent to keep her mouth shut, given that the exposed neck would be showering her with blood in seconds. That shower never came, however. Blood fired up like a geyser, rising through the air until it flowed into a thick, red bubble oozing down the street. As the blood vacated her dead attacker, a small symbol flickered into view below the remains of his neck, glowing for less than a second before it faded from sight. Dapper Doll shoved the corpse off her, careful to avoid the knife, and pulled herself up to see what was happening.

All along the street, gang members were sinking to the ground, heads neatly parted and blood draining from their bodies. Every drop of it flowed toward a figure walking calmly down the street. Her raven-black hair was held back by a helmet which matched her armor, all the exact color of the blood seeping out of her headless victims. She paused her saunter to reach into the bubble of red liquid that trailed her. When her hand emerged, it gripped a massive scythe, far larger than she should be able to wield, and the bubble grew a bit smaller.

Turning with her new weapon in hand, she and Dapper Doll at last locked eyes. Her gaze housed a pair of sclerae that were full of blood, long streams of it running from their corners and soaking her face.

"Morgana La Faye. The Blood Witch," Dapper Doll whispered. Though this particular villain had come along before Dapper Doll joined the AHC or was ever a meta-human, she was still famous, even decades later. With the power to manipulate blood, even as it pumped through other's bodies, she was regarded as one of the deadliest meta-humans in known history. While others might have been stronger, Morgana could kill with a single thought.

"I thought you were dead." Dapper Doll wasn't sure if she was about to die or not. The adrenaline from her last encounter was still tingling in her veins as she stretched her fingers and prepared to go down swinging.

"Get ready for a lot of that today," Morgana replied. Her voice was surprisingly pleasant, given that she was walking amid a sea of corpses that she'd created. "But you don't need to be so tense. My orders are to deal with the violent criminals. Capes are off-limits unless they make themselves a nuisance."

With the body of her would-be killer still laying at her feet, Dapper Doll felt certain that she'd rather have the Blood Witch on her side, at least until they restored some order to the streets. Maybe someone could bring her down later—Erinite didn't have any blood, so he could give it a shot—but Dapper Doll getting beheaded in the street wasn't going to help the AHC or Ridge City.

"With you as backup, I think we'll make short work of this," Dapper Doll said at last.

Morgana smiled, a feature that would have seemed gentle if not for the bloody tearstains framing her face. "I am only the first of our backup. Rest assured, very soon Balaam's followers will see why our guild has so few uprisings." She swept her blood-scythe through the air, testing its heft.

"This is a mistake that I will make sure no one is ever stupid enough to repeat."

Chapter 87

Chloe didn't really have much of a plan as she raced forward, watching with wonder as Beverly clotheslined both of the bigger metas into a wall. Even the fire-pants thing had just been a stroke of luck. How could she have known that the woman in the weird dress and shoes would be a braggart? Still, she would take luck over nothing, especially after watching that woman kick a freaking dragon across the street. One of those attacks and Chloe was a goner. She really needed to think of a phrase that lent itself to being indestructible. Especially as she ran forward with no actual idea of how she was going to stop this woman.

The fire was slowly going out; Chloe's best guess was that it needed fresh lies to keep it fueled. Nevertheless, her enemy was still distracted. With nothing else up her sleeve, Chloe decided to play the odds. If she was making a stupid, suicidal rush anyway, she may as well get some cosmic aid on her side.

"Fortune favors the bold," Chloe whispered. Instantly, the flames upon woman's leggings went out. She looked around in surprise just in time to see Chloe run up and shove her in the chest. It was a lot like shoving a brick wall and had the predictable result of sending the barista sprawling to the ground instead of her intended victim, arms already going numb from pain.

"Well... I suppose that happened." That darling smirk was back in place as the woman moved her platform shoes closer to Chloe's splayed form. Behind her, Beverly was fighting for all she was worth, slowly getting the upper hand. The other two criminals would probably be down soon. Just not soon enough for Beverly to help save Chloe.

Desperately scanning her surroundings, Chloe looked for anything she could use to defend herself. All that was in arm's reach was the parasol fancy-dress lady had dropped when her legs caught fire. If it had been powerful enough to stop Beverly's claws, it might be enough to ward off one of those deadly kicks.

"I can see what you're thinking, but don't bother." The woman's voice was sickly sweet and teasing, like she was explaining things to a toddler. "That weapon will only serve its master. In fact, I think I'll—"

Just as she reached toward the parasol, which had begun to float up from the ground, her wolfman accomplice was hurled away from his fight and slammed into the back of her knees. She windmilled her arms, trying to catch her balance, but the ground beneath her had been shattered by the earlier fighting and gave way, tipping her forward.

Warning forgotten, Chloe grabbed the nearby floating parasol and tried to use it as a shield to keep the powerful meta from falling on top of her. For all she knew, the lady in the dress weighed ten thousand pounds and that's why she was so strong. The parasol refused to open, though Chloe kept struggling with it until she felt a sudden pressure slam down on top of her.

Staring down at her from only a foot away was the heavily made-up face of the woman, whose pink and black dress was now stained with fresh blood. She'd fallen forward, directly onto the unopened parasol, which had run straight through her chest. Over the woman's shoulder, Chloe could just make out what appeared to be most of a heart wedged on the parasol's tip.

It was impossible to say which of them was more shocked by the turn of events. The woman's shaking hands began to rise, curled into claws meant to grab Chloe's neck.

"You... bitch... kill... you..."

As the hands grew closer, Chloe tried to twist away and accidentally succeeded in the task she'd failed before. The parasol opened, seemingly unbothered by the body wrapped around it. Instantly, the woman was gone, replaced by a rain of gore as her torso was disintegrated by the suddenly-expanding parasol. Chloe clutched the murder weapon over her head, trying to stay safe from the brief downpour of blood and organs. Somehow, she succeeded, and when the last of the splattering stopped, she pulled the parasol away to see that she, and somehow it, were both unstained.

"Holy shit, Chloe." Beverly slammed the bug-eyed meta down on her knee, eliciting a loud snapping from its spine before tossing it to the ground. "Do you have a phrase for making people explode?"

"N-n-no." Chloe's body was so full of adrenaline that her teeth were chattering. The urge to vomit kept rising from her stomach; only force of will and a healthy amount of denial kept it in check. "I-I just got lucky. I was bold."

"Yeah, I'm going to want some explanation on that later. For now, are you okay?" Beverly stepped over the bloody legs that were all that remained of the woman and the unconscious wolfman to kneel next to Chloe. "Did you get hurt?"

"Just my arms a little, when I shoved her." Chloe could barely feel the pain anymore, though she knew it would come shooting back when she finally calmed down. "I think I want to go home now."

"Probably a good idea," Beverly agreed. "Are you okay to get there by yourself?"

"Sure, **it's just a hop, skip, and a jump away.**" Chloe slowly pulled herself to her feet, using the parasol as a cane. When had it closed up again? She didn't remember pulling it down. Then again, her mind wasn't exactly running on all cylinders at the moment. "Do you want to come too?"

"No, I can hear more fighting going on," Beverly said. Her green scales were beginning to turn white, and already her body was shifting in size. "I've got a guild to look after."

"Be careful," Chloe warned, though seeing as Beverly had actually won her fight and Chloe had just gotten lucky, she wasn't sure why she was worried about the dragon.

"You too," Beverly replied. Then she leapt into the sky, newly grown wings catching the air. In a few flaps, she was gone.

Chloe looked down at the parasol still in her hands. It was oddly comforting, but also a reminder that she'd accidentally killed someone. Gently, she laid it down near the legs of its original owner, and then did her hop, skip, and jump back to her apartment.

She made it back safely, which was nice. Somewhat less comforting was her discovery that her entire apartment building was currently engulfed in flames, with a whole section already caved in. She stood on the street, staring up at her burning home, racking her brain for a saying that would put out fire. When her eyes finally left the building, they found a new, somehow more disturbing sight.

Resting against a busted mailbox, just within arm's reach, was that same pink and black parasol.

*　　　*　　　*

"Down!"

Cyber Geek fell to the concrete seconds before the laser blast burned through the air above him, saved only by Medley's warning. He jerked his gun upward, trying to find the automated cannon that they'd caught sight of, only to discover it was already frozen in an unmoving hunk of ice. Just for good measure, he squeezed off a few shots to destroy it completely, then got back to his feet slowly in case any more traps had been activated.

Between the energy fences, automated cannons, sizable attack-robots, and sonic tasers, their group was looking pretty roughed up. It was only by luck and persistence that they'd made it so far—at least one of them had had the power to handle every trap they'd encountered so far, which had bailed the less-well-equipped out. Cyber Geek was beginning to see why the defenses worked the way they did: almost every meta had some weakness, which the traps would eventually hit. But if a team came through, they could cover each other, which meant AHC members could eventually power past if needed. Of course, that

576

worked off the assumption that criminals were loners, which was proving to be shockingly untrue in light of the day's events. Still, the guild might be more anomaly than rule.

"We're getting close." Hat Trick limped as she spoke; the large tear in her sparkling pants almost hid the burn mark on her leg where she hadn't quite dodged fast enough. Cyber Geek's esteem for their newest teammate had risen; in the time since she was injured, not once did she hint at the idea of turning back.

"Which is both good and bad. There's a reason we had to keep civilians several blocks back. The farther in we get, the more dangerous it is." Medley was largely unharmed, though that was thanks only to his healing and toughness. The truth of the matter was that he'd easily taken more blows in their trek than anyone else, throwing himself in harm's way to keep everyone else safe. Without Medley, Cyber Geek doubted they would have ever made it this far— not with all of them still breathing, anyway.

"At least we're alone," Pest Control pointed out. He was right, too. While the gang members might be spread across town causing trouble, none of them were stupid enough to actually try and approach the AHC headquarters.

Nope, only Cyber Geek and his friends/temporary non-enemies were idiotic enough to take on that sort of task.

They reached an intersection that marked the last street between themselves and the AHC headquarters. While the dome stretched down around the building, the outer fences and gates were still unshielded. No one needed to say what they all knew: the lesser defenses were the ones that had been tucked away on public streets. On their own property, the AHC had no doubt constructed one hell of a counterattack system. As soon as they got closer, something was going to trigger, and none of them had the faintest idea what it would be or if they could survive it.

"You could shoot from here," Cold Shoulder suggested. "I mean, you're obviously close enough to hit."

"If this thing works, the most it will do is make a hole," Cyber Geek told her. "We'll still have to get up to the dome to go through. So I may as well be right next to it to give the charge as much oomph as possible."

"How many of those barrier breakers do you have?" Hat Trick asked.

"The game only gives you one because that's all you're supposed to need." Cyber Geek cycled through his ammo options, confirming the lone shot as he spoke. "Technically, I can get more by dismissing this blaster and pulling out a new one, but that's going to take a lot of time. Way more than we probably have."

"In that case, let's make sure your first shot does the job." Glyph walked over to Cyber Geek and held up his wand with the glowing purple tip. "With your permission, I'd like to put a rune on your gun."

"What will that do?" Medley didn't actually step forward, but the slight lean to his stance made it clear that he could be on Glyph in the span of a heartbeat.

"It should give his shots extra power, though I confess I've never tried using a power-augmentation rune on a gun summoned out of a video game. It's supposed to be for weapons, brute strength, and spells. But it works on mundane firearms, so the principle is sound," Glyph said.

Cyber Geek considered the offer, carefully examining the weapon still clutched in his hands. Even aside from the risk of treachery on Glyph's part, which was a very real possibility, mixing meta abilities was dangerous stuff. Technically, neither Cyber Geek nor anyone else at the AHC had figured out what made his power work, and if it was some method that reacted poorly to magic, then adding a rune could dissolve the gun, or blow it up, or any other outcome. However, it could also make the difference they desperately needed. Maybe he could punch through the AHC's dome on his own, but that seemed pretty unlikely. If Glyph could give them even a slightly better chance of succeeding, then it was worth taking the chance.

"Go for it," Cyber Geek said. Glyph didn't hesitate, drawing a strange symbol on the gun. It began to glow in mere seconds. When he stepped back, Cyber Geek cycled to the blaster's standard destructive ammo and let off a few test shots into the street a few feet away.

The ground exploded into miniature craters, sending dust and debris spraying up into the sky. "Looks like it works on the small scale," Cyber Geek noted.

"We'll have to hope for the best on the barrier breaker," Glyph replied. "Thank you for trusting me, by the way. Right now, I don't even think many members of my own guild would do that."

"You keep doing right by us, and we'll keep giving you the chance to prove yourself," Medley replied, though it was hard not to notice the way his claws flexed as he spoke.

"All right, time is against us, people; we need to get a move on." Cyber Geek did a quick sweep to make sure everyone was ready and found that all five of the others were attentive and resolved. All they were waiting for was his order. For a moment, he wondered when exactly he'd become the default leader of their group; Medley seemed like a far better fit for the role. It was something he'd have to contemplate later, though, as right now, they were looking to him. He had to fulfill the role.

"Everyone stay safe, prepare for anything, and watch each other's backs. Now, let's move!"

*   *   *

A soft blue glow surrounded Miss Teresa, matching the one that those with the right sort of meta-senses could see surrounding Helen's house. Her eyelids slowly pulled themselves apart, and she gave a weary nod to Helen and Penelope.

"The barrier is created. Only you, I, and Penelope will be able to pass through, at least until someone manages to overpower it."

"Which has almost never happened in our world's history," Helen replied. She laid a hand gently on the older woman's shoulder. "Thank you so much for this, Teresa. I know it takes a lot out of you, but I couldn't... with the way the city is, I had to make sure she was safe."

"Silly girl, how many times have you saved the entire planet?" Teresa said, swatting the hand away in a manner that somehow still managed to be affectionate. "I owe you my life and the lives of everyone I love. If I can help, I must. And what's more, I take pleasure in it. Even if I wish it were for a happier occasion."

Helen nodded. On the television, news crews had stopped showing the fight between Fornax and Apollo, which she hoped meant Ivan was back under control. Regardless, it didn't change the essence of her duty. Capes, guild members, and common meta-criminals were all brawling in the streets. Professor Quantum seemed to be giving as many shits as usual when a situation didn't directly affect him, and Quorum was stuck in the headquarters building. Ivan had done a good job for a long time, but the day had finally come. There was no getting around it, no one to cover for her. The world needed a hero.

It needed Lodestar.

Bending down gently, Helen took her daughter by the shoulders and looked her in the eyes. "Penelope, Mommy has to go out for a while. And when she... when she comes back, she's going to look a little different. But I'll still be me, okay? I'll still be me, and I'll still love you more than anything. So don't be scared."

For all the cheerful flippancy Penelope usually showed, her face was abnormally serious. She leaned forward and wrapped her arms around Helen's neck, hugging her with all the strength her tiny body could manage. "I won't be scared. I'll never be scared of you. I love you, too."

Helen wanted to cry, but instead she just embraced her daughter, savoring the last moment of normalcy they would ever truly have. Then it was

579

over, and the hug broke apart. "Go over to Miss Teresa, honey. She'll keep you safe while I'm gone."

Penelope did as she was told, making her way slowly over to Miss Teresa, who gently took the small girl's hand. Helen looked at them both and smiled with a joy she didn't really feel. She took several steps away. It had been a long time since she did this; she needed room to work in. Standing ten feet away from Miss Teresa and Penelope, Helen reached into herself for the power she'd been pushing down for nearly a decade.

It flowed through her instantly, the same energy that the comet had crackled with as it came down on top of her suffusing her body. Her skin glowed as her chestnut hair turned a translucent-white. Beneath her closed lids, her irises shifted to a stark lavender that was both gorgeous and terrifying to see. Most striking of all, however, was the change that rippled through her actual flesh. Her muscles toned, her spine shrank, and small details altered all over her face as the last seven years melted away. Helen could age normally if she didn't call on the power, but Lodestar was forever nineteen, trapped in the day the comet hit her, and when the power faded, that's where Helen would be again. Just one use of the power, and her whole body reset.

As she gazed out about the room, she saw Penelope peeking in wide-eyed wonder at her. Part of Helen had been terrified that no matter what promises were made, Penelope would be afraid when she saw who her mother truly was. Instead, her daughter looked awestruck, like a priest given a glimpse of their god.

"Be good for Miss Teresa, and you two stay safe," Lodestar ordered. She took a few steps, noting that once again her costume fit perfectly. "There are people out there that need Mommy's help, and she's already kept them waiting for much too long."

Chapter 88

Putting together this much chaos had, humorously enough, taken a ridiculous amount of forethought and planning. Gathering the guild members who could be trusted, secretly reaching out to the most vicious meta-human gangs that hadn't been wiped out, and, of course, getting everything coordinated with Apollo... all of it had just been so much work. Yet as Balaam made his way through the streets, watching buildings lit on fire and capes struggling to beat back a horde of destructive criminals, he felt the warm glow of satisfaction that told him it had all been worthwhile.

The glow was aided by the ripples of power that were flowing into him, coming faster by the minute. Hunting down the Brand of Kurmtis had taken him years—he'd begun the task long before the signal was ever given to actually start the ball rolling on today's festivities—and it had been time well-spent. Even the effort of convincing the gangs to let him use it on them, annoying as it had been, was paying off. And he hadn't lied when he said that being branded would give them a bit of an increase in their power. He'd just skipped over what the other, more important side effect was.

Nearby, a cape that Balaam recognized as Kicknominal delivered a strike that sent an acid-breathing meta-human in a leather jacket careening through the air to where they landed hard on the ground. Though Kicknominal didn't notice, the impact broke the acid-breather's neck. On the exposed flesh just below the break, Balaam saw one of the countless Marks of Kurmtis flicker as its true purpose took effect. Moments later, the power of the dead criminal flowed into Balaam, and he suppressed a shiver of delight.

All these criminals killing themselves off, just for him, and with every death, his magic grew a little bit stronger. It was a ritual sacrifice, one they didn't even know was taking place. Only a few minutes into the fray and Balaam's skin was already tingling with new power. By the time the guild finished wiping out all his pawns, Balaam would be the most powerful meta in history: stronger than Fornax, or Doctor Mechaniacal, or even Lodestar. He would be unstoppable.

It would be good to be so powerful when presiding over his new guild. If things were going to plan, the *true* members were getting their recruitment speech right about then, and while everyone would agree to join, there would doubtlessly be a power struggle. With this new fuel, he would easily crush any opposition and take his rightful place as their ruler.

Kicknominal, having finished with the lesser criminals, took off toward Balaam, no doubt intent on doling out more physical punishment. Balaam gave a minor wave of his staff and Kicknominal literally exploded from the inside, sending a spray of his internal components across the street.

Balaam looked from the cape's remains to his staff and back again. "Huh. Guess I've got more power than I realized." Just for good measure, he gave it another wave and finished off the gang members that Kicknominal had subdued. They burned to ash in seconds, and an instant later, Balaam felt their energy come rushing in.

Every little death helped, after all.

*   *   *

The left arm was shot and several of her systems were offline, but to Tori's surprise, the meta-suit wasn't completely a lost cause. She scrapped the rest of the left arm and sealed the gap with a focused flame, a terrible attempt at spot welding that would just have to suffice until she could get it to a lab. Having no room for an entire arm would have been a serious issue if she weren't free to reshape herself as living fire. It took some wiggling and a few tries, but eventually she managed to rise from the ground once more as Hephaestus, albeit Hephaestus with a lot of bangs, dings, and one arm fewer. Her legs were barely functioning as well, though only able to take small steps, but mercifully, the flight system still worked. While there wouldn't be any more hairpin turns, she could still take to the air.

In the few minutes it had taken her to get back into the suit, Apollo had filled Ivan in on everything: the plan to cause a revolution, Balaam's betrayal, Balaam's *second* betrayal where he'd brought in dozens upon dozens of metas to fight both the AHC and the guild, and, of course, Quorum's incarceration. Ivan took it all relatively calmly, though Tori couldn't help wondering if that was only because he'd already beaten the living hell out of Apollo and doing more would just be excessive.

"What's the plan?" Hephaestus asked, slowly making her way over to them. The legs were going to need to be rebuilt almost from the ground up. Actually, by this point, that might be true of the entire suit.

"Clearly, Balaam expected me to be a bigger distraction, that I would keep the strongest of the AHC's forces occupied as I killed them off one by one," Ivan said. "But since that's no longer the case, I think the capes will be able to rally and take control of things, eventually. Our guild is no doubt also getting into gear; once the councilors arrive, it will take less than an hour to purge the streets of every low-level meta who thought to raise arms against us."

"So, that's it? Turning you back gave us the win?" Hephaestus asked.

"No. That's what bothers me. Even if you hadn't gotten through to me, it was only a matter of time before Lodestar would have arrived and removed me from the equation. Sooner or later, Fornax was going to be out of play; there were just too many ways for it to happen for Balaam not to have accounted for that. He's a bastard and a traitor, but he's not stupid. We have to assume the best of our enemy in order to not be overtaken by him. So, if Balaam knew I'd eventually stop rampaging and the guild would mount a counterattack, what does he gain by having his forces wiped out?"

"I know I'm not exactly the most trustworthy person here, but have you considered the possibility that these aren't all of his forces?" Apollo asked. "As someone who actually sees the numbers on this stuff, there are a *lot* of low-level meta criminals out there. This might seem like a big chunk, but it's barely the tip of the iceberg. And that's not even counting the bigger fish we've already locked up in Rookstone."

Ivan's eyes went wide, a very disconcerting image since his face was still plastered with blood. "That's it. Balaam doesn't want a gang of incompetent street-level crooks. He wants a guild strong enough to rival ours. And there are only a few places in the world with enough criminal meta-humans who have that sort of power. Imagine how grateful the worst of the worst in Rookstone would be to get suddenly handed their freedom."

"Rat bastard," Apollo spat. "He's keeping us distracted. With the AHC on full response and the building sealed up, the security at Rookstone is minimal. Even if a distress call went out, we might not get it. But how can he be there and here at once?"

"We know he's turned some of the guild against us, why not more?" Hephaestus said. "Not everyone would have been in the base when your people attacked, and of those missing, I'll bet a few are with Balaam, helping with the breakout. He might have cherry-picked the gang members with potential to help out too. While he puts on the show, they do the real work. It's actually standard guild tactics, when you think about it."

"Somehow, that pisses me off even more," Ivan said. "We need to ruin his plan."

"I can fly to Rookstone," Apollo offered. He caught sight of the skepticism in Ivan's bloody face and quickly continued. "Look, we both know I'm done no matter how this plays out. Between your guild and the AHC, there's no place I'll be able to run. I messed up big time, and I'll have to pay for it. That said, Balaam screwed me too, so if I can spend my last hours as a cape repaying the favor, I'd like to do it."

Ivan looked at Hephaestus, who gave a small nod. Apollo might be a piece of shit, but he was a fast one and had the right connections to perhaps make a difference. "Fine," Ivan said. "Go now. Keep Rookstone secure. We'll find and stop Balaam."

Apollo's golden glow began to return, and he lifted slowly off the ground, hovering for a few seconds before firing off into the sky. They watched him go, the small streak of light fading into the distance. Within seconds, he was out of sight, and soon his light trail had vanished as well.

"Think he'll be able to handle it on his own?" Hephaestus asked.

"If the jailbreak has already started, then it's doubtful. That's assuming we were even right about Balaam's plan. It's entirely possible that he'll arrive and find nothing out of place. But if we were right, then he's in for a hell of a fight."

"At least he's strong," Hephaestus said. "Not Fornax strong, obviously. You whipped the shit out of that guy. But still... strong. Maybe he can handle himself."

Ivan shook his head. "Some of the meta-humans in Rookstone were put there by the sole cape that *could* beat them. Apollo is good, but there's only one Lodestar."

"Um, yeah, speaking of, do you see that?" Hephaestus pointed into the sky. What appeared to be a second sun was falling downward, burning so brightly that it seemed like the very heavens were crashing upon the Earth. Ivan had once told her there was no feeling like seeing Lodestar descend, and as the burning ball came further down, she finally understood. There was something about it, something impossible to describe, but when she looked into the light, Hephaestus knew beyond any doubt that the woman within was on a whole other plane of power.

To her surprise, she felt Ivan stiffen as he watched the light descend. His head fell several inches, and a slight whisper escaped from his lips. "I'm so sorry, Helen."

Hephaestus decided that this was probably not something she needed to comment on, at least not while a giant brawl was still going on, so instead, she slapped Ivan on the back with her suit's remaining right arm. "Since Lodestar is here, I doubt we'll have to mess with the small fries much. Let's go hunt down a traitor."

"I like that idea," Ivan said, raising his head once more. For a split second, she thought she saw the wild grin try to slip back into place, but then it was gone, if it had ever really been there in the first place. "I like that idea very much. Let's go remind Balaam what happens to those who break the code."

*   *   *

584

Greasy Gary, a nickname that had stuck with the slimy crook since falling into a radioactive oil puddle had turned him into an ever-slick meta-human, tripped as the others turned a corner. He was a few steps behind, as usual, but it would be fine. With his gang, they were unbeatable, and they'd taken down three capes already to prove it. He slid around the corner, expecting to see Tam and Kel punching people into submission.

Instead, he rounded just in time to see Tam's skull get vaporized. She fell to the ground, one more headless corpse on a growing pile. With horror, Greasy Gary realized that those bodies belonged to the rest of his gang. But... how? Ten seconds. That's how far behind he'd fallen; ten seconds, at most. What on earth could have mowed through them with such incredible speed?

His answer came with the sound of more shots being fired, and for the first time, Greasy Gary looked upward toward the source of the noise. Hanging there by means of the jets firing from her feet was a metallic woman with cannons on each arm, blasting away. There were also guns poking out of her back, chest, and a pair framing her head as she spun slowly in place, shooting without error at every single non-cape or guild meta-human on the street. She'd just turned away as he came into view, which was likely the only thing that had saved him from sharing the others' fate.

Greasy Gary didn't waste his chance, spinning around and dashing back down the alley he came from. Was that someone in a meta-suit? If so, they'd put a weirdly expressive face on the front. He could have sworn that thing was smiling as it killed wave upon wave of metas. To be fair, even if he were a better student of history, Greasy Gary likely wouldn't have recognized Xelas. She'd been through many an upgrade since leaving the public eye.

Running back to the street he had just left, Greasy Gary skidded to a stop just as a hybrid car crashed to the ground near him. Another flew through the air, smashing into a small cluster of other criminals that had been trying to flee. It was impossible to miss the one doing the throwing: a giant creature with stone gray skin was easily hefting parked vehicles and tossing them at every criminal in sight. One brave group of metas tried to charge it, and they were quickly smashed into putty beneath its giant hands.

The sound of a rocket drew Greasy Gary's attention upward again. The unmistakable form of Doctor Mechaniacal soared through the air, firing a laser that neatly sliced in half everything and everyone it touched. More split-open corpses tumbled to the ground, small bursts of light flickering on their necks as they passed from one world to the next.

This... this was insane. Balaam had assured them they'd have the upper hand, that their numbers would let them take the capes by surprise. Greasy Gary slid backward, hoping to get out of sight, and bumped into an unmoving figure behind him.

"You all really put your dicks in a hell of a beehive." A dainty hand grasped his shoulder. Greasy Gary tried to slip away but the fingers didn't budge, not even as he secreted as much oil as possible. It was such a gentle grip, just firm enough to hold him in place, but nothing he could do made the fingers even so much as twitch. A new hand came around from behind, carefully slipping itself across his throat.

"Honestly, did you all really believe Balaam when he told you that you could win? Did you never stop to question just how we'd held our position on top for so long? I'm disappointed, more than anything. I'd really hoped that the class of common criminal was a little smarter than this." The grip tightened, and much as he clawed at it, Greasy Gary couldn't get it to lessen. It was like the woman behind him didn't even feel his struggling. She didn't even seem strong. Just... immovable.

"Then again, maybe what we're seeing is natural selection at work," she continued, even as the pressure on his throat built. "Surely there were some of you smart enough to reject the offer. Maybe we'll be able to fish out of those pools for future members. And if not, if all of you were really so stupid to believe you could stand against our guild and survive, then at least the example we make of you will ensure the next generation makes smarter choices."

Stasis realized that midway through her speech, the slimy man in her hands had gone unconscious. She kept her grip for a while longer, making sure the deed was properly done as Gork and Doctor Mechaniacal swept up the rest of the street. Nearby, she could hear the screams of Xelas and Morgana's work. They needed to hurry things along; everyone had seen Lodestar drop into the heart of downtown minutes prior. Once she took control, the capes would start trying to take prisoners, and by that point, it might be prudent for legendarily dead or wanted criminals not to be so visible.

Her hands opened and Greasy Gary fell limply to the ground, one more dead body to show everyone what happened when people crossed the guild. Stasis stepped over him, looking for another straggler to pick off.

There was so little time to work with, and such a big message to send.

Chapter 89

Lodestar was a blur as she whipped through the streets, striking every meta-human throwing punches with a careful two-fingered strike to the temple. It was a technique that had taken her years to master, reigning in her tremendous strength to deliver a non-fatal knock-out blow. Despite her fears that she would be out of practice after so long on the sidelines, her form was still perfect as she downed criminal after criminal. Professor Quantum had once speculated that no amount of control should be able to produce such an effect, and that her technique only worked because she believed it should. It had been in one of their many discussions and speculations about the exact nature of her powers, and while she never entirely agreed with his theory, she was thankful for the ability to bring people down without killing them no matter what its source.

Of course, not every meta-human was so easily felled; as she zipped into a crowd swarming a cape, her first attack bounced harmlessly off a thick skull. The man whirled around, showing his bulging bones and misshapen muscles. Not all meta-humans got to keep their appearances when the change came, and it was no wonder someone who looked like this had decided to take it out on the world. He reared back and threw his fist at her, no doubt failing to recognize just who he was attacking. Lodestar caught the blow easily in midair, then punched him in the head again. This time, she used a fist rather than two fingers, and he slumped to the ground in a limp heap. She preferred to be gentle whenever possible, but time wasn't on her side.

Moving swiftly, she began knocking out the rest of the group, leveling bodies so quickly that she soon revealed their target: a crouched figure clad in an eggshell-colored meta-suit. Sparks and dents came off it as the familiar figure of the Whitest Knight rose from his knees and stared at his savior.

"Holy crap! Lodestar... you've come back." Even through the metallic hood that covered his face, she could see the shock in his eyes.

Without so much as a pause, Lodestar drove her fingers through the metal helmet, cracking Whitest Knight on the skull and sending him tumbling limply to the ground, his breath shallow but constant.

"*Whoops*, guess I didn't notice you were on our side. That sort of thing happens when you insist on dressing like a racist di-, um, jerk." Lodestar looked around to see if there were anyone to witness her words, only to realize she'd already knocked them all out. There was almost no chance she wouldn't get some heat for that, but she'd do it again if given the chance.

The area around them had been almost completely emptied as Lodestar tore through, felling opponent after opponent. Now that she was on the ground, however, her enhanced senses could pick up far more details than she'd seen on the news. The criminals were being beaten—murdered in the streets, really—as the guild's heavy hitters finally showed up for a counterattack. The rest of the AHC was regrouping—evacuating citizens, capturing gang members, and minimizing the destruction before fires or collapsing buildings could cause any more casualties.

Outside of her immediate vicinity, about a mile or so away, she could feel Ivan as he raced across the city blocks. If a meta was powerful enough, they created a sort of ripple she could sense, though usually only when she was looking for it. What surprised her was that he was on a crash course for someone else strong enough to be felt. Balaam, probably, but since when had he ever been this powerful?

She was tempted to hurry over and help but decided against it. For one thing, Lodestar and Fornax fighting together, especially after the latter went on a rampage, would raise a lot of questions in the public's eyes. Things were already going to be bad when this was over; the AHC would need a few capes who could prove they still deserved the public's trust. More important than that, though, going over would be poor resource allocation. Ivan could handle Balaam, even if the mage was sporting some extra mojo. She should focus on making a difference elsewhere.

With the streets falling in their favor, the logical step would be to break open the dome and go get Quorum. Much as she trusted Ivan—and Wade to a lesser extent—having all of the guild's councilors on the streets felt a bit disproportionate. Better to have another legend alongside her, something to encourage them to not get ambitious when the common enemy was defeated. Besides, she trusted Quorum's judgment, and he'd no doubt have insight on how to properly quell the fighting.

Moving at speeds that left her looking like a blur, she raced through the streets toward the AHC headquarters, pausing for milliseconds to knock out every criminal she met along the way.

*   *   *

The explosion blew off Cold Shoulder's arm. Or, rather, it blew off the arm of the ice construct she was currently encased in, sending freezing shrapnel across the battlefield. The mine launcher spun around from its armored bunker on the ground, taking aim at her once more.

Cyber Geek dashed forward and jammed the barrel of his blaster through the small slot in its hull, firing off several rounds until the mechanism stopped moving. The strategy worked, but in trying to pull his gun free, he

588

realized it was stuck. Not a good sign: being stationary in this fight could very well cost someone their life.

Everything between the AHC's gates and energy dome seemed designed to kill intruders. More laser cannons had sprung out to fire at them, this time joined by small nodes that blasted everything around them with enough electricity to stun an elephant and almost enough to stop Medley. There were more attack-robots as well, along with new toys like the mine-firing systems which were too accurate for anyone's taste with explosions that were almost impossibly disproportionate to the mass of the fist-sized mines. The worst of it was the unseen system above them, though, well-positioned on nearby buildings or some satellite in the sky. All they knew was that if they stood still for too long, blue bolts of piercing energy would rain down. Medley had taken the first of them and gotten a dime-sized hole through his shoulder. Since then, they'd made a point of staying mobile while fighting their way closer to the dome.

Cyber Geek kicked on his suit's thrusters, giving himself enough force to pull the gun free mere seconds before one of those blue beams hit the ground where he'd been standing. Sweeping around, he scanned as he ran to see who needed help. As deadly and insane as the situation was, there was also an odd sense of familiarity to it. How many times had he guided digital avatars through situations just like these? Keep the party alive, minimize damage, meet the target goal; he'd drilled for this countless times at his computer. Yes, the stakes were much higher and the skills needed were far different than when it was pretend, but the strategic part remained the same.

Hat Trick used her multi-colored scarves to cover the camera-eyes of an attack robot, allowing Medley to sink his claws into its metal hide and tear out its innards. Pest Control was swarming the cannons with his wasps, digging them into the circuitry and slowly destroying the guns from the inside. Glyph stood behind the cover of Cold Shoulder's giant ice construct, but he was doing far more than merely taking cover. His wand swished through the air; when he stopped, a new rune glowed on the lower calf of Cold Shoulder's frozen armor. Instantly, the ice darkened several shades. The next attack failed to do more than even chip the exterior. Cold Shoulder returned the blow, shattering the offending robot into debris with a single blow.

Just as Medley pounced onto a laser cannon and Hat Trick filled a mine-shooter's bunker with playing cards, Cyber Geek saw a path. It was thin and risky, but his teammates and the two villains had successfully managed to open a small avenue forward. Donald would have debated the idea, wondering if they should keep pushing back the forces to try for a more secure opportunity, but Cyber Geek didn't have room for hesitation in his plan. He barreled forward, cycling through ammo options as he ran. The rune from Glyph still glowed on

589

the side of his gun, and as the icon with only a single bullet appeared in his display, Cyber Geek said a silent prayer to the gods of video games that this would work.

He darted past Cold Shoulder, who threw an arm out to intercept another mine before it could land and explode in his path. This time, the explosion only took off some of her icy fingers. She stomped the bunker down with the new magical strength in her frosty legs. Medley darted ahead, triggering an electric node that Cyber Geek had missed and then crushing it in his claws despite the voltage racing through him. Hat Trick flipped her top hat around, unleashing a dule of doves that flew above Cyber Geek's head. Their beating white wings probably weren't that strong, but hopefully they'd offer enough cover from the sky beam for him to take the shot.

Then, almost at once, he'd arrived. The crackling energy of the dome was only inches away from him, a barrier strong enough to keep out meta-humans far more powerful than some upstart with video game powers. Much as he might have liked to indulge in self-doubt, it would have to wait. Right now, his team was counting on him. Cyber Geek raised his gun, got it as close to the dome as he dared, and fired.

A blast of purple energy erupted from his gun, slamming into the yellow barrier with a symphony of hisses and pops, like a computer shorting out from a voltage spike. The collision burned with a phosphorescent glow, forcing him to turn away. When he was finally able to look back, Cyber Geek could barely believe what met his still half-blinded eyes.

It had worked. There was a human-sized portal in the barrier, tinged with purple edges, just like it was in the game. He'd managed to break through the AHC's dome, something designed by *Professor Quantum*, using only his power and a little extra juice from Glyph. Cyber Geek spun around to tell the others, cycling back to regular ammunition so that he might eventually cover their run to join him. But as he turned, he realized that while he'd been burning a hole in an impossible barrier, the entire landscape of the battlefield had changed.

Everything was broken. Every robot, cannon, mine bunker, electric node, and even the massive drone that accounted for the strikes from above, all of it was shattered and spread out in front of the AHC headquarters. The only things still standing were his teammates, the pair of surprisingly helpful villains, and... Lodestar.

She ignored the awed stares from the others, who were no doubt partly wowed by her legendary status as much as the destruction she'd visited on obstacles they'd seen as deadly. With a brisk pace, she walked over to Cyber Geek and examined the hole in the barrier.

"Did you do this?"

"Yes, ma'am. I mean, I did, I'm sorry, but we needed to get to Quorum, though I know I probably shouldn't be breaking the barrier. I just—"

"Relax." She held up a hand to quiet him, attention still on the break he'd created. "I'm not mad; I was going to shatter the thing anyway. I'm actually impressed. There are a few metas who can overpower the field, like me, but breaching it like this was supposed to be impossible. Professor Quantum is going to be annoyed that you showed him up, and that's a show I always like catching."

"I... thank you. Ma'am." It felt strange to be saying ma'am to someone who looked half a decade younger than he, but there was no doubt in Cyber Geek's mind who was more senior. He'd seen pictures of her flying around since he was a child, though she'd appeared older from a distance.

"Thank you, this saves me some time," she replied. "Tell your team to get inside; most of you need medical attention, and we're already well on our way to taking back control of the streets."

"Yes, ma'am. Um, what about the two villains? Am I... should we bring them in?" Cyber Geek dearly hoped she wasn't going to say yes, but at the same time, he couldn't very well hide the fact that he'd led criminals up to the AHC's front door.

"The warrants issued to arrest the guild were provided under false evidence created by Apollo. By now, I bet they've already been suspended. So far as we know, those two were just a pair of meta-humans in the wrong place at the wrong time. We are the law's enforcers, not the law itself, so I can't see any reason to detain those two young men, especially in light of the assistance they offered." Lodestar turned back to the starstruck capes and motioned for them to come forward. All three complied, while Glyph and Pest Control headed back out toward the street.

As they were leaving, Cyber Geek caught Glyph's eyes and gave the fleeing villain a small nod. There was no doubt these two had been at the museum robbery, but Lodestar was right: they didn't have any proof or warrants, which thankfully meant there were no grounds to arrest either villain. One day they might have to meet one another again as enemies, but Cyber Geek would be content if that moment never arrived.

Now, the dragon and Hephaestus who'd humiliated him and Medley, those were different stories. But as Hat Trick limped forward and Medley weaved about, Cyber Geek's mind fell away from things as petty as revenge. He had a team to take care of. That was his real job.

Cyber Geek ran to his team, dropping his gun and letting it dissipate, then sticking an arm around Medley and Hat Trick, helping them both through the hole in the barrier. Cold Shoulder was on Medley's other side in a moment, doing all she could to support his sizable mass. By the time the hole in the barrier collapsed, they were all safely inside, and Lodestar was on her way to free Quorum.

It wasn't until several hours later that Donald remembered he was supposed to have a coffee date with Tori, though he took comfort in the fact that he had one hell of an excuse for missing it.

Chapter 90

Part of Hephaestus wanted to be surprised that amid a sea of battle, blood, and chaos, Balaam was waiting for them in a small park, an island of tranquility maintained only by his power. But she wasn't. It was the sort of piss-poor theatricality that wannabes like him reveled in. He'd probably picked the spot out ahead of time, selecting it specifically in case Ivan managed to regain control, knowing full well that he would be the first target of Ivan's wrath.

Ivan didn't seem fazed by it either, his face inscrutable under the thick coating of Blunderbuss's blood. She'd sort of expected him to wipe it off after coming to his senses, but he'd left it in place, perhaps for intimidation, or simply because he didn't have a mask with him and this offered at least some concealment. As she started forward, he held up a hand in front of her.

"This is as far as you go." Ivan turned to her, somehow staring into her eyes through the helmet between them. "He's dangerous and even stronger than normal. I don't want you getting hurt."

"What the hell? Why did you tell me to follow if you weren't going to let me help?" Hephaestus demanded.

"Because your suit is one good punch away from falling apart, and if I hadn't dragged you along, you probably would have thrown yourself back into the fray." Ivan smiled—not the wild, deadly grin of Fornax, but the gentle, wheedling smirk of her teacher. "And besides, I assumed you wouldn't want to miss this. Or would you rather just *hear* about my fight with Balaam?"

"Okay, point taken. I guess it will make for a good show," Hephaestus agreed.

"I'm sure it will; just don't try to become a participant. No matter how things go." The smile faded, and Ivan looked as serious as he had on the first day he'd warned her about messing with his children. "I've already lived through the pain of losing family once today. Don't make me repeat that experience."

Before she could respond, Ivan was gone, walking across the street to the modest park where Balaam waited patiently. The sorcerer seemed to be all but glowing with power, waiting as Ivan stepped onto the soft grass. Hephaestus backed up several feet, then thought better of it and flew upward, landing on top of a nearby building with perfect line of sight of the impending show.

"Should be quite interesting."

The voice had come from behind her, and Hephaestus whirled around to find a pair of kaleidoscope eyes looking past her to where Ivan and Balaam were slowly drawing closer. Nexus ignored the gauntlet she had pointed toward him, stepping to the edge of the roof for a better view.

"Even imprisoned, Quorum made quite the difference. His words softened Apollo, and his imprisonment gave the AHC hope that he could be freed. Although you showed some rare results as well. Generally, when you try that plan, Fornax kills you. You aren't a unique by any means, but you *are* interesting, Hephaestus."

She was tempted to press for more, to find out what Nexus knew, but Stasis's face flashed before her eyes, that look of lost terror when she'd talked about dealing with Nexus. No. Hephaestus didn't need his kind of knowledge, and it didn't matter, anyway. Whatever other versions of her he was talking about were irrelevant. She wasn't any of them. She was her own Hephaestus, with her own path to forge. And she was going to start by bearing witness to Ivan and Balaam settling their score.

"Why don't you shut it?" Hephaestus snapped at Nexus. "My teacher is about to whip the shit out of this traitor, and I want to enjoy every minute of it."

* * *

Ivan came to a stop twenty feet away from Balaam, who hadn't moved once during the approach. His red irises were gleaming with a power that poured off him in waves, like heat from summer asphalt. While Ivan didn't know exactly how Balaam had gained such a dramatic increase in his power, it didn't surprise him. If he didn't think he had the upper hand, Balaam would never have allowed himself to be found. The man was a snake, but also an experienced strategist and a survivor. Even now, seemingly ready for a final battle to the death, he no doubt had a few dozen tricks up his sleeve.

"Pity. I thought I'd be facing Fornax," Balaam said, breaking their silence.

"I'm sure you hoped for it. A brainless monster you could use your magic to outwit, maybe even trick into serving your purposes. No, Balaam. No Fornax for you. No Pseudonym either. Today, you fight the man whose guild you betrayed, whose apprentice you ambushed, whose children you tried to murder. Today, you fight Ivan Gerhardt, and he has no mercy in his heart for you." A nearby tree wilted as Ivan's power fluxed slightly out of control. All that lecturing to Tori about keeping her heat in check, and here he went and let such amateur mistakes happen. Truly shameful.

"Loud barking as always, but I wonder how you'll back it up without Fornax's bite." Balaam turned his staff through the air, pointing it at Ivan. "That version might have been a brainless monster, but we both know what he's capable of when properly harnessed. You're in a precarious position. Hold back and you'll die; use too much power and the real you will shine through. Show him to me, here and now, because it's your only chance at survival. I'm too strong for even you right now. Ivan cannot defeat me. Fornax might have a chance."

"That's your problem, Balaam. You always thought Fornax was the more powerful one. You never understood that control is far more important than brute strength." As Ivan spoke, runes covered his skin for the second time that day, dark magic bubbling to the surface. He drew it forth carefully, in far smaller amounts than earlier. It wasn't like before—at least, today's before. No, this time the power served Ivan, not vice versa, and he could think of far better ways to use it than taking wild swings at his target.

"Well then, let's see you put—"

Balaam's reply was cut off as Ivan slammed his foot to the ground, sending out a wave of energy that had the dirt erupting from the ground in a massive brown cloud. Balaam fell back immediately, raising a spell of protection with a single flick of his staff and preparing a magical blast for his counterattack. The dirt swirled, twisting and expanding, blocking any view of his surroundings. After the first ten seconds passed without an attack, he switched tactics, summoning a mighty whirlwind that blew away enough dirt for him to see. What met his eyes was Ivan neither lining up an attack nor moving into a defensive position.

Instead, Ivan had his hands pressed to the ground, muttering under his breath as magic poured out of him. Balaam fired the blast he'd prepared, but it was too late. Ivan leapt aside, letting the ground scorch in his place. A ripple of red energy flowed outward from the spot he'd been touching, across the park's grounds and up into the sky, forming a perfect half-sphere around them.

"A ward? You cast a *ward* in the middle of a fight? Half of your fighting style revolves around short-range teleportation!" Balaam's smug veneer vanished as he probed the barrier sealing him off from the outside world. It was rudimentary but strong. Busting through would be no small task.

"I didn't want you trying to cast a teleportation spell if things didn't go your way," Ivan replied. "Like I said, Ivan is far more dangerous than Fornax. He knows how to anticipate his enemy's plans. Though that's not to say Ivan can't also get into the fray, when properly motivated."

While he didn't actually vanish—his magic barred such techniques from him as much as Balaam—Ivan did close the gap between them so quickly that it almost seemed like teleportation, striking at the sorcerer with a blow powerful enough to have knocked Apollo off course. His fist slammed against a different kind of barrier, though, one that flashed into existence several inches in front of Balaam's face. The sorcerer didn't waste the opportunity, jabbing his staff into Ivan's ribs and sending him tumbling several feet back.

"You must have put a lot of magic into that thing," Ivan remarked, rubbing his side. It didn't hurt, just mildly tingled. Balaam may wield enough force to move him, but injury was a whole other matter.

"I have spent decades reinforcing every enchanted item I own, and with today's ritual, I can fill them with more magic than I ever dared dream." The air around Balaam flickered as large, bat-like wings grew from his back. The shadows at his feet rose from the ground. "Come and see what a true master of the arcane arts can accomplish."

Ivan watched as Balaam's spells snapped into effect one after the other. Protection charms, shielding magic, metamorphosis, shadow-summoning, fire-warding, and a dozen smaller ones that Ivan didn't even recognize. By the time it was done, Balaam the sorcerer was unrecognizable. He'd turned into a winged demon hovering in the sky, surrounded by flaming orbs and dozens of sharp-clawed shadow minions. This was Balaam as the capes had once fought him, a master mage whose talents had earned him back his freedom when a stolen artifact threatened the world. This was Balaam at the strongest they knew of him, and Ivan was certain that there was still more to be seen.

With a small exertion of will, Ivan called on more of the dark power buried in his soul. Around him, the grass died and the ground splintered. This was dangerous; he'd already used too much of the magic earlier in the day. Bringing forth too much could cost him his control once more. Still, he pushed on, determined to see this feud finally drawn to a close. His rune-covered eyes met the burning irises of Balaam, all that was recognizable in this new form aside from his staff, and Ivan smiled with perhaps just a hint of Fornax shining through.

"Show me what you've got. Show me *everything* you've got."

*　　　*　　　*

One by one, the guild members were disappearing from the streets. Johnny Three Dicks and Thuggernaut finished off a small cluster of crooks then hopped into a sewer entrance tucked inside an alley. Glyph and Pest Control were ambushed by a gang of eight, which would have been a real issue if a giant white dragon hadn't landed nearby, quickly turning green and evening the odds. Minutes later, they were clutched in the once-more-white dragon's claws, being flown out of town as fast as she could flap. The Bytes found a fast food restaurant with free Wi-Fi and minutes later were picked up by a town car service, all being addressed by new names that matched their fresh identities.

Morgana was the first of the councilors to disappear, simply walking down a dark alley and not emerging. A lovely woman with raven-black hair did come out the other side; however, since she wasn't surrounded by blood or wielding a scythe, no one paid her much mind. Xelas vanished next, literally turning invisible after she paused long enough to pick up Gork and Stasis. Soon the three of them were tearing through the sky toward a safe house. Doctor Mechaniacal was the final member to depart, seeing things through to the end. Only when the vast majority of gang members were dead or apprehended and when the capes began to look at him with increasing scrutiny did he activate his own shielding system and fly away.

He did linger long enough to see Lodestar and Quorum out on the streets together, organizing the broken ranks of the AHC superheroes and spearheading the organization. Neither of them would give the order to fire on him, at least not today, but tensions were running high all over Ridge City. A secret guild of villainy had been uncovered, a trusted AHC leader turned out to be a criminal, thousands of civilians were dead or injured, and the city was facing millions in property damage. It wasn't the sort of place that was secure for a meta without AHC approval. It might not even be safe for the capes, once the dust settled.

Scanning the area as he moved, Doctor Mechaniacal made certain that every guild member he'd been tracking was out of the brawl. Some were in custody, arrested before Balaam's betrayal, but he would free them through the legal system—already he had lawyers ready to tear apart the false case Apollo had built against them. Others were dead, killed by capes or gang members—it was impossible to tell. They'd done their best to make Balaam's pawns pay, and there was little sense in trying to pay back the AHC for anyone they'd killed. Capes would be going in the ground too; this day had left a wake of loss for everyone. Better to put them back on the path of peace, if it was possible. Otherwise, there would just be more graves to dig before all was said and done.

Just to be on the safe side, Doctor Mechaniacal took the long way around Ridge City, making sure that none of the countless capes had the ability to track him back to the lair where his fragile human body was waiting. This route had the added benefit of taking him past the riverfront docks, where he caught sight of a remarkable ship pulling into harbor. It was massive, protected by an energy field and spinning turrets, fashioned from a material not even his sensors could identify. There were only a few people in the world with both the mind and the resources to create a vehicle like that, and since Wade hadn't done it himself, that narrowed the list considerably.

Unless Tech Lord had found a very well-paying job or Tyranny had decided to leave her nation to invade foreign soil, it looked as though the

Champions' Congress would soon be in complete attendance for the first time in over a decade.

Professor Quantum was back in Ridge City, and that presented a slew of problems all its own.

Chapter 91

Of all the abilities Ivan had—and there were more than anyone else actually knew about—flying wasn't among them. True, he could cast a spell of flight that allowed him to slip the bonds of gravity, but the process felt unnatural and gave him a queasy stomach. Flying simply wasn't in his repertoire, which was why he used a different method to take to the skies as he cannonballed around the park.

Ivan leapt through the air, twisting about and conjuring a small circle of force beneath his foot when he wanted to change direction. Using it as a midair stepping stone, he would thrust off with his incredible, magically-augmented strength. While the method was imprecise, that flaw could be compensated for through lots of training, which Ivan had certainly acquired in his more mischievous days.

This method also had the benefit of making his movements unpredictable, which was clearly frustrating Balaam to no end. He threw spell after spell at Ivan, only for Ivan to jump out of the way at the last moment.

The shadow minions clawed at the tatters of Ivan's suit as he moved, shredding what remained with their knife-like claws. He smacked them away off-handedly, destroying the annoyances easily. They were meant to distract him, not to do real damage. Balaam knew his opponent wouldn't be defeated by minions.

On the other hand, Balaam's fire wards were causing Ivan more trouble. Whenever he managed to duck an attack and draw near, one of the burning spheres would launch itself between him and Balaam and then explode. They didn't do much damage, but the burst was enough to let Balaam slip away. The sorcerer was employing a smart, strategic method. Ivan's weakness had always been that he lacked much in the way of ranged tactics—the few spells he had took too long to cast, and Balaam knew how to ward against them. To finish the fight, Ivan would need to get in close, and that was exactly what Balaam was preventing. He probably planned to keep firing long-range spells, wearing Ivan down bit by bit until either the ward or Ivan fell.

Ivan landed on the shattered ground of what had once been a lovely downtown park, though it was no longer recognizable as such. Now the grass burned, the earth cracked, and the few surviving trees were warped and misshapen. This whole place would be the magical equivalent of a toxic spill-site for years to come; Ivan's wards were the only thing keeping that energy from leaking out into the rest of the nearby city. They couldn't go on like this for long. Sooner or later, the capes would finish up their work, and when they arrived, Balaam would try to use them as hostages. That was assuming they didn't come for Ivan first, since he was still wearing the blood of a murdered cape on his face. No, he couldn't let Balaam have his way.

Above him, more flame spheres dripped from Balaam's staff, replacing the ones Ivan had already detonated. Shadows reformed, pooling into bigger, hungrier monsters. Balaam flapped a bit farther away, keeping a wall of defenses between himself and Ivan. Despite all this casting, his magic didn't appear to be depleting in the slightest. Whatever source Balaam had drawn from, it clearly wasn't running dry anytime soon. Tiring him out was off the table.

The whispers in his ears grew louder, and Ivan pulled more power from within. It was restless; having tasted freedom so recently left it stirring for more. Part of his brain filled with gleefully bloody images, but Ivan shoved them aside. He had the focus of battle upon him, and the weight of those counting on his victory helped him stay in the proper mindset. All along his skin, the etchings glowed brighter.

Balaam's staff was pointed toward him, a spell like black lightning glowing on its tip. He would release it any second, forcing Ivan to dodge, to stay off-balance. All his little tricks to manipulate the battlefield. All the scheming and thought. Ivan would have found it impressive were it not turned against him. Instead, he just saw them as petty, childish tricks. Balaam had wanted to see Fornax so badly, to reach the same legendary status as his idol.

It was time to show Balaam exactly what a legend was made of.

This time, when Ivan leapt up from the ground, it crumbled beneath him, leaving behind a small crater where nothing would ever grow again. He soared upward on the momentum of his jump. Balaam grinned as he fired off the spell. Ivan could see it now—Balaam knew Ivan would dodge. His spells were meant to control him, not injure. They'd both been trying to wear the other down before attacking in earnest. The difference was that Ivan knew how to discard a plan when it wasn't working anymore.

Ivan wove a shield of magic around his arm before throwing it in front of him and taking the black lightning's strike just below the wrist. Pain—how long had it been since he felt *that?*—burned his flesh, yet Ivan's course didn't waver. The shadows sprang forward from the sky, but this time, he didn't let them get close. Ivan released a pulse of the dark magic that dwelled inside him. For a moment, the whispers were so loud he couldn't think, but then mercifully faded. Short as it had been, the pulse was enough to rend every one of the shadows apart; they fell to the ground, twisting and burning as they landed.

Balaam's altered face wasn't smiling anymore. He waved his free hand, putting all of the flame spheres between him and Ivan. Rather than take another shot with his staff, Balaam turned upward toward the ceiling of the ward

600

trapping them. It didn't take much to figure out his plan: Balaam wanted to knock Ivan away and then break through the barrier. Once he was free, he could slip away. He'd be free to do more scheming and attack from the shadows. He'd be free to come after Ivan's family again.

"No, Balaam. We finish this today."

The first sphere hit Ivan dead in the face, but he conjured more discs of force beneath his feet and shoved off just as the shockwave struck. It took almost all of his strength, but he pushed through, refusing to be knocked aside. Regular fire couldn't touch him, but the magical flames burned at his clothes; some were even powerful enough to singe his flesh. Ivan paid the charred skin no mind. His eyes were on the next sphere, ready to jump through it, and then the next, and the next. Ready to do whatever it took to stop Balaam for good.

Later, Tori would describe it as seeing the flaming visage of Death burst forth from within the final sphere. Ivan had fought his way through five of them—five that had burned his skin and turned his clothes into scarcely more than ash. His undergarments survived, thanks solely to the fact that a life in villainy had taught him the importance of extra-durable boxers, but otherwise, all that could be seen was fire, skin, and blood as Ivan sprang through the final explosion.

From Ivan's perspective, all he saw was a tremendous amount of fire, and then suddenly a demon slicing at his barrier with its staff. Balaam was so focused on the task that he didn't even notice Ivan until the man's bloody hand closed around his gray, muscular shoulder. Balaam's head, now with a thick brow and a pair of horns atop it, whipped around to find Ivan staring at him, strands of hair smoking and the blood burned to a copper-brown on his face.

"First off, you have a terrible idea of what real demons look like." Ivan's punch landed directly in Balaam's face. Whatever protection the demonic form offered, it wasn't enough as the two went tumbling down, Ivan refusing to yield his grip now that he finally had the sorcerer in his clutches.

"Secondly, you would dare turn on our guild? After everything we did for you?" This time, the punch was to the stomach just as they were landing, putting Balaam's gut in a pincer maneuver with the earth. Though he was coughing in pain, Balaam swept his staff around, trying to knock Ivan away and regain his distance.

"Not happening." Ivan caught the staff in his free right hand and wrenched it from the sorcerer's grip. With a mighty squeeze, he snapped it in half, letting loose an explosion of magic that left everything up to his forearm smoking and bloody. The staff's destruction caused Balaam to ripple as his demon form melted away and revealed the familiar face of the guild's traitor.

"How did you—"

Ivan jerked Balaam up from the ground before he could finish, clenching the gory remains of his right arm into a fist once more. "Third, you tried to kill my apprentice. My student. My friend." This time, there was a scream, along with a bloody stream of vomit, when Ivan slammed his fist into Balaam's stomach.

It was so loud, in fact, that Ivan didn't hear the sound of his own barrier being broken.

"Your organs are more pulp than anything right now, but I'm sure you've got enough magic left to keep yourself alive, so let's move on to your biggest mistake of the day." Ivan reached forward and wrapped his fingers, some of which were so sliced up from the exploding staff that he could see the bones, around the top of Balaam's head.

"Please, Ivan, we can make a deal here," Balaam pleaded, the blood of his vomit staining his teeth red. They matched his irises.

"*Four*, you tried to murder my children. We're both going to hell, Balaam, but you're going today." Ivan tightened his fingers and began to squeeze when a gentle hand fell across his forearm.

He was so shocked to see someone else there, his powerful wards effortlessly destroyed, that he nearly flexed his fingers and ended Balaam quickly. Only Ivan's exceptional self-control kept his grip steady as he turned to look at who had made it through.

"Ivan, your anger is righteous, and you have undeniable cause to kill this man. But while you only believed your children dead, others are not so lucky today. Please, if you will, I ask that you yield his punishment to me."

If he'd been asked a moment prior, Ivan would have said there was no one else in the world he would allow the pleasure of killing Balaam. But that would be because in his rage, he'd forgotten one of the guild's most quiet, dangerous, merciless members. Kristoph stood before him, all sense of childlike wonder wiped from his face, his hand resting on Ivan's battered forearm.

Balaam looked between them, the resignation of death quickly turning to panic. "Wait! Wait, I didn't kill them. That was Bombastic; I made sure he was the one who did the deed, not me."

"And he is answering for his sins," Kristoph replied. "But it is the fault of the man who wields the knife, as much as the knife itself, when a life is taken. You gave the order, Balaam, and now your soul bears the mark of your sin. But I will not steal from one with a righteous claim to vengeance."

Behind him, Ivan could hear Hephaestus land. Some apprentice, ignoring his explicit directions yet again. She was safe, as were Rick and Beth. When this was over, no matter what happened to him, Ivan would go on knowing the people he cared about were okay. But from what Kristoph said, not everyone in town would have that comfort. Balaam had robbed at least a few parents of that, and tempting as it was to crush his skull, that torture would be short-lived.

"Kristoph, I'll yield my claim to you on one condition: nothing quick. Make him suffer."

"He will taste a hundred times the agony he has unleashed upon the world."

"Still feels low, but I guess it will have to do. He's all yours, Kristoph. I yield my claim of vengeance to you." Ivan released Balaam, who tried to scramble away, waving his hands in a desperate attempt to call forth a magic that would see him to safety.

Kristoph simply shook his head. "No magic can save you now." From his back, the pair of wings began to grow, stretching into the sky. But they were not the bat-like wings that Balaam had fashioned for himself, nor were they the fluffy white wings that people associated with angels.

No, Kristoph's wings were made of blades. Stained straight razors, chipped scissor halves, rusted butcher's knives, they all rattled in a soul-quaking symphony as they stretched behind him, drops of blood falling from each of their tips. Slowly, Kristoph reached down and plucked up Balaam from the ground as if he weighed nothing at all. With a look to Ivan over his shoulder, Kristoph flapped those nightmarish wings once, and the two of them were gone.

"Um... Ivan." Hephaestus approached his side slowly, as if she was afraid Kristoph would reappear to snatch her as well. "Do we really have no idea what Kristoph is?"

"He'll tell you, if you truly want to know," Ivan said, flexing his hand and realizing for the first time how much it hurt. It would be at least a day before the thing was fully healed, maybe a day and a half. "But no one ever does."

"Then, how do you know he'll tell you?"

"Xelas asked once, back when we first found him and figured out what he did," Ivan explained. "She took him into a room and politely asked for an explanation of exactly what he was and how his powers worked. And he told her, after which Xelas went straight to Doctor Mechaniacal and had him purge the memories of the entire day from her hard drive. All she would say is that there are some things she's happier not knowing about the world."

"Xelas did that?" Hephaestus looked at the empty spot where Kristoph and Balaam had vanished. "Yeah, I think I'm okay with that bit of mystery in my life. What's the plan now?"

"The capes are probably restoring order, which means we need to be out of here before they start wondering about that guy who was beating the shit out of Apollo," Ivan said. "I'd like to get home, take a shower, and then go check on my kids."

A sound like worried breath being let out through someone's teeth, and then run through a voice distortion program, came from Hephaestus's helmet.

"Yeah, about that shower. I might have forgotten to mention that before I went to save your kids, there was something of an... incident at the house."

*   *   *

Apollo saw the smoke before he ever got close enough to make out details, but he still held on to hope. An attack was always possible; it didn't mean the jailbreak was successful. He doubled down on his speed. The worst of his injuries from the fight with Fornax had already healed, which allowed him to fly faster as he raced the trouble that Rookstone was facing.

It was a race he'd lost, he discovered as he floated down to find whole sections of the upper jail destroyed or burning. The few guards who were still alive were seriously injured, and even with swift medical attention, making it through the night looked to be a long shot. Apollo canvased the area as fast as he could, searching for any sign of the criminals that had caused such damage. When none met his eye, he found the door to the lower cells, the giant vertical tunnel where the more powerful metas were stored. Normally, one needed clearance from three different sources to access the area. That was less true today, as the massive door had been blown apart, leaving a giant hole into the prison's depths.

Apollo descended carefully, for not even he could take a whole jail's worth of metas on by himself. A few guards were still alive, and it seemed like a majority of the cells had gone into automatic lock-down mode. Some were ripped open or just unoccupied without explanation, but plenty others still had their prisoners safely stored inside. He continued to go lower, all the way down to the bottom of the shaft.

His greatest fear was confirmed as he landed. All of the cells here were empty, torn apart through various means and emptied of their contents. This had been the true target, the bottom floor, where the most dangerous metas ever captured were stored. Some had been powerful enough to wipe out entire cities in the fight to bring them in.

And now, because of a plan he'd played a part in, they were all loose on the world once again.

Epilogue

"The jailbreak wasn't a complete success in that many of the less-powerful prisoners remain, but in terms of freeing dangerous metas while simultaneously making us look incompetent, it did a five-star job."

Professor Quantum flipped through the report, sitting where his remote terminal had once been. Three days after the battle for Ridge City and they'd finally finished putting together a comprehensive report of the damage, coupled with exactly who'd been sprung from Rookstone. Unlike Quorum and Lodestar, who sat across from him, Professor Quantum was actually marginally showing his age, a smatter of gray salting the temples of his dark hair. Otherwise, he looked exactly the same as he had for the last several decades, even wearing the lab coat he sported in place of a cape.

"Do we have any idea what they're up to?" Lodestar asked. "Balaam was going to lead them, but since our reports say he was... extradited... that seems unlikely."

"We've gotten a few accounts of sightings and smaller jobs from across the globe," Quorum told her. "The best guesses of our analysts are that without Balaam as a uniting force, they'll probably all scatter and hatch their own plans. Few of them were ever team players to start with."

"Which makes hunting them down all the more difficult." Professor Quantum turned a page, a motion that Lodestar and Quorum followed. While it was tempting to dwell on the jailbreak, they had a lot to get through; besides, with no information to work on, they would just be spitballing. The chance to recapture the freed metas would come eventually. They just needed to be patient and prepared.

"On the subject of team players, I trust you all have noticed we're being barraged by lawyers regarding bids for the freedom of the few guild members captured during the fight. This seems utterly mad to me, seeing as we have record of them fighting against AHC-sanctioned superheroes on dozens of cameras."

"They're claiming they were exercising their right to resist an unlawful arrest," Quorum said. "And since every bit of footage we have shows them merely trying to incapacitate, even against some of our more aggressive, newer members, they've got a very strong case. Add in Apollo's confession from two days ago confirming that the warrants were based on falsified evidence, and our own lawyers don't think we have much chance of making any of the charges stick. If anything, we'll be lucky not to be sued for wrongful arrest, though thankfully, we're insulated for excessive force."

"We must have something to throw at them that will stick." Professor Quantum lowered his papers, looking between his fellow members of the Champions' Congress. "I don't agree with his methods, but Apollo was right to be bothered by our tolerance of known criminals. He's presented us with a golden opportunity to topple that guild, and I simply cannot believe we have to let it slip away."

"They've already taken some serious blows," Lodestar replied. "Several of them died in the fighting, their headquarters was broadcast on international news, many of those thought to be dead were caught on camera, and to top it all off, the world now knows their organization exists. He shone a giant light on the shadow where they hid, and that's going to make things a lot more difficult for them in the future."

"Which may not be entirely a good thing," Quorum added. "With so many less-restrained villains now running about, we might have benefitted from the quiet peacekeeping they did behind the scenes."

"No, Quorum, we need to move past depending on that." Coming back had given Lodestar perspective that she'd lacked while living in the suburbs. While the guild had ultimately served the greater good in some ways, she didn't like the way it was shaping their city. "The Alliance of Heroic Champions will be the ones to keep the people safe again. We'll clean up the mess that one of our own helped make. No more depending on villains to police themselves. It's time to stop being backseat leaders and take charge of things once more."

"Couldn't have said it better myself," Professor Quantum agreed. "Nice to have you back—all the way back, Lodestar. And on that matter, I have another boat coming in a few months' time, one that contains some experiments that should be of great help in reestablishing order. Until then, we need to sort out who our best people are and put them to work. Right now, the world has a lot of distrust for the AHC, and having our capes out keeping them safe is the only way to rebuild that trust."

"Apollo kept detailed records of everyone's strengths, weaknesses, and best role when put into a team," Quorum said. "He also has assessments for all of the new recruits we got from that last confluence. Some have already debuted, and others were getting prepped for it. We can have a wave of fresh faces on the street in a week or so if we push it."

Professor Quantum frowned. "I've heard about the hand he took with training our fresh capes. For him to be so involved with them, it might be prudent to assume their loyalty lies with him, not the organization. Perhaps it would be more prudent to simply cast them out before they have the chance to do more damage."

"Forget it," Lodestar said, her white light growing a touch brighter. "First off, Apollo has been the head trainer here for over three years, so you'll need to expel a lot of people if you don't want capes he taught. Secondly, I saw some of those rookies in action myself, and they've got their hearts in the right places. Plus enough power to back it up. Or are you just sore that one of the new teams managed to make it past all your defenses and break through your dome?"

"I will remind you that the system was in testing mode, which greatly reduced the power of the offensive countermeasures," Professor Quantum snapped. After a moment, he composed himself and continued. "But getting that far is still no small feat, especially for rookies. I find myself fighting disbelief at the idea that one of them could actually rip a hole in my barrier. I'll need to study this 'Cyber Geek' more closely. In fact, I believe I have a new device for him, one requisitioned some weeks ago."

"I'm impressed you didn't put it off longer," Lodestar said.

"My equipment duties take second place to my research, but I do get around to them eventually," Professor Quantum informed her. "At any rate, I suppose you're right about the breadth of Apollo's influence. The new recruits can stay, but I'm going to have them under close supervision. Any hint of sharing their teacher's turncoat nature and they'll be lucky to only get kicked out from the AHC."

"That's as fair as we're going to get with this situation," Quorum said.

"Agreed," Lodestar added.

"Very well then, next topic." Professor Quantum flipped the page again, bringing up a whole new sheet of names and numbers. "It looks like all of our people have finally been accounted for. We lost many, mostly our untrained rookies on crowd control, but some were only injured. The pieces of Erinite were found in a neat stack outside the front door yesterday, so he's being taken to space to heal. Stalwart Iron is more problematic, as his core remains intact but the majority of his body was destroyed. A new body will need to be fashioned from the ground up before he can serve again, which presumably will fall on me to create. The rest are in respective healing bays and surgeries, and prognosis for all those still alive looks good. That reminds me: Quorum, book me a surgery room for this afternoon."

Lodestar raised an eyebrow in confusion. "You're going to pitch in on stitching people back together?"

"Obviously not; we have people for that. I just wanted to get Cyber Geek's upgrade installed as soon as possible, as it will also give me the chance to examine the power that bested my protective dome," Professor Quantum explained.

"I thought he just pulled digital items from a computer," Lodestar said.

"Exactly," Professor Quantum agreed. "But he's been using a wrist model, much too cumbersome and limited. I have a far better idea, one that will be portable, accessible, and greatly increase the variety of items he can wield. Plus, by my calculations, there's only a twenty-two percent chance that the surgery will blind him."

Lodestar made a mental note to chat with Cyber Geek and make sure he knew exactly what risks the "upgrade" would entail. Professor Quantum was brilliant, no one could dispute that, but he'd also always been a lot better at relating to numbers than to people, which could be a bit off-putting, if not dangerous.

Then again, Apollo had been great with people, and look where that got them. Maybe numbers weren't so bad, after all.

*   *   *

Tori stood in the afternoon sun, watching as crews sorted through the remains of Ivan's home. Behind her, a moving company was packing the last of what they'd been able to salvage into a giant truck, one that would soon head to a lovely townhome rented under a perfectly legal comprehensive care package provided by Vendallia for personal emergencies. She had to tip her hat to Doctor Mechaniacal—putting guild members into normal, boring jobs with actual insurance was a much easier way to help them out when things got crazy.

As a conversation with the foreman wrapped up, Ivan walked over and stood beside Tori, listening as the crews debated how to go about fixing a house that had walls punched through and a giant energy beam fire from the center. It hadn't collapsed completely, but Tori had done enough structural damage that they may just have to tear it down and rebuild from the ground up.

"What did you end up telling the neighbors, anyway?" Tori asked. She could see them peeking out from behind their curtains. A few had brought Ivan pies and baked goods while expressing their condolences. None of it seemed like the actions of a street that'd just found out a resident was a legendary villain.

"That the men who tried to rob Vendallia turned out to be part of an organized gang. They wanted a combination of revenge and to finish the job, which hatched a plan that centered on kidnapping me. One of them was lying in wait for me to come home, but a rival gang tracked them down and ended up slugging it out on my front lawn."

"And all the wards that Rust Tooth cut through?"

"No idea." Ivan gave a shrug. "Must have been set by the crazy criminal in the metal armor, probably to keep me from calling for help. This is all just what the AHC told me in the after-report, anyway. Only so many details provided."

"Well, they seem to have bought it, and that's all that matters." Tori looked around the peaceful neighborhood, remembering how dull it had seemed when she was first driven in. "I'd hate for you to lose this place."

"That might be inevitable," Ivan said. "With the guild exposed and Fornax publicly seen alive, it might be too risky to keep living in an area like this. When Doc finishes the new headquarters, I might take him up on a residency there." Neither he nor Tori worried about discussing these matters so close to the workers. Everyone, from the movers to the construction crew, was in Wade's employ. Tori suspected some of them might be mechanical, but hadn't been able to get a good enough look to be sure.

"Don't live in the guild. You'd hate it there," Tori told him. "Keep being Ivan. That's what makes you really happy. And besides, how would your kids visit a room in the guild?"

"I'd probably keep the townhouse for appearances, but as I said, this is all conjecture. Right now, there's no headquarters to live in; the whole place was purged as soon as everyone left the building. As for visitation... Janet is less than thrilled that my past brought Rick and Beth into harm's way. Somehow she's even blaming me for Beth's powers."

"Did you ever figure out when those happened?" Tori asked. Evidently, Beth's abilities had manifested only two weeks prior, well past the last confluence. But confluences were just events that spiked the meta-human population; there were plenty that came into being between confluences.

"Not yet, but we will," Ivan said. "Beth and I, and Janet, had a long talk. She's going to be getting the help she needs to control her abilities. Although my ex-wife isn't keen on the idea, even she can see that Beth having blades in her body that she can't control is too dangerous for everyone, especially Beth."

"Is she... I mean, will Beth be joining the guild?" Tori shuffled uncomfortably, picturing the sweet girl she'd met having to pass the trials or be put in the ground. Worse, she imagined the poor bastard who actually tried to see that threat through and had to go through Ivan to do it.

"God no. I love my daughter too much to ever let her be a part of all... this." Ivan gestured to the wrecked house, torn apart by a member of the very guild that he was supposed to be able to trust. "She'll be working with some old, non-guild friends. People I trust."

"That seems like a better fit," Tori agreed.

"What about you, though? I heard they were able to get a lot of your lab out last night, but I doubt there's room for it at the hotel." Ivan and Tori had both been put up in rooms at a local mid-range hotel while their living situation was worked out, along with dozens of other displaced Ridge City residents.

"It's in private storage for now," Tori said. "I actually just came to grab a few tools I forgot, and then I'm off to meet Beverly. She's been poring through real estate ads, as well as talking with the council, and she says she's got a few leads on places that will fit our extra needs."

"Pick something affordable," Ivan cautioned. "With the guild as it is now, there's not going to be any easy jobs for a while."

"Evidently, Beverly negotiated a bit of a stipend from Arcanicus, and we've still got our heist money. And I do get a paycheck, you know. Or I will, once Vendallia reopens." Every business in the downtown area was closed for at least the next week as they waited for cleanup crews to clear the streets of debris. The AHC had capes helping around the clock, though people weren't always happy to see them.

"Well then, I guess I'll still see you around the office," Ivan said.

"Damn right! Didn't think you were getting rid of me that easy, did you?"

"When I heard you'd been attacked, I confess there were some worried moments there." Ivan glanced at her then looked at the remains of his house. "I see now how truly foolish that was."

"What can I say? I'm kind of a badass." Tori slung her backpack, filled with tools to patch up the remains of her busted meta-suit, over her shoulder. "Though, I admit, having a good teacher helped."

"And you weren't the worst student I ever trained," Ivan said.

"But I did set one hell of a high bar for whoever comes next." Tori took a few steps away and threw a leg around the used motorcycle she'd picked up on the cheap. It needed a lot of work, but that would have to wait until she actually had a garage or driveway again. Hopefully Beverly was on the ball. "I'll see you next week at the office, Ivan."

"Try not to be late," he called as she slipped her dark helmet over her head.

Tori merely waved, a noncommittal gesture that she certainly felt didn't constitute a pledge of promptness, then gunned the engine and drove out of the driveway, past the staring neighbors peering from their windows.

*   *   *

Donald felt like he'd gone ten rounds with the Trolls of Elgthok. He had been in his bed all day, leveling up a new character in *Legacy World* and trying not to wince every time he moved his shoulder. Evidently the suit from

Blaster Brahs absorbed a lot of the lethal damage with its shields, but the small-scale knock-around stuff still got through. While an hour or so in the healing tanks would have left him good as new, Donald didn't bother trying to requisition one. For one thing, they were all occupied, filled with people who'd taken far more serious damage than he had. More importantly, Donald had seen some of the injuries capes came back with. He'd be damned if he was going to complain about something as mundane as soreness.

Even his own team had taken more damage than he'd realized. Hat Trick had been limping along with almost half the muscle fiber in her leg burned away; if the beams hadn't cauterized as they burned, she likely would have bled out on the street. It was only thanks to Professor Quantum's return that they'd been able to fully heal her leg instead of giving her a mechanical replacement. Medley had taken enough damage to kill a normal person five times over, and only his rapid healing and thick hide had kept him alive. Apparently, both factors were still getting stronger as the mutation in his body evolved to keep pace with the trials he was enduring. Cold Shoulder had actually collapsed from exhaustion once they got through the door; she'd pushed herself so hard and used her powers so much that her body had nothing left to give.

And Donald, the one who'd been acting as their leader, had walked away with only scrapes and bruises. The guilt churned his stomach. Why had he made it through relatively unscathed? He wasn't stronger than them, or better, or probably even smarter. No, he'd made it because they were taking the bigger blows to protect him. Protect the gun that could punch a hole in the barrier, really. His team had beaten themselves to hell to keep him safe, and now Donald could barely stand to look at himself in the mirror.

That was why he'd agreed to Professor Quantum's upgrade, even as Lodestar gently explained all the risks that came with it. If it could make him stronger, he was on board. Donald didn't want to come back from another mission with his team, his friends, barely surviving. He didn't want them to be the ones protecting him. He wanted to be able to protect himself, and the people around him.

Right now, Cyber Geek was just a guy with a weird ability. If Donald ever wanted to push himself to be a true hero, then it would mean sacrifice and risk. Getting the upgrade was just one part of it. He'd officially sent an e-mail to Vendallia accepting their offer for early retirement. It was time to stop living with one foot in both worlds. If he wanted to be like Lodestar, to be a real superhero who could make a difference in the world, then he would commit to it wholeheartedly.

Nearby, his phone vibrated. With a glance, he saw it was a text from Tori. She'd completely understood why he'd had to blow off coffee; in fact, she'd been taking shelter when the attacks happened anyway. Part of him wanted to rebook their meeting so badly, but not yet. Not until he'd made real progress, gotten a plan in order. Until then, he had to focus, prioritize training over his crush.

It was time to start seriously leveling up Cyber Geek. That was the only way Donald could look his injured team in the eyes again.

*   *   *

"Current estimates show we can have one of the backup headquarters functional in five weeks, fully operational in ten," Xelas said.

Wade nodded thoughtfully. This was not a meeting, per se, in that none of the other councilors were present. It was more like a summary of the actions before them, conducted by the two people who would actually have to put in much of the work to see things done. While Wade appreciated the need for the rest of the council in large decisions, the minutiae of rebuilding was better left to swift decision-makers rather than a committee.

"Let's go for the ten. Might as well welcome everyone back to a proper home," Wade said. "Speaking of, where are we on tracking everyone down?"

"Almost everyone has checked in after they scattered, as per protocol." Xelas skimmed her mental memory banks, seeing who was still unaccounted for. "We're missing a few of the ones that have been confirmed as traitors and some with allegiances unknown. Want me to get people hunting?"

"No, let's wait a little longer." Wade drummed his fingers on the back of the couch, staring out at the city from his luxury penthouse perched high in the sky. An array of papers was spread out on the coffee table before him, only a fraction of the paperwork and issues currently facing him. It was why he'd been stuck in the office for days, having to rely on Xelas as his eyes and ears. She sat in a nearby chair, unfettered by anything as mundane as pages cluttering her immediate area. Wade technically had the digital option as well, but he'd long ago found that having something tactile to sort through helped him think.

"Some might need more time to get safe and check in, and for those who never do, we can offer hunting them as jobs when the guild reopens its doors. There are several members I prefer to have occupied whenever possible, and that's a task which is unlikely to raise any AHC alarms. Speaking of traitors, how's the magic division adjusting to their new councilor?"

"The division is fine," Xelas said. "Arcanicus damn near founded that division, so everyone is good having him lead. He, on the other hand, keeps nagging me about finding a new councilor, saying he's too old for the job. I can bully him along for a while longer, but it's not a permanent solution."

"None of the options before us are," Wade replied. "Tell him it's just until the guild is running properly again and we can have a proper election. After that, we'll coerce him into keeping the job by other means, but it should buy us a couple of months. By the time he really wants to quit, hopefully a successor will have revealed themselves. Moving on, have our incarcerated guild members been freed?"

"There was a lot of hemming and hawing along with more than a few tails and wiretaps after they left, but yes, the AHC has been forced to drop all charges on the ones they captured." Xelas tapped her fingers together, replaying the press conferences in her head at lightning speeds. "They weren't happy about it, though. We should probably keep a low profile, at least for a while."

"That won't be a problem." Wade rose from his couch and walked to the window, peering out at the evening sun shining over Ridge City. "With no guild, our people will keep their heads down on their own. Even once we're reformed, I plan to stay off the AHC's radar. It occurred to me that perhaps we've been doing our civic duty a bit too freely, keeping the worst of the scum off the streets and letting them snatch up the easy pickings. Now that the AHC has been publicly weakened and the shadowy guild of rumor publicly exposed, I have a feeling we'll see a big upturn in meta-human crime, and that's not including all the criminals who escaped from Rookstone. Sooner or later, they'll realize that having one spider in the house kills a lot of the lesser insects."

"You want to wait until they ask us to work?" Xelas said.

"Ask? No, nothing that easy." Wade turned from the window and walked back to his couch, picking up a pile of papers. "I want them to beg for us to take up arms again. Until then, we focus on only doing smart jobs and keeping ourselves safe. Without a guild to keep peace in the underworld, this planet is about to get a lot more dangerous."

*   *   *

The force of nature that was Penelope slammed into Ivan's legs. She wrapped him in a small hug even as her yell of "Uncle Ivan!" was muffled by the fabric of his pants around the knees.

Ivan smiled and gave her a few small pats before turning his attention to Helen, who stood a few feet back. She was lovely, of course, though personally, Ivan preferred it when she was further aged into womanhood. Even without the glow of Lodestar, she was still nineteen again, no older than the day she was struck. It would be her age forever, or at least until she managed to completely stop calling on her power.

"Glad to see you as you," she said, giving him a strong hug. While they hadn't met on the battlefield, she'd no doubt seen the news and read the reports of what he'd done while out of control. Deep down, part of Ivan had expected her to be waiting as Lodestar, ready to ambush him and drag him back to Rookstone.

"Glad to be me," Ivan replied. He finally extricated himself from Penelope and Helen, and then reached into his back pocket. "And that reminds me, I brought gifts. One for you, Penelope, and a matching one for your mommy." Ivan plunked a small necklace into Penelope's hands, enjoying the sight as her eyes grew wide with wonder before handing a larger version to Helen.

"Thank you, Uncle Ivan!"

"Why don't you go try it on in the bathroom, and then you can come show us how you look?" Helen suggested. The words were barely out of her mouth before Penelope was off like a shot, moving at the speed only metas and children could manage. With her daughter gone, Helen's face turned skeptical as she looked at Ivan. "Spill it, what are these?"

"Hers is a shielding charm that Arcanicus whipped up," Ivan said. "It will give her some protection if she's attacked and set off a beacon if she's put in real danger. I had him key it carefully to make sure some kid pushing her down on the swings wouldn't set it off, so it reacts to the attacker's power and intention. Also comes with a minor compulsion enchantment to make sure she always wants to wear it. My kids got similar presents yesterday."

"And is mine a shield, too?" Helen chuckled at that; the mere idea of her needing protection magic was beyond laughable. So far as anyone knew, while Lodestar could be beaten, even knocked out, nothing had ever managed to permanently kill her.

"No, we know how magic works around you. Yours is just a piece of jewelry." Ivan pulled another object from his pockets, a dark case that he handed offered to Helen. "These, however, are something special."

Helen accepted the case and gently pushed it open, revealing a pair of thickly-rimmed glasses. "Oh my, these take me back. I haven't worn a pair of glasses since the early days, when I was still worried about people connecting me with the glowing woman in the sky. Were you feeling nostalgic?"   "A touch," Ivan admitted, "but that pair is something Wade whipped up special. If you'd be willing to humor me for just a moment, please try them on."

Helen looked a bit uncertain as she pulled the glasses from the case and slipped them onto her face. There was no distortion around her eyes, as the lenses were there purely for show. No part of Lodestar, or the woman who

614

hosted her power, was weak or lacking. Once she was done getting the glasses into place, Ivan continued the explanation.

"Feel the small indentation on right side near the lens? Press it down for three seconds."

Helen complied, and at the end of the third second, a shimmer surrounded her. When it cleared, he was once more staring at the Helen he'd known for the past few years, aged past that fateful day when she was nineteen years old. She caught sight of herself in the mirror and gasped, then whirled around to face Ivan.

"This is too much. A miniature holographic projector like this probably cost in the millions."

"Only if you pay retail and don't have a friend who spent a few weeks making the technology more cost-efficient," he assured her. "And what use would giving it back serve? Do you think there's someone else who wants to look like you?" Ivan quickly realized how that sounded, and began to hurriedly backpedal. "I mean, certainly countless women would like to look like you, but would you want them to? Not that we're mass-producing these or—"

"It's fine, Ivan, I got the gist of what you were going for," Helen said. "But I'm not sure I should accept this. I had a long talk with Penelope the night after the battle, and I'm not going to hide who I am from her anymore. She knows the truth now, and she'll grow up with the mother she actually has rather than who I wanted to be." She started to take the glasses off, but Ivan stopped her.

"I'm not telling you to wear them around Penelope, or when to wear them all. But the illusion might come in handy if you want to take a normal job again, or meet with her teachers, or do anything that revolves around not always looking nineteen. That's why there's an on/off switch. There's also a dial on the bottom that will move your age up and down. It's just a tool, one to help you have a small piece of the normal life you lost."

"Thank you, Ivan." Helen adjusted the glasses slightly then pressed the button again until the illusion vanished. "You know you don't owe me this, though, don't you? What happened wasn't your fault. Sooner or later, I was always going to have to come back."

"But if I hadn't lost control, it might not have been so soon," Ivan whispered, turning his face from hers.

"None of that, now. What you thought happened... I don't know that I'd have behaved any better, and I don't have that thing inside me. The AHC isn't even trying to press charges for the murder of Blunderbuss. You were a victim of Apollo and Balaam, just like the rest of the city." Helen gently took his face in her hands and turned it so that they were looking into each other's eyes. "I wouldn't lie to you about this. If I thought you were responsible, you know I'd have to bring you in. Trust me, Ivan. Trust my judgment and my actions. Don't let this eat you up inside."

"Even if I wanted to, I don't have the luxury," Ivan said. "Too many people counting on me, a meta-daughter not the least among them. That's what the necklaces and glasses are, officially anyway. Thank you gifts for agreeing to teach Beth."

"Then you really shouldn't have. Even if you hadn't done so much for us, I'd still consider it a pleasure," Helen said. "Truthfully, it's gotten me thinking that maybe the AHC needs to offer a more detached training system, something for meta-humans that want to get control but don't necessarily want to be superheroes. Especially for younger people. Something funded and helped by the AHC but remaining legally unaffiliated, so that no one would need to worry about getting recruited."

"Hey now, keep thinking like that and you're going to dry up all the recruits from our pool," Ivan told her.

Helen's face turned serious, and she glanced down the hall to make certain Penelope hadn't returned yet. "I know you're kidding, but you need to understand that things have changed. You all got away with a lot of stuff while Professor Quantum and I were on our sabbaticals, but all that came to an end three days ago. Your internal revolution spilled onto the streets, and while I'll own that some of ours helped cause it, that means we have to fix our system as well as yours."

"With Lodestar back, I'm sure we'll be needed less," Ivan replied. "But don't expect us to suddenly stop existing. If anything, what happened proved the need for our organization. You saw what happens when meta-criminals aren't properly disciplined and the upstarts aren't quelled. There's a meta ecosystem, and we play a part in it whether the AHC likes it or not."

The sound of Penelope's feet racing back down the hall forced them to pull apart, only now realizing how close they'd allowed themselves to stand.

"I can't protect you, Ivan. Not from the law. If you all slip out of line, you'll be on your own."

"That's perfectly all right. We can protect ourselves," Ivan assured her. "So if the AHC decides to make a real move, tell them to bring the best they've got. Wade has already prepared a slew of slander and harassment lawsuits based on what we endured this time around. The law cuts both ways."

"Why do I put up with you again?"

"Because once two people have beaten the living hell out of one another then helped save the world together, there's a bit of a bond there." Ivan got in the last words as Penelope came rocketing around the corner, showing off

616

her new piece of jewelry that she'd finally managed to get fastened around her neck.

Even if she hadn't appeared, neither would have said the real reason they put up with one another. Some words were just too dangerous to speak, for the ones uttering them as much as the ones listening.

*   *   *

"What do you think?" Beverly spread her arms out, gesturing to the open-concept living room housed by brick walls and the kitchen that was almost as big as Ivan's. From her vantage point in the doorway, Tori could already see into one of the bedrooms, which did look sizable and had more brick walls inside. It had taken several hours to get an appointment with the property manager, and Tori was half-convinced that Beverly had ended up employing threats, so she'd been expecting something amazing. This was... less than opulent.

"Well, I like the location; we're in the heart of what's left of downtown, so that will be cool when it's fixed up," Tori said, trying to be positive. "But it's the fourth floor in a walk-up, which is going to get really old when we're lugging in groceries. The warehouse decor isn't bad... little more modern than I like, but I can deal. My main problem is that it's really pricey, and even with a third bedroom to use as a lab, splitting the rent two ways might get taxing."

"Oh, that third bedroom isn't for you," Beverly said. "But you do have a lab. This place has personal underground parking garages: surrounded by concrete, inaccessible except through the building, and up to spec for retrofitting with lab equipment. I ran it by the council, and they're willing to purchase and renovate three of them to give you the space you need as part of our home-loss compensation."

"That's... actually a perfect fit for what I need." She looked at the apartment with fresh eyes, imagining being able to escape to a new subterranean lair at the end of each day. Bonus: if the guild was paying for it, that meant they could have more cash for rent. But there was still no sense in spending money they didn't have to. "Are there no two-bedrooms we can see for a cheaper rate?"

"Not many. This place took some damage, so space is limited," Beverly explained. "Besides, I thought maybe we could put someone else in the third bedroom. Split rent and bills three ways, if you're into it."

"Who?"

"Chloe. Her place got pretty much torched in the fire. She's been crashing with some friends, but it doesn't sound comfortable. I mentioned I was apartment-hunting for us, so she asked me to keep an eye out for any studios that might be in her price range," Beverly said. "This seemed like a better option all around."

"Is she okay with our... affiliation?" Tori knew that Chloe was now informed about their membership in a guild of villains and that she'd evidently had taken the news well, but there was a big jump between acceptance and wanting to bunk with confirmed criminals.

"I floated the idea past her, no promises made, and she seemed excited about it." Beverly walked over to the living area, looking out to see the bustling streets below them. "We can find another place if you want. It's just that I've always lived with a lot of family nearby. Moving to the guild was scary, but there were always others around. I thought it might be nice to have three of us starting out together, sort of a support net in case we need it."

Tori ducked into the nearest bedroom, checking out the size and closet space before noting the private bathroom. The next room was roughly the same, as was the next. Though their shapes were a bit different, the sizes seemed consistent. Well, that was one fight they didn't need to have, at least.

"A private attached bathroom for every occupant. That's pretty swanky," Tori said. "It looks like you put a lot of thought into this place, and they have a lab, so why the hell not? If nothing else, I know Chloe can make a good pot of coffee every morning. Just one thing, though, what's the policy on renovations?"

"I thought you might ask that, so I checked," Beverly said. "Upgrades are fine, as long as you don't knock out any walls."

"So much for the indoor tennis court, but I think I can make it work." Tori wrapped her arm around Beverly's shoulders and steered her toward the door. "Come on, let's go try and terrify a property manager into giving us cheaper rent before we sign the lease."

"See, this is why you need roommates," Beverly said as they stepped through the door. "There's nothing like teamwork for properly instilling fear in someone's heart."

*   *   *

Nexus stood on the roof of the building where Beverly and Tori were currently heading down the stairs. His attention was not on them but on the bustle of people moving through the streets of downtown: some cleaning, some commuting, some taking pictures for their online lives. It was a curious sight, which was why he bothered showing up for it.

618

This was not the first world where Fornax was stopped, the riots halted, and Balaam punished. But it had sustained far less damage than almost any other in the process. The AHC still stood, the guild was more than a cemetery, and Ridge City wasn't razed to the ground. Many universes were reeling by this point, destined for years of struggle before any sense of peace reasserted itself. Of course, in the realities that did find their way onto this path, it wasn't like the show was over.

Quite the contrary, really. Like here, the tension simmered beneath the surface. Instead of an all-out war, these tended to have smaller skirmishes, at least until the tension reached its breaking point. *Then* things got interesting. Nexus was quite pleased that this, one of his favorite dimensions, had happened upon the more interesting course of events. If it had ended in the more common way, there would have been a great spectacle and then lots of boredom. This way, he was going to be treated to a much more fascinating turn of events, one he'd possibly never seen before. It would take time, but things were going to get very interesting again. Soon, the old grudges and locked away secrets would come rising to the surface, and when they did, he'd have an excellent vantage point to watch from.

All he had to do was be patient. And perhaps cause a little mischief of his own when the occasion demanded. After all, the most fun part of all shows was being allowed a little participation from time to time.

But for now, the world was boring, and there were other universes to watch. One of which was especially entertaining. Three of him were already there but more would soon join. That little gem was too special to miss even the smallest bit of, one of those rarest of instances that required careful observation.

In a far-off world, history had been made. For the first time in all of the multiverse, someone had successfully killed a Lodestar.

End of Book 1

About the Author

Drew Hayes is an author from Texas who has now found time and gumption to publish a few books. He graduated from Texas Tech with a B.A. in English, because evidently he's not familiar with what the term "employable" means. Drew has been called one of the most profound, prolific, and talented authors of his generation, but a table full of drunks will say almost anything when offered a round of free shots. Drew feels kind of like a D-bag writing about himself in the third person like this. He does appreciate that you're still reading, though.

Drew would like to sit down and have a beer with you. Or a cocktail. He's not here to judge your preferences. Drew is terrible at being serious, and has no real idea what a snippet biography is meant to convey anyway. Drew thinks you are awesome just the way you are. That part, he meant. You can reach Drew with questions or movie offers at NovelistDrew@gmail.com Drew is off to go high-five random people, because who doesn't love a good high-five? No one, that's who.

Read or purchase more of his work at his site: DrewHayesNovels.com

CPSIA information can be obtained
at www.ICGtesting.com
Printed in the USA
BVHW031757250421
605823BV00014B/189

9 780986 396847